Birth of Destiny

G. A. Jensen

The Shepherd Saga
Book 1

This is a work of fiction. All of the characters, organizations, and events portrayed in this novel are either products of the author's imagination or are used fictitiously. Any resemblance to real persons, living or dead, is purely coincidental.

Birth of Destiny

www.gajensen.com

Map illustrations by Olivia Shreve

Book cover by Lyriakey on Fiverr

This book is unashamedly dedicated to the One who authored this story in my heart long ago, and who saved me from the sea by the sacrifice of His Son, Jesus Christ.

Contents

Acknowledgements

First and foremost, I would like to thank my best friend, Jon Shreve, for helping me bring this story to life. The Shepherd Saga would not even exist without Jon and the years we have spent building this world together. From the battles, characters, lore, and everything in between, along with refining my creative ideas and writing, Jon has unequivocally delivered what Birth of Destiny and all of Scissalan needed to be born.

This dream would also not have been possible without the continuous support and encouragement of my wife, Megan Jensen. Through every prayer, nourishing meal, and all of the heavenly rest that she faithfully provides, I have been able to pursue this story that our Lord placed on my heart.

I also want to acknowledge my sister who has been one of my biggest cheerleaders ever since I started writing this story way back in 2018. She has been with me through every season of my life and helped me become the man of God I am today, while also encouraging me to believe that my writing is worth something.

Deepest of gratitudes to Olivia Shreve who breath-takingly brought the maps of Scissalan alive, along with Jesse Muller who thoroughly edited this tome of a manuscript. I am extremely grateful to all of the Beta Readers including Jon Shreve, Olivia Shreve, Megan Jensen, Madison Jensen, Isaac Muly, Adam Muly, Jesse Muller, Nolan Hopkins, and Steven Hopkins. The cover art is by the wonderful artist Lyria. There are probably a few names that I forgot to mention and thank, and I will be sure to include them in my next book.

I couldn't have gotten this far in writing my story without the immense provision provided by my parents, my grandparents, my mother and father in law, and all of my family through my beautiful wife.

Finally, I give my ultimate thanks to my Heavenly Father who deserves the highest praise, for He is the One who began and finished this good work within me.

Map of Scissalan

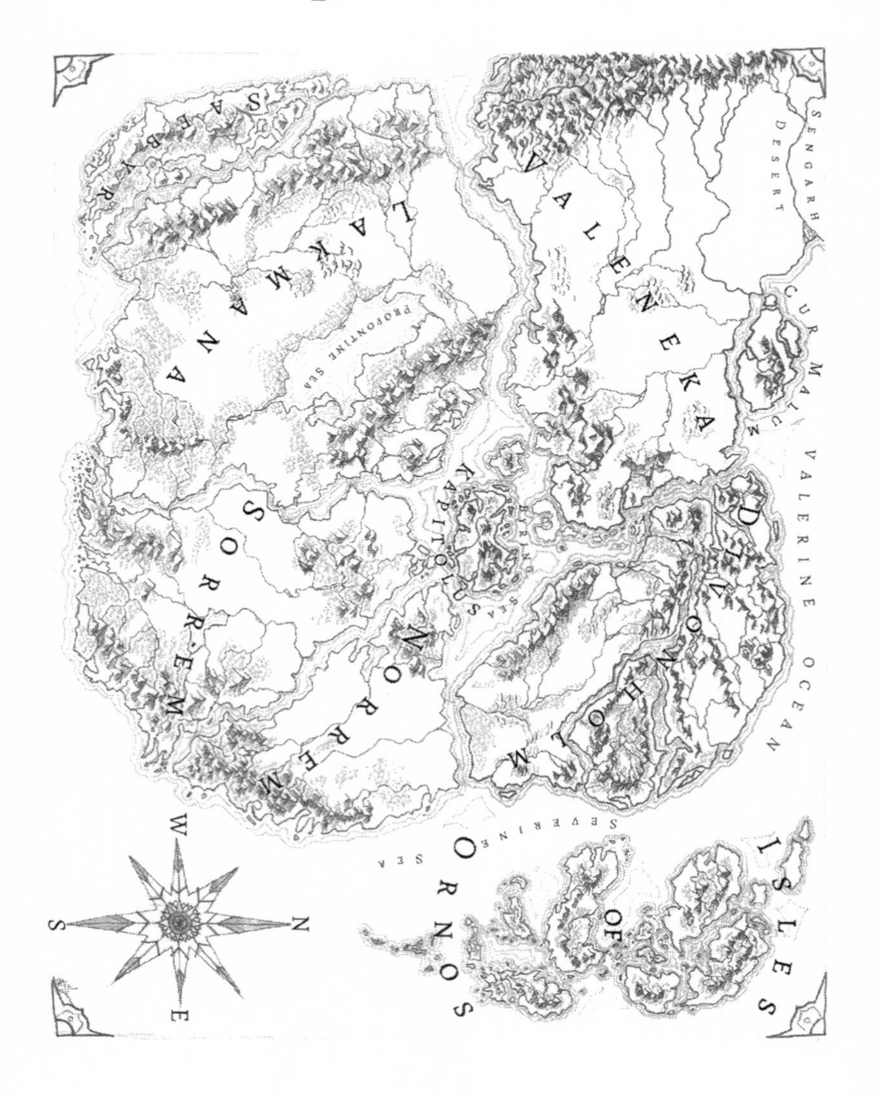

Map of Empire of Renborg

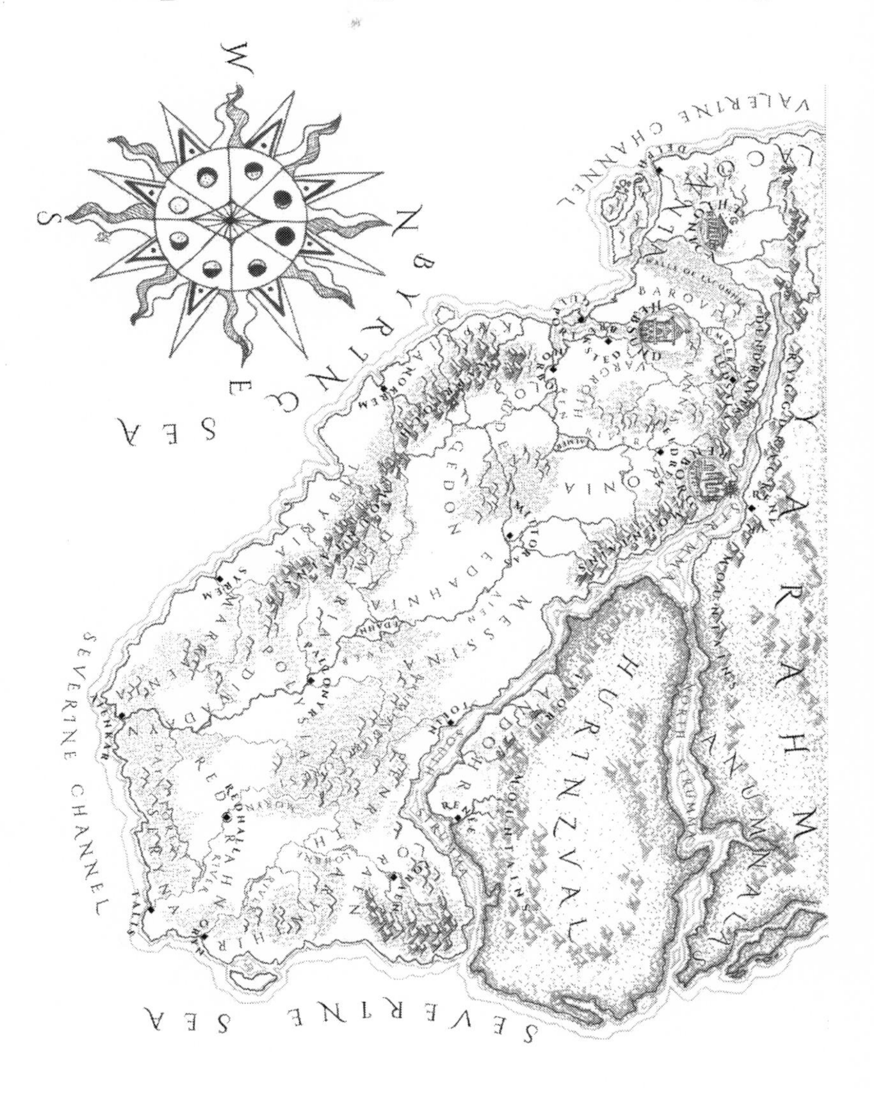

Birth of Destiny

Part I

The Fall

Chapter 1
A Shepherd's Destiny

The colorless waves thrashed against the rocks, tempting me to fall with them and sleep forever beneath the sea.

Like the sirens who haunted its endless fathoms, the roaring tides sang their deafening song of relief as my feet trembled forward unexpectedly on the ledge of the Asculum Cliffs.

Within my pounding heart there pushed a silent urge to fall.

My eyes strained upwards to see a glimpse of sunlight through the gloomy clouds, but there existed not a single ray for me. And though I pulled back to avoid the watery grave that was its own reward, my reluctance to do so last sol has haunted my every breath.

The shame and doubt from wanting to extinguish the meaningless flame of my life tore at the very fibers of my heart.

Every day.

Every single moment.

The agonizing pull within felt like a knife being plunged slowly, unremorsefully into my shivering flesh as I stood upon the same cliffs looming over the Strumma Sea, drawn to its bitter melody once again yet tormented all the same.

Nudging a pebble over the edge, I watched it plummet with the rain, disappearing in the waves that frothed against the rocks and eternally forgotten to the land of the living.

Just as magic and wonder had been many millennia ago.

The story of Amon II resurfaced in my mind at the whispers of the past that I knew all too well, more than most. The very cliffs my tears died silently upon were the same that the child Emperor of Cypheria was tossed off of at the treachery of a petty rebellion long ago. No one today, not even the Elves, remembered or cared about the usurper General Navarrian and how he carried out the uncaring will that history often had upon its victims. But his story still resonated with me as the waves roared hundreds of feet below me.

Despite such a grisly end, I envied the boy's fate.

It was so easy for him.

He didn't even have to make the conscious choice to be swallowed up by the sea; it was simply given to the child, like a gift from the ancient and endless grave.

I wondered if Amon's mother was able to witness his unexpected peace from her abrupt hanging on the castle walls.

Peace. Rest. Relief.

Nerves danced throughout my cold hands as I wrestled with the desire to join with Amon II and the countless others who drowned from the Primarchal Wars in these waters.

With hesitant tears they would soon be relieved.

Although I didn't want to acknowledge it at first, thinking it only to be a flight of fancy that spawned from the pit of my depression, I had come to wearily accept the yearning of my soul. No matter the time of day nor the quality of the moment, the seed of my being which failed to grow into anything of significance begged to be drowned in the empty harmony of death.

However, before I let those thoughts bring forth a harvest of decay, I retreated from the cliff to my room in the royal keep; my soul would have to thirst for just one more dawn.

In return for delaying the inevitable, I promised the conclusion of my story would take place at the start of my brother's marriage tomorrow night. The wedding would be a cause of celebration for the two realms now united under oath, but it would be especially for me, as I would slip away from everyone who never cared nor understood.

Lucien was the only exception, but even he couldn't hold back the hopeless waves that quietly swept away my reasons for living, day after day, until there was nothing left but the empty sands of my skin.

A cry erupted from the room next to me as I prepared to drift asleep, jolting my thoughts, followed by another cry in the room. With a deep breath, I shuffled wearily to the room of my youngest adoptive siblings.

Philomela was squirming as I picked up her fragile body and held her next to my heart, while Sigmund got up from his bed and laid his moonlit hair along my lap. A smile blossomed within me as I gently nestled Philomela's tiny blonde scalp with my hands and hummed to Sigmund, perplexed that I didn't look away from my deformed fingers while they returned to sleep. Though we did not share the same scars or a blood relation, my heart could not help but treat them with the kindest care ever since they were born.

There was such a beautiful innocence to their souls that was so absent in this world, like two flowers that had miraculously bloomed within a barren field which I did my best to water.

A soft coo emitted from Philomela as she preciously slept in my arms next to her brother.

Choking on my tears, I gently kissed Philomela and Sigmund before returning to my room.

The storms in my mind quieted to a soft roar as I laid my head down for the last time in my room. Surprisingly, I drifted to sleep faster than I ever had in my seventeen sols of existence. I couldn't tell if it was from the Hurinzvalese fur that smothered the cold or from the sheer exhaustion that accumulated from staring for hours out at the sea, but it was rest nonetheless.

That was until the soundless vortex of my mind emerged into a dark and polluted atmosphere, the sour taste of the air and the complete lucidity of my actions a haunting sign that this was too real to be considered a dream.

The only thing I couldn't explain was how I was flying.

Hundreds of feet below me were charcoal mountains vibrant with patches of green fur that shivered in the breeze, completely opposite to Renborg's cherry-stained Bludhlands.

But the foreign mountains weren't the only indicators that this was a part of my slumbering mind, as I could also tell from my hands, or wings rather, which were illuminated in the moonlight. When I clapped them together to fly, feathers, not flesh, fluttered in the night sky. Even though I far preferred this alternate reality of my physicality, it was with mourning that I accepted that this could only be a product of my nocturnal machinations.

At least I didn't have to see what they really looked like.

Inclined to not let such a lucid experience slip through my talons, I brought myself lower to the mountains that sprawled with trees hissing from the morning winds. The terrain was unfamiliar to me, but I recognized the lands of Yarahm in an instant when a herd of native Anakrum gobbled ferociously in the valley, their beaks more capable of granting death than the spears of those who typically rode them like horses.

It seemed that Piluch's lessons weren't so useless after all.

But any thoughts of Lucien's and my professor were abandoned as a sea of Ronian soldiers appeared in my elevated peripheral, their mounded camp walls and torchlights visible markings on what appeared to be the Morian Hills of Madea.

Curiosity took flight within me. Carelessly, I bent my wings inward to fall and receive a better glimpse of the seven Ronian hosts that glittered with their hundreds of torches and campfires in the night; I was also curious to see where my foster father was. Even though it was just a dream, the King had been gone with his army for several months now and I wanted to see if my subconscious would imagine him the kind and jovial man he once was.

Or would he be the sorrowed man he had become after burying his eldest not a few sols ago? However he would be, my depiction of him would be a bit more generous than Lucien's.

Before I could get any closer to determine the validity of my mind, an arrow whistled past my face.

It was not alone.

Multiplying in the uncountable hundreds, they snuffed out the moon's light, passing by me like a bitter storm. The quiet Ronian camp below was ignorant to the rain of death that was about to befall them. All except for one man who seemed to be unaware yet screaming about anyway. He was one of the three Kriga who had joined King Gulmund, Paulus Falco, who was recognizable from his tremendously long sideburns that hugged his chin.

"Where are those damned guides?" Paulus shouted, weaving frantically through the sea of white tents. "Guards! Find me those Drakin and Dwarven traitors! I will—"

Paulus finally heard the torrent of death as a few arrows sheathed into the dirt beside him, but only too late.

"Arrows!"

Dread squeezed my heart as the arrows barraged their sleeping targets across the camp. Paulus was similarly unfortunate, whose neck was lacerated in seconds as he failed to grab a shield to protect himself, laying just out of reach from his twitching fingers.

Chaos erupted all over the Ronian camp, men and horses screaming from being torn apart by the reeds of war coming from the nearby cliffs. In morbid fascination, I watched the death that came for them so unceremoniously. So many of them probably believed themselves to be the deliverers of death and not its recipient, to come home heroes and not laden upon their shields. Unfortunately for them, as all life was, their disappointment had only just begun, for that's when the Drakin decided to grind them into the dust.

Like a swarm of lightning bugs, the flaming Drakin revealed their fiery heads that were hidden in their Gyldur hoods and roared from the outskirts of the camp, their numbers stretching across the soon to be blood-drenched horizon and seemingly without end like the ever-growing population of stars. As death comes unexpectedly and defiant of any resistance, so too did the Drakin who charged into their surprised victims, their cavalry and infantry cutting down their foes without mercy.

It was impossible to tell who was gaining the edge in the battle or who was slipping closer to the empty Void that came for us all.

Though the illumination of the flaming-haired Drakin brought light, the chaos that ensued smothered any clarity in darkness. It didn't help that my vantage point below the clouds was continuously hindered by the winged Eldrakes who provided aerial assault on the helpless and crying men, gouging out the eyes of those who wept with their hybrid, Dragon claws before flapping their leathery wings into the sky to escape the Ronian spears.

Any sense of smell was not present in this dreadful dream, and for that I was glad. The air would have been rancid with blood and urine as the souls of many were ripped violently from their hearts.

Everything within me wanted to close my eyes and not behold the slaughter, to ignore the reality of blood rising to the ankles of both armies as their lives sank into the Void.

But I couldn't look away.

If anything, it reinforced and reminded me of my choice to close my eyes forever.

There was a dark resolution that validated me as I focused on the Ronian screams of fear, their eyes widening in horror from facing the brutish reality of life being so short and not at all heroic like the poetic Skallgends described. The urgings of the sea were not malevolent in wanting to hide me from the tragedies of life. If anything, my doubts about leaving this pointless world were diminished at the ghastliness of this Holy War that unfolded before me.

I doubted that the Ronian King Magnicus IV had such revelations when he condemned history with this needless conflict a century ago.

Without care, I let the air in my lungs escape as I descended to be closer to the battle, the fiery breath of a Drakin burning through me onto a Ronian knight. War was not as romantic up close, the magmic intestines of another Drakin spilling out in front of me while two Elves and Dwarves who fought for Yarahm speared a fallen Ronian into the bloody ground.

The Ronian was no older than I. Blood clogged his final breaths.

Though my mind was filled with history in which I often escaped to, the cycle of destruction and war that seemed to infect every race throughout time forever continued to escape any justification.

Tears glistening with fear were my only response to such a meaningless, ever continual tragedy.

Before I could sink deeper into the darkness of my mind, a force stronger than the wind gripped my wings and yanked me upwards to the shadowed heavens above. The air was knocked out of my lungs as I burst through the clouds, my feet gracing their fluffy puffs that were soaked in the luminous glow of the moon. Above me was the sun of the night, and across from me standing upon the clouds was a hooded figure with their back turned to me, their robes more white than milk and just as fluid.

"Hello?" my voice croaked.

A gust of wind was my answer, rustling my feathers and parting the cloud between us to reveal the fate of the Ronians below.

"Morgan Krios." The voice was deep and feminine.

My knees buckled under the weight of her words and dented the cloud. It didn't seem to come from the figure in front of me, but from all around and even within me. Fear danced its way through my being. I didn't recall drinking any juva before bed, the only explanation for a dream like this that shook my very essence to the core.

Perplexed, I said, "Yes?"

"I have called you by name."

"F-for what?"

And then I saw him through the opened clouds before me.

Riding towards the back of the Drakin army was the Grand Derasar, the elected military leader of the Drakin, dressed in golden armor that mirrored the sun's radiance. His black cape draped the winged Kiagor I had only heard about in ancient stories, its white form resembling that of a lion but parading three times as large, and horns terrifying even the Anakrum riders around him. The leader was dressed in splendor and stood out from the other commanders, his scaled gauntlets squeezing the reins of his Kiagor in frustration.

From what I could tell using my knowledge of the Domerian Tongue and the supernatural hearing in this dream state, the Grand Derasar was receiving a report from a group of Dwarves and Drakin that King Gulmund was absent from the dead.

Dismissing the scouts with a decisive flick of his hand, the leader puffed his chest high as he gave orders to his Eldrakes and cavalry in the Drakonnian tongue. The specifics of his commands were made clear when they departed to silence any Ronian who escaped the butchering, and they carried out the will of Judux et Cadullum with immediate results.

"Sleepless death," the powerful voice said as I beheld Judux in his terrifying glory.

My eyes trembled as I looked up from the clouds and upon the back of the ethereal figure before me, who was still watching the horizon in dedicated silence.

"I don't understand," I said. "You've called me for sleepless death?"

"Will you Shepherd my Shadow of Cypherus?"

At the reference to the mythic hero of Divonholm, confusion brewed with fear inside my stomach. I didn't have to be a Valkryn scholar to know the significance of being named Cypherus' Shadow and what they feared of his fabled return, but unlike the priests and their sheep, I did not kneel before such prophesied nonsense.

"You have me mistaken for someone else. Who are you?"

"Before the founding of the earth, I knew you."

Those words thrust like a terrifying gust of wind into my heart: terrifying yet refreshing. Such intimacy bled from each syllable and echoed throughout the cotton mountains above the earth, so much so that I began to choke on the lump in my throat which emerged from such an understanding that I never knew existed.

"But, what do you want from me? I am not some destined monster, nor do I have anything good to offer."

"You have all that I need!"

The words of power boomed from the Void and struck my chest, the weight forcing me to my hands and knees on the cloud. My eyes dropped to the glowing warmth that was my heart, which beamed with light more wonderful than the brightest sunflower in the fields of Feldrem.

Whatever was in my heart, it was beautiful beyond words.

The feet of the hooded figure clothed in milky robes turned to me in the moonlight. Lifting my head to his eyes, all I could do was stare at the beauty of his design. The glowing figure was contrasted to the now blood-red moon behind him, which was not darker than a pomegranate before. His face was like that of a man but not made of flesh; rather, like the ethereal swirls of the cosmos, ever-changing and translucent, his eyes burning like the sun in all of its brilliance.

"But I am nothing," I stuttered, my lips trembling in the scarlet moonlight. "I-I am no one, not high born nor anything of value, and I am certainly not the demented return of Cypherus. I just want to be left alone."

My words barely escaped through my silent tears.

"I am no Shepherd that you speak of."

A seismic boom erupted from the bloody moon behind him, a colliding star of falling grace, and it headed straight for the clouds where we braced for death like bride and groom at the altar.

Or for life.

The man of light paused for a moment, but not out of fear, then met my eyes calm and assured.

"You shall be."

The shooting star followed his words by incinerating the clouds and everything on them, my sight becoming nothing but a searing white light, the burning pain of which I could feel deeply in my thundering heart, causing me to scream myself awake. My chest ached from how fast my heart beat within me at the terrifying dream. But in the same breath, there hummed such a beautiful note of peace that my mind could not understand.

The word "Shepherd" hung faintly across the looming shadows of my room, its powerfully feminine tone a mystery, or madness.

Chapter 2
The Blade They Fear

The blood of the deceased gods still remains a mystery to us. Even though its purest Klyr state and corrupted Nox state are both rarely seen today, its natural and most prevalent Bludh state has affected this world and our empire greatly.

Though the art of using the language of the gods has been lost for almost a thousand sols, the few Godstone-filled souls the world has left have forever marred the kingdoms with a dark fascination of the unnatural. Its power to transform the wielder into a hybrid of man and beast has been one of great controversy. These Averitic races *and their dark temptations of nature's transformative abilities have caused friction to the Valkryn Faith and have even began to infect the studies of the College. I pray the return of Cypherus does not unleash another plague like this upon our world.*

Chronicles of Renborg: King's Edition
"Godstone and the Forgotten Tongue"
Piluch Joffersun: Master of Histories

"M**organ!"**

Lucien burst into my room, the scarlet light of his Godstone necklace exploding into my den of shadows like the sun upon the dawn.

The hue from my matching necklace glowed, vibrating in response to my soul Wyling in its ancient emptiness, like inhaling breath that circulated through the lungs to give life to all of my being. Unfortunately, its vessel and its power were just as hollow as most Godstone had become since the Red Death. All this fabled blood of deceased gods did was expose my body in the dark, which was drenched in sweat and shame.

"Is everything alright?" Lucien said, his voice soft and gentle like a youthful breeze.

Pushing down my fears to steady my fragile breath, I forced a smile at my brother, whose white and messy hair shone in the moonlight and reflected upon his smooth face. Seeing his silver locks reminded me of the cosmic man I saw beneath the bloody moon and the woman's words that shook the foundations of my being.

With haste, I turned to look out of my window to see if it was just a dream after all: unfortunately, the moon's grey flesh proved my dreams to be just as lifeless as it was.

"Morgan," Lucien repeated, drawing closer to gently hold my trembling hands that clung to my favorite gift from him.

With his other hand, he traced his matching Godstone amulet that sprouted a tiny Wolfwood tree upon its ruby surface. Ours were alike except for the sun and moon emblems on either side of the tree, where my sun was filled with Godstone and his for the moon. Together they completed the Tree of Truth.

"Are you well?" he whispered.

"Yes… I am well," I croaked, my deepening voice filling the empty bedroom.

Lucien muttered something under his breath. "Fine, we're doing it."

Without asking, he yanked me to my feet. Instantly, I recoiled to bathe my skin back into the liquid shadows, ashamed of what he would see but already knew from our sols of growing up together where no secret could hide.

"Would you put a shirt on at least?" Lucien said, blushing and turning away.

"For what? Where could we possibly be going at this hour?"

But Lucien only waited.

Obliging him, I dressed as quickly as my body would let me. With my heavy heart concealed under layers of egg white silk, Lucien grabbed me again by my hand, this time gloved, to lead me through the midnight halls of Renborg's castle, Caer Mordrake.

"You didn't answer my question," I said.

My nerves were still shaking from the dream, my mind rattling from images of the spectral man's eyes and the pointlessness of the lives that dissolved into a sea of blood in which I saw my reflection.

I don't think I was blessed with a nightmare from a whispering Mara, as the man's robes were not webbed with shadows, nor was the darkness inside me anything new. As for being called Cypherus, my nocturnal luminations could have been influenced by my midnight readings of the *Chronicles of Renborg*, which was filled with lamenting references to the fabled return of Cypherus' Shadow.

But still, it had felt all too real.

Drawing me out of the chaos of my mind, Lucien's calm and kind voice was soothing enough to make the mental Mara of my imagination somewhat less of a burden.

"Shut up and you'll see," he said, smiling darkly.

Well, mostly.

The anxiety coursing through my lungs was eased from Lucien's presence as we descended the stairs of our bedroom wing of the castle, plunging into shadowed halls below with torches flickering just enough light to guide us. It was at night that the repressed thoughts surfaced to haunt me. My forehead would often cringe with pain in trying to deny their existence, such as the tragedy that befell my mother when I was born that left me alone.

I was reminded of her death every time we passed the long abandoned room which had once held her upon the bottom floor of the bedroom wing, the scars from the flames long since scrubbed clean from the walls.

"When you're ready, she left something for you in there,"

Lucien's mother had said many times throughout the sols, her tone always heavy and eyes flooded with empathy.

But no matter how much Valena had encouraged me to find closure behind that door, I could never bring myself to go through it. Part of me hoped that I would find something that would justify my suffering existence, and another part of me feared that what I would find would justify nothing at all, only coming to agreement with the colorless waves.

Valena's words never seemed to disappear as I passed by the room every day, but my worthless father learned that art more than her words ever could.

"What was the dream about?" Lucien said as we continued to navigate the halls, his airy voice a small but lovely flame giving me warmth.

"I-I don't remember," I said, rubbing my arm as my mind returned to the present.

"Oh come now," Lucien said, pushing me as a smile dawned on his face. "You know what, I bet it was that *Tales of the Old World* book I found your nose in the other week. You should really go back to reading your hundreds of other books I've given you. That thing's ghastly enough to give anyone bad dreams. I mean, just the art of Thadius is enough to make your skin crawl."

A genuine smile reached my lips. "You know, I remember my dream now. I think it was about you marrying a Sukkatling and she sucked all of your blood out on your wedding night."

"Mother above, Morgan," Lucien said, looking pleased in making me smile, "no hour seems to constrain your black humor. But then again, your dream might just be prophetical."

A laugh erupted from my chest, the warm sensation a beautiful melody.

"I don't understand why you're not ecstatic to marry her.

The whispers at the court are that she glows with a humble beauty far beyond her sols."

"Only if you find hairless cats beautiful."

"I don't see why that matters."

"Well, even if she was attractive, which she's not, the way her mother negotiated the marriage with Gulmund makes me shudder that Egret is just as controlling as all the other Skyyan women."

"I hope she forces you to ride the waves with a Poecampi," I said as we entered the royal treasury of Renborg, my eyes drowning in the sea of the empire's most valued treasures while avoiding my reflections in the gilded mirrors. "But what are we doing here?"

"You'll see," Lucien said, slipping from my hand to trace the ancient shield from Mythraelyon I's ship that displayed proudly before us. "You know, maybe you and I could take a ship while Gulmund is gone and sail away to Issoken and live in peace? I would be free of this marriage and you could keep us alive with your feverishly warm flesh. How does that sound?"

"And be devoured by the Trolls of Udd?" I said, managing a smile and soaking in the once bronze but now green and ancient shield that had belonged to Mythraelyon I, the savior of the Cypherian Empire.

My hands passed slowly over the coarse grooves in the shield, making their way carefully to the center where there appeared the faintest outline of the word that many believed had granted Mythraelyon I all of his historic success.

My hand rested on the ancient and unknown symbol.

Part of me wanted to believe that heroes of old could really control the power of the sea to wash the darkness away; that there was a grander world beyond the limited one in my mind; that my story could mean something like Mythraelyon's. But the world of magic was long dead and forgotten, just like Mythraelyon's supposed spear of light that could bring absolute healing; all mysteries and magic were locked in the past, the key forgotten during the plague which reminded everyone that life was terribly short.

Fire pulsed in my fist as I curled it unto itself as I stood in his great shadow, drawn to the seas which he so easily conquered.

"It's better than being chained to a wench," Lucien laughed softly, his blue eyes wandering from the array of numerous treasures to mine. There hinted a glimpse of sadness on his face that melted with a forced but cheerful smile. "You know, all of this talk about marriage makes me wonder if there's anyone on your mind who you're interested in."

"Oh please, nobody has been or will be into any of this."

"Oh I wouldn't be so sure Morgan," Lucien jested. "Who could ever resist your olive skin and tousled midnight hair? Your eyes of fire practically scorch all who fall beneath your gaze, as I'm told."

"You know, now that you mention it, one of the Queen's royal guards looked lovely if I might say."

Lucien stopped. "You jest, right?"

Shrugging my shoulders, I continued my walk through the treasury. "I don't know, those antlered helmets look quite inviting."

"Yes, you're full of it. But if you ever decide that you want deer for children, let me know and I can arrange a meeting between you and a Suffra!"

His white teeth flashed in a smile that I couldn't resist with my own.

"You're insufferable," I said, joy returning to my lips.

"My humor comes from you, dear brother."

"Quite a statement. If Gulmund would have foreseen that, he wouldn't have adopted me then."

The joy on Lucien's face flickered out for just a moment.

"I don't want to imagine that."

His words felt like ice sprouting from the inside of my heart.

"Forgive me, I didn't mean to jest."

"I mean, if you weren't here, then Sigmund's and Philomela's nurse would actually have something to do, even take them on frequent walks! I can't imagine the thought of such tireless labor of one employed by our sober King."

With a subtle yet firm push, I propelled Lucien into the mummified and towering corpse of Bakara the Beast, the ancient Averite giving Lucien a terrifying and unwanted hug as he fell into it. Lucien screamed, scrambling away from the monster whose head bore the severe trauma from its fatal fall hundreds of sols ago.

For my kindness, Lucien blessed me with a blow to my arm.

"You know I hate that one," he said, trying his best to conceal a smile which cracked at the corner of his pale lips.

Laughter couldn't resist its escape from me at such a sight.

"It still amazes me that this creature's fall almost severed a Ludsalan bridge," I said, calming my laughter.

"Yet it still has more in its head than you do," Lucien said.

"So, what did you really bring me here for?" I said, looking upon the stained glass windows that circled the towering treasury room, void of any light.

"Come, let me show you."

Lucien's pale hand took mine again and led me past the

worthless trophies and treasures of the Mordrake dynasty to Renborg's most highly exalted prize: the blade of Cypherus the Great. My eyes gravitated as they always did to the ancient yet untranslatable engraving in the swords' handle, its meaning a mystery:

"*Sleepless death*," echoed in my mind as thoughts of Cypherus' Shadow emerged, but I drowned them out by focusing on the statue of the hero who wielded Renborg's most treasured possession. Cypherus the Great stood triumphantly over the stone head of a Dragon that lay cold and dead beneath his feet. The Godstone gauntlets of Kyllian Mordrake I wrapped around Cypherus' hands, in which the statue held the sword that sheathed downwards into the Dragon's skull.

A twisted desire to touch the sword and hear the whispers of the Dragon's soul within the blade emerged, becoming overwhelmingly strong, but any chances of doing so were halted by the ten guards defending Solstein. Their armor clinked together as they bowed at our approach.

"Good morning, Your Highnesses," they said.

"Greetings to you," Lucien said.

"Offly early at this time, isn't it?"

"Indeed it is. If you would hand me the gauntlets and blade, I would be most satisfied."

The guards looked at each other in confusion but obeyed promptly. Strapping the ruby gauntlets onto Lucien who carefully took the family sword, they made sure the Klyrstone only touched his protected hands so as to not scorch his heart from its purity.

"Don't worry, I won't break it," Lucien said with a smile that quickly turned stern. "But do not under any circumstances tell the Queen or I swear you'll be flogged and demoted."

"As you wish," they said with a surprised face, mirroring my own.

"Why are we taking Solstein?" I said as we left the treasury, exiting the palace walls to stroll through the royal district's vast and multi-tiered gardens where the wedding would take place later in the night. "Are you trying to get us killed?"

"When has that ever worried you?"

Any response caught in my throat as I looked at him bemused. I guess my humor had been infecting him more than I thought.

"Oh you know I'm joking. Come on, just follow me before we miss the dawn!" And with that he ran ahead awkwardly with the sword, begging me to follow him so as to keep him from killing himself.

"Never fails," I moaned, with the slight hint of a smile. But for the slightest moment, my joy was marred by the stories of Cypherus' return, the unknown vessel of his Shadow destined to wield Solstein for *sleepless death.*

I pushed the fantasies of the Valkryn and Navakosh priests out of my mind, uninterested in worrying about an ambiguous drama crafted by those who were bored of looking upon the empty stars and similarly empty holy books.

At least my last day on this earth would be interesting.

The sweet, honey aroma of freshly baked flavah buns and trollof bread warmed my nose as we walked through the very vibrant and festive streets of Renborg.

The recently reconstructed homes of the nobility and government officials were drenched in the forest green banners of Solstein surrounded by two coiled Dragons. Even though the sun had not yet risen, the newly paved streets were already crawling with Visians setting up their shops and businesses for the wedding celebrations that all of Renborg would partake in. Representatives from the neighboring realms were also scattered among the native olive-skinned peoples.

Barrels of wine, meats, delicacies and treasures for sale clogged the widened streets as we made our way to the Western Gate, lengthening the time of our journey to stretch almost an hour as we walked accompanied by a host of Ronian soldiers.

It amazed me that so many of them could be so blind in their happiness.

"Morgan, did you hear me?" Lucien said as the lords and citizens of Renborg bowed as we passed.

"Hmm? Sorry, what?"

"I said at least I will get to inherit a rebuilt empire. Are you sure you're well?"

The roaring whispers of my mind wanted to tell him so many things at once, like how I was mourning that I would be leaving him, to how he was the only light that kept me tethered to this empty life, though it would soon snap into darkness forever. In this way, perhaps I wouldn't be the opposite of Cypherus, destined to drown this world in death as their mystics believed.

No, I will not cave to such religious fantasies.

Mentally grabbing those worthless speculations, I destroyed them in the fires of my mind, annoyed that those words kept drawing to the surface like worms before the storm.

"Of course," was all I could manage.

Lucien said nothing as he looked at me, but in the doubt

of my answer he pushed forth a genuine smile to trace his rosy lips, as if to encourage me.

"We're almost there," he said.

The sun was just about to peak over the Ryggdrack Mountains when we finally left the bustling city and strolled through the farmlands surrounding Renborg's walls. Just as the sun began to spill into the Ren Valley in which the capital city was enthroned, we at last reached a blood red tree that bordered on the precipice of the Asculum Cliffs, its roots starving for the Godstone deposits that used to give it vibrant life so long ago.

Lucien had told the Ronian escorts to wait by the gate, much to their frustration, though we were well within sight.

But finally, we were alone.

"You first," Lucien said, gesturing towards the trunk with Solstein.

"As you wish, my Lord," I teased.

With two quick strides, I leaped onto the Bludh tree that was surrounded by a sea of scarlet grass, reaching its low hanging branch in a matter of moments. As Lucien struggled up the tree, I watched as the winds of the sea flattened the Godstone-drenched hills, bearing the same image of blood coursing from the eyes of the Ronians whose lives were spilt without reason or glorified purpose in my dream.

Lucien huffed in relief as he pulled himself onto the branch next to me, placing the sheathed Solstein in his lap before wrapping one gauntleted arm around my shoulder, silencing my barrage of thoughts.

For a moment, nothing was said as we waited for the sun to rise above the sea, together.

It wasn't long before the sun rose east over the Strumma Sea between the Ryggdrack Mountains, basking Renborg in its pale light, blinding us in its morning shine. The tingling warmth on my cheeks from its rays felt exactly like the ethereal light in my dream that replaced my heart as I knelt before the hooded being, questioning the voice's declaration of my worth and calling.

Breathing in the warmth and exhaling only a cold breath, I accepted the fact that my mind was probably doing everything it could subconsciously to keep me from the sea. And so I let my eyes drift down from the dawn and to the Ren Valley below, letting them sink all the way back down to the Cliffs of Asculum hanging over the frothing seas.

"I could just do this every day," Lucien said, looking past the sun and gazing far in the distance, but not really looking at all. "The peace of it all, the weightlessness of the world, it's so freeing."

Lucien's shoulders relaxed as he spoke, along with the brief surrendering of the man he was becoming through the harshness of his father.

For a moment, I could see the boy who used to play with me and Kyllian V, so careless and free, focused on the arts and wonders of the world as he rode upon the shoulders of his stronger brother named after one of Renborg's heroes. My heart pained for those moments, for everything became darker once Kyllian was slain, and it was Lucien who Gulmund begrudgingly had to groom for the throne, along with all of its burdensome responsibilities.

"So," I said, "is that why you brought me out here with Solstein? You're serious about taking the sword and running from your wife and the crown?"

"No, you fool," he said, shoving my shoulder. "I will accept my lot by dealing with this Princess. I actually came out here for you."

"What do you mean?"

"Here, put this on."

Carefully, Lucien inserted my right hand into a gauntlet of Kyllian I, clothing it in the surprisingly light glove of Godstone.

"What are you doing?"

"Something a little risky," Lucien said with a smirk while he put the other one on his left.

With his gloved hand, he held Solstein, and with his other, he unsheathed it.

The crystal-white blade in its bronze and leather handle glowed dimly in the morning light. The Klyrstone weapon that Cypherus used to erase the Dragons from history whispered before me like the sea, only darker, its burning light reflected in my eyes which beheld it, not knowing whether to revere it or flee.

Almost immediately, the wraith-like whispers from Solstein became louder, lulling my thoughts into their unintelligible proclamations while shivers crawled through my flesh.

It was only the second time this had happened.

The first was when a few traveling scholars from the College of Man had been showcasing their prized and ancient souls not one sol ago.

I had taken Sigmund and Philomela out for a walk amongst the city streets of Renborg, as I usually did, when I noticed them. I couldn't help but draw closer to their demonstration as I held the hands of Lucien's siblings. As I came closer to the soul that had been captured from the ocean long before the Red Death, a shrill and exhausted cry pierced my ears as I touched the crystal cage that the sea monster had been locked in for an eternally long time.

Though my flesh was not wounded, it had felt like my soul was suddenly gripped by its feral nature, my mind its dominion in which I had little say.

It wasn't until Sigmund pulled my hand away from the Godstone artifact that my mind was freed.

"Think of Godstone in terms of nature," Piluch had instructed when I brought up my strange encounter with him, our greying mentor deviating from his usual teachings of Lucien and I about statecraft, history, and kingship. "Bludh, the natural state of the gods' blood, is like the land which absorbed it: it harbors a spirit with ease, containing it like gold beneath its surface, though the gold is unable to remove itself. I assume that is what this sea monster was in.

"And just as the land can tremble at the Mother's whisper, so too can a soul of great strength breathe its influence through its cage. Though this cannot be true if the cage is Nox, the rare corrupted state of Godstone, for it will freeze the life of a soul within its cold embrace, much like the ire of a forgotten woman."

"You speak with experience, Teacher?" Lucien had jested.

"Only some," Piluch said, slightly smirking as he probably remembered an old flame.

Was there one? The old man never did explain why he remained unmarried.

"Morgan, can you remind us of Klyr Godstone?" Piluch had said.

"Of course, Teacher," I said, recollecting his lessons in our book-filled study. "Klyrstone is Godstone in its purest form… like the sun, in a way. But the only way Godstone can become like the sun is for the wielder to become pure. Nothing can withstand its purity once it is, except for those who share in its likeness. Which is why souls are unable to be held in its purest form, nor in its corrupted state."

"I didn't realize Sh'eol was so pure!" Lucien said, leaning back in his chair. "Maybe Solstein made the Dragon pure? Perhaps we can touch father's heart and he will be just as cheery."

"*My Prince*," Piluch said, casting a disappointed glance to him, "do not forget the nature of both your father's crown and Klyr Godstone: only the strongest are able to endure their burden, and one does not remain unchanged by their nature."

Lucien reddened at the rebuke.

"So Sh'eol is strong enough to endure in Solstein?" I said, redirecting Piluch's attention. "Is that how the last Dragon survived its purity for thousands of sols?"

Piluch's expression softened as he looked at me. "There are some in this life that see death as a hindrance to their glory, who refuse to die. The Dragons were notorious for this. But to deny death or to seek its embrace early are not the ways in which one should conduct themself. There is a path that runs true between them, one of meaning that celebrates the light of life while contending with its shadow. Like all things of worth, it is possible to find if you trust in Her Light."

Piluch's words had given me hope that life did not have to be a ceaseless torture like the one Sh'eol was fated to.

This hope, though not placed in his religion but in his wisdom, was initially strong. However, that hope weakened every time I passed my adoptive brother's grave who met his bitter end trying to calm a distant rebellion, every time I was mocked for the immutable characteristics of my flesh, and every time I failed to find this supposed path in my lonely and meaningless existence.

"I bought some books from the College of Man to research how Klyrstone could heal people," Lucien said, returning my thoughts to the present as he placed the sword's pommel in both of our gauntlets. "I figured today would be the only day I have the freedom to try. Now, I know I'm by no means an expert, but I think I have a pretty solid grasp on the material. For instance, the healing will be able to flow from the Klyrstone through the bronze hilt, even though it is not of the same substance, but because it is bound together from being so close. I don't know exactly how it works, but I assume it is similar to how our Bludhlands were formed."

No words could form from my surprised heart.

"I-I, no, you can't!" I said. "Are you jesting with me? You'll get yourself killed. I can't let you do that!"

"And I can't bear to watch you try to kill yourself again!"

Both of our eyes stung with tears, and I looked away in shame.

"Morgan, you know how much I love you, and if there's even a chance that I can help take your pain away that has burdened you for so long, then I will absolutely do whatever it takes."

The love overflowing from his heart was too much for mine, and with my emotions jolted from the nightmare and the plans for sleeping forever tonight, my gloomy facade broke down into the tears that held it together.

"I—I don't know what to say."

"You needn't say a word, but we must do this quickly before mother realizes we're gone; with Solstein for Mother's sake!"

"Very well," I said, brushing my leaking face against my shoulder. "Perform whatever it is quickly."

Lucien and I locked eyes, and with his other hand that was barren, he grabbed my free hand and placed them both upon the handle, our faces cringing from the immediate pain as the Klyrstone began to vibrate slightly.

And that's when I heard him.

The voice of Sh'eol was even more twisted than I imagined, and old, very old. So ancient in sols that his language was unintelligible to me as I writhed in pain, the sheer purity of the Klyrstone coursing through my heart and burning it within. Even though the Dragon was speaking Shiveric, the mental images and feelings I received from him were so distorted and nonsensical that I knew at once that this being had been driven mad from the thousands of sols it spent in this blade.

The sickening chaos of images that surged through me were like frothing waves in a thrashing sea, with ancient symbols that looked similar to the ones on Solstein in all of them.

But in those distorted memories, one person was the focus of them all.

The man was entirely coated in fire-scorched bone armor, forged from the Dragons he personally slew as he rode a fearless white steed that was similarly armed. In the memories where he was on foot, he seemed to move faster than the wind as he slew Dragons with a burning white Solstein that cut through every one of them with ease. The earth would rise at his command to shield him from Dragon blows, and even the Dragon flames would seemingly pass through him as though he were made of air.

The most painful memory to Sh'eol seemed to be when the hero quickly drew a glowing white symbol in the air as he faced the Dragon on a mountain, his dazzling white horse rearing at the oncoming fiend in the sky:

There was fear in the Dragon as he saw the lightning from the storm surrounding them strike the Godstone sword which the man wielded. In one swift motion, the fearless man channeled the electric bolt and his sword straight into the heart of the ebony Dragon who dove in malice towards the hero.

Cypherus the Great looked much more terrifying and heroic than the statues and monuments that littered Renborg in his honor.

Though my dream was just that, I guess I was his opposite as the powerful voice had said I was: lifeless, unheroic, unable to slay the Dragons of my mind, weak, unnotable, and soon to be, forgotten.

Sh'eol didn't seem to take pleasure in my ruminations, as the sight of Cypherus only made the ancient Dragon seethe with excruciating rage. My heart burned within me, the complete opposite of the peaceful sun that I saw and felt in my dream.

Lucien felt the same, evident through his feral cry that pierced my ears.

We both yelled in agony and thrust the white-hot blade against the tree, which cut through it like butter but also set the bloody leaves alight like a torch. The tree erupted into flames and I almost fell backwards over the cliff's ledge, surprisingly thankful when Lucien grabbed my arm to steady me. But staying in the tree would be even more dangerous, for it became a roaring blaze because of the dryness from the hot summer sun.

Without waiting for an answer, I pulled him out of the tree with me and down to the Ren Valley below, landing way too close to Solstein which had sheathed itself to its hilt in the ruby grass.

My eyes darted to Lucien's once we recovered from our fall, who shared the same look of disbelief as we crawled quickly away from the flames.

"What book did you research from again?" I said.

"Do you feel any different?"

Once we were far enough away from the burning tree, I checked the inside of my gloves, and it was still the shame that I woke up to every morning, with the only thing being different was my heart which felt like it had been left in a baker's oven from touching the pure Godstone.

But before I could answer, the moon above us boomed like two ships colliding into one another as it turned as red as Bludhstone, and a milky white streak of light birthed from it and shot towards the city.

"What a day for a wedding!" Lucien said.

"It's coming for Renborg!" I screamed, and as it blazed

towards our massive city, I shielded my eyes from the blinding light.

I guess this is it.

But a familiar sound like boulders crashing into the sea exploded beyond us. Since my body didn't feel like it was pulverized, I opened my eyes slowly to look for the strange light that streaked across the sky from the moon. Smoke was rising to the south of the city and yet not one stone had been touched from Renborg's double walls. However, I was not drawn to the strange cosmic event that had eclipsed the burning of the tree from Solstein. No, my eyes were drawn to the city's western gate where a small band of cavalry dressed in Renborg's forest green capes had bleached bear fur around their shoulders, emulating the ancient hero in whom they were named after.

The horses of the Knights of Kyllian were startled by the sign from the heavens, as were our escorts whose faces were stretched in shock.

But not its leader.

Instead, the man leading them was galloping furiously ahead of his guards, spit drenching his beard as he yelled at us. I could barely sustain my disbelief, for the Holy War had only just been reinitiated and there was no way he could be back so soon from his campaign in Yarahm. For a moment, he reminded me of Judux gripping the reins of his Kiagor after learning of the King's absence in Madea, something I could not explain my mind predicting or imagining.

The only thing I could do was stand paralyzed with fear as he rode towards us, his singular eye seething with disappointment. It was an ugly look Lucien and I recognized all too well ever since Lucien's older brother, Kyllian V, had passed. That look was usually accompanied by the hand that the King so often raised in his newfound habitual, drunken rage.

Glancing back to the moaning sea, a plea of desperation

surged within me, my heart shattering along with my plans for escaping this world on this most peculiar day.

The only thing that did not falter was the newfound fear of my dream becoming disturbingly true with each strange occurrence.

And for the first time in my short and colorless life, I regarded the Valkryn prophecy with serious contemplation; not because of what it meant for me, but for what it meant for Lucien, who, as the soon to be King of Renborg, was the fabled victim of Cypherus' Shadow.

Chapter 3
Failed Expectations

While the recent death of her late husband King Tarsicus remains suspicious after his failure for losing Karthos in their civil war, what is clear is Queen Nera's grand vision for her coastal kingdom: an egalitarian society built off of the profits of Godstone. A very profitable future is certain.

Your Grace, Grand Kriga Kolstok and I suggest we forge a military and trade agreement with Skyya through the marriage of Prince Lucien and Nera's eldest daughter, Princess Egret. The Faith won't like her reforms on allowing their Averites into the military, but the gold and peace we will accrue through trade will silence them. Nera is in need of political legitimacy and Godstone, and we are in need of a naval ally to thwart Yarahm's aggression, along with more shipments of the inextinguishable vori sap to defend against any Laconnian incursion (if need be). All of which will add to our fortitude against Kapitol's ambitions, adding a silver sword of defiance to all of our enemies.

Transcript of Council of the Masters Meeting
Thaedum 17th of Lakburry, 998 DE
Master of Coin Lord Tiberius Cilvahan

"I am *severely* disappointed!"

King Gulmund's remaining right eye twitched as we cowered before him in the Councilroom of the Masters, his breath reeking of wine through his snarl.

"Both of you, but especially you."

The King's meaty finger pointed to Lucien, who sat gripping his chair in silent anger beside me, the wood creaking inside his bone white fingers.

Solstein lay naked on the Wolfwood table beside us as evidence for his growing disappointment. The map of Renborg suffocated beneath it as it threatened to melt the wax figurines of troops surrounding it. The table was the only thing that separated us from the King, but it did not spare us from the vitriol that spewed from his mouth like an open grave.

My head drooped low to avoid his glare. The weight of my fears from what he would do to us kept it from rising. But that did not stop Lucien, who I could see staring right back at his father with fierce determination.

"What were you thinking, boy?" he said, spit emphasizing the only term he ever used to describe his son as of late. "You disgrace this empire with such foolishness."

The King's words fell heavy on my heart as well, for it was not long ago that he used to smile more than he did scowl.

Lucien gave him no answer, which only amplified the roaring anxiety in my thoughts. I was still trying to keep all of the pieces of my mind from falling apart at the strange dream that seemingly predicted the cosmic event of the moon and what that meant about my fate, but Gulmund's unpredictable rage jarred my contemplation.

The King could either keep the door open to leaving this life or make sure it remained closed forever.

"Do not make me repeat myself or so help me I will have Qai'phus force a lamb's heart down your pathetic throat for dishonoring me!"

The disturbing thought of the Primarch doing that to Lucien, whose hypocritical chair he was sitting in, was a defilement that sent shivers down my spine.

"Why must you question me?" Lucien said, his voice shaking but striving for confidence. "As the heir of Cypherus, Solstein is my birthright once I take the throne, so why must you berate me like a child—"

"Because our enemies will not fear a child who sits on the throne, which you are entirely capable of demonstrating to be the case. It is far beyond the time to grow up and become a man like Kyllian! Your life doesn't belong to you, it belongs to *Renborg*."

Rising my eyes carefully to Gulmund's gilded and forest green chest, I could see him clutching his stomach at the last word and his grinding teeth, the noise of which filled the otherwise silent room. Even though my sight didn't reach the bottom of his scar that gouged his left eye, I could see that the King looked pale and weak, sick even, but that didn't stop his words from being as strong as his fists which he often spoke with instead.

"I swear," Gulmund continued, "you make me wish Morgan was my son, as I'm sure he only followed in this foolishness at your direction."

Tears threatened to spill through Lucien's eyes. "So, is that why you're here? Did you realize you failed as a father and needed to raise me properly during your *little* war?"

"Lucien," I whispered, but he gave me only a quick glance before returning to his father's hateful embrace.

"*What*... did you say?"

"I think you heard me, Gulmund. You didn't even ask me of my thoughts before you forced me into this marriage, for you were only thinking of what you could gain, just like you did with mother after your first wife died. So why did you even come back? Were the Drakin you raped not as pleasing as the mistresses you abandon mother for?"

Gulmund's hand struck as hard and fast as lightning upon Lucien's face, the outline of his hand a dark blush of beet red.

Lucien buried himself in my shoulder, his tears soaking my colorless tunic. Gulmund shot up from his seat and leaned over us, digging his finger into Lucien's chest as his wine spilt from the table and poured all over me.

"Listen carefully, *boy*. You will treat your *father* with respect and not question my will. Though you are too weak to understand, know that I am trying to make a king of you! You were not supposed to inherit this empire which I have sacrificed everything for, nor do you deserve it, but I will raise you to administer this divine authority like your brother should have!"

Gulmund grabbed his stomach again in pain, coughing like a withering animal whose belly was punctured by a hunter's arrow.

Though it was a painful form of justice, it was near impossible for me to take pleasure in his suffering. For though Gulmund had become a hardened man since the fatal rebellion of Rene in which Kyllian was slain, I still remembered his deep laugh that would fill the halls of Caer Mordrake when we feasted together.

"*Raise*?" Lucien said, unearthing his tear-stricken face from my shoulder. "Raise me? How can you even say that? You were never around to raise me, nor Sigmund or Philomela. If anything, Morgan is more of a father to them, and Piluch raised us both and was in every way the father that you failed to—"

But Gulmund's fist squeezed the last of his words from escaping, violently squeezing his son by the neck and thrusting him violently against the wall.

"Gulmund!" I screamed, struggling to rise and help my brother whose feet kicked with a fury, but the five Knights of Kyllian burst through the Councilroom door and blocked me from intervening.

Lucien's panicked eyes flickered to me in fear, and all I could do was watch helplessly like too many times before. Although Gulmund looked sick, he was surprisingly strong like Bakara, looking more ferocious than the beast who also lost his eye during the Siege of Feldrem long ago.

As Gulmund heaved in his breathing, the line between villain and hero looked more like a mirror for the King.

"This will be the last time you dishonor me," Gulmund said, his voice growling over Lucien's gagging.

The King threw him to the floor in front of the royal guards like some despised criminal, their Godstone blades sheathed but still within a moment's reach.

"Sir Valrok," Gulmund said, indicating the knight with the falcon's crest upon his helmet, "take yourself and Sir Remah to escort the *Prince* to his room before we will go together to the Hall of Judges. Tell Master Joffersun and Monroe that we will arrive shortly to speak with Queen Nera."

When Lucien raised himself to go out the door, his father halted him with one last word.

"And as for you, *boy*, you will know every word of the Silver Sword Pact that you've neglected to take seriously, and from now on you will behave as a king! When I am ready, you will officially read it before the Skyyan Queen and the Judges so that she believes her daughter is not marrying some worthless, incompetent boy, though I doubt she will ever be convinced. Do you understand me?"

Lucien's ocean blue eyes looked like they would cause a hurricane from the thunderous glare he gave to his father, but he nodded out of submission.

"Good. Leave us."

The two knights escorted Lucien out from the room. Rather, they did their best to catch up with the Prince, who stormed away from them before Gulmund had dismissed them.

The door closed gently while the other three knights stayed behind, leaving me alone with the King.

My pounding heart was gripped in anguish as the silence filled the room in Lucien's absence.

And my heart was torn for him. To see him so abused by his father, and to see the hardened shells of men that they both became, was beyond any tragic description. The harsh realities of life had propelled Gulmund to the insatiable numbness of the cup, and had ripped youthful, careless joy from Lucien's days.

Their relationship, or lack thereof, was a poisonous cycle that dragged everyone around them into it. In the public eyes, Lucien was honored to soon bear the mantle of Cypherus the Great, as every Ronian king had before him. This mantle would show his absolute loyalty to defending the empire against the foretold Shadow's return as he served her people with honor. But in private, Gulmund treated Lucien with more callousness than the genocided Dragons that Cypherus himself erased from history.

Or at least that's how it felt for Lucien, who related Gulmund's treatment to the ancient slaughter on the nights when the King's drinking spiraled from obnoxious to destructive.

The venomous relationship between them almost made me feel glad that I didn't have a father, for if I had anything nearly as toxic as theirs, I might have killed him before drinking the poison of bitter reality and succumbing to its eternal stupor.

Gulmund sat down with a pained sigh, still looking at me with a degree of anger, albeit a lesser one than that he had delivered to Lucien.

"I'll make this quick. Morgan, you shall—"

A sharp knock at the door interrupted the King.

"Yes?"

"They have the soup and dust," Sir Esus said behind the doors.

"Ah yes, bring it in."

Sir Esus opened the door and in came the Dwarven royal cupbearer carrying a steamy and muddy wehstryn soup, along with a leaf pouch of faery dust.

Anger and shock were the only two emotions I could comprehend within me as I looked at the King so freely accepting the very substance that he strictly forbade in the empire.

And punished, severely.

But to remind the King of his hypocrisy would be in itself its own punishment.

"Thank you, Eruch," the King said weakly. "And please stay in the room, I will need Sommerian wine to wash this down when I'm through."

"Yes, Your Grace."

Instantly, my nostrils flooded with the beet and amber stench that the sap of dedrim trees exuded from the invigorating soup, but mine were not as busy as Gulmund's, who was inhaling the addictive and crushed faery wing dust through his reddening nose. In seeing his gross indulgence that would've resulted in the hanging of anyone who wasn't royal or of the nobelic Marqs, I felt a strange peace in my analysis of life that even the laws we were demanded to live by were just as pointless as life itself.

Gulmund shivered after he finished gulping down the wehstryn soup, resorting to his somewhat usual look of gloom, but this time with his eyes fixed open.

"I will make this quick so that I'm not enamored to you by this damned dust," the King said.

"Do you have the same bowel issue as your father?" I said, throwing off his thoughts to avoid being lectured.

Gulmund looked shocked. "A wise guess, which is unseemly from your foolish actions today. You've been reading the *Chronicles* again?"

"I have nothing else to do."

Gulmund broke a small grin through the beads of sweat on his pasty face, answering my speculations which were evident in their family's history. At least I had one answer to this climactic day, explaining why he needed the invigorating soup and euphoric dust to push through the disease; but this revelation was marred by the more pressing concern of how I could've dreamt that he had left the war and that the moon would explode in blood.

"Well," Gulmung said, grabbing the wine goblet that Eruch finished pouring, "at least one of you has their heads in the right place, which is more than I can say for Qai'phus. *Melai*! That perverted fool will barrage me to death with his theories of this damned blood moon."

"Lucien is trying."

"Renborg doesn't need a king who can try, it needs one who can rule!"

"Does not his willingness to marry the Princess count for anything? He's been trying to please you ever since he became the heir to the crown. Kyllian's death was hard on him too… on all of us."

The silence was thicker than trollof bread as the King's gaze bore into my soul. But finally, there was a weak smile that sprouted from him, and he nodded.

"I will admit, I'm proud that he has taken on this task to forge our two realms in this critical time, to do what is absolutely necessary for Renborg. It will be his first test of kingship that he must bear for all of his life, and it is *crucial* that he not fail where most would: when faced with doing what is needed.

"This crown is just too heavy to bear for those with weak spines and ill-tempered manners. We are at *war*, Morgan. Those insufferable *drowners* are relentless. You think I wanted the Primarchal Wars to resume? There's something you must learn about the Drakin, Morgan, and it is this: they will never stop until they are brought to heel. If Piluch's taught you any of their history, then you would know that."

"I do," I said, not wanting to think about their destructive and conquering origins from the Dragons and Elves.

"Good, then you will understand that I will not subject this empire to desolation from ineffective leadership that befell the

Cypherian Empire. Which brings me to my second point. I cannot have my son distracted by your reckless abandon of life, which is evident from your little act with Solstein today. You have no idea how fragile the peace with the Lacconians is, nor the stakes of this war, and I will not have you weakening the crown that holds it all so *frustratingly* together. And so, you will now have Sir Alduaura escort you at all times to make sure you do not try anything so foolish again."

"But we were just—"

"No, Morgan! I will not tolerate whatever excuse you have. Regardless of your intentions, I will not have your blood on my hands." Gulmund pulled back in his chair, pain evident underneath his beard as he whispered, "There's too much of that already."

"Your Grace—"

"That is final."

The silence was deafening, but I relented when I couldn't figure out whose blood he was referring to, me or his soldiers, for his weathered and downtrodden cheeks implied both.

My voice was hardly audible. "I'm… I'm sorry."

"Don't apologize. I didn't raise you to be weak."

If being strong was like him, then I'd rather be weak.

For even though Gulmund's eyes were wide from the Dust, his eyes seemed to fidget with the beginnings of tears, but because of his pride, he did not weep. That didn't stop mine from leaking with misery, as my sols stretched unbearingly long before me if I couldn't end it all tonight.

And that was a tragedy.

My flesh brimmed with anger for the man that treated Lucien and I so harshly, threatening to explode like the volcanoes of Yarahm.

The foreboding dream crept back into my mind as well, satisfied that I could not throw away its peculiarities and haunt anytime soon, twistedly destined to become true in this lucid nightmare.

And yet, I did not let my anger explode.

Despite his abuse, I could still see a very small part of Gulmund that was love, buried deep beneath his exterior layer of hardened masculinity and brooding. I knew that he cared, though he refused to show it. It wasn't that long ago when I would catch him and his wife Valena laughing together at the feasting hall during the banquets held for important guests. Furthermore, his fierce devotion to Renborg's people kept the empire out of most conflicts as he attempted to preserve peace and prosperity for his subjects.

After all, it was Gulmund who protected me from my father who tried to kill me when I was born, picking me up tenderly from my mother's charred ribs to save me from the fire.

Or so Valena would tell me, for Gulmund was not known for vulnerability; even his annual Skallgends only reflected on how he was grateful that the Mother preserved his empire thus far.

However, regardless of any love or attempts at love from Lucien's family, none of it was enough to make existence bearable.

To my greatest loathing, the guard would ensure I was kept a prisoner to this life and whatever the unexplained shadow decided to poison my life with. Yet, part of me was glad that I didn't have the freedom to close the door to my life quietly in the darkness.

The agony of either choice ripped my soul in two opposite directions.

I needed to find a quiet place to think and cool off.

"Now if you'll excuse me, I must be off to the baths to heal and let the dust wear off," Gulmund said, standing up as he motioned for me to leave.

The door to the Councilroom opened and Sir Alduaura was already standing there, vigilantly waiting to make sure I wouldn't flee the realm of the living.

Before I left with my unpleasurable escort, the King said, "And Morgan?"

Turning reluctantly, I said, "Yes?"

"Please don't be late to the ceremony. Lucien will need you there tonight. As do all of my children."

My aimless feet dragged me from the castle into the courtyards before it, adjacent to the gardens that would host the wedding later that night. I had no destination before me, but there was one place in mind that usually helped me to think. But before I could leave the royal district citadel, I heard my name.

"Morgan!"

Turning around, I could see Lucien waving a sparring sword in a smaller courtyard that we used often for swordplay. Lucien was accompanied by Sir Valrok and Sir Remah who sat silently on the stone benches beside him. Though I couldn't see underneath their helmets, I imagined they were not at all pleased that Lucien defied his father's will and came to the courtyard instead of his room.

"Morgan, come join!"

"I thought you were supposed to be in your room studying for your speech," I said as I moved to join him.

"I am!" he said, motioning with his sword to Piluch who sat previously beyond my sight as Sir Alduaura and I entered through the gate of the courtyard, our mentor's grey beard bristling in the soft breeze as he nodded to me. "Master Joffersun made a compromise to recite to me the speech while I blow off some steam. And I think I have a fair grasp of it. Come! Let us do it together and not think of that old fool."

A sword sliced through the air and sheathed itself in the grass between Lucien and I's feet. We both looked to Piluch in confusion who had moved swiftly to his feet to strike the blade before us. Though he was old, there was much within the Master of Histories that he often did not display.

"Old fool?" Piluch said, eyeing Lucien who shifted on his feet uncomfortably. "Do you believe your father to just be some *old fool*?"

Lucien cleared his throat. "I—"

"It was this *old fool* who spared Renborg from the costly Primarchal Wars after his brothers were slain by a Drakin mystic, sparing both Renborg and Yarahm from needless slaughter. So foolish he was that he began to partner with our former enemies like Laconnia and Sommer, making trade deals with them that enriched our empire and fostered peace that was once unknown between us.

"All of this foolishness led to more resources and improvements in the city's roads and infrastructure where before it was once falling apart from idle leadership. And now, as we face war with Yarahm's upheaval towards us, he seeks allies in Skyya in which he will bind us together through your marriage tonight, all of which was made through his *brash* mind as he navigates the Marqs, the Visians, and the Primarchs who have sway over Renborg's politics.

"Quite foolish, is he not?" Piluch said as he gently shoved the sparring sword into my hands, looking at us both with disappointment and love. But as his gaze lingered, his furrowed brow and his tone softened, his eyes instead creasing together as if remembering a terrible dream he had wished to forget. "There are a great many things you do not know about your father, nor what he had to do to preserve Renborg. And I pray your swordsmanship lessons are not as lacking as your understanding of our history."

Lucien looked at me and shared the same speechless reaction I had to Piluch's lesson as our often witty yet humble mentor sat back down on the stone bench. Though I didn't want to admit it, and especially Lucien whose cheeks were flushed with irritation, it was a humbling reminder of the respect owed to Gulmund, though the King often abused it in his drunken spiral that of late consumed him.

"Are you going to stand there or train?" Piluch said, and at once Lucien leapt forward in a precise low lunge that I barely swept away before again parrying his swiftly accompanied overhand strike, his face red and flustered, yet silent.

In a breath, Lucien sprung several feet away before dancing, light as a feather, slowly in a circle around me. Standing stiffly in the center, my sword loosely gripped at a low angle as I suffered not to find the most defensible guard.

Lucien kept his crystal blue eyes locked on mine, watching my every move with an irritated brow. Without warning, Lucien surged forward and unleashed a flurry of tactical strikes, snapping his wrists and sword left and right, with most of the blows finding their mark upon me as I made little effort to avoid them.

"Will you not advance on me?" Lucien said, before stepping quickly forward to swing his blade to my sword arm, which grazed lighter against me than the ones before it.

"Is that what the Princess will say tonight?" I teased as I swung my blade carelessly to land a stern blow against his midsection, knocking out his breath.

Lucien wheezed at the thoughtless blow and returned a precise one to my thigh that I moved too slowly to avoid. Though the strike sent fire into my leg, I feigned to be crippled from the attack, dropping my sword to the ground and holding onto my thigh in pretended agony, releasing a most convincing gasp of shock.

"Are you well?" Lucien said, dropping the sword as he ran to hold me.

As soon as his hands grabbed to support me, I swept my foot underneath his own and threw him to the ground, knocking the breath out of his surprised face as I pinned him down with my arms.

"I think I'll be fine," I said, offering Lucien a smirk while he wrestled against me in anger.

"Very unchivalrous," Lucien said before grabbing his sword to jam its hilt into my side, stealing my own breath as he slithered around me to reverse our positions, placing the tip of his sword at my throat as he stood before me.

"Yield," Lucien said, unable to keep the smile from his reddened face.

Sighing, I pretended defeat. "Yes, my Lord."

A sharp kick to his loins was swiftly followed by my surrender. As Lucien barreled over to the side of me, gasping in pain, I jumped to my feet and pushed him gently to the grass with one hand where he laid in agony and clutched his wounded pride.

"How thoughtful of you," Lucien said in writhing gasps.

"I thought you'd need some encouragement for tonight," I smirked.

"Speaking of which," Piluch interrupted, "Lucien, your father will be at the Hall of Judges here shortly. We should be going."

Helping Lucien to his feet, my brother sighed.

"Very well," Lucien said, looking at me with a sadness as we both knew that this marked the end of our childhood, as we likely would not see each other till the wedding.

And afterwards, never again.

Even if I did choose to stay, it would be a shadow of what once was.

I would miss him though, along with his siblings. But I knew in time that I would be forgotten as the pressing world and all of its chaos would force them to think of it more than my fading memories we shared, until I was only just a mournful thought that would arise if they ever thought about their childhood.

Thinking of only the now, I buried the emotions that threatened to burst from the seams of my aching heart that didn't want to hurt Lucien or Sigmund and Philomela. But I saw no other way forward in the turbulent and uncaring seas of destiny.

"Goodbye, brother," I said as I embraced him with all of my strength.

"Oh my," Lucien said as he stood in surprise to my embrace, before wrapping his arms tightly around me. "See you soon, dear brother. I'm thankful I won't have to endure this journey alone."

As Lucien and Piluch and the other knights left, leaving just Sir Alduaura and I alone in the courtyard, I mumbled too softly for anyone but myself to hear.

"Please forgive me."

Casting my eyes to the towering library in the distance, I moved my feet, one heavy step at a time, to reclude to the only place where my mind could breathe.

One last time before the sea.

Maybe within its shelves of solitude I would find in my mind the key to opening the door of eternal rest that was for now painfully locked by the King.

I hoped so.

And yet, part of me wished I would not.

The streets of Renborg were even busier than they were earlier this morning, many of the faces of Ronians and Elves and Dwarves smiling and conversing with joyous anticipation for the night to come. There were countless couples as well within the bustling crowds, all of them showing affection to their lovers and holding each other tightly as their worlds appeared to be perfect and lacking nothing.

Their joy forced me to close my eyes, as my soul could not bear to see others so happy and one with their beloveds. The light of their love was so bright that it made the shadow of mine ever darker, ever lonelier.

My fists squeezed in the bottomless pain from the absence of such a beloved for me.

Even Lucien would have someone to call his own, and in time he would grow to love her as he should. I often dreamt of what my life would be like if I too had someone to love and behold, and I wondered with great desperation if that would make a difference to how I felt about the significance of my life, and if it would alter the path that my soul seemed to be dragging itself down to with and without my permission.

Memories of Karlata intruded themselves into my mind yet again, but with spiteful haste I discarded them, for I did not wish to think of the humiliation I suffered from her lust. She was truly the mere Shadow of what could even qualify as someone to love.

And yet, she was the only one who ever inclined towards me.

These thoughts consumed me as I walked underneath the colorful forest-green banners of Renborg that hung from every door and terrace of the shops and homes that were packed tightly together. Sir Alduaura, whose metal greaves clinked on the freshly paved road behind me, followed close by. Drowning in these black thoughts silenced the greetings of the Ronians and Visian nobles we passed by. Though I heard them not, I smiled in return from such a repeated practice of showing the world what it wanted, and not what was inside.

After what felt like an endless walk, we finally passed the great homes and market square of the nobility, reaching at last the grand pillared entrance to the Great Library of Cypheria.

I always felt dwarfed by the knowledge contained in this massive tombstone of a library, its scroll and book cases towering four levels above me to reflect their belief in a deidic hierarchy. Thousands of candles oozed with wax and hopelessly flickered light into the library's vast sea of shadows as a result of few windows for light, much like the world which the builder Cypherus V tried to emulate. Despite its religious significance which I had no care for, it was my second home, as I spent most of my time here devouring wisdom and the past to fill an insatiable hunger I could not name in the present.

Purposelessly making my way up to the Archgod's floor, I traced my hand lightly over the wide staircases that weaved throughout the temple of knowledge from its center, resembling the spiderwebs of a coffin. Leather scraped against wood as I let my gloved fingers drag across its carved railing like a veteran soldier who is called to fight in a battle that he knows will most likely be his last, absorbing the memories of his home one last time.

Sir Alduaura did not find my somber reflections particularly amusing, as the Archgod's floor was up three flights of stairs, and they were great steps indeed. He huffed with impatience as I weaved slowly through the whispering Ronians and maze of bookcases looking for something to bring peace to my warring thoughts.

Maybe he would grow tired of escorting me and leave. Then again, any man who denied his family and name in order to adopt the sacred identities of the Kyllian Knights, thus entirely devoting themselves to protect the royal line, would be a man of inescapable dedication.

Nevertheless, as my mind burned with formulating various

escapes from my unwanted escort, I decided to peruse the Holy Light collection of literature in a feeble attempt at answering the devouring mystery of my dream.

It wasn't hard to find the prophecy section I was looking for, as there were centuries of research and speculations into the final words supposedly uttered by the Cypherian god after the Red Death almost a thousand sols ago.

I did not know exactly what the prophecy looked like or said; all I knew was that it mentioned something foreboding of Cypherus' Shadow. Thankfully, I didn't have to scour the entire library, as I easily found it within the first few pages of an authorless book I picked at random labeled The Hidden Shadow of Scissalan.

In the dusty book, it read:

"Cypherus, savior of souls, ruled as your thesis,
His shadow, sleepless death, will reign antithesis."

A chill trickled down my spine.

How could I have dreamt *sleepless death* so precisely if I've never even looked at the prophecy?

My stomach soured at the idea of being shackled to such a fate. Every story of old spoke of divine and unchangeable fate, but I did not incline to be such a slave.

Desperate for answers, I skimmed the book, looking for anything that would at least give some knowledge to this haunting peculiarity. After a few minutes of reading, the only thing I understood was why the book lacked authorship. The anonymous author painted vividly monstrous descriptions of the mercenary leader of the Black Legion, whom he thought to be Cypherus' Shadow incarnate.

Though the author's accusations were disturbing, his analysis of this leader being the opposite of Cypherus was comforting: along with a very detailed and gruesome list of how evil this man was. In contrast to Cypherus, the leader seemed to be impossibly immortal, hence *sleepless death*, which would be opposite of Cypherus' natural life. It was impossible to be a Human and live for hundreds of sols. That was something only the Drakin and Elves could achieve, but somehow this man had been the same leader for the Black Legion for the last three hundred sols.

A breath of relief flowed through me, even though there were still fears that this theory was inaccurate.

Regardless, I did not intend to find out.

Having somewhat doused the greatest anxiety burning within me, I decided to drift into the Holy Dark section to comfort my mind. By heart, I knew where my guilty pleasure, *Tales of the Old World*, would be.

As I entered the candlelit aisle, I could hear the Skyyan language being spoken on the other side. To know that any of Queen Nera's company would be interested in knowledge was a surprise, but given they were surrounded by the seas, I could understand why they'd want to hide away from the ocean's whispers and explore the worlds beyond, all within their minds.

Sir Alduaura and I also passed by a winged Fhaolin, most likely from the College of Man, his talons clawing an ancient scroll and making me nervous. The owlish Averite looked to be a pupil of the Cordis sect from the College, his midnight robe and white gilded hood distinguishing him as such, but I shared in Renborg's disgust for those who turned their bodies to beasts using Godstone.

Shuddering, I realized it was because I hated my own disfigurement.

Drifting by the Averite-like smoke from a funeral pyre that soon disappears without a second thought, I picked up one of the numberless chambersticks for light to find an ancient tale of sorrow that my heart of ink often bled for to escape from reality. The copper handle was too slippery for my gloves, so I had to take one off to ensure a good grip. I didn't want to burn down the only place of significance in my life, even if I despised some of the people who frequented it. To my chagrin, however, it also revealed my shame beneath which my eyes immediately averted.

It was doubtless that Sir Alduaura could see my flesh through his helm in the dark library, but I still held the candle close to my chest to avoid his sight nonetheless.

The flickering shadows swam around me as I approached the stone shelf where the *Tale of Turrok's Night* was held inside of the leather bound *Tales of the Old World*. It was just another book on the shelf and just as forgotten as all the rest.

Few would ever care to read its story.

Setting the candle aside on the floor, I thumbed through the brittle yet familiar pages, skimming past the Lycan's cultic origins and moon worship to the most brutishly realistic story that put to shame tales from even renowned Human storytellers.

At least that was my opinion, but I was probably right.

The strings of my soul were unweaved as I read the laments of Turrok, who weeped from the fate of his soul being eternally banished to the Abishx because of his wolfish inheritance, wishing he never had to suffer such a tragic existence. My being was refreshed with hope in seeing he had found meaning in his mate and their son they had together, but they too were taken away by the cruel hand of fate that cares not for one's soul. Even Turrok's revenge on the mercenaries who kidnapped his family proved fruitless when he found his son Jerok beheaded and his beloved Kaia dying like a fire, choked of all oxygen and innocence by the lustful hands of men.

My eyes graced the last line in his beautifully dark tale that gripped my worn heart and solidified my lonely pursuit of death, quieting any doubts that my soul had about being snuffed out like the flickering candle that gave me futile light in the library of shadows:

"His mate's breath did not return from the moon, and the last embers of Turrok's hope turned to ash."

My irises swelled with the familiar hopeless—

"Since when did Ronians have sunflowers for eyes?" a woman said on the other side of the stone bookshelf, her Skyyan accent awakening me like the cold spray of the ocean.

My eyes locked with hers across the sea of books, and only her eyes were I graced with. Even in the dark candlelight, I could see the depths of wisdom in her glimmering emeralds. She must have been a noblewoman from Skyya here for the wedding. It was very verboten for me to speak with her given my lowborn status, but I couldn't help but feel intrigued.

"I was unaware the Skyyans were blessed with such cunning intellect, and eyes that would make the forests of Laconnia jealous."

The mysterious woman stifled a laugh, which I could tell from the raised laughing lines near her perceptive eyes. Her voice was most definitely Skyyan as she spoke the Ronic language, with the roots of the beautifully elegant Velian tongue of the eastern Elves and the pridefully crisp Oarnic tribal tongue evident in her speech.

"I pray you are as intelligent to answer my question then," she said.

The tiniest smile flickered across my face.

"Well, if it pleases my lady, I am no Ronian."

Together, we walked in synchronous pace on opposite sides of the long bookshelf, our eyes holding fast to one another as they danced in the flickering shadows of the candle I quickly retrieved.

Sir Alduaura and my miseries were completely forgotten behind me.

"No?" she said. "Then where are you from?"

"My mother was purchased from Karthos, and I am a product of that." It was blunt, and perhaps too much too fast. She would most likely excuse herself from the conversation now that I revealed my worthless status, even though I was adopted into the nobility. But it was honest, and something within me wanted to be a transparent book that she could read.

"*Karthos?*" she said, disgust hidden but slightly evident in her tone. But the repulsion didn't matter to me, for she surprised me by continuing our conversation instead of leaving like all the rest would have. "Interesting, and who does she serve?"

My breath shook as I gulped down the sorrows that rose in my throat. "Sh-she has served the grave since my birth."

The air changed between us as we walked in silence.

"Forgive me," she continued, "but be strengthened by the nobleness of your life."

"There's nothing noble about being a slave's bastard." My words came off too quick and full of surprising venom. Even I recoiled at the harsh tone of my words towards her.

She took a moment before responding, almost as if she was trying to deliver her words carefully. "You have risen above that fate to honor your mother, have you not? I would say that's honorable."

"And how would you know?"

"The knight seems to be your slave, which would reason a higher status than most, especially of slaves or freemen."

The soft clinking of metal greaves behind me proved her point. Although, it felt like I was the slave in this particular situation, but nonetheless, an acute observation.

Is that why she stayed then? Was it only because she perceived me to be of the same pointless status that she found me worthy to speak to?

"And what about your father?" she persisted.

"I think it is only fair if I get to ask you a question."

"Please."

A smile danced lightly on my lips.

"What made you want to explore the Library of Cypheria?"

She paused.

"Are women not allowed to read in your empire?" she said, this time with her own tonal edge. It was strong, unwavering in its delivery. Fear crept into my heart that I had potentially upset her. But I wanted to know, to see if there was more beneath the surface of the usual pretentious nobility.

"Of course they are," I said, smiling as I tried to lighten the conversation, "we want all of our citizens to produce more taxes."

A typical noblewoman would have gawked at the comment, offended by such truthful insensitivity. But she did not. Instead, another suppressed smile sprouted near her glittering, green eyes as our synchronous walk resumed again, together.

The meaninglessness of titles and rules appeared evident to her, though she did not fully display it.

Maybe that's why she chose to speak with me.

"If it is not your realm, then it is your perception of mine. Are you afraid of a woman who can handle a sword or tame the seas better than most men?"

Part of me wanted to laugh, but as the memories of the largely female Thallasiun guards who protected the Skyyan fleet on their sea-bearing Poecampi horses emerged in my mind from several days ago, I reconsidered. The gilled and lankishly tall Averite guards had proved quite a stir on their arrival amongst Renborg's city guard, and I did not wish to become their enemy.

Especially if I encountered one in the waters.

"I'm not afraid of anything," I said, opening further the book of my heart.

"Even death?"

"Especially that." And though it was mostly true, there were times when it was completely the opposite.

As was the case for this moment.

Her eyes squinted at my comment. "I've never met a man who seriously meant that. So then, what makes a woman in your eyes? Is it her strength that gives her worth?"

Before answering, I took a deep breath in contemplation.

"The composure of one's body does not make one beautiful. It is what guides their heart that makes them so."

We came to the end of the bookshelf.

There emerged a peaceful rest in our conversation, and it carried no awkward overtones. Instead, it was like we were soaking in every word the other had said and letting it sink into our troubled hearts to determine if the other's organ of love could reciprocate the drummings of our lonely souls.

Like the intense hunger of the poor, I yearned to know more of her priceless heart that was so clearly evident in every nourishing word she said to mine.

She was refreshingly different from the rest.

"I'm surprised to say your answer doesn't reflect the animalistic desires of other men," she said, just out of sight in the shadows.

"I guess we have both proven there is more about the other than our eyes can perceive," I said, which I imagined she smiled at.

"Tell me, what is your name, boy from Karthos?"

I let my eyes fall to the barrier of books between us. "My name is Morgan."

"And what is your family name, Morgan?"

"Krios. But that doesn't really matter. Who might you be?"

The faintest whisper of Skyyan drifted through the shelves, belonging to another feminine voice that was much darker and somewhat masculine, a growl even. Carefully stepping back to glimpse who was behind her, all I could see through the spaces between the books was what looked to be a warrior with a horned helmet.

Why does she look so familiar?

"I must leave, Morgan," she said, awakening me from my thoughts. "I pray you don't drown in these books. The world would be a much darker and less joyful place without your light."

Before I could respond, the mysterious woman and whoever was with her disappeared in the library's maze of stories.

I almost broke my honor, whatever good that was, when I tried to run to the other side of the aisle to catch a glimpse of whoever carried this life-giving heart, but Sir Alduaura created a stoic and unmovable barrier with his hand to save my respect for her wishes.

The candle almost dropped from my hand when I realized it had been laying against my forearm after I stopped paying attention to it from our conversation. Looking at my flesh, I grimaced at the daily remembrance of the Hagroak magic and what it did to me. The unnaturally empty feeling of pain from the flame soon filled itself with the daunting loneliness that had fled while I talked to her.

Unlike Karlata's flesh, I was encapsulated by the intrigue of who this woman was and the glimpse of beauty from her heart that I was fortunate to discover.

Did her soul yearn to see the dawn like my own? Free from the everlasting night that our souls were born into, alone, to bask in the intertwining warmth of another?

For a brief moment, the peculiarities of my dream and the weary steps I would take to the cliffs tonight were all but forgotten.

Chapter 4
Before Death Let Us Part

Renborg is a proud and industrious empire. Standing twelve million strong, the Ronians are devoted to education and establishing a prosperous economy. Most elites and the slowly emerging middle class have their children educated through tutors or the College of Man to teach them science, history, politics, poetry, literature, and philosophy. Unfortunately, few families task them with the study of Solbok anymore. Since writing Skallgends is an annual tradition due to the state-sponsored Valkryn Faith, literacy rates are astoundingly higher than any other kingdom or empire, rivaling that of Kapitol. Even the lower classes know the basics of reading and writing, though less artistically, as Skallgends are highly valued in Ronian society and are read with great fervor and fascination.

Renborg is largely multiethnic with many territories, with races consisting of Humans, Dwarves, Elves, Averites, and Drakin (though Drakin are barred from citizenship and many are slaves). Ronians strive for perfectionism and structure, managing time to the most minute detail and organizing every dimension of power. This ideal leads many to dread failure and to hand out compliments only when perfection is clear, which is why most are never late.

Chronicles of Renborg: King's Edition
"The Culture of Renborg"
Piluch Joffersun: Master of Histories

I was late to the wedding.

Time slipped through my fingers as I sat in the lengthening shadows of the graveyard of knowledge. Perplexion gripped me after glimpsing the faintest hue of a star upon the darkest night of my life, who, to much misfortune, also slipped through my fingers and only added to the growing Shadow of that night.

When she left, whoever she was, the roaring tidal waves of my mind came back to haunt me with all of its whisperings from the sea. I was alone again, save my unwanted escort who stood unmoving beside me.

A collection of whispers and hushed laughter broke through from one of the lower levels of the library, drawing my attention. When I leaned over the railing out of curiosity, all I could see were two young and finely dressed Elves who were becoming familiar with one another in the shadows of the library, indulging in their lusts with an abundance of joy.

Together.

With a great sigh, I declined into the shadows of my mind again.

Alone.

The leather of my gloves squeezed against itself as I devised a plan to uncheck myself from the cruel move played by Gulmund on this board of fate: I would attend the wedding as promised, but then I would escape from these shackles of life.

At last I would finally rest.

But my heart returned to its anxious state when the windows to the library became darker than my mood, indicating my heavily shunned tardiness to what would be my brother's worst but also best night.

With Sir Alduaura acting as my silhouette, we immediately flew down the winding and candle ridden stairs to leave the heavy stone walls of the library.

At once, an explosion of colors, lights, laughter, and eclectic music engaged all of my senses. The streets were packed almost shoulder to shoulder with every kind of Human, Dwarf, Elf, Skyyan, and even Laconnian, from all parts of Divonholm and its neighboring borders, here to celebrate a grand wedding that had been in preparation for months. Or to make a profit from it, as sprinkled throughout the hordes of people were various shops that had been erected for this very day to serve glowing foods and smoking wines, along with selling strange gifts to inebriated guests like severed unicorn horns that had long been extinct but were most certainly authentic.

"I guarantee it!" a Hurinzvalese seller proudly claimed beside us, twisting his handlebar mustache as two Dwarves dressed in gilded leather examined the horn, trying their best to hold it in the light in their drunken state.

All of the chaos was almost overwhelming, especially since I was late.

"Try to keep up," I muttered to Sir Alduaura before pushing my way past the two Dwarves who longed for the false immortality of the horn and into the massive crowds, becoming quickly consumed in the sea of flesh as I tried hopelessly to run to the palace garden.

My nose flooded with every odor of perfume as I weaved through the elites of Divonholm who had just enough gold to come here to celebrate but were not invited to the exclusive wedding party that was meant for the highest of royalty. The crowds noticed me not as I slipped through them, sprinting through the openings where none gathered.

At last, we finally arrived at the palace's Garden of Truth while the sun was dying beneath the Ryggdrack Mountains.

My lungs struggled for breath after running without end to reach the wedding in time. We were greeted by a large procession of Watchmen who guarded the entrance of the garden and parted at the sight of us, but one man would not move out of our way.

Piluch's grey beard huffed in disappointment when he saw me approach.

"Have you forgotten the essence of manners?" he said, leading me briskly into the enormous garden of glowing trees.

Piluch splashed hurriedly through one of the five streams that came from the center oak, leading me into the great congregation of Renborg's royalty, richest nobles, and ambassadors from other kingdoms. Their powdered eyes glossed over me like I was some lowly servant, their painted lips thirsting for the wine to be poured in order to smoothen their political machinations that they were undoubtedly weaving.

"I apologize, sir, I was—"

"Far away in your books, I know. But never mind that, go and sit by your family! Gulmund will be most displeased by your tardiness."

Bowing my head low, I tried walking past him but was stopped when he gently raised his hand. Looking at Piluch in surprise, he gently smiled.

"If it lightens your heart, you won't have to worry about Karlata tonight."

Blushing, I said, "I don't know what you're talking about. Did Volsung refuse to come?"

"The King thought it would be best for him to stay in Hebsund to monitor the Lycan's lunar festival. You know how wild they get on the eclipse, let alone the bigger celebration they'll have with the solar eclipse later this sol."

Imaginations of their zealous orgies that they considered worship revolted me, and how far they had degraded morally was insulting.

I guess the Lycan and the Ronains shared something in common, after all.

"And the real reason?"

Piluch sighed at my expected inquisitiveness. "The King invited Orpheus Talon and his brother, Menander, but Volsung refused to even be in the same vicinity as the Lycan Ambassadors. Volsung's stubbornness might appear threatening to the Lycan, but maybe we will gain some more silver in negotiations of our lands with his sterner edge. As Solbok teaches, 'Politics is battle without blood.'"

Piluch gave me a grin before sending me off into the crowd, as if he expected me to find his political lessons humorous.

He was right, but I didn't want to show it.

With gentle steps, I parted through the crowd to where the royal family stood, my expression a colorless grey as I forced a smile at the noble Lords who recognized me. Though I wanted to be alone in my thoughts, I was thrust into unwanted conversations that were absolutely and tiringly mindless. Though, I was able to endure the false niceties of the nobility by glancing upon the lamps hanging like golden apples above us from the trees that encircled the hallowed one in the middle.

The colors were beyond beautiful. To fight the tears that emerged from glimpsing upon such beauty was a strenuous task. The Garden of Truth hosted a vast array of green and purple flowers throughout the rings of stone benches, of which wedding guests were standing near or already seated.

The lovely palette of lights and flowers that were absent in the sea were briefly forgotten as I made my way to Valena and Sigmund, passing by those of high *importance.*

"I heard Jean-Marque amassed his own forces despite his father's will," a Hurinzvalese noble said, twirling his large mustache. "Something has gotten into the Prince's head. Does he not think his father will grant him the throne of Hurinzval?"

"Do you think Nera killed her husband?" a lanky Elf said in another conversation.

"Gulmund finally did it," the Master of Kin whispered to himself, his Kapitolian accent and words catching my thoughts in curiosity.

My eavesdropping faltered when I accidentally bumped into the Laconnian ambassadors, spilling the wine of the tallest Lycan. His fur was grey and his robes a darker shade of the moon. Backing away from the Lycan whom I had run into, I gave the wolfish hybrid a curt apology as he brushed his garments in annoyance. The Lycan was about to say something when his wolven eyes saw my royal cape.

"Ah, you must be the boy the Mordrakes adopted," the grey Lycan said, offering me a smile with his sharp rows of wine-stained teeth instead of his previous snarl. "I am Orpheus Talon."

"Pleasure to finally meet you," I said, though I cared not. "Gulmund speaks highly of you and your moderate faction within the Pentarchy."

"I wish his brother would think the same," Orpheus said. "However, perhaps Volsung takes too literally the motto of our faction to *never forget*, as I see he is not here for the wedding."

"Perhaps it is best, brother," the midnight Lycan said beside Orpheus.

Orpheus turned sharply upon the darker Lycan, though in best efforts to remain polite, steadied his voice. "Menander, our growing population must do its best to make peace with our neighbors if we are to have the land we need to survive."

"Forgive me, brother," Menander said, bowing low to his kin. "Shall I fetch you another wine?"

Orpheus Talon hesitated. "No, I will be well. The wedding is about to begin. A pleasure meeting you, er…"

"Morgan," I said as Orpheus gave a nod of farewell.

The Lycan returned their attention to the sea of wedding guests and the coming procession as I began to walk towards Valena, all except for the midnight Lycan who stood quietly beside Orpheus. Feeling watched, I risked a glance behind me to find Menander's scarlet eyes fixated upon mine. He stood like a predator watching its prey, but I quickly looked away, not caring to play games of ego with whoever this Menander was.

Most likely someone of unimportance like everyone here, though all their egotistical pride would claim otherwise.

Sir Alduaura and I squeezed next to Valena and Sigmund at the front of the crowds. Sigmund's boyish face exploded into joy upon seeing me, jumping into my arms as he usually did.

"Morgan!" Sigmund whispered.

"I'm here," I smiled faintly, which was true for just a few more hours. "Where is Philomela?"

"Sleepy," Sigmund said before nestling into my chest.

"Do you always have to be late?" Valena whispered harshly, the few remaining black hairs on her head most likely greying at the stress we often caused her.

Almost immediately, Valena gave me a quick hug and ruffled my hair.

She meant well despite the constant stress we caused her.

The other half of her anxieties stood quietly at the altar. When Lucien's eyes caught mine, his embroidered royal cape seemed to deflate as he let out a sigh of relief, along with a quick smile.

Standing next to his father inside the garden's hollowed oak, Lucien looked nothing like the King; Gulmund appeared tired as he braced himself against the tree, but still managed to display his chest high with confidence before the nobles which ruled the empire but whom he ruled. They were both dressed in Renborg's green tunic and black surcoats. Lucien's joyful face was in sharp contrast to his father as he waited patiently beside him, but I could recognize he was forcing the emotion as it was the unnatural expression that I also wore to cloak what hid beneath.

His hesitation to marry the Princess perplexed me, who I could barely see standing with her back to Lucien in the hollowed tree. Like most of my thoughts, I didn't believe my opinion on her was reliable since I had not seen what the Princess looked like when she and Nera arrived on their Carrack ships a week ago.

Instead, I had been in my room when they arrived, perfecting the letter I would leave for Lucien tonight. In the tear-soaked Skallgend, I explained my decision to quietly close the pages of my story and place it amongst the countless others who were similarly forgotten in the uncaring oceans of time that took us all. But in my final words, I also wrote of how much I loved him, Sigmund, and Philomela, and how I was sorry to disappoint them once again.

I wouldn't ruin his wedding by giving it to him in person, but part of me wanted to so I could hear how much my life mattered to him; perhaps a feeble attempt to stop the torrent of worthlessness that would eventually swallow me.

The doubts and turmoil that flooded my mind were only briefly stopped by the one thing that was absolutely clear to me and which I had discovered in my thoughts within the library: I knew where to leave my letter for him, which was exactly how I would escape to the colorless and eternal waves.

The muffled talk of the crowds abruptly came to an end when Piluch, joined by five trumpeters who stood over each stream coming from the center tree, ordered them to blow their instruments for attention.

"Welcome everyone, welcome," Piluch said, circling the streams while his fluffy grey hair tousled in the ocean breeze that swept its way upwards from the sea below, as if a dark reminder for me.

"Thank you all for coming to this historic wedding," Piluch continued. "We are here to celebrate the union of not only two souls, or two families, or two generations, but of two realms. The significance of this day cannot be more exemplified.

"Today, Thaedum the 21st of Valqr, the day of the summer solstice, will be a day remembered for centuries to come. Today is the end of our religious differences and the beginning of our new lives as we stand boldly in this dark world, together, and uphold the Mighty Mother's values that unite and give us purpose. Bond bearers please!"

A female servant from Skyya and a male from Renborg approached Piluch on either side, carrying the Godstone wedding armbands for Egret and Lucien. Piluch unsheathed the Sacred Blade of Asculum I, holding the twisted Dragonstone blade high for all to admire.

Paying little attention to the replicated blade, I instead watched the rising fear in Lucien's inflating chest.

The pain he was about to endure would not be trivial.

Lucien and Gulmund turned to face Egret and Nera at Piluch's gentle insistence. As they turned, I was finally able to see what my brother's bride looked like. To say I was perplexed would be an understatement.

She wasn't stunning like the women of Hornsvall around me, who were most likely judging Egret for her complete lack of hair next to their brutish men who sprouted spruce mustaches. Instead of hair, she displayed a white headdress with lapis lazuli jewels sewn into it. It was surprising to see a princess without hair, mostly because it would have made anyone who wasn't royal unable to wed, for hair was believed in Renborg to grow and reflect the heart. Those without it were believed to have hearts of dangerous mystery.

But it was as if Egret was proud that she defied what many of us were expecting of a princess. She stood with her shoulders back and exuded nothing less than the fierce bravery of an Akaidian warrior.

And though her bravery was honorable, I began to understand why Lucien was hesitant in marriage because of her stark lack of exterior beauty, though her slender face and sharp eyes hinted of potential wonder underneath. But to even judge her for her appearance was hypocritical for me, for I shared an undesirable flesh as well.

In a way, I guess I pitied her, though in her apparent strength she appeared to need none of it. There was something *familiar* in the way she held herself.

"And now," Piluch said, holding the twisted knife between them, "I ask you, Lucien Mordrake of Renborg, the heir to Cypherus and the defender of his Shadow, do you take Egret Thyna of Skyya to be your wife, forever intertwined like your blood will be now and even beyond your destiny in Solæf?"

Lucien hesitated for the briefest moment as his eyes flashed to look up at Egret, but quickly said, "I accept the Mother's fate."

Piluch nodded and cut from Lucien's lower left wrist down to his bicep, being careful to avoid most of his veins, which was followed immediately by the Ronian bond bearer who clasped the golden ring upon his bicep. Piluch asked the same of Egret, who bravely said her vow, her voice not shaking, and she received the same cut along her arm, looking to Nera for approval who watched like a predaceous hawk behind her.

Strangely, Nera didn't look concerned at her daughter's oozing wound.

"Now," Piluch said while taking a small step back, "embrace your bride and be united in the blood of your new family, blessed and made sacred by the Mother!"

Blood splattered Egret's sea blue dress when her's and Lucien's bleeding arms clasped together, their fingers treading each other's wedding armbands and permanently marking their fates. The crowds erupted into celebration at the marriage of Renborg and Skyya, with Gulmund presenting his son's bloody hand victoriously, albeit roughly, in the air for his empire while Nera turned around and did the same for hers.

Sommerian wine, juva, flavah buns, and even my favorite vybernut pastries were soon dispensed to the array of guests who were enjoying themselves too much already. Along with a horde of other desserts and alcoholic drinks, the guests descended upon all of it at once, leaving the rings of ceremonial benches for the tables draped with nourishments just beyond them.

It would be a while before Lucien was free for my final

goodbye, so I quickly departed from Valena and Sigmund, giving Sigmund a crushing hug and Valena a true smile before leaving to devour the crushed walnut and the honey-like vybernut pastry, promising to return.

By the time Sir Alduaura caught up to me, I had already finished it and was drinking my final mug of juva, savoring its golden nourishment. It was a strange feeling to be drinking the awakening brew for the last time, for the milk of the foreign, golden beans had kept me up throughout the endless nights of my life to write poetry no one would ever know or to read stories from history that would be like my own: forgotten.

Discarding my empty cup amidst the basket of other mugs drained of juva, I shuffled my feet to say goodbye to Sigmund who came running to my arms through the horde of guests.

"Where are you going?" Sigmund asked, his voice full of innocence that I wished could remain forever.

"To get some rest," I said, loud enough for Valena to hear as she approached us.

"He means he will be up till twilight," Valena said, smirking as she came to hug me. "Don't do anything foolish now."

"I won't," I lied.

Tears began to swell in Valena's eyes as she looked at me. And though I had no idea what thoughts ran through her mind, I knew that she loved me like a son; for though Lucien and I brought her much stress, she was the only continual presence who encouraged and loved us throughout the sols. It was especially apparent in the ever-growing absence of Gulmund, who had reclined more and more to the shadows of himself after the early demise of Kyllian.

"Best run along now, Morgan," she finally said. "But not too quickly!"

Weaving through the crowd of colors and races before my eyes burst forth with my own emotions, I raced to reach my brother.

Piluch and Lucien were engaging with the many royalty of Sommer, Hornsvall, Skyya, and even the Dwarves of Anumnalas, doing their best to tirelessly thank them for coming.

Gulmund had disappeared to the tables of wine where he was indulging with Renborg's Grand Ambassador Monroe, though the King was not laughing from the Dwarf's latest immoral conquests in the red streets of Kapitol he returned from and promptly told of. The King just continued to drink quietly, alone in his misery that he so often hid in order to rule.

By the time I reached my brother, Nera and Egret had already left and were heading towards the royal palace with their elite guards, the Suffra encompassing them like a defensive ring of horns with their antlered and decorated helmets.

"Morgan!" Lucien said, interrupting a conversation with Orpheus and Menander. Lucien looked grateful to escape, wrapping his pale arms around me in embrace. "For a moment, I thought you were going to pass on my wedding."

"Of course not!" I said, squeezing him a little tighter.

Lucien's arm was wrapped in a bandage to stop the bleeding, but I didn't care if the blood got on my clothes. I was wearing black anyways, and the oceans would wash it all away.

"Your Highness," Piluch said as he guided the Lycan away to give us some privacy, the dark Lycan never letting his cunning gaze leave the Prince, "the Queen and her daughter will not be pleased with waiting. I suggest you head there straight away."

"Of course," Lucien said, slowly pulling away from me as if in pain. "I'll head there in a moment."

Piluch scrunched his face like he didn't believe him but ultimately gave us a little privacy in these last moments.

"So, you're a man now?" I said, trying my best to act like everything was normal.

"If according to your primal definition, then not yet."

"Must you be so ungratefully vulgar?" I teased.

His rosy lips stretched across his glacial skin to form a smile, a real one this time.

"I won't be long I imagine," Lucien said. "Once I'm through, how about you and I take a dip in the Strumma like we used to?"

"Near the cave?"

"Like always."

But before I could respond, Gulmund staggered towards us and hooked his meaty hand into Lucien's shoulder, his breath reeking with debauchery.

"Time to seal the marriage, son," Gulmund said, laughing to himself while pushing my brother forward to the royal palace.

"Wait!" I shouted as I grabbed Lucien's hand, yanking him back into one more embrace. Gulmund moaned with annoyance and he could probably suspect something was off, but I couldn't let him taint our last memory together.

"I love you, Lucien," I said, my lips trembling. "You're going to make for a great king, I just know it."

"Thank you, Morgan," Lucien said, nestling his head into my midnight hair one last time. "Promise me you'll be here when I get back?"

My eyes twinkled from the fading sunset as I pulled back.

"I promise," I lied.

Gulmund said something in anger before dragging Lucien away from me into a destiny with Egret in which he did not want, for whatever reason. As for me, I wasn't chained to any responsibility, expectation, or worth, so I was free to choose what I wanted to do.

Turning to the dying sun as it sank beneath the mountains, I knew in my fading heart where my path lay, where the trail would end when the song would cease.

It was time for the death of destiny.

Chapter 5
Whispering Waves

O bitter blade, song of Dragon bane,
Whence shall you cease, shall I share their sleep?
As their bones shall bend, so shall my story end
Forever forgotten when the sea consumes the sand.

Solbok
Eldren Wars, 40:10-11
"The Grief of Cypherus"

The roaring sea churned in bitter excitement at my internal approach, beckoning me forth with each heavy, fearful step that lumbered up the stairs. The bedroom wing of the palace came ever closer, my feet ever slower, surer, yet anxious nonetheless.

Upon opening the stair door, I wasn't surprised to see Queen Nera and her Suffra standing outside of Lucien's bedroom next to mine, but they gave me a curious glance at my arrival since I wasn't the Prince that Egret was waiting for; their disappointment would soon fade away.

After an awkward greeting, I told Sir Alduaura that I planned to retire for the evening given my feigned exhaustion from the wedding, his silent glare telling me that he didn't believe it, but he relented. Once I thanked him and locked my door, I waited quietly at my bed for what felt like forever, blowing out the candles in my room and ruffling my sheets to make it sound as if I were asleep. Hearing not a sound, I softly opened the rusty window, the hinges creaking much to my anxiety as they swung outwards.

There came no reaction from the hall.

Breathing a sigh of relief, I climbed up into the window

and settled my feet carefully on the outer ledge, this time being cautious not to fall. The stone wall was mostly flat by design, save for the small ledge that connected the bedroom windows. During the day and from below, the ledge looked much simpler to traverse, trivial even. Looking down in the dark, what was once the easy path was now dressed in shadow, begging me to fall. Its whispers were only marred by the drinking and roaring of the wedding guests just beyond, their joy so ever out of reach.

Moving carefully along the ledge to the bedroom window of Philomela, I hugged the cold wall as tightly as a newborn did their mother.

At last, my shaking fingers clawed their way through Philomela's window, pulling it aside and letting me in. My eyes almost broke with tears when I saw her face. Philomela was wrapped up in a cloud of blankets to keep her cozy on this most lonely, cold night.

Such an innocent bundle of life deserving nothing but love.

A hiss from the shadows made my skin crawl. The royal family's cabat coasted across the room to chase after a mouse, her feline wings giving the rodent probably more of a scare than me. The anxiety caused by the castle pet melted away at the tender sight of Philomela whose snores fluttered from the crib.

Caressing her pale cheeks, I tried not to wake her up to this cruel world. Bending down, I gave her a kiss on her forehead, but when I stood up, her tiny fingers tried to clasp onto my nose.

My heart folded into silent sobs as I pulled away.

One day she would cease to reach upwards because she found nothing to cling to, no wonder in the stars to look forward to. Her own empty whisper would be the only response as the stars failed to catch her breath. She would come to the bitter realization, just as I had, of the empty void within that could not last and should not be.

Or maybe she would be blind to it as so many were and would be.

If I could pray for anything, it would be for the latter. For though Sigmund and Philomela both had my heart, there was something so precious about Philomela and the light that sparkled in her eyes, brighter than the stars.

Maybe she would see that the lights in the reigning night above merely tried to reflect her own wonder.

If she would grow up to overcome the darkness, I would know not.

My hands shook as I took the Skallgend I had written for Lucien and placed it beside her. It unfurled amidst the shadows and I could barely see my writing, but I knew it by heart, for that was the origin of the pain that drenched the scroll in unrelenting anguish:

Shadows dance across the flickering walls, their source of illumination a mystery.
Shackled like the sleeping slaves, I tried to find truth in the shifting silhouettes.
Wisemen say choose any contour, worship at the altar of my own understanding.
I listened; desperate hands with veins of hate unable to grasp the vaporous shapes.
Here one second and gone the next, like our lives on this planet: meaningless.
My tears are the only truth I can feel, Lucien, but even they soon evaporate.
The meek and mindless act content with their formless truth, but not I.
No, I will wrap these chains around my neck to be free of my failures.
My mother died while giving me life. In a snap, I will return it,
A gift broken by my father and deemed unworthy by men.
I know my departure will hurt you, but please forgive,
For the pain I feel with each breath is unbearable.
Your faithful love has carried me all of my life,
But the burden of purposelessness is too heavy.
The shame of imperfection, a crushing weight.
If I can ask for anything, please grant this:

Guide the children away from this darkness.
Be the calm in the storm of their thoughts.
Collect their tears so that they ~~believe~~
Know that their souls are important.
Give them hope that life
Is worth living.
I love you.
Morgan.

The ink of my sorrows dripped and smudged in some places because of the tears that spilled from me. However, the rivers of suffering would be even deeper for Lucien, who undoubtedly would find my note to be selfish and agonizing on the day of his wedding.

It… is better you don't know, I thought, crushing the Skallgend as my tears wetted its worthless words. The hearth in Philomela's room soon relinquished such pain from Lucien as I cast it into the fire.

Instead, I hastily wrote a note that would still convey my eternal absence but that would suffer Lucien the least:

Lucien,

I have to leave Renborg, but my heart will be with you forever. I am sorry, brother. You are going to be a great King. I love you.

Morgan

As I set the new note beside Philomela, my weeping became a howl, loud enough that would wake up even the farthest dogs of the empire.

And they did.

The tears of my heart were hardened when Sir Alduaura suddenly burst into her room to apprehend me, startling Philomela into a terrified fit.

With no time to lose, I took one last look at Philomela so I could have peace of my approaching night before jumping back to avoid the knight's grasp that pierced through the shadows. Before he could ensnare me back in chains, I leapt out of the window and aimed to land onto the ledge.

Though I should have been slightly more careful.

Completely missing the ledge, I almost plummeted to the ground below if it weren't for my immediate reaction to grasp the ledge as I fell. My gloved hands almost slipped as I frantically moved between the ridges of stone to escape Alduaura. I risked a look back and locked eyes through the slit of the knight's helmet, who ducked back into the room, most likely running to catch me at the next window. But I had planned for that, because the bedroom he would try to catch me crossing was—

And then my heart stopped, as did the soft weeping of the woman with emerald eyes who captured mine at her window.

My heart did not prepare for this.

For a moment, all we could do was hold each other's gaze in the candlelight like we did in the library. But my eyes betrayed me when they drank their fill of her exposed vulnerability that was reserved only for her husband whom she was waiting for. My heart became a storm of lust and shame that threatened to tear it apart in that one enduring moment.

When my eyes returned to her familiar emeralds, the fear in them was replaced with rage, her veins spreading across her smooth scalp like lighting. There was commotion at the door behind her, but Egret paid no heed to it and was already moving. In one seamless move, she covered herself with Lucien's sheets and threw a Godstone knife at me. The blade whistled through the air, sheathing itself where my hand was moments before. Luckily, I let go before it did, but that left me without a grip and only a fall from grace.

My body crushed through the limbs of a nearby tree, landing with a thud to the Bludhgrass garden below. The shame was as heavy as the force that knocked out my breath, weakening my resolve to live even more. Wheezing, I shakily rose to my feet.

Everything inside me was on fire.

Sir Alduaura would not stop until I was enslaved to this life again, so I had to move.

Until I could run, I limped to the gates of the government district. There was no way I could scale the royal district's wall to jump to the waves below, so the government gate leading out to the open Bludhlands would have to do.

The Ronians were oblivious to me as I ran through the parading streets dripping with wine and inebriated dancing. Any who did notice me would soon forget my passing. Even the Watchmen at the royal gate didn't seem to mind that I was running from my life.

The only exception was a handful of Watchmen who seemed alarmed that I was running, despite the other guards around them who were distracted by the dancing Elven courtesans arrayed in their garments of glittering feathers. I almost stopped because they seemed ever so slightly out of place, just like the Elves who were seducing them. And for a moment I thought I saw one of the Watchmen whisper something to the one next to him, their focus trained on me in case I tried to ruin their night. But behind me I could hear the clatter of metal greaves hitting the road and getting closer, so the mystery would have to wait indefinitely.

I don't care to find out anyway.

At my current pace, I would never make it to the ocean. So to quicken my speed, I ran to a Ronian soldier who was transporting Drakin slaves in chains. Against whatever was left of my morality, I pushed the soldier off his horse and took off with his stallion towards the final gate.

I almost plowed through a group of Visians when I shot a look of concern back at the soldier and his slaves. But in risking a look back, what I saw mystified me even more than the Watchmen and Elven courtesans: the Drakin slaves and their master glared at me in unison, with the Ronian not worrying about his back exposed to the flaming-haired slaves who crowded behind him.

If I didn't know they were slaves, I would've guessed they were the soldier's friends.

The night couldn't get any stranger, but at least it would be a memorable one. Then again, all memories are temporary and soon forgotten. Only the sirens of the deep would know my story.

Charging the horse through the last gate that led to the Bludhlands, I came upon the same scene of dancing Elves and several Watchmen who were looking at me more intensely than usual. Shaking my head in disgust at them, I abandoned the wretched city of Renborg and all of its pretentious citizens behind, the fog swallowing me in my only comfort.

The tree that Lucien and I burned this morning appeared in the far distance and was like the embers of a dying fire; a leap from its cliff could hasten my fall to sleep, but any miscalculation could also pierce me upon a rock.

Maybe that's what I deserved.

Perhaps in cowardice, I avoided the charcoal tree and led the horse down a different path on the sea cliffs to the foaming Strumma below. It was too dark to see the hidden path that Lucien and I always took to play in the ocean, but thankfully the horse had better eyesight than I and guided us safely to the rocky shores.

As we descended to the sea, the fog opened slightly in the distance. Through its web of mist, I saw a handful of dark ships gliding silently through the waters as they neared Renborg's seaport. Anxiety pounded in my heart at the eerie sight of the torchless ships.

They are most likely Ronian ships returning from the Drakin siege of Madea in Yarahm, I thought.

Though, that mattered to me not, nor did the dream in which I had of its future. I would never understand what it all meant, and part of me was fine with that.

Breathing a heavy sigh, I reached the site of my eternal departure, the colorless tides frothing in excitement at my solemn decision to sink beneath its waves.

It was time, at last; yet, fear still remained.

Letting the salty air soak in my nostrils one last time, I dismounted and gave the steed a quick brush along its coarse mane for doing me this merciful favor.

"Thank you," I whispered with a shaking breath before turning to the inky waters, leading the horse in tow.

My feet were as heavy as my thoughts as I lumbered to the ocean grave with the horse at my side.

No one had ever actually helped me in ridding myself of this pain. When the King or whoever he hired tried to help me from the well of my thoughts, all I was told was that I was selfish for thinking about ending the pain, that I had everything I could ever want in life. If only I could see how much I had to live for, then I would be free of this burden that visited me every night and every moment alone.

It was just as useless as telling a blind man to just open his eyes so he could see.

However, it would be unfair to discredit Lucien who was the only one who really tried. Memories of our childhood danced freely in my mind as I placed my head lightly against the steed.

In that moment, I also deeply missed the playful innocence

of Sigmund and Philomela, who always without trying made me forget about the aching within.

My tears drizzled down the bridge of the horse's snout.

Facing the water, I nodded my head in acceptance of my fate while I undressed myself of gloves and boots. I could barely see my deformed extremities in the ghostly moonlight, which I was grateful for. As always, the cold water took my breath away as it kissed my abhorrent toes. The thought of my father who cursed me with such depravity aroused anger within me, causing my toes to curl in the wet sand.

How someone who supposedly loved his beloved could kill their child without hesitation was beyond me.

Then again, I had followed in my father's footsteps by invading the privacy of a woman whom he found beautiful. The thought of causing Egret shame fostered more hatred for myself, rivaling the hatred I felt for my father.

Perhaps this cruel prophecy of Cypherus' Shadow wasn't really some foreboding terror that would wreak an antithetical havoc upon the masses through me or any other unfortunate soul. Maybe it was a proverbial destiny meant for anyone who strayed too far from the personified light that Cypherus characterized.

No more, I thought, squeezing my temple at the invasive and persistent thoughts of that malicious prophecy I couldn't care less about. My mind was becoming too burdensome to bear any longer.

It was time to sleep and be at peace.

Pain shot through my cracked feet as the icy water fully submerged my toes. I tried to face my death bravely by embracing the torture of the ocean. Fortunately there didn't seem to be any patrols on the beach at this moment, which was unusual, but I was spared the embarrassment of what they would've seen.

Instead, my thoughts turned again to my brother who would

be broken at the news of my eternal farewell. Lucien would never understand that this would allow him to become an even greater king, for he could only carry one burden at time. My heart tightened and my tear ducts loosened at the thought of my brother's reaction in realizing I was gone forever, but the water was already up to my neck.

There was no turning back.

My breath quickened in fear the further I brought myself out in the foggy sea, its currents humming to me like a lullaby, but my body now resisting its dark allure.

I tried to ease the doubt in my mind by pivoting to look at Renborg one last time, assuring myself that this decision was correct given its finality.

Was it?

In an attempt to stop the waves from smothering me in its shallow kisses, I dug my foot into the dark sand to pull back. But the more my soul merged with the waters, I found that they brought peace instead of tragic humor, easing my flesh from clinging onto the empty air within.

For once, this decrepit vessel realized it couldn't bear the shame of a failed destiny, and to go on would only result in more disappointment that this world was better off without.

Letting the air out of my lungs like the vapor that was purpose, I held no substance within me and sent it back to the stars from which it came. Tears fell like ropes to the sea, pulling me down to be eternally silent like every other soul before me that has ever been damned with the burden of living. All the pain and suffering they endured and caused others to bear for them was so tragically pointless.

All of it.

At least Philomela and Sigmund would have Lucien to love and Egret to strengthen them. From this, I made peace with my bitter fate, letting the waters consume me as I thought of the last part of my intended Skallgend to Lucien:

Give them hope that life is worth living.

And so, it was finally time to rest.

Unlike Sh'eol, I wasn't trapped inside the soul realm of Solstein to writhe in painful anger and loathing at a fate that was entirely in the hands of someone else. To be dead to the world but to be fully alive with nothing but the agony of consciousness forever was not something I would wish upon the most evil of people. It would be a mercy to release the tormented Dragon, and I knew that, if he were in my position, he would hunger for the sweet relief of death that trickled into my mouth from the ocean.

What a pity to have sleepless death.

A part of me hoped my eyes would glimpse the stars just one last time as the rocky waves sloshed above me, but the uncaring fate that mistakenly molded my deformed clay decided I was not worthy of such an honor.

My eyes closed in defiance of not letting fate shackle me to its morbid destiny of Shadow. But the brief moment of sleep was stripped away when through my eyelids appeared what looked like a star. Opening my eyes carefully, I couldn't see what it was at first, my irises burning at the light that was brighter than all of the constellations combined.

It was almost unbelievably bright. Death was postponed temporarily as I kicked back up to the surface to see what it was.

I was at a loss for words.

There appeared a milky white light shining upon the lip of the seaside-cliffs high above me. Whatever it was could not be a star, for it wasn't in the Void above but looking down upon me from above.

There seemed to be an array of colors ebbing through the glowing being.

Before I could make out what it was, something jabbed me in my side, the pain shocking my focus out of place. Cursing, I turned to see a piece of wood floating away from me in the foggy water, followed by a plethora of debris that appeared to be from a ship's remains.

"What in the Void?" I said, fear rising in my heart.

Bobbing through the dark waters, a Drakin corpse was my answer. It took everything within me to contain a scream.

The Drakin floated lifelessly on a tattered plank of a ship, his normally flaming hair only a dying ember that stuck lifeless-ly to his dead and cracked flesh. The current from the waters pushed against me again and I felt the hand of a dead some-thing stroking my foot, which I couldn't restrain a scream from.

As in response, the fog cleared just enough so that I could see I was surrounded by the corpses of Dwarves, Elves, and Drakin.

The dead were everywhere.

The seawater filled my lungs and I began to panic, thrashing in the polluted shores. Suddenly the urge to live became very strong as I did not want to join the deceased around me.

Water choked in my lungs as I struggled to make it back to shore, my lack of aquatic navigation becoming annoyingly apparent as I struggled to the beach. The current must have pushed me a little downstream from where I left my horse as I crawled on the sands before the Cave of Lost Lovers, exhaust-ed and shaking with horror.

Turning quickly around, I could see more of the dead pol-luting the rocky waves, and the stench became ever so sharply pungent and apparent.

"Hel…" someone said in the cave behind me, startling every thought of the deceased from my thoughts.

"Who's there?" I said, standing wearily to my feet and peering into the dark cave, my stomach sour with anticipation.

A bloody hand crawled out of the shadows and into the sand, followed by a punctured man bathed in the foggy moonlight. The movement of the Ronian soldier looked slow and painful. It was one of the beach patrolmen who had been absent earlier, though there should have been more than just him. The slowing of his strained eyes told me he didn't have long, so I lowered myself quickly to hear his faint whispers.

"What happened to you?" I said, gasping at the severity of his injuries; blood flowed from too many gaping wounds for hope of survival to be allowed. His solemn eyes told me that we both reached the same conclusion: he would not survive the night.

The Ronian looked at me in trembling despair.

"They're here."

My heart flooded with fear.

"Who?" I whispered, but my dream told me the answer long in advance.

"The Drakin."

Chapter 6
Through the Fire

The first of the Drakin were born unto ten Elven mothers at the direction of the Elvish King of Ezorelai, Elduin Tokindell. They were conceived in the Dendravik Mountains in the ancient Dorian Kingdom after mating with Sh'eol the Great. They were initially named the "Dravakin" since they were born in the mountains of Dragons, which morphed into Drakin over time. How or why King Tokindell convinced the Elven mothers and Sh'eol to mate is unknown. Some Sefir have speculated that it was to preserve the Dragons' powerful seed as Cypherus the Slayer was, by some wicked magic, genociding the last of the Dragons and destroying their precious eggs throughout Divonholm, even the ones who did not side against the Humans.

After Cypherus slew Sh'eol and plundered his horde of gold, King Tokindell fled with the ten Drakin babes across the Strumma to his fortress of Moer in the Ryggdrack Mountains. There he left them with his regiment of Ezorelaite warriors to raise the new race. They were headed by the Valkryn Priest Josefa to guide the children into the Valkryn Faith and loyalty to the Ezorelai Empire. Little did they know that the Drakin cannot be chained. We would conquer Ezorelai and any kingdom like it for their arrogance, for our ancestors ruled the skies.

Scrolls of Yarahm
Dawn of the Drakin: 1,484 - 1,435 AE
Safira Seraii et Elishem

My heart pounded in my throat as I ran. It was the only thing reminding me that I was not sleeping beneath the sea, along with the dead floating in their aquatic grave behind me.

The soldier's dying words reverberated through my mind as the waves of stress coursed through me. All of those little signs came flashing back to me, my only hope being that they weren't true. From the out of place soldiers at the gates, to the Drakin slaves looking too comfortable in those chains, my mind was reeling from who they actually were.

The most harrowing of these thoughts was the conclusion that my dream was never a nocturnal hallucination but a demented reality that became increasingly true.

The last part of the dream to become real was the sleepless death I was meant to suffer.

No.

There was no time to let those thoughts consume me, so I placed them in the corner of my mind to deal with later. If the Drakin were truly here, then Lucien and the children were in danger, and, Shadow of Cypherus or not, my life could serve at least the noble purpose of sparing their innocent souls from whatever was coming.

Breathless, I almost scared the horse as I came running to it, rushing with panic to put on my boots and gloves as fast as I could. But as I steadied the beast and prepared to jump on, I looked up the sea cliff to the walls of Caer Mordrake looming high above it, reconsidering my course: if the Drakin were here, then they would have climbed to avoid being seen, taking the faster but more dangerous route to reach the royal keep, which would be an obvious target given its supply advantage from the sea.

And if I took the horse all the way around to the city gate, an invasion could be well underway before I ever reached them.

The wall was dangerous, deadly even, especially in the dark. Panic seized every breath of mine in trying to decide. Every moment that passed was a moment closer to peril for the few I loved.

A slurry of curses flew from my mouth as I abandoned the horse to race to the cliff wall. The lack of certainty for this path further declined as I stepped over the crushed heads of

Drakin who had fallen from the perilous climb and lay dead in the sand before me. Before the rising fear could dissuade me, I leaped carefully onto the wall and began my ascension in the dark, hoping this time not to fall.

My hands shook as I struggled to find footholds in the path with only my memories with Lucien to serve for finding the hidden trail that would lead upwards. The climb was slow and arduous, painful even with my gloves on, but as I found my footing in the dark, it became easier to navigate the higher I climbed. Death almost had its way with me as I pulled myself up onto a ridge that sat just beneath the one in which the walls stood upon; for as I came to its surface, there lay another dead Drakin before me, terror rivetting through me again as I came face to face with him.

"Don't look, don't look!" I whispered to myself, climbing over the dead Drakin and grabbing onto the wall ahead, perplexed that the Drakin's hair had not died down like the rest.

A shout erupted behind me and a hand wrapped around my foot, almost yanking me off the wall.

"Ahh!" I screamed, kicking with all of my might and aiming blindly for the Drakin's head.

The iron grip finally ceased after several frantic stomps, and I wasted no time in looking back as I fumbled over the last of the sea cliff. As I lay panting on the ridge just before the castle wall, I could see that I had indeed chosen the right path: there was a rope dangling from the wall.

The Drakin were already in Renborg.

Fear seized my heart and refused to let go. If I was too loud, my light might be snuffed out before the rest of Renborg's. How quickly my priorities had changed, though the darkness that sung to me from the sea was still there, ever tempting and ever growing to escape Cypherus' Shadow.

Giving the rope a tug to ensure its safety, I dragged myself up the wall, the task more laborious than the previous climb and proving far slower. Reaching the top with shaking arms, I collapsed over the parapet and onto the walkway. The exhaustion was too heavy for me to react immediately to the dead Ronian guards who littered the walkway, but it did encourage me to rise to my wobbling feet and run as quickly as I could to the staircase that fed into the garden of statues below.

Sprinting across the shadows of the royal district, I rushed past the marble statues of famous kings like Hezekias II and Cypherus I, my panting chest rising as quickly as their empires and my inner screams as silent as their fading legends.

I could scarcely breathe when I made it back to the gate of the royal palace, the Garden of Truth with the wedding guests drinking about just ahead, oblivious to all of what would come next.

The Watchmen looked at me curiously when I approached them struggling for air.

"Guards," I said, holding myself up on my knees, "p-please, they're here! The Drakin are ambushing us!"

All of them laughed and told me to lay off the drinking.

There was no time to argue. Shoving past them, I swam against the sea of guests whose dull roar drowned out my voice from making it to Gulmund, who was now drinking with the Grand Kriga, Servilius Kolstok, beneath the hollowed oak.

"Pardon me!" a Skyyan woman said as I bumped past her.

"He must be drunk," a Dwarf said.

"Gulmund!" I yelled again when I burst through the guests before him, knocking over a nobleman's drink to the floor in which he cursed at. "Gulmund, please listen to me. The Drakin are—"

"Enough about those damned Drakin!" he said, his breath reeking of wine as he waved me away. "They've already t-taken so much, too much from me. Come now, where is your brother—"

"Kolstok," I turned, focusing on the more competent of the two, "please, this is urgent! The Drakin have sent an invasion party on the banks of the Strumma and have killed the patrols. I saw it with my own eyes. They've just climbed the royal district's walls. We need to gather the troops to defend the city!"

Kolstok looked at me with a dead seriousness, his bold mustache crinkling against his studious frown as he analyzed my words. "At once, Your Highness. Baeros, Felman!"

His captains came at once and their men around the garden perked at the seriousness of the moment. My panic eased seeing that the Grand Kriga trusted my words. Although Kolstok didn't know the depths of my churning soul, our bond of trust was strong from the numerous sols of training he had given me with all of his finest swordsmen to fill my endless days.

Though I was not the best, I took comfort knowing I could somewhat defend Lucien and my siblings if it came down to wit and steel.

Kolstok moved quickly to assemble the troops, the Knights of Kyllian forming the closest ring around the King and his children, along with myself. Sir Alduaura was also here, making sure to stand as close to me as possible as he delivered a steely-eyed stare for successfully escaping from him.

To my surprise, I was relieved at my unwanted escort's presence.

The sudden movement of troops caused the wedding guests to stumble around in confusion and fear. Kolstok began shouting for everyone to remain calm in an attempt to ease their tensions while the guards secured the premises. Gulmund was not too pleased that the wedding, or more likely his drinking, was ruined. In his spittle and rage, he turned to grab me by my shoulder cape.

"What in the Void are you doing, boy?" he said, shaking me as my eyes threatened to spill tears.

"I-I—"

"Do you know how much our reputation will suffer because of this foolishness of yours? I swear I'll make you *wish* you could kill yourself."

There were no words for his remark.

"Let go of my brother you damn drunk!"

Lucien stormed up to Gulmund and shoved him forcefully aside, freeing me from his iron clasp, though my heart still felt the King's fist around it. Gulmund snapped to his son, his face as red as the lips of wedding guests who were shouting in a raised tenor of terror.

The alarm bells across the city started ringing; the invasion was well on its way.

"You are a weak, and worthless son!" Gulmund said, ignoring the bells and screams of the guests running into each other around us. "You should have taken *Kyllian's* place in the grave."

Kolstok tried to get hold of Gulmund's attention but the King just shrugged him off.

My hands were weak with anger at the King's behavior, and I was paralyzed to respond. He didn't mean the words he said nor the way in which he was acting. Perhaps the evil in which he burdened Lucien with was why I almost didn't notice movement in the shadows on the walls across from us. An emerging darkness from the night crept in direct contrast of the figure of light I saw before my attempted end.

"I hate you!" Lucien screamed.

And then I saw him.

The shadow's face was concealed beneath a rusty orbed helmet and hood, where five downwards claw marks must have given him sight. And in his hand was a long and curved bow, the wooden shaft mirroring the now yellow moon above his shoulder.

Time slowed as I realized who he was aiming at.

Before I tackled Lucien to the ground, I saw the assassin make the slightest nod of his head, like he was whispering something to himself.

"You forever disappoint m—"

But the King would never finish his final rebuke for his son.

The sad man who was once the King stumbled over his words repeatedly when the arrow sunk into his eye.

One could have mistakenly assumed he was incoherent from the drink, but when he fell over dead in a pool of his own weeping blood from the last of his good eye, they would've realized he was just another man who had died bitterly and regretfully, though in retrospect they would have seen that he had been a great King for Renborg. For a moment, Gulmund's slumped shoulders reminded me of his troubled love that he had shown me so many times before, along with all the joy he had shared with Valena and his son Kyllian before vanishing in the bitter winds of life that took his greatest treasure from him far too soon.

And though I knew he loved Lucien and I in his own way, especially since he saved me from my own father when I was born and did his failing best to raise us, whatever love that was contained in his stubborn heart oozed out along with his blood, his tormented soul extinguishing forever.

"Gulmund!" Valena said, who came running into the scene of his death with little Sigmund in tow. She crumpled next to his blood-soaked head and heaved a mourningful cry.

"The King!" a chorus of cries erupted from the wedding guests.

"Reia's mercy!" Orpheus Talon screamed, and even the eyes of Menander looked surprised at the fallen King.

Everyone exploded into a frenzy of terror at his assassination.

As the crowds ran into one another in panic, I looked

underneath my arms at Lucien, but all I could see was a chillingly cold stare as we lay huddled on the grass in silence at the tragedy that had befallen.

"Arrows!" Kolstok roared.

Without a moment to lose, I grabbed the nearest table to shield Lucien, Valena, Sigmund, and I as the rain of steel fell upon us. A barrage of screams pierced the raging sea of destruction as those who were not so lucky were pinned to the ground and drowned in their own blood. Sigmund cried as I crouched over them, but we were spared.

A row of shields surrounded us as Kolstok ordered his men and the Knights of Kyllian to surround their new King, allowing me to throw the table off and yank Lucien to his feet and help Valena and Sigmund to theirs.

"To the castle!" Kolstok said, but his words were deafened by the screams that erupted from behind us.

The guests found no escape when they tried to leave through the garden's southern gate. Instead, they met the sword of about twenty Drakin who came pouring in without mercy, their flaming hair a burning signal of their rage. The guests stood no chance and were cut down left and right like insignificant wheat from a sickle, being hacked to death with ease as they were packed too tightly to flee. Blood began to spray across the garden as people tripped over one another in a desperate attempt to run away from the Drakin butchers.

I stood frozen in shock and revelation: they were the same Drakin slaves I saw from earlier.

The rusty orbed assassin wasted not the surprise and continued firing his barrage of arrows at the Knights and Watchmen who surrounded us. The assassin's arrows met every target and dropped the Watchmen like flies, but the Knights held their ground with their oval shields and Godstone-laced armor.

"Quickly!" Kolstok said, grabbing Valena by the arm while leading us towards Caer Mordrake beneath the Knights' shields. "We must make it through to the military district!"

The Grand Kriga was wise to lead us through it. Before we made it into the stone walls, I could see what looked like man-sized Dragons in the night sky soaring towards the nearest victims with their leathery wings and vicious teeth; the Eldrakes would be best avoided, but many of the guests were not so lucky, including an Anumnalasi Ambassador who was taken abruptly to the sky only to be dropped to his death, followed by a deafening crunch once he violently landed.

Soon all I could see was the cluster of metal armor protecting us. Clashing through Drakin steel, we hurried into the royal palace to reach the other gate. There had never been a reason to truly appreciate the Kyllian Knights before, but I was thankful for them now as their Godstone blades and armor kept the Drakin at bay, the magmic skin of our enemies glowing like cracked fire as they hunted us into the castle.

"My Lord!" a Ronian lieutenant yelled, running from the other side of the castle to us.

"What is it?" Kolstok said, halting our group for just a moment while our guards behind us warded off any of the enemy.

"The Drakin have also infiltrated the Sea Gate!"

The memory of the shadowed ships that sailed silently over the black waters when I descended to the ocean came flooding back to me, turning into dread in my heart.

Kolstok cursed under his breath before looking wearily at Lucien and Valena.

"We must flee the city!" Kolstok said, pain throbbing in his eyes as he said the words.

Lucien looked aghast. "We cannot just abandon Renborg!"

"I know my King, but in truth, I cannot yet tell you whether a thousand or ten thousand Drakin have infiltrated our fair city.

I must get you all beyond these walls and on the road to Brannfalt or Hebsund if we are to ensure Renborg's survival!"

Lucien was speechless as Kolstok nodded for his men to keep moving us forward, but as we did so I realized we were short two people.

"Philomela and Egret!" I said, letting go of Lucien's hand who looked appalled that I did. "They are in the upper rooms! We need to rescue them before we leave!"

"We don't have time!" Lucien said. "We need to retrieve Solstein first if we are to abandon Renborg. It must not fall into their hands again!"

Kolstok ground his teeth in contemplation while we hurried through the soon to be desecrated halls, weighing both paths but presumably not wanting another Soul War with Solstein in their hands. Both were the right choice in his eyes since his duty was to both, but the lives of Egret and Philomela were far more precious than any sword.

"Sir Alduaura, take five of our soldiers and escort Morgan up to the bedrooms to retrieve the Queen and the Princess. Meet us in the armory, and if not there, reconvene at Hebsund."

Valena sighed as she carried Sigmund.

"Thank you," I said, hugging Lucien quickly before he could protest and sprinting towards the stairs that fed into the bedrooms above, followed by Sir Alduaura and five of the Ronian infantry.

"Morgan, wait!" Lucien screamed, but I refused to turn around, no matter how much it hurt my heart to do so, for Egret and Philomela deserved to live.

If anyone should survive this night, it was them.

Before I could even open the wooden doors to the bedroom chambers, they were bashed open and I was thrown to the ground, my nose throbbing while the spears of the antler-helmed Suffra scraped my neck.

Just the slightest pressure and my throat would drain my life out in a million different places.

Sir Alduaura and the soldiers who followed immediately drew their swords upon the Suffra. Upon recognizing me, Queen Nera shouted something in Skyyan and the Suffra withdrew. Sir Alduaura relaxed his guard, only slightly, and helped me to stand to my feet.

"Thank you," I muttered, my eyes wandering to Egret who was standing clothed and bitter behind her mother, the only thing exposed being her shaven head.

It looked like they had been arguing seconds before I arrived.

"What in Aryarc's name is going on?" Nera said, her eyes searching me for the smallest detail of what would give her a clue.

"The Drakin have attacked, and we need to retreat!" I said, pushing myself through them and leading my escorts to Philomela's room.

Upon hearing her familiar cry as we walked in, my heart rejoiced in knowing she was alright.

"There there," I said, quickly stuffing my note into my pocket before carefully picking her up in her feathery blue swaddle which I had bought for her so long ago.

Philomela cooed in my arms and fell back asleep, warming my heart which could barely understand what was going on. Gulmund's death was still fresh on my mind, but knowing Philomela was alive helped to calm me and refocus me.

Before I even turned around, I felt a familiar Godstone knife at my stomach. Egret wielded the blade, thankfully not throwing it at me again.

Though the anger rippling across her face suggested she was not far from doing so.

"If you so much as look at me like the way you did, I will burn your insides more than a Drakin ever could!"

"Egret, be silent!" Nera yelled from the hall.

Egret took a deep breath and gripped her fingers which grew white from squeezing them so tightly.

"Forgive me, mother," she said as I followed her out of the room with Philomela. In a whisper, she said to me, "But you will never receive my forgiveness, lowborn."

My voice stuttered as I tried to apologize. "Egret, I—"

The doors crashed open again. This time, Valena came rushing through the hallway.

"Morgan, we need to hurry, they've almost made their way into the castle!"

Upon seeing Philomela, Valena sighed, thanking the Mother repeatedly while she scooped her daughter from my arms.

"Thank you, Morgan," she said before turning to Nera. "Nera, we must flee the city! Follow me and I will explain."

"Flee the city?" Nera said as we hurried through the hallway towards the stairs, about to pass my bedroom door at the end. "Why not hold them off in the keep?"

"The Drakin have made their way through several entrances to the city, including the royal keep. The Grand Kriga is taking our troops to the military district where your forces are in order to hold for an evacuation."

"Abandon the entire city?" Egret said, almost in disgust.

"No, just the royal family," Valena continued. "We will use our combined effort to hold them here while we gather reinforcements in the neighboring cities."

"How many are there?" Nera said. "I thought your husband was fighting them in Yarahm. How are they here?"

"I don't know, it was all so—"

The door to my room swung open and threw two of the Suffra aside, stumbling into a few of the Ronian soldiers nearby.

Out of the darkness came the silent assassin who killed Gulmund, his scarred orb of a helmet bashing the last Suffra by the entrance, stealing her life's breath with one forceful crunch. A trembling song of fear played in my heart as I put myself in front of Egret and tried to protect Philomela, but Egret shoved me out of the way and went to engage the hooded Drakin with the spear of the fallen Suffra.

"Egret, no!" Valena screamed, but Nera let her daughter fall into danger.

Egret wasted no time to test her opponent's fighting style. Rushing forth to attack, Egret barely dodged the Drakin's axe as it nearly missed her unarmored body several times. She danced to avoid the Drakin's blows, her body moving swiftly past each swing of his axe to pull herself closer. The Suffra also converged on him and were about to assist her, along with Sir Alduaura and the Ronians about to strike.

The Drakin would be overwhelmed in seconds.

But the doors of all the other bedrooms flew open before they could slay the assassin. Multitudes of Drakin poured out from the rooms, taking some of the Ronians and Suffra by surprise as they buried their swords in their backs, dividing our group in two from the chaos. Philomela began to cry as Nera was forced towards the back of the hall with a handful of her Suffras, while Egret and the remaining Suffras continued their deadly engagement with the assassin.

I lost focus of them as Valena and I were forced to move towards the stairs by the oncoming Drakin. Thankfully, we were joined by two Ronian soldiers and Sir Alduaura, who disengaged from the assassin to protect us; the massive Knight silently and swiftly beheaded two of the Drakin who came running at us in one swipe of his sword, while the Ronians held off the other Drakin who poured endlessly through the bedrooms.

To even the numbers, I grabbed one of the Drakin swords for myself as the flaming-haired assailants surrounded our two groups.

Egret screamed again, this time rolling past the assassin and thrusting her spear into his side. The assassin roared in response, turning to shatter her spear with one downwards strike before kicking her halfway across the room into our defensive ring.

"Egret!" I said, running to pick her up while the Suffra engaged the assassin, who paused for a moment to assess their moves, waiting patiently and decidedly to strike as the battle with the other Drakin and Suffras continued around us.

Egret weakly pushed my hand away and stood up on her own, but her disgust for me vanished when she saw the assassin faint an attack to the left guard of the Suffras. All mistakenly took the bait as he nimbly lunged into a closer range to negate the reach of their spears. With sickening ease, the assassin hewed three of the Suffras with his axe across their chests before they could react, bursting open their flesh and armor with successive strength. For the two that remained, he grabbed one by her horned helmet to ram into another victim, unstoppable in his horrific prowess as he slaughtered his way towards us.

My vision was briefly obscured as a Drakin slipped through Sir Alduaura's defenses, seeking to impale him from the side. Valena responded quicker than I, grabbing a nearby vase of water that she subsequently broke against the Drakin's skull, crippling him as he fell to the ground in anguish over his natural enemy.

Valena took Egret's hand and led us towards the stairs, pushing us in front of her while she carried a screaming Philomela, with only our Knight following us quickly behind.

"We must go before it's too late!" Valena said.

"We cannot abandon my mother!" Egret resisted.

"They won't kill her, but we need to go! Lucien and Kolstok are retrieving Solstein, but I fear the Drakin already know. We must find them and escape the city!"

Egret and I risked a glance back at Nera who stood with her hands raised in surrender at the swords of the Drakin, along with her group of Suffra. Her face portrayed a look of severe disappointment, one that looked strikingly familiar to Gulmund's who looked down to Lucien for not being the son he wanted. Nera's gaze looked harsher, resentful even. And it wasn't until I caught the glimpse of Egret's eyes brimming with tears that I realized Nera's displeasure was intended solely for her.

Like her mother expected failure.

Nera's chilling stare was interrupted when the orbed helmet streaked through my vision. Its target was Valena, who crumpled lifelessly with Philomela to the ground as blood gushed from her head before the doorway to the stairs, the child bathing in her mother's suffering and screaming beneath.

"No!" I yelled, but before I could turn back to help her, three Drakin came between us and forced us to the doorway, Sir Alduaura managing to hold them off with depreciating success.

Through the Knight's tiring battle, I could see the Queen stagger from the blow but stood shakily to her feet. To my greatest relief, Philomela was not crushed but had been cushioned by the fall in Valena's arms.

"Valena!" the now helmetless Drakin roared, but to call him a Drakin was almost incorrect. His cracked skin was similar to the Drakins' grey hues but different in his sickening resemblance to a Human; his veins bulged a darker red instead of a fiery channel of his life essence, much like his beet red hair which was braided like a Vilderman warchief's and not flowing in flames. His eyes were what gave him away as one, which were fiery like all Drakin, except it looked more like the yellow tip of the flames rather than the red heat of a roaring blaze.

"Rolloc, you sick bastard," Valena said through broken teeth as Egret and I pushed against the stair doors.

"Valena!" I yelled, desperate as Rolloc approached her, his Godstone axe poised to strike. Philomela squirmed and cried in her mother's bloody arms, completely unaware of what was coming.

"You know your sin, and this is your penance." Rolloc's voice was deep and calm, as if his voice had been seeping in hatred that aged him far more than time ever could.

Egret and I both stood in shock as Rolloc swiped Valena's life away with his axe, blood painting the bedroom hall like a canvas of an unknown tragedy. Rolloc went in for another strike, presumably for Philomela who I couldn't see through the clash of steel before me. In desperation, I screamed and tried to push through to save my baby sister, but the wrath of Rolloc's axe found its home as more blood covered his midnight cape.

My mind went into total shock at the sight.

Before my tears could fall, the remaining Drakin before us parried the blows of Sir Alduaura and unleashed a spew of fire from his charcoal lips, his neck and chest glowing like embers beneath his cracked and grey skin.

I jumped back from the flames and through the doors, slipping over the step and tumbling down the long flight of carpeted stairs, taking Egret with me away from the carnage that bloodied my soul.

If fate was kind, it would let me break my neck on the way down.

For some cruel and unhumorous reason, I lived.

As did Egret, who struggled to stand up, bruised from the fall like I was. Though as she wearily held herself upon the wooden railing for the stairs, I could see her body was more purple than mine.

The heaviness of Egret's heart was a mystery, but mine was like that of a millstone which had been dropped to the depths of the ocean, where I wished I had drowned before witnessing the death of my innocent sister and the family who had adopted me into this cruel life. I couldn't dwell on it. That much misery and sorrow would be enough to cripple anyone with an irreversible finality.

But before I would let this sleepless death, this unwanted doom from such a cruel god, have its way with me, I had one last task to ensure: to make sure Lucien was safe.

Though we couldn't see him, he was probably only a few halls away at the treasury right now. The room which, as my panicking heart realized, was in clear sight of the upper bedroom hall where the Drakin Valena had called Rolloc and his beasts were. It was only a matter of time before he would see my brother and slay him like he did his mother and sister.

But Egret had other plans.

"What are you doing?" I said amongst the shouts of wedding guests running past us while I grabbed her arm, holding her back from going back up the stairs.

"Let go of me, lowborn!" she said, slapping my gloved hand away. "I cannot fail my mother nor my people!"

Egret tried again up the stairs, this time grabbing the sword I had retrieved from a fallen Drakin. Unfortunately, the weight of the sword and the damage from the fall prevented her zeal, forcing her to limp heavily one step at a time. Grabbing the sword to stop her, I quickly pulled her back down into my arms. Egret weakly resisted after stepping on her bad leg, the skin of her hairless head contorting into a silent scream.

"We need to escape with the King," I said as she shrugged off of me.

"You are ignorant of the responsibility I carry for my people. But why should I expect you to understand? You are nothing but a perverted peasant who cares only for himself."

The volcanic eruptions in Yarahm, with their horrendous magmic fury scorching all who dared to be in their presence, were cold in comparison to Egret's incinerating words.

A perverted peasant? While accidentally true, she proved no better as a pretentious Princess.

Keeping all but my embarrassment hidden from her, I said, "*Princess*, can you not see in your royal wisdom that you are unable to fight in this condition?"

Egret looked at me with an intense annoyance before looking down at her bruised self, her mind a silent whirlwind as she collected herself. She closed her eyes and nodded slowly, accepting the truth of the situation, albeit begrudgingly.

"I will slay you for this," she whispered through gritted teeth while using me to support her weight. "And it's *Queen* to you, lowborn."

With great pain and struggle, we hobbled quickly through the crowded and chaotic hall to the royal treasury, every step aching as the sounds of Drakin breaking into the castle echoed through the hall.

The screams of death behind us only made the tumultuous hurricane of my mind even more fragmented with grief, fear, and despair, mixing violently with anger and sorrow that almost collapsed me; seeing Valena and Philomela cut down like insignificant casualties of war was too horrific to bear, too gruesome to even imagine. The only thing pushing me forward was the deeper than flesh desire to save Lucien and Sigmund.

To spare at least one from this ever unfolding nightmare.

In what felt like my first stroke of luck ever, we caught up to Lucien and Kolstok with their Knights and soldiers. Oddly, they were at a standstill outside the treasure hall.

Why aren't they grabbing the sword? I thought as we hobbled to them, the wedding guests screamed past us with no regard but for their own.

Lucien cast me a look of relief as he saw us, though his face darkened from the absence of his mother and sister. It was not the time to talk about such things.

Kolstok gravely nodded at me as we drew into their group, most likely guessing what had transpired only minutes ago. As Egret and I came into view of the treasury, I understood why Lucien and the others didn't dare enter: inside, Piluch stood bravely as a last defense for the ancient blade while ten fierce Drakin clad in scarlet armor surrounded him, their bloody scaled armor darkly beautiful in the window dome's reflections.

Kebri Knights.

Piluch yelled something in the Draconic tongue, causing the Kebri to step back in fear as he held the blade high as a warning. And though I understood not what he said, it would make sense if he threatened to release the Dragon soul within; it was a cunning move since neither Ronian nor Drakin wanted the Dragon's soul released. The Drakin especially did not want this, for they undoubtedly wanted to create more Eldrake Averites and use Sh'eol's great power for themselves.

With just a look, Kolstok ordered his soldiers to slowly circle the red-scaled Kebri as it was clear they wouldn't harm Piluch, while Lucien and the rest of us were left outside to be surrounded by the Knights of Kyllian. The Kebri raised their Godstone swords against Kolstok's men. Time moved slower than the trickle of sweat that crawled down my deformed back.

"Drop them," Kolstok growled, but the Kebri refused. "*Fine.* Piluch, release Sh'eol from their hands forever."

Piluch looked like he was actually going to go through with it as he stood unshaken and brave with the ancestral gauntlets of Kyllian I to hold the famed blade. But before he could, a shadow darkened the window behind him. Without warning, we were all blinded by a falling rain of glass as someone burst through the windows.

It was Rolloc.

The hybrid Drakin pounced onto Piluch's back with the help of an Eldrake who screeched behind him in the air.

The Ronians immediately clashed with the Kebri. A bloodbath ensued as the men of Renborg were cut down with haste by the scarlet armored Drakin. The Eldrake gouged out the eyes of a Ronian soldier before Egret grabbed one of the fallen soldier's spears and impaled the beast mid-flight, even in her battered condition.

Piluch tried to raise Solstein in defense but Rolloc clove his hand from his wrist with his ax, the blade they feared clattering to the ground amongst a horde of treasures and blood. Piluch looked back in desperation at Kolstok, but his friend issued a cowardly retreat. The Knights of Kyllian began to herd us towards the castle's exit while the other soldiers gave us cover with their lives. Lucien clung to my arms like he always did, but I was not going to let that monster escape; he killed my sister, and he would join me in the Void to suffer the nothingness of death forever.

And so a sleepless death would be forever rebuked.

Leaving my brother for the last time and unhinging myself from Egret, I slipped through every Knight's reach and rushed into the battle, not caring if my life would end but *when*, hoping I would be released from these chains of life only after dragging Rolloc into my fate.

Lucien, Egret, and Sigmund would be safe with Kolstok, as safe as they could be in this situation. I took comfort in that, but I had failed Philomela, so it was time I made up for it.

Defying death, I ducked beneath the sword of one of the scarlet Kebri who had just finished crippling a Ronian soldier by a blow to his neck. Not wasting my dwindling time, I bounded for Rolloc through the storm of fighting around me, swinging my sword with all of my might at his own hands.

Rolloc recoiled as my blade smacked into his gauntlets, giving me time to reach for the burning Solstein so I could plunge it directly into his heartless being. But Rolloc recovered faster than I thought he would and moved swiftly to stop me dead cold in my pursuit of the sword.

His rusty plated hand grabbed my face and threw me to the ground, my head throbbing beneath the bronze Mythraelyon shield mounted on display. Piluch shared in my moans of pain beside me, though I could offer him no aid. All I could focus on were Lucien's cries for me which grew ever fainter as the final note to my worthless destiny loomed over me, the murderer seething with anger while he yanked the shield to deliver me to an unavoidable and meaningless end.

"*Pathetic*," Rolloc said, accurately summaraizing my reasons for suicide right before crushing the shield against my temple, slamming me into the darkness.

Chapter 7
Well of the World

The Soul, eternal words of character
Remember the One who writes it
The Heart, ephemeral pages of history
Remember the One who reads it
The Blood, purloins ink and imprisons biographies
Remember the One who drains it
The Cannibal, swallows stories for unforgivable strength
Remember the One who devours it

Solbok
Laws of Light, 24:17-20
"Author of Flesh"

T**he** prison of my mind awoke in an inferno of pain that scorched throughout my body in the awakening dark. Time itself was lost as my aching brain tried and failed to determine where I was and what had happened.

Upon recognizing my conscious thoughts, I was perplexed to find myself alive.

And it was quiet, strangely silent.

Where am I?

My senses slowly began to wake up again. The feeling of something cold against my flesh became evident as I realized my heart was beating wildly in my chest.

With excruciating effort, I opened my eyes to the silver glow.

The midnight light coming from the window showed me that I was in one of the castle's privy chambers.

"What?" I said, stumbling to my feet which ached from laying for so long.

And then the memories came flooding back violently, tormentiously.

Gulmund choking on his own blood, Valena and Philomela being cut down like wheat by Rolloc.

Fire, panic, death.

Invasion.

Egret's eyes flickered in my thoughts in both the library and the bedroom, weighing my heart and finding it repulsive. And then there were Sigmund and Lucien, both of whom were afraid as I left them to face Rolloc.

"Pathetic!" he screamed before bashing my head to the floor.

My heart almost capsized from the panic that took hold.

The world was quiet. I was alone.

"Lucien!" I shouted, at once wrestling with the door handle to try and open the solid wooden door to escape.

It was locked.

"Lucien!" I yelled again, bashing my aching body into the door repeatedly to no avail.

Terror devoured me with its hopelessness as I sank back to the floor.

Where were they? Were they alive?

To my agony, it seemed my dream was becoming ever more prophetic. By Cypherus' Shadow, would it mean that I would become only a Shadow of a being who lived forever a prisoner, unable to die?

The world was too dark and uncertain to know.

Like a dying animal, I curled into myself as my mind raced with panic in the shadows. My moans of pain withered into sobs of suffering as I lay shivering from tears on the stone floor.

Death seemed like a distant dream of rest that avoided my remembrance.

Though, the strangest part was that I wasn't sure if I wanted the sweet embrace of such a sleep.

There was a tear in my soul between two destinies which were now entirely out of my grasp. Humiliated and hopeless, I was now enslaved to a far darker destiny than I had ever wanted. I was too weak to try and find anything to grant me eternal rest or to live with a purpose. Giving up, I slipped into what I hoped was a coma, the memories of battle and terrified guests becoming a dull lullaby in the Void of my mind.

The symphony of death carried me to a dream where the man in milky white robes and a cosmic face stared into my very soul, like a seamstress examining the fibers of someone else's creation. The blood moon shone brightly above him as his burning suns for eyes studied me, the depth in them reflecting the look Valena often had when she watched every move her sons made, or didn't.

His swirling stars for a mouth silently whispered:

"You will be!"

And then, in a snap, he was gone.

The moment his image left me, I felt my eyes begin to open, slowly and against my will. They were open to an entirely new world. It was as if the dream in my mind leaked out through the open wound on my temple because the bathroom was now awash in the morning light that was even more silent than before.

"Ahhh," I said, pushing myself up. Blood pounded my aching temple, my fingers jittering as if I had too many cups of juva. Gently, I fingered my matted hair from where I was struck: blood had long since dried. The sharp pain that pulsed in my head was only paused when I felt the cold Godstone necklace brush against my chest.

An eternity passed by as I realized there was still one possible way to escape this fate; albeit as unlikely of a chance at ending my miseries now.

With trembling hands, I held my Godstone tree necklace

before me. Like a locked door without a key, the lack of my soul's name made it impossible for my soul to enter, and I could only pound on the Godstone's door to let me into its crystal embrace.

Will that even end my life? Or will it just be another prison?

Shouts of a familiar Drakin and scraping metal of the bathroom door interrupted my brief lament.

Rolloc.

Without a word, the red-haired hybrid barged in, his yellow eyes boring into my soul. Before I could even respond, Rolloc yanked me by my inky curls to drag me into a blood-drenched hallway, forcing me to stand as he pushed from behind.

"You're a monster," I trembled.

Scaled Drakin soldiers enclosed behind me, their flaming hair weaved together like bands of fire beneath their helms.

"I will bring you to the Abishx with me for—"

Rolloc's fist interrupted my threat, a crunch emitting from my jaw. He didn't say another word as he led me through the desecrated Caer Mordrake, not caring to avoid the dead Ronians who littered the ground like sewage in the streets.

It was *harrowing* to see all of the dead. Though I had never cared much for them before, seeing them now so lifeless and pale was horrifying.

Death was less enticing with each corpse in our path.

Entering the massive throne room overlooking the capital, I was both relieved and afraid when I saw the city.

Through the towering windows that dwarfed us on either side of the throne, I could see everything beyond the Sovereign Square was still in Ronian and Skyyan hands. Comfort only came from knowing that there was a chance Kolstok had guided Lucien, Sigmund, and Egret to safety from the city, but there was no way I could be sure.

The dread of the unknown was almost too much for my tired heart to bear.

Any solace I received became an unexpected weight when I glanced at the opposite windowed arches. The Strumma Sea was glittering in the sunrise, but it was marred by a fleet of hundreds of trireme ships that were fast approaching Renborg's docks; they were not Ronian.

Speechless, I stood perplexed. Nowhere in history had the Drakin ever assembled such a fleet, if any at all. They avoided the water like the plague, but now they were pridefully showing off the defiance they had mustered against their fatal limitations.

Now, they had a fleet like never before, with my brother's empire as its target, revenge its goal, and death its appetite. Only a fierce political leader amongst the Drakin tribes could organize such a massive unified war effort with such bold ambition.

"You will bow when he enters," Rolloc growled before shouting something in Drakonnian to the hundreds of Drakin soldiers and priests who waited patiently, expectantly in the throne room.

All of the Drakin moved to either side in unison, creating a path to the empty throne.

Rolloc forcefully guided me to one side and ordered something to his soldiers that followed us, and soon their spears surrounded me as a cage of steel.

The hybrid Drakin soon departed us to stand at the end of the room by the marble-green throne. In the blink of an eye, Rolloc handed something dark that glowed with deep shadow to a Drakin priest nearby which he had withdrawn from his satchel. The priest, completely garbed in a golden metallic robe from head to toe, took the dark object that was given and folded it into his heavy robes.

What is that?

Any question I had, which continued to ever grow in this

strange new reality, was unanswered as we all waited in gripping silence.

Before long, my mind began to dance with fear at who we were waiting for, my imagination doing more harm than good as I remembered my dark dream and the fearsome leader of the Drakin.

Then, I heard it: a snarling growl emerging from the halls, causing the hairs on the back of my neck to stand up in fear.

A heavy pattern of footsteps echoed on the stone floors, metal clinging with each fearsome step. The shadow of something large and terrifying flickered from the entrance of the throne room, growing closer with every bated breath. The white as snow maw of the Kiagor came first through the opened doors of the throne room. The Drakin standing towards the entrance recoiled slightly in fear as the massively terrifying beast of myth came crawling through in its ancient dominance.

Even though I was safe from its reach, I found myself backing away ever slightly at the creature that I had seen in my nightmare. And riding high and proud upon its mythical back was the very focus of my dream, arrayed in golden-scaled armor meant only for the Grand Derasar.

Judux et Cadullum.

The entire throne room exploded with thunderous applause as Judux rode the legendary beast which roared in response, its pearly white fangs reflecting its silver fur and majestic wings.

In one command, it could kill me.

Sleepless death...

Judux waved almost humbly to his warriors on either side of him as he passed them by.

Did he plan to look surprised? He definitely sold the expression that he had not been expecting such a royal welcome.

As Judux approached the throne with his Kiagor, the Drakin priest who received the strange dark object moved quickly to stand beside the throne, gesturing to Judux and announcing something in their language that I figured was an invitation to claim it.

Judux frowned slightly upon his Kiagor as the Drakin cheered him on to claim the throne. For a moment, Judux hesitated. Though I knew not a comprehensive understanding of Drakin history and culture, I did know that what was unfolding could either be Judux's greatest moment, or most foolish; the Drakin were not fond of kingship before, and any attempts at claiming to be king could have a Drakin quickly drowned.

Judux dismounted from the Kiagor to approach the marble-green throne. Carefully sitting himself on the throne, the golden-robed priest immediately waved his hand to silence the still cheering crowds.

The room became deathly silent again.

Judux's fiery eyes flashed to mine for a breath as the world was but a whisper, an intense sense of regality and reverence passing before him unto me.

The Drakin priest broke our connection when he began to speak through the golden mesh that encapsulated his entire being, speaking at length in a grand tone that I could only guess was praises for the Grand Derasar as he paraded before him. When the priest finished, he withdrew the dark object that Rolloc had handed him from his robes, holding it high before Judux and for all to see: it was a crown, darker than midnight and seeming to suck in all of the light around it.

Something felt strange about the crown, but it was beyond my shattered concentration to understand its mystery. One thing I did know for certain was how it made me feel: the crown sparked a kindling of *fear.*

The priest lowered to his knees as he tried to give Judux the crown. Judux at once refused the crown with a raised hand, looking to the crowd as if he were determining if it was a test. The priest spoke loudly again, and the Drakin crowds erupted into applause and heapings of praise in their native tongue. A chant took hold of many of the Drakin, their deep voices echoing through my soul as Judux watched carefully.

At last, Judux bowed his head to receive the crown.

The crown of shadows kissed Judux's steel hood as the priest placed it upon him. A twitch of pain flashed across Judux's grey face as the crown sealed itself on his head, but the Grand Deresar betrayed that feeling no longer as a look of supreme confidence and royalty overshadowed the pain.

The throne room sang again of applause as his subjects cheered his regal acceptance. As his audience praised their lord, my eyes drifted to Rolloc standing behind the throne, where a brief glimpse of a grin almost broke on his pale face.

In a display of his increased power, Judux waved one hand to silence the crowds again, and almost immediately all became unnervingly still.

The silence was broken as Judux pointed towards me, his bold voice crisping through the room in my Ronic tongue.

"Bring forth the boy."

Judux was silent as he watched me from his newly claimed marble green throne, his molten lips betraying no emotion as Rolloc departed from behind the throne to return to where I was standing under guard. The hybrid Drakin roughly placed himself behind me, leading me past the torch-lit arches and crowds to stand before the Drakin leader and his terrifying pet.

Judux appeared calm, cold, meticulous as he made no move

to speak, waiting patiently upon the throne as he studied me. The golden-scaled Derasar sipped from a boiling cup of water that was handed to him after his acceptance of the crown.

Another Drakin draped in silver robes stepped before the throne, clearing his throat before speaking roughly in the Ronic tongue.

"You are graced with the mighty presence of Judux et Cadullum, elected Grand Derasar of the Yarahm tribes, The Great Defier of Renborg, Hero of the Wars of Deliverance, The Silver Hand of Laconnia, and The Shadow of Cypherus. Kneel to your Lord."

Before I could defy the order, Rolloc kicked the back of my legs, my knees slamming into the stone floor and burning with sudden shock.

"You must be our brave hero I've heard so much about," Judux said in a surprisingly soothing voice, leaning forward into the smoke from his boiling cup. "Tell me, where is the King of Renborg?"

My eyes caught those of a calm Piluch who sat boundless beside the Kiagor, his head shaking carefully as a warning. I hadn't seen him until now, but I was relieved to know he lived. He held his posture confidently with just one hand, Solstein mockingly held by a red-scaled Drakin beside him to display a continuous reminder of all that was lost.

"I have no idea," I said, my voice catching in my throat as the nerves coursed through my veins.

Judux shook his head as he calmly placed his boiling cup of water on the arm guard of the throne, taking a moment to himself before looking at Rolloc behind me with his fiery gaze.

"Are you sure this is the boy, brother?" Judux said, oddly still in the Ronic tongue.

Brother?

There was a look of annoyance in Judux's eyes, a slight

sense of distrust in the way his cracked eyelids squinted underneath his hood and dark crown.

Rolloc growled something in the Drakonnian tongue behind me, pushing me to the floor with his Godstone axe before finishing in the Ronic tongue. "I know what I *saw*."

Judux snapped.

"*Rolloc*, you will stay your hand or I will drown you myself! Is not the King and Queen's blood enough for you? Are we as uncivil as they are?"

Rolloc was as silent as the grave.

"Forgive me," Judux said, his igneous eyes looking at me with curiosity as he calmed himself. "We did not come here to slay them. My brother forgets his respect, and his *restraint*."

Rolloc sounded as if he were about to say something but Judux cut him off before he could.

"You will speak when spoken to, brother! Now, tell me, young man, with whom do I have the pleasure of speaking with? You must be of some importance given your clothing and proximity to the King."

Anger swelled within me. "I am—"

"A Knight of the Akaidian Order," interrupted Piluch, who gave me a pleading look to keep quiet. "Brother Kaselot is the Prince's… the *King's* greatest personal friend and loved deeply in the realm. King Lucien would be rather upset and less agreeable to any terms if his sworn brother was treated dishonorably like his mother and father, which would be mirrored by the rest of Kaselot's brothers in arms who would seek retribution."

Piluch's lie confused me. What danger would there be in just saying I was only some royal adoptee which would grant me safety as a prisoner of war?

Unbeknownst to his reasoning and not wanting to compromise his words, I decided to trust Piluch. His wisdom was far greater than mine, despite his blind loyalty to Renborg.

"An Akaidian," Judux said, his brow lifting slightly at the word before he rose from the throne, descending slowly, carefully to examine me, his molten eyes locking directly with mine. "I've had the pleasure, or displeasure rather, of meeting your brothers in battle on more than one occasion. The finest lancers in all of Divonholm. Perhaps all of Scissalan if the tales of their greatness are to be fully believed!"

Straightening my back, I attempted to stand taller in hopes of masking the growing fear within as Judux paused in his speech to bore his eyes into me. The Grand Derasar tilted his head slightly as his next question burrowed beneath my skin to stir the growing fear that I could not hide.

"I was not aware they recruited ones so young as yourself. You must be quite an accomplished man to forgo the customary sols of study and training before one may be named a brother of the great... *Akaidian* Order."

Judux could see right through the lie.

My heart quickened as I stood helpless before him, waiting anxiously to hear what mine and Piluch's fate would be in the discovery of our deception.

"I pray Her Fire doesn't cause your brotherhood to foolishly side with the Ronians," Judux continued, his tone dripping with both mockery and seriousness, "for I've dreamt of adding the Akaidians to Yarahm's might. You would teach our Elven and Anakrii riders great wisdom for battle."

"A shame your term ends too soon to see it through," I said, to which he smiled. "This desperate grab for power will only bring about more unnecessary death. Your Council will reel you back in like a fish, ready to replace you with a less ambitious Grand Derasar who actually pays his taxes."

"You think this is about power, *Kaselot*? Or wealth?"

"You proved it when you raided Laconnia's silver stores to fuel your military campaigns. I don't see how this is any different."

His smile only strengthened, as if talking to a child in which he controlled the conversation.

"Let me give you a nuanced perspective then."

Judux strode back to reclaim his throne, his midnight crown glowing softly, darkly as he relaxed in the marble seat.

"Ever since our conception by the Mighty Dragon Sh'eol and our Elven foremothers, my people have fought every day to avoid drowning in a sea of relentless enemies like Renborg, your people, who want nothing but to douse our light out of jealousy. If we are ever graced with a brief respite, my people abuse it to destroy one another in pointless ambitions to be the true Tribe of Sh'eol and gather hordes of gold like our ancestors did in the mountains; which your people stole from us.

"But the Winged One, out of Her fiery mercy, did grant us peace after all of this suffering to finally unify as a country and to build a realm for our children to call home. But then your people robbed us of our chance with these *Primarchal Wars* which you declared on us unprovoked. We have lost *countless* of our Drakin sons in this endless war which your people hath wrought on us, even two of my own."

Judux paused for a moment, closing his eyes as if in pain of the past that he mentioned.

"Now I ask you," Judux continued, opening his fiery eyes, "who here is really the villain?"

Despite Judux's own loss in the hundred sols of war, to think he was some martyr whose current evils were justified was incomprehensible.

"You can't claim to be the hero with the blood of innocents dripping from your sword," I said, harshness biting my words.

Judux nodded in agreement.

"You raise a good point, Kaselot, and you are right to be skeptical of my motivations and how I will achieve them for my people. But as in every struggle for freedom against one's oppressors, casualties will inevitably occur on either side, good and evil, their sacrifices a necessity. Even if you see me as evil and wicked for doing what is right for my people, you too would commit the necessary evils in order to restore peace. There is no other way."

"That's no excuse."

"Oh, really? Tell me then, do you think I want to kill your people? Do you think I am oblivious to the Ronian children who will grow up resentful knowing that their mothers and fathers were slain? Do you have any idea what I've lost from your people's war? How short-sighted you are! But then again, I expected nothing less. It is easy to arraign the actions of the powerful when you are powerless. Every option seems so much better than the one chosen for them. But when you are in my position, you do what is necessary for those you love. No cost is too great."

"The war you came for refutes that."

"Kaselot, I did not come here for war. I came here for peace!"

Standing quiet like a lamb before the butcher, I was unphased by his lies that the cleaver he held was meant instead for shearing.

Seeing my disbelief, he sighed.

"I cannot undo the work of the past," Judux continued, "but I can remedy the wrongs that are present, something your King should clearly see when all of this is through. Your ancestors genocided ours, but out of my mercy, I will not destroy your people. No, my purpose is to save my people, to unify them against the Ronians' insistence on our destruction, and to bring about justice for the sins of the past.

"Yarahm will be respected and left alone after this war, and our people will finally thrive in peace, and so will yours. Once we capture your King in his cowardly retreat to another city, we will simply require only a fortune of reparations and an acknowledgment of submission, and then we will leave."

"You speak with such false boldness, as if you know where they will go."

Judux grinned.

"I did not know previously if he had fled, for he could have equally stayed here to battle our forces in the streets, if he were a real King that is. I thank you personally for saving me the trouble of searching for him here. General Kesch, assemble one hundred riders to capture the King at once."

Terror and shame withdrew the fiery blood within me at my blunder.

I exposed Lucien's flight, I thought, tears swelling my eyes at my ever-growing failures. *I would be responsible if they were captured.*

My fate was becoming ever more like the sleepless death that my dream warned of, the noose around my neck not a tool to escape but a shackle to this death sentence.

Unknowingly, I helped tighten it.

"You don't seem too uplifted by my words," Judux said as his General departed at once. "Perhaps I will let you soar the clouds with me after I put Renborg in its place and there is peace in the land once again. Maybe instead of your Brotherhood wearing wings while riding your horses, you can be true Akaidians while riding the wings of *Dragons*."

Dread plummeted any hope in witnessing Judux's devotion.

He wasn't lying.

"W-what are you talking about?" The words could barely escape from my trembling mouth.

Judux's smile only deepened in his Gyldur metal-weaved hood.

"In time you will understand. But, as you're well aware, there's a war to be won and a mighty destiny to be fulfilled. Rolloc, take our honored guest to the royal bedrooms to wait out the war, and send that Dwarven doctor to bandage his wound while you're at it. We can't have our relationship strained with the Akaidians now. Once you are finished, report to General Kesch for the retrieval party of the King, whom you are *not* to slay."

Piluch looked relieved as Rolloc led me out of the throne room, but inside me was a raging storm that reflected the opposite; Lucien's death would be on my hands, and possibly Sigmund's and Egret's too.

I didn't want to live anymore. Before, it was a trembling and temptatious end; now, it was the only thing I could desire, for I didn't deserve to exist.

But I had no choice, for Rolloc yanked me to my feet to lock me away in this Shadow of a destiny.

The halls were silent as Rolloc forced me along them, save for the Drakin guards who followed, their metal grieves clinging with each step as they marched behind us.

Panic and dreadful sorrow raced in my heart from the bleak fate that I was being led to.

It seemed this nightmare would never end.

Before we reached the hall that contained the staircase to the royal bedrooms, Rolloc spoke something in Drakonnian to the scaled guards who followed us. They abruptly turned away. I was confused why the red-haired half-breed was directing the guards away until we took the staircase leading downwards into the belly of Caer Mordrake, directly opposite of his brother's commands.

The only reason for this would be to kill me.

"I plan to kill you," Rolloc said in Ronic, hiding nothing as we descended into the torchlit hallways drenched in shadows.

"Did the baby's blood not satisfy you?" I said as he prodded me along with his Godstone axe. Philomela's screams that his blade silenced only hours ago were still hauntingly real in my mind. Everything in me *hated* him. "Your brother won't tolerate your disobedience."

A sharp sting erupted on my back as Rolloc used his axe's handle to jab me to the ground. Giving me no time to writhe in pain, he picked me up by the collar with his almost unbearingly warm hands to force me again on this death march.

"He is but a pawn, much like you. I swore only to spare the Prince and his wife, but I will do everything I can to make the Mordrake family *suffer*!"

The fire that achingly spread across my back was too much for me to utter an inquisitive response. The meaning of the Drakin's words escaped me, but any efforts to grasp understanding were snuffed as he shoved me towards the dimly lit entrance to Gulmund's bathhouse. No one besides the former King had ever been allowed in, as it had been locked and reserved only for Gulmund. My heart quickened in fear of such a gruesome end that awaited inside the shadows of death before me.

Without a word, Rolloc knocked the steel door down to the bathhouse in two swift blows of his axe. The light emitting from Rolloc's hair and skin were enough to let me see the empty circular pool where its supporting pillars disappeared in the darkness beyond.

And in the center, where the drain usually was for Ronian pools, were two steel trapdoors, their rusty handles locked with one of the biggest chains I had ever seen.

"Do you know what this place is?" Rolloc asked while prodding me forward to the trapdoors.

"Your new pleasure room?"

"*No*, you child! This room represents Renborg's hypocrisy, and it will birth the suffering of your new *King* when he finds out the truth of his father and the demise of his greatest friend."

"I don't understand," I said, attempting to stall as I searched the room for a weapon. Scanning the area for anything of use proved fruitless as he quickly broke the chain before us. All there was in the pool was a wooden stool that was propped before the trapdoors, to which Rolloc yanked open with ease after cleaving the chain in half.

The room became bone-chillingly cold.

Before me was a pit devoid of any light and sound. It was darker than night itself. I couldn't even tell how far of a drop it was. The darkness was too thick to be penetrated from the dim light outside the old bathhouse.

The fate Rolloc planned for me was as void of light as the pit.

"Did Gulmund ever tell you how he ascended to the throne?" Rolloc said, pushing me ever close to the edge with his axe that hummed with the energy from the Godstone.

"Why?"

"I want to hear the hypocrisy; it will make it sweeter."

The nerves in my body shook my voice as I tried to speak calmly.

"His older brothers were slain in the Primarchal Wars."

Rolloc laughed darkly.

"Of course," he said, hatred and glee dripping from his words behind me like honey from a rotting hive. "What your King forgot to tell you was that he hired a Drakin sorceress to kill his brothers to end the *Primarchal Wars* he so hated. But against his knowledge, she stole their souls in order to kill them, wanting to torment her captor for the grisly deed she was forced to do."

"And what makes you think I'd believe that?"

"Because he used me to *feed* them!"

The pit before me reflected how I felt within: void of light and certainty, if this monster was to be believed.

"I was one of the Drakin that they captured in their brutish conquest. The sorceress Gulmund used was someone I had known all my life. Upon seeing her potential, Gulmund didn't hesitate to use her for his own, as he did with any woman he saw. However, Gulmund didn't have the spine to kill them himself. Instead, he gave them a fate far darker than sleepless death, and he used me as his slave for many sols to keep them hidden, for he was too cowardly to take care of them himself."

A shrill riveted up my spine at his words.

Every word that Rolloc had said up to this point was something I detested and did not find trustworthy. But the plausibility that Gulmund would have done something so impossibly horrible was not far from the mark. Gulmund was a man whose face gloomed with sorrow in having to do what was necessary as King.

Do all of those with power rape the grave to birth life?

"That fool took everything from me," Rolloc continued, almost to himself. "But it is vanity to explain my decisions, when you can see what Gulmund did yourself!"

I was already grabbing the stool to deliver a blow to Rolloc's temple before he finished speaking, but the Drakin was too quick and delivered a crushing kick to my back.

Launching forward, I fell headfirst into the well of the world.

There was no time to scream as the darkness swallowed me whole, the end nowhere in sight.

For a moment, I thought I was going to be blessed with a bittersweet ending by falling to a crushing death; but because life had always been so unreasonably cruel, my body crumpled into a pile of what felt like timber and kindling, all of it cracking beneath my weight.

The pile felt too slimy for wood, too cold.

The trapdoors above me slammed shut. Any light that there had been was suffocated by the dark.

I'm almost glad I didn't have any light, for my hands slid over the teeth of what definitely felt like a jaw, confirming my fears that it wasn't kindling nor wood.

"What in the Void!" I said, kicking and screaming on the sea of bones, panic consuming me.

I couldn't tell where I was in this hidden grave until I anxiously rolled off of it onto what felt like a dirt floor. All I could do was hopelessly fight the fear swelling within me like a roaring wave that threatened to capsize a lonely and hopeless schooner caught in a storm too large for it to even see.

How many died in this pit, and for what purpose?

I didn't want to know.

And then I heard it: a wheezing laugh echoing in this chamber of death. It was soon joined by another just as horrible.

Against my best wisdom, I performed Wyl on my necklace, breathing nothing into my soul as my empty Godstone emitted a bloody, pulsating hue. At first, I didn't see anything beyond the pile of bones that were now painted a bloody red, but I could still hear the backwards laughter coming from behind it. As a precaution, I frantically searched the pile of bones until I found myself a femur for defense.

It was no sword, but it was better than nothing.

"I don't know who you are or what you want, but I will k-kill you if you come any nearer!"

Only the same backwards laugh was my answer.

My skin crawled as I listened like some caught prey to the very things that nightmares were made of. There was a rustling in the bones like that of a reptile slithering its way patiently but with excitement through a pile of leaves, hunting carefully but not afraid to make a little noise to leave its victim petrified.

And then I saw it.

Emerging into the bloody light and crawling on the bone heap like a spider, the first thing I noticed was its wicked grin. Its smile completely lacked teeth and stretched across its rotting flesh. Even more ghastly were its eye sockets which were as hollow as the grave it should be in. The creature was dead but very much alive as its flopping tongue, hanging unnaturally long from its mouth, suggested.

"Aaaah aaah ah aaah!" it laughed, jumping onto the sea of bones like a child while its friend joined behind with its own gumless and feral smile.

"LLik su, llik su!" they screamed in unison.

Curses flew from my mouth as they pounced upon me. With only a leg bone to protect myself with, I started swinging without abandon, forgetting all that I had learned of swordsmanship and defense from my sols of training in those heartbeats of fear.

"What the Void are you!" I screamed, bashing their festering heads left and right as they scurried around to try and add me to their decaying collection that I had disturbed.

There was something about these demented creatures that seemed so insanely familiar but was hard to remember in those precious seconds of survival. It wasn't until my bone sword began to cave in the familiar shapes of their noses that unlocked my recognition: they looked exactly like Gulmund's and Lucien's, small and buttoned.

I'm beating the corpses of Kyllian IV and Aedon!

"Aghh!" I screamed in the revelation.

There was a whole new meaning to this fight that eluded my understanding but started to make sense from Rolloc's twisted words.

How had they been alive for over twenty sols? What could Gulmund have done that made them as hideous as his soul? If they were without souls, how did they live?

The monsters were uninterested in my inquiries and fought with a feral vengeance. No matter how hard I hit the smiling creatures, they continued to claw at me and laugh, unphased by the pain and driven by such a deep and unyielding hunger.

For the first time in my short life, I fought with ferocity against the literal faces of death, having no desire to succumb to them.

Despite my zeal to live, what strength I had began to dwindle against their unrelenting hunger, their incessant attacks causing me to slip on something and fall on my back. The howling creatures took advantage of this and pounced on me like hunting dogs tearing apart a wounded pelafahn downed by a hunter's arrow. Their leathery fingers tore into my skin and held my squirming body with an iron grip.

The one closest to me, Aedon it looked like, clasped my throat with its nails and slammed my head against the dirt, stars erupting in my reddened vision. My jaw was too weak to fend off the slithering tongue of Aedon as it crammed its inky black snake down my throat. Fear as thick as glaciers from the polar regions of Udd filled me along with its tongue that wiggled its way beyond my throat and towards a destination I did not intend on it reaching.

Light flickered through the cracks of the trapdoor above.

With the full knowledge that I would probably regret it, I bit down while kicking the other brother with my foot. The creature screamed and laughed at the same time while releasing its grip. Turning my head, I vomited its revolting acidic tongue that it so blessed me with. Bellowing pure rage, I headbutted the disgusting thing, following with a crushing blow to its jaw with my fist that separated it from its chin.

"Llik su llik su llik su llik su!" they chanted still.

"I hate you!" I yelled while bucking them off and wrestling to my feet.

Snapping the femur bone in one violent motion against my knee, I used it to spear through the gaping mouth of what used to be Aedon, pushing the laughing creature into his former brother and mirroring their screams.

The other was too fast for me, dancing its way behind me where it wrapped its poisonous tongue around my arm and yanked me back to the ground. Slamming into the floor knocked the breath from my lungs, my heart beating ferociously in fear to not have another disgusting tongue forced down my throat. Before I could fight back, it pounded my more sensitive regions and left me completely deflated, vulnerable to its mindless machinations.

Moaning in agony, I was helpless as its dripping tongue began its descent into my quivering lips, its tongueless friend coming to join as it rose from the bone pile I forced it onto.

The fear was so capsizing within me that I froze with terror and uncertainty in what to do.

Just as the maniacal corpse was making its tongue slither into the back of my throat, the trapdoors above us boomed. It was enough to make both of the monsters stop and look up. The silence was followed by another boom which shook the room to its very core, but this time, the trap doors exploded off their hinges and plummeted to the chamber floor, one of them even decapitating the tongueless one by surprise.

Landing gracefully like a dove upon the door which had speared the monster, the majestic being from my dreams stood taller than a stallion in his cosmic display of colors. The mysterious figure from my dream glowed like the stars in this well of darkness. I could only see my savior's eyes from the floor, and they burned like radiant suns of hope.

The remaining monster bounced to its feet and screamed at the cosmic being.

"Llik su, llik suuuu!" it screamed before rushing him.

And then my guardian of light did something I couldn't even begin to understand.

As the demented figure sprinted towards him, the cosmic man simply held his colorful hand out in front of him, unafraid of the eyeless monster who leapt into the air to devour him.

The creature fell directly in the path of his hand. Like a bird swimming through the clouds, the man's hand phased through the creature's head where it abruptly stopped halfway through, catching the monster in mid-air. I knew my head was sinking towards darkness, but I could swear the man's hand went through its face like a spirit, like he had caught hold of its brain and was threatening to crush it. All that the shriveled husk could do was gasp the same "Llik su" phrase over and over, the phrase repeating faster and faster in a frantic excitement.

A wet crunch came from what was left of Kyllian IV's brain like celery being snapped, leaving it to dangle before the colorful being, completely lifeless.

That's also how my brain felt in seeing this mysterious figure of galactic light perform such an impossible deed. I tried standing to my feet, which were shaking in fear, but all I could manage was to rise to my knees as my head swam deeper into the darkness of pain.

"W-who are you?" I managed to say through my aching mouth.

The one from the moon discarded the dead creature and walked slowly towards me, his ethereal light illuminating my darkness. He said nothing as he approached, choosing instead to lock eyes with me as he leaned his galactic face towards me. It was like staring into the vast cosmos of stars as I gazed at the ones swirling around his burning eyes.

Strangely, just like in my dream, I felt a surprising peace; it almost felt natural seeing him.

The wonderful being reached out to touch my chest, something I felt incapable of resisting as I watched in wonder and fear. It was only then that I realized he wasn't trying to harm me, but instead was reaching for something within me as his sunkissed fingers gently graced the doors of my heart, like someone who was eager to be let in.

"Yield to the Light," he whispered.

And at his quiet knock on my heart, my thoughts and vision turned white as snow that melted before the spring.

Chapter 8
The Sunset and the Dawn

They watch over us, we sleep
Our Eternal Womb finds relief
For from Her tears were they formed
Like water they move, pure as falling rain
They guide the shattered earth, kissing its pain
Hidden from the eyes like dew in the morn'

Solbok
Dawn, 3:24
"Tears of Guidance"

It felt like my soul was on fire.

No, probably a more accurate description of how I felt in the depths of my tumbling mind was this: it was as if lightning was being stitched into my being.

Slowly, carefully, one thread at a time.

I don't know if I was actually screaming, but I wouldn't be surprised if I was, for the pain was beyond any magnitude I had ever experienced before.

Before I could find out, my thoughts plunged back to sleep in the coldest depths of my mind, exhausted.

Sleepless death finally had its way with me.

But then, I felt three heartbeats instead of two.

A candle flame sparked in my mental vortex of darkness. In the fire, I could see images flashing through: a silver and smooth temple that looked like nothing I've ever seen before, surrounded by a canvas of stars.

The flame grew brighter.

What started as a tiny flame soon became a roaring fire that consumed my entire unconscious vision. The images were larger now, many of which showcased the same galactic being that rescued me from the backwards smiling creatures, but there were more than just him. There were dozens.

And some were hooded with robes of white, covering their naked spirit.

Each moment that passed before my mind's eyes were incoherent and random, and the same silver temple appeared in most of them. Perhaps the strangest of them all contained a luminous and luscious moon surrounded by an inky sea twinkling with stars. I have never seen it before, but there was something distinctly familiar about the place.

If I didn't have the slightest of grips on my identity, I would have thought these moments were my memories.

But the memories came to an abrupt halt when a burning red line began to form in the corner of my mind. I could feel the line being scraped across the strange moments, the searing line almost throwing me back to unconsciousness as it painfully completed foreign yet familiar symbols that flowed more elegantly than the tides of an eclipse.

Perhaps the strangest part was not those symbols, but the fact that I could understand what they meant: Human.

The ancient markings became so bright that I could feel my whole being squirm under its radiant power, the inner fire torching my eyes like a pulled muscle.

The unbearable pain awakened every part of my being like cold water drenching my slumber. My senses were rudely awakened by the symbol that seemed to burn within me and before me.

Though the state of confusion was disorienting, one thing was clear: I was not asleep in the eternal Void of death.

With a steady caution, I opened my burning eyes to adjust to the blinding light that immediately flooded them. It was daylight.

As for my ears, they heard screaming.

"Please, please!" said a bloody and garbled voice, sounding older than my history books. I could understand he was speaking the Elvish tongue of the Vivekians and not Ronic, which was strange because I've never learned that particular dialect of the Elves, for there were many tongues of their kind, even in Renborg. Yet, it was as clear as the crisp morning air flooding my lungs.

"I know you speak Drakonnian, Sarrus," an elegant but sharp voice said, typical of the Drakin tongue which I clearly understood, adding to my confusion. "I'm sure you've taught it to the rest of your greedy children you've spawned. By the way, how are they? The ones you rape and sell that is? Hmmm?"

A bone-crushing thud filled my ears, followed by a crusty welp from what sounded like Sarrus.

"Disgusting," the Drakin continued, "I make an oath in Sh'eol's name that every part of your withered body will feel my blade, and you will soon feel the scales of His judgment against your wicked acts. And if you don't tell me where you've hidden our shrine, then I swear by His wings that I will personally erase the Cilvahan family from history! Actually, Zora, go ahead and find his son. Tiberius shouldn't be far from the castle's vault. It's past time that we show this plant breeder how hot a fire bath really is; I'm *done* being patient!"

My mind drowned in confusion.

On the one hand, I couldn't understand why I was comprehending this exchange between two languages I have never mastered. Both tongues sounded easily distinguishable, like I've known them for a long time and could fully understand their differences. On the other hand, it felt like my mind was continuing the story of the Great Temple Sacking that the Cilvahan family committed on the Drakin almost a thousand sols ago, which for some reason came to life in my chaotic thoughts.

Was this a nightmare of the many stories I had read at night from the history books I drowned myself in?

Perhaps the biggest mystery was how Gulmund could be such good friends with that shriveled and pedophilic Elf, for he was supposed to be a King of justice.

Gulmund… Drakin… invasion!

My mouth erupted into a gasp as it all came crashing in.

With the functions of my body and mind kicking in, I thankfully grabbed the marble pillar to support myself as I jolted backwards in confusion and fear.

I was hundreds of feet in the air.

All around me, the city of Renborg was blackened with smoke and the scars of war.

This was no dream.

The pillar I was grasping onto was part of the tower that sprouted from the domes of the Hall of Judges. From my vantage point, I could see the source of the interaction between the Drakin and Cilvahan was coming from below, for Sarrus was laying on the street in front of the Hall's entrance. The Elf was beaten to a pulp by a burly Drakin who glowered over him.

I was not in Gulmund's demented pit anymore either.

The thought of those eyeless and laughing freaks invaded my heart with fear and drowned out the Elf's sorrows. Memories of their hollowed eyes and backwards laughter invaded my mind like their rotting tongues did. Perhaps even more harrowing than their discovery was the revelation that they were undoubtedly the King's deceased brothers. Or formerly deceased.

What were those things?

I did not know nor did I want to. To my own peril, my analytical mind scoured all of the stories I've read to make sense of the monsters. From their appearance to how they moved, I couldn't help being reminded of one of the darkest myths in the library's *Tales of the Old World.* It had something to do with Godstone, and possibly sorceresses if Rolloc was to be believed, I just couldn't put my finger—

"They were Soulis," a deep and stoic voice boomed.

I froze; the voice didn't seem to come from behind, but within. Snapping my head back, I covered myself with my hands for protection, but there was no one there.

"Hello?" I said, being careful not to yell too loudly because of the Eldrakes patrolling the upper districts where the Hall was located. I pulled at my face in the fear of losing my mind. "Nox! Please don't lose it."

"You are not lost."

The cosmic being who had saved me from the Soulis appeared alongside me, his stars and brilliant array of colors that comprised his flesh painting the air beside me.

My heart skipped a beat and my flesh jumped out of its skin. Dashing to the other side of the tower's domed turret, I cowered behind another pillar.

"Who are you?"

The glowing figure stood up and folded his arms, almost amused as he studied me. "Do not fear. I am Aquilla."

Scrunching my forehead in uncertainty, I said, "And what do you want, Aquilla?"

"To stop you from achieving your destiny."

The voice from my dream came rushing back to me like the anger of a hurricane, its wrath terrifying and dreadful. Words were as sparse as water in the Seng'arh Deserts, my heart just as dead as the myths who had once slithered deep within them.

"Sleepless death?"

"That is what the Author of Light has written."

Aquilla sat down cross-legged in the middle of the tower walkway, completely vulnerable to me. His suns for eyes stared at me curiously, as if he were a Cordis student from the College of Man who was just beholding Godstone for the first time.

"I believe destiny to be of your own hands," Aquilla continued, "that the Void is not an unwanted destiny, but a choice."

My hands slipped from the pillar and I fell to my knees. The revelation of gods and lunar beings was like a storm of trebuchets to the fragile castle of my mind. The immense amount of questions and complexities that arose were daunting.

What I wouldn't give to be swallowed by the simple sea.

"Everything in my dream becoming true proves otherwise," I said, my voice weak, tired and shaking as I tried to wrap my mind around the ever-growing list of questions. "If this god of yours is real and intent on damning me with this destiny to be the wicked opposite of Cypherus, then it's better to die. There's no point in even trying."

"Not even for them?"

Images of Lucien crying flooded my mind; he was rocking back and forth in his ash-torn wedding robes next to his younger brother Sigmund who wailed in some encampment. No sounds emitted from Lucien, but his mouth was drowning in tears. And next to them but far apart was Egret, her eyes alert but ringed with fatigue and painted with sorrow.

Seeing them tore my heart. They did not deserve to suffer.

"'A river which flees to the sea will wither its banks left behind,'" Aquilla said, quoting Solbok.

Before I could respond, Aquilla abruptly stood and pierced the air with his finger, an ethereal line glimmering like crystal forming behind the pattern he drew. The Godstone around my neck hummed in response to the spiritual command before me. With surprising speed, he drew a word I had never seen before, but that I somehow already knew:

"I am a Medjaib," Aquilla said, "born from the Author's tears to guide you. And this is the name of my being."

The glimmering symbol consumed my vision.

Though I've read hundreds of stories concerning the lost magic of souls and the power of names, its true power was as evasive and unclear as the mist the symbol soon became before evaporating.

There was only one thing about these words that was more certain than death itself: the power before me could steal souls. It was the kind of power that Cypherus wielded as he stole the souls of Dragons and became strong enough to save his family. But it was also the same power that led to the Age of Ashes where war and disease burned over a third of Scissalan, including any knowledge of the dark power that was lost.

And maybe it should have remained so.

So before me was a power that would either raise me above a shadowed destiny or quicken my descent towards it.

"How do you know this dark magic?" I said, my mind unable to believe even the conversation I was having with this luminous being. "And how do I know what it says? I could even understand what the Drakin were saying."

Aquilla nobly bowed his head. "We are bonded, Morgan. My soul has intertwined with your own. My knowledge is your knowledge, as is my power."

The memory of Aquilla's hand phasing through the Soulis before crushing its brain replayed vividly in my mind, but not by my own volition.

Without his ethereal lips moving, Aquilla said, "We are one."

His voice was a cold but pleasant breeze in my mind.

As if he understood my confusion, Aquilla pointed to my heart, his finger phasing right through. Gasping in preparation for pain, I felt nothing. But then I understood without any words: his heart had truly intertwined with mine.

"But not completely," Aquilla said, the feeling of three heartbeats resurging in my core. Though they beat at a similar rhythm, they were not one completely in tune. "Once you yield entirely to the Light, I shall show you the path to saving your family, and I shall keep you from becoming the Shadow of Cypherus."

The words of the strange being were refreshing. But the cynical part of my mind found them dangerously appealing, like a false chance of freedom that would consume me ever further once I committed to its lie of hope.

Did not my prophetic dream say that I would be sleepless in my grave?

Storms of doubt clouded my mind again.

How could this Medjaib not believe the words of his god?

"I do believe them," Aquilla said.

He can read my thoughts?

"Only if you trust in me your thoughts, and not keep them hidden from me," he said, answering my question. "As for your heresy, do not hold to such false truth so tightly. I believe every word the Author has written, for, 'The quill of Her words is a spear, and the ink of Her truth pierces every story.' You should not be so hasty to make conclusions, young Morgan. Her prophecies have been vague before, for others have been the true recipient, or even things! You cannot control the pages of destiny the Author has given to you, but you can control what is inscribed upon them."

Aquilla's suns for eyes twinkled as if he saw something that I was unable to see. With grace, he drew closer to me, showing me his humanoid head whose features were defined by a purple hue of galactic colors and swirls, his eyes the burning focal points of a canvas of stars and cosmos that composed his translucent skin.

Aquilla's face was beautiful, mesmerizing, and, surprisingly, young.

"What you glimpse is my spirit," Aquilla said, gazing into my soul. "In time shall you be able to move through this world as a Medjaib, without hindrance to things that are not of spirit as we strive to save your family. You shall wield the power of souls as Cypherus did, and together, we shall ensure sleepless death shall be the fate of our enemies, not ourselves."

If I couldn't have felt Aquilla's heartbeat next to mine, I would've thought I was dreaming of this colorful being and his strange dialect.

Looking out to the Strumma in bewilderment at the collision of the Medjaib's world and mine, I was barely able to hold it all together with its implications and questions more numerous than the stars that flickered through Aquilla's skin, all of it barely wrapped in my mind with a thin string of belief. Dropping my gaze down at my gloved hands and back towards Caer Mordrake where the monsters who had killed my baby sister and threatened the lives of my brothers were waiting, I felt a growing seed of angry confidence within.

For what felt like the first time, a hopeful reason to live began to sprout from my broken flesh like a budding rose in the summer rain. Though the thunderous storm of destiny looked deathly black and its ending unclear through its painful torrent, there bloomed a chance of surviving this fated darkness from above, and blessing others with the same chance.

And although I wouldn't know what being the opposite of Cypherus would entail, if it meant saving Lucien and Sigmund, then it was worth it. In rescuing them, I would also be sparing Egret from Judux's ambitions, and part of me felt I owed her just that.

"Very well," I said, filling myself with air as I pulled myself shakily to my feet. "What shall we do?"

"If we are to be formidable against the rising darkness, your heart must become one rhythm with mine."

"How so?"

"All you must do is recite the *Heart of Stars.*"

I frowned at his odd request.

"Forgive me, how is reciting that poem going to align me with you?"

"It shall inscribe these words of light upon your heart, which shall allow our hearts to move as one. For now there is only darkness, and as the shadows dance before the dawn, your soul scurries away from my own."

"Well, then you will have to find another way to grab my soul. I am not uttering the words of those priests."

Aquilla turned away to gaze upon the Drakin lines that were battling the Ronian forces in the streets. "You *must*, Morgan. Thus is the beginning of our journey, which is why we must begin now to prepare for what is to come. Even if you could phase as I do, your lack of training shall doom us if we engage Judux and his Drakin. And from what Judux has warned of, we face insurmountable challenges if we do not become one."

"You believe he can bring back the Dragons?"

Aquilla was silent for a moment. "I know not if the Drakin speaks truth, and that is what worries me. Godstone can only merge two souls together in equal harmony, so he should not be able to create anything more than one Eldrake with Selstenos."

"Selstenos? Do you refer to *Solstein*?"

"Ah, yes, *Solstein*. I forget you Humans love to change your words. Nonetheless, *Solstein* is indeed a powerful tool in Judux's hands."

"But there's more to Godstone than just its power over souls?"

Aquilla nodded grimly.

"Indeed. But he spoke boldly of his determination to bring them back from death, the knowledge of which is beyond my understanding if he has found a way. 'The grave never sleeps,' it appears, and so it shall be that you must recite this Skallgend, for the darkness of ages past has come to devour us beyond our current power."

"I-I… I will not," I said, my words as heavy as my steps to the edge of the tower, my resolve to live weakening as the rains of doubt pummeled the birth of my fragile rose.

"Why not?" Aquilla's voice was impatient.

Staring at him with disbelief, I said, "How can you expect me to recite an oath of allegiance to a god who sentenced me to a *sleepless death*? Even if my hopeless destiny is not as clear as rain, she has unequivocally fated millions with the same. I do not wish to serve her."

The air was thicker than the reeking blood rising from Renborg.

"Then there exists no hope for Lucien or Sigmund," Aquilla said after a long pause. "Shall we resign to watch the King and Queen become martyrs?"

Anger flooded my cheeks as I strode to the edge where Aquilla stood gazing beyond the city. Standing beside him, I scoured the Ren River looking for Lucien. But it was impossible to tell.

"They have already fled," Aquilla said.

Aquilla's memory of the King's banner fleeing from the outskirts of Renborg flooded my mind with relief.

Finally, I could breathe. "Kolstok probably sent them to Feldrem to reinforce with the city's Provincial Kriga and to keep them safe from the siege. They will be more than fine."

"Look again, Morgan. Do you see them riding along the river towards the city?"

Squinting to look closer, I saw there was no one along the river, which is where they should have been if they were traveling to Feldrem. However, when I looked west, I saw a host of Ronian's and their green banners heading away from the path to Feldrem, even departing from the Dragon Highway. And just a few miles behind them was another host, though smaller, but I could spot the flaming-haired Drakin and their Eldrake easily from afar.

"They're directing them away from Feldrem," I said, my stomach turning sour. "They're not going to make it to Hebsund either at that pace."

"And Ludsala is their only refuge, which I am sure you have heard the stories of. They are doomed either way without our help. They need us, as does the empire."

A storm of emotions thundered within me, the rose within swaying in the winds of fate. The Medjaib's words made me shudder at the thought of Lucien, Sigmund, and Egret being trapped there in that den of evil long forgotten. That is if they even made it. As for how I would be of any use was the question, as to serve a cruel god was against my very soul, and to reject her meant I would lose all anyway.

But there seemed no other choice in saving them. Their lives were more important than mine, and they deserved to live.

If I failed, then I would sleep and not become any doomed shadow eternal.

That was enough for me.

And so I chose to forgo the sunset of my life and stumble into the dawn of some new meaning, the rose within basking in its glorious light of possibility of saving the ones I cared about; for now at least.

"Very well," I said, shaking my head clear of any darkness and trying to fill it with a plan.

Aquilla's galactic face hummed a warm orange, his soul telling me that he at least approved that we were making progress towards what he wanted. "And so our story begins."

"But how do we escape from the city? We're trapped between hundreds of Drakin and Renborg's double walls."

Aquilla hesitated before responding. "You shall not be fond of my proposal."

"Why?"

Aquilla nodded towards the Eldrakes screeching in the air, and my stomach plummeted in reading his thoughts which he made readily accessible.

"No! That… no, I'm not doing that!"

"We can lure one here to have a gentle descent into the river, where there is bound to be farming horses we can borrow to save your family."

"Gentle descent? That's if the Eldrake doesn't drop me from trying to claw out my eyes. I'm without a doubt that it won't be too fond of your idea."

"Do you see another way?"

I grunted in frustration.

It was a horrible plan, and one where death seemed likely, but he was right that there were farms sprawling outside the walls of the city and bordering the river.

There would be horses and provisions at any of the farms, which would provide us with what we needed to rejoin Lucien and Egret.

Or at least attempt to.

Taking a deep breath, I filled my lungs for the life I was about to enter or escape from.

"Let us be done with this."

My lips sang a piercing note that immediately caught the attention of the nearest Eldrake. The hybrid roared in response as it was swooping over the ancient Hippodrome. I took one last glance at the southern half of the city where the Ronians were battling the Drakin street by street in a feeble attempt to take back the city.

Little did they know the fleets of Drakin that were coming for them.

They would be crushed.

"Wait, how do I grab hold of the beast?"

"Wait for my command to fall to the floor. As he passes by, grab his foot and let him carry us over the walls and towards the river, for he shall move in that direction."

Attempting to steady my breath proved impossible, for my heart began to race as the Eldrake called more of its friends to its aid. Even the Drakin patrolling their portion of the city looked towards the Hall of Judges as the Eldrakes came flying in. There was only one chance if I didn't want to be devoured by the Eldrake's companions or shot by the Drakin.

"Three… two… yield!"

Obeying the Medjaib's advice, the Eldrake scraped over my back, but not before I could grab a hold of it's plantigrade foot that was typical of the Drakin peoples from their Dragon ancestry. Gripping with all my might, the Eldrake yanked us forward from the dome and over the city with blinding speed.

Or me, *as I didn't know how to describe the being living inside me.*

"You can say *us*," Aquilla said as the Hall of Judges became a blur beneath us.

The Eldrake screeched while it tried to shake *us* off over the surrounding buildings of the government district, the double walls of Renborg approaching with speed at the Eldrake's aerial path.

No, us *is too much,* I thought, hiding it from Aquilla.

"Fiend!" it screamed in a dialect I had no time to identify but could immediately understand.

"Hold!" Aquilla said.

Our friend didn't sound to be enjoying our unapproved flight as we frighteningly descended towards the Ren River, barely making it across the city and towards the farms below. My feet even kicked the battlements that lined Renborg's walls like teeth.

"Hold tighter still!" Aquilla said as my arms burned from having to squeeze onto our rambunctious friend. All I could do was try not to look at the dizzying ground below that could very easily deliver me unto a black fate.

Another Eldrake arrived to ensure that I reached it.

"Gahh!" I screamed as the other one tore into my back with a powerful swipe. "I cannot hold on any longer!"

"Hold!" Aquilla yelled, the other Eldrake looping around with jagged teeth glinting in the sunlight. It looked hungry for my back which dripped with blood like wax from a dying candle.

"Foolish child!" the other one screamed as it tore through the sky, my deformed flesh its target.

"Now!"

My gloved fingers slipped from both of the Eldrakes feet before its aerial friend could destroy me, and I plummeted to the sloshing river below.

With my detestable home behind, a galactic being from the moon within, and the last of my only family being chased to the lair of shadows ahead, I plunged into the waters of not my death, but of my uncharted and unwanted destiny.

Part II

The Light

Chapter 9
Worlds Beyond

To Wyl
Breathing peace
Feasting knowledge
Drinking wisdom
Divine

To Wae
Exuding purity
Feeding guidance
Draining evil
Destiny

Scrolls of Akhorus
The Medjaib Code

"W**ith** haste, Morgan!" Aquilla said, the heart of the stolen horse drumming faster than mine while it raced through the Bludhfield farms outside of the city.

The Eldrakes screeched just a stone's throw behind us.

"I'm trying!"

I could barely hold onto the reins of our terrified horse as it fled from the flying creatures who pursued us with gnashing teeth. Its bucking and whining almost threw me off as it ran desperately for its own life away from the city. The fields became a steady blur of rosen wheat in this nightmare which had no end.

A rising torrent of anxieties and questions and fear threatened to snuff out every breath that escaped from my panting lungs as we rode for our lives. Nothing made sense anymore. The bleak world which I had known had been violently taken from me with no remorse, no remedy. The chalice of my mind was overflowing with questions that had no answers, the chief of which was the cosmic being inside of me whose presence was contradictingly intangible yet undeniably material.

But to survive the present danger, I shut out every question from my thoughts like a hastily closed book.

"There, into the mountain forests!" Aquilla said. "We shall break from their pursuit— Morgan!"

My stallion barely avoided trampling the Dwarven farmers running through the dense Bludhfields, their lives almost eternally sifted like wheat from my reckless pursuit to save the ones I loved. If it wasn't for Aquilla, even more would have died because of me.

"Ssstop or they die!" one of the Eldrakes roared.

Knowing they would die either way did not remove the raging guilt that dominated my mind as we tore away from the open fields to burst into the dense woods of the Dendravik Mountains. The Eldrakes screamed at our defiance and made good on their promise to draw us out by slaughtering the Dwarven family, knowing just as well as we did that they would not be able to hunt us in these tightly packed woods.

The blood-curdling screams of the Dwarves were thankfully filtered through the dense foliage.

"Let us not ponder the inevitable," Aquilla said as my borrowed steed galloped tirelessly through the sun-choked woods. "Our triumph will come to pass, and their sacrifice shall we avenge."

If only that was true.

Our words were mute like the sounds of the Eldrakes soon became as we traveled west, using the mountains that loomed beyond the trees as our guide forward. Like a brook moving swiftly and quietly through the forest, so too did our steed help us disappear unnoticed in the overgrowth of trees. But as the shadows of the woods lengthened throughout the unending ride, I had to grip tighter onto the reins to keep myself awake and to distract from the chaos of my mind.

Despite my intermediate imprisonment and concussionary

limbo, I was exhausted, afraid of the dreams and horrific memories of the last day that would come to haunt me.

After several hours of riding, without realizing it, I found myself slowing our horse into a quiet part of the forest, my fingers shaking from lack of rest.

"Why have we stopped?" Aquilla said. "Is not your family in need?"

"I cannot keep this pace any longer, I need a moment to rest," I said, the simple words sapping the last draught of strength within as panic began to shake through me again from the crushing exhaustion and terrors I had witnessed. "And I need to think."

"Rest? Think? How can that be so? Has night yet fallen?"

"I need a brief respite, spirit, lest I be useless in the time of need."

"Aquilla," he corrected. "And it is so that, 'The Light of Her nourishment strengthens the soul awake.' How are you unable to endure while the day is light?"

"*Endure*? My entire home has been invaded, my family slaughtered and scattered, I have recovered no strength over this endless night, and you ask me to endure? You've gifted me with nothing except your simplistic Solbok for a mind, with only the possibility of being useful through your god. How can I even stand a chance if I can barely see from my weariness?"

Aquilla said nothing in response.

Slipping off my horse in tired frustration, I tied him to the nearest tree which I sat down to lean against.

I was alone in the forest.

Aquilla emerged from my vessel to stand beside me, his galactic radiance helping slightly to remove the feeling of solitude that threatened to overwhelm me amidst the silent trees.

As I rested against the tree, Aquilla walked around to observe the trees and vibrant flowers that blossomed around them, his curious composure reminding me of Sigmund and Philomela looking at the colorful foods and gifts from foreign kingdoms when I would take them to the marketplace.

"The world is so… vibrant with color," Aquilla said, almost to himself as he fingered a golden flower that sprouted from the forest floor. "I do not understand why many sleep when there is an entire realm to explore."

His inquiry intrigued my dozing mind, but there was no more strength left within me to respond.

Exhaustion soon enveloped me and pressed its uncaring foot down upon my chest, along with the endless array of questions and fears that I tried to force out of my mind during our flight; there was no escaping them now. Looking at Aquilla only confirmed that all that had come to pass was unnaturally real, that this wasn't just some nightmare after all that I could wake up from, to emerge back into a world where I could hear Lucien's laughter and hold the small and innocent hands of Sigmund and Philomela.

At the thought of them, I crumbled into tears, wailing pathetically as the creeping silhouettes of the forest began to close in on me.

Aquilla turned to look at me, but it was hard to understand what his thoughts were, for he did not share them with me. Instead, Aquilla tilted his swirling head as if in curiosity of what to say.

"If you need rest, then rest. Should trouble arise, I shall wake you."

It was impossible to respond through the aching cry that consumed me, but Aquilla seemed to read my worried mind.

"No, I cannot physically protect you now that we are one. Our souls are interwoven and impossible to separate, lest I should be eternally banished. What you perceive is but a projection of my spirit, while the vessel of my being remains sewn to yours. It is because…"

Aquilla stopped as my mind's drifting comprehension of his words was taking on a severely diminishing return. "We shall discuss it further upon the dawn."

I didn't respond.

Closing my quivering eyes to Aquilla and the world that continued to never make any sense, I let the tears fall and dry without care.

The darkness of the forest sang to me a lullaby of loneliness as I curled myself up and listened, my conscious thoughts drowning in the blackest parts of my tumultuous mind and begging to never be resurfaced.

There was too much change and chaos to grapple with, none of which I understood, so my tired soul decided to ignore all of it in order to survive.

The whispering trees soon hushed themselves as the darkness consumed me, and then there was peace.

At last.

But a silver light began to glimmer through my eyelids.

Curious, I opened them, only to discover that I was no longer in Renborg and its dark forests: I found myself meditating in a field of silver and white roses. Unlike the nightmarish vision I received before the wedding, this dream felt real, like it was something that once was. It felt ancient and as far away as worlds beyond.

But instead of the moon above me, it was the earth.

My eyes trickled with wonder at the peculiar replacement of the moon in the vast ocean of stars above me.

Where am I?

The only reason I knew it was the earth floating far beyond me was because of Renborg's recognizable form that bordered the Byring Sea with Kapitol's unique fixture in the middle.

The lands that stretched beyond them were entirely foreign to me, and much larger than I could ever imagine. The unknown lands of the earth looked like shattered clay formed hastily back together, and they were much larger than Renborg.

In fact, Renborg looked to play only a very small part in the vastness of the earth.

Looking down from the earth, my hands sparkled a translucent hue, no longer a hideous shell but a beautiful glass. Through my glittering flesh, I could see the dirt was not earthen at all but instead reflected the same haunted glow which shepherded the night from the Void above.

Fascinated with my spectral form and the reality my mind was conjuring, I tried to force my eyes to look around this lunar atmosphere. But it was like my eyes were glued to whatever this spectral vessel I inhabited decided to look at. For one moment, I was looking across the vast and mountainous craters of the moon which were spotted with marble trees to then return my attention to the earth above, completely out of my control as I, or we, sat on our knees with hands relaxed and our heart positioned to the stars.

What is this?

"Aquilla."

My naked but colorful vessel turned slightly to the voice as if to not break the deep meditation I was in.

"Prucios," I spoke, the name vibrating across the air before me as someone who looked exactly like Aquilla weaved through the silver roses towards me, sifting through like a spirit in a brilliant display of colors.

The looming mountains where Prucios had come from nested a mystical glass temple that stretched over its vast peaks. It glittered like ice from the starlight.

My mind's imaginings were beyond perplexing.

"The Iyrah have summoned you, friend."

Closing my eyes, I sighed. "They shall wait."

"Aquilla, be not foolish in rejecting their summons."

Taking a deep breath, I stood to face Prucios. "Mindless chatter and aged pride are not what I seek. I know what they wish to proclaim."

Prucios had no face, just like Aquilla, but a swirling cosmic purple flustered over where his eyes should have been.

"You must not let naive zeal blind you! To perceive every rarity as revelation for the *descension* is foolish."

"But Her vision *confirms* it!"

Prucios shook his head.

Aquilla let our eyes drift towards the larger mountain opposite from the glass temple that rested just beneath the distant earth. The hand-like monument on top of the mountain gave the appearance that it was holding the entire planet in its hands from our point of view. Somehow, something within me knew it modeled the female hands of the Valkryn god he proclaimed to worship, its purpose a mystery but of tremendous importance to the Medjaib whom my mind appeared to be imagining with explicit detail.

"Prucios?" Aquilla said, turning back to his friend.

"Yes?"

"I cannot help but wonder…"

"What?" Prucios said, his eyes locking with the blazing suns of Aquilla's.

"Do you believe the Iyrah still know the Author?"

Prucios tilted his swirling head at Aquilla's words.

"Do you question our brothers' purity?"

"Prucios, they seek nothing but control, and they deny the Mother's vision—"

"Not for ill motive do they seek to control their destinies. Do you so easily forget our brother Elios? His suffering has not ended, nor will it till the Mother's justice. A desire to usurp freedom with control comes when seeing only the wickedness of the world, not the light that prevails underneath."

"My memory serves me well, but what they desire is corrupt!"

"They desire from pure intentions. As for us, we shall let the Eternal One decide who shall descend."

"We shall never receive their blessing, nor shall they believe Her vision!"

"You must be patient for Her will!"

Aquilla sighed, and the silver roses sang a somber melody from the vibrations of his labored breath.

"Do you truly believe my soul was graced by Her Glory?" Aquilla said.

"I… it is not impossible that it is so. But it is not for me to say."

"So I stand alone in belief."

"Aquilla, you cannot blame them for caution. Do you not believe they are eager to see another descension since your arrival?"

"My eyes do not lie Prucios! How can you doubt Her wonders?"

"It is not that we doubt Her blessings of visions, it is only—"

"Do not waste your breath with the same excuse."

Prucios lowered his head as if burdened by a heavy guilt.

"My apologies, friend. They delivered me no choice."

Before Prucios even finished his words, a ring of Medjaib dressed in silver robes sprung up around us with crystal-like spears.

Aquilla tensed himself as he surveyed the guards that closed in on him without warning.

"Forgive me, Aquilla."

Aquilla was silent as Prucios stepped out of the way, letting the guards escort us to the glass temple in the distant mountains. A look of betrayal was all Aquilla gave to Prucios as we were forced to walk through the silver roses and marble trees, the temple awaiting us as judgment.

Aquilla remained silent as we were forcefully marched up the grand steps of glass beneath the towering and transparent pillars of the shimmering temple. Since their feet emitted no sounds, the only thing I could hear was the white rivers that poured on either side of the staircase down into the lakes below, for Aquilla spoke nothing either. He didn't have to speak for me to know that his heart turmoiled with hurt from this betrayal and an ever-deepening loneliness.

The familiarity sent chills into my ethereal state.

Once we reached the top of the stairs, I was bewildered by the lack of any doors, for all that was before us was a sheer wall of glass with ancient symbols inscribed upon them.

Strangely, I could understand what they meant: *The Eyes of Akhorus.*

Without hesitation, the guards began to phase through the solid glass wall to the other side, and Aquilla and I followed against our will.

It was strange, to say the least, to be able to move through something that was more dense than ice like it was only water. Inside, their flickered white flames mounted along the massive halls that dwarfed us. Though I wanted to stare in amazement at the impossible architecture of the temple and its dizzyingly endless array of halls and rooms and artifacts, I was robbed of this leisure as we were led to a dome-like room in the middle of the temple.

Once we were forced into the circular room and to the singular stand in the middle, I could see hundreds of Medjaib sitting above us. They appeared to be floating because of the transparent rings of glass that constructed the dome-like tower in which they sat silently upon. Most of them shared the naked exposure of their galactic skin like Aquilla and Prucios, but there were a handful of them at the first ring of chairs above us who were draped in milky white robes, their cosmic skin hidden beneath as differing crowns of silver and glimmering lights nestled on their hoods.

Prucios approached to stand beside us before he spoke.

"Great Council of Iyrah, Aquilla has accepted your summons and awaits your counsel."

"Without his own will, it appears," said the robed Medjaib with the largest crown.

"I know what you shall say, so deliver unto me your disbelief," Aquilla said.

"How dare you!" said the Medjaib of the smallest crown, his words rippling across the air like stone struck water. "Do you question the wisdom of the Iyrah? Are you eldest in age and wisdom?"

"It is not my intention to display disrespect, but the Eternal One's vision was—"

"Do not spew your blasphemy in this holy refuge!" the Medjaib of the largest crown said. "We have considered your *declaration*, and we have found it to be *false*. You shall speak no more of this heresy, lest you wish to be banished to the Shadow."

Aquilla took a deep and heavy breath. "It is my destiny to obey only my Creator, for in Her Voice alone do I trust. Do with me as you desire, but know that you move against Her will. 'The oak stands rooted against the wind, and it shall be proven unshakable.'"

"Your vision is false, as is your misuse of Her song!" the Medjaib with the largest crown said, but just as his words were uttered, a sudden hue of blood bled through his ethereal face and over his milky robes, along with every Medjaib in the Councilroom. It wasn't because of a change in his cosmic composition that he now mirrored the translucent Godstone, for even the glass temple around us glowed scarlet.

No, it was because the entire moon had turned as red as an apple.

Panic seized the glowing eyes of the Iyrah as realization dawned upon them, and as Aquilla glanced at Prucios, there seemed to glimmer regret on his friend's face as they all shared in the revelation that Aquilla's dream had been true.

"Seize him!" the Iyrah shouted.

Aquilla waited not to be seized and dove through the temple floors, phasing through a dizzying array of glass to roll upon the moon floor hundreds of feet below. Not wasting time in looking back, Aquilla sprinted with all of his might, taking me with him to the mountain opposing the temple.

There was a commotion of shouts and anger behind us as most likely we were being pursued by the Iyrah and their guards.

"Aquilla, wait!" Prucios yelled, his pace quickly matching ours as we ran.

"Leave me!" Aquilla said, but Prucios caught up to us, though not to apprehend.

"Forgive me, friend," Prucios said. "I was wrong to doubt you."

"To doubt *Her*!" Aquilla said.

"Save your breath for the climb, you fool!" Prucios said.

Our hands quickly became as clear as glass and lighter than air, the rest of our body soon following which Prucios's also mimicked. It was like we were leaping without gravity as we bounded towards the mountain, the silver roses beneath us barely affected by our footsteps because we merged the two concepts of running and soaring in the skies together.

It was the most freeing and exhilarating feeling I'd ever experienced.

Though the mountain was miles away before the moon turned red, it now was only as far as a few leaps.

But we were not alone.

As soon as our feet hit the mountain which was now surrounded by dark clouds flickering with red lightning, a spear of light impaled the lunar tree beside us, inches away.

"Halt or face banishment!" a Medjaib said behind us but to no avail, for Aquilla and Prucios only quickened their pace up the dark mountain, leaps and bounds taking us through the trees at a frightening pace.

Aquilla looked sharply behind to see who had followed us. It was the entire Council, and then some.

Everyone was running to the mountain.

"What shall the other do if not chosen?" Prucios said, the trees melting into a blur as the hands holding the world became closer.

"Pray for the one who is!" Aquilla said.

For a moment, I felt that the Medjaib chasing us would catch up due to the thickening storm that choked all of the light from the sun, but he too was slowed down in the storm. Aquilla and Prucios struggled with every fiber of their being up the stone path on the silver mountain, the winds tearing bitterly at their galactic skin. As they reached the last bend in the forest, steady but careful steps taking them ever closer to the hand-like monument holding the world, it seemed that victory was certain for Aquilla's machination as they wrestled with the winds.

Prucios was not so fortunate.

Just as Aquilla came within a few feet of the obsidian structure, a gust of wind swept the feet of Prucios right out from under him and took him hundreds of feet back into the forest, almost throwing him off of the cliff entirely. For a moment, the winds looked like a hand that was keeping him and everyone else surging up the mountain away from the altar.

"Prucios!" Aquilla said.

"I am well!" he said in the hardly visible storm. "The Mother has chosen you! Bring Her glory, be not like the elders who have failed before! Stay rooted in Her song, and you shall stand triumphant!"

"I shall not fail, my friend!" Aquilla said, though I could feel the glimmering tears in his eyes. "*Until eternity*!"

"*Until eternity*, Aquilla. Now go!"

With a deep breath, Aquilla made his way into the hands' structure, this time with no resistance from the wind, and placed himself firmly in its grasp.

Before he could even take a breath, Aquilla began to float in between the palms.

"Aquilla!" a deep and powerful voice echoed from the Void above. Her voice seemed familiar, instilling both a fearful awe and a desire to hear more.

"Here I am."

"You have been chosen, your fate has been decided, your destiny awaits."

"I am honored, Eternal One. And my bonded one, is it the boy from the sea you have shown me?"

The voice responded with at first only a picture that consumed our mind, but it was enough to make my soul gasp in wonder.

"This is truth. The boy by the sea, the one who will know me, the Shepherd of Cypherus' Shadow I receive. Vow to me that you'll make him strong, and through you both the world will sing a new song of my wonders."

It was me.

I almost didn't recognize myself as we stood beside my trembling soul that longed to be washed away by the sea, the colorless waves crashing, chaos down below.

"Does he believe?" Aquilla said.

"Not yet."

"Then why him? He appears to long for ending his life

rather than devoting it to Your Glory. And how will a destiny of the Shadow be of encouragement? Is he not destined for darkness?"

The storm was interrupted by what sounded like the heat of a teapot escaping a kettle. Our eyes returned to the present where a star was streaking across the heavens to the moon, and we were without a doubt within its path. Strangely enough, I didn't feel any fear in Aquilla as the comet hurled its way towards us, growing closer every second.

No, there was only calm assurity.

"Please, grace me with understanding Your Will."

The burning star was seconds away from colliding into the hands of the Mother, the earth waiting behind us as the only destination. Although I couldn't see the woman who was speaking to Aquilla, I could feel a mixture of peace, power, and joy all around us as she talked to him.

Just like the voice before the fall.

"Must I use only the mighty stones that make up the face of the mountains for my glory? Must I use only the rarest gold for my wonders? Did I not create both the stars and the dirt as my masterpieces? Do you question my methods, Medjaib?"

Aquilla fumbled at the weight of her words, his head cowering in fear and shame.

"Forgive me, forgive me."

"The birth of destiny can be born in even the darkest of places; sometimes those are the brightest, after all."

And then the comet collided with Aquilla and I in the hands that upheld the world, and from the moon my mind was propelled back to the dark unconscious abyss, the woman's words echoing in my soul like the wind chimes of an ancient temple in the distant mountains.

~

A scraping sound jolted me awake.

My eyes burst open to the sight of a red elk brushing its twisted horns against a tree. At the sound of my awakening, the elk froze and locked its cherry eyes with mine.

"Strange," Aquilla said, appearing from the woods to run his swirling hand slowly across its rigid pelt, "yet brilliantly designed."

"Reeekkk!" the Eldrakes screeched not more than a mile away, the sound of which startled the animal. The elk bolted into the foliage away from Aquilla and I, reminding me that the nightmarish existence was a reality.

"It is time," Aquilla said beside me as he listened to the skies, confirming my fears. "Come, you have slept for two days. We should leave at once."

"Two days?" I whispered, unable to comprehend what the spirit was saying as my body and my soul raged against my sudden awakening.

It felt like I hadn't slept at all.

Bleary-eyed and with a mind as cold as my muscles, I unhitched the startled horse from the tree. In frantic exhaustion, I pulled myself up onto the steed and kicked it into a gallop. My stomach growled with hunger and my bones ached from fatigue, but my fleeting strength would have to do as we raced against time. It wasn't until we hit a steady pace and the fears of the Eldrakes diminished that the memory of the strange lunar dream I received came roaring back into my awakening consciousness.

"Wait, did you make me see that?" I said.

"If you mean my memory from before, then yes."

"Was… was that your world? The moon above?"

"It is. That is where my brethren have watched your kind for thousands of sols. It is a testament to the Mother's everlasting love for Her creation, and it is more fair than the purest silver that can be mined on earth. You would most enjoy reading in the Spiral of Wisdom, Morgan, as did I. You can see every river which flows from it that would bless you with Her eternity."

"Eternity?"

"But of course. How else would we watch you until we are chosen for the descent?"

A moment passed between us as the gravity of his words sank into my soul. Another planet, unknown spirits watching us from above. For eternity. Where the water would not drown you, but would sustain you forever.

Is anything real anymore?

Knowing not how to respond to such revelations, I said, "Well, that was brave of your friend to join you in the end."

"Indeed," Aquilla said, his mind drifting from mine as memories flashed of their friendship. There were many kept within his heart. "He was my closest companion for over seventy sols."

"What will happen to him now?"

Aquilla trembled in his sigh. "They shall likely cast him unto the Shadow if I fail in the Mother's calling."

"The Shadow?"

"Where the Light of Her Glory is eternally unknown."

"Why is that to be feared?"

A brief image of a mountain range on Akhorus flashed through Aquilla's mind. The dark and eerie mountains bordered the edge of the moon's light side, but instead of a gradual diminishing of light to shadow, the two opposites were starkly separated. Though the memory was brief and quickly hidden, I was able to glimpse the edge of the mountain range: it looked like a fingernail.

"It is a place that is darker than the Void, serving as a reminder to what shall be if we fail our purpose."

"What is it?"

Aquilla shuddered within me. "It is better that you do not know. All that matters is that you know I understand your longing to save your brother, and I want to help you spare him of the Shadow."

The image of the jagged fingernail stretching larger than a river continued to sicken me with fear. "I… I always thought there was nothing there. That it was just lifeless, empty."

"There are many things which you cannot see, young Morgan. It is perhaps because you keep your eyes closed for too long."

"*What?* I needed to rest. I could hardly function beforehand."

"Morgan, your eyes were closed for two rotations of Akhorus. Upon the second night I gave you my memory."

"To awaken me?"

"No, to show you the world from my perspective."

"Why would I need that?"

"Because you lack understanding of the importance of your soul, your worth in the Mother's eyes."

"And what worth is that, exactly? To be the one fated to drown in darkness? Forgive me for not recognizing the vast gravitas of such a destiny."

Aquilla sighed. "Morgan, I do not fully comprehend Her Majesty—"

"Clearly."

"—but that does not mean we can assume ill motives behind Her intentions. She sees far more than we could imagine, so we must trust Her sight to be true and meant for your good."

"If she sees so clearly, then why did she not inform you entirely of her plan to ensure its fruition? Why leave so much to assume if she loves us so much?"

Aquilla stuttered for a moment before a heavy sigh overtook

his words. "I do not know, Morgan. I often wish for complete knowledge of Her plans as well."

My cheeks flustered with anger. "Can you not see how this changes nothing?"

Aquilla's galactic swirls frowned. "Why does it not?"

I couldn't believe the Medjaib's arrogance.

"Morgan, you simply misperceive the path before you—"

"Nothing changes that I was born unwanted! I have drowned every day in that undeniable truth! And if there is such a creator who would force upon me such a dedric destiny that let my real mother burn into an unrecognizable husk… for me to drown hopelessly along with her on such a fated gloom, then I would rather let the sea fill my lungs than bow my head in *thankfulness and worship*. You are the one who cannot see."

Aquilla said no more, and was silent for the rest of the day, the horse's relentless gallop the only thing filling the mountain forests. However, my mind was a torment, no, a battle against disparaging thoughts of my deformed and useless self, the pain of their truths piercing my tiresome heart that was failing against and falling under their arrowy storm of misery.

Even this god believed so.

I knew Aquilla could hear every thought, and I let him. Maybe then he would understand how ignorant he was to take such a grave matter so lightly, as if I were a child that needed only to straighten my behavior in order to be rewarded. He didn't even have a plan to begin with, let alone a sufficient understanding of our hopeless purpose.

To the Void with such worthless mediocrities.

When my blackest thoughts become painfully unbearable, I distracted myself by keeping an eye out for dedrim trees and faery hives, not wanting to meet death's crushing or frightening embrace that often came for those who lacked caution in the woods.

But even in this distraction, the darkness found a way to seep back into my mind, my thoughts morphing into fears of losing Lucien and Sigmund. He must have felt devastated in thinking my demise was certain, and my heart broke in thinking of his suffering. To see his family slaughtered before his very eyes and to also lose me, his repeatedly proclaimed rock, his heart would be burdenly heavy to carry as they fled from the Drakin's jaws.

I could only hope that they made it to Ludsala safely and that the Drakin had lost them by now, but I feared I was too quick to believe in such a foolish hope. For the forest in which we travelled was thick and the road wove endlessly through, no straight path ahead, making our journey of solitude unbearingly slow. Thus my hope diminished evermore as the journey to rescue them stretched from unbearable hours to days, and from a blurring of days to weeks in the lonely forest.

"I will not fail you," I whispered as time scoffed at me.

I would have lost track of time entirely if Aquilla hadn't reminded me a week later to at last replenish myself of food.

"Is it not written that 'Man eats a cow a week while a Lycan consumes a herd a day'?" he said, startling me from the pit of quiet despair as I rode bleary-eyed through the endless maze of rock and trees, desperately hoping we were not lost as we ventured west towards Ludsala.

"Where have you been?" I said, my voice tired and irritated after the endless hours, endless days of our silent pursuit of Ludsala.

"I have never left you."

"You have for the last several days in this blithering forest."

"I have read that Humans need time to mourn and are usually emotionally unstable within the first week, which you demonstrated after my memory of Akhorus. Hence why I have left you to your thoughts, though my spirit abides with you every moment."

"Isolation was exactly what I needed," I mocked, my fatigue and bitterness too overwhelming to speak truthfully.

"I know," Aquilla bowed, further increasing my annoyance. "But now you are ready to yield to the Light in order to save your family."

"Aquilla, I already told you that I am not reciting that foolish Skallgend."

"Does not the wisdom of the Drakin Prophet Sefirus et Um'manda mean nothing to you? That 'Mine eyes are blinded by the smoke of war. I seek Thine Holy Flame to save me from its pathless grave.'"

"You truly believe I would trust in the words of Drakin prophets?"

"Of course! Sefirus was chosen by the Mother to bond with a Medjaib, to lead his people away from death's embrace. He could not have done so in rejection of the Light."

"I do not reject 'the Light,' *spirit*, I simply reject your god. I will make the light myself in saving my family."

"That is impossible, Human. Light only comes from Her Song, which we *must* sing!"

"How about instead of singing, you help me through this forest with 'the Light' which you claim to have? I cannot see in this forest of shadow."

Aquilla sighed, his soul heavy alongside mine. "Very well, Morgan. As I promised before, I shall guide you unto your destiny. But first, I believe you should eat. Though I do not know where you will find provision, for I have not seen any cows."

"Humans eat more than just cows," I said, searching through the dense forest in hopes of finding a hive of honey that was most probable.

Thankfully I didn't have to search long, for one was buzzing low in a tree. Quickly, I scooped several handfuls of its golden nectar before being stung, riding away as quickly as I could. The honey was restoring to my soul, reviving me greatly. Though it wasn't bread or meat, it would sustain me for now, along with water from the brooks and rivers we passed by.

All that mattered, all that I cared about, was saving my family. Especially if they were forced into Ludsala, into its haunted labyrinth of a city long abandoned for good reason.

And we were nearly there.

By the fifteenth day of our silent journey from Renborg, I had almost given up.

Though I was extremely fatigued and starving, Ludsala was too close to stop now. In fact, as we surpassed the second River Grelohm and emerged from the forest hugging the lip of the Dendravik Mountains, I could see the tips of the abandoned city's rotting spires just beyond the whispering trees.

Hope rekindled my weary soul.

Kicking my horse to push past its limits, we reached the Osatven River by nightfall, discussion scarce with the spirit within me. The mountainside was drenched in shadows in which we lurked. I could only see because my eyes were accustomed to the darkness, but my ears startled me when Aquilla spoke again, appearing beside me like a midnight wraith and just as unwanted.

"We near Ludsala, Morgan, and there is something we *must* do before arrival."

"No, I cannot. You have tried to convince me for the last two weeks, but I know the nature of my feelings, and they cannot change into what you seek—"

"I do not ask you to build trust based on the fleeting security of your shifting mind."

"Then *what* do you want from me?"

"For your friends and family, and for the millions in the empire, I ask you to trust in me. It is only in this trust that we can help them. All you must do is recite the *Heart of Stars*, that is all. Nothing more, nothing less."

"Would you kiss the blade that slit the throat of your loved one and scarred you beyond redemption?"

"Morgan, your mother sleeps with the Eternal One in Solæf as we speak, and she would—"

"Don't you dare speak about my mother! You have no idea what it's like to suffer."

"But your family shall if you do not yield to the Light. Say it for them!"

Tears began to spill as the horse's gallop yanked them out from my eyes, my hopes and dreams falling with them. And as they disappeared into the soil below, unlovingly discarded by the eyes of the beholder, anger swelled within me that such a proposed being had the audacity to so carelessly throw life to the grave and expect those who suffered to read the memoirs of its blackened heart.

I will honor my real mother.

"We… we shall find another way," I said.

"Morgan! There is no other way! You must yield to the Light if we are to save them! Even if you could save them alone, we must prepare for the unknown poison that Judux is concocting for this world to drink!"

"You are ignorant, Medjaib."

"Morgan, the ignorance lies within you! Judux has Solstein, and with the soul of Sh'eol and the darkness that surrounds him, we are blind to what we face should we save your brothers and Egret!"

Aquilla threw himself in front of my steed, locking eyes with me as we raced down the river under the lonely moon.

"Morgan, look at me. Look at me Morgan! You must hear

my words within your heart, and not your mind. We draw near—"

But my ears stopped listening to his words, and my eyes looked beyond his spectral form to the ruins of Ludsala that loomed from the Osatven River like a rotting yet massive oak. The river gushed like waterfalls over the countless broken bridges and mossy stone terraces that formed the backbone of the ancient city, the oily night weaving a web of its own terrors beneath the abandoned buildings and eroded streets. The unknown and mythic nightmares of what hid beneath Ludsala would have been enough to freeze anyone in terror upon first glance, but my weakening heart trembled for a different reason.

The Ronian banners streamed fearfully across the crumbling bridge of the southern gate to the city, and a host of hundreds of flaming-haired Drakin were biting at their tails on their own heat-protected steeds.

Without hesitation, I kicked my tired horse relentlessly to gallop into the darkness that I was all too familiar with, with only the dwindling hope that Lucien, Sigmund, and Egret had not succumbed to it.

Chapter 10
What Lies Beneath

Long ago in the land of Ludsala
Six priests were drunk in the haunting hour.
In a pub they drank their vows away
'Till a lustful lad led them astray.
"Come play in the dark while the night is young."
To a well he lured them, but not for fun.
He pushed them into the well below,
Throwing them Godstone and a soul he stole.
"To climb out, you must transform like I did,
Treated with disgust from the faith you live."
They resisted 'till they began to starve,
But when they Wyled the soul, their hearts grew hard.
To their great ire, they became spider,
All from being blinded by desire.
So they hunted the lad, dragged him down below,
Shamed to resurface, damnation their woe.

Tales of the Old World
"Spindler Lullaby"

Our horse thundered across the decayed bridge, its hooves clopping wildly against the ancient stones that were joined by the shouts of pursuit ahead in the ruined city of waterfalls. Ludsala was a behemoth of a city that loomed many tiers above the river that wept beneath it which we now crossed.

The moonlight that was once our guide was now drowning in the mountainous shadows of Ludsala's ruins which engulfed us like the grave. The lack of light almost led to our premature demise when Aquilla shouted at the last moment to avoid the troll-sized hole on the southern bridge. Utilizing nothing but the rawest instincts, I blindly yanked the horse away from the drop that would've left us plummeting to the Osatven River below.

"Hence is why you must yield to the Light!" Aquilla said within me. "You could've seen with mine eyes and avoided such careless tragedy."

"It wouldn't have made a difference," I said, but within I could feel my bones shaking from the fear of death for the first time; for now there was something to live for, and I almost let it slip through my shameful gloves.

The hundreds of Drakin beyond us recentered my focus, their appearance like a swarm of fireflies on their cushioned horses charging up the spiraling ruins of Ludsala. They took no efforts in hiding their flaming hair from Lucien and his Ronians now that the chase was revealed. As for my brothers and Egret, I could only imagine that they were just ahead of them, for it was too drenched in shadow to perceive them, but I could fairly predict that they were barely avoiding the bite of the Drakin spears licking their heels.

The chaos almost distracted me from the little flames that silently made their way around the mountain, strangely away from the pursuit.

"Where are they going?" I said, but my tightening gut gave away the answer.

"It appears they intend to surround them, but how is unknown," Aquilla said, leaving my stomach to clench in fear at the thought of the ensuing slaughter that would become of Lucien and Egret.

"We have to warn them!" I said, weaving through the eroded yet cluttered streets and graveyards of mossy buildings, all while avoiding the occasional stream of water gushing from the plethora of waterfalls that bathed the forgotten city.

"Ludsala I have not explored in great detail, for there are a great host of evils whispered of these ruins. I have only seen the city from above, and if we are to be of aid to your family, we must—"

"I can see well enough without your eyes!"

"Oh, have Humans suddenly been granted the ability to perceive the darkness?"

"Just tell me where we need to go!"

Aquilla made what sounded like an annoyed groan within my soul, but nonetheless led the way, departing from my vessel to run past our horse as an apparitional guide through the silent streets bleeding with water.

"If this Kolstok is of wisdom," Aquilla said as he sprinted past the empty shells of buildings, "he could know of the cavern that weaves through this maze of ruins. It leads to the northern bridge where they can flee in the darkness."

"How do you know that?"

"It has been known and avoided by us for a long time."

"Do the Drakin know of this place?"

"Unlikely, but if guided also by wisdom, your brother could be fleeing unto a trap."

"So they will have an ambush awaiting even if they escape the jaws of death."

"Unless we warn them."

The futility of our plan caused me to groan in frustration. "Even if he did know of it, why would Kolstok hope to lose them in this cavern instead of heading straight to the northern bridge?"

Aquilla hesitated but said, "If I spoke of it, you would not enter. If the scrolls of Akhorus are to be believed, Kolstok is a foolish gambler in leading the Drakin there, but I see no other way."

My mind reeled in trying to think of any legend or story that would shed light on this tale of gloom that Aquilla refused to share. All I could remember was an old lullaby that Lucien and my nurse would make us read every time we got caught climbing the rooftops of Renborg at the break of dawn, annoying and awakening everyone beneath our feet.

The warmth of those memories helped to quell the fears of what lay beneath the city and what we could be running towards.

"Take the alley!" Aquilla said, interrupting my thoughts as we pounded up the glistening cobblestones that once carried the souls of thousands but now bore only the whispers of evil and our anxious breaths.

The zealous screams of the Drakin pursuers faded as we disappeared further into the skeletal remains of broken pillars and collapsed houses, the worthless remnants littering the streets. Aquilla's guidance proved fruitful in leading us on a quicker path to catch up with Lucien and his soldiers, for as we rounded the corner of a forgotten temple, we could see the tail end of the Ronians making their way into a pyramidic structure surrounded by a graveyard of statues.

"We have bested the Drakin, but they are close behind," Aquilla said, and he was right, for their candlelight aurora of death was warming up the nearest alley. The roar of clopping hooves shook the road in fear of death's arrival.

Without hesitation, I spurred our steed into the mouth of the pyramid's pillared teeth, unable to read the sign above that was written in ancient dialects unknown to me. Although it felt like we were being swallowed by the eternal Abishx, I could see lights ahead that illuminated the just wide enough tunnel with walls covered in even more statues.

"What did the sign read?" I said as I tried to encourage our horse to go forth, but the lack of sight left the beast too terrified to move.

Anxiety flooded my soul upon hearing the Drakin approach ever closer.

"Move, you foolish beast! Move!"

The horse only bucked its way backwards, but as the sounds of the Drakin came closer, it started to move forward again, as if the darkness were best compared to what was behind. But as the steed moved closer, I began to Wyl my Bludhstone necklace into my soul out of sheer panic from the approaching Drakin.

The rosy light glowed from the pulsating stone.

I wish it had not.

The red hue from the Godstone brought to life the mummified and deteriorating corpses that lined the walls, many of them bearing a half Human-half Dragon copper skull. Skeletons of every race with scraps of festered clothing numbered in the hundreds along the pyramid's domed tunnel. Standing in rows with unnaturally large spider webs for company, the dead appeared to be grinning at me.

"The sign read, *The Catacombs of Behl'amon*," Aquilla said as he stood in disgust before the row of corpses, but his words were the furthest thing from what I wanted to hear since it was the last place I wanted to be. "Humanity's fixation on death is rather perplexing."

"We can discuss this later!" I said, kicking the horse with all of my might in a desperate attempt to flee from the rotting fingers of fate.

And none too soon.

A spear impaled the jeweled skull of what looked to be a man of great renown from centuries past, the decorated corpse almost collapsing onto me before I reared back on the horse.

"Kaselot!" Rolloc roared behind me, and with a snap of my neck I could see he was the one who almost ended and began my eternal night.

"Morgan, we cannot linger!" Aquilla said, and my stammering heart was in complete agreement.

Gripping the reins, I charged the horse down the descending path into the stomach of this house of death, not wanting to join the sea of forgotten souls that silently screamed around us.

"There's nowhere to go but down!" I said as the horse awkwardly and fearfully made its way down the sloped path.

"There shall be a way!" Aquilla said, but it sounded more hopeful than certain.

"You don't know that! Your god did not make you omniscient of my fate nor this grave. You are just as blind as me!"

"You must trust me, Morgan!"

To our great fortune, Aquilla's blind optimism proved right when we reached the bottom of the tunnel.

Our path opened up to a massive cavern with hundreds of pillars reaching to the stalagmites above, looking like the bones that fortified their structure. The only way I could see in this sea of silenced sorrows was by the torchlight which flickered from the Ronians ahead of us and by the moonlight pouring in before them. And towards the exit, I could see and hear the soft roar of a waterfall.

But that's not what consumed my thoughts.

As we hurriedly navigated the maze of bones filling the cavern like piles of dusty gold, I could sense something above us. I made the mistake of looking up. My skin crawled at the sight of the wallpaper of webs drenching every inch of the cavern's ceiling, and even most of the bones around me.

Our horse began to panic at the death all around, and was joined by Lucien's and his Ronians' horses who also began snorting and bucking in fear. I could barely hold onto my horse as he continued to grow in panic beneath the beam-like silky chords that crisscrossed the air above us.

"Whoa boy!" I said, failing in my efforts to calm him.

"Why are the horses dancing?" Aquilla said.

"They smell death," I said, gazing upon the dangling clouds

above as the sounds of horses colliding into one another filled the catacomb.

I swear I could see shadows twirling about them.

"Boy!" Rolloc said as he and his Drakin vomited from the tomb's staircase like magmic faeries.

"Lucien!" I said, no longer worrying about concealing myself as I tried to encourage our horse to move through the darkness. "Lucien, it's Morgan! The Drakin have an ambush ahead!"

"Morgan?" I heard a collection of voices say, the most startling of which were behind me.

But those voices came to a crashing halt when my horse collapsed its head mid-gallop into a pile of bones, causing my anxiety-riddled body to slam into the cavern floor, crushing all of the air out from my lungs. From my writhing position on the ground, I could see the Drakin spear protruding from the tail of the horse's spine that just missed my nether regions.

"Leave the King and his Queen alive, and signal the others!" Rolloc said in Drakonnian as he dismounted his blanketed steed before me, his warriors charging past him and I to carry out his will like an impending wave of fiery stallions. A horn blasted from one of the countless mounted Drakin, and with it I had no doubt that their allies would hear it from beyond the tomb and come to their aid to trap my family.

"Morgan, recite the Skallgend!" Aquilla said, his voice frantic as I failed to rise from the blood-soaked ground that Rolloc wasted no time in reaching, his Godstone axe unsheathed and ready to taste my blood, or my soul. "*Heart of flesh rots to—*"

"Kaselot!" Rolloc interrupted, planting his muddy boot firmly on my chest and squashing any chance of escape. "Or should I call you Morgan?"

"*Ignite with love of Light above—*"

The sounds of battle echoed throughout the cavern as I

looked into the fiery eyes of who I presumed would be the one to send me to the Void forever. I gritted my teeth in the fearful anticipation of a grim fate, my aching and pathetic hands scrambling to grab onto anything to thrust into the Dedric beast before me.

"*Heart of fire world is—*"

My efforts ceased when I felt something like saliva dangle into my mouth.

"I guess it doesn't really matter," Rolloc said, heaving his axe to cut the withered string of my life. "Your life is just as nameless as mine. I will spare you of that painful reality."

"*Shine forever in—*"

Twisting my head back, I gazed just in time upon the salivating creature that descended inches from my face, its thick, ropey web dangling above it. The shadows danced across its slimy white skin as four tiny claws emerged from its chest, followed by eight pincers that surrounded it like a cage of death, the dark being shivering in the shadows in anticipation of feeding upon its prey. Its sickly but muscled form was far larger than my now still horse which breathed its last beside us. My mind broke as I stared into the countless orbs that covered its furry and somewhat Human face, but whatever trace of Humanity it once had was lost eons ago.

The Spindler hissed as it prepared to bite my sanity away with its curved forks for teeth.

Before it could tear me apart, inky blood spewed from the gouge made in the Spindler's humanoid face by Rolloc's ax. The spider-like monster screamed something closely resembling the Adamic language, dousing my soul in complete fear.

"Anaki!" Rolloc said, yanking his axe out of the withering Spindler which collapsed onto my chest, enclosing me in its gooey embrace that entangled my entire body, leaving me drenched in its midnight blood.

Rolloc cursed again in Drakonnian and left me beneath the freakish Averite, blinding me both with its pungent smell and its miniature arms from its chest that squirmed across my face.

I was tempted to scream as I panicked underneath the slimy Averite, but it was the sounds that kept me silent. Humming like cicadas on a summer night, I could hear hundreds of Spindlers descending from their cloudy webs, excited for the feast set before them. Thankfully, the Drakin and their horses would draw most of the attention to them, but that did not mean Lucien or Sigmund would be spared. My heart leapt at the thought of them and Egret being paralyzed by these ghoulish freaks which lost their souls and their minds long before we arrived in their den.

"Morgan, you must recite it!" Aquilla said as I tried to push the Spindler off of my wheezing chest. "There is no time to avoid it! Yield to the Light and acquire my strength and sight!"

Fear and anger clouded my mind, and the Medjaib's words of turning to the Mother were the furthest from appealing.

Drawing from the depths of sheer rage and terror, I shifted the Spindler off just enough for me to scramble out from underneath its corpse. When I rose to my shaky feet, I almost lost the strength to stand in seeing my nightmares come to life. Spindlers fell on the Drakin riders like flies swarming on festering flesh. With their ghastly pincers and claws, they snapped off limbs like carrots and tore off magmic flesh with their black maws, their horses being equally as unspared from their ferocity.

For the Ronians, their horses proved no less reliable, for they were bucking off their riders and crushing into one another out of pure fear and desperation.

Chaos consumed everyone.

"Flee, Morgan!" Aquilla said, his galactic face just as horrified as I was.

This time I listened.

My tired feet pounded on the outskirts of the slaughter as the soft red glow of my Bludhstone lit the path before me. The Drakin riders didn't even give me a second look as they fought back against their overwhelming enemies; their forces depleted faster than sugar in steaming juva and their demise just as pointlessly sweet.

The worst was a Drakin who fell off of his horse into a pile of bones trying to escape a grinning Spindler that bit the legs of his horse, but the pincers of the abomination forked his tender neck. The screaming Drakin was dragged to its oily teeth, dripping with hunger as it found its nourishment.

"Grab his spear!" Aquilla said, and I obeyed with trembling fingers, quickly grabbing the fallen Drakin's weapon to strengthen our chances of survival in this dark nightmare.

Only one Spindler stood in my way that I barely had time to register any fear for, and, with the purest instinct along with Aquilla's immediate advisement for the blow, I swiped its snarling jaw away from me and kept running without missing a beat.

Rounding the last pillar of bones that towered before the exit, my feet came to a halt when my eyes gazed upon the carnage before me.

Though most of the Drakin were being consumed by the Spindlers, a good portion of them surrounded the Ronian flanks at Rolloc's lead, the sight of swords and bloodshed filling the northern mouth of the catacombs.

In the few seconds that passed in indecision, I could see Kolstok hacking with all of his might against Rolloc, the old man struggling against the hybrid Drakin's swift blows as he was supported by the Knights of Kyllian who fought with cold determination.

To Kolstok's back were Lucien and Sigmund who were sheltered by Egret, who fought with an unyielding bloodlust as she defended their flank from the tunnel's exit. Her headdress must have fallen in their flight, for I could see her blood-splattered veins flexing through her scalp as she decimated the Drakin reinforcements that arrived from the other side of the catacombs.

"They have them surrounded," I said, all hope escaping my heart with each word.

With heavy strides I ran foolishly to the death that awaited me with open arms.

"Morgan, there is no time," Aquilla said, "*Heart of flesh*—"

My *heart of flesh* ignored the useless pleas of Aquilla when my eyes locked with Lucien's. His eyes were filled with fear and hopeless desperation as Kolstok received an axe blow from Rolloc to his chest, the blade sweeping him off of his horse as if he were only made of straw. Such meaningless waste of life only solidified my resolve to not yield to any being that claimed to be the paragon of light while allowing for such tragedies.

Ignoring Aquilla's fanatical recitations of monks who never understood the realities of life, I used every bit of strength I had left to sprint and throw my spear at Rolloc's back, whose outstretched arms attempted to grab Lucien and Sigmund. The spear found its home in the hybrid Drakin's ribs which caused him to fall, allowing me room to leap through the chaos and onto Lucien's horse.

"Morgan!" Lucien said with eyes drenched in fearful yet thankful tears.

"Morgan, you lived!" Sigmund said, tears billowing from his puffy eyes.

"Ride!" I said, attempting to grab the reins around Sigmund who sat between Lucien and I. Every second was precious in the struggle to break through the Drakin who blocked the entrance.

Egret and the few Ronians who survived the front flank were being pushed back into the catacombs, causing the entire regiment of Lucien's troops to suffocate against one another. Further adding to the chaos were the horses from both our own and the enemy, all of them bucking in fear and snorting with terror from the battle surrounding us and the Spindlers who sang of death.

"Spindlers, Morgan!" Aquilla said.

More of the spider Averites descended around us, breaking the Drakin line and giving us an opening of escape onto the waterfall bridge where we would lose our flaming pursuers.

Not failing to seize our chance, I spurred Lucien's horse along with Egret's to push forward through the sea of Spindlers and Drakin towards freedom, silently thanking the Ronians who would be left behind to give us cover. The horses resisted my motivations at first, but when one of the Spindlers bit the leg of Egret's horse, they quickly changed their minds.

"The King is mine!" Rolloc said from behind, stopping our horse's momentum with a sudden iron grasp that crushed my shoulder.

"Let go!" I heaved with all of my might, but even then it was not enough.

Spindlers were scurrying all around us like a writhing sea of arachnids, and I would've drowned in their inky jaws if I hadn't been holding onto Lucien.

In seeing my terror, one of the Spindlers crawled onto my back and began snipping with its mandibles at my head, the only blessing it provided being the release of Rolloc's grip.

Aquilla help me!

"*Heart of flesh rots to—*"

Egret's Godstone knife punctured the foul beast's skull with one precise thrust. Free at last, our horses continued to terrifyingly make their way through the bloody storm of spiders and swords.

"No!" Rolloc said, his voice frantic, grabbing my leg in desperation.

Our horse was unable to pull the added weight of Rolloc, who had made his stand on the ground near us as the last of our Ronian troops met their demise. I kicked ferociously at Rolloc, whose mouth bled from his wounds but remained carved with hateful determination.

The Spindlers moved to surround him and us.

"Morgan, the poem!" Aquilla said. "Do not let your ignorance be your family's doom. Say it now!"

Kicking the bearded face of anger that was Rolloc, I tossed aside Aquilla's thoughts and landed a blow directly on the Drakin's nose. A crunch ensued, though Rolloc did not pardon my leg from his shackle-like grasp.

"Morgan!" Aquilla said. "Now!"

But then Rolloc released me, causing our horse to buck forward, the shock of his sudden release causing Sigmund to fall as the horse bolted forward.

In total shock and disbelief, I watched Lucien's little brother whom I've known all of my life be swallowed in the uncaring darkness that our horse fled from.

In desperation, I tried throwing out my hand to him, wanting to save his precious heart from the evil around us, wanting to carry him on my shoulders as I've done all of his innocent life.

"Grab my hand, Sigmund!" I screamed, so I could hold him safely in my arms like he trusted me to do whenever he had nightmares and couldn't fall asleep. Memories of his pure joyful soul were a strengthening light that empowered me to reach for him, almost causing me to fall off the horse in desperation to save him, to spare him from the death that so ruthlessly devoured his sister and his mother and his father.

But he was just out of reach.

Rolloc was able to fend off the flood of Spindlers, but Sigmund could not, whose screams pierced my soul as we were unwillingly separated.

The Spindlers' hesitation lasted less than a second.

With relentless pace, the monsters tore into Sigmund with their inky teeth and silenced his screams forever upon the third bite.

The rest of the world became as silent as Sigmund's corpse as Lucien and Egret's horses broke through the carnage onto the bridge. I couldn't even feel the waterfall that we galloped through or hear the voices of Lucien and Egret who kept looking back at me, both with worried glances and tears of disbelief.

Even Aquilla was still.

But not my mind, which roared with one inescapable truth:

His shadow, sleepless death, will reign antithesis.

Chapter 11
A Choice

Derasar Zeliuh's choice led to him and his remaining 10,000 Drakin to flee Laconnia after the Lycan routed him at Kerax. Zeliuh fled past the walls of Laconnia with his warriors to the Brehnok River, but they were stopped by a Ronian host near the grand Umber Lake. While the Drakin fought bravely, many were forced into the watery depths when their lives were taken and destroyed, and too many would drown that day. To our shame, the Ronians would rename the lake to Ember Lake, for the vast number of Drakin corpses were like Kaffah plants glowing in the lonely night.

Only a small fraction of Drakin sent on this fruitless war returned home in the sol 814 of the Dawning Era, and there was great anger not only towards the Laconnians and the Ronians who lured us into this greedy conflict, but also from the Council who wasted so many lives under Zeliuh. To honor their precious lights that had been snuffed out, we deposited hundreds of Ethudera memorials to their shameful graves during the endless nights without them, allowing the waters to be forever scarlet and alight as a reminder to the cost of choosing a destiny without concern of others.

Scrolls of Yarahm
The 1st Silver War: 807 - 814 DE
Safira Seraii et Elishem

Failure.

Mistake.

Worthless.

… nothing matters.

Sleepless death.

Sigmund's hopeless and innocent face being torn apart burned in my mind like a branding iron, every minute, every conscious and unconscious intolerable second, more excruciating than any physical torture.

Our flight from Ludsala persisted throughout the night like a nightmare which knew no end. The waterfalls pouring loudly throughout the decadent and cursed ruins that loomed extravagantly around us were not enough to quiet my mind, though I wish they could have.

Once we escaped Ludsala's clutches, Egret took the reins in leading us along the Osatven River towards Ember Lake. She was relentless in making sure we did not stop nor risk the chance of being spotted by any Drakin, despite her baggy-eyed fatigue which we all suffered.

"Lucien," Egret said wearily in the Ronic tongue, "is this the path towards Hebsund?"

"Yes," Lucien said, his voice almost a whisper.

"How are we to cross the waters?"

"Just… follow the river."

Lucien spoke no more to Egret nor to me.

Egret looked at me with a hint of concern as we rode silently beside the river of shadows, though it quickly devolved into frustration when I caught her eyes.

I deserve it.

Sigmund's death had been completely avoidable, and like everyone I knew, I failed him.

And for what cost?

The memories of chasing a cheerful Sigmund around the castle, tucking him and Philomela into bed every night, of Valena's small gifts for me whenever the seas became too daunting for my soul, and even the sparingly few moments of Gulmund giving me silent praise with a smile before his sobriety ended.

All of those memories that once warmed me like the dawn now made me shudder more bitterly than the night as they surged through my weakening mind. They were all reminders of what was lost, of those I did not truly appreciate until they were murderously stolen from me.

I miss you. I miss you all.

It was not until dawn that I realized the tears stopped shedding from my swollen eyes. Not once did I hear Lucien cry, for his composure had been as still and emotionless as a gravestone as we rode along the grey morning river.

"Lucien?" I whispered to him, but his gaze was set upon the endless river ahead.

But he did not appear to be really looking at all.

As I cast my own eyes down in crippling shame, it was then that I realized how strangely quiet it had been in my mind.

Aquilla?

Nothing.

Aquilla? I know you can hear me.

My mind was void of any life.

Answer me! *You cannot just leave me alone after this! What kind of monster are you?*

Not a word came from my thoughts except my own. Instead, all I could see was myself reflected in my mind, and I cringed with disgust at the sight.

At the sight of a true sleepless monster.

Of failure.

The silence loomed thicker than the dark clouds that began to form above us when we stopped our horses to briefly relieve and refresh ourselves. It wasn't much, the little wine and bread they had left from the Ronian host, but it would sustain us.

"We need to be going," Egret said, keeping an eye on the darkening clouds above us as Lucien and I scarfed down what little our stomachs could hold. "This storm will help to give us more distance if the Drakin are still pursuing."

"Can we not *rest*, Princess?" I said, my voice stinging with bitterness as I wearily set aside my portion which I could barely ingest. "We have been without a moment of respite since the invasion, nor have we had a moment to process all that we have lost."

"And do you think you are the only one?" Egret said, her brow furrowing which caused her veins to spread like lightning across her bald scalp. Her headdress was nowhere to be found and I felt a slight shudder of appall within me. "We can rest when we reach Hebsund, and you can find whatever pleasure you need in its *streets*, peasant."

Our eyes locked again as they did in the library, but this time, there transpired only bitterness and annoyance, which left no room for reconciliation.

"Very well," I said, remounting our steed in frustration while Lucien silently wrapped himself around me.

While Egret said nothing more, her emerald eyes cast a suspicious and concerned glance towards her husband, but when hers rose to meet mine, she quickly turned away.

Thankfully, the lightning-filled thunderstorm drenched and drowned any inflamed conversation that could have arisen as we continued our journey near the river, and it helped me not to think of Sigmund and the others who forcibly slept in the grave. The rain consumed every thought I had, washing away all of my strength and soaking my heart with hate of its misery.

By the third night, the river finally fed into the glowing Ember Lake that spread vastly before us, illuminating the small Ronian village that nestled beside its waters.

As we arrived on the outskirts of the village farmlands that were elevated greatly above the lake, I could see the Amon Bridge through the rain stretching high across the Jöarmellan river that churned far below in the steep chasm.

"We need rest, so we will cross the bridge tomorrow at dawn," Egret said as she led us hurriedly through the rain to an abandoned hut bordering the wheat fields that she spotted.

Although Lucien and I didn't say anything, it was fair to assume that he was also thankful to give our minds rest from the drainage of suffering and sleeplessness we endured. Tying the horses to the wind-groaning trees, we rushed into the hut and found as comfortable places as we could on the rotting floor to sleep on.

Egret sat apart from us without a moment's consideration, and Lucien surprisingly kept his distance, huddling himself into his knees as he shivered for warmth.

Though they didn't say it, they were both freezing.

As for myself, though my garments were soaked, I was not shivering; I never did, as long as I was not consumed by water. It was the only time in my life that I thanked the Hagroak witches for their black magic which saved my charred flesh from the fire. But this unwanted blessing did not extend to others, and I could not bear to watch them freeze.

"We need a fire," I said, catching their sullen eyes with my intrusion of the raining silence.

"That would be pleasant," Lucien whispered through shivers without looking at me.

"So, let us build one," I said.

Lucien shifted his strained eyes towards me in question.

"The fires were always built for me..."

A weary glance towards Egret proved just as fruitless.

"We do not build fires on our fleets," she said, as if it were obvious.

They both looked at me with royal expectation.

"Are you serious?" I said, frustration dripping from my words as they expected me to do it.

"What did you expect?" Egret said, her tone mirroring mine.

"So you're telling me you've never made a fire before? Have you even prepared your own meal in your entire existence, or put on your garments by yourself?"

"Such tasks are beneath us, peasant, such as our responsibilities are above you."

"You're right. I shouldn't have expected you to actually understand the people you rule, nor to care for anyone but yourself, *Your Majesty*."

Egret's face contorted in anger, but before she could say anything, I rose to my feet in my reluctant quest to build a fire. The only pleasing part about my task was the temporary distraction from the horrors we had witnessed. In a way, I was glad they were unable to help, for it meant that I had something useful to offer.

Thankfully, our hut provided shelter from the ongoing rain, leaving the ground devoid of moisture.

I mindlessly cleared an area between us of debris as they watched, the task occupying my thoughts that threatened to consume me. Our source of kindling was not far, for a table and some chairs were the only furniture in this forgotten home, this abandoned hearth. The limbs of the old furniture were easy enough to snap, and I did so with the rising anger within.

It felt good to break them. To feel *control*.

Once the pieces were assembled, I withdrew a knife from our satchel and carved strips of wood from the broken table, gathering them into a small pile before Lucien and Egret as I added some dry leaves that were near the entrance. Carving a divot into the butt of a chair, I began rubbing one of its legs into the hole in the desperate hope of sparking an ember that would kindle a flame.

Lucien's teeth clattered in the cold, yet Egret did her best to hide her discomfort by pulling herself deeper into her cloak. A hidden sense within me felt her eyes watch me closely, but I chose not to meet hers as I worked.

The wooden leg groaned in my hand as I twisted ever faster and pressed down into the hole, rage and pain burning within me as I rubbed my skin raw in the desperate attempt to not fail them. I lost track of time as I twisted the wood furiously in my hands, feeling no pain from the heat it produced on my skin.

"Come on!" I yelled, every fiber of my being wanting to quit, to cave into my failures.

When I was about to give up, a spark emerged.

Not wasting my efforts, I blew gently into the kindling, cupping my hands around it to contain the heat.

It worked.

The leaves began to catch fire, and my hands helped to spread it to the carved strips. With dedication, the fire began to grow, and I began to feed the withered furniture into it. Lucien and Egret moved closer to the growing warmth, the orange heat reflecting off of their faces as they stared solemnly into the blaze, the shadows dancing around us as the rain pounded above us.

Breathing a sigh of relief, I was comforted to at last provide something of use to my family as their shivers began to dwindle.

My family…

Staring into the fire, I could see Sigmund's helpless eyes looking at me, pleading for my help.

The countless hungry eyes of Spindlers replaced his, devouring him without a second thought.

And then, fiery red hate that were Rolloc's eyes who removed the eye of Gulmund and cut the jaw from Valena before slaughtering Philomela. I could see his treacherous eyes in the fire, and hate grew within, barely eclipsing the hate for myself. Suddenly, Rolloc's eyes became the charcoal and cunning embers of Judux, and then the fiery rubies of a Dragon of which he promised to revive from history, and its rotting teeth declaring the decrepit value of my—

"Lucien, how are you?" I said, the words a brief respite from the prison of my mind.

"What?" Luicen said, stirring from his own gloom as he looked up at me through his white bangs and with his blood-shot eyes. "Oh. I am well, Morgan."

"You are?" I said, not believing him.

Lucien nodded slowly, carefully.

"Thank you for the fire."

Lucien turned away and resumed his gaze into the flames.

In the corner of my eye, I could see Egret looking at me. I turned to catch her glimpse, but she returned her eyes to the fire as well.

For hours we sat around the fire saying nothing.

I continued to feed the fire as Egret fell asleep hugging her knees. Lucien wrapped himself in his cloak and laid down by the fire. I was still for an endless stretch of time as I stared into the flames. For a while I thought I was the only one awake, but then I heard the softest cry coming from Lucien. I made no move to comfort him, though I longed to. He needed rest more than anything, and the guilt I felt in failing his brother hindered me from speaking more to him, adding more to his pain.

I was thankful when his tears ceased and he fell asleep hours later, but every second that passed in hearing his pain felt like a repeated plunging of a knife into my heart.

The fire was my only company in the dark storm as I continued to feed it with the dwindling furniture. But before long, my thoughts became ever more consuming than the fire. My soul was beyond tired, my mind racing and refusing to let me sleep, for the evils I had witnessed kept resurfacing in the churning seas of memories.

To save myself from losing my mind, I quietly stood to my feet and left the glowing hut, needing to be alone.

Immediately, the darkness swallowed me, the rain-drenched me, the cold seized my breath, but it was nothing compared to the wars in my mind.

Useless.

Pathetic.

I shook my head to clear the thoughts, walking faster through the forest to focus on anything but myself.

Sigmund.

My heart clenched in thinking of him as I stumbled through the wet forest, draining what little strength remained in my legs and causing me to crash into a mossy tree. Blood dripped from my nose as I tried to steady myself from its crushing embrace.

It became increasingly harder to justify holding myself up.

With laden feat, my soul drifted through the weeping trees, aimless and weak as the wind and leaves violently slapped my face. It was too dark to see even my gloved hands before me, my blindness leaving me prey to a nameless brook that I fell into. Now I wished for the strength to rise, for even though I could barely see, the shadow of whom I hated was apparent in the brook's reflection, the one whose sleepless death was not meant solely for himself.

"*I hate y-you*!" my vessel screamed to the reflection of my soul, and to any being, if there were any, that orchestrated such an existence of pointless suffering.

My chest heaved and struggled to breathe amidst the shameful sobbing that followed suit, misery beating my neck to the ground more than the raindrops that were endlessly being spit from the Void above.

"Why did they have to die? Why…"

The torrent of tears overwhelmed me, shaking me violently.

Even when I could breathe again from the agony of remembrance, I would catch the silhouette reminder of my existence in the water, bringing back everything which I tried to suppress. My eyes became like fire with hate for the shadow that was my soul, and the brook became the outlet of my corrupted rage instead, my anger uncaring if the blows from my fists met stones underneath. My eyes were too swollen from the sorrows leaking from them, but I could feel the blood from my hands filling the gloves more than the rain as I relentlessly marred the mirror image.

Time was irrelevant as I failed to beat the monster who dragged everyone around him to the same place of loathsome suffering that he endured every moment of his life.

It wasn't until my tattered gloves slipped off my hands that my muscles gave up, for the sight of my flesh made me weak with loathing.

My charcoal fists clenched in hatred for their deformity.

"Failure," I said, a hoarse whisper from my strained throat.

This is why the sea calls to me, begs me to sleep beneath the waves. It's the most selfless thing to do.

The world is brighter without my destructive fire.

I laughed softly at first to the twisted version of Aquilla's poem which he thought would save me from the fact that my life has been and always will be worthless. If anything, the Mother's words only confirmed what I've already known. These revelations made me roll in laughter at the truth which was so simple. How I had foolishly thrown away the chance to be forgotten at the thought of some lunar being living in my mind.

"Aquilla?" I tried again, but to no surprise, there was only silence.

This only led to more laughter, most undoubtedly coming from the depth of my exhaustion which made me feel drunk with fatigue, but also from the idea that such a life as mine could be redeemed from a predetermined suffering.

As if I could be saved.

I may have lost my senses, but there was still time to remedy the mistake of my life before Lucien and Egret would suffer a similar and inevitable fate.

Looking at the water, longing for its release, I let my vessel collapse into its freezing visage. My lips kissed the icy waters, swallowing me only halfway, but it was enough to drown.

Closing my eyes, I held my breath, ready for the painless sleep that had so long eluded me.

❧

"Rise, Morgan."

Light burst forth from the dark clouds of my mind at the sound of the familiar voice.

Terror gripped me as I wrestled in a sea of confusion, my surroundings unknown to me but feeling exactly like I was underneath the weight of the oceans.

All I could see were the burning symbols of what was written on Solstein, its peculiar waves whispering in the abyss of my mind. Its sound was like an echo in the wind, too faint to decipher.

"Where am I?"

"Rise!"

My eyelids thrust apart at the shock of his voice. Perched in the swaying oak above me was Aquilla, his fiery red suns in replacement of where his eyes should be glowing brightly. They were almost a substitute for the cloudy morning but with intentions the opposite of joy.

That's when I realized I was not in the freezing blankets of the waters from the brook surrounding me, but instead laying beside the water. Scrambling to my feet, I found it to be a shocking relief that I did not die.

I tried to kill myself, but I lived.

Standing wearily on numb feet, I felt both fear and relief at those conclusions, though I wasn't sure which emotion related to which truth.

Aquilla suddenly dropped to the forest floor to meet me, and words were empty in my lungs.

"Follow me," he said, turning quickly away to stride through the grey forest without waiting for my response.

In disbelief, I watched him pace to the town surrounding the Amon Bridge that was now illuminated in the sullen dawn.

My heart hardened with rage in returning my focus to the apparently real Medjaib. Having no idea where I was or where Lucien and Egret were, I ran to catch up with Aquilla to settle both of these crippling factors warring within me.

It was harder than I thought.

My mud-caked body and sore legs caused me to stumble repeatedly, the lack of food and energy within making my struggle to even walk almost unbearable. It felt like I was carrying boulders in the mud trying to follow Aquilla, but I could feel the weight was actually coming from within.

"Where were you when I needed you?" I spit, my words almost breaking.

But the Medjaib was silent as I followed him through the sleeping cobblestone town. And it was while we threaded through this graveyard of shambled buildings that I saw the rotting corpse of a sparrow that lay in the street's gutters with wings crushed and mud covering its cold eyes.

It broke me.

The storage of my tears seemed to be without end as I

wailed throughout the quiet streets, Aquilla's gait unhindered to my wallow.

It wasn't long before we reached the steps of the Amon Bridge stretching over the glowing outlet of Ember Lake. Bracing for the pain, I forced myself up each step which felt like their own mile, the straining of my cold and tired muscles almost too much to bear. Time was only measured by the labored breathing of my lungs as we crossed the chasm, and before long we stood hundreds of feet above the soft glowing pockets of unattainable Godstone at the depths of the lake below.

It was at this point that Aquilla finally stopped.

"Climb," he said, nodding up the slick granite wall that framed the bridge.

"What?"

"Climb," he repeated, no change in his authoritative tone.

For a few moments I stared into his swirling eyes so he could feel my anger.

"For what purpose? Do you want me to die?"

"I want you to learn!"

"Learn how everything is meaningless like your p-pathetic advice? I already learned that when your supposed god sent you here *without* a plan to reverse the irreversible."

"Morgan, you will climb for your failures."

The audacity.

The arrogance, the belligerent pride stole the words from my mouth.

"Morgan," he said softly, his cosmic face seeming to reflect the lonely stretches of the stars in empathy, "trust in me."

Aquilla leaped to the top without waiting for a response.

I was tempted to think his promise was pointless. But the curiosity that was sparked from the Medjaib's words began to warm in my heart, like the reversal of a dead fire whose embers began to glow after ceasing their flames.

If his words were nothing, all a mirage of hope, there was always the height of the bridge that would end my fall from grace.

So I climbed, drying back the tears with the strain of my aching muscles and pulling up my broken vessel to sit beside the strange being whom I could not comprehend. Seeing the height produced fear in my heart at the thought of falling to my death, throwing me off balance as my mind was indecisive of what fate it wanted.

But then, I could see the first glimpses of light breaking through the cloudy storm, and my tears disappeared in the light rain.

"Why did you bring me up here, spirit?"

But Aquilla did not look at me or my tattered hands. Instead, he was as silent as the grave, not moving for what felt like hours as he looked upon the glimmering waters, almost as if he were more interested in that than in me. All I could do was watch the sun begin to rise on the horizon of the glowing lake, keeping my arms between my legs to hide them.

"You know very little of your worth."

My fingers scraped the charred scales of my forearms. "I have an accurate estimation according to your god."

"Morgan, what is it like to feel the heat of the sun?"

Words were impossible to grasp as I balked at the question, expecting something else entirely.

"I… what do you mean?"

"To feel the sun, the heat that is produced for life—"

"I know what you meant, but—"

"Then why did you say you did not comprehend?"

"No," I said, recalculating my response. "What I meant to say is, why do you ask?"

"I have always wondered what it was like to feel it. Everything appears brighter, warmer, and in want of the sun, from the flowers of the fields to the animals that awaken to frolic in its splendor. Even the Dwarves follow your race in seeking the light, waking only when the day is of the sun, and hiding while it is gone. Yet, until now, you have kept yourself entirely cut off from its nourishment, hiding your flesh from its grace. Is it because you are afraid of its glory? Is that why you sought the cold sea to be shielded from its reign?"

"I am not afraid of the sun!"

"Then why must you hide your flesh? Why seek the waters where the sun cannot be? 'Only the shadow flees from the light, as does all wickedness which spawns from it.' But you are not wicked, Morgan, your heart is warmed by Her light. It is as bright as the sun in the way you care for others."

My eyes stung with tears at the obvious truth which he was oblivious too.

I knew if I tried to explain the abhorrent hate in which I had for myself, the complete lack of care for my soul, I would be nonsensical through the tears that would erupt. Instead, I let my memories speak for me, allowing one in particular to show to Aquilla whom I had shut out until now.

The memory that began the downward spiral to the colorless waves emerged from the depths of my mind: with innocent and oblivious joy, I looked upon the reflection of my five sol self in the waves of the Strumma, my body disfigured from the flames but my youthful self seeing nothing wrong with it, only a burning curiosity. Valena had told me that the Hagroak witches were able to hide the scars from my olive face, but the rest of my body resembled a log left in the fire pit too long: charred and broken.

At the time, I thought it was rather intriguing, something unique that set me apart, as I was too young to understand the gravitas of suffering that came from my mother that led to my disformity.

The memory shifted to Lucien's cousins, Karlata and

Seifred, who came to swim with us in the ocean. It was the first time we met, and it was the first time someone other than Lucien and Valena saw my flesh. At once, Karlata began to laugh, pointing at my flesh and asking why I looked so *disgusting*. Her brother joined in on the mockery, and I stood speechless as my naive innocence was stripped away and never restored.

Trembling, I moved quickly to submerge my shame in the waters, feeling the relief that I would grow to yearn for over my darkening development.

I hated her, but not as much as I hated myself.

The tears burned against my frigid cheeks as the pools of depression and hatred crashed against my heart like a torrential storm.

"Let me see your hands, Morgan," Aquilla said, disengaging from my memory.

Whether it was from the weakness of my cries or the abandonment of hope, I slowly let my hands unfold from my lap to be exposed before the Medjaib, who tilted his transparent and colorful head slightly as he examined me.

"Your hands, Morgan, are nothing to be ashamed of. It is an honor to even have flesh, to be able to feel the wonders of this world that the Mother has given to us. They were uniquely crafted to carry the Light that this world needs, especially in the time of now. I do not know why She allowed such tragedies to carry out upon your soul, nor do I understand the entirety of her will for you, for us. However, I do know that in your hands lies a choice to make your own destiny, for, 'All of creation shares in Her unshackled gift to create.'

"So, before you are two paths that were established long before you were ever born: to let the shadow consume you, or to drown the darkness in the sunlight; and so, let these ancient words rekindle the flame of hope within you:

"Dancer of dawn, sunflower my soul
Feeding from your light, freedom from my night
Blooming brighter than gold
Reforging my mind with Dragon might
Painting my scales: priceless, beautiful
Destined to fly, worthlessness take flight."

The words burned in my heart like a hot blade disinfecting a rotting wound. The Skallgend reminded me of the Dragons Cypherus slew long ago, and in their reflection I remembered how I paled vastly in comparison to him.

But I wanted to believe.

A small, gasping part of me wanted to fly, to bloom brighter than gold. To be worth something. To be beautiful.

"What is your decision?" Aquilla said.

"I don't… I don't understand what to do," I said, my lips weak with the words I was trying to produce.

"*Trust* in me."

"Why should I?"

Aquilla turned his head to the side as if it were obvious.

"Because you need a Light in this dark world to follow," he said, standing to his feet and offering me his spectral hand as if I could take it. "Fly with me, Morgan."

"How?" I could barely say, rising to my feet.

"By making a choice."

The wind was picking up as the morning dawned before us across the horizon. Like a tossing sea frothing back and forth, I couldn't decide if I wanted to resist the wind from this fatal height, the river sloshing in the chasm beneath us.

But the Medjaib's words were like an anchor that kept me grounded despite my indecision. Part of me prayed, no, *begged* for there to be validity in them.

Something was better than the nothingness of the Void.

"The Mother's words may seem ominous," he continued, "but we are the hope of Renborg, Morgan. Only we can do this in your surrender. *Yield* to my heart so that we can move as one, so you can move in spirit as I do. It is the only way to snuff the flames of Judux and his knights of Sh'eol. If you are to save the ones you love."

Something about his words continuously struck the chords of my heart like the fresh strings of a harp about to produce a somber yet beautiful melody. The song it would play sounded like something I already knew but was struggling to remember: a memory that hasn't yet happened.

And my eyes watered in hope at a destiny that wasn't so meaningless; that light bloomed more beautifully in the shadows than it ever could in the day.

But the opening acceptance of this world I so hastily shut before was now brewing another storm in my mind. Stories of gods, kings, and dragons rushed into my thoughts all at once from my endless hours of studying what I thought was once mythology. The crushing weight of the unknown pressed onto my chest like the claw of a Dragon, the world birthing an even stranger one than I could ever comprehend.

"There is much to learn of this world, Morgan. That is why I am here to guide you. If you do not wish for a destiny of drowning Shadow, then take this leap of faith with me."

Instead of just being metaphorical, his galactic head nodded towards the ledge.

"*You* want me to jump?"

"Yes, I want you to fly!"

Fear filled my heart as I let my eyes wander across the glittering drop below. Ember Lake was glowing now from the rising sun that brought warmth to my flesh, but that didn't ease the coldness in my feet at the thought of plummeting to my death.

But in those revelations, warmth flooded my heart as a new hope emerged within it: an overwhelming desire to live.

"S-so why can't I just say the *Heart of Stars Skallgend*?" I said, avoiding the edge as much as possible. "This height will kill me."

"Not unless you recite the words before we hit the water."

"That is the furthest from comforting."

"Morgan, you do not have to understand why. All you must do is trust in me! This shall only work if you are in a complete state of dependence, for that is when your heart is most open."

Breathing became laborious as I wrestled with his words. The finality of such a trust was more promising than what I had concluded before I dragged myself to sleep under the waves, but that didn't make the jump any less terrifying.

With a shaky breath, I said, "Very well. I am ready."

Aquilla repeated the *Heart of Stars Skallgend* so that I would be ready before the waves, and I clung onto every word like the debris of a capsized ship in the middle of a storm, hoping to live to see the dawn.

"Morgan," Aquilla said, his spirit hovering over the air in front of the ledge as I braced myself for destiny or death, faeries filling my stomach in nervous anticipation. My eyes locked with his fiery suns and for a moment we stood in silence, but then we spoke the same two words with our hearts that were about to fully embrace: "Thank you."

Taking a foolish and hopeful breath, I leapt off of the Amon Bridge. The wind took away my breath as I plummeted towards the blood-red waters that glimmered below between the rocks.

The feeling of elation as I fell was exhilarating, soaring through my entire being and almost making me forget about the only thing that would save me from adding scarlet to the lake and company to the dead.

"Morgan!" Aquilla yelled as he fell with me.

The waters reached out to me with their wet arms for a crushing embrace.

"I know, I know!" I said, wrestling with the pivotal moment of my existence where my life would be lost if I held onto it with bitter hatred but would find it in surrender to this Medjaib like a sheep does in trust of his strong though young shepherd. I don't know why I smiled at the irony of it all, but in this strange understanding of my soul's meaning, I found peace at the prospect of giving up my light to make it worth shining for.

Placing the poem on my lips, I found them arduously difficult to say.

The proof of any benevolent cosmic source behind the words of my story and worthy of my worship were scarce and bordered on non-existent, but the desire for the truth to be found so that there was even an inkling of meaning behind the tragedy of existence was stronger than my disbelief.

Though just slightly.

I took one last glance at my charcoaled skin that was about to be doused in the stone-like surface of the cherry waters, and despite my abhorrence for it and everything underneath, and my failures, and my worthlessness, and my betrayal from the world and anything that could have caused it, I let my soul deliver one last cry of desperation.

Seeing the poem before me in my mind, I charged the words and wrestled with them with all of my might, hoping to either prove them false or be submitted to their freedom.

"Heart of flesh rots to death,
Ignite with love of Light above,
Heart of fire world is brighter,
Shine forever in surrender!"

And with a deafening smack, my heart stopped as I tore face first through the waters.

But rising from the bloody lake was a sparrow set free.

My heart found its beat again but almost stopped as I soared weightlessly above the lake, my form similar to that of a Fhaolin but instead of real feathers for wings, they shone with glassy wonder that guided my flight towards the clouds.

A reflection of my dream before the flames.

"Aquilla?" I said, stopping my aerial journey just before the departing clouds to take in my surroundings from a new perspective.

Everything was so much simpler up here, trees as small as the cares of this world. And my soul felt light, like it had been set free from a dark and miserable prison.

"I feel so… free," we said.

Like two water droplets diverging from one, Aquilla's soul morphed gracefully out of mine as we stood upon the air which held us.

"Well done, Morgan," Aquilla said, "you are now a Shepherd. Though we still have a long journey ahead, these are your first steps."

I stared into his swirling eyes that were as translucent as my entire body.

"What… how?"

"We have named it *Soul Sleep*! This is how the Medjaib watch the earth from the moon. We leave our physical bodies behind as our soul wanders the earth, always tethered to our heart where every soul belongs."

"But why do we have wings?"

"Every soul has wings, Morgan. How else would they learn to fly?"

Aquilla moved in sync with me above the waves, stretching out his arms. A glorious pair of crystal wings rose from him, like an eagle rising for the flight of dawn. For the first time in my existence, I felt free. The fearful-joyful sense within me was burning throughout every fiber of my body, tremendously more than any cup of juva could provide. But the elation came to an abrupt halt as I flew unstoppably and blindly towards a fisherman making the early morning rounds on the water.

"Watch out!" I screamed as I braced for impact, but only the sound of Aquilla's laughing could be heard as I continued my flight unhindered.

Daring a quick glance backwards, I could see the tan-skinned fisherman was not only unphased by my flying through him, but he also seemed oblivious to our flight and my screams.

"Do not fear, Morgan," Aquilla said as I regained control of my wings and rested gently above the waters. "While we are in Soul Sleep, no one and no thing in the physical realm can see us or feel us in the spiritual realm. Our worlds are completely separate from each other, but we are linked nonetheless."

"Like a mirror?" I said, catching my spectral breath and seeing no reflection of us in the waters.

"Exactly, but only from our point of view. To them, we are nothing but whispers in the wind."

"So, if my spiritual form is like a mirror in this realm, does that mean…" I said, letting my eyes wander to the lake where a Human-sized form was floating in the waters.

"Forgive me, I almost forgot!" he said.

"I'm drowning!" I said on the way down, instinctually using my feathered arms to fly like I had in the nightmare.

Aquilla chuckled as I tried to touch my soaked body with my vaporous fingers. "Do not fear, Morgan, the Mother's breath sustains us while we sleep."

"How do I get back into myself?" I said, jarred by the peculiarity of that sentence.

"Simply knock on the door to your heart, which is your home in this life."

Immediately, I was pulled into my body like a draft of wind slamming a door shut. Water also followed my reentry, unfortunately to my lungs, and as I swam to the shore and cleared the lake from my chest, existence felt heavy again; but to my relief, not as burdensome as it was before.

"How do you feel?" Aquilla said as I rested upon the sand, my mind whirling to understand this new world that I had just graced the surface of.

Looking at my hands in the morning light, I was still appalled by what I saw but for the first time in my life, I knew that there was something even more beautiful inside of me.

"I… I do not know. There is an unfamiliar sense of peace in me that is hard to describe."

Something appearing like a smile crested through Aquilla's colorful spirit.

I found myself smiling alongside him as we watched the sunrise together on a new day, one of promise and hope. The waters before me looked uninviting now as I began to contend with the possibility of saving Lucien and Egret from Judux and whatever he was planning, all of it a form of redemption for my failures for Sigmund and Philomela.

Their deaths plagued my mind ever still, along with their parents' gruesome demise, but like the sun, a chance at life worth waking up to was visible and bright. All I had to do was rise with it. And growing from this nourishing potential, embedded deep in the rocky crevices of my heart that had been crushed and withered from the hatred for life and myself, was the first seed, though incredulously weak and insignificantly small, of love.

"So," I said, my heart filling with hope, "what do we do now? How do we help Lucien take back Renborg? Can this defeat any Dragons if Judux is able to—"

My words came to a halt as my hand gave out its support. When I turned to look at it, my hand wasn't there. All I could see was my arm protruding into the red sand that was unearthed. And when I pulled it out, my hand glittered transparently like Aquilla's.

"At last," Aquilla confirmed, moving from my center with his hand that I was just beholding. "You have begun to trust in me."

Excited wonder boomed in my soul as I looked from my now deformed hand to Aquilla, and to the clouds where we flew and back to my hand again. "H-how… how did I do that?"

Aquilla's eyes blazed with intensity. "This is only just the beginning."

Chapter 12
Reigniting Embers

The Mother's Skallgends imply that Her Holiness became sad after looking at the empty void She had created, all alone in Her beautiful Solæf. Her poems show that She created the Earth in the middle of the Void to cure Her loneliness, but it did not, as it was lifeless and dry. She then created a being like Her but different, so that they could enjoy each other's company. She bore him from the earth and made him powerful so that he could impact the world as She could. She designed him as the most beautiful creature, adorning his scales with gems and gifting him the breath of fire, and he was her most treasured possession.

Thadius was the name she gave him, which means "Sun of Dawn". We believe that the Dragon Sunflowers Skallgend refers to this fallen god, but it is uncertain. From Her last Skallgend's on the Birth of Existence, it is clear that the Mother and Thadius lived happily for thousands of sols as they reigned over the Earth, filling it with wonders beyond belief before the Battle of the Gods that tore the world apart.

Holy Reflections
"Commentaries on the Mother's Skallgends"
Qai'phus Giabhor: Primarch of the Valkryn

"You shall not tell them, Morgan. Again!"

Fiery pain erupted in my charcoal hand as it collided with the dark oak near the moonlit waters of Ember Lake. And just like the last twenty-two times, to much throbbing disappointment, it did not phase through.

"Aghh!" I said, crumpling to my knees in painful exhaustion. "*Very well*, I will not. But I do not think I can keep punching this dedrim of a tree!"

"Be thankful it is not, that would be a disturbing fate."

I shook my head, not wanting to think of being snatched by

one of those forest predators and filled with its harrowing seed to become just as miserable as they are. Though it wouldn't be far from the misery I was experiencing now, with every bone in my cracked hand aching with white-hot severity.

"Speaking of suffering, my hand cannot take another mistake. I tried Wyling into our souls like you said, but it's not working."

"It is for one simple reason: trust."

"*Trust*?" I said through gritted teeth.

"Yes. In order for there to be harmony between our souls and for our spirits to move as one, you must trust in me. Clearly, you do not."

"But you knew this whole time?"

"Of course."

"Then *why* did you not tell me this morning? Wouldn't that make me trust you less?"

"I do not see how, for I trust in the Author though I know not the entirety of Her plans. I had to ensure that you would not speak of this to Lucien or Egret after our flight. I must also trust in you if we are to move as one."

I couldn't see Aquilla's face because his soul was vibrating through mine so I could phase. For the briefest second, as my hand throbbed with pain after beating a tree, I believed my mind was truly becoming sick; that I was rationalizing a spirit who told me my life had purpose after witnessing the slaughter of my family, friends, and home.

If Egret or Lucien were to see me now, they would probably believe it as well.

Steadying my breath and curling my fist yet again, I positioned my heart to trust more in Aquilla this time, though it was more of a seed than it was a sapling of trust. Breathing in, I Wyled my soul unto Aquilla, and swung at the tree, though much more gently this time. To my surprise, my fist phased through the trunk, but it stopped abruptly at my wrist. As I pulled it out, Aquilla's hand flashed for just a moment before returning to mine.

"In time you shall trust me more," Aquilla said, "and learn to strike more powerfully."

"Trust goes both ways, spirit."

"*Aquilla.*"

Immediately after our brief flight in Soul Sleep, we had returned to Lucien and Egret who were still sleeping by a lifeless fire, the embers of my care a soft glow beside them. But as soon I opened the rotting door to the hut, Egret immediately opened her eyes and grabbed her knife, bracing herself to kill.

"It's me!" I whispered harshly, waking Lucien from his slumber.

"Where did you go?" Egret said, her sleep-crusted eyes full of speculation as she reclined back to the floor.

"I had to relieve myself," I lied.

Egret nodded slowly, but it didn't appear that she believed me.

"Do we have any more food?" Lucien said, his eyes gaunt and red from a night of sorrow.

"I believe not, but there is a town nearby," I said, my stomach groaning in a shared hunger, though probably more severe than both of theirs.

It had been weeks since I had eaten a full meal. The shaking of my hands was not only coming from our training, but also from how starved I was.

"Why must you eat again?" Aquilla said to me, staring at Lucien. "Did you not eat yesterday?"

We did, but it was nowhere near enough.

"Must you consume as much food that was present at the wedding?" the Medjaib said, his voice one of astonishment. "It is only Lycan that need to consume a herd of cattle a day."

"We should remember we are still being hunted and in the middle of a war," Egret said, rising in frustration to leave the hut for the crisp morning forest.

Lucien muttered something under his breath and turned to look at me with desperation. "I will faint if we do not have something of nourishment, Drakin or not. We have Drakmun in the satchel to purchase something in the town before we reach Hebsund."

"Very well," I said.

Lucien returned a brief smile in a show of my support, and he rose to embrace me.

"Thank you," he whispered, though my intuition believed it was not just for taking the initiative on settling our food shortage.

As Lucien departed quickly to leave the hut, my soul grew heavier in seeing him suffer beneath the evils that had unfolded upon him and his family which he dared not to speak of or share.

In a way I could understand, for I would crumble in despair if I thought too much of the deaths that had occurred before us.

There was a deep and heavy silence over the village people as we rode in, many of the Humans and Dwarves clearing to either side of the town's road to avoid us as we searched for the right merchant.

I couldn't understand why they acted so strangely to us, and then I saw that they were all looking at Egret, whose bald head shone appallingly in the light since she had lost her headdress in the invasion. Egret strained to keep her head high as we passed through, but her perception of their reactions to her was clear by the way her neck tightened and her jaw clenched, as if she was battling to stifle angry tears.

"I never realized there was such distaste for those who hailed from Skyya," Aquilla said.

It is not because of her heritage. It is because she lacks hair, which is something they are probably not used to seeing.

"But I share with this Egret in my lack of hair, yet you did not find me repulsive when we became one."

I didn't say I found her repulsive.

"Then of beauty?"

I didn't say that either.

The words choked within me, for I had seen a glimpse of something more within her when our souls encountered one another in the library; but when I realized who she was, I shied away in both my shame of exposing her and from her strange appearance. However, the chasm of my mind was too distraught to even think about such things from the nightmare in which I found myself in, along with the being from the moon who relentlessly questioned the world and my sanity.

With the Drakmun they had managed to save from Lucien's former soldiers, we were able to purchase a map of the lands, rye bread, a block of cowurt cheese, flasks of boiled water, and apples from a scarcely stocked booth near the bridge. Strangely, when we tried to acquire fish, the merchant gave us a fearful look.

"The water is cursed!" he said through yellow and rotting teeth. "All which flows from its waters are poison!"

The villagers halted in their mundane tasks, their attention drawing to us like children hearing of horrific tales before bed.

"He is of a simple mind, for things cannot be *cursed*," Aquilla said, watching the villagers closely.

The villagers soon resumed their simplistic existence, and instead of fish, the sun-scorched merchant gave us the mushroom heads of the Mycelvik creatures, which was the furthest from appealing but which we begrudgingly accepted for nourishment.

"Excellent," Lucien said as we remounted our steeds and

began to ascend the Amon Bridge. "Instead of food, we receive the heads of the mushroom folk."

"These are not for… stew?" Egret said, watching me examine the bodiless Mycelviks in horror as we rode gently across the chasm and to the sloping forest beyond. "Or for bait in catching the fish they fearfully refused to retrieve?"

I refused to look while I tore it to shreds with my teeth, passing some to Lucien who quietly refused. "We don't have time to make stew, as you said."

The ridges of the heads were revolting, but it would be filling.

"Why are your people so averse to selling us fish?" she said, her eyes squinting in annoyance at my comment. "I don't recall the *Chronicles of Renborg* ever mentioning that. What curses are they afraid of?"

"Yes, what myths do they believe the Mother cannot undo upon these waters?" Aquilla said.

Though my soul was weary, I remembered well the story of Ludsala, longing to think of anything besides the nightmare we continued to endure. Lucien's heavy soul before me also indicated that he was loath to speak, especially to his wife, so I chose to spare him from explaining.

"Ludsala was… constructed many sols ago at the height of an empire which came before Renborg, built at the expense of the citizens who were squeezed and starved to build for its pointless extravagance and spiraling towers. Once it fell during the Red Death, the kings who rose afterwards condemned the corrupt city as a reason for the plague, abandoning the city ever after to the shadows in which it was birthed. From my understanding, the villagers believe that the water which passes through it is also tainted with shadow."

A heavy silence whispered through the trees as we said nothing for a time, the memory of Ludsala and its evils overshadowing our minds that I longed to leave behind.

Sigmund's demise flashed through my memories, and I squeezed my eyes shut to avoid them.

"I do not understand," Aquilla said as we rode. "Can the kings of Renborg not rid the city of its shadows easily with their armies?"

The collective myth carries more weight than logic.

"Strange…" the Medjaib said, waving his hands curiously through the trees we passed by, his inner thoughts unknown to me.

"Let us be rid of this place then," Egret said to my heart's agreement, withdrawing the map we had purchased. "According to this map, Hebsund should be about… a nine day's ride. Let us be going then, we are on a tight schedule. We should not tarry in the forest longer than we need, unless you need more time for finding mushrooms to eat, lowborn."

"Tight schedule?" Aquilla said as Egret cast a look of mistrusting annoyance to me before kicking her steed into a gallop, a slight smirk hidden beneath her glance.

More time for mushrooms? I thought, flustered and giving no response to Aquilla's inquiry as I encouraged mine and Lucien's horse to follow Egret, sharing her frustration we had with each other but nonetheless wanting to outpace any Drakin pursuit.

~

After a full day's worth of riding in silence, we made another fire beside Ember Lake. Sharing in a meal of internal solitude, we had a greater sense that there were none who followed us.

Lucien smiled softly at me as he took just a few bites of bread and steamed Mycelvik beside the moonlit fire.

"Goodnight, Morgan," he said, quickly giving me an embrace before wrapping himself in his cloak to sleep.

"Goodnight, brother," I said, my words but a whisper as they painfully formed from my lips.

My heart bled in seeing him suffer alone.

Egret was similarly quiet as she knelt to pray before turning to sleep, tracing water in each eye as she stared into the Void above through the trees. Though I didn't understand why she prayed, it was hard to deny her admiring faith.

"Give me sight," she whispered to herself in Skyyan before turning to me, her face immediately morphing into one of annoyance in being watched. "Wake us if we are encroached upon, *Krabios*."

"Krabios?" I said, confused. "It's *Krios*, Your Highness. And that's not even how you pronounce that sea creature. It's *Krabourak*."

"Whatever you say, Krabios."

Aquilla was silent as she prayed and I fumed, watching her with a burgeoning curiosity in which I could also feel within me, though it was tempered by annoyance in being compared to a miserable sea monster.

Egret's emerald eyes caught mine for the briefest of moments before she laid to sleep. In her ocular seas there glimmered an intellectual intensity that must have been refined and strengthened from life in the courts of Skyya, along with a hint of humor that defied the darkness around us. And though I wanted to make amends from betraying her, her eyes and wit perplexed me with an intimidation that was frustrating to solve.

Her sense of humor was similarly aggravating, though a welcome distraction to the chaos of our current situation.

Aquilla waited over each of them until he was sure they were asleep, and then in the darkness, he guided me through the forest to a clearing not far from our encampment to practice. For hours, we practiced silently the same strikes against a tree, in which he encouraged me to trust him further for more control of his spirit.

"This is still relatively new to me," I said, a small part of my arm beginning to phase but not entirely.

"Again, Morgan!" he repeated, never leaving me alone to my mind.

As my hand dove repeatedly through the tree like water, my wearisome mind repressed the growing frustration of not having any privacy from this spirit. Every waking second, when I wasn't consumed by the memories of the invasion or the present danger at hand, I could see and feel and hear Aquilla as he investigated the world, the drummings of his mind a distant song that I was slowly beginning to become familiar with.

Forced to become familiar with.

Despite this, there was a peace in knowing Aquilla could not see my innermost secrets and ponderings before I could even articulate them with words. Only the thoughts in which I wanted to express could he see.

Yet, in some strange way, it was comforting to not be alone, both within my mind and the world.

It helped to cure the loneliness I felt in the shadows.

When my wearied body could take no more for the night, we returned to the soft glow of the camp.

Aquilla said nothing as I withdrew my flask of water to revive myself, my eyes drifting between Lucien and Egret who laid on opposite ends of the camp. Though they were married, they acted the furthest thing from it.

"You look at the girl often," Aquilla said. "Is this what your kind refers to as love?"

I came to an abrupt halt.

What? Of course I don't love her! She is… well, she is… not the kind of woman I would fancy.

"I see," Aquilla said, his tone one of genuine fascination

as we walked beneath the stars. "So, when she caught our eyes earlier, I felt your heart quicken and your blood rise… from disgust?"

The incoming swig of water from my flask exploded from my mouth from Aquilla's cosmic candor.

Lucien stirred abruptly from his rest to look at me in startled reaction, Egret rising as well.

"Are you well Morgan?" Lucien said, squinting at me through his moonlight bangs.

"Yes… p-please forgive me, I choked on my water," I sputtered through sporadic coughs, catching Egret's ire as I felt the lightest of smiles from the guest within me.

Damn that curious prodder, I thought instinctively as Lucien returned to sleep, fully wishing Aquilla to hear that specifically. But if he could, he did not remark of it.

"*You* are late, Krabios," Egret said, intruding my thoughts as she stood up to fulfill her watch for the night.

"Forgive me," I said as I went to stand beside Lucien who looked confused at my apparently new name, "I didn't know you wanted to take the watch so soon. After all, such a task is beneath you."

"There is an ocean of wealth you do not know about me," she said, bitterness lapping behind each word as she brushed past me into the forest.

Sighing, I looked down into the cooling embers of the campfire as my annoyance burned into shame.

"Is that how all Skyyans act towards men?" Aquilla said.

Grabbing one of the burning embers with my ungloved hand, I looked at him with a tired glance.

No… she is upset because I mistakenly saw her, uh, undressed on the wedding night.

"So she was of no clothing as I am?"

Well, yes, but to her it is completely different.

"How? Are we not one?"

My cheeks flushed at his naivete.

Yes… but not as... ah!

The ember crushed in my irritated hand as I threw its remains back into the fire.

To see a woman's beauty underneath is an act of intimacy meant only for her husband. For me, it was a crime.

"Why did you look upon her beauty underneath if it is a crime?"

I did not plan to. I stumbled upon her privacy before the invasion.

"Shall you not then resolve your miscommunication with her, if it was merely a stumbling? For is it not so that, 'A mighty sword can conquer a kingdom, but only a gentle word can win a woman?'"

I'm not trying to swoon her! And where did you learn that? That's not in Solbok last I checked.

"It is a proverb from Egret's ancestors on the Isles of Ornos. I found it to be appropriate."

It will change nothing, I thought, looking at Lucien cringe in his sleep, alone on the dirt. He seemed to be fidgeting in terror, sweat beading off of his pale brow. Sorrow eclipsed my heart in seeing him drown in his dreams.

Aquilla moved between Lucien to look deep within my eyes, and as I stared into the swirling stars that ebbed through his face, I found a curious wonder inside of them.

"Just as you were only a few words away from receiving the gift of Light that is now at work within you, so too are you only a few words away from creating trust with her heart, Krabios."

You know, it sounds worse when you say it.

"My argument remains."

She doesn't want my trust to begin with.

"Is it not in our interest, in Renborg's interest, that your family builds trust with Egret and her kingdom? Even if we are to save Renborg from the flames, there must be the unified pillar of their marriage to support it. And as it is now, Lucien has abandoned the task and effort, leaving it to us."

The Medjaib's words were uncomfortably right, though I didn't want to admit it. If anything, my words could aid in her loneliness which she undoubtedly suffered in this strange land, away from her family and joined to one which did not graciously accept her.

And if we were divided against the Drakin, we would fall.

Wasting not another breath, I took one last look at Lucien before turning to disappear into the forest, desperately looking for her in the shadows.

"Do you expect to find her in the darkness?" Aquilla said as we blindly ran through the trees.

"I can see just fine," I said, just as a branch appropriately struck me in the face that was invisible moments before.

"Use my eyes so you shall not stumble," Aquilla said, the smallest bit of humor evident in his voice.

"Do I just—"

"Same as before, Morgan. Breath into our soul, focus the Wyl towards your eyes, and *trust* in me."

The forest immediately morphed from the darkest of shadows to an oceanic landscape of crystals. Everything around me was void of color but differed in their shades, allowing me to see every tree and branch with clarity more arguably than a Fhaolin could at night.

It was all so… *beautiful.*

Little crystals of red rummaging about in the trees above and on the ground below appeared as I ran through the strange forest. The bright contrast caught my attention, and as I looked more carefully upon them, I realized they were in the shapes of birds and rodents.

Life truly glowed all around me.

"Is this what you see?" I said, looking up at the sky to see it was a dazzling canvas of white with pepper-black stars.

"Yes."

"Are the animals red because of their souls? Like Bludhstone?"

"Precisely."

"And why are the stars black?"

"Those are not stars, Morgan, those are the souls of the banished."

My stomach grew sour in thinking of the Valkryn stories of those whose songs did not please the Mother. It was difficult enough wrapping my mind around everything Solbok proclaimed to be true, and all I could feel was pure fear in the knowledge that I too could join those banished souls, alone forever in the Abishx if my song was found wanting in its harmonious melody.

"I don't ever want to be alone up there," I said, my words shaking from my lips as I wrestled with the gravity that this new world continued to deliver.

"And you shall not if you continue to yield to the Light within me."

"And that will be enough?"

"It is not how bright you shine that spares you from such a fate, it is in your dedication to Her of a pleasing melody that makes it glow."

"How could I even begin without the lyrics?"

"That is what we will learn, *together*. 'From the nest a bird shall fly, though untaught it shall not die.'"

Sighing as I leaped over a log, I made my way through the forest into the upcoming meadow. "I don't think this god of yours would even forgive—"

Fire erupted in my nose and reverberated throughout my

entire head that was forcefully thrown onto the moonlit grass. Losing focus on my Wyl, the world suddenly became night and full of shadows again, but light came before me from the shiny surface of Egret's head from the moon.

"Oh," Egret said, standing above me with a branch that most likely had my blood on it, along with her Godstone knife, "I did not assume I was going to be stalked by you, Krabios. But then again, I should have known what to expect from a lowborn. You are graced with the Mother's fortune that I did not let Kalypto pursue your throat next."

"What are you doing all the way out here?" I said, pushing myself up to sit as I tended to pulling out the splinters from my face, thankful that it wasn't her ornate knife marring my flesh.

Aquilla sat silently beside me, unknown to Egret as he watched us both, carefully.

"I could ask the same for you."

She was still holding the branch in her hands, the walls of her heart just as evident in her defensive posture.

"I wanted to apologize," I said, my words a sigh of surrender.

"For which offense?"

Lifting my eyes to her forest gems, I could feel the iron doors of my own heart start to tremble beneath her fierce intimidation and the weakness within myself.

"*All* of them," I said, my words agitated yet heavy enough to drag my eyes back to the dirt in shame.

Tears burned at the edges of them.

Squeezing my eyes shut kept them locked away from her. The guilt of causing her shame was like a bitter thorn in my flesh, especially after receiving the regal glimpses of a strong yet gentle soul.

"Morgan," Aquilla said, perking my attention back up to Egret who had sat down in front of me and was studying me with an acute gaze. "Open your heart to her. Then, she shall trust you."

The doors of my heart were grabbed by my deformed monstrosities that were my fingers and yanked open without remorse, all in the effort of giving at least some peace to her; to remedy the ever-growing list of mistakes that I continued to make, even with divine aid.

"I-I'm… I'm sorry, Egret. I know nothing I can say will remove the embarrassment I caused you to suffer. To see you was not my intention, and I wish I could take it all away."

"What were you doing by my window then?" she said, her words as sharp as a sword and as painful as it would be to be honest to her. "Do you think I do not know the bestial nature of your kind? To be so foolish enough to accept any other weak excuse for your animalistic desire to indulge your senses? I should have known that the words you spoke in the library were nothing but a ploy to swoon me as the enemy so often employs."

I stumbled for words. "I was—"

"No!" she interrupted. "It matters not what you say, it will not change how criminally you looked upon your Queen! If it wasn't for your brother, I would have you tied to the end of a Poecampi and—"

"I was trying to kill myself, Egret!"

The words hung before us like the physically de-hearted criminals of the Valkryn Faith after they were sentenced to the rope: just as heavy and appallingly dead. Although I could not see Egret's expression as the tears welled up inside of me and began to stream from my eyes, I could feel a well of empathy from Aquilla, whose soul I could sense looking at mine with quiet sincerity, though I knew he would never understand.

As the silence weighed heavily on our conversation, I dried my eyes so I could see again.

Looking up to Egret who stood awkwardly, unknowing how to respond, our eyes reconnected for just a moment. But just as quickly, Egret looked away from me, as if glancing at me was a mistake. And it was. I was nothing but a lowborn as she was fond of reminding me, and she was of the highest of births in her kingdom. If anyone else saw us alone in the woods together, it would be a cause for great shame and speculation for her status.

"I accept your apology, Krabios," she said, the tiniest hint of a smile flickering from her rosy lips. She looked as if she wanted to say more, but after a brief silence, she added, "and I pray you are not still tempted to end your life. I cannot watch after the King alone, and he would surely die without you."

Managing a faint smile, I said, "I think he can take care of himself. He is stronger than you know."

Egret cringed slightly at those words before recollecting her composure. "You would say otherwise had you seen how he handled himself after we retreated from Renborg without you."

"How so?"

She paused before answering as if reflecting upon those moments. "Let us just say the King was fortunate to have Lord Kolstok as an emotionally *stable* counsel."

Looking down upon the trampled blades of grass, my heart felt pangs of sorrow in knowing how the Grand Kriga met such a gruesome end in the Spindler lair.

Images flashed in my mind of all of the Ronian soldiers I saw torn to pieces, excluding Sigmund whose death I tried to bury in the furthest recesses of my mind. Despite this, I couldn't conjure up the memory of Kolstok biting the steel blade of death. But even if he was alive, it would be a worse fate for him, for the wisest thing for the Drakin to do would be to use his knowledge against his own empire in the coming battles.

"Well, I am thankful he had Kolstok… and you."

Lifting my eyes, I found them locking in place with her emeralds again, and this time she did not look away.

"Was it you?" I said, rubbing my glove against my shoulder in remembrance of being pulled out of the creek in my failed attempt of drowning. When she said nothing, I added, "Sparing me from the storm, I mean?"

"Can I ask you something first?" she said, hesitating before she spoke.

Aquilla folded his arms beside me as a silent warning to any answer I might try to give.

"Of course."

She looked deep within my eyes as she measured her words in her mind. Not even the slightest detail of my answer would escape her hawkish eyes that searched for truth. Tension rose within my chest as I tried to calm myself to give her the most honest answer I could provide, though the limitations of which were unbearable.

"Who have you been whispering to along our journey?"

To not betray her trust again, I wanted to tell her of Aquilla's existence, but just one look at his fiery eyes reminded me that such truths were only for us to share.

"To myself," I said, lowering my gaze to the dirt.

The sound of a twig breaking in the distance snapped my attention back up to where Egret was sitting that was now empty.

Egret was already heading back to the camp.

"Egret… wait!" I said, jumping to my feet to catch up with her. "Egret, I promise, I have not gone mad—"

"I know you have not, but that does not mean you are honest."

Her words stopped me in my tracks, shame berating me for my perpetual disease to disappoint.

"We cannot tell her, Morgan," Aquilla said as I Wyled my

eyes to see her in the night. "Nor anyone, as we have discussed."

"Why? What's the harm in telling her? Egret and Lucien are the most—"

"Be still!"

"Excuse me?"

And then I saw it.

Drifting through the trees was a shadow blacker than Noxstone itself. The fullest of its features were impossible to grasp from the field of trees that separated us, but from what I could see, a smoky essence that was its demented form backed slowly into the looming shadows, its hood covering its darkness. And although I could barely see it, I could faintly hear the clinging sounds of chains coming from its direction.

"Morgan, speak only to me in your mind from now on. We are not alone in these forests."

What is that thing?

"The very reason why we cannot tell anyone of my bonding with you. At least not yet, for we are far from ready to face them."

Face who?

Aquilla penetrated my eyes with all of the seriousness that Piluch would have when describing the horrors of the past.

"The very eyes and ears of Thadius, the father of Sh'eol."

Chapter 13
The Dragon King

Judux was seen as a populist candidate who had a vision for Yarahm; a vision to be united beyond their petty confederacy with its archaic laws and civil wars. Helping to achieve this vision and the hearts of Yarahm was his successful history in the Primarchal Wars. Judux had won many important battles for Yarahm and was petitioned by the people to become the Derasar in 980 DE. As the embers of the Primarchal Wars were still hot, Judux knew that Gulmund would surely return one day when he had gathered Renborg's economic strength, or at least one of his descendants would.

This was the reason for his famously daring two sol campaign in Laconnia from 982-984 DE, where he and his hired mercenaries successfully raided and plundered at least half of the treasury of Lucca's silver stores in order to build up Yarahm's first professional standing army. This conquest single-handedly made Judux the richest and most powerful person in Yarahm and played a decisive role in his unrivaled political domination. By the end of his term in 985 DE, he was so beloved in Yarahm that the Council elected him into a newly created position, "Grand Derasar". This was meant to last for twenty sols, which is why he renewed the war with Renborg in the eighteenth sol of his term. He believes that if the invasion is successful, and if he can bring back Sh'eol, then the people will cry out for him to be crowned as king and hailed as the chosen one which he alleges he is: to bring about a new era of Drakin freedom, prosperity, and security.

Scrolls of Yarahm
Draxian Reforms: 980 - 998 DE
Safira Seraii et Elishem

Every shadow we passed by I thoroughly examined. The next two days to Hebsund were unlike any other day in my existence. Now, I was seeing the world through Aquilla's eyes.

Though we did not see any more of those nightmarish

shadows, or Mara as Aquilla called them, it still felt as if we were being watched. I was careful to keep my conversations with Aquilla in my mind as I searched through the varying shades of grey that he saw through his galactic eyes.

Even when we trained at night beside the Brehnok River, we did our best to speak only in our thoughts. In almost every moment, I watched carefully for any of the monsters who were once of fables but now scoured the lands in search of providing nightmares to the vulnerable.

Had I been prey to their wicked designs? Was it their haunting lullabies that lured me to the sea?

"They exist to also pervert the plans of leaders for their master," Aquilla said as we practiced breathing and focusing my Wyl the next night.

How many of them are there? I thought while balancing on one foot and attempting to phase my head.

"That knowledge eclipses me. We observed at least hundreds of them from Akhorus, but there could be thousands. And that is just in Scissalan alone."

What lies beyond our world?

"More than you can bear at this moment."

Sighing, I accepted his deflective answer, as any more information might've capsized my already swelling mind which continuously struggled to not slip back into the shadows of my memories.

What are they? I thought, following the combative pattern Aquilla showed me in my thoughts. *It looked like a spirit wrapped in chains.*

"Don't be fooled, they are lesser than that. They were once flesh and blood like you. Human, Elf, Dwarf, Drakin, and even Averite, but in the twisted use of Godstone, they lost their physical form and their souls along with them."

Frowning, I thought, *What soul can you use to become completely spirit? There's none that I know of with those properties.*

Within Aquilla's spirit I could feel hesitation as he guided me in footwork that was far more graceful than what Kolstok had taught Lucien and I. Before the moment grew awkward, he relented and said, "What other spirit do you know that can phase besides my kind?"

My flesh phased back to normal as Aquilla stepped out of me. *They stole the soul of a Medjaib?*

Aquilla looked away from me and towards the distant tree line which were the Walls of Laconnia. "Indeed… Tolemic, his name was. The enemy uses his soul to spawn more of these shadows with each day that passes."

What happened?

Shaking his head, Aquilla said, "Tolemic and his Bonded One, Hasadum, were led into a trap by a Neluhmite deep in the Frystan Forests. The demigod giant, Kaw, had learned of the Shepherd's spiritual abilities from a Thadanite—"

A what?

"They are the leaders of Thadius' cult, in charge of the Mara and directly responsible to their decrepit master. Hasadum and Tolemic were careless and soon became known for their unnatural prowess, clearing out Troll dens and plundering the keeps of demigods for the honor and rewards embellished upon them by kings and men of great repute.

"But in doing so, the Mara noticed and reported back to the Neluhmite, and there was nothing we could do as we watched the Thadanites unleash devastation upon Hasadum's friends and family through Kaw the Neluhmite. Hasadum would only be free from his misery when Kaw ripped out his heart and had Tolemic siphoned from it while it was still beating."

The image in my mind was too much to bear as each word he said was carried out in my conscious thoughts. I almost wretched at seeing the ghastly sight of what I presumed to be a Thadanite, a figure in black robes with a large skull with horns for a head staring deep into my soul, its eye sockets darker than midnight at a graveyard.

Why didn't he just phase his heart to prevent Kaw from grabbing it? I thought, shaking my mind free from those demented images.

"Because it is the only part of the body which cannot be phased, for it's the very home of the soul."

Then how can the Mara completely phase?

"Because their souls are kept in the belly of Thadius, whom they swore their souls to in order to receive such power. Their hearts are empty, with their beings kept only alive by his dark power."

"Thadius?" I said, the name heavy on my lips. "The father of Sh'eol?"

"*Be quiet*! Do not say his name out loud, only in spirit!" Aquilla paused to look around the whispering trees. "We do not know which shadows listen from the darkness."

Aquilla's words caused a shudder within me, and I viewed the dark forest we camped in with increasing scrutiny.

Why do these Mara and Thadanites work for this god?

"I do not know. They know of Akhorus and our sleepless search for their cult, but they operate with great caution, using the darkness to conceal their wicked schemes."

The purpose of which is unclear?

Sighing, Aquilla said, "Unfortunately. But we know it has to pertain to the eradication of life, henceforth our urgency."

Do you think this god seeks to bathe the world in flames through Judux's resurrection of the Dragons?

"Thadius does not wish to destroy what he loves," Aquilla said, observing something through the trees.

What?

Aquilla phased back into me and silently directed my eyes to Wyl into his. "Look, beyond that tree there. Do you see it?"

In his crystal sight, I could see the cherry red outline of a doe nestling one of her young in their den.

"Thadius was the first god to be created by the Mother, and in him She filled his heart with all of Her creative glory. They spent eons together, with Thadius forming the world and sculpting many of the lifeforms you see today, like this doe. He took great pride in his work and was joyous to please his Creator, especially in his creation of the Inor."

The Inor exist?

"Of course they do," he said, as if it were obvious that everything of fable and myth were completely true. "Thadius created an immortal kind of each creation so that they could guide their own while he sang more of the world into existence. Which is why many of them took his side in the wars against the gods and all of creation that shattered the earth."

But not against the Elves? I thought, remembering the tense but polite debates Piluch was often invited unwilling towards by the prideful Adrian Elf, Tiberius Cilvahan, who, even when Piluch was in the middle of tutoring Lucien and I, would insist that we would be taught the full truth of history; primarily, of the Elves.

"Correct," Aquilla said, the word ringing of distaste. "Most of the Elves began to idolize their seemingly immortal lives, longing for the everlasting blood from the Inor that granted immortality. They forsook the Author and the love of Humans and Dwarves, though in their pride they twist such stories."

I do not know what to say, I thought, my mind barely able to grasp the ever-expanding world in which Aquilla painted with his words. *The thought of an immortal being is… strange.*

"You have already seen one in your lifetime."

The memory of Judux's Kiagor formed in my mind, its glimmering silver pelt an indicator of what I once thought was myth.

Was Cypherus' steed an Inor as well?

"Yes, Buetarus was the finest of them all."

Sh'eol's memory of Cypherus riding his dazzling white steed escaped my attention when I held Solstein in what seemed like a lifetime ago, but now I could remember seeing the Klyr blood that leaked from the immortal Buetarus' mane as Cypherus slew the aerial serpents.

I was stunned.

This world is larger than I once perceived.

"That is precisely what Thadius believed too, as his primary aim is to rid the world of the sentient creation that the Author sang into existence."

Why? Does he think we are inferior?

"No, not at all. It is because the life that She breathed is far too capable in destroying what Thadius created. From festering cities to destroying forests and slaughtering his beloved animals, he thinks you should be purged from his masterpiece."

Why not help us to better take care of it instead?

Aquilla stepped out from my body, his galactic skin hued red as he turned to look deep within my eyes. "As the Mother spoke unto Anya I'lyanova Valkryn, 'The birth of life came forth from love. In love's absence, jealousy desireth its death.'"

Compliance with Aquilla's wishes to remain silent on his existence and our purpose was not trivial, but I managed. If not for myself, then for Lucien and Egret, who were oblivious to the dangers around them as we journeyed alongside the Breh-nok River towards the city.

Egret was still thoroughly suspicious, though slightly less hostile to me now, and I caught her numerous times throwing glances of speculation at me as we rode in silence beneath the shadows of trees.

The rest of the time she gazed at the free-flowing river.

"Do you Ronians not tire of all this land?" she said, her question not particularly clear in its intended recipient.

Lucien only looked at her with a heavy annoyance, declining to respond.

"I don't see why the land would be so tiring," I said, enjoying the cool of the shade and soft roar of the river. "Do Skyyans not often venture inland?"

"She is unimpressed with the Mother's creation?" Aquilla said, similarly confused.

"Of course we do," she said. "But the sea is where we spend most of our time, out on the open, free waters. It is more of a delight than this."

"What's so grand about the sea?" Lucien said, sharing my thoughts, though his tone was more bitter.

"You are not confined to the limitations of land," she said, not bothering to look at him. "The ocean has no trees to hinder your path. Only your strength will determine where you go, nothing else. Once you see the sun melt its golden crown across its blue horizon early in the morning, or its heart spill blood in the evening sky above it, then you begin to understand the wondrous freedom that the Mother has created for us."

Egret paused for a moment, joy beginning to flicker on her face as she reminisced of the ocean. Her longing for the sea was innocent, though I hated the sea entirely.

"That's true," I began to say, "but—"

"The ocean is also unpredictable, and often sends violent waves of storms that mercilessly tear apart those in its waters," Lucien interrupted, his voice wavering and unstable. "Like the storm that tore apart your father's fleet in the Karthosian Rebellion, which comes to mind."

Egret's face reddened, her fingers squeezing her steed's reigns.

"The land is more predictable anyways," I said, attempting

to divert Lucien's unsubtle attack. "And the shade of trees is welcome when the sun raises its heat."

"You Humans speak so much of the earth," Aquilla said, completely oblivious to the meaning of the conversation beneath.

"Predictable indeed," Egret said, regaining control of her tone, though the hurt was evident. "But I don't care for that nor the shade of trees, for there are too many of them. So rigid and tall, full of themselves even, yet covering themselves in shadow nonetheless, hiding their roots beneath the scorn of the sun. Whereas the river runs so freely, not hindered nor controlled by anything but itself. Nor hiding anything beneath its clear surface."

Lucien refused to respond further, as did I.

Egret's ire was clear in its direction towards Lucien, and especially towards me, understandably so. Sighing, I wished to explain myself further to her, to regain the trust that we had almost established, but one glance from Aquilla, who sensed my yearning to expose him, silenced such words within me.

Maybe it was better that way. Besides, we were of completely different worlds. We owed nothing to each other now, and one less friendship to worry about would be a relief.

The rest of the journey was completely silent, with the only words being spoken when we reached the small town of Yulsa at night, a six-day journey from Hebsund.

"We shall have separate rooms and our horses stabled," she said as she paid the wrinkled innkeeper. "And a meal for each."

"We need to stay *together*," I said through my teeth as the aged woman handed Egret two keys and three steaming drunkard pies.

"No sorcery in here, or we'll call the Watchmen," the aged innkeeper interrupted, pointing with the prunes she called fingers to Lucien's Godstone necklace I was wearing, before returning her gaze of speculation to Egret, whose head was covered.

Not wanting to draw attention, I nodded politely and tucked the necklace under my shirt as we walked away.

"We should eat within our rooms," Egret said, moving towards our quarters upstairs with her wine-soaked pie in hand. "We are not yet safe in Hebsund, and the Drakin are sure to have spies that are not of their fiery flesh."

"A wise guess," Aquilla said as he trailed behind our heavy feet to the tavern's second floor.

Stopping at her door, Egret said, "I will wake you both at dawn. We should be safe from any Drakin, but keep an eye out just in case."

"Thank you," I said as Lucien's gaze hung heavily to the floor, ignoring her.

Egret looked at him with a sort of pitiful disdain before closing her door, offering me no glance.

Upon seeing our beds, I sighed in relief at the prospect of rest. Though I wanted to eat, my flesh was too weary, and so I set my pie aside before I laid my head down. It was beyond relieving to not have to think of Dragons and gods and being some destined Shadow. Although it was loud from the drinking guests downstairs, it was the most comforting sensation to hear laughing while having a pillow to rest on after what felt like a never-ending nightmare.

Lucien climbed silently into the bed next to mine, setting his untouched pie on the floor and covering up his marriage armband with the lamb skins draping over his bed.

"Do not become too comfortable," Aquilla said as he paced the room. "There's something we need to do when his soul falls asleep."

Groaning, I relented, sitting up in order to stay awake.

Very well, spirit.

Unfortunately, Lucien was also unable to sleep.

Sitting on his bed, his eyes wide with fright, Lucien stared at the floor's dark and splintered planks. Slowly, he sputtered the first words he had spoken in hours. "I think… I think the world is falling apart, Morgan. They're dead… they're all dead."

My stooping head was lifted by the words as his soaking and bloodshot eyes met my own.

"Father was right. I'm so weak, Morgan, so… *weak*."

"Lucien, you're not—"

"Those *animals* butchered them and I did nothing!"

Everything within my trembling heart wanted to comfort him, but all I could do was weep and listen as I moved to sit on his bed beside him.

"Every night I see it," Lucien continued. "That arrow in his eye, that ax in her neck, those—"

His body began to shake as he struggled to speak.

"Those *things* in his… little chest."

Again I tried to speak, but nothing of comfort could form.

"Why is this happening, Morgan? Has our Sovereign Creator abandoned us?"

Aquilla, kneeling in the corner of the room, lowered his head and hid his thoughts from me, but I didn't need them to feel his doubt, his uncertainty.

"Lucien," I said softly, "it's my fault, not yours. I failed them, Lucien. Maybe Sigmund would still be alive if I had just… just—"

"Just what?" he said, the words birthing from pity that showed on his tear stricken face.

"I don't know, just… something."

"Morgan, those *half-breed* abominations did this, not you!"

Looking down in unbearable shame, all I could see was the dark and splintered floor.

I could have done more. I should have done more.

Aquilla said nothing as my thoughts spilled before him. But I could feel him analyzing my worthless ruminations.

"Father was afraid when he died," Lucien said, his voice almost a whisper. "I couldn't see his eyes but—" Lucien choked a raspy breath. "But the way he grabbed me at the end…" His eyes stared at a horizon beyond me that wasn't there. "I never wanted to be king, and he never wanted me to either. It was always Kyllian who was supposed to be in my place. He was born for the role, ready for it. I always had this peace knowing Kyllian would be king. He would have been better for Egret, too."

Lucien's breath rattled as he inhaled deeply and closed his eyes. "I… I hated Gulmund because I just wanted a father, but he needed a king. Renborg needs a king! But… but it's not me… not as I am."

"What do you mean, Lucien?" I said, shaking my head.

"You'll see… they'll see."

The solemn yet sullen words hung in the stuffy air as he rolled over and laid himself to bed; soft tears drenched his pillow as he did his best to shut out the world.

"I thought I lost you, Morgan," Lucien muttered. "I don't know what I would do without you."

His silver hair felt greasy as I rubbed it to comfort him.

"You're all I have left, Morgan. I can't bear to lose anyone else."

Words were impossible to articulate as I mourned the loss of his innocence, as I longed for the times that once were: for when Kyllian would wrestle Lucien and I in the cherry fields of Renborg before a smiling Gulmund and his once loved Valena, for the hours of tutoring Sigmund to begin writing his first Skallgend while Philomela rested softly in my arms, and for the times that Lucien would unearth one of my many Skallgends and read them dramatically in my room while I unsuccessfully tried to retrieve them.

But those times were gone, just like our family was.

Just as Lucien was becoming.

The Shadow of this unwanted fate seemed to grow evermore, being nourished by my own failures with each passing day.

In the corner, Aquilla was no more as I rose from Lucien's bed to return to my own. Yet even as my vision faded with exhaustion, his glowing form was not hard to find. On the windowsill, staring out at the night, he sat in utter silence as he searched the ever-growing stars above.

"Goodnight," I whispered to Lucien before I nodded off into the dark recesses of my mind to hide from the pain of the present.

~

"Rise, Morgan."

Aquilla's voice startled me awake, leaving my head swimming in confusion. Hearing Lucien's gentle breathing in the darkness, I quietly slipped out from underneath my sheets and got to my feet, remembering my promise to Aquilla.

Very well, I'm awake. Where are we going?

"You shall see," he said, though there was panic in his voice.

Is something wrong?

"Yes, but it's best to see what has become with your own eyes."

Aquilla immediately sat down into his meditative form, and I quickly mimicked him, my legs tucking into my lap with my hand over my heart.

"Quickly, Morgan," Aquilla said as he phased into my body.

What did you see? Was it Judux?

Aquilla was silent as he tried to control the stream of thoughts in his mind that surged alongside mine. "Time will be wasted in an explanation in which you shall soon receive. Now, Wyl and touch your heart with my hand. This shall open the door of your vessel so you can Soul Sleep again."

Just like before, my soul burst out of my flesh like water flowing freely along the river. Along with Aquilla's spirit, we soared through the inn's roof to the midnight skies like two cosmic eagles. If the Fhaolin could've seen our spectral forms, they would've mistaken us for their gods. As we flew, I could see my glittering wings out of the corners of my eyes, and it would be no wonder such creatures would revere us, even worship us had they seen such beauty.

It was a feeling I was not used to, flying so freely above any and all turmoil on the lands of Scissalan.

If I could remain in the skies forever, I would.

"Quickly, Morgan," Aquilla said.

We surpassed leagues within seconds using the wings of our souls. Trees and rivers were just a blur as we flew at breakneck speed. I could hardly believe it when we found the Dragon Highway and, soon afterward, the rosy and lush vegetation of Renborg's Bludhlands. It was a peaceful distraction of normalcy before the war-torn capital city of Renborg came into view.

The royal sector surrounding the palace was on fire, and the flames were surrounded by a differing array of uncountable Drakin banners; a mockery to the rest of Renborg, which hadn't been overthrown yet due to its massive size and impenetrable defenses. Despite this relief, the royal district was littered with crispened soldiers and civilians, their steaming corpses blacker than any land drained of life by Noxstone. More deathly silent.

Adding unto the sorrow were the thousands of remaining Ronian soldiers who were encamped in the outer rings of the city that surrounded the royal sect, along with the even more numerous citizens who appeared ragged as they tended to them.

It would take months for Judux to completely take over Renborg, street by street. However, it seemed that Judux averted this time-consuming and bloody task, at least for the time being, for there appeared two growing walls encapsulating the outer walls of Renborg. Tirelessly working through the night were hundreds of Drakin building the two walls while being protected by thousands of Drakin soldiers from the Ronian guards who patrolled the walls.

And to starve those caught in between into submission.

The military tactic in which Judux employed was hopelessly impressive.

"Why is Judux building two walls?" Aquilla said. "Does he not wish to take over the city?"

"No, the dual walls will serve to entrap the Ronians inside and protect Judux's supply lines for his garrison."

"Which would free him for other pursuits in Renborg."

"Exactly," I said, my soul an anchor that threatened to fall without hope upon seeing the brilliant mind who stole everything from me.

Adding to the pain, there were hundreds of Ronian men being herded by the Drakin from the royal sect into the Hall of Judges.

Prisoners without hope, without purpose.

My thoughts were bleak and heavy as I looked upon a paradoxical reminder of the *merciful* god they worshiped.

Their fates would lead them to the same conclusion in which I was prevented from suffering.

And as I looked up to Aquilla hovering beside me, I could see and feel that he also shared the same questions that berated me. Yet, there seemed to be an almost childlike acceptance of what he did not know as he watched them file into their makeshift prison to be robbed of all purpose; like sheep before the slaughter, yet in this case, sheep in which they knew that they would meet the knife, not the shears.

"'The pure shall perish and the corrupt may flourish, but the Author remains holy as She writes their stories,'" he said, quoting a famous yet contradicting proverb from Solbok as we flew closer to the royal sect. "Hence is our purpose Morgan: to prevent this evil from happening."

"Why didn't this god of yours stop this evil herself? Can she not, in her *great holiness*, write a different story for the wicked?"

Aquilla sighed. "I… I do not know. The Author's Story is one too large to see in its entirety, too eternal to understand its beginning or end. All I know is why I am here, and it is not to force you to our destiny, but to guide you through it."

"To sleepless death."

"To *avoid* it."

We drifted solemnly over the fractured city that was once so beloved by the Ronians, that I once raced through the streets of myself.

Questions and chaos and bitterness swelled within my mind to the point of capsizing at the illogical reasonings behind every pointless tragedy, all of it made worse at the thought that the stories of gods fragmenting the earth and almost destroying life itself was true. Overwhelmed was not even close enough to describing the crumbling state of my sanity, but it was because of these whirlwinds of chaos within me that I almost didn't see the strange white light emitting from one of the many towers of the royal sect ahead of us.

"What is that?" I said as we drifted towards it like moths to a torch fatal to our existence. "Have they taken the Morythia Priestess from her temple?"

But Aquilla was quieter than the emptying streets, feeding

the fear in my heart that the ethereal light was not coming from the Mother's oracle that Renborg long proposed to have. Besides, one glance at the Morythian Tower behind us proved that she had not been taken, for her Bludh figure was still present near the Valkryn Temple which remained in Ronian hands from the ongoing invasion.

"Sh'eol's darkness," Aquilla finally said as we stepped through the tower walls of Caer Mordrake to witness the birth of an abominable destiny.

"You must quicken his growth," Judux said in the Drakonnian tongue, his broken crown immediately drawing my attention as he leaned over what looked to be the pale corpse of a woman, its dark hue casting a shadow over her. "But if you kill another Ronian, I will have your scales peeled from your thighs to remember their deaths in every waking moment. Do you understand? We are not here to destroy them. We have a higher *purpose*!"

Dry blood drenched the floor upon which Judux and four of his priests stood, the thirteen of them circling the dead woman.

For a moment I thought I could see Aquilla and I in the reflection of the golden metallic robes that draped the Drakin priests from head to toe, but, as we got closer, I could see the light reflecting from their Gyldur garments was from Solstein. And holding onto Renborg's most treasured possession was another Ronian man who feebly screamed as the purity of Solstein was most likely burning through him. His shaved head distinguished him as a soldier, but I was distracted by the path of Sh'eol's soul that coursed from his heart to the—

"Dragon," Aquilla whispered.

Judux stepped aside, and at first I thought it was yet another dream, for before me was the misty energy of Sh'eol's soul from Solstein surging into the fresh veins of the blood-soaked baby Dragon, which lay nestled in the carnage of its mother's exposed ribcage.

"I… I do not understand," I said, the sea of my mind churning upside down as the world in which I knew continued to become stranger and darker.

"And every moment, the Dragon grows," Aquilla said.

That's when I noticed the fiery red muscles of the Dragon twitch and grow ever slightly as the Klyr wisps came from the man's twitching hand. But the wisps came to an abrupt end as the man released an exhausted cry and collapsed into the arms of a Drakin soldier who dragged him away, only to be replaced by a younger man whose petrified eyes made up most of his pale face.

"This one should last longer," one of the Navakosh priests said to Judux, "and the other will recover."

"Good," Judux said, nodding as he grabbed the hand of the younger man. Switching to the Ronic tongue, he said, "My boy, do you know what you are about to be a part of today?"

The young man answered with a stream of tears and a wobbly shake of his head.

He was no older than Lucien, most likely just having joined the ranks of Renborg's soldiers.

Judux smiled. "No need to fear, your mind is much too young to understand the significance of this moment. But, do not be alarmed, you will be alive to see the dawn of this new era unfold before your very eyes, and your hands will have helped to shape it. It is a destiny of peace and hope for not only my people, but for yours as well. It is the end of these pointless Primarchal Wars."

The young man crumpled before Judux and began to wail. As he wept, Solstein was brought carefully to him from a priest, who held it before the Ronian whose flesh shivered with fear.

"Now," Judux continued, "all you must do to see your family again is breathe the Dragon's soul into your own as you touch the child. Understood?"

Nodding as his lips drowned from his eyes, the young man quickly grabbed both Solstein and the child. At once, the familiar burning of its purity surged into his heart, and before he could collapse from the pain, the white wips danced from his chest to the Dragon as he screamed.

Lightning was the Dragon's eyes that flashed awake in its mother's womb.

The Ronian backed away as the red Dragon rose shakily to its feet in the carcass, its pomegranate eyes ignoring the young man's and looking up directly into Judux's.

"Aquilla," I whispered, not knowing what to say at the myth being born before us.

For a moment, nothing was said as the two stared intently at each other.

Aquilla and I watched with bated breath at what was about to unleash itself onto the world. Even the priests seemed terrified as they hastily ordered for the weakened man to be restrained by a Drakin guard next to them, and their faces were entirely covered in their gilded robes.

In what sounded like roaring thunder, Judux slithered a quick and indecipherable word to the baby Dragon.

"That was... *Shiveric*," Aquilla said, his galactic skin becoming white, his fear rising alongside mine in both mind and spirit.

For a dreaded moment I thought Shiveric would be beyond his understanding. However, when the Dragon responded again, its singular word sounded chillingly clear to both of us.

"*Thade*?" the Dragon slithered.

Judux shook his head. "No, my name is *Judux*. Welcome, my child."

Looking at Aquilla, I saw the same panic in his eyes that were in mine.

Thade?

But Aquilla was as silent as the grave, his skin becoming a ghastly white.

Instead, I turned to look into the fiery red eyes of the Dragon, and how they so perceptively gazed upon, almost worshiped, Judux.

"What am I?" the Dragon slithered in its thunderous Shiveric tongue.

Judux smiled as he attempted to stroke the beast across its horned snout, but the Dragon snapped at him, removing his smile.

"Be calm, my child! You are the start of a new chapter in our great history. One of freedom. One of choice!"

The Dragon looked confused as it turned around and looked achingly at the deceased Ronian woman it lay in. "But what am I? Is she my mother?"

"No, she only served to harbor the mighty seed of Sh'eol," he said pointing to Solstein, "of which I used to bring you to life. You possess his vast wisdom and are shaped by his ancient soul."

A shiver ran through the Dragon as it shook its head. "But why did you bring me to life, if only to take away another?"

Judux shook his head. "Your purpose is of more glory than this woman ever could have dreamed of. Though, her sacrifice was unfortunately necessary.

"But rejoice, my child! Your life will save countless more. I gave you life to end first our suffering and also theirs. They do not realize the gift of peace I am creating for this world, but they will soon be grateful that the Falm Baqira has brought true deliverance from the sickly light of Renborg. You will have your place alongside me in bringing justice to your ancestors slain by Cypherus, and Divonholm will be at peace like it once was when our ancestors ruled the skies."

Aquilla's eyes met mine, and they were just as mortified.

He thinks the prophecy is of him. And he revels in it.

Looking at Judux, I could see why he would think so. He was a leader, someone with an inherent purpose that was far grander than himself. Being the Derasar already granted him fame and honor more than most could ever achieve, and with his people's differing interpretations of Solbok and their tainted history with Renborg, it wasn't a wonder why they would believe the Shadow of Cypherus would bring good to this world; nor that Judux could fulfill the role.

And he would do so with the abomination wrapped in a bloody carcass before him.

Though, upon seeing the Dragon's untrusting eyes and how it snapped at Judux, it seemed possible that the relationship could change as the beast grew more powerful than Judux.

But what made the Dragon look upon Judux with reverence only moments before?

Leaning carefully close over the detestable creation, the broken crown on Judux's head seemed to almost cast whispers around the Drakin leader. It was such a small and fractured crown, yet it somehow seemed larger than him.

My eyes were drawn to it like the many times I stared into the fatal depths of the sea.

"What shall your name be, young Dragon?" Judux said.

The Dragon looked back at the dead woman whose open corpse it was resting in, and it lowered its eyes to the ground in shame. Before speaking, its lips quivered with indecision, a look I shared when staring at the sordid reflection of my broken vessel I so often avoided.

"*Belial*," the Dragon said, its voice growing in anger as it looked blamingly at Judux, "for I am stained by the blood of a meaningless death… and life."

It was as if my soul was being pierced and yanked from my heart in hearing Belial's words.

The crushing worthlessness Belial felt was all too familiar as I looked pitifully upon the baby Dragon; it was also ashamed of the unchosen vessel and existence handed unto it.

These brief feelings of understanding turned venomously sour in seeing how it also killed the mother of its inception, the death of whom would only sow the destructive seeds of Lucien and Egret's home. And now that a Dragon had darkly awoken, countless stories beyond Renborg would end in meaningless tragedy, like a dark comedy that made one laugh through bitter tears at its painfully bleak truth.

Rising to his feet with eyes closed, Judux's volcanic stress lines mirroring the parental frustration I often saw on Valena's, he said, "I too despise needless bloodshed, which is precisely why I have created you, Belial. You should be *thankful.* If you have lived half of the centuries I have, lost the sons in worthless wars fought for pride, you would see the totalic good I have created within you, for all of Divonholm and even Scissalan. Your fiery might will silence the sorrows of Sh'eol and deliver their hearts from the depths of destiny."

I was about to speak to Aquilla when Judux laid his hand on the priest holding Solstein and said, "How long till he is of age?"

Stumbling over his words, the golden draped priest said, "It d-depends on the recovery of the Ronians. It would be faster if we didn't stop when they were only halfway—"

"No! We will not be draining our kingdom of its subjects, nor the ransoms we will earn from their soldiers' captivity. Have the Derasars round up the raiding parties and bring to me as many Ronian men you can find, even the Elves and Dwarves you find too. We cannot delay his growth."

"Yes, Falm Baqira."

Aquilla looked at me with concern in his eyes, nodding his head towards the window as if to leave. As we prepared to fly, I could feel the weight of my soul burdening me to the floor.

I felt… heavier, disgusted and… relieved?

Relief that someone else, no, *something* else felt the same tremblings which my heart had felt every moment of my existence, even when I was asleep.

The gnawing ache of shame for oneself did little to encourage any worth that could be found within, if that was even possible. Although, the light of Aquilla driving me towards some greater purpose beyond myself was like a torch being dropped into an abyss, lighting the way forward in the dark unknowns of destiny and self-worth that I had yet to discover in such an unsolvable dialectical prophecy.

Now I had the smallest chance of discovering a hair of light peeking through the blackest clouds.

I felt a sense of peace when I looked upon Aquilla despite the radical shift of hopelessness that we now faced with a Dragon growing by the souls of Renborg's—

"Rolloc," Judux said, interrupting my thoughts, "bring in the girl."

My eyes found Aquilla's, but this time, any peace that I had felt was now torn apart like Sigmund, swiped away like Valena, gouged out like Gulmund. And when I saw Rolloc carrying her alive and without harm into the room, I think my heart stopped beating.

"Ah, there she is," Judux said, smiling as he took a tired and cranky Philomela from Rolloc's arms, her greasy locks a wrinkled mess on her forehead.

She was alive.

"Philomela!" I screamed, but only to be noticed by Aquilla who threw me a deathly stare to be quiet.

A chaotic storm of relief and fear rose within me.

I stood in utter shock, unable to determine which emotion was justified in seeing her alive. To be alive meant that there was still hope in the world: that I had not failed everyone. But to be in Judux's hands next to a Dragon which he somehow used the souls of men to create, I was left horrified in the unknown.

Despite this, I wanted nothing more than to slay them.

To run freezing water over each of them until they stopped breathing. I wanted to watch the fire in their eyes cool with their dying gasps.

For the first time, thoughts of falling asleep beneath the sea diminished to a dull roar as I felt the deepest and rawest of anger swelling within me at seeing these children harmed under such a pathetic monster.

They were all monsters, and they all deserved to drown.

If my life only amounted to sparing Philomela from a fate worse than death, that would be a life worth living.

And then I remembered Lucien was counting on me to help him, and that meant helping Egret as well. The fight before Aquilla and I suddenly became a lot more clear; and now, for the first time in my weightless existence, I could feel my feet being drawn forward.

Towards a purpose. Towards destiny.

"I do not understand why she must live," Rolloc said.

"No, you do not," Judux said, turning away from Rolloc and looking upon Philomela, as if in deep thought.

As if uncertain, his furrowing brow saying as much.

Rolloc grunted. "She is too old to create a mate for—"

"I *know*, Rolloc, I heard them clearly. We shall find another with child when it is time."

Belial stood on its wavering legs, inching its head to look at Philomela in Rolloc's arms. The baby Dragon cocked its head as it studied her. Philomela saw the Dragon rise, and in turn, reached her hand out to the Dragon. The whole room was silent as her tiny hand graced the snout of Belial who rose up to her, the beast seeming to warm at her innocent touch.

"Very well, Judux," Rolloc said, confusion shrouding his face as he removed Philomela from Belial, the Dragon immediately glowering at her forced departure. "Have you spoken to the Lycan?"

Judux snapped his hand to silence him, his face briefly contorting with fear as he startled Philomela. "We will speak of this later. Here, take the child—"

The sound of a sword clinging against metal sounded, followed by a piercing scream from the enslaved young man.

Aquilla and I looked to Belial where the boy was wrestled to the ground by the red-scaled Drakin knights, in his hands a bent sacrificial blade from one of the priests.

Belial looked shocked but nonetheless unaffected by the blade. Though in the Dragon's eyes, there appeared a confused hurt that I had often seen when Philomela was upset and uncertain of a situation.

"My boy," Judux said in Ronic, handing Philomela to Rolloc as he stood over the child. "Did your parents never tell you of the Dragons your ancestors *erased*? That nothing, not even the strongest steel, nor even Godstone, can cut through the hide of a Dragon? Or did they tell you another story?"

Judux held the whimpering man in his arms. "Usually, kings would execute citizens for such a treasonous offense. But I am not like most kings. No, my destiny is to save you, to save every single one of you. But, that does not mean I can let you go unpunished, for I will stop at nothing to save your soul."

The man's eyes grew in fear as Judux stepped away and looked at Belial.

"Time to display your loyalty, Belial. As this child tried to steal the life I have given you, so must you deliver retribution.

For the hands of a thief are better off taken away than their whole soul being drowned in the Abishx."

Judux turned away from Belial. For a moment it seemed that Belial would not do so. But when Judux cleared his throat, a snap of obedience was delivered by Belial, who ripped off the right hand of the child in unwanted submission.

I couldn't force myself to watch as his blood bathed the floor.

As the young man screamed in blood-curling pain, the doors from which Rolloc had entered brought forth another Drakin priest, draped in golden robes who boldly approached Judux. Strangely, all I could hear from the Drakin's footsteps was the slightest clinging.

Like the sounds of chains.

The faceless priest leaned over to whisper in Judux's ear.

"The Dragon bones speak of Cypherus' spirit," whispered the priests, the words slithering through the robes. "They speak of his *return* to defeat his Shadow."

A flash of pain burst across Judux's face, the crown tilting with his shaking head before he concealed the unknown pain with his hardened yet fiery glare.

Judux quickly thanked the priest before sending him away.

But as the priest departed, his masked sight rested briefly on where Aquilla and I stood.

"Everyone, leave us," Judux said, abruptly waving his hand for their dismissal. "Escort the young Dragon to the throne room. And Rolloc, see to it that she is properly taken care of, and not lost like our former prisoner."

Rolloc muttered something under his breath before leaving, but not before casting a careful glance at his brother.

The room quickly emptied of Judux's servants who followed after Rolloc, along with my heart, who was carried violently away next to a snarling Belial, though the Dragon softened as it looked to Philomela.

I want to kill him, I thought, my hands trembling as I watched Rolloc leave, Philomela writhing in tears in his pale arms.

The doors boomed shut as we were left alone with the true monster who stood rubbing his hand over his fiery eyes.

Aquilla and I made not a sound as Judux stumbled to the water basin beside us, passing through our spirits.

Judux gripped the stone rim of the basin, his head lowering to the water as the dark crown loomed upon his head, Judux grinding his teeth in pain.

All Aquilla and I could see was his reflection.

"The Dragon is more rebellious than I imagined," Judux whispered. "What have I done in opening this dark portal which resents my command? What shall become of me once he is grown? I *am* the Falm Baqira! Damn Rolloc and his friends! I cannot fail my people…"

The water before him began to churn, as did my skin begin to crawl. Aquilla held a hand before me to stay any thought of movement to investigate.

"To ensure victory," the reflection of Judux said, "you must use the wisdom of the past."

The water rippled again, and this time, strange markings that glowed as dark as his crown appeared.

"Once they know of your knowledge, they will *kneel* to you, oh Shadow of Cypherus; even the spirit of Cypherus who hunts you."

"How will they know?" Judux continued, his head lowering further before the basin as if the entire world were pressing down upon him, crushing him before the strange symbols.

The reflection of Judux rose his head, but not Judux himself. Instead, the reflection's eyes were not of fire but of a black Void, looking directly into my soul before his words slithered into my ears.

"They will *know*."

Chapter 14
The Dark Path

On my sixth day of exploring the largely untraversed and rumored Wolf-woods, there was a dense and wet fog on the road that disappeared beneath the sea of trees. The path had led me to a dip in the road with wooded slopes on either side. I was taking a leisurely pace on my horse when suddenly the silence of the trees was broken by a low and bone-chilling growl. I stopped immediately and looked about… nothing. Then suddenly, the mist cleared in front of me just enough to see the figure of a large wolf fifty paces down the road. Or so I thought it was a wolf.

Then it stood. It began to walk, and I began to cry. For the life of me, I could not move; transfixed in toxic fear gripping every muscle and thought. But then I remembered my sidearm. I am no warrior but I drew my sword. It was thirty paces away and closing, but even through the fog I could easily make it out to be at least ten feet tall. When it came to be but five paces from my horse, its eyes lay above my own, blinding me to the hundreds of shadows that waited silently amidst the trees. Then shockingly… it spoke.

"Put down the blade, or for you, we shall."

Reign of Renborg: King's Edition
"Discovery of the Lycan"
Reynhalt of Divonshire, 112 DE

"T**ell** me you saw the same thing!" I said as we burst through the midnight clouds in our flight back to the inn.

"I did," Aquilla said slowly, his mind pondering deeply within me.

"What dark magic was that? His reflection even had different eyes!"

Something of which I could not unsee.

Aquilla turned his head to me as we flew. "Do you remember the story of the Mara and Thadius I told to you?" he said.

"How could I forget? Was that priest one of them?"

"All I can gather is but a theory, and it is this: like the leaders of this world, I believe Judux is under the hand of Thadius, or *Thade* as he is also known, whispered to not only by a Mara, but also something of a deeper shadow, of a darker design."

"The crown," I said, the memory of its darkness a stain in my mind.

Even in thought it drew me into its unknown abyss like a deadly current in the sea.

"Indeed," Aquilla said. "I assume this crown allowed him to speak the language of the Dragons."

"No, he should be able to speak Shiveric without it."

"How so? Do you know of Shiveric?"

"Piluch taught Lucien and I that the most devout Drakin priests and scholars studied the dead language."

"And why would they devote such time to a consuming task?"

"In hopes of one day bringing back the Dragons," I said as we returned to the inn. "And if he believes he is the Shadow of Cypherus, then why would he not want to know the language of the race Cypherus destroyed?"

Aquilla said no more as we emerged into our soul's vessel.

Laying still beside a restless Lucien, I desperately tried to close my eyes to receive some amount of rest.

It was useless.

Philomela's frightened heartbeat drummed through my mind throughout the cold night. The oceanic comfort I felt in knowing her heart still beat washed my warring mind of its thoughts. Still, the tides of my mind repeatedly surged with fears that her fragile soul would drown in the cruel fate of Judux's monstrous ambitions, the machinations of which were beyond my comprehension, and Aquilla's.

"They will know."

The mysterious ancient word shown to Judux and the unknown identity of the Drakin's counsel were overwhelming in their potential for darkness.

And then there was the Dragon, the skin of which could not be penetrated, the eyes of which were fascinated by Philomela.

Countless myths and ancient stories glorified the use of Godstone and the commands that could be wrought upon them for powerful effect. The memory of Cypherus shielding himself with the earth and calling forth lightning from above with the strange symbols he wrote thundered through my mind as I wrestled with the manner of Belial's birth. But I saw not one symbol of the ancient language used in Belial's creation, for it seemed to be a simple Averitic transformation passed on from the host who Wyled into a recipient.

Not only was Belial's mind not broken from infancy, as it would be for any bestial mind merging with that of a child's, but the Dragon shared no resemblance of its Human origins.

Belial was wholly Dragon.

If this Dragon was immune to even the strongest blade, how in Scissalan would we even dare to stand against one that was fully grown?

"I… I am uncertain," Aquilla said. "I must ponder upon it more."

Were you not prepared for this in your decades of preparation?

"Against a resurrected Dragon? No, not in particular. But take heart: Belial did not appear to enjoy the leash Judux bound it too. There is the possibility that the beast could rebel against its master, though we should prepare if Belial is bound in obedience."

Closing my eyes, I longed for the darkness to wash away my warring thoughts, the anxious fear that danced in my mind at the thought of having to face a Dragon; I didn't even have a sword to fight Belial, let alone an army to take on Judux's forces that would most surely unite as they clenched Renborg in their molten grasp.

Helplessness anchored me to the bed in waves of heavy depression, crushing my will to live.

It wasn't until the early morning light from outside burned my weighted eyelids that I realized I had received no rest at all.

Egret, on the other hand, did.

"Come now," she said as she burst uninvited into our room carrying her satchel and knife. "We must go."

Lucien groaned as he sat up.

"I could feel that you did not rest," Aquilla said as we retrieved our two horses from the inn's stable.

I wonder why, Aquilla.

We took a steady pace towards Hebsund in the misty morning, the sun unfolding itself slowly over the forest green hills on our right shoulder, the sparkling yet quiet river on our left.

Before we departed, Egret looked at me as if she wanted to ask me a question, suspicion briefly clouding her squinted eyes. However, her face quickly changed into one of stern determination, and so she abruptly took the lead on the hillside road towards the city that was only six days ahead of us.

Lucien's arms around me tightened as I led our horse after her.

"Were you able to rest?" Lucien said.

"I was," I lied, fighting to keep my eyes open.

Our ride was eerily silent as we followed Egret in the early morning, the looming forest walls of Laconnia coming ever into view like a shadow in the distance.

And in that silence, my weary mind wrestled with how to slay Belial.

I don't understand, Cypherus used the forgotten words and Godstone to slay the Dragons.

"He did," Aquilla said within me.

Then why did the Godstone blade not harm him?

Aquilla waited for a few seconds. "What state is the Godstone of Solstein in?"

Klyr.

"Precisely. It is only a Klyr blade that can cut through the hide of a Dragon. The natural Bludh state is like straw to its might, and even the corrupted Nox state merely scratches its scales, though the force behind it could possibly break the beast's bone. But such ways are not for us."

Hopelessness stole the breath from my lungs like a blade slipped between the ribs.

And Judux has Solstein, and there's no other Klyr blade in Renborg. So it's pointless?

"No. There is hope yet."

Is there another blade?

"Yes, but… it is not in Renborg."

Where is it?

His colorful swirling eyes met mine within my mind, full of absolute seriousness and dread.

"Cur Malum."

Cur Malum? The place where children are taken to be sacrificed?

"Those are just stories from the College of Man. Cur Malum is the home to the Ora'suns, and they have the only other Klyr blade I know of."

My mind reeled at the thought of the feared assassins guild having such a rare blade. It would explain the almost impossible assassinations that were thought to be of them, from the Vaerosian bankers to the Queen of Kadush, all of which were marred by the rumors of a white spear that cut through both steel and bone like butter.

"Let me show you something," Aquilla said.

An image of a spear made entirely out of Klyr Godstone filled my mind. The weapon was held by a man whose eyes were fiery white while dark shoulder-length hair graced his royal armor. The man's face portrayed strength yet a divine humbleness, and his ears were like that of the Elves.

The ornate shield he carried was painfully familiar.

"The Spear of Mythraelyon was made long ago during the Melain invasion that overtook all of Scissalan," Aquilla began. "Of which Mythraelyon created with his heart of service as he defended all from the barbaric sea peoples. After he received the gift of death, the spear was given to the Taldarii Order. The Ora'suns later took the spear from the Order. It is their most treasured possession, and from what I can recollect from the histories, they guard it with their life."

And what makes you think they will just give it to us?

"The Ora'suns are a very… ritualistic collection of people. We will challenge the Order for admittance, and with my training, we will prove our purity to take the spear, thus becoming their lord, for they seek the Shepherds of the earth and will serve us willingly, for it is in their creed. And there is no need to fear. I am able to hold anything that is Klyr because of the purity of my nature. The spear will not burn you as it did the victims of Judux."

Rubbing my gloved arm, I remembered the fiery pain that roared in my heart whenever I accidentally Wyled in Solstein with Lucien.

It felt like an entire lifetime ago.

Why don't we just make our own Klyr Godstone? If your heart is as pure as you say it is, then we can just create one right now.

Aquilla paused. "Though our hearts are combined, it is not

as pure as it needs to be in order for it to change the Godstone. It is already next to impossible to create a Klyr state, especially with the condition of your heart. 'From a fresh well can only fresh water flow.' It would take a lifetime of dedication and righteousness to earn a pure heart that would transform Godstone into its clearest state. Cypherus was a husband and a father before he ever purified Solstein. No, your heart, as it is, is unable; so we shall go to Cur Malum."

His words burrowed deep in my heart which he so accosted. I closed my eyes to the rhythm of our horse, comforted that Lucien's arms were around me. I turned around to see he was looking at me, intently, and flowering on his pale face was the faintest of smiles. Warmth flooded my cheeks in knowing that at least he believed in me.

The thought of Lucien reminded me of the pressing war.

Wait, we do not have time to travel to Cur Malum. That would take weeks!

"Judux's forces shall take time to come from Yarahm, and Lucien will need weeks to summon the Kriga and their hosts from the provinces. War takes time, Morgan, so we shall be back when they need us most."

How do you expect me to leave him behind? He cannot do this without me.

"Very well. Tell me, how many men shall perish from Belial's impenetrable might before Lucien surrenders?"

The heaving breath of mine and Lucien's horse was the only sound I could hear in my refusal to respond.

"This empire shall be lost if we do not have the spear. Your brother must learn to lead on his own, Morgan. He is Renborg's King now, but we shall be their *savior*."

Hanging my head low, I accepted his words with bitter anguish.

I did not feel like a savior, nor did I feel ready to challenge some cultic leader for their greatest treasure.

Least of all, I wasn't strong enough nor ready to kill Belial, and he was just an infant. And to leave Lucien, to forsake him to this ever-darkening world, seemed like a fatal cure to the incurable disease of fate. As the thoughts darkened my mind, I gripped the reins with crushing anger as we passed under a growing number of trees spotting the hills of Hebsund.

Aquilla sighed alongside my soul, his mind probably sensing the heaviness of my own. For a long time he did not speak. The pounding of our horse's hooves led my mind in a downspiraling abandon.

At last he spoke.

"You may feel powerless. But I can teach you the power that has been long forgotten."

You speak of the ancient words?

"Indeed."

So you know of them? Why did you not tell me what word was given to Judux?

Aquilla looked off silently for a long time to the increasing woods around us as we drew closer to Hebsund. "Because I have never seen that word before, and I fear what it may be. And though my knowledge of the words will aid you, I severely warn against it."

Why? Wouldn't conjuring lightning and manipulating the earth to our will do us good?

Aquilla sighed. "In many ways, yes. But the cost of your mind would become a sickening consequence."

What do you mean?

Aquilla's galactic eyes focused on mine with absolute seriousness.

"The language of the gods will consume you."

~

The rest of the journey to Hebsund felt like a dream. Ancient stories of the Ora'suns and their persistent atrocities against Kapitol filled my mind with a hazy mist of terror.

The fear that I would only be venturing towards a pointless end once we left Lucien and Egret behind with his uncle Volsung was unshakable. However, those concerns were replaced by the much larger threat that became visible as we ascended a large hill six days later: in the far distance, the forest Walls of Laconnia loomed like mountains.

Stretching across the entire horizon that would be taller than Renborg's doubled walls, the impenetrable forest was thick in its darkness many leagues from us.

As we turned the corner of the river where the Brehnok's mouth opened, our sunlit city finally came into view. Hebsund was a relieving sight for our sore eyes, yet what we saw both welcomed and worried us. Situated on a large peninsula cut at the neck by a wide moat, Hebsund surrounded itself on three sides with the dazzling waters of the small Lake Hebron. A large military camp was situated just a half mile away.

Memories of warm, carefree summers long past flooded my mind: images of glimmering water on moonlit nights brought strength to my heart as I remembered Lucien's and my childhood. However, those days of old seemed like centuries removed from the grim reality of the now. Drawn ever back to the present, I began to notice something strange: there whispered a disturbing quiet, even in the military camp.

"Does this Volsung not know of the war?" Aquilla said.

The invasion should be known to him, I thought, looking behind me to see Lucien sharing the same dread on his face from what his uncle's delay could mean.

Had they already left for the siege of the capital?

We followed Egret onto the oncoming highway that fed into the walled city of Hebsund. As we merged onto the road, we fell behind a band of traveling Valkryn priests, their heads bowed low and voices murmuring tearful prayers. Though Egret was of the Lilithian Sect of the Faith, she nodded to them in respect for their prayers.

Lucien's grip tightened around my waist, but I felt comfort knowing we were surrounded by life, by a sense of normalcy, no matter how somber it was. However, that comfort only went so far, as there persisted an eerie feeling of being watched in the thickening fog that descended upon the quiet hills surrounding Hebsund's moats and dark blue lake.

Looking briefly through Aquilla's eyes, there existed no Mara we could see, but the strange feeling did not flee from me.

"Why is it so quiet?" Egret said as we neared the drawbridge.

"The Lycan feast upon every morsel they can find, and they often purchase all of our livestock we have to spare," Lucien said, bitterness drenching his words.

"This is true, but there is much hate in his words," Aquilla said. "Do all Ronians share in his distaste for the Averites of wolf?"

Most do.

The Lycan's persistent threat was evident in the towering battlements strengthened by stone, Wolfwood, and archers, all a necessity to defend against the Delphian bows of the Lycan that, with a clean shot, could tear through a fully plated man at arms. Even a glancing blow carried the authority to break bones.

"And his uncle?" Aquilla said.

Even more, I thought, relaying a memory to Aquilla of Volsung's son being torn to shreds by their arrows many sols ago.

Being so close to their Lycan confederacy shed a new understanding of why Volsung was so persistent in always wanting more resources, more men, and stricter trading measures to the wolven peoples who seemed to double in numbers and meat consumption every decade. And, knowing the lengths I was prepared to go through for Philomela, I could understand why Volsung was so relentless in wanting any chance for retaliation.

In many ways, it began to make sense why Volsung was always so isolated and bitter. The cruel and unexplainable destinies forced upon us would drive anyone to question the point of it all.

Did he share my sentiments?

A shouting of soldiers broke my thoughts as a group of lanceliers took notice of Lucien, upon which an entourage of infantrymen was ordered to surround us.

"Halt!" one of the lanceliers said as we were surrounded, the spears of the infantrymen encircling us. "State your business!"

"Do you not recognize your King?" Lucien said from behind me. "Who is your Cavalry Marshal?"

The lancelier who spoke to us was about to say something when another soldier on horseback broke through the line.

"King Lucien?" the man said before opening his helm. "Morgan?"

"Mathis!" Lucien said, the anger in his voice being replaced with relief as we slid off our horse.

"Stand down!" Mathis barked at the infantrymen, who stepped aside as he ran to embrace us both.

Seeing the Marshall whom Lucien and I had known for sols was desperately relieving after being on our own for so long, through so much unspeakable suffering.

"My Lord!" Mathis said as he held us tightly in an embrace. "I am grateful to the Mother for letting me see you both again, to know you are safe from Ludsala!"

Mathis pulled slightly away from our reunion to look at Egret. "My Queen, I am humbly at your service."

Egret gave Mathis a polite nod of respect.

"Were you preparing to leave Hebsund?" Lucien said, nodding his tired gaze to the thousand lanceliers surrounding us.

"Indeed, Your Grace. Volsung has ordered us to join with Kriga Kelmont's forces in Ren Valley to attack the Drakin's supply lines."

"He sends you with only a thousand men?"

"I did not question his orders, Your Grace."

"Of course," Lucien said, his fists clenching tightly.

"But I will see to it that you are escorted to Volsung. Tolrik, take fifty of our lanceliers to escort the King and his companions to Volsung. Rendezvous with us after ensuring their safe delivery."

"Yes, Marshal," Tolrik said.

"I must leave, Your Grace," Mathis said, bowing his head in reverence for Lucien "For Gulmund."

"For Gulmund," Lucien said, though his words were dry.

"Take care of him, will you, Morgan?" Mathis said, his tone one of joy as he led his thousand lanceliers away from us.

His remark did not leave me with joy as we remounted our horse.

As we were escorted into the city by Tolrik and his men, I tirelessly restrained the tears that threatened to fall at the thought of failing someone else who trusted in me, who depended on me.

The dwindling path of my thoughts began to steer towards the depravity whose name was truth that I shuddered to accept, but an image of Philomela burned brightly in my mind. I don't know if it was from myself or from Aquilla, but the sight of her being held by Judux and the fate she would suffer without my intervention fueled me with shaking determination to do what was necessary.

Even to leave Lucien behind.

Even to learn the ancient language that would consume me if it gave them a chance.

It was worth the sacrifice.

Sensing my thoughts, Aquilla said, "You ponder the ancient tongue?"

Yes, I thought, my soul longing to accomplish what was necessary to save them.

"I will teach you, Morgan, but only when we are alone."

Nodding in acceptance, I understood that patience was prudence. Still, it did not remove the anxiety which churned within me at being so far behind in skill and knowledge of powers long unknown and forgotten. We were blind to what we stood against with the unknown word shown to Judux, and what it could mean for Renborg.

What it could mean for Philomela.

"The Mara which we saw further proves the cult of Thade is behind this," Aquilla said. "The crown's purpose and power are unknown to me, though it must have a darker purpose than I can conjure in ponderance. As for the word shown to Judux, I still do not understand it, though it did not resemble any element of life that one can write and control."

Is there not a record of the language on Akhorus?

"All knowledge of the language's power and *vast* complexity was burned during the Red Death of the Age of Ashes. We Medjaib only remember the basics of the words, and even that dwarfs the knowledge of everyone in Scissalan."

Apparently not.

"Even more reason why we must leave. We shall go once we have reunited them with Volsung."

My soul dragged like an anchor at the painful yet ever-increasing validity of his words.

The four of us were silent as Tolrik led us through the

multi-walled city, both the new and old sectors quiet like the lake adjacent to Hebsund. Faces of Ronians hung low as we passed by them.

It was like looking into a sea of mirrors.

The gripping fear so often accompanying war was clear from their melancholy. News of the Drakin must assuredly be here, but the unpreparedness from Volsung continued to be unsettling.

As the lanceliers escorted us to the higher rises of Hebsund, I couldn't help but look to see the small island in the middle of Hebsund's lake. The upper classes of Ronians lived there, only connected to the mainland by the extravagant Lauront Bridge.

I hoped to not have to deal with the Lauront family, as they were quite entitled and annoying in their wealth.

But my attention returned to Hebsund's Hall before us, where adjoining its Wolfwood structure sprouted a stone tower that was moon washed in ground silver.

The tower glimmered as a painful reminder.

Switching to Aquilla's eyes, the world became as grey as rain. His sight was becoming more and more familiar to me, and when I wasn't engaging with Egret or Lucien, I peered into his world to make sure we weren't being followed by a Mara. Thankfully we hadn't seen many in Hebsund, just a few on the outskirts of the city. This time, however, in the middle of the tower, there appeared a Bludh red figure, curled upon a bed.

Motionless.

Looking closer, I could almost discern something trickling down from the figure's face. They looked like droplets of light.

Aquilla hummed. "Who is that?"

Karlata, I thought while anxiously sighing. She must have come back from the College of Man.

"Who is she to you?" Aquilla said as he could feel my growing nerves.

Volsung's daughter. Someone I'd rather not deal with unless we have to.

"Why is that?"

You'll see.

Any fearful thoughts of her lust vanished as my eyes met Egret's, her eyes studying me with an almost accusatory zeal when we unsaddled in the military stables we were led to.

Shrugging my shoulders to her, she frowned, her face flushed as she turned away, similarly annoyed.

"Interesting," Aquilla said.

What?

"You two look at each other with a great intensity."

Wait… what are you speaking of? No we do not!

"I am not making any accusations. Simply an observation. You Humans are inconsistent in your emotions."

Whatever, I thought as the guards opened the Wolfwood doors to the dimly lit Hall of Hebsund. The massive Hall looked like an upside-down ship from the inside, with shields and Ronian banners draping the oaken walls next to flickering oil lamps.

Accompanying the lamps were an array of Lycan heads mounted like trophies, the greatest being the midnight fur rug that lay stretched out before Volsung's empty chair. His prominent station was raised above the grand feasting table that encompassed most of the Hall. The sight of Firnox's cold and silent eyes delivered like always a creeping cold in my flesh. It was like a whispered threat to all who dared to oppose Hebsund's lord, a morbid promise from Volsung that anyone who would cross him would become like the rug who stole his son from him: skinned and flattened.

The guards gave us seating at the head of the long table, near Volsung's empty chair, before leaving to return to Mathis.

Lucien looked at me with nervous uncertainty as time burned slowly like the candles illuminating the great table.

And so we waited for the wolf of Hebsund to return.

Chapter 15
A Wolfish Threat

In 798 DE, the Remulan scientist and archeologist Joras Inaeos of Naxos, in search of the truth, discovered the black mark of Lycan heritage. In a cave deep in the Remuloi Mountains, he found evidence of a cult that dated back to at least the first century of the Dawning Era. From the writings discovered in this cave, it was revealed that this cult was known as The Children of Reia.

The Reians were fanatical worshippers of the moon (Reia) who sought to transform themselves into the wolves that praised her. By using Godstones, over five hundred humans took for themselves the souls of wolves by using the now forgotten word for "wolf" in the ancient language of the gods. Together, they began a week-long process of Wyling the transformation to completion. Once the Averatism was complete, they left inscriptions on the walls, telling of what they had done, but letting the word "wolf" be forgotten like the rest of the powerful language in the Age of Ashes so that none could rise up to oppose them.

And so the Lycan were born.

The Histories of Laconnia
"Origins"
According to Karnax of Ehlonica, 996 DE

We must have been waiting for Volsung for at least three hours, but it was impossible to tell as the night from the windows showed no difference.

"We should go, Morgan," Aquilla said. "Cur Malum awaits. We waste our time in wait when they are safe in Hebsund."

It is not the best time to leave without any explanation.

"Then when is?" Aquilla demanded.

Soon.

"What could be his reasons for delay?" Egret said well into the night, her flustered cheeks a stark contrast to her forest green dress and head covering, both of which were weaved of silk that she was provided to change into upon our arrival.

Much to her displeasure, of course.

"He is not known to be late," Lucien said, sharing the same agitation.

"It is likely he is caught unawares of our arrival," I said, fingering the weathered carvings of the rustic table. "He was probably attending to something concerning the Lycan. It has been his obsession of late."

"Because of his fallen son, Aether?" Egret said.

"How did you know of that?" Lucien said, his tone hostile as he cast her an irritated and tired glance.

"Did you not read of Skyya's politics before you married me?" Egret said, returning him a sharp glance.

"Are angry words how one communicates the need for intimacy?" Aquilla said, his glowing eyes watching them carefully.

What? No, not at all. Why would you think that?

"I studied Gulmund briefly before my descent, and he often became of the same flesh with other women after he argued with Valena."

That is… unfortunately true, but that is not what love looks like.

"I am curious to see how it appears."

You may never see it, I thought, the words hurting me more than I thought they would.

Lucien sighed before looking at me.

"Morgan, how should we proceed when Volsung arrives?"

"Proceed?" I said, leaning back into my chair. "Hmm, I'm uncertain."

"Do you not know of your uncle's behavior?" Egret said, challenging us.

"We come here every summer, *wife*," Lucien said. "I think we have an accurate assessment."

"Apparently not," she quipped.

"The uncertainty lies within his reaction to his brother's death," I said, hoping my words calmed the storm between them. "Volsung was always a kind man towards us, but there brewed a hostility between him and Gulmund after Aether was killed."

"Because Gulmund sought peace with the Lycan?" Egret said.

"Precisely," I said. "He may be irrationally upset when he arrives, though relieved of our survival. However, we should garner strength beforehand."

Waving one of the servants towards us, I quietly asked for food and refreshments to be brought while we waited. As we ate our fill with tired mouths, Egret slowly became overwhelmingly pampered by the stewards who continued to bring her juva and trollof bread.

Insistently so.

"I do not need anymore," she had said as they asked her for the fifth time. "And I can prepare my own bread!"

Egret's intolerance to pampering drew amusement from me, but I concealed any display of it so as to not draw her ire.

Lucien did not share in my concealment, as he gave her a look of annoyance as the servants left.

"I do not understand their love," Aquilla said as Egret took a sip of juva before puckering in disgust at the taste.

"Vorim!" she cursed, roughly setting the drink aside. Then, in Skyyan, in which she thought no one would understand, she said, "He is as delightful as their sewage drink."

I don't understand either, I thought, my eyes lingering on her dress and the way it formed around her toned waist.

An abrupt sound of door hinges creaked through the massive Hall, captivating our attention.

"My dear nephew!" Volsung said as he came running into the Hall, worry striking many lines across his face as his hair parted down the middle like wheat from a gust of wind.

A soft roar of footsteps followed quickly behind him.

Jolting from my seat at the table, I stood groggy and half awake.

Lucien and Egret did the same.

"*Uncle*," Lucien said as he embraced Volsung. "Uncle…"

"I am so terribly sorry, Lucien," Volsung whispered as he held Lucien in his wiry but firm arms, his sea blue eyes watering with pain. "There are no words… but I rejoice in seeing you alive, my King, along with you, Morgan. Come, let us feast in remembrance of your father and mother."

Volsung gently eased into the chair at the head of the table as we returned to our seats, along with the host of commanders, marshalls, guild keepers, and other men of repute finding their place at our table around us.

Along with Lord Arkon Lauront III, a thin yet sullen man dressed in fur brooched in silver who sat a few seats from us.

A deep sigh overcame me at the thought of having to listen to the grievances of that man's family again.

"Please forgive me for my delay," Volsung said, his eyes weary and burdened. "There were some troubles at the border that needed to be dealt with immediately."

Lucien nodded in forgiveness, but his eyes showed that he was silent with frustration.

Aquilla emerged from my flesh and sat on the edge of my seat next to Egret who sat by my left.

What are you doing? I thought, making every effort not to look at him.

"What? Must I always be trapped inside you?"

No, I just… ah, very well.

Moving slightly to the middle of my chair to retain my forgotten independence and sense of normalcy from his spirit proved pointless when Aquilla filled the gap a moment later.

A sigh flooded my lungs, and I could just glimpse a grin coming from his cosmic face beside me.

Joining Volsung on either side, Karlata and Seifred held their heads up high, posed with the same cunning their father shared, but distinguished in their appearance that seemed to attract the eyes of both men and women in the Hall. Attention to Seifred or his finely groomed brows I did not pay attention to, as I seemed to be nothing but a bore to him, a waste of space and time.

Why even *bother* with a bastard?

It was Karlata whom my eyes gravitated towards instead. Her charcoal eyes found mine and smiled, like a fox sizing up its prey.

Karlata tugged at a corner of her velvety black locks seductively.

Shamefully, I didn't look away.

Out of the corner of my eye, I could see Egret's eyes boring into both of us. Closing my eyes briefly, I pretended to breathe. It wasn't enough to break Karlata's spell, but it was a temporary measure. A bleak part of me wondered if Karlata would be an obstacle that I had to avoid in deterring the shadowy prophetic fate of Cypherus.

Aquilla looked at me inquisitively from his imaginary seat at the table next to me, but I turned away to avoid him, not revealing my thoughts entirely to him.

Taking a careful sip of wine, Volsung paused before he spoke, lifting a hand to cease the mutterings of those who joined us. As the silence settled the trophy-ridden Hall, Volsung looked at Lucien with the most studious of gazes through his matted and straw-like hair.

"It pains me to hear Caer Mordrake was lost to those savages," Volsung said. "As if the night could not grow darker, I am most grieved of the King's passing, the last of my brothers, along with Valena and Philomela. A toast in their name! May the Mother show favor to Her children as they rest in Solæf."

The men around us joined us in raising their mugs to glance off each other, along with Lucien, Egret, and I.

"Why do you touch your mugs together?" Aquilla said as everyone drank. "Do you think it brings forth a blessing from the Eternal One?"

It is done so out of customary respect for the fallen.

"Hmm. Useless, I suppose, but intriguing."

"Thank you, uncle," Lucien said as he finished taking a drink, his cheeks flustered. "But why have you not readied your own forces to march to Renborg's aid? From what we saw entering the city, you must have at least twenty thousand men camped in the southern hills."

"Lord Kolstok is already on his way to reinforce them with Kriga Kelmont, along with Mathis and his division of one thousand lanceliers to break Drakin supply lines. Through what I've been able to surmise from a flood of reports, they should be able to gather eight hosts and more than a few divisions of cavalry, at least by the month's end. I think forty-five thousand men should do the trick, don't you?"

"Lord Kolstok?" Lucien said, his blue eyes wide with shock that mirrored mine. "He lives?"

"Indeed. He and two Kyllian Knights, Sir Valrok and Sir Alduaura I believe, arrived last night, battle weary from their survival and flight from Ludsala. Despite this, he left this morning to join Kriga Kelmont, heeding not my advice to rest and recover his strength. His leg was badly wounded you see, as well as was his heart which grieved tremendously in belief that he failed you. He will be blessed to know you all live."

Deafening silence fell upon us as Lucien lowered his head in shame. Volsung raised a concerned brow in confusion as he looked to me to explain.

"Not all," I finally admitted.

The realization swept across Volsung's face as he clenched his eyes in pain before opening them with soft tears.

"Servillius had believed you perished. But when they told me you three had entered the city gates I had hoped… I'm so sorry, my boys. I know all too well such pain."

Lucien lifted his eyes to his uncle and nearly whispered, "I should have, I could have—"

"No, let us not ponder such darkness," Volsung said, his weathered lips pursing before he raised his hand. "Come, nephew, let us regain our strength and celebrate your deliverance. The Mother is merciful."

At a snap of his hand, Volsung's stewards brought in steaming plates of roasted lamb, vegetables, cowurt milk, sommerian wine, and even more juva and trollof bread. Volsung's guests quickly diverted their attention from Lucien and began to gorge themselves on the food brought steaming before them. Lucien's face betrayed confusion, but he said no more and joined in the feast.

"I am amazed that Kolstok lived," Aquilla said, surveying the table as I emptied a mug of juva.

Me too, I thought, using every ounce of strength to repress the memories of the Spindlers tearing apart their victims, dooming Sigmund.

"Though what is more staggering is how much you Humans eat… and drink, especially juva."

Do the Medjaib not eat?

"Why would we?"

The lamb chunk halted before my mouth as I turned to him in surprise.

Then how do you—

But my thoughts became consumed with Egret who sat beside Aquilla, her form visible through his glowing flesh. She was sparing nothing on her plate, most of which was meat, and it soon became as bare as her toned scalp.

"She consumes more than you," Aquilla said in wonder.

Indeed, I thought, amazed at her ferocious hunger for the bloody meat on her plate.

Before I could return to my meal, Egret slid from the folds of her dress a dark green flask, which she slipped quickly into her drink before concealing it again.

"Was that green juva?" Aquilla said, his cosmic eyes missing not a single detail.

No, juva is only golden. It must be a tonic of some kind.

"Hmm," Aquilla said, returning his gaze to Lucien and Volsung who spoke quietly. "Well Morgan, we have ensured your brother and his wife's safety upon their deliverance to Hebsund. Time is of the essence, so eat your fill before we venture to Cur Malum tonight."

Tonight? We do not even have the supplies nor a plan for getting there.

"Very well. We will leave tomorrow night. How will you inform Lucien?"

I—I'm still sorting it out, I thought, dread rising within me at the thought of crushing Lucien's heart with the Skallgend I had written. Would my fabricated death cause him to lose focus of the war at hand?

There has to be another way.

As we internally spoke, I could hear Lucien growing restless beside me. He cleared his voice to speak, but before he could do so, Volsung interjected.

"Apologies for not making introductions sooner," he said to Egret, looking past both Lucien and I. "This is my son Seifred and my daughter Karlata. You must be Princess Egret."

"*Queen* Egret," she said, holding her chin high as she looked down at him.

"Forgive me, my Queen," Volsung continued, drooping his head low in a humble posture. "As I'm sure you've heard, I am Volsung of house Mordrake, Marq and Kriga of Barovia."

"Both Marq and Kriga?" she said, her airy tone feigning naivety. "Under Renborg's laws, are not those authorities forbidden to intersect in one man but the King? Was this not established by the reforms of my King's ancestor Tormund V?"

Volsung leaned back in his chair and smiled at her as she took a sip of her wine.

Without looking, I could also see that Lauront III halted his attention to his friends around him as he eavesdropped with an intensity upon the question he had asked all of his life since his father was stripped of Marqship. The memories of Gulmund's mood souring at having to deal so gently with their pride, along with doing what was necessary for Renborg's safety from the Lycan, returned to me. At the time I didn't agree with Gulmund's decision, but as Volsung had proved throughout the sols, he had indeed been the right choice as Renborg's buffer to our wolfish neighbors.

Noticing Lauroun t III and perhaps wanting to keep the conversation light, Volsung chuckled lightly, clapping his hands together and turning to his King.

"What a formidable wife you have attained, young Lucien. I commend your father's choice greatly. You are quite right, my Queen. Marqs are given the task of governing while Kriga are granted generalship. These roles have not intersected ever since King Tormund V so wisely recognized the danger of ceding too much power to duplicitous Lords that may govern their own lands and raise their own forces as they see fit.

"This was the way for hundreds of sols. With cunning and

mortar of blood, he relaid the foundations of Renborg's crumbling house brick by brick."

Egret looked intrigued but not satisfied. "And your position?" she said behind her cup.

"Yes of course, your question remains. Barovia, my Queen, is not an ordinary province, with wolves like these to the north."

Volsung gestured to the snarls mounted on the walls. Their presence was unnerving, yet I felt a great pity for their current state.

"The previous Marq, Arkon II of house Lauront, and Kriga, Dorian Sigmar, lost too many lives and could not do, as few men can, what was necessary to keep our people and our border safe."

"Preposterous!" Lauroun III whispered harshly, though all could hear it.

Perhaps to prove his point, Volsung ground his foot into the stitched fur rug of a Lycan that ran its length beneath the long table.

"But I *did*," Volsung said.

"And now I am sure you will bless our efforts to repel the Drakin?" Egret said.

Volsung nodded his head humbly.

"Of course, we will discuss this after you have rested from your journey."

"Rest evades me, as does your reasoning for stalling our response. We should aid Kolstok's forces for combined strength, for the Drakin strike Renborg united. We should respond the same. What could keep us from responding appropriately?"

Egret's statesmanship was intense, though unrefined. Still, her cunning and boldness were impressive.

"Father was preoccupied with the repercussions of Gulmund's trust in those bestial savages," Karlata said, her brows furrowing in frustration at Egret.

"Daughter," Volsung said, holding his hand before her to remain silent.

Seifred laughed, pushing an attractive bardess off of his lap and focusing his hungry eyes on Egret. Blood rushed to my gloved hands that curled at the thought of what disgusting sewage was filling his mind.

"The reason for my delay is this: our caravans were ambushed in the Wolfwoods on their way back from Delphius two weeks ago. The Lycan Council insisted they had no hand to play in it, but a thorough investigation was needed, as there has been nothing but tension since the war, despite our *treaty* with them. Then came their mindless festival, so we had to ensure that they wouldn't attack us in their bestial lust as they indulged, and as they prepare for another one soon.

"And with the Drakin invasion, they have even more incentive to provoke us, to tear apart our backs that will be turned to them as we fight the Drakin. We mustn't divert all of our strength to one front of Renborg, Your Grace, lest we allow all of our enemies to steal our homes left unprotected."

Egret looked confused at the politics he was suggesting at, though I couldn't tell if she was pretending to hide a lack of knowledge by taking a bite out of her bloody lamb.

Looking back to Lucien, I could see he was not looking so convinced by Volsung's explanations, for his face remained furrowed.

"Investigations or not," Lucien said, "there is no excuse to keep your men here idle while we are at war! As your *King*, I demand—"

"Do you know what would happen if I withdrew my men from my border, my King?" Volsung's voice was barely a whisper now to avoid being overheard. "Your father may have failed to warn you of the serious threat that the Lycan are and have been since those wolf lovers decided being human was not enough. They grow in number every *single* day, nephew, like damned rabbits breeding in the spring with their twins and triplets!

"And they are smarter than they look. They spread their festering colonies across Valeneka thanks to Kapitol, and they know we are under invasion. And can you guess what would happen if I pulled out the only thing protecting this empire from those beasts? We would be fighting a war on two fronts, something your father refused to—"

"I heard you went through Ludsala on your way here," Karlata said, distracting Egret and I from their conversation.

"We did," I said, not wanting to remember it.

Her eyes lit up in fascination. "So, it's true then, about the Spindler lair?"

Grimacing at the memory, I nodded.

"I'm sorry to hear that, and for Sigmund's fate," she said. "I always thought those things were just myths."

"She's asking so she can have something new to study for her program," Seifred said, rolling his eyes as he took another bite from his honey-glazed trollof bread.

"Seifred!" Karlata said, throwing daggers with her eyes.

Lucien grabbed the table forcefully. "We can deal with the Lycan after we have—"

"Why are you so interested in the Spindlers?" Egret said, tearing into her lamb with her knife as she looked at her.

Karlata smiled. "Like my father said, I've just returned from the College of Man. We usually have a break in the months of Valqr and Echrine, but I'm using this time to find something of a phenomenal discovery. Anything concerning Godstone will do, and the competition is rigorous, so I need something of significance to study. It's the only way to be promoted to a Cormag."

"I can see why you don't like her," Aquilla said, an image of the winged professors flooding my mind, along with his disgust towards them. "Though I don't understand why your body is reacting so… warmly towards her."

The blood in my flesh colored my cheeks red as I tried to ignore him and the memories of her own.

"Have they not twisted the world enough with their worship of Godstone?" Egret said.

"They have," Aquilla silently agreed.

"Well," Karlata said, "it is all a matter of perspective."

Egret was about to respond when Karlata looked at me, her eyes batting slowly as she pronounced my name with what sounded like yearning. "Morgan, I am very glad to see you're alive. It's been so long since we last…" she let the silence imply the regrettable shame, "well, since we last saw each other. I missed you. After dinner tonight, how about you stop by my quarters and tell me all about your journey—"

"Your Grace, would mutton fulfill you?" a servant said while approaching Egret, who, from the corner of my eye, waved him away in frustration, though she took the mutton from him anyway.

Resisting a smile, I cleared my throat as I returned my attention to Karlata, who grinned in waiting. "Well—"

The sound of crushing bone snapped the words from my lips. Even Karlata halted our conversation to find the origins of the interruption.

Egret's eyes met mine as she quickly placed the mutton leg back on her plate. The bone of the meat was somehow scattered in shards before her.

"A broken leg," Seifred said through a grin.

"Must be," Egret said, politely pushing back her plate.

"Does meat not satisfy you, my Queen?" he said.

"Of course it does, and greatly so, but it is the life of the sea rather than of the land which brings me most joy."

"The Queen hails from Skyya, brother," Karlata said, annoyance treading her tone as she refused to look at him. "Her Grace is probably more familiar to their native krabourak and fish than our elk and lambs."

Karlata said no more as she returned to her food before her, though she merely picked at her plate as I watched from the edge of my sight. Several times I caught her eyes looking towards mine, but she never lingered, only turning away before I inquired to meet her gaze.

She seemed… different than before, though I did not trust those lustful eyes.

It was a foolish mistake before.

"Well, I pray you do not bring a vision of conversion as your ancestor Aryarc Thyna did," Seifred said, flashing his teeth. "For I would most likely perish in my insufferable appetite of the land, the life of which brings me pleasure, greatly so."

"You will be relieved to know that it is not my intention to divorce from such traditions," Egret said, casting her eyes humbly downwards and away from him. "Nor to convert all of Renborg to the Lilithian belief of Solbok and prophecies."

"There is only one belief that is correct," Aquilla said unbeknownst to her.

And that is?

"Neither the Novamiric nor Lilithian sects of the Valkryn Faith."

How very helpful, Aquilla.

"What? It is clear with even the simplest reading of the Author's Story."

Seifred smiled at Egret as he took another sip of wine.

"It gladdens my heart to know that you only share the beauty of Aryarc and not her conquering zeal," Seifred said.

"I wouldn't be so quick to make assumptions, though your words are kind," Egret said.

Lucien broke briefly from his conversation with Volsung, looking to Seifred and Egret, but his tired gaze showed he did not care what they were discussing. As Lucien turned his uninterested gaze, Seifred watched, nodding ever so slightly at Lucien's withdrawal, pulling his chair closer to the table.

Closer to Egret.

Egret's eyes also lingered on Lucien, though she uttered not a word.

"No," Volsung whispered harshly as Lucien returned his focus to him, "I will not hear anymore—"

"Well spoken, my Queen," Seifred said, regaining Egret's attention. "I will assume no longer, but if you are ever curious to taste more of what Hebsund has to offer, you have but to ask."

"He speaks of meat with such... *intensity*," Aquilla said, studying Seifred. "You Humans perplex me with your love for food."

Seifred masks his true thoughts with other words because his mind is twisted with indecency, I thought, an unexpected rage filling my chest as I pretended not to look at Seifred, whose intentions were absolutely, disgustingly clear.

How could he even dare to advance upon her?

"I do not understand," Aquilla said as Seifred returned his hungry gaze to Egret.

Seifred is... known for his exploits of the flesh in Hebsund.

"Exploits of the flesh?"

But I did not reply to the spirit, as I was speechless but not surprised that Seifred took such a hidden interest in Egret. She was truly unique with her lack of hair and composure of unyielding fortitude, but it made my stomach churn that he would try to steal her from my brother.

The Queen was, without question, untouchable, but that didn't mean he wouldn't try.

The *insufferable* audacity. Did he not know his place?

"You will be pleased to know that I am curious of your home, Seifred," Egret said, her tone a bit louder as she offered a smile in return.

I thought the words originating from her were an illusion, for I couldn't believe that she would play this obvious game with him which he contrived with double meanings right before Lucien and Volsung.

"Really?" Seifred said, excitement illuminating his lips. "From your conversation with my father, it appears you already know much about our empire."

"It is my duty to know my subjects," she continued. "But what I know least of is your knowledge of the sword, of battle."

"What do you mean?" Karlata said, her gaze rising from her nearly untouched plate. "Why would that be of importance to know, my Queen? We are not soldiers."

"Of course, but death can easily meet us unprepared and away from the battlefield. It is prudence to know the blade, to be prepared for the moment where your life depends on your own strength and not an army's. Did not your mother prepare you in the wisdom of Liberio di Montarii, the master swordsman who has held great sway over Renborg's finest knights and nobles?"

Karlata squeezed her eyes shut as Seifred's face reddened.

"No, she did not," Seifred said after moments of silence between us were drowned by the noisy crowd, a sudden melancholy overtaking his once eagerly lustful gaze.

"That saddens me to hear, for I wished for a partner to spar with who could meet my needs."

But Egret did not sound displeased. Rather, it almost seemed that she wanted to hear that he could not match her, which he most assuredly could not in anything.

Egret was fascinatingly frustrating.

"She… she took ill to the plague many sols ago. Thus the way of the blade is unknown to me," Seifred said, the words forced from his lips.

"Oh," Egret said, her bold demeanor diminishing. "Forgive me, I did not—"

"I assume your mother taught you the ways of battle, my Queen?" Karlata said, her words communicating kind curiosity, but her tone implying grievance underneath.

"She did. Every morning before the dawn she would have me trained, along with the ways of the Skyyan court."

"Do the ways of the Skyyan court require head wrappings as well?" Seifred said, his words similarly innocent, but his pained face portrayed that he longed to regain his pride in being shown unworthy of Egret's attention.

"How about you tell me what you think," Egret said, her voice carrying no reaction to his words as she took another bite from the mutton.

Intriguingly, she did not even bother looking at him, as if he weren't deserving of her eyes, just like she did at her wedding with Lucien.

Seifred's smug grin wavered as he sipped more of his sommerian wine, but he quickly regained his composure. "I would say, and this is only a guess, it must be because you are without hair. However, I cannot imagine why that must be, for it is of tremendous worth to a woman." Receiving nothing but silence, he quickly added, "Though, you are still exceptional without it."

His first mistake was letting the drink poison his mind. The second was thinking that a woman's worth was found only in her outward beauty which contained the priceless treasure within. And though Egret's lack of hair was something I did not find beautiful, to blindly say that her worth came from her appearance was both foolish and wicked.

If Seifred had shared in my deformity, I wondered if he

would keep such a prideful stance on women. But alas, Seifred pursued whomever he wanted and suffered no need in this life, no imperfection or shame. Yes, his mother's passing was tragic, but so was mine. Yet it didn't seem to give him pause in how he chased women so relentlessly like a hound hunting for game in the forest. The very thought of his words angered me, disgusted me, made me long to squeeze Seifred's smile from his face.

To save Egret and Lucien the embarrassment, I restrained myself by placing them under the table.

Aquilla hummed as he watched me, ever curious.

As for Egret, her face became as hard as stone, though she still refused to look at Seifred.

Clearly he had struck a nerve, but it was a question I doubt she would give an answer to.

And though I hated to admit it, his question made me wonder why she chose to have no hair. Or was it hereditary? I knew the Skyyans focused on raising warriors from their youth, with little girls now able to join because of Nera's reforms. And though less hair was advantageous in battle, none of Egret's Suffra nor her mother were without hair. In fact, even her younger sisters and brothers were said to have golden locks that came from their ancestor Aryarc Thyna, mirroring Nera's.

Egret was the only one who lacked.

"Why have you not asked her of this mystery?" Aquilla said. "Is it because your being warms to Karlata as well?"

Excuse me?

"What?" Aquilla said. "Do your heated physical reactions not mean love?"

There is so much more to love than… than physical attraction!

"Hmm," he said, and through my unsettled spirit I could feel him seriously pondering the notion next to my mind.

Egret paused from her food to look at Seifred with an intimidating yet careful gaze. "I will let you ponder such a question further, Seifred, for to understand what makes a woman beautiful is not simply found in the eye."

Seifred said no more as Egret returned to her food, closing the door completely which she pretended to open. Seifred's pride led to his fall, and his attempt to regain his injured ego with a calculative strike of his own revealed his shallow character.

And though it was beneath me, I couldn't deny that seeing Egret shut him out of her heart gave me an unexpected relief.

Mixing uncertainly with this elation was the knowledge that she knowingly or unknowingly referred to our first conversation in the library, her purpose unknown as she hid her heart from everyone around her.

"Morgan," Karlata whispered amidst the awkward silence, "I know you need rest from your journey, but if you would like after dinner, please stop by my room." Her soft hand reached out for mine which hid underneath the table, sulking in their gloves. "I can make us juva while we catch up, like before."

Aquilla groaned. "That would be unwise, Morgan, especially with the emergence of those imaginative thoughts in which you are attempting to conceal from me."

Go away, I thought, my mind scrambling to reason a painless rejection for her.

Clearing my throat, I failingly tried to pull my gloved hand from her lusting shackles. "I think it would be best—"

"Uncle, I will command these men myself if I have to!" Lucien said, his near yell breaking our conversation.

All of our eyes turned to witness Lucien, his cheeks reddened with anger before a calm but weary Volsung who looked tired from the negotiations. My focus broke momentarily in the sense that I was being watched. Turning my head slightly, I could see Egret was staring not at her husband, but at me.

And like the riptides that pulled one into the watery unknown, so too did our eyes gravitate towards each other in the silent room, though there were dozens.

She looked away after what felt like an eternity, as did I at last. I slowly released the breath I had unknowingly been holding.

"Lucien," Volsung said, his tone delicate yet strong as the entire table listened, "it pains me that there is no path to spare any more men. I will do my best to coordinate with the other Kriga so that we can repel the Drakin while keeping our borders safe from the *Lycan*."

A collective murmur of agreement sounded throughout the Hall, especially as Volsung said *Lycan* with such vitriol.

"Uncle, I am your King! Do you want Seifred to die just like Aether?"

Volsung looked like he'd been slapped in the face. The tension in the Hall weighed and blackened every breath, thicker than the smoke from Dwarven forges.

Lucien cleared his voice before continuing. "That is precisely what will happen without your men. You are going to—"

"The King is ready for bed," Volsung said, his voice strained while lifting a hand between them. "Escort the King and his Queen to their chambers. They have had a long ride and a hard journey. We shall talk tomorrow, Your Grace."

Egret began to protest that she did not need rest for the second time, but the moving crowd drowned out her voice as Volsung dismissed his guests. Egret threw a quick glance towards me, her brow furrowing as her new world seemed to be falling apart and she had no control to stop it, or even guide it. Despite the looming tidal wave of politics in which she had no control, her face showed staunch determination to somehow find a way to rise above it as she stood abruptly from her seat before pushing past me.

"Well, until tomorrow," Volsung said, departing from us without another glance. "Come, children, let them rest."

"Yes, father," Seifred said as he and Karlata rose to follow.

As Karlata walked slowly past me, she let her hand lightly caress my shoulder. She began to say something but held back with a fragile smile before curtsying in departure.

"Lucien has much to learn," Aquilla said as I breathed again. "However, we shall not waste any more time. Belial grows every day, and Lucien is safe with his uncle, no matter how young of a King he is. Let us prepare for our departure. Have you thought of how you shall explain your disappearance tomorrow night?"

Yes, I thought, guilt drowning my breath as I looked at a frustrated Lucien, who gave a flickering smile upon seeing me. Opening my mind, I showed Aquilla what I would do, how I would do what was painfully necessary.

"Indeed, that shall crush him," Aquilla said, "but it shall ensure we are left unfollowed."

And unloved, I thought, dreading what I was about to do.

Chapter 16
Victims

'Mor y Thaea', meaning 'Mouth of God', refers to the Morythia, who exist as the Mother's chosen oracle on earth. Through her, the Mother speaks prophecy to prove Her Will is undeniable. When a prophetic word is given, the Morythia's eyes shine a blindingly white light, she levitates from the ground, and speaks in a voice that combines her own and the much more powerful yet feminine Voice of the Mother. This Voice emanates power that can be seen through the vibrations of the air and surroundings. For as long as they speak the Voice they are referred to by their title.

Morythian prophecies come without any forewarning and thus it is required that ten priestesses, called prisorai, first sisters, must follow the Morythia wherever she goes to inscribe any prophecy uttered. They even go so far as to sleep in the Morythia's tower in a room adjoining her own, divided only by a semi-sheer linen cloth. These ten women, chosen by the Morythia herself, adorn their heads with white linen cloaks, a deep red waist wrap, and a white linen cloth two inches thick that forms a ringlet about their foreheads. When the Morythia begins to prophesy, the light is so bright that they must pull this linen over their eyes and write what they hear without sight. This practice this skill daily so that they are prepared to transcribe at any moment. However, doubt of the Morythian prophecies has grown over the last few centuries, especially as they have served primarily for Renborg's involvement in the Primarchal Wars and were the reason for the birth of the faithless Lilithian Sect.

Chronicles of Renborg: King's Edition
"The Voice of the Mother"
Piluch Joffersun: Master of Histories

"It's done," I said, laying the inked feather down next to the scroll that would make Lucien weep.

"It will suffice," Aquilla said.

"I—I know," I said, my breath shaking in having to crush the only one who trusted me.

"Come, Morgan," Aquilla said, standing to his spectral feet in my personal lodging that Volsung provided. "Let me deepen your knowledge of my spirit to give peace to your mind while the moon reigns. You shall need it for Cur Malum."

"What do you mean?"

"You shall see."

Pushing aside my tired soul, I followed Aquilla out into the shadow-drenched halls and into the surrounding courtyards dedicated for prayers. A few Valkryn priests were still awake at the twilight hour, looking deep into their holy fires in hopes of learning the Mother's Will.

Does the Mother communicate through the fires of the priests and the oracles? I thought as Aquilla stopped to look at them.

"The idea of the Mother speaking through the flames was one of false invention by the Morythian oracles, who have not had the Mother's voice spoken through them for generations," he said, moving his hand down the middle of the fire and causing it to split.

The priests fell back from their stools, their eyes wide in both fear and awe.

But She spoke to you, I thought as Aquilla walked away, leading me deeper into Hebsund's tight and winding streets that were hidden from the moon, the strategically tall structures engulfing us in its shadows.

"The Medjaib do not make false prophecies for themselves."

But they attempt to control the ones they bond too?

Aquilla stopped at the gate of one of Hebsund's many city walls, turmoil cresting the waves of his soul next to mine as he turned to look at me.

"They do. And it is a great burden."

Are Medjaib incapable of trusting those below them?

"Only the eldest of the Medjaib, the Iyrah. I have chosen not to follow in their ways."

Does their lack of trust have to do with the name mentioned by your friend?

"Who?"

Elios.

A visible shudder rippled through his swirling skin.

"*Yes*, and no. The Iyrah have long mistrusted the children of creation, and the tragedy of Elios only further serves their agenda. However, I shall not darken your mind with such wickedness. Fear not, Morgan, I will not attempt to control your destiny. I am your guide, not your master."

Aquilla resumed his pace through the gate, not waiting for my response. His transparent steps were heavier, weighted even. Whatever was troubling his soul, he did not share.

The streets were quiet as we traversed to the middle of the city, the full moon high above us, though I could barely see it. Aquilla kept his gaze upon the moon for most of the walk, paying no attention to the towering homes in the bordering Visian district that he walked unhindered through.

After what felt like an hour of solitude with a silent Aquilla, we approached a quiet and walled courtyard adjacent to a glimmering tower. Seeing not a soul, Aquilla drifted towards it beneath the stone arch, stopping just before a familiar statue that stood at the courtyard's center.

It was a thin but strong man wrestling a Lycan.

I believe this is a replicant statue of the one on Lauront Island, the island we saw upon our entrance. The man wrestling the Lycan is Larion, the ancestor of the Lauront family. This Visian house must be a patron of theirs.

Aquilla said nothing as he looked upon the display of distrust before us.

Aquilla?

But his silence scraped across my warring mind.

Before I could retort, Aquilla abandoned the statue to approach the tower that shined like smooth silver beside it. Aquilla traced the silver-painted wall, watching it glimmer through his spectral and transparent flesh. Despite its dazzling glory, I was not as transfixed as he was, for even in this Visian courtyard I could see Karlata's tower looming at the edge of the city by the Hall.

Her tower also shone silver paint, but it was dark, mirroring her heart.

Aquilla turned his head slightly to me.

"Much races in your mind, though I cannot read it."

What happened to Elios?

"No, we shall not speak of such evil. We are here to practice something that was once impossible."

Aquilla motioned to the gleaming tower, but I made no move to join.

Do you not trust me, Aquilla? What story is too dark that mine would shy from?

"I—" Aquilla began, but hesitation halted his words. "No, I do not believe that delivering such an idea to you would be wise."

Do you think I would do something to harm you Aquilla?

"Not intentionally, but your flesh may. And it is your flesh I do not trust, for 'The flesh is weak to the woes of the heart.' That is why we are here: to let the Light which is in me descend into yours. Let us begin to build our trust in one another."

It is difficult to do so when one fears the other will commit some evil that occurred in the past.

"Trust me, Morgan, this is the only way."

I see a plethora of other options.

"You do not trust in your own flesh concerning Karlata, so why should we trust what your flesh desires in this moment?"

Taking a step back from Aquilla, disgust contracted my face.

The furthest thing from my heart is a desire for Karlata.

"Then why does she intimidate you?" Aquilla said. "Your vessel reacts the same as it does with Egret, only there is fear that labors your breath when you see Volsung's daughter."

Sighing, I closed my eyes to try and forget the memories that blackened any innocence I once had.

I do not wish to speak of it.

Aquilla's spectral face clouded a disappointed blue that glimmered with a thousand stars.

"You prove my point, Human. But nonetheless, let us begin our climb. Tonight you shall learn to overcome any mountain that lays before you. Take off your gloves and boots."

My steps came to a halt.

Why?

"You shall not be able to phase through with material objects, only your flesh."

Won't my fingers be visible through this wall?

"They shouldn't be. It looks thick enough."

Hesitating, I did not want to look at my shame anymore than was necessary. But Aquilla had already seen my flesh, already seen the worthlessness that was scarred in my hands and feet that reminded me of painful truths.

No. I needed to focus on what I was called to do, not this Shadow of sleepless death who I was right now.

"Remember, trust in me," Aquilla said as I breathed in and let my unsheathed fingers melt slowly into the wall. "You need to unphase your fingertips while leaving the rest of your hand in my spirit. This will allow you to hold on to the inside of the wall as you climb."

Closing my eyes, I concentrated on my fingertips. But it felt like I was trying to push blood into my fingers, something that was not even close to my control.

How do I do that?

"You need to focus more on trusting me."

You do not make this task trivial, I thought, my fingers barely feeling the stone. *Why is this so much harder?*

"Because it requires more concentration than simply phasing, and more trust. It is like delicately lifting the strings of a puppet for precise movements of its body, but that comes only with getting closer to the one who shows it how to dance."

Trusting Aquilla was the last thing I wanted to do, but there appeared no other way.

My feelings of mistrust stood in the way of climbing the wall, so I let a deep breath flow from my lungs as I separated myself from my feelings. Within my mind, I took a step back away from my emotions to examine the logical insanity of what I was doing: talking to some spirit from the moon who was showing me how to climb a wall.

If Aquilla was truly real, and if I was not losing my feeble grip on reality from witnessing the demise of Sigmund and his family, then this new world in which Aquilla spoke of, guardedly so, was beyond my comprehension. And though Aquilla did not trust me, I loosened my grip on pride for his assistance in navigating such a dark and confusing world, especially if it meant avoiding some fate of Shadow and saving Lucien and Philomela.

Stone began to rub against my fingertips as I dwelled more on surrendering to his spirit. Encouraged, I pulled myself up. My fingers burned under the straining of my weight, as it didn't feel like I had gotten much of a hold for my hands, but it was something. Redirecting my attention to my feet, my crispened toes slid through the stone like dipping them in water. Once they were in, I hardened my toes and pushed up, repeating the same pattern for my fingers as I reached up for a higher hold.

The climb was excruciatingly taxing on my body, the pain of which was like fire in my hands and feet. The world of Aquilla would take some getting used to.

"You are doing well," Aquilla said, but even he had uncertainty in his voice.

Halfway up the tower I felt that my arms were going to explode from the strain within. Tears brimmed at the corners of my eyes.

"Trust in me, Morgan! Yield to the Light."

I'm trying!

My mind scrambled to continue its submission to Aquilla. But then I looked at my hands, the charcoal skin that looked even darker than the night we were submerged in. No kind of hopeful destiny was enough to remedy such a broken vessel, such a fated Shadow. It was like pouring new wine into a broken wineskin, and I didn't even know if the wineskin I had been promised was to be anything but endless death after all.

How does anyone expect me to be able to carry such a load under a rotted interior?

My mind was a shifting sea, thoughts of trust shattered under the wind and waves of my turbulent mind. All I saw was my brokenness. All I could think of was how I would break the trust of Lucien after I abandoned him to go off on a suicidal quest hundreds of miles away to destroy another abomination. He would be left with worry, confusion, and anger. Justifiable anger.

Lucien would be the one with sleepless death, not I.

I would be seen exactly how I saw myself when I let Karlata take my innocence in the most shameful way imaginable: with hatred.

What did Aquilla even *see* in me? Could I even trust this dream he painted with silver?

Pain erupted in my hands as my feet slipped out from underneath me. My hands had completely unphased as I choked upon the hatred for myself.

"Morgan, stop thinking! Trust in me!"

I wanted to respond, but fear mixed into my heart as I dangled high in the midnight air.

I can't—, but my hands blinked through Aquilla's, and I fell to the gravel below, fiery pain erupting in my back.

Air was nonexistent in my lungs like the empty vessel of a Soulis. Aquilla tried to say something to me, but the amount of pain that ruptured in my back was too loud to hear through. But what I could begin to hear was a hurrying of footsteps behind me, followed by an amber light that bled into the night and cascaded upon me.

"Morgan?" Karlata said, stepping from the shadows into the glimpse of moonlight with her lantern, her hair draping over me as she knelt down in front of me. "What are you doing? Why were you climbing a tower?"

Her cheeks blushed scarlet as she caressed my own. As much as I wanted to turn away, I could feel the familiar sensations she lured me with so many fateful sols ago. It also didn't help that I had no breath even to speak. In that moment, all I wished for was that Aquilla had taught me the power to shield myself with the earth like Cypherus did so I could hide from her predacious eyes.

"Here, let me help you up."

Every part of me wanted to resist. Instead, she helped me to my feet, almost gleefully leading me into her den.

It was exactly as I remembered it, but just a few more books were added to her bookshelves of oddities and trinkets from around the world. And by her Wolfwood bed tucked in the corner of the circular room, a leather journal lay open on an ornately carved bedside, right beside her ivory Castle Chess board.

"Sit here," she said, pulling up a chair by the center hearth that glowed with warmth. "I know you never get cold, but I, for one, am freezing."

"What is she talking about?" Aquilla said.

She knows of the Hagroak magic that affected my body.

"The powers of those who lurk in the shadow are indeed a mystery," Aquilla said as he sat unbeknownst to Karlata near the hearth, "but to say they wield *magic* is only to admit that you know nothing of what they can actually do; for all power comes from the Tongue of Creation which binds our existence together."

If you are so informed, what can the Hagroak witches actually do?

"To that, I am uncertain."

"Here, drink this," Karlata interrupted, handing me a cup of juva as her olive skin glowed in the firelight. "I have a little bit of drunkard's pie if you want."

"I'm not hungry, but thank you."

Sipping from the stimulating gold drink, its heat adding more warmth to my perpetually hot flesh, I tried not to think about the honey pecan pie that was drenched in oaky wine. I was hungrier than I thought, but I didn't want to indenture myself further to her.

"Morgan," Karlata said, sitting next to me in another chair that she pulled closer to mine. My eyes mistakenly glanced into hers. Surprisingly, there seemed to be tears in them, and I couldn't look away from those charcoal pits. Instead, she did, looking down almost with sorrow.

"Morgan, I'm so glad you came to Hebsund."

"Why?" There was more venom in my voice than I intended.

Karlata raised her velvet black eyes to mine again, and they looked to brim with tears. She gently reached for my free hand and held it.

"I just wanted to apologize. For everything. I know it's been four sols since… well, since then. And I feel horrible for doing what I did to you. I'm sorry, Morgan, truly. I was only of fourteen sols and it was a mistake born out of ignorance and youth. I've changed so much since then, and so it seems have you."

Pulling my hand away, I leaned over my cup and placed my head in my burnt hand. My mind felt like it was being thrown back into the sea while my body was anchored still to the cliffs. Nothing was making any sense.

Aquilla hummed in confusion as he watched us.

"So… she is not evil?" he said.

"Morgan," she said, grabbing my hand again and stroking it with her smooth fingers, her familiar tips touching my own as she looked at them studiously. "I was wrong to say those harsh words, only to steal your innocence for my own pleasure. I was young and reckless and selfish, and if I could take it back, I would, as you deserve so much more."

She pulled herself closer, her violet scent luring me closer. "But," she whispered, "part of me is glad that we did."

I looked up again, and this time her eyes were leaking. She reached to stroke my own eyes. I was also crying.

"You're just as lonely as me," she said.

My eyes closed at her first words of truth.

Karlata pulled herself closer to me, her breath hardly warming my constantly feverish skin. Her words were more beautiful than a dangerous fire, and I was an ignorant moth.

"Do not forget our purpose, Morgan," Aquilla said, abrupting my thoughts. "It was unwise to be led here. We should go, you need rest before tomorrow's journey."

Opening my eyes, I gracefully tried to pull away, but she held my hands in place with her smooth olive fingers. Silence was stronger than an iron rope; I was captivated.

"There's something I think you should know," Karlata said, her gaze penetrating like arrows from a Lycan bow. "In my time at the College, I've had ample time to study the strangest of creatures living in Scissalan. I've examined the gills of the Fish Folk, and even the lifeless cadavers of those acclaimed to have been drained from those mythical blood-sucking Sukkatlings.

"I've seen a lot Morgan, but never once in my studies did I see anything magical about the Hagroaks and their healings. Yes, they produce the strongest potions and poisons given their resistance with their amphibian Averitic form, but not a single one I've met can do what King Gulmund claims happened to you. They say the healing you received is *impossible.*"

Impossible?

I flexed my burnt hands in the hearth light, feeling their almost gravitational pull towards the fire.

Is it impossible?

Aquilla didn't say anything. Fear rose in my chest at the unknown.

My voice was hardly a whisper. "What are you trying to say, Karlata?"

Her button nose brushed against mine. "I'm saying that they *lied* to you, Morgan. The fire that killed your mother most assuredly happened, and those are definitely burn marks on your body from the flames that your father started, whoever he is. But there's something else about you, about who you are, about what's inside of you, that is so beautifully different."

My voice was hoarse. "Like what?"

Our lips were a breath away now.

"Let's find out together."

Fire blossomed in my heart as our ember lips ignited in embrace. Time burned in the flames of our familiar connection, and, in the blink of an eye, we were on her bed. Aquilla's voice drowned in the roaring smoke of lust that crippled any reasoning. We only stopped when I heard a gasp come from Karlata, and it was not out of ecstasy.

"Morgan, your eyes…"

It was only too late when I realized Karlata glowed a crystal red like Bludhstone; she had seen Aquilla's eyes.

"I'm sorry," I said, jumping out of the bed and making my way to leave. "I—"

Karlata caught my hands, back in their normal state now. "Morgan, please, it is well. I don't know what's going on with you, but I'm not here to pressure you. You can trust me."

Her eyes pleaded for me to stay, opposite of Aquilla's who glowered for me to leave.

"I have to go, Karlata."

She looked down, hiding her sorrow. "I understand." When she looked up, there was a longing in her eyes; they mirrored mine. "Will you come again?"

As much as I didn't want to do it, I nodded to conceal the fact that I would be leaving for Cur Malum.

Karlata gave me a kiss on my forehead. "You will always have a home with me."

❧

Sleep evaded me.

Again.

And again, this vicious cycle went.

Was this the ill-avoided fate of a sleepless death? Was I already becoming Cypherus' Shadow in my ever-growing betrayals to others and myself?

Despite Aquilla's persistent demand for my rest before our departure in the morning, I laid awake with all of the memories of Sigmund and slaughtered Ronians coursing through my mind. Philomela drifted closer to Judux's unknown scheme with every second we wasted, every moment I took to rest; her screaming innocent face petrified me in my troubled dreams.

The worst part of the night was seeing the tactically brutal executions of Valena and Gulmund replay in my mind, the cold eyes of Rolloc seeping in vengeance. Crouching on the castle walls, bow taught in hand that would silence the drunken stupor of Gulmund, whispering obscurities that my amnesiac mind could not decipher but could fairly guess: Rolloc had sought revenge for his enslavement to feed the Soulis.

And Judux had been so vehement in his anger towards Rolloc for killing the King. Did not the conqueror want the heads of royalty beneath him?

Arguably the most troubling was Karlata and her revelations. I couldn't make sense of her now that so much had changed. Old feelings sprouted their poisonous vines through the fractures of my heart that she once crushed with her abusive lust, and, like before, I could feel myself lowering my neck to have them wrap around me, ready for the guillotine of her desires. At least if she crushed me again and drove me back to the cliffs, I wouldn't have to worry about the meaning behind the Hagroak lie that Valena had told me.

The more I thought of my flesh's story, the more I hated it. Had I been the decrepit creation of Godstone manipulation like Belial? Was that why I was so monstrously hideous and unwanted that my mother was burned to death?

Countless questions seeped back to the corners of my darkening mind, all of them shadowed by the dark word that Judux was shown by his lurking reflection.

What fate was being concocted? What wicked scheme was in the twisted mind of Thadius?

When I groggily stood to my feet before dawn, Aquilla was quieter than normal as I got dressed.

Is everything well?

Aquilla hesitated for a moment, then said, "Yes, of course."

I felt you leave my body last night. What were you doing?

"Just studying more of your kind."

I shrugged in acceptance of his unconvincing response, but then he quickly added, "I just am anxious to leave, for Judux's designs grow on my mind."

I know, me too.

I stuffed extra clothes into a leather bag, both of which I found in my room. As we were about to leave, I heard a commotion outside our door. Phasing just my head through the door, I could see Egret being chased by three servants who politely though insistently hounded her with the offerings of food and beverages.

"For the last time, I can take care of myself!" she yelled, desperation and irritation vibrant in her voice. "If I am asked again, I will bury those refreshments where the sun cannot be seen."

It was a very humorous spectacle to see, but I felt sorry for her as she left the Hall. She was out of place in this new world, chained to her unfortunate situation that was forced upon her, just as I was. She longed to be free like the ocean.

The brisk morning air met us as we departed from Volsung's Hall shortly after. The sounds of grunting and metal clanging emerged from the training grounds a stone's throw from us. Curious, I climbed the ramparts of the walls.

"What are we doing?" Aquilla said.

Just getting my bearings.

Invisible on the walls, with only a few guards passing by me on patrol, we watched in silence as the bald but zealously determined warrior from Skyya beat the armored practice dummy into submission with a Ronian sword and shield. She hadn't bothered changing from the dress she wore when she was chased by the servants not long before. Even still, her form graced elegantly from different thrust and blocking movements, her eyes never leaving the straw man before her. Egret would occasionally grunt and roar as she pulverized her target in the early grey dawn.

Determination was her spirit. She was impressive, admirable even.

"Our schedule is squeezing," Aquilla said, motioning for us to move.

What?

"Yes, squeezing. Or as you say: *tight*."

No, you meant that we have a tight *schedule.*

"Are squeeze and tight not the same? If someone's neck is squeezed, is it not tight?"

It is, but that's not how you use it. You're supposed to say, 'We are on a tight schedule.'

"You Humans have too many words."

As I shook my head in frustration, Egret did something peculiar. Looking around to make sure she was alone, Egret pulled out the dark green bottle. In a matter of seconds, Egret drained the last of the flask. This didn't seem to please her, because she quickly followed by smashing the bottle against the armored straw man.

"She seems fond of that elixir," Aquilla said.

The questions I had were so overwhelming that I almost didn't notice the scurrying and shouting of the guards behind us.

"What is that?" I said, turning to determine the source of chaos behind me.

And then I saw them.

Leaping over the wall, not more than fifty feet away from us, were two dark shadows. Sprinting faster than pelefahn across the morning plain, the two creatures howled in victory as soon as they disappeared into the Walls of Laconnia. Whatever scroll was in their claws was not important, for we had almost been devoured by Lycan.

How did they get in here? I thought, feeling the terror of almost facing death so abruptly.

"It matters not," Aquilla said, almost too quickly. "We need to leave as soon as we can."

With a shaky breath, I nodded. I turned to look back at Egret, but she had also disappeared. With nothing keeping me here, we went forth in preparations for our departure.

The sun was just beginning to set over the Walls of Laconnia by the time we finished gathering enough food, water, Drakmun, and supplies for our journey from Volsung's munitions officer. The spotted horse we borrowed was saddled with our gear, along with a steel-tipped spear from Volsung's barracks.

The lie I told the stout man watching Volsung's stables about needing the horse for a messenger was easy enough. He had recognized the green slanted cloak of Renborg's royalty that I never used, but obeyed without question. It was a time of war, and messengers were commonplace to be sent between the holdings of Renborg, as with any kingdom in similar circumstances. The officer had probably heard of the Lycan who had been in the city earlier, which only increased his diligence to give us everything we needed.

Of course, Lucien would be informed of this, but not until later. Before the sun even rose, he was occupied with meetings upon meetings over strategy and messaging efforts to the other Kriga with Volsung and his staff of commanders.

The hardest part of all was waiting for darkness so we could leave under its shroud, knowing that Philomela grew closer to some bestial fate with every second wasted.

But to leave in the light would spoil our plan, so we waited.

Finding a secluded garden in the upper districts of

Hebsund, Aquilla and I practiced climbing up its walls. Uncertainty flooded my mind as I tried to phase into his flesh and climb, but I feared the thought of falling again and crushing my back, which still ached from the night before.

"Trust in me, Morgan!" Aquilla said as I leaped to phase my hand through the moss-ridden wall, but my fingers jammed into the stone and I fell down into the grass in failure.

I need a break from this, I do not know why I cannot phase as I did last night.

"It is because you fear falling. You must trust in me that you will not fall."

I sighed, rubbing my eyes in frustration. *Can we begin learning the ancient language instead while we wait? Something that involves no chance of falling?*

"No, we are too exposed. We shall not risk the chance of your generation learning of such power."

My broken hands trembled with frustration. *Then what do you propose we do, spirit?*

"Tell me about your father," Aquilla said as I sat up from the grass.

What? Why?

"I am curious."

Sighing, I thought, *I don't know much about him, other than he killed my mother when I was born.*

"I thought your mother was a slave from Karthos."

She was.

"How did she conceive you?"

I cringed at the thought, almost oblivious to the sound of movement behind the garden wall. I brushed it off as being merely a squirrel, but it happened to be a cabat who flew past me to catch a squirrel.

I don't know how that happened. All Valena told me was that he washed up on the shore one day and took an interest in my mother.

"What is her name?"

Joanna.

"Joanna… so, Joanna conceived you with this stranger, but your father did not wish to have your birth?"

You're smarter than I thought, spirit. He tried to kill me so that he wouldn't be charged with sleeping with the King's slave. But in doing so, he caught her room on fire, killing her and burning me inside her corpse that kept me alive.

"I sense hatred in you?"

Of course. Without question.

"Then why do you hate yourself?"

His words caught me off guard.

I come from the most disgusting man who, because of my birth, caused my mother to die and is now nothing but a pile of ashes swept away and forgotten. And you ask me why I don't love myself? What is there to love, Aquilla? These scars are an ugly reminder of the truth that I am nothing and unwanted, regardless of how I received them.

"But Gulmund and Valena lied about your birth."

I—, but my thoughts ran short. I didn't know how to respond to that revelation. Nothing was making any sense.

"Regardless of your birth," Aquilla continued, "you forget the most important aspect of your determined existence. 'The birth of destiny is known to the Mother long before we are ever born.' She knew of your song even before the Prophet Bards sang of your life to come. You have purpose in that! Avoiding the Shadow that consumes most is not something to be dismissed. We must *rise* to our worthy calling, be strengthened by it!"

"Do you think I care about being important?" I said, forgetting to speak in my mind. "That I desire to be fabled and remembered like Cypherus the Great and not his Shadow?"

"Of course! Why would you not be?"

"I could care less about being like him. My worth does not come from some old man's songs or what your god says."

Aquilla looked perplexed. "Then where does it come from, Morgan?"

A Godstone knife whistled past my face and stuck into the stone wall beside me.

Egret looked furious as she stormed up to me, her emerald eyes strikingly deeper in their hues of green. "Either you are losing your mind or you are hiding something from me."

My words choked in my mouth as I stood to my feet, flustered for almost being impaled again. "What are you talking about?"

"Is this her doing?"

"Whose?"

"*Karlata's.*"

She said her name with an unexpected amount of bitterness.

"I don't know what you're talking about. And you don't have to throw your knife at me every time you're upset, you know."

Egret marched up to me and pinned me to the wall, her hands on either side of me. Fear sparked in my chest at her intimidation.

"I know that you visited her last night." Egret's face looked almost hateful as her bald head furrowed in anger.

"Be careful with your next words," Aquilla said.

Aquilla—

"Has she involved you in her darkness? Is it the College that she's roping you into that makes you speak to the shadows?"

Breaking away from her hold was impossible, so I relented to her peculiar strength. "No, Egret. We were merely catching up. And sometimes I speak to myself when I'm alone. Is there anything wrong with that which you would like to accuse me of?"

Egret's face seemed to display a bitter annoyance at my answer. Her furious gaze lowered to my hands that were exposed to the air, and for the briefest moment, a look of compassion resurfaced on her face. Egret let me go of her hold, grabbing her gilded Bludhstone knife and sliding it back into her ornate sheathe.

"I'm glad you have someone to talk to, Krabios, both real and imaginary," she said before walking to the iron gate to leave the garden, her steps heavier than the gate itself.

"Egret—"

"And just so you're aware, you were almost killed by Lycan prisoners that escaped."

"Those were prisoners?"

"Yes, and they almost killed you for watching me again."

"I almost wished they did."

Egret brushed her fingers against her smooth scalp, her face concealing what looked like pain. Instead of words, her sea green eyes met mine. There was an ocean beneath the surface, one that was confusing, frustrating, and stubborn; yet, sometimes humorous, admirable, resilient and… *familiar.*

As our eyes locked yet again, seeing which would spar next in banter, she hesitated briefly as if to say something. But as the moment became laden with silence, she gave a slight nod to excuse herself and left hurriedly without another word.

"Egret's actions are not making any sense," Aquilla said.

As always, so helpful, I thought, the sun descending over the Wolfwoods, along with my hopes of not failing Egret and my brother any further.

The sunset was another painful reminder that we were running out of time. My exchange with Egret was the furthest from pleasant, and though she meant nothing to me, part of me wished it had not gone so poorly.

Another part of me thinks she felt the same way.

"Let us not dwell on these matters further," Aquilla said. "Come, it is time we depart for Cur Malum, and at last learn the language of the gods."

Chapter 17
Ill Forgotten

The Black Legion was founded in 697 DE by a mysterious man whose name has been hidden in the shadows. Their exact strength is unknown but it is possible that they boast numbers of men at least twenty-five thousand to an astounding sixty thousand strong, making them the largest mercenary army in all of Scissalan. Although Icarus, their believed base of operations, is officially under the domain of the Kapitolian Republic, in reality it acts more as a city state ruled by one. Under this shadowed reign, the city has become the unofficial capital of Scissalan's black market dealings; of which it is widely supposed that their leader receives a generous percentage.

Many believe their leader is of Human descent and has led the Black Legion since its conception and to this day. I suppose this theory was weaved to garner a reputation of imposing legend, due to most men not living beyond eighty sols. However, my hypothesis is marred from several Elvish accounts who report to have seen the same man over the last hundred sols. Some have even joked that he is an Elf himself who has "clipped his ears". Another clue is the complete devotion unto death all of his closest followers show him. His generals and lieutenants obey his every command without question and even seem to treat him almost as if he were a god. The man remains an enigma.

Chronicles of Renborg: King's Edition
"The Black Legion"
Piluch Joffersun: Master of Histories

As we practiced by our makeshift camp, my hands phased deeper in the silent hum of the dark grey morning, the red wisps of my Godstone creating a glowing trail through my fingers to write my first word of the gods.

"Good," Aquilla said, his robes mirroring the moonlight as the creek before us began to churn. "The water before you is under your command. Now, as is the opposite of Wyl, Wae the water upwards into the air, slowly. Instead of your soul breathing into the Godstone, let your soul breathe out through it, and focus on where the breath of your soul shall flow."

Though I could barely believe my eyes, part of the creek began to flow into the air before us as I breathed out to perform Wae, the Godstone vibrating in response. In a state of disbelief, I twisted my galactic hands and imagined the water wrapping around them. The shimmering water slowly but surely concealed my arms of Aquilla in its splendor.

I truly laughed for the first time.

"This is incredible!" I said, Waeing the water to stretch from me towards the treeline above us.

"Now, Wyl it into your Godstone to store its essence. But do it very slowly, and not all the water at once."

Excited by the new challenge, I began to Wyl by breathing in, and the water started to disappear inside my glowing red Bludhstone necklace, watering the carved tree on its emblem.

The possibilities seemed limitless with such power; to at last be lord over the sea instead of letting it lord over my life. Suddenly, the threat of Judux and Belial didn't seem so bleak after all. To have such power over what was once uncontrollable filled me with courage. And though Philomela's life reached ever closer to an unknown plot by Judux, the fleeting spark of hope within me was beautifully bright nonetheless.

Without realizing, I began to pull in more and more water from the creek, thirsty for more control over the chaos that flaunted itself through its previously unhindered stream. As I did so, the image of the ancient word began to emerge in my mind, slightly burning, until my conscious vision was dominated by its strange markings like a hot branding iron sizzling through flesh.

"Enough!" Aquilla said, the water dropping as I obeyed, along with the word for water from my mind. "You must be careful with such power, Human. You have now stored the water within your Godstone which we can use later, but you have tasted of its initial but growing consequence."

"The burning of my mind?" I said, standing up from the muddy bank where we practiced during our brief rest.

"Yes. That power was meant only for the gods. It was never intended for the creation to use the power of the creators, hence why you must use the blood of gods to even birth such power. Most will go mad if they delve too deeply with the language of the gods."

"The Tongue of Tihrrvyith?"

"Correct. The Tongue of Creation."

"If that is true, why did Cypherus not lose his mind? I saw him use the language to channel lightning into Sh'eol and raise the earth to shield him. He looked sane to me."

"Nazrioch shielded him from the Tongue, prolonging the degrading effects that Tihrrvyith has on the mind; mainly, its consumption of the individual. But Cypherus was not completely spared. As written by Kapitol's infamous Aldomhir Daggerlad in *The King*, 'There are some men who wield gleaming armor only to hide the vulnerable broken underneath.'"

"So I will be broken then?"

"Not as fast as those without a Medjaib's purity, hence why it was a blessing this power was erased in the Age of Ashes. I shall protect you as best as I can. But we must use this power sparingly."

Readjusting my supplies and the sack of Drakmun on our Hebsund horse, I mounted and kicked our steed into a gallop, eager to not think about the Medjaib's damning words and to put more distance between Hebsund and us.

The clinging of Drakmun was a pleasant distraction as we rode again. Before we had fled into the night, against Aquilla's wishes, we had stopped by Volsung's treasury within the Hall to provide us with more Drakmun to pay for the naval passage to Cur Malum.

And maybe for some juva along the way.

"A bit excessive, Morgan?" Aquilla said when I had poured hundreds of Drakmun into my pouch.

We'll need it. And he has enough silver to get by.

Aquilla insisted that we did not visit Lucien before we left, who was asleep after another long day of negotiations and planning with Volsung, but I refused to leave without seeing him one last time. Unsurprisingly, Egret was absent from the room; any trace of her belongings was nonexistent.

I would never understand him.

I stroked a white lock of hair from his forehead before kissing it. The anguish and pain he would feel at my vague note of departure, which I laid to rest on his bedside table, would be immense, as would my grief in placing him in such agony.

But it would keep him focused on the war.

As I turned to leave, the faintest whisper escaped from Lucien's mouth, but it was enough to stop me in my tracks as if a force held my heart in place.

"Morgan," Lucien said, his voice unconscious as he appeared to be dreaming.

"This is what I warned you of," Aquilla said.

"Morgan… please. *Please…*"

My heart stretched at the seams in the amount of love I had for him.

An invisible grip released its hold on my heart as I pulled away from him. Thankfully, he didn't ask me to stay. I don't know what I would do if he knew I was leaving.

"His love for you is… *different*," Aquilla said, his voice trailing as I felt his cosmic mind whirring inside of me.

Aquilla would need another seventy sols to learn the basics of Humanity and all of our idiosyncrasies, but he would need a millennium to understand Lucien; not even my personal knowledge of my brother would suffice. So many times I would catch him looking at me, his gentle smile showing me how relentlessly much he loved me, yet displaying pain all the same.

And though guilt berated my soul as we left him, knowing he was surrounded by an army and strategic leaders brought me peace of mind as we rode throughout the cold night, the dark road bringing us ever closer to the Aerothred Port. At least my life would amount to the good of securing my brother's political future. At least now Lucien had a chance. That gave me peace and, refreshingly, even the smallest amount of pride.

I could feel my shaking hands steady at the fact that they weren't so worthless after all.

We didn't risk stopping for the night again, as Lucien would most likely send a search party within Hebsund's radius in denial of the written wish to not search for me. So to voyage through the drenching dark, I used Aquilla's eyes to see.

Aquilla was silent as I navigated our steed through his glassy vision, his thoughts obscure to me in his attempt to hide them, but I figured they surrounded the gloom of using the Tongue of Tihrrvyith.

Fortunately, the road was void of any marauders, Lycan, or Mara. Only clear, glassy, diamond-like trees and hills consumed my vision. Sometimes I would have to blink back into my own eyes because the Medjaib's world looked too much like the crystalline sea, the Asculum cliffs still singing their haunting siren to lure me back. Gripping my hands tighter on the reins, I continued to practice phasing, determined to pour out my life for Philomela and Lucien.

And Egret too, perhaps, though our personalities clashed just as well as water and fire.

Nonetheless, degraded goods traded for priceless innocence were worth any sacrifice.

To guide my thoughts, I repeatedly recited the Sunflower Skallgend, letting my thoughts flow from the ancient words to focus on phasing and trusting the Light in Aquilla. And though my focus was strong for the beginning of my practice as we rode, my phasing routinely stuttered to a halt at the ugly reminder of Cypherus' Shadow that did its very worst to consume my destiny.

Sleepless death…

Shaking the dark prophecy from my mind, I glanced to the white treeline stretching beside us. Before I resumed my attention to the road, a glimpse of red caught my eye: one that was moving fast. Looking again, I could see a red figure moving through the crystal trees at a distance, only for it to disappear when I focused on it.

It wasn't the first time either since we took off on the road.

"It was most likely an animal," Aquilla said, dismissing my worries and speaking up for the first time in hours.

I grunted in agreement, but what I saw looked larger than an animal. I couldn't shake the feeling that we were being followed.

Or hunted.

For five cycles of the moon being drowned by the sun, when we were not practicing phasing or the Tongue of Tihrrvyith, I found my aching thoughts drifting once again towards the Mordrake family that was now almost entirely decimated.

Memories of them were allowed to breathe along the wind-swept and quiet road beside the Brehnok River, my mind having no distractions as I reminisced of the boar hunting that Gulmund would take Lucien, Sigmund, and I on with his favored son, Kyllian. The procession was precisely the opposite of the quiet forest now, as Gulmund would take hundreds of his soldiers to escort us into the forest as he sought to strengthen Kyllian for his inheritance of the crown. The boredom on Lucien's face always made me laugh, as did Sigmund's childish taunts.

"Does hunting make you sad, brother?" Sigmund said, the words barely forming from his young mind.

"Lucien is just afraid the beast will hunt him instead,"

I jested, prodding Lucien in his side, bringing great annoyance to him.

"Don't listen to Morgan," Lucien said, sneering at me. "Morgan can hardly think with the ladies of the court pursuing him. Isn't that so, Morgan?"

"Ladies of the court?" Sigmund asked with innocence. "What do they want from you, Morgan?"

What Karlata began, I thought, not wanting to darken his innocence with the shameful lust that had begun to dominate me with his cousin.

I closed my eyes to the memory, regretting the many pursuits I had taken to fill the need of my lonely soul which Karlata had exposed and exploited. And the thought of Sigmund and Gulmund burdened my heart ever further. I could think of them no longer.

I wonder how Lucien thinks of them, I thought, grief berating my mind for his family. It was devastating enough for me, but for Lucien, I couldn't even fathom the darkness that encroached upon his mind. Thinking of his family also reminded me of Egret and her mother, Nera. Guilt rose within me as I realized I hadn't thought once of Nera since the invasion, and she had most assuredly been captured by the Drakin. It hadn't occurred to me that Egret would be burdened by her mother's capture; no one had even asked her.

Next time I see her, I will inquire of the condition of her soul, I thought, affirming a plan to resolve the guilt I felt in not treating her with a kindness that most deserved.

"I sense your thoughts of Egret," Aquilla said, his galactic and winged being beside me interrupting my isolated gloom. "Your thoughts continue to gravitate towards her, I've noticed."

Your thoughts never seem to leave mine in peace, I've noticed, I thought, shaking my head in annoyance at his continual disregard for my privacy, and for his unnecessary conjuration to appear as flying in my spiritual consciousness.

"It helps to break the illusion of isolation," Medjaib said as I stared at him.

Thankfully, our journey was not halted by Ronian scouts from Hebsund who Lucien most definitely would have sent out by now in pursuit. It would have been trivial to remedy the anxiety I felt from the thought of being followed by a quick flight in Soul Sleep to Hebsund. However, each and every time I asked, my pleas were halted by Aquilla who insisted we used our time of resting from horseback to train both in the physical ways of combat and in the ethereal gifts of his spirit and Tongue of Creation.

"We won't be able to train as frequently once we reach Aerothred," Aquilla said early the next morning as sweat dripped from my fingers in following the Window Guard on my right side with the steel-tipped spear.

My right hand remained steady next to my ear as I held the spear behind my head like a sword about to strike, waiting for Aquilla's cue.

"Strike and phase!" Aquilla said.

Stepping forward with my backfoot, I struck diagonally down and across, keeping the head of my spear as stable as possible. Stepping forward again, I phased my hand through a tree before solidifying it as Aquilla did to the Soulis; however, my grace did not match his, and when I tried to pull out my hand, it remained stuck, jolting my focus.

"Again!" Aquilla persisted.

Whenever we would finish our arduous guard and strike movements with my spear, Aquilla relentlessly forced me to practice climbing the trees bordering the Brehnok River, along with the occasional use of the Tongue.

I never received a break.

"Pour out the water from your Godstone by focusing on Wae," the Medjaib instructed, to which the water poured too quickly out of the red wisps from my trembling fingers, only making myself wet and miserable.

"You are too tired," Aquilla said, to which I collapsed onto the soaked plain that was thankfully being warmed by the sun.

My broken body should have felt relieved in finally receiving a break from my unrelenting tutor, but my frustration remained from being unable to Soul Sleep. A gnawing feeling in my soul yearned to see Lucien and Egret once again to see how they responded to my note; to see if they were okay; to see another face besides the cosmic swirls of my *inner* Mara.

"I am the *farthest* thing from a Mara," Aquilla said as I let him read my mind, hurt noticeable in his tone as he sat down beside me. "I shall grant you rest, but just enough. The port city should only be a few hours from here, so our time waiting should be minimal, especially since we are being followed."

"So you finally admit to seeing it," I said, dragging myself to retrieve some trollof bread from our supplies that rested near our steed who fed on the grass.

"Yes, but whoever it is has not caught up to us as of yet, though they are very careful."

"Is it a Mara?" I said, phasing into Aquilla's eyes to scout the glistening hills that bordered the Brehnok River, all of which were now glassy with the occasional blood-red hue of an animal or bird.

"No, its heart would have been Nox."

"Why don't we just Soul Sleep to see who—"

"You need your rest more than anything," he said, forcibly phasing his spirit from my eyes and sitting back down beside me.

"Whatever," I said, tearing a huge bite of trollof bread as we both mused in our own frustrated silence.

Though I was grateful to take a break, the lack of intensive training allowed the tidal thoughts of hopelessness for our suicidal quest and the bottomless depression of loneliness to surge back in.

Longing to submerge these wailing echoes of my soul and to think of anything else besides our current misfortunes, I said, "What was it like on Akhorus?"

Aquilla's galactic swirls of eyes hued cyan blue in surprise.

"Do you forget the memory I showed you so quickly?"

"I remember what it looked like," I said, rolling my eyes as I recalled the moon's silver fields of roses and glassy temple. "I'm asking you what life was like for you?"

"Hmmm," he said, stroking his cosmic chin in contemplation which I could feel within me. "It was engaging."

Always so direct.

"How so?"

"Well, like we are doing now, I spent most of my time training in the combative arts, of which I followed in the teachings of warriors we gleaned from thousands of sols in observance."

"Did you ever sleep?"

"I Soul Sleep every day."

"That's not what I meant."

"If you're referring to wasting a third of the day with my eyes closed like Humans and Dwarves do, then no. We are the eyes of the world, Morgan. The moment we close them, Thadius moves with blinding speed to spread his wickedness, which is why we spent all of our time watching your world, reflecting on its history, and preparing for our time to guide you. At *any* cost."

An image of a spiraling tower of glass emerged in my mind, of which Aquilla's memory showed him reading from translucent books with languages of every kind. The memory shifted to him practicing the Tongue of Tihrrvyith in solitude, using careful eyes to ensure he wasn't being watched.

Was it not allowed?

"Akhorus is the memory for a world which forgets its past and blindly falls into the future," Aquilla continued. "Hence our purpose: to guide each race to the Light, and thus to their respective eternity of blessing that the Mother longs to give."

"Respective? As in several eternities?"

"Yes; one for the Elves, another for the Dwarves, and one for your kind; Solæf, as you call it. Each with their own god who created them. Such division of race was deemed necessary by the Author, as in their unity did they bring destruction to the earth, and still do."

"And what of you? You are none of those races."

"Eternity is a gift in which I must earn with you, Morgan. Should we succeed, I shall be granted the privilege of sharing Solæf with you, shepherding the new earth that Humans shall rule without need or suffering."

"And if you fail?"

Aquilla paused as he looked at me, his swirling eyes darkening like Shadow as he pondered the thought.

"Should I fail, I shall be returned to the Mother's spirit, where my essence shall be given to a Medjaib who is more worthy of Her calling."

"You would cease to exist… forever?"

"It is more desirable than the judgements of Her Wrath for those unworthy of their Paradise or the melancholic Void. Such as being reduced to a conscious stone for the Dwarves, for instance."

"That is far worse," I admitted, my flesh cringing at the abysmal and lonely thought, though I could think of many who deserved it.

"And that is what must be, for existence was forged by Her Truth, and its fruit shall either sustain or destroy us. But the Mother is merciful, and She longs for us to be nourished by Her nature, which is why we Medjaib were born from Her tears."

"Her tears?"

"Of course. How else would one react to seeing their creation tear the world apart in ignorance and pride?"

"The Battle of the Gods…" I said, remembering the fabled tale of the world being fractured by the gods and thus Scissalan's unique shape, their blood saturating the dirt that would later become Godstone.

The Valkryn Priests loved to spew this story as a dire warning to those who sought to abandon the Mother's teachings, like Lucien and I most often did. Those abandonments of the law often left me with a smile.

"So it was real? Godstone is truly the blood of gods?"

"Yes," Aquilla said. "And Thadius was solely responsible for that devastation."

"Why? Didn't that kill thousands?"

"Millions."

Aquilla's words sank deep and heavily into my heart.

The world which I used to know felt so small and insignificant compared to the gravity of the past and the eternity of the future.

Looking to the faded stars in the Void above, I almost felt sick in realizing that all of those twinkling lights were the banished souls of those who rebelled against the Mother, including the gods who created and almost destroyed the creation. Thadius, the preeminent example of those gods, whose constellation of the Seven Lamentations was akin to a scholar pridefully praising his written work, making an idol out of what was created.

If I failed to avoid this destiny of Shadow, would my sleepless death be like theirs? Watching forever the world which I corrupted, eternally alone?

"So," I said, "Thadius convinced the gods to kill each other in hopes of destroying the other sentient beings the Mother created, including us?"

"Yes, knowing full well that the creatures and Inor he created would survive the earth's shattering and even multiply in the wake of sentient life being forced asleep forever."

"He was that jealous?"

"Jealousy was assuredly part of it. But Thadius felt alone, Morgan, and betrayed; as if his whole world in which he prized had become completely corrupted."

Though Aquilla was discussing Thadius, a memory of his glimpsed through his guarded subconscious to show himself alone in the silver rose fields of Akhorus. Soul Sleeping far away from those in the temple who vehemently rejected his vision from the Mother, he sat himself rejected.

"Is that how you feel?" I said.

Aquilla bowed his galactic head, his emotions weighing him down. I could almost feel his burden.

"A Medjaib is not guided by temporary feelings, but an eternal purpose," Aquilla said, avoiding my question but answering it with his initial hesitancy to respond.

Letting moments drift between us, I said, "If you received a vision from the Mother, then why did they not listen to you?"

"Because they are *prideful*," he said, almost too quickly. "Eons ago, the Medjaib were but servants to the Author and the ones She chose to join our stories to. But so much time has passed, so much evil has been wrought onto the world, that they wish not to be servants of the misguided creation, but their masters."

"And because of Elios."

Aquilla paused. "And because of his betrayal."

"What happened to him?"

Aquilla bowed his head, his thoughts hidden from me.

"So, just as your brothers do not trust creation, neither do you."

"I…" Aquilla began, before finally sighing and surrendering. "Very well, if you must know. But guard your heart against what I am about to say to you, and remember it well, for I shall not repeat it."

"My ears are open," I said.

"What happened to Elios happened long before my arrival. Elios was sent to guide a boy, a child with no name nor significance, but a child who had been born corrupted and twisted since his upbringing on the streets of Kapitol. When Elios bonded to his heart, the child, by the strength of his wicked heart alone, suppressed Elios, forcing the Medjaib to be in service of his designs, enslaving his spirit to his own instead of trusting one another to carry out the Mother's Will."

"What became of Elios and this boy?"

Aquilla sighed. "The boy hid from our sight, and Elios was lost ever since."

"So because of one child, the Medjaib don't trust us?"

"Nor do they trust me."

"That seems very shortsighted, for not all Humans long to consume the souls of others. I thought the Medjaib were pure of heart."

"'Even the purest with our righteous intentions can lead others astray,' including ourselves."

"Aquilla…"

"Yes?"

"Do you trust me?"

For a moment, Aquilla's only response was the careful swirling of his galactic face as his cosmic eyes seemed to almost frown.

"Morgan—"

But then something closer than a whisper invaded my ears.

Añaer…

"What was that?" I said, thinking first it was whoever was following us.

Springing from the muddy grass to scope the largely treeless plains around us, fear surged through my beating heart that was so rudely awakened.

There was nothing.

Aquilla looked at me with pity as I calmed myself down, realizing that no one had whispered that word to me, though I still felt like we were being watched.

"We must be careful, Morgan," Aquilla said.

"Is it that thing which is following us?"

"No, but we should finish our journey to Aerothred now, for whatever is following us is getting bolder, getting closer."

"Then what just invaded my mind?"

The usually cyan hue of Aquilla's cosmic eyes burned a dark red as they focused on me as if in a warning.

"The Tongue of Tihrrvyith."

~

Aerothred came into view after a desperately needed stint of rest, its cracked marble buildings and temples stretching vastly across the Komner Channel as its countless wooden docks surrounded it like a cage. Though dusk was fast approaching to smother the city in darkness, the ancient Elvish port was still bustling with trade, the coming and going of merchant ships from all across Scissalan creating a dull roar of a world seemingly untouched by war.

As we rode through the arching columns of the city's Western Gate near the docks, I was overwhelmed by a foreign sense of normalcy. Seeing hundreds of Humans, Dwarves, and Elves exchange goods in the streets, little ones play fighting with wooden swords and unrobbed joy, and even Averites like the winged Fhaolin selling red elk and pelafahn pelts in the square, it all almost didn't seem real.

We dismounted and began leading our steed through the crowds.

"I don't know where to begin looking for the right ship," I said. "What soul will take us to Cur Malum if all fear it?"

"We should start with transportation to Valeneka," Aquilla said, "and quickly."

"Quickly?"

I turned to look at Aquilla whose cosmic eyes were focused on the Western Gate. Our eyes merged as one as I followed his gaze, trying to decipher between the sea of glassy Bludh and Nox hearts before us. I almost gave up until I saw a familiar crystalline figure weaving carefully throughout the crowds until it stopped upon seeing us.

For a few heart-pounding moments, we were locked in a gaze.

Then, the hooded figure began to run.

"Time to find a ship, Morgan," Aquilla said as we both jumped back on our horse, the figure making depressingly significant progress as we struggled to move away.

"Why don't we confront it?"

"You're not ready, and it could be a spy from Hebsund, meaning you would either have to shed innocent blood or reveal yourself, neither of which are an option."

There was no time to think as we frantically searched for a ship that could simultaneously board us and depart immediately.

But who would openly and quickly accept someone who came flying in on a steed, no questions asked?

And to leave so soon?

"We might have to stow away," Aquilla said as we narrowly avoided running people over in our pursuit of ships leaving the docks.

Many gruntles and shouts occurred as too close of calls were made by our stampeding steed. We even received a warning from a Ronian patrol who were unhappy at our carelessness, but as I scanned the crowd, I could see it paid off, for our pursuer was nowhere to be found.

"That doesn't mean they are not there," Aquilla said as we at last reached the swarming docks of commerce.

"There!" I said, pointing towards an Ornosian carrack ship.

The golden vori flame banners of a Merigold Company ship were glowing bright as it was preparing to untether itself from the docks and set sail northwards away from the sunset.

"How do you know it will go to Valeneka?"

"The Merigold are from Karthos, so they are likely making a return voyage northwards."

"And stopping in Valeneka's city of N'ahl Juvara?"

"It would be foolish not—"

A knife whistled past me, kissing my lips before burying itself in a wooden support beam of the nearby shop.

Our pursuer had caught up.

"Flee, Morgan!" Aquilla said.

With no time to waste, I kicked our horse with all of my

fleeting might, and we flew down the docks paying no heed to the crews who scrambled to avoid being trampled by us. Another knife screamed past us and nicked my shoulder.

"We won't have time to stop," Aquilla said as we neared the Merigold ship.

Not wanting another knife to find its premature home in my pounding heart, I hastily wrapped our gear around my back and gripped the spear with all of my might as I jumped off of our breathless steed before the end of the dock. With no time to lose, I sprinted with all my might, leaping off the docks and onto the departing Merigold ship, much to the shouting dismay of the onlookers behind me. My gloved hands almost slipped as I climbed the wooden ridges with a spear in tow, but before my strength gave out, I tumbled over the side.

Any feelings of relief were immediately dashed when sailors of the Merigold Company drew their swords at my neck.

"Wait!" I said, indicating my sack of Drakmun at my waist. "I'll pay for passage."

"Admiral Akoshka!" an olive-skinned sailor shouted.

"What, pray tell, is your grand plan now?" Aquilla said.

Remain calm and hope the Admiral is favorable towards her countrymen.

The Admiral was quick to deal with my sudden intrusion, her feet pounding as she immediately descended the helm, her dark blue and yellow flowered cape billowing behind her as she approached. Upon sight of my Karthosian olive face and Nox wavy hair, Akoshka, to our great relief, was merciful but accepted my full sack of Drakmun instead of a more reasonable one hundred Drakmun for passage.

"I would have slain you and taken your Drakmun had you not been of our kin," the Admiral said in her thick Ornos accent, helping me up with her hand. "But we of Karthos must stand strong together."

"And broke," I muttered.

"Excuse me?"

"Nothing."

"Hmm. Luckily for you, I have a storage room you can sleep in down in the lower deck. We will be in N'ahl Juvara nine days from now, so I hope you packed enough provisions to last. Otherwise, enjoy your fast."

"Thank you," I said, giving a courteous bow as the Admiral and crew returned to their duties navigating the ship from the port.

Grabbing what little we had, we stood for a moment gazing upon the shrinking port of Aerothred. Any signs of our pursuer were nonexistent, though I could see some wayfarer rejoicing in his new stolen steed which we left behind.

"I doubt we will be followed," Aquilla said as we descended the ship's stairs to our dusty and crowded storage room. Thankfully some light shed a path for our feet from the open window. "But we must continue to be careful. Whoever was following us might very well be a spy from Thadius, though their heart was not yet Nox."

"I think our biggest problem we face now is more of a financial one," I said as I gloomily closed the window and any feeling of hope. "The Admiral took all the money we had, so say goodbye to hiring another transportation. And even if we had more money, who in their right mind would take us to Cur Malum? We might as well just try swimming across the Praetar Shores—"

A red and very familiar Godstone knife emerged from the shadows and pressed across my neck, elegant fingers grabbing my chin to hold against the knife, leaving me helpless.

"Before you do that, Krabios," a beautifully feminine yet terrifyingly recognizable voice said, "first explain who your invisible friend is here and why you so callously abandoned us?"

Aquilla's cosmic eyes were startling white with surprise.

"Egret?" we said.

Chapter 18
Castle Hearts

The youth who are chosen are put through vigorous training, where they must kill a krabourak with their bare hands, successfully navigate a ship, survive on a ship for a week in the middle of the ocean with no food, be drowned and revived, and successfully ride a Poecampi. The successful are given honor and celebration amongst the community, where they go on to join the elite Queen's Navy. Those who are weak return to Skyya shamed and are delegated to economic and government functions.

After twenty sols of service, the Skyyans who served in the military are allowed to return with their pay and are granted land and a ship. They are then eligible to enter politics in the government, which many do.

Strength and perseverance are what Skyyans prize, and weeping for anything other than a fallen Skyyan is seen as weak and is justly mocked. While Skallgends are written as per Solbok regulations, they focus primarily on triumphant feats and battles that the Mother has guided them in for that sol.

The Ornosian Histories: 'Royal Edition'
"Culture of Skyya"
Penned by Matheos of Thylios

K**alypto** pierced through Aquilla's cosmic face not a moment after he reluctantly revealed himself to Egret at my request, the knife sheathing itself into the storage wall behind him.

"Mara!" Egret screamed, her veins lightning across her bald scalp.

"Be still!" Aquilla said, his tone full of authoritative fire as he stepped effortlessly away from the knife. "I told you this was foolish, Morgan. Did I not warn you of this needless exposure?"

"What black magic is this?" Egret said, advancing with zealous anger.

"I am no Mara!" Aquilla said, his luminescent face shining a blinding white that caused Egret and I to shield our eyes from. "I am a Medjaib from the moon, Akhorus, sent by the Mother Herself to aid Morgan in his destiny."

"And what might that be?" Egret said, shifting her inquisitive wrath to me. "Did this spirit advise you to abandon your brother and your empire in their most perilous hour of need?"

"We are not abandoning them," I said, "we left to save them."

"For Cur Malum? To learn some more sorcery with this dark phantom?"

"This is why it was foolish to reveal myself," Aquilla said.

"No," I said, sitting down on one of the barrels and checking the storage door again to make sure it was closed, and though it was, I lowered my voice. "Cur Malum has a Klyr spear which we need in order to slay Belial."

"Belial?"

Taking a careful breath, I said, "The resurrected Dragon of Judux."

Egret's small yet powerful hand left a stinging mark across my face as she spoke without words.

"Do you make me to be some brainless krabourak?"

"What Morgan speaks is true," Aquilla said. "Judux appears to be in league with the fallen god Thadius, who has taught him how to raise a Dragon from the seed of Man using the soul of Sh'eol."

"Within Solstein," I added. "And the only way to slay Belial is with Klyr Godstone that is found in Cur Malum, and we must do so before Belial is fully grown."

Egret looked the furthest from convinced; for a minute she was speechless. Wanting to ease her lack of trust, I offered my hand.

"Hold it," I said, unsheathing my hand from its glove, revealing its charred flesh to her eyes.

Strangely, it was easier to expose myself to her.

"What?"

"Just trust me."

"Why should I touch the hand of one who is not my husband? Do you forget decorum?"

"It will help to understand, and I think our current situation disregards such formalities, my Queen."

With an oceanic amount of caution, she gently placed her delicate fingers within mine. Through Wyl, I breathed my soul in to let Aquilla's hand phase through mine, which he allowed to be visible to her eyes alone besides mine.

"*Vorim*!" she said in Skyyan, sharply rescinding her hand from mine.

"Do not fear, I am not a Vori in the flesh," I said, laughing to myself that I would even be considered to be one of those seductively deadly water spirits. "It was Aquilla's hand you felt."

"How?" Egret's dark green forest eyes pierced mine in longing for understanding. Then, switching to Skyyan, she said, "And how can you understand my tongue?"

"We are one," Aquilla and I responded in Skyyan, reclining on the ship floor. Then, taking over, I said, "Aquilla is fluent in many languages, including Skyyan. I am able to understand and speak your language through him."

Egret cautiously sat down beside me, the look of confusion and contemplation painted on her elegant face but covered with a natural facade of confidence.

"If what you say is true," she continued, still in Skyyan, "then why did you lie? Why not tell your brother of the Dragon and let him give you aid to this godless island you speak of instead of abandoning us with no explanation? All you left in your letter was that you must 'leave Renborg,' which only provides us the knowledge that you are a coward who can't explain himself and simply chooses to flee from his duty."

Egret's words felt like a knife plunged into my feeble heart, twisting with the hurt evident in her voice. Even though we barely knew each other, the intensity of her glare betrayed that she abhorred being lied to; was this a familiar sorrow?

"Because Lucien wouldn't have let me go."

"And that was the only reason?"

It was primarily the reason, though there was a small part of me that felt I would've stayed if she asked me to, for my darkness towards her had already been too great, and the thought of openly abandoning her would only crush what little trust I had earned. If I could mar one less soul in this life, that would at least somewhat halt my consistent failings.

"No," I said, though without strength.

Egret's forest eyes widened in shock for a brief moment, as if understanding what I meant. Her eyes rescinded to the gentle yearning which she yielded in the library before, inquisitive of what lay beneath the surface of my own. In that moment, I was grateful she was here, for being with someone familiar as I ventured into the chaotic unknown was surprisingly relieving.

But these thoughts I kept to myself. Egret's eyes quickly snapped back into defense as the silence grew between us and I yielded no clarification.

"You know," she said, "I would almost believe you if you hadn't visited your lover, who needs something *novel* for her studies."

"What?"

The only word I could manage without breaking was dry, empty, devoid of life. How could she assume that I left for Karlata? And if so, why would she care?

Aquilla's swirling eyes widened in shock of her stinging remark.

"I was correct," he said.

"Excuse me?" Egret said.

Before any failure of a response could form within me, Egret made for the door in both fury and fluster.

"I will not partake in your foolishness! I shall return to Lucien to inform him of your shortsightedness and betrayal."

"Wait!" I said, feebly grabbing her wrist which she spun out of and attempted to smack me with, but her hand phased through my pain-stricken face.

"I do not deserve your forgiveness—"

"Absolutely right."

"Nor can I excuse my shame with Karlata—"

"You must have a *wise* teacher."

"Egret, *please*. Despite my many flaws, I cannot bear this journey alone, nor its surmounting burdens."

For a moment, a look of understanding passed between us.

"You have me," Aquilla said, red hues flourishing in his cosmic face. "Besides, Egret is the Queen of Renborg, and she does not belong to this adventure. Her place is with her husband."

"I am not a slave to that loveless boy!"

"Yet you return to him," I dared, the words painful but entirely true.

Egret was stunned by my remark, her mouth agape as she stumbled for a response.

"I return to him because it is of my own choice, and I have a duty to Renborg and my mother."

"A duty to be pampered like a child? What good will any of that be when he won't even look at you? Why not use your strength to help me truly save Renborg and her people, instead of waiting to be told what to do?"

Egret's scowl appeared only moments away from slapping me again. But before the temptation was too overwhelming, she resumed her stride to the door.

"So is this goodbye?" I said, fear choking my words.

Egret paused, looking down to the floor in thought. It felt like an eternity passed before us as she contemplated her fate.

"No. I just need some fresh air."

"They will throw you overboard if they see you," Aquilla warned.

Egret turned her glare to Aquilla. "I do not fear some Karthosian rebels, spirit."

"Egret, please… stay," I said.

Egret hesitated before the door. Fortunately, wisdom prevailed and she sat down again, albeit unpleasantly so.

"Very well. I will join you on your foolish quest, regardless of what your spirit friend says, for my mother will not be proud if I let our ally be crushed in the hands of Judux and his vorim Dragon, if what you say is true. And for the life of me, I will not sit idly by as your foolish brother's wife, waiting so desperately for her husband to relieve her of the slightest need by his impotent servants, only to watch helplessly as our empire falls apart."

A sigh of relief escaped me, along with a slight laugh.

"Thank Juva," I said.

"Morgan!" Aquilla said. "Do not utter that false god's name."

A smile threatened to grow from Egret's rosy lips as well, but she turned before it fully blossomed, mirroring mine.

And so our journey became of three.

Impatience began to slowly choke the dwindling hope that fought to stay aflame within me as we sailed to Valeneka, the nine days that it would take to reach the conquered lands of the Elves feeling like nine sols. Every day that passed by was another day closer to Judux's dark design, the fate of his spectral word unknown to us.

Judux's ploy was only kept off my mind with the relentless

training Aquilla had me do in our little storage room away from the prying eyes of the Merigold crew. Only Egret witnessed our activity as she mostly avoided being around her native enemies, thankfully working through some hand-to-hand drills with me that Aquilla guided us through so that I could receive realistic practice.

Even with Aquilla's phasing abilities, she was a terrifying sparring partner.

"Egret!" I yelped as she swept her left leg behind mine before Aquilla gave the cue so I could counter it, throwing me to the ground where I phased my head to avoid the wooden sting of embarrassment.

"How did you not sense that?" Aquilla said.

"I would say I'm sorry, but I'm not," Egret said, still favoring her Skyyan tongue when we spoke. She held out a hand to help me up, though obviously fighting a smile.

Much to her surprising dismay, I gave her my hand in a plea for help; only to phase as she began to pull me up, throwing her forward and off balance where I quickly laid my own leg for her to stumble and fall over, which she humorously did while expositing a few unsavory words.

"You sure take after the Karthosians for their trickery, Krabios," Egret said as she rose, reddened and flustered while trying to reinstitute a confident composure.

"Please forgive me, my Queen," I bowed, albeit slightly in a mocking manner while grinning at her perpetual effort to showcase her strength.

"You know, I can't decide if I am annoyed or pleased that you can speak with me in my native tongue," Egret said, readying herself for another duel.

"You wanted better communication between us, right?" I said, lunging to strike.

"You're beginning to understand the ways of a woman," she

said, effortlessly parrying my blow. "Though, you have much to learn!"

Aquilla was silent as he watched us spar, his thoughts increasingly kept hidden from me. I could feel him humming within, watching our every step, every word, ever carefully.

On the ninth night as we neared Valeneka, after another long, bruising, frustratingly constructive, yet humorous session with Egret, Aquilla taught me to write the word for fire before a rustic lantern.

"Look carefully into the small fire with my eyes, and you shall see the word which comprises it, which you must write to wield it," Aquilla said as we sat before the lantern.

For the longest time, my sight was only filled with the flame, but as I steadied my thoughts to Wyl into Aquilla's eyes, its name flickered brightly before me.

"Good," Aquilla said as I drew the name of fire in mid-air, the red essence of my Godstone necklace lingering before me and reflecting the name within the fire. The flame shivered as I touched its essence. "Now, Wyl the flame into your hand."

The bright fire danced slowly from its wick to my hand which wrote the Tongue of Tihrrvyith. Unsurprisingly, I was not burned.

"Interesting," Aquilla said, "there must be an explanation to your flesh and its idiosyncrasies to fire."

"Unfortunately, the only explanations were slaughtered by

Rolloc," I said, breathing the flame into my vibrating Godstone necklace. "This flame will be useful, though."

"Indeed, but for what purpose are you thinking?"

"To find Egret in the dark."

"She will return. We should stay here and continue to train."

"We've been training for hours," I said as I opened our storage room door. "I need to make sure she's alright."

"Morgan—" Aquilla began, but I refused to heed his command and submerged myself into the darkness of the hold.

"Egret?" I whispered, performing Wae to let the flame trickle to my fingers and rest in the palm of my hand, the sudden light piercing the sea of shadows which I hoped she would see.

"Use my sight instead!" Aquilla said, to which I did listen.

The flame wouldn't have mattered, for Egret was nowhere to be found in the hold of the ship through Aquilla's crystal sight lens. All I could see through his eyes were a mixture of Bludh sailors slumbering in their cots, with the occasional Nox sailor who slept peacefully despite their corrupt hearts.

"She might be on the ship deck," I said as we made our way up the stairs.

To my desperate relief, she was at the helm of the ship, unrecognizable to all else for the hood she wore. As we approached her, she was oblivious to our approach, focussing on chugging something from a green bottle before throwing it into the ocean.

Egret cursed under her breath, her fingers clawing into the railing in complete agitation.

"Egret?" I said, startling her.

"*Morgan*," she snapped as we joined her on the ship's railing, "what are you doing out here?"

Upon seeing my confusion, Egret composed herself, trying to regain her calm.

"I could ask you the same question," I said as we looked out to the starry sky that danced above the inky sea.

"It is unwise to be on the deck," Aquilla said.

"Most of the guards are asleep," Egret said.

"What were you drinking?" I said.

"It was just some water," she said quickly, her forest green eyes shining a deeper, denser green hue than normal.

Relenting for her sake of comfort, I declined to press further.

For the longest time, the three of us rested against the railing. Aquilla was somewhere in his own mind, thinking and pondering beyond my sight. As for Egret, her eyes were swimming in the sea of stars that glimmered above us. My heavy heart anchored my eyes to the aquatic graveyard that stretched endlessly before us. Though it was void of light, my eyes picked up the slightest movement of something bobbing from the waves.

Was it a Fiskan? It very well could be, as the water-breathing Averites tended to form their communities away from land, far from those who would hunt them. Underneath the waves was a mysterious and dark dungeon I would never explore alive and consciously, but maybe that was the point, maybe it was better that way—

"Does it amaze you that the stars grow in number every day?" Egret said, drowning my thoughts.

Following her gaze, I beheld the mesmerizing Void above.

"I never really paid much attention to them."

"The souls of the banished are there to serve as a warning," Aquilla added.

Egret was quiet for a while before she spoke again.

"I guess it feels different now."

"How so?" we said.

"I don't…" she began, but before the gates to her heart were fully closed, our eyes gently interlocked, and she eased her defenses. "I just wonder if my father rests in Solæf."

"What was he like?"

Egret's emerald eyes alit as if on fire with joy.

Before she spoke, Egret weighed her words carefully, until she could no longer hide how she felt. "Everything a father should be."

"Do tell, as I have no father to relate to."

"Well, I wish you would have had him for a father then. Even though he was King of Skyya and had most of his time consumed with politics, especially when those Karthosian scum rebelled, he would always prioritize time with me, even if it was just for a little bit of the day."

"What would you do?"

"So many things."

"Name your favorite."

"Hmmm. I would say Poecampi riding was probably my favorite thing he taught me."

"But you don't have gills like your Thallasiun guards do. Wouldn't you drown riding one of those sea horses?"

"Can you not hold your breath?" she said, her voice dripping with humor.

"I don't care much for swimming."

"A shame. You probably wouldn't like riding Poecampi then."

"It sounds horrifying," I said, a smile breaching my lips.

"What's horrifying is wrestling a krabourak to prove yourself after thirteen sols. Their slimy shell is abhorrently difficult to grab onto."

"I'm sure it wasn't too difficult for you."

"The Mother's wisdom refreshes you!" she said, my humor reflecting in her own smile which burst forth elegantly.

"It seems you were blessed with a true father, Egret. He raised you well."

"May he sleep in Solæf," Aquilla said.

"Thank you," she said, her joy now fleeting and resolving into her usual defense of stoic strength. "He was a great teacher, taken too soon. Thankfully his presence abides in my Poecampi."

"You have your own?" I said.

"Yes, my father trained me with him every morning before dawn. Just the two of us…"

"What was your Poecampi's name?"

"Palamaius," she said, her eyes and her words drifting and swimming far beyond the inky waves before us. "Though I fear he was slain by the Drakin in the invasion."

"We will find Palamaius once we've won, along with delivering your mother."

Egret labored a heavy breath before she spoke, her tone hardening like ice but displaying a familiar formality.

"Yes, we will make sure Nera is safe."

"Do not be fearful," Aquilla said. "Judux would be foolish to harm your mother and threaten himself with the Skyyan Navy."

"I do not fear for her," Egret snapped. "She is more resilient than you could ever dream to imagine. I doubt she would even hesitate to marry one of my younger sisters off to my *beloved* husband if we don't return from this reckless adventure."

Egret was silent as the night slowly sank away, leaving me to my ever-growing curiosity for her lonely yet steadfast spirit.

She was more familiar than I had realized.

"Egret?" I said, startling her from her melancholy.

"Yes, Krabios?" she said, looking at me once again.

"Do you hate Lucien?"

Egret turned sharply to me. "Hate? That is a strong word to use."

"You do not speak of him in kinder regards," Aquilla noted.

"That is because he does not speak to me at all, even in Ronic!" Egret said, shifting her glare to the Medjaib. "The most he has spoken to me were his vows. He speaks to you, Morgan, more than anyone else."

"That's different," I said. "We have been close since birth."

"Clearly."

"Just give him time," I pleaded. "Lucien is a good man, though willfully annoying sometimes, I admit, and difficult to understand. We've all endured so much recently, him most of all with the fall of his father."

"We've all lost someone," Egret said softly.

"Then you know what he's going through. He will warm to you in time, I promise. He just needs space to mourn his father and time to fully embrace the relinquished role of his fallen brother."

"You speak of Kyllian V?" she said, her tone softening. "I read that he fell during the rebellion of Rene."

"He did," I said, my words catching in my throat.

"You miss him too?" she said, her eyes pouring into mine.

Nodding, I looked away from her to hide the tears beginning to brim. "He was one of the best men I ever knew. He taught Lucien and I so much when we were younger. He was like a father to us in a way. We all believed he would be king. Everything was so much… warmer, in those days."

"I know what you mean," Egret said softly.

"You know, Lucien laments that Kyllian was not the one to marry you."

"I already know he despises me."

"No, it's because he believes Kyllian would have loved you better, as you deserved."

Egret was speechless at the revelation. We did not speak again for a long time as our ship sailed across the inky sea. Even Aquilla was silent beside us.

"Please don't tell him I said that," I finally said, returning my gaze to her. "He would be most upset."

"I won't, Krabios," Egret said, smirking.

"Egret?"

"Yes, Morgan?"

"Thank you for joining me. I—I'm glad you're here."

Egret smiled, truly letting her joy be known without any reservations. "It is... pleasant being able to speak to someone who can speak my tongue, who can understand me. I missed it." Perhaps realizing the vulnerability of her words, Egret quickly added, "I was tired of sitting around anyways. Besides, someone needs to make sure you don't get yourself killed on an island filled with sorcery and assassins."

"My thoughts exactly," I said, unable to stop the grin from spreading across my face as we looked out to the sea in peaceful silence.

But that peace soon washed away as my mind became more turbulent than the waves licking the ship; for land was soon approaching, and two problems emerged simultaneously to consume me in shadow:

We would be without money and ship to reach Cur Malum upon the morrow, and we were worlds away from Lucien, the only hope I had left for him left in the careful hands of Volsung.

Chapter 19
The Wolf Within

To settle for humanity is to enslave our potential, but to embrace the inner wolf is to be set free. The old morality devised by the weak only wished to restrain our nature, for they feared the rightful rulers of the forest and thought it unjust the natural hierarchy in which they found themselves inferior. Let us return, brothers, to the greatness we once enjoyed, for kings do not ask for permission; they take what is rightfully theirs.

Wild Heart: Untamed and Unbound
"Rumok Doctrine"
According to Jor Exos of Feralacum

The grand port city of N'ahl Juvara burst into view as our ship sailed through the towering monoliths of its eastern sea gate. Two opposing statues of the goddess Juva, standing at least two hundred feet tall, each upheld a handful of the golden narcotic beans famed for bearing her name. Though I was mesmerized by their grandeur, I couldn't help but notice Aquilla's obvious disdain, made quite evident by a startlingly odd rattling sound he speared at the towers as we passed underneath.

"Hashan Faen!" he hissed under his breath.

Intrigued by the apparent vitriol in what sounded like a curse, I turned my eyes back to him and said, "What is a Hashan Faen?"

Aquilla exhaled heavily. "Not *what*, but *who*: a false prophet who poisoned many minds with a twisted doctrine and an addiction to the undiluted spice of the juva bean some two thousand sols ago. The Elves of this Kapitolian province are fools to continue its false worship, and they will suffer the judgment in abandonment of the Mother and the god Valen who created them."

"What judgement is that?"

"To forever remain in the exact moment of their death, timeless in complete consciousness and pain, as they fully deserve."

The idea of such an eternal suffering was unbearingly atrocious, and pity found my heart for the Elves who were sentenced to such a fate, even for Sarrus Cilvahan who perished at the beginning of my shadowed doom. Was that what *sleepless death* alluded to in my unwanted destiny?

Not longing to devolve further into such bleak thoughts, I returned my mind to the present; however, I could not help the feeling that we were the fools for entering this foreign city with no money and no idea of how to reach Cur Malum.

I presumed the "fools" he was truly referring to were the largely Elven populace of Numeria, who had once created an empire founded on the profits from the exclusive trade of the juva bean, native to the northern Amahri Mountains.

The wealth was evident not only in the towering statues, but also the looming fortress above the city.

Elevated and walled over hundreds of feet high within the city was a great fortress, supported by a pyramid of ornately carved temples that spiraled pointlessly into the clouds. Despite such stunning glory, their ancient grandiose was smothered by their irrevocable conquest by the Kapitolians. Their bloody golden banners of a Kiagor dancing within were mockingly draped over every dry stone building, like decaying white flesh ladled with the fresh blood of defeat.

"We must be careful here," Aquilla said as the three of us descended the Merigold plank into the bustling market square, Kapitolian guards patrolling the populace with careful eyes. "Kapitol is zealous in its pursuit of slaves and control. They embody their ancestral Aldomhiric philosophy, 'Knowledge by stability, stability by strength.' We will not have the grace to make any foolish mistakes here."

Nodding to Aquilla's worries, I took in the foreignly oppressive surroundings.

Although I had read about the brutally swift and efficient Republic that controlled nearly all of Valeneka and most of Lakmana, Aquilla's words didn't fully sink in until we saw two terrifyingly tall knights towering over a finely dressed Elf. A slaver's carrack rocked behind them next to the pier, with a net in tow that looked to contain captured Poecampi.

Egret seethed in seeing her native sea creatures treated so harshly, the bones of her knuckles turning white as she squeezed her bag of belongings.

"May the Mother erase their stories," she whispered harshly.

Our passage through the bustling and finely dressed crowds became easier as the Elves and Kapitolian soldiers halted their trade and traversing upon sight of the heated exchange. As we drew closer, I could see why: the two knights draped in blackened steel and carrying bats with embedded Nox Godstone were Brutes.

"Who are they?" Egret said.

"They hail from the Order of the Black Rose," Aquilla said, his disdain evident in his words. "They are trained at the College of Man in hatred and malice, and they serve both Kapitol and the College."

"Are they not different entities?" Egret said.

"Not in their outward appearances."

Switching to Aquilla's galactic eyes, I could see underneath the frog helms of each knight, and their hearts were blacker than the Nox studded upon their Koba bats.

"You have failed us!" said one of the Brutes in a language that I presumed was of Numerian origin of Valeneka, threatening his Koba near the neck of the rich Elf. "Where are the other fifty Drakin we paid for?"

"We were interrupted by those damned Ra'sghalians!" the

cowering Elf said. "They took one of our ships as we fled Yar-ahm's shores, but we were able to instead capture some of the native Poec—"

The Elf's words were crushed as the Brute squeezed him with his blackened gauntlets, forcing the squirming Elf against the drystone wall.

"You have *failed* us for the last time."

Quickly turning to make sure Egret was safe, I was met only with air from where she was before. Panic ensued within as I searched desperately through the stilling crowds. Relief flooded me when I found her: she was descending quietly into the pier waters, making her way carefully and unseen to the net which held the Poecampi as the entire city seemed to be focusing on the increasingly deadly altercation. My heart immediately began to pound with anxious fear for her, but as her eyes caught mine, she raised a finger to silence and beckon me towards her.

I think Egret has found a ride to Cur Malum, I thought, making my way slowly towards her.

"Morgan no," Aquilla said. "We need to find a ship, not steal—"

But before I even took three steps, an ear-piercing boom rocked the market square, throwing the crowds into a panic. My head snapped to see the building crumble around the now headless Elf as the two Brutes stepped back from their carnage, blood and brains dripping from their Kobas. The repulsion from such needless death and the ease at which the Brutes delivered it was almost too much to bear, but I focused my attention on diving into the waters as chaos erupted around us.

"Quick!" Egret said, grabbing my hand and pulling me onto the slimy Poecampi that lunged forth from the now severed net that previously held it captive. Thankfully she used part of the net to create reigns for the sea horse; otherwise, I would have drowned then and there.

One of the Brutes noticed our apprehension of the Poecampi and roared, his hand a blur as he javelined his Koba at us.

Egret instinctively ducked and I phased my head just in time.

The Noxstone bat whistled through my face and exploded into the now decimated slaver's ship. To our great fortune, the Poecampi was swifter than the horse of an Akaidian, and we surged past the docks and even the city's towering sea gate before the debris of the desecrated ship could litter the waters.

Aquilla at last broke the silence once N'ahl Juvara was far behind and our hearts began to feel peace.

"That was extremely reckless, and this even more so. What if you lose control of the beast halfway across the sea? Do you expect to swim to Cur Malum?"

"I don't recall you offering any solutions to reach this island of assassins, spirit," Egret said, mastering the reins with ease to keep the sea beast from submerging us.

"It's Aquilla," he grunted with disapproval, but Egret was right. No matter how much I would loathe this wet and draining voyage by a Poecampi, it was our only ride to Cur Malum.

As I predicted, I hated our mode of passage to the island wrapped in mystery and shadow.

Every endless moment.

"You certainly did not inherit the Skyyan stomach for the sea," Egret accurately pointed out as I hurled what little remained in my stomach.

Again.

"I need to see something else besides the sea," I said, my arms shaking as I held onto Egret a bit more tightly, desperate not to fall off.

Aquilla wanted to say something, his thoughts reflecting upon how much food I ate in his eyes and its consequences, but he chose not to speak since we left the port.

Egret, however, cast a quick glance of concern back to me, only for her thoughtfulness to degrade into a humorous grin.

"Oh Krabios, one day I hope you come to visit my people. They would enjoy seeing your love for the sea."

"I'm looking forward to it," I trembled.

After a day of riding the slippery Poecampi and trying my best to squeeze my tiring legs to stay on, I was exhausted. Despite this, Egret seemed to be invigorated by the sea, empowered by the openness of the path before her. Even more perplexing was how she was able to sleep peacefully the first two nights we were at sea. The fear of drowning in the watery depths from falling off mid-slumber was enough to keep me restless and irritated when I attempted to sleep.

It was maddening to say the least. How I longed for dry land again.

Aquilla probably shared in my longing for land, but if he did, I could not tell, for he was largely silent as we rode for the three days we were at sea. I assumed it was because he was annoyed at both the plan of taking this sea horse to Cur Malum, and because of my avoidance of anything to discuss with him because of my waterlogged condition.

On the third night at sea, to remedy my cold and aching bones, I performed Wae on the flame within my Godstone, letting the little bright fire dance within my burned palms as we glided through the now inky sea of stars, my Godstone pulsating upon my chest quietly. The fire was a great relief to my skin which had only known the ocean for three days.

Egret turned to me, her eyes a lighter shade of green and painted with panic.

"Why is there fire in your hands?" she said.

Even the Poecampi turned its long neck towards me in surprise of the flame.

"It's very comforting to me, especially in the cold, lifeless waters."

"But how did you make the flames appear? Is this some magic the Ronians know? Or is this the Medjaib's doing?"

"Neither," Aquilla said, to which he succinctly explained the Tongue of Tihrrvyith. "It is a power as old as this broken world."

"And you will share in its broken fate because of its use," Egret said, her emotions uncertain with her back turned to me, but there was a familiar tone in her words that seemed just beyond my grasp.

"It's worth it," I said.

Egret took a steadying breath as she said, "Do you not fear the breaking of your mind and body?"

"The composure of one's body does not make one beautiful," I said, a slight smile resonating on my blued lips.

"I pray what you say is true."

As she spoke, I realized what the familiar tone in her voice was: sorrowful fear. Though it did not make sense to me, for what did she have to be afraid of? And why be aggrieved with sorrow? Her intellect and fearsome strength gave her no reason to fear or to be weary with sorrow, for what was I to her?

Whatever she feared, it eluded my understanding.

Strangely enough, what didn't escape me was a growing fear in Aquilla's spirit, though he declined to share it or even verify its existence when my subconscious pressed upon it, trying to find an elusive door to see inside; but I could sense it, though I knew not what it pertained to. It seemed that I was the only one who was truly threatened by the waters themselves as we traversed the dark seas that threatened to swallow us if our seafaring creature abandoned us.

Aquilla had been disgruntled at my lack of heeding to his advice, so it may have sprouted from that, but its dark fruits seemed to be much more ominous.

What did they both fear?

Unwillingly, I Wyled the flames back into my Godstone necklace; my spirit needed a break from this heavy gloom.

"Egret, Aquilla and I are going to Soul Sleep for a while, so don't be alarmed if we are temporarily unresponsive."

"What?" Egret and Aquilla both said.

"My body will remain with you, but our souls will be traversing the spiritual realm—"

"Morgan," Aquilla interrupted, "we should be present in case of danger on the seas."

"Egret's more than capable of ensuring our safety. Besides, I want to check on Lucien and make sure he is well."

"You can travel that far in your spirit?" Egret said.

"We can, but we mustn't Morgan—"

"Why not? Your reasoning eludes me, spirit. Before, you wouldn't let me because we needed to train before we left Renborg. Now, I see no valid reason to impede a quick flight in our souls to make sure Lucien is well."

"Morgan, I need you to trust me."

"I have been."

"No, your heart is still stubborn to my guidance. We must remain conscious in case of danger. We must be alert."

"Any pirates we encounter can easily be outrun by Egret and our faithful steed here."

"It is not what lies above the water that concerns me so. The deep holds more than mere fish."

"Then we will make it quick," I said, opening myself to Soul Sleep. "We will be back, Egret."

Egret began to protest, but my vessel collapsed onto her before she could.

"It shall not matter at this point!" Aquilla said as my soul's wings glittered above my body.

My eyes locked with Aquilla's, who watched me with the frustration of a parent beholding a disobedient child.

"What won't matter now, spirit?"

But the Medjaib was silent.

"Aquilla?"

My spirit soared across the ocean at the Medjaib's ominous warning, the waves a blur as the shadowy lands of Renborg soon emerged and were similarly a blur beneath us.

"What are you not telling me?" I yelled, my frustration bleeding with hurt at whatever he was hiding from me. "Is it about my brother?"

Aquilla's voice was heavy with guilt as he flew next to me. "Possibly."

"And what, pray tell, is it?"

"You shall see."

Aquilla's words were surprisingly painful in his delayed relaying to me; his purposeful hiding of my brother's lack of safety in his cosmic heart, for whatever good intentions he would manifest, were bitterly cold to my aching heart.

"What have you kept from me, spirit?" I could barely say as Hebsund came within sight, the Walls of Laconnia a distant yet ever-present menace.

"It was the only way."

"According to *who*?"

"It appeared wisest in memory of your repeated failure to listen to me in our most dire hours we have shared together."

"So to keep me from a destiny of Shadow, you concealed the truth from me, thus forcing that destiny to Lucien instead?"

"You would not have left had you known, and Lucien and all of Renborg would have shared a worse fate than yours if you persist to distrust—"

"Enough! Must you suffer me with your feigned reform? It

is you who persists in following in the footsteps of your controlling brethren!"

"I am nothing like—"

But Aquilla's half-hearted denial was silenced as we phased through the Halls of Hebsund into Volsung's Councilroom where I hoped to find Lucien.

Lucien was nowhere to be found.

Instead, warmly lit by hearth-light, we found a quiet and contemplative Volsung, his dirty blonde locks hanging over a crude but detailed map of Renborg, along with an even harsher map of Yarahm before his gaze. Wooden figures carved and painted with standards to represent their respective hosts of infantry and divisions of lanceliers dotted the map at what must have been strategic points. Renborg, surrounded by black figurines, still held green soldiers at its capital, though what I imagined were Judux's forces were growing more numerous around the city as they were reinforced from Yarahm.

As I drew closer to Volsung, I also noticed a crown with wings in the center of Hebsund.

The Councilroom door opened abruptly, causing me to jump. A servant whispered his apologies before rushing to Volsung, speaking inaudibly to Volsung, who nodded gravely at his words.

"Thank you, that will be all," Volsung said, motioning for the servant to leave at once as he returned his attention to the map.

Volsung sighed heavily, bowing his head into the palm of his hand before dropping back to his chair.

Aquilla stood beside me, and I turned to inquire if he heard what the servant said, but we didn't need to. Volsung plucked the wax crown from Hebsund and carefully placed it into Laconnia's capital at Ehlonica, along with a new piece which he pulled from his robe: a black Lycan's head.

"What is he doing?" I said, anger and fear confusing my mind. "Where is Lucien?"

Aquilla was treacherously silent like Volsung.

Spectral tears flooded down my cheeks as I launched through the walls with my aching wings. Desperation channeled the weakening strength of my soul in my search for Lucien, his room seconds away from my paranoiac flight.

Relief threatened to drown me when I stumbled into his moonlit room: Lucien was asleep in his bed, still in Hebsund.

He was safe.

Though as I knelt beside him, I could see he was not sleeping restfully, for in his hands were clenched my note and his matching Godstone necklace of the Tree of Truth. Soaking his sheets were tears that still drained from his swollen and shut eyes.

My harrowing tears drowned with his.

"Oh, Lucien!" I cried, my soul shuttering with shame and sorrow for abandoning him when he needed me most.

All his world had torn asunder, and his only brother was hundreds of miles away.

"I'm sorry for hurting you…"

Aquilla stood silent beside me, a monolithic mockery of the uncaring fate that befell me and Lucien. Though I could feel the cold throbbing within his own soul at the choice he made for us; it made little difference to the pain's resulting effect.

"I'm sorry, Morgan," Aquilla said, "this was the only way."

My spectral wings flustered in anger at his poor excuse, but as I turned to rebuke him, all words froze within me at the terrifying sight of the glowing amber eyes of a Lycan.

The Lycan was no manifestation of my mind.

The monster quietly pulled himself into Lucien's open window. The grey Averite, dressed in similarly colored and tightly fitted robes, towered at least three heads above me, leaving me breathless. Quickly and just as carefully emerged another Lycan, equally as fearsome in its towering stature, coarse black fur, and amber eyes dead set on Lucien.

A flash of pain erupted in my mind as I stood petrified at their arrival.

Aquilla's voice was drowned as I heard a deeper, more ancient and terrifying whisper ricochet through my tormenting mind:

Uwitheejuwik…

Lycan.

But there was something else ebbing from their Nox hearts as they creeped before Lucien's bed, and the whisper of the Tihrrvyith word penetrated my soul:

Laeyeth…

Complete Zeal.

Time to contemplate the dark mystery of these two Lycan vanished almost as quickly as they did, for the first beast smothered Lucien with his clawed hand and tossed him like a bushel of wheat to the other Lycan by the window, all within seconds. Before Lucien could even attempt a muffled scream, they had vanished into the night.

Lucien's matching Godstone necklace was the only thing that remained of him as it crashed, helpless and lonely, to the floor.

"Lucien!" I yelled, bursting through the window in pursuit.

The Lycan vaulted over Hebsund's walls and were soon at the edge of my sight, bolting incredibly fast across the plains. With every drop of strength within my weakening soul, I soared across the night in hopeless pursuit for many miles. But before I could reach them, Lucien and his captors were swallowed by the fog surrounding the Walls of Laconnia, the impenetrable Wolfwoods shielding them from both mine and Aquilla's sight.

"No!" I screamed helplessly.

Sleepless death…

All I could hear in my mind was the arachnid truth of Rolloc as Spindlers of shame devoured my will to live, my failure to save Sigmund and Lucien crushing my soul into the dirt, and I fell from the empty night in sorrow at the abysmal truth that began to infect me: Lucien was gone.

I had failed them all.

Chapter 20
Cur Malum

The thirty men who fought bravely with Cypherus in the Eldren Wars were known as the Companions of Cypherus, or, in Cypheric, as the Taldarii, who helped Cypherus lay the foundations of Renua. Cypherus' friends revered him as he fulfilled the prophecies spoken by the Morythia, seeing a holy man mighty in gifts; thus, they founded the Taldarii Order, swearing to guard Cypherus and his divine progeny, of whom would become the emperors of Cypheria.

Over time, the blood of Cypherus was seen as sacred by the Taldarii, who viewed the Cypherian emperors as more than mere men; thus, their doctrine grew just short of worship. Growing from a handful to hundreds, these carefully chosen protectors were revered for their skill of arms, stealth, political maneuvering, and espionage. They were granted access anywhere in the empire. Their presence was seen as that of the Emperor, and any harm that befell them was to be treated as an attack on the Emperor himself. They also carried some of his authority, and their presence in a foreign court was often seen as an act of protection by the empire over that state. All grew to fear and respect the Taldarii Order, and none opposed them.

Chronicles of Renborg: King's Edition
"The Taldarii Order: Origins"
Piluch Joffersun: Master of Histories

The fog of Cur Malum was thicker than my grief. Our Poecampi departed mournfully when Egret let the sea horse loose shortly after our arrival, allowing us to wade onto the silent beach before the arid mountains that were grey in the gloomy dawn.

The Kapitolian ships near the shoreline watching for pirates along the trade route were similar in their absence of sound.

It was too silent.

"I can barely see," Egret said in Skyyan, stopping for a moment in the sand to observe the fog-soaked mountains.

Initially, I assumed she was taking in the haunting view that befell us, but as I looked closer, I could see that she was shaking, her fingers squeezing into a fist as if to hold onto her strength.

"It is the Author's veil which keeps the island hidden," Aquilla responded in her tongue as we usually did whenever we spoke with her. "Though as to why She continues to protect a branch of the original Taldarii Order, I do not know."

"The Taldarii Order?" Egret said. "Was it not Cypherus who started that cult?"

"Indeed, though the founder of the Ora'sun sect was named Aela Zaeim, who fled to this island when the Taldarii were betrayed and hunted in Scissalan."

"And this is as close as we can get?"

"Yes, for the Temple is hidden deep within the desert mountains to avoid those who dare hunt them. If we get any closer, we will be met with ballistae."

"Are not those machines of war known only by Kaptiol?"

"The Ora'suns have been quite resourceful in their crusades, learning from all to do what is necessary."

My entire being raged within me to rebuke Aquilla for believing that what he did was necessary, keeping me hidden from my brother's demise so that I would not abandon this foolish quest for Cur Malum, but all of my strength was depleted after a sleepless night in agony. So in fuming silence, I followed behind Egret and Aquilla, the Medjaib leading the way into the foreboding mountains, the gloomy fog swallowing the sea behind us in a manner of seconds.

For three days, we hiked in the mountains of the desert. Though we were beyond exhausted, we were unable to sleep on the whispering island.

Before the island, Egret's and my banter in the evening was usually filled with questions about one another, filling the silence of the night with jovial inquisitiveness and the occasional mockery. But now, being clouded in vision kept us awake and silent when we rested, for we could barely see two steps in front of us from the all-consuming fog, and every little sound that echoed in the night provoked fear.

Egret, being staunch in her resilience to fear, attempted to conversate with me despite this. However, my mood was blackened by Aquilla's betrayal, and my responses were short, leaving her many times confused by my sudden shift in demeanor.

When guilt arose from how quiet I was to her, the memory of Lucien's captivity was quick to make me forget, replacing sorrow with anger and hopelessness.

Being largely without sight almost led to our quick demise as we were on the steep incline of the mountain path on the third day. A Feary nest glittered between two fir trees not a stone's throw from us, hauntingly beautiful as it caught my weary eyes. But lying cold beneath it was a corpse draped in strangely dark yet ornate gambeson, whose markings were foreign to me but evoked a sense of terror.

At the fallen warrior's hips were a dual set of wicked, short blades.

"What is that?" Egret said, but Aquilla held us up with his cosmic blue hand. "Were the lights responsible for that person's death?"

"Yes, which is why we must go a different path, lest we want to be frightened to death by those dark imitations of light," he said.

We carefully heeded Aquilla's advice to avoid the fate of the strange corpse and that of many children of Renborg who suffered in the alluring and evil tidings of the Ilyrien Woods.

The lack of sight only added to the feeling that we were being watched, for we were trespassing not on ordinary grounds. This was the voiceless maze of mist that the Ora'sun assassins thrived in to conceal their ambitious plotting. Gripping my spear tightly, I attempted to let Aquilla's eyes guide me through the fog, but it was just as obscure in his sight.

"The fog hinders both material and spirit," Aquilla said without my inquiry. "We shall not be able to Soul Sleep here. We must trust in the Author's promise that She 'shall inscribe your path clearly as a river carves the stone.'"

Despite my deafening silence to anything he said, I let my mind focus on Egret before me, her steps becoming more labored and tiresome as the day stretched quietly to night.

Egret was surprised when we came back to my body after Aquilla's betrayal before we reached Cur Malum, for though I spoke nothing, my silent tears said enough. She chose not to inquire of the suffering that Aquilla had bestowed upon me, and I was grateful for that. For though she could be abrasively honest at times, she knew when not to push when one was at their weakest.

Aquilla shared in my silence when I had scoured the thick Walls of Laconnia before returning to my body that night, which proved fruitless like my fate. The dense Wolfwoods revealed nothing despite my agonizing search. Though because of Volsung's treachery, I knew Lucien would be taken to Ehlonica, eventually at least.

And I knew the Lycan responsible were identified by their Nox hearts, full of complete zeal.

Laeyeth…

Anger seized my mind, but the waves of fear and doubt also began to clash against it: must all those near to me drown in my fate of Shadow? Was there zeal from the Mother to birth me a destiny of darkness that consumed all, saving me for last?

It seemed that I could not avoid this sleepless death that so perilously plagued me. There was still Philomela to save, for she was not yet consumed by the unknown fate in which Judux schemed with Thadius. However, that fate came closer with each passing second.

If only I could see Philomela again, my soul would take renewed flight.

To know that she was safe, to know that I was not a failure.

The weight of my afflicted soul dragged me at last into the dry path of the eerie mountainside where I sat motionless.

"Morgan," Egret said, halting our climb to sit beside me.

Egret's voice was soft and gentle, and her face, which glowed in the dim sunset, seemed relieved to pause this enduring excursion, for her breath was shaking as if she were beyond exhausted.

"Morgan, what happened the other night?"

My bloodshot eyes grappled with her faint green irises. Genuine care rested within them. She could be trusted.

"Why not ask the *Medjaib*?"

"Morgan," Aquilla said, "forgive me at last for keeping it from you. We need the Ora'suns—"

"You didn't even give me the chance! We could have ensured he was safe before we left!"

"You would not have left—"

"You are *just* like the other Medjaib in your lust for control!"

"Morgan…" Egret said, weakly.

Aquilla's galactic eyes were huing red with fury.

"You *need* my guidance if we are to—"

Our words were cut short by Egret, who, crashing into the arid path, revealed the veins of her quivering scalp to glow a sickly, faint green.

"Egret?" we said, to no response.

~

Egret didn't arise until the morning three days later, all of our progress lost in the exhaustion we had previously tried to endure. Seeing her move again steadied my heart, but she was a shadow of her former strength. Her words came as forced and weak, her eyelids heavier than the pull of a Delphian bow.

"Morgan..." she said, her eyes strangely a pale blue in the campfire I had created with the Tongue of Creation.

"Egret, what happened?" I said in Skyyan, handing her some of the last rations we had to regain her strength.

Aquilla observed in silence from the corner of our makeshift camp beneath an overhang of the mountain that was nearby where she fell. We had spoken nothing to one another after she fell, but in determined prudence, we had trained nonetheless while she slept, for we were at the mercy of the hidden Ora'suns, wherever they were.

"I... I am unsure," she said, scarfing down the piece of bread I gave her with shaking hands. "I think... I was exhausted from riding the Poecampi for three days without rest."

Though that most certainly contributed, I could see something else that weighed her down when she tried to push herself off the floor but failed at the strain, her eyes no longer green but a sickly blue.

"Egret, please tell me what's going on. Something is affecting you; I can see it in your eyes. They're no longer green."

Moving closer, my hand unknowingly held her hand to comfort her tired soul.

"Morgan, I am married," Egret whispered, slowly withdrawing her hand from mine.

"Forgive me," I said, looking away in shame. *What am I doing?*

"It is well. It's just—" she tried to say, tears bursting from her eyes. "I am weak..." she said, her words hardly pushing through her torment of tears. "All of my life I have been so... *pathetically* weak! And now... *now* you see the truth of it."

"Egret, we are both exhausted by our journey, and so much has happened—"

"*No*, Morgan, you lack understanding," she said, sitting up and reigning in her tears. "I was born with an illness that eludes all understanding and healing. From the time I was born, I had to have the most insufferable servants do everything for me, from feeding to washing, while my sisters got to train and play whenever they saw fit. I was helpless, Morgan. If not for the pity of my father, I would still be this way, and in fact, my body is returning to its pathetic state without the medicine he helped find for me to make me strong."

The memories of seeing Egret drink the mysterious green bottles throughout our journey came flooding back to me.

"What was it?" I said.

Egret looked down like one who was undeservedly beaten.

"It was… dedrim sap."

Aquilla burst from his quiet observation to interject.

"You've been drinking from those wicked trees?" he said, swiftly moving to us. "Do you not know the darkness within those lost souls?"

Enraged, I shot Aquilla with a look of frustration, both physically and mentally, but Egret deflected his criticism with her resolve.

"It was the *necessary* cost," she said, her mirroring words silencing Aquilla's rebuke.

"So," I said, not knowing what to say in the silence that followed, "what happens now?"

"I'm sorry, it… it was a mistake for me to come. I will be frail and useless, a burden to you on this journey. Though, my hair will finally grow back while I am without it. So the Mother blesses me even in the darkness."

A smile seeped its way to her cracked lips as she spoke about her hair, and a surprising pain found its way into my heart to hear how she so longed for it as if she thought she wouldn't be beautiful without it. It was joyous to see her smile, to see her soul peeking through her fair eyes as she dreamt of a fate more caring than this one. Without realizing it, my eyes slipped into Aquilla's. My thoughts became gently consumed by her, by the bold courage of her heart despite her condition.

Like the Lycan, I began to see and hear her soul's name through the quiet Tongue of Tihrrvyith that seemed to slowly be invading my mind:

Oohitheekleea…

Woman.

But there was more to Egret than just being a woman, and I could see it ever slowly, ever more, every day that she was with me. I could almost hear the words of the ancient tongue that described her soul perfectly.

"You are the furthest thing from a burden to us, Egret," I said, "and you do not need a drug to be strong."

Egret looked askance, as did Aquilla.

"It is… comforting to not be alone in this burden," she said, her words ending from her lips but lacking any finality to them as if there was more she wished to say.

But the weariness of the withdrawals dragged her eyelids down with exhaustion.

"I hate that I have hindered your quest," she barely uttered.

"You have not. I will carry you myself to the Ora'suns if I must."

"You will do no such thing!" she said, struggling to her feet in an attempt to ward off any sight of helplessness.

As she rose, her body threatened to fall until she grabbed me again for support.

"The secrets of the Ora'suns are many," Aquilla said. "They may be her best chance at recovering her strength. But we cannot linger here if we are to find them. Our time is running ever so thin while Judux and Thadius's plans continue to progress."

"Then let us go forth," I said, my hope weakened by Egret's suffering but strengthened by her will.

What rekindled hope we had in Egret's recovery was soon extinguished in our resumed journey through the impossibly thick mountains of fog of Cur Malum.

Ten weary days and sleepless nights had passed in the now whispering darkness that surrounded us. Though as we delved deeper into its shadows, we encountered more signs of life, particularly flickering lights in the distant caves and evasive, Elven sheep herders who scurried quickly away from us. At times when it was quiet, I could swear to hear an incoherent chanting in the wind, sending shivers down my spine.

Even stranger than the unknown tribal Elves, an abnormally large and dark raven flew nearby, which had begun following us on our second day.

"We must not let our guard down," Aquilla said, who kept a careful eye on the bird as we hiked in the arid mountains, "for though the Mother protects the island with Her mist, many evils have hidden themselves in Her covering."

Evil indeed used the covering of the fog to remain concealed, for though I tried several times to pierce through the thick veil with Aquilla's eyes to glimpse at the raven which seemed to stalk us, it proved fruitless each time. It was impossible to determine its corruption from afar, but a safe guess was that it was.

Though our progress was significant into Cur Malum, it

came to a depressing halt as Egret collapsed again later that day, nearly slipping from a mountain ridge that would have had her impaled on the arid forest floor hundreds of feet below us. Egret's eyes were relieved as I caught her, as was my heart, for that grave misfortune would have been too much to bear. In light of this, or in its darkness, we decided to finish our journey for the day, though it had only just begun.

"You've never told me much about your mother," Egret said as she sat down along the mountain path, obviously wanting to talk about anything besides her condition.

Aquilla was silent as he watched us.

"There isn't much to speak of."

"Did you not know her before she returned to the Mother?"

"She died in childbirth," I said, the words callous and unfeeling. "Though, she chose to give birth to me, knowing its cost."

"A sacrifice only few would make," Egret said, her words becoming slower. "Many would trade everything in the world to have a mother that so loved her child as yours did."

Egret's words were heavy, her eyes looking away from mine as if she was speaking to herself for a brief moment.

"What was her name?" she said, her eyes closing heavily.

"Joanna."

"Joanna," Egret said, a soft smile blooming before she entered into a deep sleep against the wall of the mountain.

It pained me to see her so fragile and tired, curled softly as a dove resting in its nest, though beaten from the winds of fate.

Egret… *deserved* a gentler life, and it hurt to witness destiny's denial of it.

"As Egret said, it was a mistake to allow her to come with us," Aquilla said, breaking my thoughts.

I will not abandon her as you tricked me into doing with Lucien! I thought, rage fueling the venom of my mind. *And she is far more caring than you, thinking more of me than herself, unlike you.*

"Morgan," Aquilla said, his galactic eyes closing in frustration, "I did not want to keep that from you, but—"

You had to, or so you say. I know your excuse, Medjaib, and I do not believe it was necessary.

"Morgan, pulling against one another will only aid Thadius' plans with Judux, whatever they might be. We must stand together if we are to slay Belial."

Turning away from Aquilla, I cast my eyes down into the fire which I prepared to keep Egret warm. Though I did not want to look upon the face of my betrayer, I could see the galactic swirls of Aquilla's face from the corner of my sight. His sadness was evident in his golden blue hue as he looked upon me, my feelings of betrayal completely exposed to him.

Before Aquilla could offer me more of his *guidance*, I sat myself down beside Egret in preparation for Soul Sleep.

"What are you doing?" Aquilla said as my soul fluttered from my earthly shell. "You know we cannot find the Temple because of the Eternal One's covering."

"I'm not looking for it," I said, propelling myself through the blinding fog that soon consumed me, from which we were only freed once we emerged closer to the Void above.

Looking below, Cur Malum appeared only to be a cloud consumed by the uncaring sea.

"I want to look for Lucien while we wait for Egret to recover," I said, desperate to see if he was still alive.

Remembering the small crown Volsung had placed in the center of Laconnia, I figured it could not have been a mere chance that it fell directly onto the capital at Ehlonica. It was, after all, the largest and most populated city of the Confederation, and it would serve well as the place to hide something one wished not to be found.

Aquilla said nothing as he silently acquiesced to my desire, though it did not matter if he would have, for the search was just as fruitless as before, maddeningly so.

The city of Ehlonica was too large to search thoroughly. Its relatively new architecture and buildings stretched high and proud midway upon the river Parnaxos; even if there existed no maze of structures, the tens of thousands of its largely Lycan residents made it nearly impossible to find the exact two who had kidnapped Lucien. Aquilla's eyes phased into mine to siphon through the crowds, yearning to see the word for complete zeal in their hearts.

But it proved futile.

"Morgan," Aquilla said, hesitation steadying his words, "we should return to Cur Malum, for it is unwise to be in Soul Sleep if something were to find us."

My flight stopped just above the sprawling meat market, where hundreds of merchants selling various meats were met by thousands of Lycan purchasing animals who hadn't even been skinned from the hunt. They were hungry, desperate for more meat that became increasingly sparing with their expanding populace.

They needed strength to persevere.

"I need to see Philomela before we return," I said, turning from Ehlonica to ascend the clouds.

"There is no time for that!" Aquilla said, following after me. "We have searched for hours, Morgan."

"Seeing her safe will give me the strength to deny this unwanted and unknown fate of Shadow."

Aquilla began to say something, but I silenced whatever it was by my aerial departure to Renborg.

It wasn't long before the familiar lands of Renborg came to pass below us, its cherry-rich Bludhlands bathed in shadow from the shadowed clouds above. There would be no storm, but a gloomy wind would thicken the air with its somber melody. The heaviness of my soul obscured my mind that I almost didn't notice the soldiers surrounding the farmhouse that overlooked the vast farmlands and fields of Brännfält. Instead, my eyes were drawn to the fields of steel themselves.

There appeared a sea of glittering spears and armor.

Opposing the Ronians, the Drakin stood fearless. Though smaller in number, they faced the Ronians with no hint of timidity.

"We are running out of time," Aquilla said as we landed near the Ronian leaders by the house, their forest green cloaks billowing roughly in the wind. "The war has already spread."

Aquilla's words fell deaf on my ears as I gazed in awe upon the familiar Ronian commander and his spruce mustache.

"It doesn't make sense," Lord Kolstok said as he poured over a map of the battlefield surrounded by several Knights of Kyllian. "Why do they not retreat? Judux is a fool to think they stand a chance against our cavalry in the open fields. He should know he's outnumbered and outmatched."

"My Grand Kriga," one of the Sektors said breathlessly as he galloped up towards the meeting, "their infantry have begun to advance."

"What of their cavalry?" Kolstok said while climbing onto his armored steed.

"Their left has started to advance. Their right flank, however, does not press forward… but—"

"But what?" Kolstok said curtly.

"They're just kicking dirt into the wind," said the confused Sektor.

"They seek to conceal their movements on their right through the haze," Kolstok said, turning to the only other familiar face whom I was relieved to see. "Marshal Mathis, you are master of my left wing. You must be vigilant but patient.

The Drakin may have added to the strength of their right wing, but be not dismayed. Kriga Kelmont shall aid you with his cavalry once he's overtaken their left as planned."

"Do you understand Judux's move?" I said, turning my gaze to the first flank of the Drakin who marched fearlessly through the wind-swept fields of grain, their flames for hair a glowing fire that boldly threatened to consume the Ronians.

"Judux is either foolishly brave or he is trying to conceal something we are not prepared for," Aquilla said, his spirit pointing towards the growing cloud of dust created by their right flank of zealously stomping cavalry.

There was only one reason I could guess for his boldness, and it made my heart weak at the very thought.

"Kriga Kelmont," Lord Kolstok said, addressing the seasoned general next to him. Kelmont's chest proudly hosted a Golden Rose of Valour pinned to a red sash leveled across his breastplate. "Order our right flank of Lanceliers to engage the Drakin left flank when our center line of infantry meets theirs. And make sure our concealed infantrymen behind our cavalry stay hidden; they are paramount to your success! Once we've cut the wings from their shoulders, their backs will be completely open to our lances."

"Yes, Grand Kriga!" Kelmont said as he mounted his horse to relay the commands to the army below.

"Take heart, my friends!" Lord Kolstok said as he addressed the remaining officers and mounted men of his personal guard. "Today you shall be the hand of justice that avenges our fallen King. They have sacked our fair lands and slaughtered our noble people, but I say no more, for the day of their reckoning is nigh, and the hour of our bitter steel is about to bite!

"Indeed, I wager not one of them that lie in the valley before you shall see home again; so confident am I in the strength of our arms and the will of the men who hold them.

Go forth then, and by the Mother's Will, break asunder these interlopers!"

With that, he reared his horse and roared, "For Renborg! Long live King Lucien!"

"Long live King Lucien!" roared back the galvanized officers of Renborg.

Even amid chaos, Servillius's commanding presence, if just for a moment, stilled my fear. His words carried such gravitas that I thought even a mouse would feel bolstered with courage enough to face an army of elephants. I had never seen him on the battlefield before, but as I watched the tender old man I had known all my life mounted atop his magnificent war horse, he transformed into something out of legend.

Reinvigorated with life, as though he were in his prime once more, Servillius's every move seemed like those of a man twenty sols younger.

There bloomed a hope that the Grand Kriga's words would be fulfilled.

Upon examining the field displayed before Lord Kolstok, I could see how he intended to crush the Drakin's right flank of cavalry with his own.

The subsequent charge from the right flank would then take the Drakin infantry from behind once they crushed their army's left side. And there was no doubt in mind that they would be able to do so, for Renborg was renowned for the discipline and skill of its lanceliers, something Piluch had often drilled into Lucien's and I's studies. Even with the fearless Drakin, who showed no sign of hesitation, thirty thousand against forty-five thousand were mountainous odds for any army to overcome.

"Brilliant," Aquilla said, to which I could not deny.

"Agreed. Though, something seems off…"

"I sense it as well," Aquilla said, "for wisdom and smaller forces would prove wiser to avoid the open fields and remain in

Renborg's capital. The only reason they would meet them out in the open is if they…"

"If they what?" I said, but my words were drowned in a tormentous clashing of steel and blood as the armies vehemently collided; the music of needless, sleepless death a violent, melodious reminder of the shortness and bleak disparity of life that befell before us.

"Let us hope I am wrong," Aquilla said, soaring to the darkening clouds above without warning, to which I followed with bated breath.

"Aquilla?" I said, but Aquilla's fears sliced through the clouds before us.

Like a fish's silhouette beneath the water, a large crimson shadow the size of a small trade vessel slithered in concealment behind the clouds and moved with ferocious speed.

"*Belial*," Aquilla said as we were held captive by its thunderous shadow.

What shattered our spell was when the young Dragon's scaly red back peeked through the clouds for a brief moment. I could see that it was ridden by an even crueler monster who straddled between the spikes of the serpent's wretched spine.

"Rolloc," I said, venom flooding my mouth.

The vile hatred I had for him soon soured ever more as I realized what purpose the Dragon had been serving for Judux: the abomination had clear sight over the Ronian formations and could just as easily inform Judux.

"Judux shall know of Kolstok's deceit," Aquilla said, which I could now grimly see.

"The dirt being kicked up is concealing a larger reserve of infantry amongst the cavalry," I could barely say.

"He seeks to mirror Kolstok's tactic. They shall surely overwhelm the Ronian's weaker left!"

"We need to warn Kolstok!" I said, turning from the oncoming slaughter and looking desperately for the Grand Kriga beyond the right wing cavalry and concealed infantry who charged through the brittle crop fields, the significantly smaller Drakin force of lancers awaiting them as bait before the crops.

But it was too late.

Liquid fire erupted from the clouds of death as Belial descended upon the helpless Ronians. Hundreds were instantly incinerated in the fiery heat of the young Dragon's wrath as it focused on the Ronian infantry hidden behind the cavalry.

The still charging Ronians were immediately thrown into chaos, horses trampling over one another from the sudden terror thundering from the clouds as orders to halt their advance left them in disarray. They were hopeless prey before the Drakin lancers who charged forth to skewer them in their disorganized chaos. No avenue of escape lay open to them as burning stalks of men desperately pressed from behind and the merciless charge of the oncoming Drakin was soon at hand.

With no choice left but to fight to the bitter end, a shocked but resolute Kriga Kelmont raised his lance and reordered what remained of his burned and bloodied divisions onto their death. Kelmont was the first unto the fray, and very soon, upon meeting the charging horde of Drakin lancers, he too met his end, the uncaring hand of destiny trampling his valiant efforts and crushing his life from his bones.

I wished my eyes could not see as well as they did.

"No!" I screamed, uselessly watching the Ronians' swift demise.

Countless Ronians were not gifted an immediate death in the Dragon's flames. My stomach churned in seeing some of the dying Ronians crawl voiceless from the burning carnage, unable to scream as the smoke consumed them. Others who could scream pointlessly pulled off their blazing helms from their smoking flesh before collapsing into cinders.

The fate of their burned flesh mirrored mine.

I felt empathy too great and too sorrowful for words in my weeping heart in seeing the Ronians suffer without purpose, redemption, or justification.

"We have to do something!" I said, helplessness dousing my words.

"There is nothing we can do," Aquilla said, the wind sweeping carelessly through him.

My eyes wept uncontrollably as we watched from above. The sight of my soul became like Aquilla's as I watched those who suffered before us, the souls of the departing drifting towards the Void above to be judged.

One soul took me by surprise, and he belonged to the Drakin fighting along the frontlines. The Drakin's heart was Bludh red but surprisingly tinged with Klyr purity as he fought surrounded by a special guard of Drakin spearmen.

"Advance the right wing cavalry!" the warrior yelled in Drakonnian, his Gyldur braided flaming hair and richly adorned battle armor distinguishing him as a leader.

"As you command, General Kesch!" said one of the spear Drakin, pulling out of their ringed formation to deliver the command.

Judux's plan became painfully clear at that moment.

"They're going to funnel them into the flames—"

"And rain fire from above," Aquilla finished, reading my mind with horror as we watched Belial swiftly loop in the sky to return another barrage of flaming doom.

Without thinking, I propelled my soul's wings to launch myself into the sky.

"Aquilla, make me visible to Belial alone!" I said as Aquilla hastily followed me to the sky.

"Are you foolish? Thadius shall surely know of us if his pet sees us."

"I'd rather bear that fate than let more suffer under this cruel fate of Shadow."

"We shall only delay the inevitable!"

"No, we will give Kolstok more time to recalibrate. Do it!"

With deep hesitation, I felt Aquilla make my appearance from the spiritual realm visible to the material world.

Belial flapped his wings to a stuttering halt in sight of me.

"Who dares stand before Belial the Meaningless?" Belial roared in Shiveric, its voice deep and penetrating in my mind, images and feelings of horrid emptiness flooding my soul in the peculiar Dragon language. "Are you some Fhaolin who comes to taunt my existence?"

Belial's ruby eyes of fire burned into my soul, the slight squint from its scaled eyelids indicating that it already knew the answer but was perplexed nonetheless. The torrent of war below drowned out Rolloc's frustrated screams at Belial as the hybrid was oblivious to our conversation.

"I am no Averite like yourself," I said. "But I come to question your motives, not taunt you."

"Hmmm," Belial hummed, its thunderously large wings shuddering the air with each consistent flap to keep itself afloat beneath the darkening clouds. "You taunt me yet with your deceit, for I can see the fire in your eyes."

Confused by the Dragon's words, I pressed on.

"And what do you see in yourself, Belial?"

The Dragon cringed and bore its teeth, the brief glimpse of its ivory fangs a horrifying sight as it closed its eyes in pain.

"Clearly less than you, for you know my name, strange one."

"I know a destiny of Shadow was forced upon you which you did not choose, yet you carry it out with such fervor against those who are your brethren."

Belial snorted its nostrils in apparent frustration.

"You think I have a choice, strange one? Your mind speaks

true in my unwanted fate, for I did not want to be a monster. But there are only two paths before me, and I will do what is *necessary*."

Has Lord Kolstok moved?

"Yes," Aquilla said, "he has moved the reserve troops to the thin centerline of the Drakin forces. Keep stalling the Dragon!"

"That does not excuse you from destroying the Ronians!" I continued. "Why do you serve Judux, who thrust this fate of darkness upon you?"

"*Serve* Judux? Sh'eol is a *god* that is to be served!" Belial's fiery eyes twinged and distorted before shaking its head in frustrating confusion. "No! I am Belial! I am in control! It is Thade who I revere, who gives me purpose. I will not serve this pretender, despite its cost!"

"Then tell me, Belial, why do your thoughts not align with your will? Why do you continue to bend the knee to this Judux who is not a god? Do you fear him more than Thade?"

For a moment, the Dragon looked afraid at the mention of Thade, and in that hesitation I could see an innocence that threatened to reveal itself behind the scales of the monstrosity that strangled it.

But that innocence suddenly melted into a tormented rage.

"*Judux*… he is only his puppet!"

As the Dragon hissed its words, flames spewed from its mouth upon me in sheer anger. I flinched from being completely consumed by the fire, but I was unaffected in my spiritual form. The Dragon withdrew from its molten fury after several seconds had passed, but upon seeing my unharmed form, it continued its intent of destruction, this time long enough to melt a castle. But as I knew it would, the Dragon's flames began to sputter in its force, first dwindling in its power like a dying fire until it was nothing more than a flickering flame smaller than a candle.

The Dragon had depleted its fire for today; yet another reason I was thankful for Piluch's history lessons.

Belial unleashed a horrendous roar, and the battle was halted briefly in fright.

"Deceiver!" the Dragon screamed.

"Belial!" Rolloc roared from behind the Dragon's neck. "Have you gone deaf—"

Belial snapped backwards to bite him but stopped within inches of Rolloc's face. The Dragon appeared to be held frozen in its retaliation, unable to move as Rolloc turned to look down to the battlefield below. Following his gaze, I could see Judux standing with arms raised before a Nox symbol that glowed from one hand while the other aimed at Belial; Judux's hand curled as if he were clutching Belial.

Belial's wings crumpled as he was unnaturally dragged down to the battlefield with Rolloc emotionlessly in tow. Judux seemed to be pulling in the Dragon, though much strain was visible upon his grimacing brow, along with an ever-darkening shadow on his eyes from the Nox symbol before him.

"How is he doing that?" I said, my mind scrambling to understand how Judux controlled him.

It almost looked as if he were performing—

"Wae," Aquilla said. "He is manipulating the Dragon as if we were manipulating water; bending the Dragon to his will, controlling the ocean that once threatened to drown him."

"That was the name of Belial's soul," I said, understanding now the strange symbol that Thadius had shown to Judux, which was now used to force the Dragon to the ground before himself.

"Kneel before your lord!" Judux screamed, anger fueling his words as he forced the head of Belial into the field before his feet.

"As you *wish*," Belial slithered in forced obedience.

"The vermin almost slew me," Rolloc said, sliding off the Dragon's back.

"And so shall Belial never act in such a way, again," Judux said. "You will be brought to heel since there exists no trust between us. If you dare disobey again, I will pull you down from the skies. And if the idea to cross me passes through your tormented mind, you will bring death upon yourself."

At Judux's words, Belial began to writhe before him. A dark and twisted red wisp began to emerge from Belial's chest, causing the Dragon to roar in pain as it could do nothing to stop him. Judux grimaced as he took the soul of Belial and fed it into his heart before he twisted his hand that held its soul, as if tying it together.

"If I die, you shall immediately suffer the same fate," Judux whispered as he knelt before the Dragon before releasing the ancient symbols which vanished.

Belial's scales shivered from being released. A sudden hatred glazed the Dragon's eyes as it looked at Judux, mixed with loathing and pain. It was a look that eerily reminded me of how I looked at Gulmund when he forbade me to die.

"Do not place all of your trust in the idea that I wish to live," Belial said before launching back into the winded skies.

Judux said nothing as he glared at the departing Dragon. Turning to Rolloc, he said, "You do not seem surprised, brother, by my power of the fell beast."

Rolloc betrayed no emotion as he stood still beside Judux. "Your knowledge eclipses me, brother. But it seems even this will not be enough to stay the Dragon's wrath. You will have to be awake at all times to ensure it doesn't attempt to end its life in retaliation."

"Indeed," Judux said, his hand gripping his chin in deep reflection, his molten face paling ever slightly.

"Come, let us return to Cur Malum," Aquilla said as he ascended back into the sky, which I begrudgingly followed. "We have served our purpose here, and now we know of Thadius' scheme. The enemy has granted Judux complete control over Belial's soul. There is a chance that, in time, Belial will rebel, ending both of their lives. But we cannot trust in such a future premise nor chance the lives of many more being wasted in the Dragon's wrath. We must ensure victory ourselves by claiming the Klyr spear."

I hung my head low in acceptance of Belial becoming ever more inscribed into the Shadowed fate I was burdened to endure, in which it was guaranteed that I would have to slay it.

As we began our journey back to Cur Malum, I couldn't help but glance upon the battlefield.

The Ronians held their ground as they covered their retreating forces, much to my relief. Their ensured escape, a costly one for the Drakin, was an ever-increasing possibility despite the flameless Dragon's barrages which resumed its plight against them.

Despite this, the Drakin General Kesch endured with his soldiers along the centerline. The Drakin only held on by the encouragement of their relentless General who parceled out his elite guard to wherever the battle line was most critical.

Though I hated to admit it, there was an honorable bravery in the General, one which held revered purpose that I envied despite our opposing sides. He fearlessly placed himself at great risk by limiting his own protection in pursuit of a worthy victory.

Instead of risking the lives of others, he risked himself. And for the life of me, I couldn't help but watch in wonder.

"What are you waiting for?" Aquilla said, but my words were cut short when an arrow pierced the General's calf, followed swiftly by the sword of a Ronian nobleman cleaving a fatal gash in his neck while he valiantly held the thinning Drakin front line.

"For Yarahm!" the General roared, but another arrow penetrated his horse's neck, to which he was crushed underneath in the following crash.

The General was spared from the ensuing carnage that would have trampled him by the five Drakin guards who dragged him out quickly, far against the General's will. Though, three of them fell to spears and arrows in the effort to save their beloved General.

"My sons!" the General screamed, molten tears streaming down his horrified face as he was laid to rest outside of the battle before us.

Two younger Drakin came rushing over to weep beside him, and there they held him and wept.

"Father!" they cried, hopelessly trying to stop the gash in the General's neck from bleeding.

"It is well, Jeshum, do not worry my son," the General said. "Ephraeos, as eldest, I relinquish my authority over our soldiers to you. You will let your father die with honor. Win this war for our family! Do you understand?"

Ephraeos nodded while holding back his own tears.

"Good," the General said. "I will hold on with every ounce of strength to hear of our victory. Then I will let myself rest."

Both sons wept at his words.

For a moment, I forgot they were Drakin.

"Go, my sons. Bring us peace at last for our families."

But their intimate exchange was interrupted by a sharp pain that stabbed my groin, breaking my heart's transfixion.

"That must be Egret," I said, my physical body exploding with pain from far away. "Why did she have to hit me there?"

"Either she has become strangely fond of you, Krabios," Aquilla said, "or she is in danger. Come, we must go!"

Chapter 21
Trial of Beating Hearts

The Taldarii Order was fractured when the last true Cypherian Emperor, Amon I, died. Amon II was recognized by some of the Order to be the rightful heir but a bastard by the rest. When the child King was slain at the hands of Krixus Navarrian, a choice was forced upon the Taldarii: side with Navarrian or Atreus. Both were recognized as usurpers, but the Order was without unity as to which usurper was more justified. As a civil war unleashed upon Cypheria, so did the Order face a bloody division. Underneath the grander civil war, a silent war of assassinations and espionage broke out between the Taldarii. Amidst the war of shadows, each faction struggled to find a true heir where none truly existed anymore.

After the usurper Atreus lost a crushing battle, he fled into the far reaches of the empire to gather support. However, his efforts failed when he was found and cut down by the Navarrian members of the Order. Those of the Order who had stood with Atreus were similarly hunted down or attempted to create new sects that later died from lack of purpose. The Taldarii Order thus survived, but it was a shadow of its former self. The Taldarii strove to serve the new emperors, building new cults around the bloodlines of the Navarrian dynasty and those that followed. Still, the Taldarii always knew their honor had been besmirched with the blood of their own brothers.

Chronicles of Renborg: King's Edition
"The Taldarii Order: Evolution"
Piluch Joffersun: Master of Histories

We were too late.

Upon our frantically swift return, we arrived to see Egret and myself bound in rope, carried into the fog by men of shadows.

My heart broke in seeing Egret: she was pale and lifeless, no different than a corpse.

Had we been a second later, I'm afraid we would have lost the darkly robed men who carried us, their footsteps as quiet as the Void as they traversed the silent fog of Cur Malum. The only reason I could see their faint outlines was because of their dark blue robes which bore a vivid golden sun on their chests, but even those were soon swallowed up by the vaporous air.

Except for one, whose imposing size was impossible to miss.

"You must not struggle," Aquilla said as my soul merged with my body. "They will take us to the Temple to question us, and we shall be left unharmed in the revelation of our quest to at first join them."

How do you know that?

"They would have slain us if it were not so."

And you wish to simply tell them the truth?

"It is written that 'A truthful tree will bear the fruit of life.'"

"We shall feed them both to the Valravn if they prove to be foreigners," said the largest one, in a language I knew was foreign but known to Aquilla.

What?

"Wait—" Aquilla said, but I was already moving despite his foolish plan.

Focusing on Egret, who was gently whispering my name in desperation, I phased through the bonds of my captors, dropping to the mountain path to every knights' surprise. Without waiting for a response, I Waed the fire from my Godstone necklace which thankfully had not been taken from its concealment. The fire danced in my hands as a deadly distraction, allowing me to trip my captor and free Egret from hers.

They encircled us within moments, and soon a ring of spears was at our throats, though they were cautious to the flames from my hands.

"Hold!" the tall one said, bringing himself closer to us and removing his hood to examine us.

His satin black hair was probably darker than his heart.

"So you do not slumber in death, but who are you?" the Elf said in what Aquilla said was the native Cuerian tongue of Cur Malum, his serious eyes consuming every detail. "You are clearly not native to our island." Switching to Kapitolan, the Elf continued, "Otherwise, you would not have stumbled into this place so foolishly."

"And loudly," added one of the other robed men in ancient Cypheric.

The Elf gave him a stern look before turning back to us.

"If you are servants of the Kira Naz'ka, speak truthfully and I will deliver you a quick death as was given to your brothers."

"Tell them you seek to join the Ora'suns," Aquilla said. "*Quickly*, in Cypheric. He believes you are of the Black Legion, Kira Naz'ka, in their tongue."

"We are no Kira Naz'ka," I said, carefully repeating the ancient tongue, a noticeable shock rippling through the Ora'suns' stances, even the larger Elf's. "We wish to join the Ora'suns."

The large Elf squinted his eyes as he studied me.

"What makes you think we would want someone who practices dark sorcery as you do, though you know the tongue of our ancestors?"

"Say, 'I ask for the Trial of Beating Hearts' in order to prove your heart," Aquilla said, to which I relayed in their language.

"Hmmm," the largest Ora'sun grimaced. "Very well. Since you have pleaded the Trial and know of our past, I shall bring you to be questioned by her, for this is greatly irregular. Though before you are tested, I must know your names, so if you are to perish, the Berei a'l Zaeim can pray to protect us from your unrighteous hearts."

"Give forth your name, and I will give you mine," I said, to which Aquilla and the Ora'sun balked.

"Very well. If you are so inclined to know, my name is Alcharion. I am the greatest of the Ora'suns."

There seemed to be too much pride in Alcharion's voice, but his might overshadowed the men around him, and none dared to oppose his claim.

"It would be wise to befriend him," Aquilla said.

That's what the Valenekan Elves said of Kapitol before they were conquered.

"My name is Morgan Krios," I repeated in Cypheric, showing no signs of inclined friendliness.

"And who is your companion?"

"I will let her speak for herself when she recovers."

"Do you wish to make an enemy?" Aquilla said.

If they knew they had a Queen in their midst, they might discard tradition in place of their political ambitions.

Aquilla and Alcharion were both silent as they stewed over my words.

"Very well," Alcharion said. "Krios, we will take you to our Holy Dwelling to be further questioned. But until you and your unnamed companion pass the Trial, you shall not have blades to harm us, nor shall you see whither we go, lest you truly be spies of the enemy."

Without warning, blindfolds wrapped around our eyes and arms slid underneath mine to forcefully guide my steps. One of the Ora'suns also ripped my Godstone necklace from me, along with my spear and presumably Egret's blade. Though I was physically blind, I opened Aquilla's eyes to see the crystal world of glass, which could not be hindered by the material world except for the supernatural fog surrounding us, giving me at least some sight.

Oddly enough, all of their hearts were Bludh and not Nox, even Alcharion's. When I gazed upon Egret's, though her heart was Bludh like the rest, there painted in the deepest crevices a glimmering Klyr, though it drummed ever softer in our march.

I feared she would not survive the Trial.

"She will not have to endure the Trial, and neither shall you," Aquilla said.

What do you mean?

"It is simple: we will at last reveal ourselves, and they shall kneel."

Five days of journeying slowly through Aquilla's eyes alone while blindfolded almost made me forget what it was like to see the world of non-crystalline color from before. For Egret it must have been worse, who was silently carried as our captors led us at a painstakingly slow pace.

It would have been so much faster if I didn't have to pretend to be blind.

Upon the afternoon of the fifth day, we had reached a mountain valley deep within the island where a silver river streamed gently down. With no temple in sight, I wondered if we were truly being led to any dwelling at all. That was until Alcharion began ascending a hidden path along the mountainside that weaved its way steeply upwards and away from the river. Though as to what we were climbing towards, I could not tell, for the fog was impossibly thick to see through.

We followed with cautious steps.

At last, after a long, laborious climb, we reached the end of the path that fed onto a towering plateau of sandstone ruling over the valley behind us.

Before, I could not see what was beyond the plateau through the fog, which was thicker than wool below. But now, as it cleared slightly, I could see just beyond a faint outline of the mountain spine looming higher in the distance, shrouded by the clouds and fog that enveloped us. As my eyes fell, I was surprised to see what was carved into the sloping plateau itself: a city.

There were hundreds of Elves.

The assassins have a city?

"Indeed," Aquilla said as Alcharion led us forward, still blindfolded. "It is called the Meshiac, or the City of the Chosen One."

Who is their Chosen One?

"That would be us, Morgan."

And they will just bow to me once they see you? Your plan to simply take over these strange Elves seems ever more improbable.

"Do not fear," Aquilla said, "for 'Fear is a disease that spares no man it infects.' We will rule these assassins, and they shall learn to fear us instead very soon."

And what must we do for that?

"It is simple: we must only prove that we can wield the Klyr spear. Only a true Shepherd can do so, and my face will be enough to silence any doubt."

Do they not already have an Aela Zaeim who guides them?

"No. All they have is the Berei a'l Zaeim, Seeker of the Zaeim, of *you*."

Our ponderings turned aside as I caught a glimpse of Egret, her limp body beside me like a fallen dove that had to be carried with grace.

She had been so strong once.

It was sickening to see her so broken.

"Egret?" I whispered, but she gave no response.

Instead, a shadow darkened her tender sleep as we came to the entrance of the city, gated by colorless stone and guarded by three Ora'suns who nodded to Alcharion, letting us pass through.

The music and strong musk of the city flooded our senses almost at once, coming from the bustle of intricately adorned Elves who went about their business in the sandstone market square with their sharp yet elegant language. Their strange turbans and billowing shirts were foreign to me, and probably would have been more so if I could see what colors comprised their clothing. But the Elves were vibrantly beautiful in their own way as if they weren't afraid of what made them unique.

Of what made them different, even repulsively different.

"Morgan…" Egret moaned as she was bathed in light that peaked through the clouds, the senses from the city awakening her.

"Egret!" I said, pulling myself closer to hold her, my feverishly warm flesh completely opposite to her cold skin that shivered with sickly green veins.

"What is wrong with your companion?" Alcharion said.

"She took ill on our voyage here," I said in the Cuerian tongue, not knowing what else to say.

The words themselves came out with some difficulty as it seemed even Aquilla, with his vast knowledge, had not a firm grasp on this ancient and obscure dialect.

Alcharion whistled quickly to someone in the market square that I could not see, motioning to Egret, who was now stumbling into my arms.

A strongly perfumed Elf emerged from the busy crowd with a jar in his hand. The Elf took no attention to me as he hastily spread what appeared to be a jelly over a biscuit in his hand, to which he fed to Egret. At first, Egret nibbled with little attention, but then began to awaken more and grow in hunger with every second until the entire biscuit was gone.

"Thank you, Ru'ish," Alcharion said, to which Ru'ish bowed and slipped back into the crowd surrounding us.

"Where am I?" Egret said in Skyyan, much to everyone's confusion except for Aquilla and I.

"We are in the city of the assassins," I responded in Skyyan.

"Please, do not thank me for it," Alcharion said with absolute bitterness.

It was tempting to remark something equally as disgusting as his words towards us when several Elves ran up to Alcharion from the market square. Alcharion's expression immediately melted into joy as the little girls with dresses and turbans jumped onto him like flying cabats expecting a treat. One of the little girls whispered something in Alcharion's ear before pointing to Egret.

"She wants to know how long you two have been married," Alcharion said in the Cuerian tongue, which Aquilla translated for Egret.

"What?" Egret said in Skyyan, pushing blindly away from me as if I disgusted her. "We are not married!"

Though Alcharion and the little girl could not understand, they could decipher every blunt word.

My head bent down as Alcharion said goodbye to the little girls and continued to lead us through the city.

When we came to the end of the city, I was lost in confusion: there was nothing else except the rising spine of the arid mountain before us.

"Can we take our blindfolds off now?" I asked in frustration. "It's been almost a week since I last saw the sun."

"No, we still have half a day's journey left," Alcharion said.

Half a day's journey? The war will be over at this pace!

Alcharion said nothing more as his Ora'suns guided our ascent into a narrow canyon that opened before us. Though I did not wish to be captive to the Elves, I was thankful for guidance, for the canyon weaved endlessly upwards and broke off into several varying paths that I assume would only lead to death for those who did not know the way.

True to his word, it wasn't until several hours later that at last the canyon took a sharp bend, opening up to a massive rock wall that indeed took my breath. Carved intricately upon the face of the canyon wall, there stood a weathered carving of a familiar warrior bowing his head, holding both a spear and shield before him as pillars and strange symbols surrounded him.

The shield of Mythraelyon caught my attention first, for the symbol at its center was one I could understand now: it was the word for water.

So Mythraelyon did have power over the seas?

"It is written," Aquilla said, nodding towards the carving of an apparition close behind Mythraelyon.

It looked like Aquilla.

"Aela Zaeim," Alcharion whispered, bowing in reverence before the ancient carving in the mountain.

The Ora'suns escorting us bowed as well.

Aela Zaeim? I thought as Alcharion led us into the heart of the mountain through an opening beneath Mythraelyon's feet and up a steep flight of lowly-lit and winding stairs.

"It is synonymous with *Shepherd*, named after the one who founded the Order, who shepherded its purpose."

Did she have a Medjaib as well?

"No, but she sought for the one who did."

Why?

"Aela Zaeim believed the Taldarii Order should serve the Shepherds such as Cypherus and Mythraelyon, not the corrupt officials who had the most influence. Thus, she drew many away from the corrupt Order and established her own here."

Weren't the Taldarii destroyed in her abandonment?

"Yes, but it was necessary; the path would either be continued Shadow or purging Light," Aquilla said as we ascended the mountain stairs. "It is the same with your destiny: sometimes the choice of cost is the only path of Light."

I don't believe that.

"Why not?"

But before I could answer, Alcharion stopped halfway up the winding stairs, whispering something to two of his Ora'suns. When he finished, they ran off through one of the many tunnels that pocketed the walls of the stairwell.

"Before you meet with her, I must ask and tell you something," Alcharion said. "First, what is your name, *Human*?"

There sounded a heavy distaste in the large Elf's words as he spoke of our race.

Aquilla translated for her but simultaneously warned her not to say her real name, lest she would be used as political fodder for the Ora'suns' schemes.

"Joanna," Egret said, much to my surprise.

Joanna? Why my mother's name?

Alcharion nodded and motioned to the Ora'suns surrounding us.

"Very well, Morgan and Joanna," Alcharion said. "It is time for you to meet the Berei a'l Zaeim. Should you fail her questions, this will be our last conversation. Should you be wise, I shall see you soon for the Trial of Beating Hearts."

Without another word, the hooded Ora'suns led us away deep into the tunnel before us, only taking our blindfolds off after locking us away in a dark and cold room.

It must have been hours later, or possibly the next day when our door opened again.

Though we had been left with food and refreshment, the exhaustion from the journey had wrung the energy from Egret and I like washed clothes squeezed of water. Much to Aquilla's continued confusion about our perpetual need for recovery, Egret and I rested our eyes in the dark room instead of our usual banter.

"We must not close our eyes to the darkness," Aquilla warned. "We must use this time to prepare!"

"I won't be able to fend off any shadow if I can't keep my eyes open," I said, resting by Egret, who lay silently.

Aquilla sighed. "'An ant winks not at sleep and is fortified from the storm; a cabat dwells in rest and is lost in the rain.'"

Shaking my head, I let my eyes rest from the journey that took every ounce of strength from me.

For once, I wished I had listened to Aquilla.

A rotting smell of meat mixed with a pungent perfume rudely awakened me before the sound of the door scraped into my ears. Looking at Egret, she was fortunate not to awaken from the noise or the smell.

"Quickly, Morgan!" Aquilla said, panic in his voice.

As I scrambled to my feet, the candlelight flickered silently into my eyes, almost blinding me. But it was not just one candle: there were dozens, all outlining the form of a masked figure. Switching to Aquilla's eyes, there was only darkness before me, illuminated by the smallest of lights.

A deep and heavy breath followed as the figure stared at me. All I could see was its black mask and a pair of gleaming eyes shining beneath it.

"So," the figure said, its feminine voice a raspy, gargled whisper as the door closed behind her, "you seek to join the Ora'suns?"

"Follow my words exactly," Aquilla said as he translated in ancient Cypheric, my heart beating more loudly than his words.

"I seek not only to join the Ora'suns, but to rule them," I said.

The masked figure laughed, her lungs wheezing as she almost barreled over. "Do you know who I am, young one? Do you know our roots, our purpose for being?"

"Now," Aquilla said.

Wyling in Aquilla's flesh, my face transformed into his own. Aquilla's colorful, cosmic radiance shined before the startled figure.

"I am Morgan Krios, Shepherd of the Mother, and bonded with her Spirit, her Servant. You are the Berei a'l Zaeim, Seeker of the Shepherd, of me. You will serve me, and together we will serve the Mother who is our purpose."

The Berei a'l Zaeim trembled for a moment, stepping back as she stood in awe of Aquilla's glory. For a moment, the figure said nothing, simply staring at our face.

"I… I was mistaken," the Berei a'l Zaeim said, her wheezing voice trembling slightly before hardening her stance once again. "It has been a long… *long* time since we have seen one chosen by the Mother for Her Will. Do you know who came before you, young one?"

Do you know?

"I do not," Aquilla said in my mind. "What knowledge we have of their Order came mostly from before they migrated to Cur Malum."

"I am unaware of whom you speak of," I said, to which the Berei a'l Zaeim nodded slowly.

"The one who came before you spoke of similar words to Aela Zaeim, our founder. She was shown the same face, the same power, and many believed, though not she. Aela Zaeim was slain in her disbelief, along with most of the Order; for the enemy concealed a heart of wickedness beneath, leading many of our people astray because of the oath we swore to serve the Mother's Shepherds."

"Such a tale is… impossible!" Aquilla said, anger and

confusion churning within his spirit like a tempest at sea. "If this Shepherd she spoke of truly committed a heinous deed, I would know of it."

"Thus, your words and face are not enough," the Berei a'l Zaeim continued. "You must prove your heart is pure and gain the loyalty of those who will follow you."

"What must I do then, to gain your loyalty?" I said.

The Berei a'l Zaeim took a deep and rattling breath, the potency of which was enough to make me sick.

"Tomorrow, you must prove your heart as all Ora'suns have done in the first Trial."

"Do you mean only myself in this Trial?"

The Berei a'l Zaeim looked at Egret sleeping on the cold floor, before returning her dark eyes to me.

"The girl shall be exempt from the Trial, for it is only your heart which we seek to know. However, should you fail any Trial, she will join you in death's embrace."

~

The winding stairwell opened up to the tip of the mountain, feeding into a partially exposed and hollowed peak that was the arena. As Egret and I emerged into the pit of death, I saw we were not alone: hundreds of Ora'suns surrounded the arena, draped in their dark blue and golden robes, along with the ever-present, ever- penetrating fog of Cur Malum that swirled around them. All were silent as they watched like vultures from amongst the circular stands elevated above the fighting pit.

"Do not fear. We will best any foe they bring before us," Aquilla said as Alcharion led us to the arena's opposite side, which opened up to the mountain cliffs, but even his voice could not mask the fear that also crept in my spirit.

I've never taken the life of anyone before, spirit, I thought, the very idea invoking fear into my being.

"It is necessary," Aquilla said.

"Choose your sword and shield, and wait silently for the Berei a'l Zaeim," Alcharion said, motioning to the wooden rack of weapons brought before us by several Ora'suns. "If you wish to avoid this fight, the cliff is always an option: for *cowards.*"

Though I had no temptation for the cliffs, it felt as if Alcharion wished that I would taste of its deadly fruit.

"May the Mother steady your blade, and grant you favor," Egret said, clasping her tired arm to mine. "Trust in Her, Morgan. And remember to strengthen your center as you strike. And most of all, do not even think of dying on me, Krabios."

"I won't," I said as she joined Alcharion to watch from the sidelines of the arena, her words slightly cooling the raging fire of anxiety within me.

Being more familiar with the spear, I decided to choose it and a shield, but as I reached for it, Alcharion tore off the black gloves, exposing me to all.

"You won't need these," the silver-veined Elf said, as a dark smile presented itself upon him. "Though, I can see why you desire them."

Biting my lip to keep the boiling thoughts from erupting, I quickly grabbed a shield to hide one hand, though the other remained unfortunately exposed. Hundreds of eyes looked upon me, and whispers began to waft through the crowds due clearly to my embarrassment. The attention was almost too unbearable, though one look at Egret's compassion helped enough to cool the growing flames on my cheeks.

She offered a gentle smile of encouragement, bolstering my spirit and returning my focus.

Ignore them, she seemed to say with a roll of the eyes.

Any further taunting by Alcharion or the crowd was immediately silenced by an eerie horn that blew from the central balcony overlooking the arena. All eyes fixated upon it as footsteps echoed from its cavernous dark, from which little lights began to appear. Switching my eyes to Aquilla's, I could only see two hearts emerge from the shadows: they were completely and entirely Nox.

Alcharion and all of the Ora'suns kneeled at the sight of the masked Berei a'l Zaeim who approached the balcony, along with an older Elf who helped the figure walk. The sight of her entirely exposed to the light appalled me.

Her cape of midnight cobwebs draped over a silver carcass, hiding any sign of flesh beneath. Candles protruded from the black helm of the masked and emotionless figure, and perched on her wax-ridden shoulders was a raven whose heart was just as putrid and dark as the monster it perched upon.

"Kneel before the Berei a'l Zaeim!" Alcharion whispered harshly, to which Egret and I did, though begrudgingly.

"The leader's fate is of banishment," Aquilla muttered to himself. "She is more repulsive in the light."

The Berei a'l Zaeim lifted her hand slowly for us to rise, but it was the assistant who talked.

"Welcome, brother and sister," Aquilla translated for Egret, his radiant voice a significant contrast to the ancient Elf who spoke on Berei's behalf as the figure leaned to whisper. "I, Nizari Aevina Hassan, the Berei a'l Zaeim, am the one who seeks the Shepherd of this generation. I pray the Mother gives you strength to pass the Trial, for none shall be permitted to leave with the knowledge of this place and not be Ora'sun, those who serve Her Shepherds."

Egret and I looked at each other, but I saw no fear in her eyes: only determination. She truly believed I could overcome the Trial before me.

"As a servant of Her holy vessels," the Elf continued, "we face many dangerous threats in this rotted world, for purging the land of its corrupted hearts is a task many do not wish to see us fulfill."

How hypocritical. How could this creature even speak of such a mission when their leader has the darkest one of all?

"The riddle eludes me as well," Aquilla said.

"To ensure you can bear this," the Elf said, "you will face a series of foes who will test your heart. In order to serve the Aela Zaeim, you must be strong enough to face the darkness, but you also must live a life of surrender, allowing the Mother's Will to flow through you, caring not if you shall perish; for this shall be Her glory."

Without warning, the steel gate below the balcony began to screech open. Three snarling grey wolves bolted from the shadows towards me, followed by an armed Dwarf and a lanky Elf.

Five against one.

"They shall try to flank you!" Aquilla said as the wolves pounded against my shield in chaotic unison, causing me to stagger beneath their fury.

In pure desperation, I was able to strike at the wolf closest to me. The wolf offered no more violence as it fell limp to the sand.

The two remaining wolves increased their fervent attacks on me, one attempting to gorge my feet and the other nipping at my spear hand. In my mind, I saw Aquilla jump backwards to bash one with a shield and impale the other with the spear. I attempted to do just that, but as I tried to jump backwards, I heard a terrifying roar as a spear impaled my shield. The added weight and shock crippled my strength, and my defenses fell before the teeth of the wolves.

That's when the world decided to drown me as well.

The wolves suddenly became figures threaded together by the Tongue of Tihrrvyith:

Joohihk…

Agony pounded my head as the world violently returned to normal. With a snap of my wrist, I sliced one wolf's throat, only for the other wolf to clench my hand unawares in its bloody maw.

"Gah!" I screamed, its teeth tearing into my charred flesh for all to see.

"Phase, Morgan!" Aquilla said. "Trust in me!"

His trust was the furthest from me, and I found it impossible to phase.

As I wrestled with my wolf, I saw Egret's face from afar, one of hopeless fright that would soon cease to exist should I fail. Anxiety drummed my heart as my hand phased through the wolf's mouth, submitting my lack of trust to Aquilla so that I might save her. My fingers clutched its brain and phased back again, crushing its beastly mind like Aquilla did to the Soulis.

The lifeless wolf was easy enough to throw off, but as I scrambled to my feet, the Dwarf slammed the butt of his battleaxe to my chest, crushing me to the ground in preparation for a killing blow as his Elvish ally stalked behind him.

It's over, I thought as the Dwarf grunted in the heaving of his weapon to strike.

"Morgan!" Aquilla cried desperately.

But as I looked up, I realized it wasn't Aquilla who shouted my name.

A spear whistled through the air and buried itself in the Dwarf's chest, followed by a terrifyingly ferocious cry from Egret, who rushed into the arena with a sword she had taken from the weapons rack. Egret swept the battleaxe aside with her sword, but before she could land the killing strike, the Dwarf punched her in the throat, disarming her and throwing her in rage across the arena. She tumbled before the Elf.

The Elf turned his sword to plunge it into her chest.

I was too far away to help.

What happened next was difficult to comprehend, for nothing but one word could describe what beat through my heart that allowed me to move faster than the wind itself. In one moment, I was clear across the arena, and in the next, I found myself next to the Elf, thrusting my spear into his jaw right beside Egret, as if a hundred feet were only a breath.

And my body felt lighter than such a breath.

Egret looked briefly at me in surprise, as did the Dwarf who couldn't believe I was there with them so quickly. Egret took advantage of the pause, taking my spear and launching it deep within the Dwarf's lightly armored chest who stood askance, this time ceasing his life forever as he crumbled at a distance from us.

"Thank you, Morgan," Egret said, though the words sounded labored, difficult to pronounce as she caught her tired breath and gazed in hesitation upon the life she ended.

I wanted to thank her as well, but my hands trembled from taking the life of another. There was no way to describe the monstrous guilt that riddled my soul from such an act, even though the Elf was wicked to my knowledge and almost took the precious life of another.

The gloom that threatened to overwhelm me was briefly set aside when Alcharion shouted to Nizari at the breach of protocol of Egret joining in the fight.

She had saved me, risking her life for my own.

Instead of watching me drown, she jumped into the colorless waves with me to brave the tempest of fate by my side, not caring if she would die but in the slightest hope of saving me.

"You threaten to reveal us too soon!" Aquilla said.

That is the least of my concerns, I thought, giving my arm to Egret to steady herself.

She was safe.

Sweet mountain air flooded my lungs as I breathed in a sigh of relief.

But just as we were recovering our strength, a throaty caw echoed from the balcony, piercing any semblance of relief.

Looking in expectance of the raven, I was confused to see that the foul bird formerly perched upon the Berei's shoulder was not there. The figure looked at us with a morbid curiosity from my impossible feat and Egret's unprecedented joining in the Trial. However, my inquiry of what she was thinking was halted when a plated knight darker than the sea and adorned with raven feathers was suddenly standing alone in the arena before us.

Its hand gripped a bone sword. The wickedness of its carved design mirrored the carvings on its feathered armor. It made no sound as it watched us with its beady, bottomless eyes.

"We must be careful," Aquilla said as Egret and I took a moment to prepare ourselves. She grabbed the Dwarf's fallen battleaxe and I temporarily put aside Aquilla's frustration with me for nearly revealing his power.

"Do you see any weakness we may exploit?" Egret said.

"I'm afraid I do not, but we must work together, and not reveal more of myself."

"What is it doing?" I said, ignoring his complaint.

The knight of raven feathers stood completely still. Its chest moved not as it watched us.

As it studied us.

"It taunts us," Egret said.

"Come now, don't let cowardice become of you," Alcharion jeered behind us.

"So says the *hero*," I said.

"We must demonstrate control of our power," Aquilla warned. "Let us prove of our strength to the Mother in *wisdom*."

"I do not seek such approval from these heretics," Egret said, breaking from our defense and striding haughtily towards the knight who began to copy her movements.

The knight's steps mirrored Egret's with exact precision.

"Egret, wait!" I said.

But it was too late.

As Egret attempted to feign a striking lunge with her battleaxe, the knight performed the same attack. Fear flashed on Egret's face as she changed course, deciding to swing her battleaxe towards the knight's hip. The steel found its home in the dark knight, but so did the knight's bone blade in Egret's spine.

She collapsed without a scream.

"Egret!" I screamed, my entire being pulsing with hatred for the dark creature who snapped its beady black eyes to me, moving at a rapid pace to meet my own.

There was so much vile behind the eyes I yearned to obliterate. Eyes that reminded me so much of Rolloc's, so much of Judux and his reflection.

They deserved to drown. All of them.

"Morgan, wait!" Aquilla said, his spirit standing before me and causing me to stop only a striking distance away from the foul beast.

The knight also stopped.

"He…" I said, the spear trembling in my hands, "he—"

"I know Morgan, but we cannot make the same mistake. You must listen to me, Morgan; trust in me! We must work together, wisely, to take down the knight. The creature is matching your movements, so we must do what it cannot."

Despite the pain, despite the agony of seeing the blood pour from Egret's back, the suffering almost unbearable to witness, I listened.

"All right," I said, dropping my spear before the black knight, completely defenseless in surrender.

It too dropped its bone sword.

The entire crowd was quiet as Aquilla and I walked towards the monster who made silent the strongest woman I had ever met. As the knight mirrored every step I made, I realized in that moment that I had completed the challenge they tasked us to do: completely surrender to fate despite the very real possibility of death, which is something they did not seem to be afraid of.

The Berei a'l Zaeim made a motion upon the balcony for me to stop, but though I displayed surrender, I did not feel in the slightest any morsel of mercy for such a dark being, whose Nox heart was an exact reflection of their so-called leader. The vile creature had snapped the wings of Egret without hesitation.

It deserved the same fate for such a wicked act.

My broken, disgusting, and charred hand reached towards the knight, passing its own hand and gently rested upon its plated yet feathered chest as it did the same to my shirt.

Without a second thought, I crushed its heart as it failed to push farther into my chest in response.

The Void eyes of the raven knight blinked wide in shock as my revenge snapped its life, and it collapsed dead before me.

Aquilla's soul portrayed a feeling of satisfaction in seeing the dark monster fall before me, but I felt an unexpected sense of guilt. In my mind, I saw the heart of Judux, Rolloc, and Belial being crushed in my anger as I slew the knight, but the only thing that filled my mind now was an empty silence that followed its death.

Such pointless suffering.

The creature had been completely at my mercy. I could have spared it from a sleepless death. Yet, I extinguished its bitter flame, rightfully so in my vindicated anger.

But a thought nagged my conscience: was this the path of Shadow?

Would Cypherus have displayed such ruthlessness?

"Morgan…" Egret softly groaned.

My destructive thoughts halted at once to her calling. Dropping to my knees beside her, I held her blood-soaked head in my hands. Her flesh was cold like my tears which fell heavy as rain upon her.

"Is she well?" Aquilla said.

Gently, I looked upon the wound which the raven knight had cursed her with.

Egret's spine was completely severed.

Chapter 22
The Shadows

Through the crisis of the eighth century, the Taldarii Order fractured evermore and almost died completely. Pretender after pretender donned the Imperial Robes within a short set of sols, dozens of emperors seizing and losing the throne, diluting its reverence. The Order's purpose also diluted as it went from one organization of a hundred to several organizations with many hundreds in each. They reflected private armies rather than protectors. The core tenet of reverence for the emperor's divinity soon faded. They accepted employment to the highest bidding "new" emperor and felt no conviction in killing those they were previously sworn to.

This continued until Mythraelyon donned the Imperial Robe, unifying the thricely fractured empire. When he was elevated to the office of Emperor, he purged the scum from the Order and drastically reduced their size to a mere fifty loyal members. What helped their loyalty was that many of the Order recognized the Emperor's abilities mirrored those of the fabled Cypherus; thus, Imperial divinity was bolstered once again. This was foundational for a small portion of the Order who believed Shepherds were real and the Order should serve them, not the empire. This belief was not widely held until the Elf Aela Zaeim, who arrived before the collapse of the Cypheric Empire.

Chronicles of Renborg: King's Edition
"The Taldarii Order: Revival"
Piluch Joffersun: Master of Histories

E**gret** rested in my arms for what felt like an eternity, though it was only two days.

Words were impossible to produce when the Ora'suns guided Egret and I away from the bloodied arena. Their words were lost on me as well, for I cared not for anything they had to say.

The only thing I do recall was Alcharion, who, after locking us inside a pillared sandstone bath house with an Ora'sun healer, was rather callous.

"You will wait while we prepare for your final Trial," Alcharion said.

"Are we not Ora'suns yet?" I could hardly say.

Alcharion boomed a dark laugh.

"There is more to being an Ora'sun than outwitting death. But this time, you shall receive no aid in finishing the remaining task, though I doubt she could be of use at all."

"She is stronger than you know."

"The *Valravn* would disagree."

Our eyes were locked like swords in the breathless air.

"Morgan," Aquilla said, watching us from the corner of the bathhouse, "be still. He shall be useful for us when we rule him."

In unmerited mercy, I let the Elf go without further challenge. Just barely.

The healer could do little for Egret, who remained unconscious and unmoving, the open wound across her back a scarlet tear upon olive skin. All the Ora'sun did was clean the wound and bandage it with oils and a strange smelling paste, but seeing that Egret was beyond repair, the Ora'sun left us to wait.

Egret was lighter than a feather as I lifted her smooth and soft head into my lap.

"How much longer till we become the Aela Zaeim?"

"We will simply lift the Klyr spear after we are initiated as Ora'suns, revealing your designation as Shepherd. If we are impatient now, we will be executed as if we were one of the Kira Naz'ka."

"And I will be able to lift it?"

"You shall be unscathed from its purity because of my spirit within you."

There ebbed within me a foreboding sense that it would not

be as simple as the Medjaib made it out to be, but his words allowed me to relax and focus on the flightless dove in my arms.

The dove which I broke from my destiny of Shadow, who flew to save me but was crushed in the flight.

Everything was so… quiet as she slept, her closed eyes concealing the light that had so filled them.

Egret's defying courage, our witty conversations, her surprisingly deep knowledge of politics, unwavering faith, and even the nicknames and taunts she blessed me with when we trained together, that lack of it all made the world feel horribly empty.

Agony devoured me as I beheld the broken light who was stronger than me in every way, who cared for me more than I deserved.

And more than I thought.

Egret did not deserve to lose all of her strength, and it was all my fault that she would never walk again.

First Gulmund and Valena, then Sigmund and Lucien, and now most likely Philomela; all of them, including Egret, were either dead or in a fate worse than death because of my broken being and accursed fate.

Rage wanted to blame the Mother for bestowing such a horrendous destiny upon me, to curse Aquilla for bringing me to this wretched place, but I knew that I was to blame as well.

Would it have been better if I had leaped from the cliffs before all of this could unfold?

Was it better to end the tragedy of Turrok before he became a monster and lost himself and countless others?

Was the shadowed fate of the wolf my own?

With every day that burdened my soul, I began to doubt the avoidance of Cypherus' Shadow, of sleepless death that took the innocent breath of those nearest to me. At the end of every thought, I concluded with the same dark reality that could only be: such suffering was the necessary cost.

My heart grieved timelessly for them as I wept uncontrollably over Egret, my tears bathing her pale flesh. The torrential rain that was my tears blinded me for so long, days even, that I didn't realize my soul had drifted from my being: when I opened them, I found myself at the sea cliffs of Cur Malum.

The colorless waves thrashed against the rocks, tempting me to fall with them and sleep forever beneath the sea.

Pain flared in my mind as the waves morphed into its unyielding taunt:

Hirwa…

Destiny…

Aquilla's spirit emerged from the arid rocks behind me, but I shot off beyond the fog-ridden island to escape all of the suffering from within and without.

"Morgan, where are you going?" Aquilla said, his winged spirit effortlessly following me.

In truth, I didn't know, I just knew the familiar waves of hopeless suffering were calling to me again, and I didn't want to be anywhere near those waves.

Never again.

The blurred waves beneath me quickly turned to the wine fields of Sommer, before blending in with the dark Wolfwood trees of Laconnia. Almost instinctively, I let my soul drift to their capital of Ehlonica.

"We will not find him, Morgan," Aquilla said. "We are only wasting our time."

"I will not rest until we do."

Aquilla sighed as I began my hopeless search, but he did not persist.

Instead of searching near the densely populated heart of the city, I took up the hunt towards the outer rings of the heavily fortified walls. Aquilla's world became my own as I merged our eyes together, and the impenetrable walls of Ehlonica became glassy grey in his sight. There were thousands of Bludh hearts belonging to Lycan who went about their business, from guards to hunters to nameless citizens, of all factions and every creed. There was truly a sea of Lycan, so I focused less on them and looked for those with blackened hearts.

For hours I scoured the city, dizzying myself as I looked under every stone and Lycan home. I almost gave up the search in its defiant fruitlessness. My soul was an anchor that dragged me down to the wide city streets of Ehlonica, despair threatening to crush me as I drifted aimlessly after a time.

Aquilla was oblivious to my feelings as I hid them from him, but he decided to continue searching through the crowds of Lycan and other races despite my inner turmoil. Though, our search soon came to a halt as my spirit almost collided into an enigma that had captivated a rather large crowd: a Lycan dressed in the Cleric red robes of the Valkryn Faith. His gentle sermon drew us softly as he stood high on the bridge's railing overlooking the Parnaxus River.

For a moment I forgot he was a Lycan.

"And my brothers, do not forget the destiny which befalls you should you choose the fate of the beast," the Lycan Cleric said, a visible tremor rippling across his snout as the crowd leaned in. "The Cult of Reia lied to us that we were born of the wolf, that those who were faithful to Bellatorix and Reia should hunt blissfully in the endless field of stars for the souls of the unfaithful. But that is simply a perversion of the truth: 'For those who embrace the soul of any creature shall receive its endless fate upon the earth.'"

I half expected the crowd to throw the Ilyite off the bridge for his denunciation of their long-established religion, but the Lycan were intriguingly captivated by the Cleric's words, many of them nodding in agreement.

But not all of them. There were a few Lycan whose snouts could barely restrain the fury that snarled underneath.

"The Author sends Her words to even the furthest from Her," Aquilla said as he too stopped his search and listened to the Cleric. "Out of mercy, She attempts to spare them from such a mindless eternity."

The now verified doom that Lucien and I had so often heard preached to us by the Cormarchs of the Faith made me shudder with fear. Instead of furthering hatred for the Lycan as Volsung shared, it drew my heart to pity their lost souls.

"Return to the true Mother, my brothers," the Cleric continued. "Accept the discovery of Joras Inaeos of Naxos, though it is painful. It is never too late to return to her and share in the eternal bliss of Solæf."

"And what shall we do with the Black Book of Devina and the Silver Scrolls of Aphrenios?" a Lycan from the crowd shouted.

"*Burn it*," the Cleric said after a careful pause, "along with any desire of the wolf within. Abandon the wolf, my brothers, and run to the Mother! She is the only One who is responsible for our birth and worthy of our—"

A knife whistled through the air, sheathing itself in the Lycan Cleric's neck, the force of which threw the Lycan over the railing into the river below.

A sudden fear gripped the crowd at the Cleric's swift demise, chaos propelling everyone to flee from the murder as shouts of terror filled the air.

Aquilla threw me a quick glance before we jumped into the air to see who killed him. It would have been impossible to find the murderer had it not been for Aquilla's sight, but through the glassy view of the Medjaib's eyes, one Nox, darkened heart scoured from the crowd into the darkness of the alley beside the bridge.

And in the Lycan's being, there was one word whispering from his soul:

Laeyihth…

"There!" I said, dropping from the sky in pursuit of the now sprinting zealot who threatened to disappear in the shadows of the city bathed in moonlight.

With every bit of rejuvenated might, our souls kept a steady pace, only a claw's breadth from the midnight Lycan who slithered effortlessly like an eel through the congested city. Blending carefully with crowds who were oblivious to the murder, he turned to run through the maze of alleys when he was unseen.

And being carried on his back, a grey figure showed no heartbeat. In my sight, however, it was merely a large twine bag.

"Is that a body?" I said in our pursuit.

"I fear it is," Aquilla said, the mystery of the dark zealot giving us cautious passion to trace his origins.

If it was Lucien, I would steal the Lycan's soul and throw it into the forgotten depths of—

"Morgan, no!" Aquilla said, intruding my thoughts as I revealed them unknowingly.

The Lycan skidded to a halt in an alleyway as we kept closely behind, quickly discarding his ragged cape to reveal a finely made robe that marked him as nothing more than a prosperous Lycan strolling the city streets. The zealot pretended a slow and calm gait as he crossed the busy street with the bag over his shoulder. Prominent Lycan youth were flirting with richly dressed Elven courtesans, but the zealot displayed no attention to their licentiousness, except for his Nox heart which oozed with hatred only visible in Aquilla's eyes.

With quiet footsteps, the zealot ascended the unnoteworthy staircase to one of the moderately sized pillared mansions along the street.

Aquilla and I exchanged glances of confusion before we followed the zealot up the stairs.

The Lycan stopped when he approached the double Wolf-wood doors of the quiet mansion, giving a slight knock upon its plain surface. He awaited a response with reverence.

Or was it fear?

Three downwards-facing slits opened in the doors, to which the Lycan knelt and bowed his head as the whisper of a deep voice came from the other side.

"Who seeks entrance?" the voice said.

"A son of Kairos returns to his brothers."

There was a pause before the voice spoke again, "A red hand rises in the east."

The kneeling one looked up and answered, "A white hand strikes in the west."

At once, the doors opened for him.

"Welcome, brother," said the Lycan who opened the doors, letting a warm light bathe the torch lit steps that fed into the mansion's porch.

Aquilla and I phased through the quickly shut doors.

"He is expecting you," the Lycan said, to which our zealot nodded before following him down the richly adorned hall of the mansion.

Fear impaled my heart as we followed them in spirit, for towering on both sides of the ink-soaked carpet pathway were two statues carved of pure silver, the masculine one wearing a sun wreath and his female opposite wearing a necklace bearing the image of the moon. Their size was larger than any Lycan and gave an impression of holiness that deserved worship.

And zealous dedication.

"Bellatorix and Reia are false gods who only exist in the minds of the Laconnians," Aquilla said. "It defies the mind how even the wolves know of their Author, but not the ones who pretend to be."

"I'm assuming these other statues are their *offspring*?" I said, motioning to the dozen or more smaller Lycan statues that lined the carpet path behind them.

"*Imagined* offspring."

The two Lycan stopped at the end of the hall, where our lead waited while the other disappeared through the doors beyond them. While the zealot stood patiently, I glanced upon the smallest statue hanging upon the wall above him, which silently watched us as we approached. The statue was not like the other Lycan offspring. Its eyes were darker, jetted with black amethysts that seemed so disturbingly familiar. The only indication of the statue's identity was the stone cloth that unfolded from its claws, which bore a deep etching in its colorless flesh: Tenebrix.

"Lord of the Night," Aquilla said, his disgust as dark as the statue's eyes.

"You know of this Tenebrix?"

"I briefly studied their fantasized beliefs and promised afterlife of the most faithful Lycan."

"And what is that?"

"To join the moon Reia and her children, the stars, in fighting Tenebrix, who they say *is* darkness incarnate, along with forever hunting the faithless amidst the Void above; they believe that in order to strengthen the light against Tenebrix, who they both fear and respect, the faithful must eternally devour the souls deemed unworthy and placed in the landless realms between Bellatorix and Reia."

"Who they believe toil endlessly to hold the darkness of Tenebrix at bay," I said, remembering the tragic reflections of Turrok the Lycan.

The doors before the zealot opened softly. The Lycan who strode confidently through and clasped the arm of the zealot surprised me.

"Brother Eludoros," Menander said, his snout still displaying the care and innocence he touted during Lucien's wedding.

"The Pentarch of Lucca?" I said in disarray.

"I thought he was a member of the Pax," Aquilla said in equal dumbfoundedness.

"I bring good tidings," Eludoros said while unloading the sack before him.

A pale Human hand slid through the folds of the bag, along with moonlight locks quickly after. I dropped to my knees as the corpse, unmistakably Lucien's, revealed itself to Menander, who smiled with a darkness like that of Tenebrix above them.

"He looks exactly like him," Menander said, my heart skipping a beat as I tried to decipher his meaning. "Well done, Eludoros."

"Do you think it will work?" Eludoros said.

Aquilla and I walked around the body, and to my greatest relief, it was not my brother, but the resemblance was uncanny.

"Reports have already been spread to Delphius and Nicandor of their King's disappearance," Menander said while motioning to the shadows, at which another Lycan emerged to pick up the body and disappear to most undoubtedly pursue the plot involving Lucien's replica.

"The city states are like dry kindling waiting for the spark to burn any trust for the confederacy," he continued. "Once they hear, once they see the Ronian King's blood dripping from the Deplhians' and Nicandorians' hands, then they will hate. Their hate will tear them apart, and only fear will remain. Fear will lead to their repentance, brother, to their salvation."

The zealots bowed their heads before Tenebrix above them.

"Our time is almost upon us," Menander said. "The Festival of Eros shall see what we have been waiting for: a resurgence of faith that will topple the faithless."

""Thou shalt not abandon the wolf,"" Eludoros said.

Words choked in my spirit at the revelation of the revolution unfolding before us. Such plotting was so deceptively cunning that I could hardly comprehend its existence, especially given the wolf in sheep's clothing who feigned no support of what would burn the confederation he served.

He reminded me greatly of Volsung.

And from Menander's ill omen of their lunar eclipse festival, in which they indulged in ritual procreation and satisfied every bestial desire in celebration of their gods' union, time was drawing short before their schemes would be fully enacted.

"He wishes to build upon the Pentarchy's ashes with his own machinations," Aquilla said. "And if he intends to do this on their festival, that leaves us with only twelve days after tonight to save Lucien."

At the sound of my brother's name, I felt a stabbing pain in my heart at the one jarring question that had been left unanswered despite their revealed plot: where was Lucien?

"Menander!" a familiar but strained voice yelled from behind the doors.

Menander sighed a look of annoyance.

"Why is the boy still here in your home, Menander?" Eludorus said.

"Because, my dear Eludorus, it is the last place anyone would care to look. Now go, get some much deserved rest. I must deal with the pup."

Without another word, Menander returned through the doors he came from, which fed into a moonlit courtyard walled by three pillared floors surrounding it.

And chained to a fountain at its center was Lucien.

Aquilla was the only thing holding me back from revealing myself to Lucien as I flew to him, who looked pale and gaunt in the moonlight, his face a pale rose with his dried tears being evident from the traces of dirt enveloping his bound frame.

"Lucien!" I said, kneeling in a futile attempt to embrace him with my spirit.

The darkness which threatened to consume any hope and sense of worth was stalled by the light of defiance that glimmered in his eyes. Lucien was glaring past me at Menander, who walked slowly to him. Menander was not alone, for countless shadows of Lycan moved amongst the balconies as they watched their leader confront their prize.

"My dear friend," Menander said as he towered before Lucien.

"I was not finished with you, dog!" Lucien said. "I will have you skinned like a cabat and your disgusting pelt sold to your Kapitolian masters to whom you grovel so well."

Before Menander could respond, one of the Lycan guards from the shadows cursed and furiously whipped Lucien across the back for his remarks. Several bloody gashes tore through his heaving and shivering flesh.

"Gahhh!" Lucien groaned, collapsing in his chains.

"Lucien!" I yelled, my spirit tearing at the seams from my inability to help him.

"Enough!" Menander said, halting the guard mid-strike by grasping his hand wielding the whip. "I did not have the Prince brought here to be beaten!"

"Forgive me," the guard said, pulling away in obedience.

"I sincerely apologize, young master," Menandaer said as he knelt before a trembling Lucien, staring directly into his eyes. "It was never my intention to see you harmed."

Everything within me wanted to reach into Menander's heart and crush it like the Valravn's, like the Soulis; to treat him like the lying monster he was.

"Steady your hatred, Morgan," Aquilla said, reminding me of my former guilt of such bloodlust. "Do not let it dwell."

"Is that what your masters in Kapitol tell you to believe, *dog*?" Lucien stuttered, blood trickling down his back from the several deep gashes he received. Lucien was trying not to cry, but the quiver in his voice betrayed the fear and pain within. "They must have you on a tight leash!"

"You misunderstand your purpose in all of this, and who your true enemies are," Menander said calmly. "I am no lover of any kind but my own, though I admit the Kapitolians have been a most valuable ally of convenience to Laconnia. But you should really look to your own flock for want of wolves. Your dear uncle could almost pass for one of our citizens in that regard."

"Lies!" Lucien screamed, balking at his chains. "You lie!"

"How piteous. You led yourself right into his web like a naive insect expecting comfort from a spider," Menander said, standing to his feet again to tower over Lucien. "Once the rebirth of Laconnia has passed, I will set you free to take back your crown from Volsung. He is rather unpleasant in his view of our kind."

"So that's what this is all about? You and your brother Orpheus lust to become kings yourselves?"

"Unfortunately, I am the only one who sees the truth of what is to come," Menander said, his tone melancholic as he began to pace before Lucien. "The souls of the Lycan are what I care most deeply about, thus is the thesis for all of my desires and of Kairos before me: *salvation*."

A look of confusion spread upon Lucien's enraged brow, mirroring mine. "Kairos, that heretical revolutionary, was executed nearly a century ago, was he not?"

Menander's gaze locked onto Lucien with a simmering heat, yet his words betrayed no such anger. Calmly, he began to speak once more. "One of the many great sins our Pentarchid Government has performed. Truly, there is nothing so difficult as to institute a new order. But his spirit is kept alive by Bellatorix Himself. May His name strike fear into the faithless once more to ensure the downfall of this city."

"What does the ruin of Ehlonica have to do with salvation?" chided a thin and shivering Lucien.

"Do you know what this city is named for?"

"I'm afraid I haven't yet had the time to study your history to the extent of your liking."

"*Victory at Ehlos*. That is what Ehlonica means in my peoples' tongue. Near the ruins of Ehlos, ten thousand perished by the shower of Delphian arrows, Nicandorian steel, and the aid of Kapitolian trickery. Ehlos, where the downfall of our culture began and the rise of our unequal Pentarchy set its roots. The eastfold of Laconnia burned in their conquest, including the home of our great prophet Kairos. While others bent the knee and even joined in the rebuilding of Ehlos into the abomination of Ehlonica, Kairos was given holy revelation of new scripture, *foresight* to see the danger that was born here.

"All that has corrupted our traditions and faith has spread

from this city, dear Prince; whether it be the false claims of our Averitic origins, the dilution of our faith to mere philosophy, or even the acceptance of other gods in place of our own. Ehlonica is, by its very nature, a name given to *insult* Laconnian freedom and culture. That is why Kairos sought to destroy it, and why his followers will ensure it."

"The Averite is truly lost," Aquilla said with disgust.

"*Danger*?" Lucien said. "In a century, the Ehlonican Renaissance brought the cities of Laconnia together as one for the first time in history. I see now that your forebears were right to put the axe to that heretic's neck. As he would have done, you too will dismantle the stability of this land. Then, the foreign powers of man that you so fear shall take from you all that they desire."

Menander drew uncomfortably close to Lucien, so close that his teeth were but a breath from tearing apart Lucien's slender and starved face.

"As one?" Menander snarled, breaking his composure for just a moment. "Where was the promised unity of Ehlonica when Judux plundered the east for its silver not but seven sols ago?"

"Do not mistake my passion for recklessness," the Lycan continued. "Though I will do what I must, I do not wish for the destruction of Delphius, Nicandor, nor any other city of the confederation, no matter their past follies. With due penance, all may receive Reia's mercy, and Laconnia will be stronger than ever before once our work is complete. It is only Ehlonica that must be razed to the ground to ensure the sins of the past may linger no further.

"I assure you such reckoning shall also be dealt to any who would set foot on our sovereign soil again, whether they be man or Drakin. 'Giveth but a spear unto my right hand and a shield unto my left, and a ring of corpses shall thine servant make of those who dare bear arms against thee, oh sacred Laconnia.' This is my promise from the very words of Kairos, young master. Your people will receive *nothing* from our lands, nor will we have anything to do with you after you are used to unseat our Pentarchy."

To mine and Aquilla's shock, Lucien spat in his captor's eye, who returned not even the slightest flinch.

"This revolution of yours and whatever plans you have for me will not see the light of day when my people come for me. For then you will be thrown down to your belly like the beast you are when I am rescued, and you will join your heretic as a martyr!"

"Tell me, will it be your wife who rescues you?" Menander said with a terrifying smile, rising above Lucien and wiping the spit from his face. "Or your beloved uncle, perhaps? No, I think not. A king who commands no authority or respect is nothing but a king of empty air. You would be wise to lead like a wolf, cunning and displaying no weakness, such as your father did. But you are not the man he was, only a pale reflection, weak and informidable. For your emotions will only show where your foes can *devour* you!

"I will return you to your uncle once Laconnia is reborn, and Laconnia and Renborg shall be fully separate once again. But when this life is at its end and we are called to judgement, I shall find it great sport to personally chase you in the eternal hunt ever after. Alas, that time has not yet come, for there is much work to be done and many who must die before it is finished."

At that, Menander turned from Lucien to make his exit, but not before Lucien's final rebuke made him halt.

"And what of your brother, Orpheus? Must he too fall for your zealotry?"

Menander paused.

Inhaling the reality of Lucien's words, he lifted his head, almost prayerfully to the heavens. A moment later, he exhaled as he straightened his back and turned slightly to answer. "Orpheus may share my blood, but he does not share my heart. That lies with my true brothers, and they are legion. Farewell, young master."

The courtyard emptied quickly as Menander summoned several of the zealous Lycan to follow him out. As soon as they left, Lucien collapsed back into his chains, his air of confident defiance bleeding out of him.

"Morgan, we should leave," Aquilla said gently. "It shall do us no good to remain. We should return to finish the Trial of the Ora'suns so that we can rescue your brother and reunite him with his wife."

The thought of Egret completely helpless and alone was the only thing that drew me away from Lucien's suffering, which I could not bear to watch nor look away from.

"Very well," I said, my heavy soul drifting through the wispy clouds of the night as Lucien soon disappeared from my view, though not the image of his agony.

"We are running out of time, and they are counting on us to save them," Aquilla said, images of Lucien, Egret, and Philomela flashing through his thoughts made apparent for me.

The feeling of failure was threatening to capsize my soul's vessel into the sea of worthless oblivion, but each of their eyes contained a beautiful soul that I was not going to let my damned destiny of Shadow destroy. If Aquilla was truly called to aid me in saving them, then may we be able to ensure it, though it all seemed impossible.

May Aquilla and I lift the Spear of Mythraelyon and save Egret.
May we deliver Lucien from the Lycan.
May we slay Belial and Judux to spare Philomela.
May my weak and shameful hands be successful.

Chapter 23
Aela Zaeim

Aela Zaeim, an Elven member of the Taldarii Order, believed in the Shepherds. Other sects thought they were merely a myth or that the only Shepherd who ever existed was Cypherus and possibly Mythraelyon. Aela believed not that the Order should serve the emperors but that they should serve the Shepherds. She would go on to found the Ora'suns, "Her Servants", which was meant to serve as the Shepherd's personal army. Their formation received the scorn of her brothers who shunned her from Divonholm, to where she and her followers instead founded their home in the Elven lands of Valeneka.

But the Shadow of the Black Legion arose, finding the Ora'suns and tricking many of them to swear loyalty to their leader. Many who did hated him but felt honor bound because they believed he was a Shepherd, albeit a Dark One. Aela retaliated against the Unnamed One, leading him to draw power from the Void to burn alive all but a few of the Taldarii Order, including Aela. The Ora'suns fled from their secret strongholds in Valeneka to Cur Malum, the "Isle of Weeping", where they buried Aela. It is rumored that Aela's wise mentor took her place as the Berei a'l Zaeim, "Seeker of the Shepherd."

Chronicles of Renborg: King's Edition
"The Taldarii Order: Birth of the Ora'suns"
Piluch Joffersun: Master of Histories

"M**organ?"** Egret said, her voice weak and withered.

"I'm here, Egret," I said as my body awoke from Soul Sleep, Aquilla resting beside us.

"I had a feeling you were gone," she said, her eyes closing heavily.

"Only for a little while."

"Don't… don't let it be longer next time."

"I won't."

Exhaustion painted Egret's baggy eyes, but she held in herself a display of strength nonetheless as she firmed her lips.

"What did you see?" she said.

"Too much."

"I want to know," she said, relinquishing a smile. "Let me know, so I can pray for you."

As I was about to tell her of Lucien, I realized I had not received the chance to tell her of Belial and the Battle of Brännfält. So with a heart scorched from Belial's flames and whipped from Lucien's torture, I told her everything, including my destiny of Shadow and how Philomela would be destroyed if we did not defeat Belial.

And as I finished, the agony of what had befallen me the last two months finally took its hold and shook my soul so violently, so callously, that an uncontrollable torrent of weeping overwhelmed me.

"We are going to succeed, Morgan," Aquilla said, his words more uncomforting than water against my skin.

"Morgan," Egret said, "do not lose heart yet. The Ora'suns are nearly ours, and we will save your brother and Philomela. We will find a way to not become some destined Shadow, for the Mother's song is our strength."

"What about you?"

Egret reeled back at the thought of herself, and for a moment, a flash of hopelessness and despair appeared on the soft glow of her face in the torchlight, her pale green eyes brimming with tears which she hid by turning away.

"I will be well."

The four words she spoke with grimacing pain were a lie.

Egret closed her eyes for a long pause.

The truth must have been settling in that she would never be able to walk again, that she was destined to be helplessly pushed around by servants and unable to create a family that would love her.

But maybe I could…

The idea was cast from my mind as quickly as it was made. I was of a bastard's status, and she was a Queen.

No, she was Lucien's wife.

Lucien's unloved wife.

Lucien's discarded beloved in which not a second thought was given to her.

How could he not see it?

All it took was just a glimpse, a sight I received when our eyes first met in the library, leaving not the flesh to be devoured by the eyes but the soul. Egret's loyalty, her faith, and her enduring strength continued to bloom despite our differences and frustrations, regardless of our broken vessels that did not immediately attract the other's eye.

To my greatest confusion, Lucien was blind to Egret's inner worth, which began to dawn on me like the warm sun rising after a night of cold rain.

Though he could not see it, the light of her soul deserved to be treasured.

Aquilla's eyes bore into me as he watched me wrestle with my thoughts.

"Morgan," Aquilla spoke within and to me alone, "we must not let our thoughts carry us away from our purpose. As you have said, she already belongs to a husband, and it is his responsibility to take care of her. Do not incur the divine wrath of dividing a marriage."

What is the purpose of a Shepherd, Aquilla?

"To obey the Mother's Will, of course."

Which is to take care of Her people, is it not?

"Yes, but you seek to care for her needs that only her husband can fulfill."

No… no, I seek only to repay her for what she has sacrificed for me. She is more worthy of life than I am; like Philomela.

"Egret…" I began, though the aching of my heart made it difficult to even speak.

"The composure of one's body does not make one beautiful, nor strong," Egret said with a soft smile. "It is what guides their heart that makes them so, is it not?"

Before I could respond, Egret gently unsheathed my arm from the rest of my shirt, revealing the charred skin beneath to the warm glow of our prison, much to my surprise. She tried to reveal the other arm from its sleeve, but as she reached, a pain jolted her away, and she returned to lying where she could only move her head.

Gently, carefully, I laid myself down next to her upon the carpet which was our floor, giving her space to breathe. Lying softly beside her, my heart thundered, beating precipitously as our eyes embraced.

I couldn't say where Aquilla was at that moment, nor however long the moment lasted, for all I could see was Egret. The Shadow of my destiny became a dwindling threat as Egret's eyes danced with mine.

"Look," Egret said, unable to help a smile, "we at last see eye to eye, peasant."

"You deserve to stand tall again, my Queen," I said, my face mirroring hers.

Egret shrugged. "I will accept the destiny in which the Mother finds me worthy of. As long as you save our people, Krabios, I will be content."

Egret's words lacked passion, but they were empowered by conviction. She cared not for herself, though she mourned the loss of her strength. She had lost her greatest joy to save me, forever a cripple from her sacrifice, but even then her concern remained focused on others, all of which was fueled by her faith.

Egret truly deserved to be cared for, to enjoy life to its fullest.

Despair for Egret almost overtook me until a memory sang a nearly forgotten song: a way to save Egret from this crippled life, for I had once been shown such care before.

The only way to heal Egret was to become the Aela Zaeim.

"Morgan, we shall not!" Aquilla said as Egret slept in peace beside me.

We need her Aquilla!

"And the world needs you, Morgan! You shall stand no chance against Belial if you commit such a foolish act with the spear. She is not worth the sacrifice!"

Did you not think the same of me when the Mother showed you my broken self?

"That was different."

How so?

Our internal argument was interrupted by the door of our prison cell being thrust open. Two Ora'suns marched in and plucked Egret from the ground before dragging her away with little resistance.

"Where are you taking her!" I said, grabbing the closest Ora'sun by his robed collar.

"Enough!" Alcharion said, his sword, emerging a finger's breadth from my face, glistening in the afternoon light that threaded into the cell. "Take her to the Berei a'l Zaeim and bring forth the other contestant."

"Wait!" I said, my eyes locking with Egret's panicked stricken eyes which still paled a sickly green, but again I was stopped by Alcharion who glowered between us.

"You will see her again *if* you complete the last Trial."

"Be calm, Morgan," Aquilla said as I longed to crush his wicked heart.

At Alcharion's command, we were forcefully escorted from the cell. Before I could even say goodbye, they took Egret in another direction as we descended back into the city. The last glimpse I saw of her before a blindfold was forced upon me was one not of fear, but only calm assurity. Her faith in me kept the flames alive from the hopeless darkness that threatened to smother me once again.

That darkness was ever-present. It so frustratingly longed to drown me from my first breath and until my last.

"Where are we going?" I said in darkness, but Alcharion said nothing as I was forced to follow him blindly.

In declination of any answers and sight, I opened my eyes to Aquilla's to see anything that could help. In the world of spiritual glass, I could see, and now hear, that we were descending from the mountain temple. We traversed down and through the crowded and perfume-ridden Meshiac, followed by ten Ora'suns on either side, along with another blinded Elf beside me. He must have been the other contestant.

What perplexed me was the Bludhstone glowing from Alcharion's pocket. When Alcharion readjusted his robe, the necklace became clear in its unfurling.

The Elf had stolen my Godstone necklace.

"His motivations elude me," Aquilla said.

Anger propelled me to feign a stumble into Alcharion, allowing me to place my hands upon his robes for balance. In the irritated commotion, I quickly slipped my hand into his robes to retrieve my necklace, hiding it underneath my belt in surprised gratification.

He can find his own necklace.

"Foolish boy!" Alcharion sneered, ordering his Ora'suns to help me back to my feet, completely oblivious to my retrieval and his robbery.

It wasn't until we descended the winding path of the mountain river valley that Alcharion stopped and unblinded me, along with the other Elf.

Now that I could see his face, the other contestant was a younger Elf, probably fifty sols young, his eyes a violet dark and skin a lighter shade of sand. There existed no fear in his eyes as he looked at me, only a calm intensity.

"The last of your Trial now begins. As an Ora'sun, we are both fearless of death and able to deliver it from the shadows. Your task is simple: make your way back to the Temple arena without being seen."

"Simple enough," I said.

"If you are seen, you will be slain."

"Let's begin," the other contestant said.

"And if you finish last, you shall similarly be slain. The same is true for your friend, Morgan. Her fate shall be the same as yours."

"What?" Aquilla and I both said.

A million different ways to kill Alcharion surged through my mind, but Aquilla's stern inward barrier created a mental dam to divert them away from my words and actions. But before my thoughts could breed fruition, the dark Elf slammed his fist into my stomach, crippling me to the ground.

"You may begin," Alcharion said, taking himself and his Ora'suns back along the bridge to the city as the sun began to fall in the sky, along with a storm fast approaching beyond.

The other contestant did not wait for me to recover.

"Vorim!" I screamed, scrambling to my feet and hopelessly chasing after the other contestant already bounding up the mountain path.

"Do not fear, Morgan," Aquilla said. "There is one thing Alcharion forgot to calculate for."

"And what is that?"

Aquilla looked at me with an otherworldly serenity that

transcended my fearful heart as I limped along, his galactic and transparent eyes burning like suns into my own.

"Like Cypherus before you, I will show you how to move faster than the wind."

"We've wasted too much time," I said as we abandoned the path towards Meshiac to delve deeper into the rocky, fog-ridden river valley.

As we raced with haste, the sun descended ever closer to the horizon beyond, and the other contestant sped undoubtedly far ahead of us. However, we were enveloped in the deep fog that penetrated every breath. Though I hated to admit it, we were certainly invisible to any Ora'sun above us.

"'A careful measure will ensure the scales of victory are favorable,'" Aquilla said.

"This only makes it more impossible to reach Egret in time. How are we supposed to get to the top of the mountain? The sides are too steep to climb even with your spirit. The only path up was the one in which we left behind."

"Shall you trust me at last, Morgan?"

Taking a shaking breath for patience, I relented.

"You're not easy to trust, Aquilla."

"Morgan, forgive me for keeping you in the dark about Lucien. I admit I was wrong to do so. Can you release the anger towards me from your heart?"

The immediate response of my flesh was an absolute *no*. However, time was of the essence, and Egret's life was at stake, as were my brother and sister. There was no time for petty games of the mind caused by pride and miscommunication. Instead, I nodded my head, bowing slightly.

"Let us speak openly and work together then, from now on?"

Shaking my head from annoyance, I agreed.

"Very well," Aquilla said. "For us to climb this mountain, it shall require more diligence than before. Since our schedule is *tightened*, we must lose some of your weight."

"You are truly hopeless. What are you implying, Medjaib?"

"You are strong and lean, but you would climb faster if you weighed nothing, correct?"

"Like your spirit?"

"Exactly, and you've already performed this before."

Aquilla's memory of me running to save Egret in the arena presented itself in my mind, and from Aquilla's eyes I could see the core of my body phasing beneath my clothes as I ran faster than an eagle in flight.

"Your heart removed itself momentarily from your mistrust of me upon seeing Egret in danger. Now, let it blossom fully and yield ever more, ever further into the Light which calls you from my spirit. Trust in me; let me guide you, Morgan."

This time I did not rebuke the Medjaib.

It was easier to trust in Aquilla having seen Egret on the other side of surrender. So I allowed my thoughts, my very heartstrings, my everything to hone in on the memories of Egret, particularly seeing her being cut down by the Valravn and seeing her lie helplessly in the prison cell.

Egret would be slain if we failed, as would Lucien and Philomela.

To trust in Aquilla would be their salvation.

And though Aquilla had proved exceedingly difficult to trust at first, I believed in his words, his authenticity, forgiving his naivety that misguided him at first for not wanting to be like his brothers.

In fact, I was, in many ways, glad to have him at my side.

The lightning of my soul struck upon the thought of friendship with the strange spirit from the moon, and my soul began to break free from my charred though useful vessel.

"I… I can't believe it," I said, watching most of my legs

and chest be replaced by Aquilla's shimmering spirit within me, which soon phased through most of my flesh, but not all of it.

There felt a hindrance in my spirit that I could not name. But for now, my being felt as light as a feather.

"Well done, Morgan! Now, run as the wind!"

Like Soul Sleep, I was elated to sprint faster than any winged creature ever could as I exploded forthward through the thick fog, unafraid of collision with Egret's life at stake.

My soul was more bountiful with joy than I could ever remember.

The last I had felt such pure, burdenless delight was the almost faded summers in Hebsund that I kept locked in my heart: fishing in the Lake Hebron with a jovial Gulmund and Kyllian, playing Castle Chess with Lucien long into the endless nights, and writing Skallgends that lacked in poeticism but abounded in youthful, naive joy.

And like a tea kettle ready to erupt, I leaped effortlessly into the sky and sailed far above the mountain's treeline shrouded in fog.

"Incredible!" I said, my body falling towards the ground, though I was not like a boulder plummeting towards the dirt, but like a leaf being carried gently yet quickly through the wind.

"It is indeed!" Aquilla said. "Now, let us surpass this mountain that stands proudly before us!"

I ascended a great deal of the soon to be storm-ridden mountainside before Aquilla even finished his encouragement, though I almost plummeted to the jagged rocks below in reaching my intended destination so quickly. Turning towards the steep cliff, I jumped weightlessly upon it, hardly needing to phase my hands and feet into the stone to propel myself upwards. The body I once despised before was now intertwined with the beautiful, mesmerizing galaxy of Aquilla's flesh, making my once unbearable skin now a tool for feats unimaginable.

I felt truly free; no longer an anchor in the colorless sea.

Within minutes, we reached a shelf overlooking the city that sat just beneath the opening of the arena.

"Just in time," I said, taking a second to catch my breath and readjust Lucien's Godstone necklace as the sun began to kiss the oceanic horizon, its orange rays pouring out onto the crystal blue waves like a spilled drink.

The rain also began to grace our heads.

"We make significant progress, but we must not let pride befall us," Aquilla said. "Each day that bleeds by will be a day closer for to Lucien and Philomela's demise. Let us make haste to ensure we have beaten our competitor."

"How long will it be till we rule the Ora'suns?" I said, preparing to leap onto the last ridge.

"We shall request to perform the Sundel Ritual immediately after completing the Trial of Beating Hearts. The Berei a'l Zaeim shall be there, and all you must do is wield the Klyr Spear of Mythraelyon with my purity, which you shall, and her wicked heart shall be removed for your placement as their leader."

"The Ora'suns will follow me after the ritual, even though I have just arrived?"

"That is what Aela Zaeim decreed upon the Order's founding: that all shall kneel to the Shepherd upon his finding."

"Then they will know I am the Shepherd, thus revealing us to the world and to Thadius?"

"It is... *necessary* that they know, for it is the only way."

"Then let us take the spear."

As I prepared to jump up the last stretch of the mountain, a rock cratered into my stomach but thankfully phased through Aquilla's flesh, the wielder of stone crashing down in a mighty display of strength and fury before me.

Alcharion had found us.

"I knew it," Alcharion said, spit and rain flying from his snarking lips as he raised his ornately curved sword. "You are a mad sorcerer whose only friend is the shadows you whisper to. I will not let you fulfill your intent to control us for your own evil designs as our enemy did! Stay your hand, and die honorably."

"Why do you hate me so much?" I yelled through the now pouring rain as the thunderously tall Elf rushed and swung his blade down upon me.

Phasing, I rolled out of the way upon the slick stone.

Though just barely.

"Use your surroundings, Morgan!" Aquilla said.

"You Humans are all the same!" Alcharion said, backing me against the drenched wall of the mountain. "Always wanting to use others for your own glory!"

With ease, I leapt over Alcharion just as he violently struck his sword into the wet stone, rendering it stuck and unretrievable from the sheer force he harnessed.

Every second we wasted fighting was another closer to Egret's death. Quickly, through Aquilla's eyes, I could see the other contestant had made his way to the bottom of the mountain stairs, sprinting up them quietly.

Alcharion roared in his failure to retrieve the sword. At once, he returned his fury to me. Like a rolling boulder, Alcharion advanced upon me with size and haste, the drop behind me drawing ever closer.

Moving as one, Aquilla showed me the word for stone in the Tongue of Tihrrvyith, which I drew quickly with his fingers, gripping the rain-soaked mountain before the rushing Elf's feet and raising it just a foot.

Oohm!

Alcharion stumbled past us and over the cliff as we slid out of the way, though his hand caught onto the slick ridge as he hung helplessly beneath us.

The Elf was bested. Hanging from the edge in defeat, Alcharion still held a defiant fire in his eyes.

"False Shepherd, why do you hesitate? Take my soul and be done with it!" Alcharion winced, his fingers crushing into the stone as his glare strained upon us with blood-fueled rage. "Prove you are no better than the dark one of the Kira Naz'ka. Deliver me the sleepless fate of my mother and brothers!"

"I am not here to steal your soul!" I said. "But I will not let you steal the soul of—"

Vaekee!

Lightning struck the mountainside and took our breaths by surprise. Even Alcharion's anger was subdued at the sudden intrusion of burning light from the storm. As for me, I could see the Tongue of Creation holding it all together in its terrifying glory.

But the blinding language seized my mind.

The lightning and the word transfixed and consumed me for a precious second too long.

"Morgan!" Aquilla tried to warn, but it was too late.

Alcharion grabbed my ankle with his free hand, and with all of his remaining might, he threw me down the mountain.

"Morgan!" Aquilla yelled as panic consumed me. "Phase!"

A second longer and I would have truly tasted the cost of falling from the cliffs as I had yearned to do not so long ago; but now, I wished to live. Slowing my descent by removing most of my weight, I caught hold of the mountain just in time as my trust in Aquilla strengthened.

"I have you now, deceiver!" Alcharion growled above us as he rose to his feet upon the cliff's ledge. Loosening a stone from the mountain, the Elf prepared to ensure my fate as he took aim. "Enor will arrive any moment, and you will fail."

They're going to kill Egret!

"We must hurry, Morgan!" Aquilla shouted. "Quickly, follow my thoughts!"

What? I thought, reading his mind. *I will surely fall to my death!*

"Trust in me!"

The stone hurling from Alcharion quickly extinguished such crippling fear. With everything to lose, I weightlessly propelled myself upwards and over the Elf using Wyl, the grace of which surprised both the enemy and myself as I landed behind him.

Alcharion's surprise quickly boiled into rage as he turned, lunging towards me to ensure a shadowed fate.

With every drop of strength, my mind transfixed upon Egret as I leapt weightlessly up the mountainside again, my feet just missing the Elf's hands.

The storm-ridden mountainside was a blur mirroring my mind as I soared breathlessly up the cliff, the dark clouds thundering around us. Fear and anxiety threatened to overwhelm me as we collapsed, hands shaking and sweating, into the sandstone arena.

"I'm here!" I yelled in exhaustive triumph, catching the surprise of all of the Ora'suns as the other contestant, panting but focused, sprang from the stairwell only moments too late.

The other contestant, shocked at my sudden appearance and victory, knelt and sullenly bowed his head in defeat. Though it would be a tragedy to see him die, one glance upon Egret, still alive as she lay guarded beside the Berei a'l Zaeim and her ancient assistant, made such a cost necessary.

Alcharion crawled without a word up the cliff moments after, catching the attention of all from his labored climb. The Elf's face contorted into that of hatred as he moved to stand still amongst the silent crowd of Ora'suns in the middle of the arena. But then, as the other contestant waded into the parting crowd, Alcharion began to smile.

"Well done," Nizari's assistant said, the entire arena as silent as the grave except for his voice. "Come, both of you, stand before the Berei a'l Zaeim."

"She has brought the spear in preparation," Aquilla said, nodding to Mythraelyon's Klyr spear which shone a holy white before Nizari and Egret. "She must have expected you to win."

This second Trial was not as challenging as I had assumed it would be, I thought as the contestant and I stood before Nizari and Egret. *Let us grab the spear and—*

"Morgan Krios," the Elvish assistant continued, "as the victor of the second Trial, you shall be spared from the sting of death which devours those unable to hide in the shadows. Enor Tinishar, as the defeated of the second Trial, you shall depart from the realm of the living. *Immediately*."

My eyes met Egret's somber melodies before I bowed my head, not wanting to see what would befall the Elf.

"*Morgan*," Nizari whispered harshly, "cast his unworthy heart unto the Mother's hands. Only then shall you prove to us that your heart is worthy of being a true Ora'sun, that you are willing to purge the darkness from the light."

The rain swept down upon us from the storm, drenching the candles upon the masked Nizari. The rotting odor of death flooded my nose as Nizari nodded to several of the Ora'suns to move the terrified Elf to the edge of the cliff, leaving Aquilla and I alone with him.

"What?" I said, disbelief throwing my mind into chaos as I looked in shock at Nizari. "You want me to kill an innocent person?"

"Who are you to say he's innocent?" Nizari said, her pits for eyes an abysmal dark, watching me intently through her silver mask, challenging me to disobey.

Aquilla emerged from my flesh to stand before Enor, tilting his head slightly as he studied him before casting his gaze to the moon in the Void above.

"I will not kill him," I said, my words trembling from my mouth in anger.

"Very well," Nizari said, nodding to Alcharion, who, in an instant, sprung from the crowd beside me, unsheathing a curved knife that he wrapped tightly around my throat.

"What are you doing?" I yelled, struggling carefully against his grip.

"Morgan!" Egret said, her eyes stark with terror as Aquilla rejoined my anxiety-filled vessel.

Everything within me wanted to phase, but as the blade began to bite harder into my throat, Aquilla stopped me. "No, Morgan! At this range, your blood would spill before you could even blink an eye. This one is too quick."

"One of you must embrace death in order that light be birthed from the darkness," Nizari whispered harshly. "It is the only way, Morgan. If you refuse to send Enor to the grave, then you shall take his place instead. What will your choice be? Will you do what is necessary for the light to be born?"

"Listen to her Morgan, do not hesitate," Aquilla said. "We must return to Renborg to save your brother, to save millions of lives against the plans of Thadius! His single life is not worth theirs. Think of your brother, Morgan."

The storm engulfed the entire congregation in a heavy rain that danced across the wet stone ground as I thought of my imperiled brother. Lucien, encaged by the zealous Lycan sect who saw bloodshed as the only way for the *light* to be born. Sigmund also emerged in my frantic mind, the flame of his life being extinguished before it could ever begin.

Could I do that to another? Willingly stop their heart?

Yes, I had easily crushed the Valravn's heart for harming Egret, but even then, despite its wickedness, I felt guilt for ending its life.

"Choose now or the choice will be made for you," Alcharion said, the blade tightening against my throat as drops of red stained my captor's hand.

"Egret," I said, looking to her soul's embrace as all whispered for me to take the Elf's innocent life.

In her pale emeralds, I expected to see the same begrudging answer I found in Aquilla: to do what was necessary. But that is not what I found. Instead, she shook her head, giving me the same perceptive look she gave in the library.

"I'm not afraid of anything," I had said between the sea of books.

"Even death?" she had whispered, curious if I was truthful.

"Especially that."

My eyes met Aquilla's cosmic curiosity.

"Morgan," he began, reading my mind.

You know my heart Aquilla.

"We must—"

"I refuse to kill an innocent," I said, my neck beginning to shimmer into Aquilla's flesh, preparing to fight for what was right.

"Very well," Nizari said, nodding to Alcharion.

I began to shift my feet to strike—

"Well done, brother," Alcharion said as he pulled the blade from my throat, nodding to Enor, who bowed in thanks before returning to the Ora'sun crowd. They received him warmly like one of their own.

Alcharion also joined him, though he did not seem pleased.

"What is this?" I said, standing in shock as Aquilla remained similarly confused.

"Congratulations, Morgan Krios," Nizari said, bowing slightly. "You have proved your heart to not be wicked, to not be of the corrupted nature as our enemy. The one of the spirit, who came long before you, would not have hesitated to kill his brother for his own gain, for what he perceived as necessary."

Anger reddened my face as I understood that it was merely a test which I had nearly failed. Looking at Egret, I could see in her tired eyes that she was relieved at my choice.

"Morgan," Aquilla began, but I cut him off by storming to the spear.

The Ora'suns were silent, and the gilded Temple guards stayed their blades as I approached the spear.

"As the Mother's Shepherd, as an Ora'sun who has *proved* my heart, I seek the Sundel Ritual to lead Her servants."

Alcharion gave me a look of fearful desperation as Nizari bowed her head, her wax-ridden hand pointing to the spear sheathed in the stone before us.

"Let us rise, Morgan," Aquilla said, his spirit's hands waiting like destiny upon the spear.

Do you trust me at last, spirit?

Aquilla hesitated for a moment, but at last he bowed his head.

"I do."

As one in trust, we wrapped our hands upon the cold, wet spear in the rain, thunder rumbling all around us. As one in purpose, we lifted the Spear of Mythraelyon from its gilded rock and held it before the Ora'suns for all to see: a trophy of destiny that rebuked the Shadow of fate.

It was, surprisingly, light.

One by one, the Ora'suns began to kneel. As it became evident that I could handle its purity, every Ora'sun found their knees buckled in reverence of me, of us. The Berei a'l Zaeim herself bowed as low as she could before me, and even Alcharion bent the knee in silence.

However, despite the victory in becoming Aela Zaeim, winning the fealty of a zealous army, and gaining the only spear that could possibly slay Belial, it all felt incomplete.

Egret's eyes caught mine as she sat next to me, smiling at my success. Underneath her encouraging smile that had given such speed to my flight up the mountain, I knew that she too wished once more to be able to stand so she could celebrate with me.

The Tongue of Creation sang to me as I looked upon her, and for the first time, I was blessed with seeing the name of her eternal soul that bloomed like a spring flower after a storm:

Oohitheekleea...

Human Woman...

Without thinking, my hands began drawing the word of her soul before Aquilla could register what I was doing.

"Morgan, wait!" Aquilla said, but the name of Egret's soul had been written at the direction of my heart, and every eye beheld the glowing white symbols that I drew from the Klyr spear which shimmered before Egret, whose soul I could now feel the weight of in my very own hands.

Egret must have felt exactly as I did when Lucien tried to heal me on that morning that felt so long ago: amazed and terrified.

But this time, healing would become more than just a dream.

Sheer agonizing pain erupted in my spine as I performed Wae on Egret's very being, the spear vibrating upon the command. The healing power found only in Klyr Godstone coursed through my flesh and transferred her wounds unto me in exchange for my health unto her. She deserved it. Egret's eyes were wide in shock as I took more than half of her burden unto myself so that she could walk again.

Though it was not completely severed, my knees began to buckle as my spine, now forever weakened, was unable to hold me up as it had before. It would take time to be adjusted to this new reality. But all of the pain and weakness I would suffer for such a sacrifice was worth it the moment Egret began to rise from her chair, her strength being mostly restored as tears gushed from her eyes in thankfulness.

Egret grabbed my hand and helped me to my feet, and together, we bore the same scars on our backs; we would conquer the Shadow together.

Aquilla's suns for eyes were fiery at my decision, but there seemed to be an understanding at last in my choice that was made beyond reason and logic without his approval.

"May Aela Zaeim guide us from darkness," Nizarri whispered for the first time hoarsely beside us, to which every Ora'sun repeated with zeal.

Even Alcharion muttered the mantra with respect and what seemed like awe at what had just transpired.

"Morgan…" Egret said in Skyyan, but she let her words bury in my chest as she embraced me. And though we both knew such embrace was verboten, our tears mixed together with the rain as we held each other, such worries being washed away. "I don't understand why," she barely said, tears overwhelming her words.

"Because you deserve more in life than to be left behind," I whispered in her own tongue. "The world would be a much darker and less joyful place without you, Egret. Though, it might be a bit quieter," I said with a smile.

Egret returned a small smile but pulled slightly back from me. "You care for me?" she said, her eyes undecipherable yet tinted with accusation as she sought to discern my words.

The care I had for Egret was supposed to be the same for Philomela: the one of an older brother who seeks to protect and care for his family.

After all, Egret was my family now, and it was my duty to protect her. She more than deserved that protection because of her determined and faithful soul that endured with me on this dangerous quest.

Smiling, I began to explain that my sacrifice for her sprouted only from familial care for her and our friendship, but the words immediately caught in my throat the more my heart marvelled at hers: that would not be completely true.

A river cannot help where it is to be, for it is clear for all who seek to see, I thought, remembering the Solbok proverb Lucien always quoted as I stood speechless before Egret, lost in her eyes which had drawn me in since the first day we met.

And now, it was clear why.

But my thoughts were swept aside as the storm clouds boomed a deep thunder that rolled across the dark sky.

"You are loved…" the clouds whispered through the rain.

Aquilla and I exchanged glances in confusion, but the voice was strikingly familiar.

Lightning danced from the clouds to strike the Spear of Mythraelyon in my hands, though Egret and I did not stumble.

"You are priceless…" the hot white energy sang while swirling within the Godstone.

Egret and I looked in reverent fear upon each other, but there was an otherworldly peace between us.

And that's when I felt it.

My breath became as still as the stars above as I felt an overwhelming yet powerful essence fill my entire being, and without even looking, I could feel the ethereal presence standing beside me.

It wasn't Aquilla.

Beyond any understanding or comprehension, I knew who it was that was now within and all around, as my heart knew the hands which formed it like a pot does its potter.

"You are *mine*," whispered the Mother.

Part III

The Rise

Chapter 24
The Redeemed Sun

Lycan have been, for their entire history, devout to one faith. That is until the sol 868 DE, when the Lycan Joras Inaeos of Naxos published his archaeological findings in a series of tomes entitled, "Genesis of the Lycanthropic Averite: The True History of Laconnia", in which he uncovered the secret of what many now believe was our true origin.

In a cave deep within the Remuloi Mountains, Joras found evidence of a cult. In their den were left inscriptions dating back to between 100 AE - 23 DE, detailing that they had performed an averitism on themselves to become Lycan, believing they were wolves encaged in Human flesh. Ever since Joras' research was published, he was condemned by the many Belorite Temples of Aphrenios and Devina as a liar and a heretic. Ironically, Joras was heavily conflicted by his own discoveries and did not publish them until 20 sols later. He himself had always been a very ardent and faithful Bellarite, but the response from his own religious friends and members of the faith who denounced him shattered what little faith he had left. Joras took his own life a sol later. The devoutly religious Belarites, however, believe this "evidence" to be the deceit of men.

The Histories of Laconnia
"Doubt"
According to Karnax of Ehlonica, 996 DE

The small but bright candle in the Ora'sun captain's quarters provided me with just enough light to see the Skallgend that once haunted me with no relief. But now hope flickered valiantly against the darkness, proving that the flame shared no nature with the shadow it was named to be. There existed hope that was impossible to see before:

"Cypherus, savior of souls, ruled as your thesis,
His shadow, sleepless death, will reign antithesis."

"We shall overcome destiny," Aquilla said while watching the other two Ora'sun ships sail in front of us upon the morning sun-crested waters of the River Parnaxos.

Nodding in agreement, I prayed that he would be right.

Grasping the Spear of Mythraelyon for support, the lightning within the Klyr Godstone swirling with power as a constant reminder of the Mother, I pulled myself out of my chair. Immediately the metal brace of my back dug into my ribs, grating my skin. My spine throbbed as I walked over to Aquilla to gaze upon the waves that had once been my destiny.

Each step was agonizing, but healing Egret was worth it.

Our journey to the capital city of Laconnia had taken longer than I'd hoped and carried its own risks, the chief of them being the avoidance of Kapitolian naval patrols and bribing an uncomfortable number of harbormasters for their discretion. Entering *quietly* through the port of Delphius at the mouth of the Parnaxos had been particularly expensive. However, all was worthwhile once the city of the Laconnian renaissance came into view from the side windows of our quarters.

Ehlonica's high walls and decorated towers held command of both river banks from which her dual ports would soon receive us.

It was an impressive sight to behold.

If time or circumstance were different, I would have even liked to explore the city with Egret and Lucien, as well as the hills beyond that hinted at the surprisingly rich beauty of this land. Regardless, it was a relief, to say the least, to finally be so close, yet somehow it all still felt so helplessly out of reach.

The candle wax of time was melting ever so thinly to the doom that Judux would deliver as he continued to burn the heartland of Renborg with the aid of Thadius' monstrosity, which he seemed to fully control. And as time drew uncomfortably close to the Lycan revolt that would take place during the eclipse tonight on their Festival of Eros, our chances of saving Lucien would be stolen from us if we did not stop it beforehand.

Time was running out.

The Festival of Eros, the Lycans' holy day of worship dedicated to the rarity of sun and moon becoming one, was only hours away.

Despite this, hope defiantly grew within us as Aquilla and I were given control over the fate that had so perilously tried to plague us with Shadow.

After becoming Aela Zaeim and our electrifying encounter with the Mother, which still radiated a mysterious, ethereal joy throughout my entire being, my first order as their long sought Shepherd was to completely mobilize any forces that could be spared. I planned first to bring one thousand Ora'suns with us to Ehlonica and then Renborg to face both Lycan and Drakin.

Resistance, despite my divine coronation, was voiced by Alcharion, who raised concern that we should not leave Meshiac and Cur Malum unguarded from the Kira Naz'ka or halt our efforts throughout Valeneka and Kapitol. Reluctantly seeing the wisdom in his counsel, and after a week of preparation, we sailed for Ehlonica with only three ships carrying nine Kapitolian ballistae for the Dragon, one hundred Ora'suns, and as many mounts, granting us much needed mobility. Strength reassuringly was to follow with another two hundred Ora'suns meeting us at the port of Norbo in Renborg with arms and mounts enough for our entire company.

And to my greatest joy, Alcharion publicly volunteered himself to join in our quest in *reverence* to his new Shepherd.

However, I did not believe his choice was of pure motives, but his addition and experience with the Ora'suns would make our small band of warriors slightly more formidable against our foes ahead of us.

"It will be enough," Aquilla said as we watched the first two of our ships begin to dock in the crowded port of Ehlonica's eastern bank. "We have the spear, full of lightning, mind you, and the Ora'suns' ballistae to take down Belial so we can meet him face to face."

"And what are the chances that the Ora'suns, skilled as they are, can even land a single bolt upon that serpent?"

"Morgan…" Aquilla began, but departing from him, I started to pace about my increasingly confined quarters.

"You saw yourself what speed it possesses! Even then, how are we to know if anything at all will come of it other than to draw the ire of its wrath?"

"'Fear maketh all things impossible.' Morgan, you fear for those you love, I understand. However, you must trust in the Ora'suns as they now trust in you, and in the end you must do what is necessary."

"I know," I said, thinking of the unfathomable weight of this new call to lead an entire people I had just met and barely understood, all the while avoiding the thought of ending Belial's unwanted and twisted life.

Breaking the tumbling spiral of my mind, the cabin doors exiting to the quarterdeck creaked open behind us.

Supported by a similar brace but displaying only courage, Egret strode confidently through the doors. She blessed me with a small but warming smile, her eyes glittering brighter than emeralds from the dedrim sap which Nizari oddly seemed to have heaping amounts of and gladly gave to Egret upon my request.

My heart saddened at the thought that Egret had to rely upon such toxins to feel strength again, to be of worth in her eyes. However, the joy in her recovered strength from my healing and the sap buried such lament, and I made no further complaint in her usage of it.

"Lady Nizari humbly requests your presence, Aela Zaeim," she said in Skyyan, giving a slight bow through the limits of her brace.

Rolling my eyes at her mockery, I was unable to hold back my own smile; it was truly rewarding to see her move again, to see her smile.

"Am I no longer Morgan to you?" I gently said in her tongue.

Egret stepped closer with cautious pace, her eyes furrowing as she studied me alongside Aquilla.

"You are no longer the boy I met in the library," she said, our eyes dancing as our vessels stood as still as statues.

"And you are much more than an arrogant Queen," I said, carefully moving a step closer.

"What a thing to say to your betters," she deflected with a wry smirk. "At least you say it in a tongue that I understand."

We were but a breath apart.

Eternity was grasped in the moment we shared, but it ended just as quickly as it began, for Egret pulled away and looked out upon the ports through the window.

"I will tell Lady Nizari that you wish to speak with her," Egret said, feigning me a quick smile before leaving us alone in my quarters.

The breath I held collapsed within me.

Within the almost two weeks that it took for us to reach Ehlonica, Egret had constantly been by my side as we led the zealous Ora'suns in preparation for our quest. Though we were both weakened in our spines, Egret proved more than capable. She had sparred day and night with us once we had healed enough, helping me perfect the techniques of Aquilla's phasing and using the Tongue of Tihrrvyith in battle as he instructed.

Her renewed joy from her healing was infectious, and I found myself ever fonder of her as I was blessed every day with her presence.

And when we weren't sparring or preparing for our journey, we danced with our minds as we did in Renborg's library, sharing a plethora of laughter and fascinating discussion of her homelands and her family, leaving us late into the night on many occasions.

"He was truly everything I could have wanted in a father," Egret said only a few nights ago as we both looked over the ship's railing, the stars above a glittering canvas painted far beyond my understanding.

"Did you have any siblings?" I said, my heart full of wonder.

"Four, all younger," she said.

"What were they like?"

"Well, my two sisters, Kallisto and Embria, are twins, so they got along better with each other than with me. Then there's Persius, the eldest brother, who follows in the political arts of our mother. But who really took my heart was Atheos, my youngest brother. He takes after his father, and has the most courageous spirit."

Egret was lost in thought of her family, the thoughts bringing her joy that I had rarely seen in the short time I had known her.

"Is it true that your mother intends to impede Persius' ascension to the throne to let Kallisto rise instead?" Aquilla said, who emerged from my spirit.

At her mother's mention, Egret's joy quickly sapped from her face, only to be replaced by an emotionless facade that I could not decipher.

"Yes," she said, her voice slightly trembling as she spoke, which she always did when her mother was brought up in conversation. But unlike the many times before, Egret did not refuse to speak further. "She is doing what she thinks is best."

"And do you trust what she's doing?"

Egret paused, casting her gaze deep into the waters. "My mother has plans that often eclipse my understanding… my marriage to Lucien being chief among them. But as Solbok instructs, 'I trust in the hands who formed me, in the one who birthed me.' She has never lied to me once, and she is doing what is best for her children."

"By sending you far across the ocean for the rest of your life?" I said, frustration building in seeing the deep hurt behind her words when she spoke about her mother, though she failed trying to conceal it.

"I'm of nobility, Morgan," Egret said, her voice defeated yet firm. "It is my duty to my people. What I want is of the least concern."

"But don't you miss your family? You will rarely get to see any of your siblings, friends, or your home again, except for the occasional diplomatic mission to maintain relations. How could a mother do that to her child?"

"She and everyone in the court have a responsibility you will never understand!"

Egret's tone was harsh in her defense of her mother, the reminder of our opposite positions in society a stinging rebuke. Perhaps realizing it, Egret recoiled slightly from me, looking down as she regained control of her thoughts.

"I know your heart seeks only to help. Truly, I am grateful that you speak to me in my tongue, that you would help me feel less alone in this strange new world. But Morgan, there are some things you were not meant to carry; some things that cannot be."

Egret bowed slightly before departing with haste from us, just as she did every time the courage arose within me to show her my growing devotion to her heart. Though, it never felt like she wanted to.

She was a loyal wife.

"And you are a covetous brother," Aquilla said as he so often did, not understanding my feelings at all but knowing enough about the sanctity of marriages to chide me each and every time it was brought up. Aquilla was especially fond of providing examples of history in which covetous people such as Jurgon II who "incurred the wrath of Bakara the Beast with such foolishness. Do you want to create an enemy of an empire? What peril shall that bring for both Lucien and Egret? For your soul?"

The worst part: he was right.

However, I sensed her true feelings mirrored mine in her glances upon me as I commanded Ora'suns on our voyage and when I was apart from my vessel in Soul Sleep with Aquilla. Several times we had gone to watch the war-stricken lands of Renborg only to return to see Egret gazing upon my sleepless form, lost in thought.

Guilt in trying to win my brother's wife attempted to consume me like the waves of meaninglessness did so long ago, and maybe they were of the same nature; perhaps it was meaninglessness that would devour me in the absence of sharing my heart with a beloved who cared for me and saw my broken flesh as beautiful.

Many would see such ponderings as nonsense, as I could see Aquilla's inner mind shake at mine in disapproval and confusion, but I could not refute how I felt towards her and the lifetime of loneliness that I feared I would endure without her.

Was not an instrument discarded if there was no one to play its purpose?

Though we sought to nullify the dark fate of Cypherus' Shadow that lay cursed upon me, perhaps the sleepless death was intended for my unrequited heart that drummed only for Egret.

"Such involvements of your heart are reckless and shall only hinder us further," Aquilla said. "You must not let your mind toil so endlessly."

My head bowed low in agreement.

Our conversation was interrupted by the stench of Nizari's approach, which came long before the candle-ridden leader did. Heavy footsteps thudded into the floorboards, marking her arrival.

"Aela Zaeim," Nizari wheezed through her silver and expressionless mask.

Two Ora'suns carried in a large and dusty wooden chest, laying it at my feet and returning from whence they came, leaving Nizari and I alone.

"I have something for you… and your *spirit* from the moon."

"What did you say?"

Nizari croaked a laugh as she hobbled over to a chair to sit down. Aquilla gave me a look of caution before she began to speak again. He did not make himself visible to her, but her remark gave me doubt.

"Do not pretend, Morgan. I have long lived my sols in waiting for someone to take my place, to truly lead the Ora'suns like Aela Zaeim did before me. Though the Shepherd's before never revealed their mysterious power and its origin, I know you are no ordinary Human, and that you are not alone as the Shepherd we have waited for."

Nizari readjusted her dark mask to breathe, and that's when realization struck: the mask was Noxstone.

"The sacrifices I have made to watch over my children and to provide for them are too much to speak of, but I am thankful you are here to at last ease me of them, which is why I have brought you this. Go ahead, claim it."

Nizari motioned to the ancient chest before me.

Should I open it?

"It's difficult to decipher if she is being deceitful," Aquilla said slowly, still unnerved in being known without revealing himself.

Looking quickly through his eyes, there appeared to be nothing alive or evil inside, so I relented.

With great effort, I lifted open the heavy chest lid, which brought forth a plume of dust into my face. But once the dust cleared and my coughing ceased, I saw the robes within.

"Whose are these?" I said, lifting out the old and creased robes that were heavier than I expected, their former white shine now a soft eggshell color but still radiant and otherworld-ly in their design.

The robes felt like forged steel, but of cloth-like flexibility.

"These robes laced with Gyldur ore were created by Aela Zaeim. She believed that the spirit who guided Cypherus and Mythraelyon would come again, that a new Shepherd would be born to guide us in this wicked world. In my studies, I found that she learned much from the Taldarii before they banished her, and in her writings, she discovered something which has never been corroborated: that the Shepherd's received their power from the moon.

"Thus, she created the Sundel Ritual in hopes of finding a leader pure enough to lead us, intending to discover the Shep-herd at last. And though we have added the Trial of Beating Hearts to further clarify the heart of a pure Shepherd, you have passed them both with grace, hence why these robes belong to you."

"Thank you, Nizari," I said, giving a small bow of respect.

Black nails dug into my arm as Nizari grasped me violently, pulling me closer to her. Prudence warned against cutting her down where she stood in fear of my life, for her eyes looked afraid through her trembling mask.

"Do not believe the lie that he will soon spread, lest you and the world shall rot like me," she said, her voice horse and gasping for breath. "You will undoubtedly soon face the Shadow who leads the Kira Naz'ka, the Black Legion, who lies on *his* behalf."

Aquilla looked at me with an equal amount of confusion.

"Whose behalf?"

Nizari leaned closer and muttered what was barely a whisper, the stench of which I could hardly stomach.

"The *Father* of Dragons!"

After Nizari had gone, Aquilla and I were left alone with the opened chest. Donning the glimmering armored garments, I was surprised to find them an excellent fit. That was until I recalled the somewhat embarrassing episode of an elder woman in Cur Malum insisting on taking my measurements very thoroughly after having just come out of a long-needed bath during our rest before the voyage. Although heavier than most robes, the addition of a tightly wrapped cloth about my waist stole the weight off my shoulders and left me quite comfortable.

From the little I had studied of the amazing properties of Gyldur, I knew it would grant me incredible mobility without sacrificing protection. Deceptively strong, it would not rival full steel plate, yet it far outmatched the capability of any mail. The thickness of the robes would serve well to cushion the force of most blows.

"It's a shame it lacks a shoulder cape," I said as we studied the robes in the mirror.

"It is better without a cape."

"Really? I think it would look quite good."

Aquilla shook his celestial head.

"A cape is a vain accessory to bring to battle and a sure way to get oneself killed."

"Alright, no cape then."

"The color white is a poor choice too."

"What? Why?" I asked, immediately regretting.

"As we engage in battle, there will be blood, mud, the bite of steel, the bowels of our enemies, the fire from the—"

"Very well, you proved your point!"

"It is only an observation. However, it was kind of her to give us this, though I cannot guess her motivation."

"Perhaps it was to undo the corruption of her heart?"

"Perhaps," Aquilla said, but I could feel his mind still pondering Nizari's words.

"What is it?" I said.

Aquilla took a moment before deciding, rubbing his translucent chin in contemplation.

"I am bewildered."

"By what?"

"Nizari is Human. From my knowledge, your life spans generally from forty sols to at the most eighty."

"Which makes Nizari impossibly old."

"Unfortunately, it is not."

Turning from the mirror, I looked at Aquilla to see if he was jesting.

"I am *not*," he said, reading my mind.

"How can anyone live beyond their normal sols? She must be a descendant of mixed Elven heritage."

"I have seen the archives pertaining to her, and she is Human. There is only one other way to achieve such lengthening of life, and you have done the opposite recently."

"The Klyr spear?"

"Precisely. Though you were able to heal Egret by sharing her suffering, this could only be done through the purity of Godstone. In its opposite, Nox, one can absorb the soul of another. Completely devouring that soul's existence gives its time of vitality and youth to the one who drinks its essence."

My skin shivered at the thought of having my entire existence be forever dissolved into dark nothingness. Such a fate was ever more terrifying as I slowly grew to love being alive. I pushed the thought of having myself devoured for someone else's wicked design far from my mind, for it was too evil to bear.

"So Nizari has consumed the souls of others to lengthen her life?"

"Possibly," Aquilla said, his face darkened with shadow. "There is no other explanation I can foresee, but our path will not be one of sleepless death as she has chosen."

My own Bludhstone necklace felt heavier around me in its tremendous capacity for good or evil.

"When Nizari said not to trust the lie of the Father of Dragons, what do you think she was referring to?" I said.

"I am uncertain. Her mind may be twisted from her lengthened days in this life, though her eyes do stretch far and wide across Scissalan."

"Indeed."

It still amazed me that Nizari had known of the Drakin's recent capture of the Ronian city of Feldrem before we did, as we Soul Slept almost every night to survey the shifting power structures in Renborg. Nizari had shared with us its gloom-filled capture several nights ago. My heart had since been discouraged by yet another Ronian defeat, for it meant the battle to save Philomela became increasingly challenging.

Volsung was marching there now with the last forces Renborg could muster in the north, though they too would be soundly defeated by the Dragon if we did not intervene in time.

We were running out of time; the moon and sun could see each other now on the horizon.

"It would be wise to glean more knowledge from her and to keep her long after we win back Renborg," Aquilla said. "Though she is wicked in her heart."

"I agree," I said, though I found the chance of our victory ever more trying to believe.

The door opened softly again, and like before, Egret stepped through, her radiant face betraying no hint of emotion from our previous stumble.

Or at least, my perceived stumble in which I was perhaps the only willing participant.

"The Ora'suns are ready," she said, offering a small but guarded smile.

"Good," I said.

"What are you wearing, Krabios?" she said as we left my quarters, the sun from Laconnia shining brightly upon us and revealing her playful sneer.

"What? You don't like it?"

"It's just… very foreign, all of the robes and everything," she said, nodding towards Aquilla. "Is it Numerian?"

"I think he looks well acquainted," Aquilla said, posturing his head high. "It is fitting for one bonded with a Medjaib."

Joy found its place in my smile.

"Aela Zaeim," a chorus of Ora'suns whispered as we emerged from my holdings, all of them giving a deep bow in reverence as I passed by them.

Though, from an outsider's perspective, they would have appeared as simple crewmates of any merchant's vessel, dressed in civilian garments and playing their roles perfectly. They gave no indication of their true identity. Even the ballistae were hidden underneath the ships from the Lycan patrols, who would have complicated our quest if they had instead seen three fully armed ships with one hundred warriors and ballistae arriving at port.

Everything was falling into place.

"Aela Zaeim," Nizari bowed as we descended to the docks where she stood waiting, surrounded by ten Ora'suns dressed as wealthy merchants. They concealed mail, weapons, and small shields underneath their robes.

Aquilla translated for Egret as Nizari whispered through her Nox mask.

"Your new robes and armor are very becoming of you."

"Thank you, Nizari. They were well tailored."

The ancient one nodded slowly.

"The Ora'suns are waiting for you, and they will not fail you."

"I will ensure it," Alcharion said, stepping forth from the disguised Ora'suns.

I'm certain he will.

"He shall be useful to us," Aquilla said. "The Ora'suns have faith in him, and he knows best how they go about their work."

The lantern covering of my spear that the Ora'suns had fashioned to conceal my blade and act as a walking staff was punished by my hands which squeezed it in frustration, knowing the Medjaib was unfortunately correct.

"Very well," I said, giving a slight glance to Egret for renewed strength, who smiled back in return.

"Aela Zaeim," Nizari said, "may the Mother guide your hands and render your deeds complete. For if you do not save the Prince from destruction tonight, then there will be no return from the fire that will spread from their *demonstration*. May the one you call Orpheus help you stay the tide of rebellion so that these Kairosians will not pose another threat that must be dealt with."

"I know," I said, not wanting to think about what might happen if we failed. We knew we couldn't stop everything. The boy who mirrored Lucien would be *discovered* tonight somewhere in Ehlonica. Simultaneously, priests and other zealots of

Kairos would be stoking the fires of rebellion in Delphius and across Laconnia as soon as the word had reached them.

Aquilla and I had watched the careful plot of Menander take steady fruition, and we were thankful for the good weather on the seas that had allowed us to arrive just in time to prevent chaos from consuming my brother and all of Laconnia.

Orpheus Talon was the only Lycan senator I knew with certainty had not been corrupted by Menander's plot.

It was he we would seek for aid in apprehending the plot so that we could escape with Lucien unscathed. The help of Orpheus might also prevent countless more lives from being crushed in the coming revolt that would surely be bathed in blood.

"Why not warn this Orpheus of the plot ahead of our arrival?" Egret had asked when the three of us had planned during our voyage. "Wouldn't that give us more time?"

"He is a political being, your majesty," I said. "And he is also Menander's brother. It will be no simple conversation. Even if he did believe our tale and not think of us to be some trick or phantom from his gods, a test even of his familial loyalty, he would hold power over us and Renborg knowing our secret."

"Is it not worth the risk?" she said.

"Would you trust another politician with your secrets, Princess?" Aquilla said.

"It's *Queen*," Egret muttered while rubbing her smooth head, proving his point.

With no time to waste and with shaking breath, we looked beyond the port teeming with colorfully dressed Lycan and merchants from every race and creed. Silver glimmered in the hands of many merchants trading goods from across Scissalan in great quantities for the rarities found only in Laconnia such as wolfwood and precious Ilyite crystals.

Everything was so… *peaceful*, like the calm before the storm.

The Lycan were all oblivious to the fire that was being kindled right underneath them from the religious zealots who would upend all they ever knew in a violent return towards their ancient traditions.

And we were walking right into the dry wood that would soon be set ablaze by rebellion, for the sun and moon were about to embrace above us.

Chapter 25
The Broken Moon

"Eros" is the singular Laconnian word for "eclipse", with Eroi as its plural form. Eroi are considered an extremely holy and celebrated occurrence where both the Mother and Father are united intimately again. On the day of an Eros, many festivals are prepared in every city, town, and village. Songs and poems of worship are played and read all day, and it is customary to drink and be merry and play games such as lokoi, kyros, and basilyskos chess. During Eros, one does not toil on any task that does not serve the festival in some way. It is considered deeply sacreligious to kill any living thing, and it is encouraged to seek amends with rivals, if even only for the day.

As an Eros is seen as the sexual merging of the sun and the moon, it is customary for wedded mates to engage in relations once the moon's arc commences. It is believed that any union joined in the duration of the Eros will be blessed with abundant fertility, especially if that union begins and ends within the time that the Moon Mother Reia still holds the Sun Father Bellatorix. Traditionally, this is supposed to be a custom between two oath-mates, male and female, but in the recent century, the ancient practice of mass orgies and deviations of the original pairing have become more prevalent. The majority of Lycan, being traditionally religious-minded, see this as a sign of the degradation of the faith brought on by the Ehlonican Renaissance, Neo-Bellaritism, and the loss of faith due to greater belief in the Jorist theory of Lycan Averitic origins.

The Histories of Laconnia
"Doubt"
According to Karnax of Ehlonica, 996 DE

E**gret** and I were careful shadows of Aquilla, who guided us through the largely Lycan crowds beneath the sea of colorful roofs, though only we could selectively see the Medjaib.

The buildings surrounding the wide streets were mostly of

stone and freshly wattled walls, towering tall and proud in the vast, clean city. Almost every house and street bloomed with paintings, flowers, shrines, and stands sizzling with the most savoring meats in preparation for their festival of Eros tonight.

It still amazed me that this city had been reborn and remade into such a burgeoning center point of culture within the last century.

Our ten Ora'suns, at Alcharion's guidance and my direction, disappeared within moments of my signal when we began our voyage through the Ehlonican streets. The Ora'suns mimicked the merchants and pretended to both browse the various shops and move swiftly to keep our pace at a distance.

Even more impressive, it was only through Aquilla's eyes that I could see them weaving through the crowds in unison to follow us.

They certainly lived up to their fearsome reputation.

"How far is this Orpheus that we must meet?" Egret whispered in the Ronic tongue.

"Aquilla and I found his home just beyond that temple," I said, pointing to the elevated and walled citadel district ahead of us, situated on a hill banking the river that dwarfed the pillared temple before it.

To our dismay, the towering wall was heavily patrolled by Ehlonican city guards. And before the circular temple adjacent to the wall, a Lycan priest stood atop a wooden platform giving a fiery sermon that stirred the audience's fervor and made the patrolling Lycan uneasy.

Though I couldn't hear precisely what the angry priest was saying, I could make out one repeated phrase: "Laconnia has abandoned their gods!"

"How did you plan to get through to the citadel of the city?" Egret said as we came to a halt before the mesmerized crowd.

"Still working on it," I said.

"The guards will be less welcoming of anyone trying to enter from the heated crowd, so we cannot enter through its gates," Egret said.

"Heated crowds?" Aquilla said. "You are mistaken. Only a Drakin is of a heated flesh given their blood of fire. Fur does not emit a flame."

"That's not what I meant, spirit," Egret said, rolling her eyes.

Aquilla's naivety bloomed an idea in my mind as I stared at the torches on either side of the Lycan priest.

"Egret, stand in front of me."

Aquilla looked at me as I quickly drew the symbol for fire with my fingers while hidden before Egret, my word glowing white from the Klyr spear's purity that surged through me.

"You're not going to set me aflame, are you Krabios?"

"No," I smirked.

"Whatever you are planning, fire will only draw attention to us," Aquilla said.

"Just trust me."

Taking control of the flames next to the priest, I breathed out Wae and let them dance onto the wooden platform, right beneath the zealous priest. The rest of the wooden platform quickly took flame, much to the priest's surprise. Howls from the crowd pierced the air as the Lycan priest abandoned his sermon and jumped off, much to his fortune, mostly unscathed.

The guards watching from the archway beneath the gate took notice and moved quickly to douse the fire and tame the chaos.

Our opening appeared.

"You peasants certainly know how to make fires," Egret said.

"I'll have to teach you and the rest of the nobility someday,"

I said, nodding to Aquilla. "Then you can cook your own food and be rid of your servants."

"I will hold you to that promise, Krabios," Egret said as we quickly followed Aquilla through the reckless crowd, disappearing quietly through the temporarily abandoned gate. Some of the wealthier Lycan within the government district took to see the commotion behind us as we walked calmly through.

"Though foolish, your plan worked," Aquilla said as the Ora'suns caught up behind us.

I appreciate the trust, Medjaib.

In precise cohesion, the Ora'suns formed a ring around us, each of them moving soundlessly and in rhythm to Alcharion's commands given by quick hand movements. Though the large Elf still displayed hostile relations towards me, he was keen on ensuring I was protected.

We arrived quickly at the mansion of Orpheus after a brief walk. Orpheus' guards stood atop the green mound that raised the rectangular home above the other richly decorated government homes and buildings.

"What if he's not there?" Egret said.

"He is," I said, looking through Aquilla's eyes and seeing a Lycan through the dark triangular glass that hung above the pillared and grand entrance, which I had noted was Orpheus' room in our previous Soul Sleeping reconnaissance.

The guards gave us a peculiar look beneath the Pax banners that hung from the glass room above them, the nine phases of the moon a peaceful display of balance that encompassed all sides of the night.

One of the guards marched quickly down to us.

"Whom do I have the pleasure of speaking to, and what do you seek, my lords?" the Lycan guard said in what I assumed was the Novanic tongue, the Lycan giving a slight bow of respect.

"My name is Morgan Krios, and we wish to speak with Orpheus," I replied with Aquilla's guidance.

Before the guard could falsely suggest that Orpheus was not there in order to save his senator from what he most likely presumed were traveling merchants in want of a sale, I whispered in Novanic, "It is of an urgent matter regarding Renborg and the sons of Kairos."

The Lycan's brown fur almost took on a pale sheen at the mention of the martyred prophet, and he nodded quickly before retreating up the stone steps to inform the other guards.

We waited but a few minutes before the guards let us through the gates and into the mansion's entrance. Before we could go further, the guards stripped everyone of their weapons which they felt beneath the Ora'suns robes. When they attempted to remove my lantern-covered spear, I showed them the metal cage supporting my back.

"The staff is for walking," I said. At this, they relented. I breathed a sigh of relief, for all would be pointless if the spear were lost, and even the slightest threat to it must be feverishly avoided.

"Very wise," Aquilla said, to which I nodded in his approval.

"Come this way," the Lycan said, escorting the twelve of us into the senator's spacious home.

The guard wasted no time in bringing us upstairs into the stripped Wolfwood framed room that towered above the pillared entrance, the glass wall a sight to behold as it encapsulated the grand city beyond it.

"Morgan Krios and his companions, sir," our Lycan escort said, bowing low before his senator.

"Thank you, Remus," Orpheus said, motioning with his grey paw for Remus and the other guards to leave.

The door shut quietly behind us.

"I thought I recognized that name," Orpheus said in the Ronic tongue while offering me a small bow. "Welcome, Son of Renborg. And my… the *Queen* of Renborg as well."

The eyes of Orpheus were wider than one hooked on faery dust as he beheld Egret, whose eyes were glimmering more richly than all of the world's emeralds combined.

"Greetings, Orpheus," Egret replied in the Ronic tongue.

Alcharion's dark and Elvish eyes furrowed tightly, barely concealing his anger as he most undoubtedly understood the Lycan's words: Egret was not Joanna, but the Queen of Renborg.

I would deal with his feelings of betrayal later.

"What a strange gathering at such a time as this," Orpheus said. "Please, all of you, have a seat. I am most interested in this tale of Kairos and Renborg, and to hear more of the disappearance of King Lucien and the fallout of the Drakin. As I've heard, there are even ridiculous rumors of a Dragon!"

"I will do my best to explain, though quickly," I said, sitting beside Egret and Aquilla, folding my spear in my lap while the Ora'suns remained standing behind us.

How much should we tell him?

"All of it," Aquilla said. "Except for our identity, who the Ora'suns are, and the weakened state of Renborg, along with concealing Volsung's betrayal. Although he is a leading member of the Pax faction of the Pentarchy, they could still gain a political advantage against Renborg should the temptation of Kapitolian gold arise."

For what felt like too long, I told the story of Lucien's kidnapping by the Sons of Kairos.

Orpheus' eyes widened as I told how they planned to frame the Delphians and Nicandorians, effectively most of the senate leaders, in the false murder of Lucien that would be revealed during the eclipse amidst the drunk and passionately crazed

Lycan; all of which, I told him, was being orchestrated by Menander.

Orpheus grew pale and deathly silent as I mentioned his brother's name.

"Menander will use the flames kindled tonight to fan the fire of revolution that he hopes will spread to the rest of Laconnia," I said.

"You accuse my brother of treason?" Orpheus whispered.

"With much regret," I said carefully, weighing every word as Egret looked at me with silent anticipation. "And many eastern cities of Laconnia are dry kindling thanks to the preparation of their zealots and priests."

Orpheus was silent as he looked down at his ornately carved Wolfwood desk, his mind entirely elsewhere.

"At the very least, you know I speak the truth of these Kairosian zealots," I said, not knowing their relationship beyond what I had seen. "I know it might be difficult to believe that Menander—"

"No," Orpheus interrupted, his gaze weary as he turned to look at an Ilyite stone shaped in the image of the moon on the wall, a symbol of their Bellarite Faith. "Menander is not who you think he is: he is a noble Lycan. I have known my brother all of his life, especially his faith. His passion for the gods who bore us was incessant in our youth, blind even in his desire to take Laconnia back to her founding faith.

"But he had matured beyond that when that Drakin *scourge* pillaged our silver, for that is when he ceased in making such bold proclamations of our faith.

"Even now, as a Drakin army marches through our Ilarkoi Mountains and sully our forests in the thousands, Menander does not demean their kind nor faith with his former zeal. He is more thoughtful and considerate than any Lycan I know."

"The Drakin send reinforcements through Laconnia?" Aquilla pondered.

The Ronians and Skyyans must have the Strumma blockaded, I thought.

"Have you not noticed any peculiar behavior of late?" Egret said.

"No, my Queen," he said, turning his tired eyes back to her. "The only peculiar behavior has been his increasing dinner visits, of which I have been well pleased to welcome."

"How is that peculiar?" she said.

"It is very unusual for him," Orpheus continued. "Menander hardly makes time for gatherings, let alone with me. All of his life, he's been that way. However, the last several times he's been here, which have been very frequent indeed, we have had very deep and theological conversations."

"He's testing your faith," I said, putting it together, "judging if you would join him before blood is spilt."

"Blood has already been spilt!" Orpheus said, his teeth flaring at the accusation. "He knows of my distaste for their creed, for their obsession with the past. And he knows I would never join the Kairosian Cult, as I know he never would."

"The Mother blesses Orpheus with Menander's failure to convert him," Aquilla added. "Though the brothers share in their blindness."

"Do you worship this Bellatorix and Reia?" Egret said.

"I do, but I am not alone in my… *doubts* of how our existence came to be."

"Does Menander know?" I said.

"He has always known. In fact, it was only the other night that we had a very passionate discussion about the subject. If you knew him, you would know he is very fond of saying that, 'A resurgence of faith—'"

"'Will topple the faithless,'" I finished.

Menander looked askance. "How did you—"

"'Thou shalt not abandon the wolf,'" I said, quoting their holy *Black Book of Devina*. "Orpheus, I know my brother is enchained in his palace. My sources have seen him there tied to the courtyard fountain, as well as Menander's silver statues of Bellatorix, Reia, and the rest of their children whom he zealously does all of this for."

Fear darkened the Lycan's maw. "Many have never seen his great shrines."

"Do your politicians not enter his palace?" Egret said.

"It is rare that they do," Orpheus said. "He usually travels to the other cities or will meet with the Cenarchoi and Pentarchoi in their homes. But I am one of the few who has glimpsed upon our father's shrines which were bestowed upon him."

"Why were they given to him?" Egret said.

The Lycan slowly looked to Egret, acceptance clear in his eyes, though the weight of such revelation made him look beyond tired. "For his zeal… when we were pups."

"So you realize now that he leads the Kairosians?" I said, eager to propel the conversation to one of immediate action.

Orpheus nodded grimly. "My spies warned me that the Mynkari priests have been preparing for something to take place soon. I didn't realize that King Lucien's disappearance and the ambitions of the Mynkari's Kairosian masters were connected. And to think… *Menander* behind it all."

A sigh of relief escaped me, as it did within Aquilla. "Thank you for trusting in me."

"My trust is not fully formed, young master. Menander is still my brother, and I do not take these accusations lightly, though they stand on firmer ground than before. There are very few who know of his private tongue and shrines, for he does not make his faith public except when necessary."

"Do you think his plan will prevail in usurping the government tonight?" Egret said.

"Most likely, for Menander could easily dissolve the Pentarchy for trying to start a war with Renborg, even though he himself is Pentarch of Lucca and a leader of the Pax no less," Orpheus said, his grey fur creasing depressingly around his sharp but aged eyes. "He could seek to use his authority and perceived neutrality to influence the minds of several thousands throughout Laconnia.

"His moderation, or pretensions rather, have gained him great respect amongst the majority of the people who have not embraced the doctrine of the Rumok. I have no doubt with his skill for oratory that he may achieve much of what he desires if this plan is to be carried out."

"Which is why I need your help in confronting him at his palace before he enacts his plan," I said. "In truth, my chief concern is for the safe return of my brother and Renborg's King, but if you would lend us your aid, the future of Laconnia may well also be saved tonight. At the very least, you can apprehend the Mynkari priests who seek to spread revolt. The moon has already commenced its journey across the sun. If we must go alone, then so be it, but I hope with all my heart you will join us."

Orpheus sighed, his eyes downcast as he submitted to the bitter reality of what may befall Ehlonica this night.

"Very well. I can summon a small force to hunt for the zealots who aim to plant the fallen double of the King. If he plans to frame the Delphians and Nicandorians, then he might try to stage the murder near one of their cenarchoi's mansions in the citadel.

"Alas, there is no way to know for certain, for if all of this is real, then Menander has fooled us for many sols without betraying his heart's true intentions. It might even occur in

Delphius for all we know. However, my warriors are scattered throughout the city in preparation for licentious behavior from the festival, and it will take time to gather them and coordinate a search."

"We don't have time! The moon and sun are almost one!"

"I'm sorry, but I cannot gather them that quickly."

The sunlight caught the Lycan's eye as he looked upon me with sorrow, but the light was becoming ever darker, as were our hopes in rescuing Lucien.

"You must go. His palace is not far from here," Orpheus said, motioning towards the squared courtyard home of the zealots that seemed to hide in plain sight amongst the other government leaders. "The eclipse will happen before I can muster support, but we will be there to aid you and to stop Laconnia from burning. Whatever fire is about to be set ablaze, I will do what I can to cinch the flames before they are ever lit. Now go, Morgan Krios, for the eclipse will soon be upon us!"

My heart was heavy as we retrieved our weapons and made way for the lair of the zealots, the sun and moon about to kiss. Still, my spirit was encouraged when I looked before the strength of Egret and Aquilla, who, though Shadow plagued them as it did my soul and all those who I knew, strode boldly with me to save Lucien, just as the Ora'suns did.

And now, we were not alone.

The sun and moon embraced in the sky.

We were running out of time.

"We must make haste," Aquilla said as our group moved through the shadows surrounding Menander's mansion.

Though all was quiet, through Aquilla's eyes, I could see several Sons of Kairos carefully guarding the front entrance of the pillared mansion. Alcharion pointed to a corner of the mansion beneath the entrance's staircase that was well hidden, but his plan did not make sense until he pointed to the spear and drew a circle in the dirt.

"The spear will cut through," Aquilla said, and to this I nodded in agreement.

Our steps made no sound on the lush gardens that bordered Menander's mansion. Taking my place behind the stairs, I unwrapped my Klyr spear and slid the pure Godstone into the wall.

The spear's purity met no resistance.

In one quick movement, I carved out a circle large enough for us to move seamlessly through. Once we were all inside, a few of the Ora'suns carefully slid the circular slab back into place.

"We should keep this escape in mind if all goes wrong," Egret whispered, to which I darkly agreed.

Though, a quiet hope emerged as I believed Orpheus would remove such a perilous need for escape. In stopping the staged killing of Lucien, we could leave this den unharmed and without a future need for Renborg to deal with religiously crazed Lycan.

We would solve both present and future problems for Lucien.

My ponderings froze as a Son of Kairos walked unannounced into the torch-lit hallway we found ourselves in, but before he could call for help, Alcharion threw a hidden blade into the Lycan's neck. Two of our Ora'suns dashed to catch the Lycan before his corpse hit the ground, removing all sound and tucking him away in the corner.

Such was their stealthy efficiency as we moved quietly throughout the halls. We encountered several more of the guards before we reached the inner courtyard, and like before, the Ora'suns moved as one and stole their breaths before they even realized we were there.

Egret looked almost frustrated that she was given no chance to utilize her returned strength. I was thankful, though, for taking the lives of others, wicked or not, still brought guilt upon my heart.

Alcharion sent the other nine Ora'suns to take care of the rest of the guards inside the mansion, particularly on the upper floors. That way, when we entered the courtyard, we would be met with no resistance in freeing Lucien. Much to my surprise, we received a signal that the mansion was clear shortly after the Ora'suns left us.

It was easier than I expected, and fear rose in my heart that it was almost meant to be that way.

Where is Menander?

The door to the inner courtyard opened, and all thoughts of precaution vanished when I saw Lucien; his white locks shrouded his solemn face, which hung over his bloodied and scarred chest.

The whip marks were egregious, though thankfully not fresh.

"Vorim!" Egret whispered to herself.

"Lucien!" I said, running over to him and quickly cutting the metal chains that bound him.

Lucien collapsed in my arms, his blood staining my white robes as I held him gently, as softly as Philomela, whose innocence and my heart he shared.

"Lucien," I whispered, tears brimming from my aching soul upon seeing him crushed, "please… *please* speak to me."

Lucien's eyes opened with a deep heaviness as if waking from a nightmare.

"Morgan?" he barely uttered.

"I'm here Lucien," I said as Egret and Aquilla stood behind me, the Ora'suns surrounding us as a shield.

Lucien's eyes opened wider, slowly. As his pupils focused

on me, his breath began to shake. Without hesitation, Lucien embraced me, squeezing his arms around me as if to ensure I wouldn't leave him again.

"Oh, Morgan!" Lucien cried, his tears becoming a bitter heaving until he could hardly breathe. "How I've missed you!"

"I know… everything is well now. We're here to rescue you."

Lucien retreated to behold my face with his quivering and cold hands.

"I t-thought… I thought you left me alone on this earth."

"No, I haven't, and I won't," I said, letting a smile bloom despite the agonizing guilt that robbed me of all joy in knowing that I deeply wounded him.

Lucien's eyes shifted to Egret behind me, and his confusion deepened as he saw Alcharion and the rest of the Ora'suns around the courtyard. Aquilla studied us all unbeknownst to him.

"Egret?" he said.

"Lucien," Egret said, her voice emitting compassion.

Lucien's gaze returned to me, but before he could ask anything more, I said, "I have much to tell you, but now is not the time. We need to leave."

Before Lucien could reply, the doors behind us slammed open.

"Morgan!" a somber yet relieved voice boomed, to whom I turned to see Orpheus striding humbly with a bound Menander, who was encircled by a large procession of heavily plated Lycan guards.

"Orpheus!" I said, hope lifting me to my feet to help Lucien up. "You came back so soon!"

"Indeed," the grey senator said. "I was surprised; in fact, I almost didn't believe it. I had just begun my search and gathered a fraction of my soldiers when I found Menander and several others attempting to break into the home of a Delphian senator."

Menander hung his head low, his face indecipherable as his guard readjusted his grip on him.

"And what of the staged reveal of Lucien's death?" I said.

"They will most likely relocate, but I assure you, we will snuff out any revolt they incite because of your help. And without their cult leader, the riots will crumble."

"He did not live up to the reputation which you told me," Egret said, sharing my thoughts.

"Hmmm," Aquilla said, his glowing eyes frowning in disbelief.

"I am thankful to see that you are alive, King Lucien," Orpheus said, giving a small bow. "We will uproot this radical following that endangered you and bring swift justice upon them. I pray you do not hold this against us, your Liege, as Laconnia and Renborg would benefit from a steadfast relationship renewed that your father pursued."

Rage appeared to almost explode from Lucien's eyes, but he took a staggering breath and calmed his speech. "Let us negotiate on a further date. Our hands are a bit preoccupied for the moment. I bid you my thanks."

"Of course," Orpheus said. "In the meantime, let my home refresh you before you leave."

"We would be delighted," Lucien said, bowing with his exhausted eyes.

"Very good!" Orpheus said. "Eludoros, take this traitor to the dungeons to await his hearing. We have heroes to celebrate."

Menander's guard stepped forward as if to guide the cult leader to his certain doom. Instead, he subtly and deftly loosed Menander's bonds to the ignorance of his fellow guards and the aged senator. Before I could process the significance of his familiar name or actions, Eludorus had already freed his true master.

"You have been asleep far too long, Orpheus," Menander said, his tone surprisingly somber.

In the blink of an eye, Menander pivoted on his heel, simultaneously drawing Eludorus' sword before sheathing it into the ribs underneath Orpheus' right paw.

"Forgive me, brother," Menander said as he tearfully laid Orpheus down, the dying senator gripping his familial executioner with a last gasp of shock. "I wish you of all could have joined me in seeing Laconnia reborn."

Before we could even comprehend what unfolded before us, shadows sprang from the rooftops above, arrows piercing the air even faster and finding their homes in the Lycan guards who, not a moment ago, had been confident in their rescue of Laconnia.

Alcharion and the Ora'suns surrounded us within moments as the arrows rained over us, withdrawing their shields to form a ring of wood above and below us. However, we may as well have covered ourselves with parchment for the little good it did. The arrows splintered shields and wrought armor with terrible ease, unlike anything I had ever witnessed. Two of our brothers fell instantly, and the rest would have followed had Menander not quickly shouted for them to cease.

Though my sight was limited, the Ora'suns gave me just enough room to see Menander and his traitorous pet.

Egret and Lucien both gave me panicked looks as our entire mission turned hopeless, but Aquilla whispered in me an idea that seemed even more radical than the Sons of Kairos.

"Your shields will be useless against Delphian Bows," Menander said, rubbing his wrists calmly and approaching our nearly useless ring of defense.

There existed no hint of fear in Menander's eyes as he stood proudly before us, whereas Orpheus choked on his own blood behind him.

"Lower your shields so I can see the heretics who failed to thwart the redemption of Kairos!"

How do you know it will work?

"What other choice do you have?" Aquilla said, following my eyes' surveillance of the beams surrounding the courtyard that supported the mansion.

"You have a plan?" Egret said.

"We do, but I don't trust it," I said.

Lucien looked at me, his fear giving way to a flicker of joyful hope as our eyes met. Though it pleased me to see the light in his eyes, the flame of relief within him was swiftly snuffed as he looked at Egret, who I covered with my Klyr spear. Lucien's face hardened, betraying nothing more than a stern gaze that was mute in emotion.

"I pray whatever is in your mind is something we *can* trust," Lucien said, his eyes perplexed by the Klyr spear but portraying a memorable understanding of its use that we once shared.

"Menander," Lucien continued, his eyes no longer gravitating to me for reassurance during a confrontation but focused entirely on the enemy ahead. "Your revolution is *over*. Once the Lycan see that I live and your brother is slain, they will not trust the lies you breathe. They will have you cast from your heretical throne, and you will be executed for trying to dissolve the confederacy, let alone for killing a revered senator."

Menander's teeth gleamed in the eclipse light, a dark smile its fruit.

"However," Lucien continued, "I will let Laconnia fall into your hands if you let us leave unscathed, letting the Lycan believe the lie which you so tirelessly contrived, and I will oath not to seek vengeance on this new order."

I almost didn't believe that it was my brother who spoke so boldly to the Lycan.

It was only weeks ago that he could hardly stand before Volsung as the King despite the crown, and here it was that he stood before Menander as a King despite the chains.

Brokering with the enemy.

"I cannot tell if your brother speaks truthfully," Aquilla said, and I wholeheartedly agreed.

"You have grown bold, Child King," Menander said. "No more tears do I see in you, though it comes now too late."

The doors behind Menander and Eludoros opened.

In unison, more Sons of Kairos marched through the doors, some with blood on their weapons and claws as they formed behind Menander and over the dead Lycan before them. One of the Lycan came and whispered something to the zealot leader, who nodded with satisfaction.

"I am pleased to inform you that your newfound strength does not equate to wisdom," Menander said. "You see, the fire has already been lit, and Laconnia is in an uproar over your death, which has now been revealed to be at the hands of the once trusted government. Orpheus was a fool to think he could so easily uproot what has been planted long before you were ever born."

"Shall we not fight these *dogs*, Aela Zaeim?" Alcharion said.

"Patience, Alcharion," I said, though I feared he would soon receive the answer he wanted.

"And you are a fool to think Renborg will not destroy you," Lucien said. "Your state will be weakened following your revolution of pride and power."

"That is where you are so arrogantly wrong!" Menander said. "You think this is nothing more than a vie for power, but it is not: it is a struggle for the very soul of Laconnia! As you display in your own carnal lusts, so too have the Lycan fallen prey, for the godless evil spread by Kapitol and the College of Man have taken its rot in our cities, along with Renborg's; and that rot is *deep*! It is only in returning to the true worship of Bellatorix that they will be saved, and it is worth the unwanted sacrifice of the few who stand in its way."

Menander looked briefly with deep sorrow upon Orpheus below him.

"Which brings us back to you," the Lycan continued. "Volsung sold you to us to ensure a civil war for Laconnia, but we will not kill you as he desires. You will live to ensure that he leaves Laconnia be, lest you should be found alive to take back the crown with his head. But I have no such need of your friends."

With a single nod, a volley of arrows peppered the ranks of our Ora'suns' at the command of Menander.

The storm of arrows immediately crushed the shields of most of the remaining Ora'suns, the Delphian bows showing no respect for their sols of training. Only a few remained standing from the eviscerating force that tore five of them apart.

Thankfully Egret, Lucien, and I, along with Alcharion and a few others, were only gashed and bruised from where we stood amidst the splinters of shields and arrows that now offered no protection.

Their faces of fear looked to me desperately for a way out of death's imminent embrace.

The archers above nocked their arrows almost as quickly as they had fallen, the blows of which would soon be more destructive than the kisses of lightning.

Alcharion roared at the taste of battle, and he was seconds away from leading the remaining Ora'suns into a presumably suicidal charge.

"Now!" Aquilla yelled.

Waeing forth the Mother's lightning from the Klyr spear, I

heaved with all of my might the electric light through the tall wooden pillars surrounding us.

The lightning effortlessly completed its explosive arc in one swift motion, finding its final destination in the heart of Menander, who was thrown into his guards. Fire erupted from the surging path of the lightning but was soon extinguished in the collapse of the three floors of Menander's house around us, with all of the archers above falling like bricks down into the rubble below.

A handful of the Sons of Kairos fumbled through the dust and sudden shock to form haphazardly before us. Their desperate efforts and disbelief were cut short as I nodded at Alcharion, who was surprisingly calm at this display of destruction.

"Now," Alcharion said as the Ora'suns charged to engage with the survivors, their swords effortlessly finding the crevices in the rectangular plates that armored the wolfish Averites.

But four Lycan swarmed around the Ora'suns and charged directly at the three of us.

Egret stumbled from parrying the arcing blow of a Lycan, the force of which caused her to scream from the impact on her spine. The Lycan tested her weakening limits, thrusting several times towards her, each time nicking her sword arm from his overwhelming size and strength. Luckily, a loosened stone atop the rubble plummeted behind the Lycan, drawing his attention, and she took advantage of the distraction and pierced his bowels with Kalypto.

One of the other Lycan was quickly intercepted and slain by Alcharion, but the other two rushed forth to deliver a killing strike to Lucien and I.

In the midst of battle, I forgot my spine's impairment, and as the blade of the Lycan hewed down upon me, I swung with all of the strength in my back to shatter the swords of the Lycan with my Klyr spear, which cleaved them like butter.

Agonizing pain seized my breath at the movement, and I collapsed onto the floor before the dazed but quickly recovering Lycan, who prepared to deliver death to Lucien and I with their sharp claws.

"Strike at their legs!" Aquilla said, but I could barely breathe from the pain, and the Klyr spear rolled out from my hands.

In one moment, the claws of the Lycan reached down to tear us apart, and in the next, they were completely severed from the elbows.

"To the Void with you dogs!" Lucien screamed, swiping the spear again through their hearts before dropping the pure Godstone onto the courtyard from the burning purity that was taking its toll. Lucien looked down upon me. Underneath his stern gaze was a familiar glance he had given me so many times before.

"Thank you, Lucien," I said as he helped me to my feet.

Lucien nodded but spoke not a word.

The rest of the Lycan had been dealt with by the remaining Ora'suns, though just barely. Other Sons of Kairos were still in the fire-encrusted rubble around us. But my mind was overwhelmed at the sight of what was beyond the carnage.

Smoke consumed the eclipse skyline of Ehlonica. Bloody riots and the destruction of government homes and buildings spread like an uncontrollable fire.

In their drunken and drugged and angry stupor, they had believed the lies of the wolves who wished to devour them on the false premise that uprooting their society would only lead to peace; so Ehlonica burned in its falsity. But in this destruction, the Lycan mobs saw Menander's mansion, which lay in a heap, and their enraged eyes pierced us as the enemy receiving due justice.

The mob turned on us to ensure the government's destruction in its entirety.

"We must go!" I said to the few Ora'suns who again circled us over the slain Sons of Kairos.

"Wait!" Lucien said, his eyes full of wrath and focused on Menander, who lay gasping before us beside a burning pillar, his claws grasping over his lightning-struck heart while Orpheus lay silent beside him.

"Lucien, we must go!" Egret said as Lucien knelt before the writhing Lycan, his whipped back oozing torrents of blood from the motion as he grabbed hold of Menander's snout.

"Laconnia will rue this day upon my return," Lucien whispered, his hands shaking Menander's face in rage. "I will let you live to know it, but may my eyes be the last thing you see in your wicked life!"

Menander's eyes fried like eggs upon being forced into the flames, but the leader made no sound as Egret and I repulsed at Lucien's wrath. A look of disgust flickered across Egret's face, and as our eyes met, I could sense fear within her that she tried to conceal; it was a fear I shared.

"A darkness has entered your brother's heart," Aquilla said, his voice similarly repulsed.

Lucien rose from the suffering he kindled for Menander, his eyes passing without care from Egret to me. When his eyes took hold of mine, a familiar warmth returned to them that he so often gave to me before. But now, the warmth lacked authenticity and merely appeared to be true on its surface, though there was so much more underneath that now eluded me.

We had come to rescue Lucien and Laconnia, but now we escaped from the crumbling society of Lycan with a King who resembled his wolfish captors more than his kin.

As Alcharion led us through the rioting city, the remaining Ora'suns slaying anyone who tried to harm us as we fought to return to our ships, I looked through Aquilla's eyes. Darkness had indeed infected Lucien's heart, like ink being poured into wine.

My heart crumbled like Laconnia.

Chapter 26
Betrayed

The earliest records of Godstone appear in the sol 2,350 of the Ancient Era, over one hundred sols after the Great Rift, whence the gods spilt their blood, shattering the world. Two Dwarven brothers, Halnir and Maeghir, were believed to have been led by a sorceress, whose emerging from a cave of bats terrified them, but whose skin and scent, fair and beautiful, calmed them. Deep in the mountains of Lakmana she led them, the fire from her hand their guide as she bent the flame to her design. The brother's were bewitched by such power and its potential. Upon revealing the hardened blood of a god buried in the mountain, the sorceress promised to teach of its power, to grant an everlasting kingdom over the new earth: but only to one.

Halnir, without hesitation, beat Maeghir with the blood of gods, desire betraying him for what he did not possess, though he loved him dearly. As Maeghir died, Halnir stole his soul in heartless lust, stealing even the life of the mountain in his kindled malice. It is uncertain whether Halnir learned the secrets to an everlasting life afterwards, for the sorceress abandoned him, and he was buried alive by the sons of Maeghir. His sons found more of this rare Godstone, all lusting for its mysterious power and unbreakable flesh that could only be crafted in the hottest fire.

Chronicles of Renborg: King's Edition
"Discovery of Godstone"
Piluch Joffersun: Master of Histories

A**rriving** in Renborg by the Varon River five days later, I feared we were too late: all of Renborg's hope from Hebsund had already been on the march to Feldrem while we were in Ehlonica, which now burned in the far horizons.

The Dragon's destruction of Renborg would be imminent if we were even an hour late, though I tried to hide the dark gloom from my face.

This fear was only strengthened by our delayed travel via the Varon River up towards Brannfalt instead of the quicker route of arriving at the port of Norbo and taking the Ren River. This was due to a sudden and vicious storm that surprised us at sea in Norbo's direction as we neared Renborg's shores.

Though, we would have been delayed further had we chosen to risk the storm, which had already begun tossing our ship without care, threatening total loss. While storms on Renborg's western shores were not nearly as bad as the hurricanes on its eastern side, they had the potential to last days.

We did not have days to spare.

"Fear not, Aela Zaeim, we will spare this Volsung in time from this fowl serpent," Nizari whispered through her dark mask. "And our message has reached our reinforcements that were on route to Norbo. They will wait for us at Feldrem."

"Forgive me, my Aela Zaeim," Alcharion interjected, "but how do you know that Volsung marches to Feldrem to face the Dragon? Wouldn't he have seen the scorched fields from this battle of Brännfält you claimed to see?"

Anger flustered my mind. "Do—"

"*Morgan*," Aquilla interceded, "do not spoil my presence. Though they know of the Shepherds, they do not understand your power or where it comes from. The more we reveal, the more he could twist into his own designs."

Fine.

"Do what, my Zaeim?" Alcharion said.

"Do *not* question your Lord, Alcharion," I said, anger stirring through my words. "I received this revelation from above. Volsung knows of the Dragon, but he is under the false impression that it is still a child and not full in its size because of how long Dragons took to grow in the Ancient Era. But because of Godstone, Belial grows with exceeding haste, and has roughly tripled in size since the battle of Brännfält."

The memory of Belial looming over the conquered city of Feldrem was terrifying when Aquilla and I surveyed the monster in Soul Sleep a few days before, for the Dragon was now far larger than even most mercantile ships.

The memory I cast aside, along with our merchant disguises, once we landed on the shores of Brännfält, not far from the field of slaughter that we were bound to see. Only the sullen eyes of a few Ronian guards posted at the mouth of the river were there to meet us as we prepared for the long march to Feldrem. They would guard our ships for us as we went to war.

Upon first seeing Lucien, the Ronian soldiers paid him no respect but mocked him for claiming to be the vanished King. Their mockery came to a swift end as their sergeant, who happened to recognize him, barked at them and apologized profusely for their ignorance. They bowed deeply in reverence, their faces pale and stricken with simultaneous fear and unbelief.

They must have thought they were seeing his resurrected spirit, for rumors of his return had not yet begun to spread, and he was thinner than any Mara one could see or imagine.

Seeing his withered form made me sick, but his image was not nearly as painful as his silence: Lucien had barely spoken a word to me since our flight from the collapsing Lycan confederacy.

Even as we were almost captured by Delphian ships along the coast of Laconnia, Lucien chose to remain completely silent. The Lycans were stopping every vessel from Ehlonica to ascertain knowledge of the current crisis, but we narrowly escaped because of Egret's mastery at the helm.

At first, I attributed his silence to the shock of all that had happened to him, and I gave him ample time and space to let his fresh wounds heal, days even as he rested on the ship. But even as we neared Brännfält's shores, Lucien would refuse to look at me; even when he was forced to speak when discussing our plans to save Volsung and his fifty thousand men who marched to certain death in Feldrem, he would portray a stoic look of normalcy, as if nothing had been broken between us.

I had expected him to react in anger and confusion when Egret and I explained to him our journey, especially when I shared my reasons for abandoning him. We were careful in omitting everything involving Aquilla, but I detailed who the Ora'suns were and why we needed them and the Spear of Mythraelyon to slay Belial, to save Renborg.

Despite this, Lucien only nodded, asking nothing more, not even inquiring as to how I knew of the spear nor the assassins and where they were to be found.

The only time his face broke from the emotionless and hardened determination was when the rotting stench of Nizarri flooded his nose upon meeting her. Still, even the cringing of his nose to the smell was quickly masked with tactful politeness.

"He is no longer the boy you once knew," Aquilla said to me as Egret listened nearby. "'The wine of suffering stains the teeth.'"

My heart sank in acknowledgement of the truth.

This burden was alleviated slightly when the remaining Ora'suns quickly unloaded our horses and equipment with haste. We wasted no time beginning our venture along the Vylonian Highway, though it was not nearly as fast as I would have liked.

As we rode, the hot summer breeze of the Rehmune month drenched my Shepherd robes in sweat. Though the lands were quiet, in the gentle winds there whispered something ancient, and my sight blended seamlessly with the world of the living and the world of Tihrrvyith, the language of the gods consuming the chatter of the Ora'suns around me and the internal thoughts of Aquilla.

Vaekee!

The word for lightning burned through my mind.

Nizari cocked her candle-lit mask towards my surging of pain, as did Alcharion, whose suspicious glower growed ever inquisitive.

Aquilla also gave me a concerned glance from within, and I sought a distraction from the growing power of the Ancient Tongue over my mind.

The steady rhythm of my horse was the only thing keeping my mind from not being consumed by the Tongue and my impatience, as it would take at least five days to reach Feldrem with our cavalry and ballistae in tow. By then, Renborg's end would take place if we did not save Volsung's army in time.

As would any hopes of saving Philomela.

Clutching at my Tree of Truth necklace, it weighed heavier than a boulder upon my heart in thought of her and what I must do to save her. In five days, her fate would ultimately be decided by either my failure to defeat the Dragon or our miraculous success.

"Belial shall fall to our might," Aquilla said as his spirit sat behind mine. "The Dragon, like his ancestors, lacks the Mother's blessing."

"Will you tell Lucien of Aquilla?" Egret whispered beside me as Lucien rode by himself ahead, his head held high but appearing to be weighed down just as heavily as my heart.

"He shall not," Aquilla said before I could respond.

"It's best he doesn't know," I finally said after a long pause.

"Because Thadius watches over him?" Egret said.

"Precisely," Aquilla said.

Egret's eyes beheld mine for a moment, a sense of lonely understanding passing between us before she returned her gaze to the plains of Renborg ahead.

It gladdened my tired heart to know I could trust this secret with her, and it made the prison of my mind feel less lonely. Though my entire being longed for so much more, it was just as pained by unrequited feelings that she seemed hesitant to deliver.

However, these turbulent feelings that mixed with anxiety for the battle ahead were forgotten every time she looked at me throughout our journey.

These glances and small conversations with Egret were like warm lanterns in the perpetual night of my mind, glowing brighter now since she was reunited with her husband and unable to have any sparring sessions with me.

Something is better than nothing, I thought as the sun began to settle along the increasingly familiar rolling summer yellowed hills that preceded our entrance into the Ren valley on our relentless hurry to Feldrem.

After a long day of riding, we made camp by the lip of one such mounds. We were four days away from where Volsung's camp was purported to be. Our horses snorted in relief, receiving a break from carrying the pieces of the hopefully Dragon-debilitating ballistae all day.

Strangely, as we began to set up camp, Lucien ordered for separate tents to be constructed for him and Egret.

"Do not husband and wife go to create children together every night?" Aquilla said as we watched the Ronian escorts erect each tent. "How is Lucien to expect an heir if they do not intertwine?"

Aquilla! I thought as I similarly cringed, not wanting the image of them together in my mind.

"What? I only seek to understand their behavior. She is not your wife, after all, nor shall she be. So why should their act of creation disturb you?"

Let us speak no further of this.

Suppressing those thoughts to the furthest reaches of my

mind, I couldn't help but agree that their behavior towards each other eluded my understanding.

After setting up my own tent, Alcharion roused several weary Ora'suns to scout our perimeter. Though they were skilled in the dark art of ending life, they would not be able to see as much as Aquilla and I could.

To give my heart peace, though I was beyond exhaustion, I followed Aquilla over the hill far from where we camped so that we could ensure that we would be safe for the night.

Much to our relief, we saw no bandits nor Drakin raiding parties.

Instead, before us stretched the tarnished and burnt fields of Brännfält. The battle's graveyard was more disturbing in person than it had been in Soul Sleep. From the top of the hill, it was clear to see where the main lines had met, for there could be seen a great concentration of both men and Drakin laid low and rotting in the dusk of the summer sun along a nearly two-mile stretch. The stench of Brännfält's wretched affair was perhaps most disturbing of all and had even signaled to us miles before our arrival.

Through Aquilla's eyes, I saw no life except a dozen or more animals that looked to be scavenging in the ashen fields at a great distance.

It seemed that even the dead would find no rest in this war, in this Shadow.

"We shall impede the Shadow from spreading further, Morgan," Aquilla said.

"I know," I whispered, forcing the words from my lips and my heart to believe them.

Death was inexorably ahead of us in this destiny of Shadow, no matter how hard we tried to avoid it; the burnt fields and stripped corpses were a staggering reminder. Though we could prepare to mitigate it as best as we could, and that is what

I hoped for and why we strove to train every spare second we could when all were asleep.

However, for tonight, we needed rest; the stench of the dead also made it too sickening to practice.

"You need to recover your strength," Egret said as we returned to the campfire she and Lucien were lounging beside.

My metal brace dug into my flesh as I sat down, followed by a severe throbbing in my spine.

"Agreed," I said, barely managing the word.

As we sat around the fire the Ora'suns had built beneath the edge of the cherry-red Bludhwoods that towered before us, we took part in a meal from the pelafahn meat that a few of the Ora'suns had caught and cooked for us. Because I had shared my meals primarily with Egret since she joined us for Cur Malum, I chose to sit next to Lucien, who sat all to himself at the edge of our gathering.

Before I could sit down next to him, Lucien stood abruptly and retreated into the shadows of the night.

"I must relieve myself," he said, grabbing a torch before being swallowed by the ocean of the night. Two of our ronian escorts stood to accompany him but were promptly waved off by their King.

He was obviously lying, for he had barely eaten that day.

"Leave him be, Morgan. It is better this way," Aquilla said.

His mind will not be in a place to lead if it is consumed in thought.

Setting down my steaming food, I got up to follow Lucien into the darkness.

"We will be right back," I said to Alcharion and Egret, both of whom gave me a look of perplexion as I departed from them.

Before Aquilla and I departed from their sight, I expected to meet Egret's eyes as I glanced quickly behind me, but instead

I was met with Alcharion's, whose silver eyes watched me as carefully as a wolf.

The Godstone-rich woodlands were refreshing to see after being gone from Renborg for so long. Though I had Aquilla's eyes, the trees around us glowed Bludh like Lucien's heart, which would have made my search for him in his hurried pace impossible without the torch light to guide me.

Thankfully, Lucien stopped not too far within the Bludhwoods. However, the glade in which he walked beneath the moon was far from preferable, for the rich red trees and grass suddenly turned lifelessly grey and barren.

Corrupted grounds created by the touch of Nox had only been something I read about in the moonlit hours of many lonesome nights, but now they were a bitter reality. The use of Noxstone drained all life and color from the area, leaving only a bleak sight. Who or why someone had destroyed the life in this part of the forest would forever be a mystery, for the one standing in its middle robbed me of all my focus.

Lucien awaited me in the colorless sea of the forest. His smile melted away, being replaced by trembling anger.

"I want the truth," Lucien said, his hoarse voice almost a whisper in the lifeless glade we found ourselves in.

My and Aquilla's steps came to a halt before him, my consciousness looking inward to Aquilla for guidance.

"He cannot know the truth," Aquilla said, "for the kings and leaders of Scissalan are watched too carefully and too closely by Thadius. Egret was the only exception because she forced our hand, along with the Ora'suns who have seen but a glimpse."

I don't know what to say then. He won't believe any lie we weave.

"Tell only what he needs to hear."

"Lucien," I began, my words sticking in my throat as I

searched to find the right words to say, "I've told you everything."

Lucien slapped me across the cheek, his eyes brimming with angry tears before turning to shock at what he did.

"I'm—I'm sorry… but no, I don't believe everything you said is true. It just doesn't make any sense! I know you struggled with wanting to leave this life before the wedding, but I was with you day and night and saw nothing that would suggest you would run away to join some mysterious cult and learn dark magic!"

"It's not magic, Lucien. It's the language of the gods, what's needed to use Godstone."

"And you learned this *how*?"

Words caught in my throat again as my thoughts stumbled frantically on how to avoid revealing Aquilla's presence and role in the truth of it all. Fortunately, Aquilla showed me a memory of the true monster in my mind that would help to spare the truth, but not truly lie.

"When the Drakin captured me, I was brought before their leader, Judux. Through him, I learned he planned to create the Dragon using the soul of Sh'eol in Solstein. Only another Klyr blade like this spear can kill the Dragon because of its hide, which only the assassins had."

The memory of the Soulis also resurfaced in my mind as I recounted Judux.

For a moment, I considered telling him of Gulmund's past and the dark creatures held within Renborg to further overwhelm and distract him from the absolute truth which I hid, but the thought of grieving him further sickened me, so I relented.

I would have to rid Caer Mordrake of those corpses when we reclaimed the capital to spare Lucien's mind.

It was the least I could do to recompense my betrayal.

Lucien looked at the Spear of Mythraelyon in my hands with deep speculation, but his unbelieving frown slowly gave way, leaving only some mistrust behind.

After a long pause, Lucien whispered, "Why… why didn't you just tell me? Why did you leave with no explanation? Do you even know what that did to me?"

Lucien's words pierced my heart like daggers with the simple sincerity and sorrow that permeated his voice and the knowledge of just how much my actions, however necessary, had failed him.

I wanted to tell him everything, to comfort him with clarity, and to let him into my world, thereby bridging the divide between us that seemed to widen with each step I took. But the world I was in now had no place for our former closeness. My destiny was one of Shadow, and my heart belonged to Egret, neither of which I could not share with Lucien.

"I didn't think you'd let me go," I said, our eyes locking in a regretful embrace, both acknowledging in bitter silence the growing divide.

"You're right," Lucien said, his voice shaking but solidifying in strength with each breath.

What Lucien was thinking was no longer clear, for he would not reveal his heart to me any longer. It saddened me to know that the brotherhood we once had was forever changing in the suffering of war: the childhood of warm summers in Hebsund, hunting with Kyllian, swimming in the Strumma, keeping Valena on her toes with mischief, and having not a care in the world.

Yet, even in this burial of childhood, something hidden worked unseen in our interactions that still perplexed and eluded me. How he looked at me differently, stiffened every time I drew near, tension and a slight but growing resentment visibly apparent in every breath.

"He is not ready to assume the mantle of responsibility to be a King of kings," Aquilla said. "He still lives under the shadow of his father's favored heir."

You do not give him enough credit, I thought, though in truth, I was uncertain.

"What will you do with Volsung?" I said, redirecting the conversation.

"You will see," he said, saying no more and disappearing with his torch from the glade, leaving Aquilla and I alone beneath the cold and isolated moon.

Lucien was gone from the campfire upon our return.

Alcharion and another Ora'sun were also missing, their nightly patrol around the perimeter one of paramount importance that superseded the exhaustion we all felt.

Egret was similarly absent from the fire. Instead, Aquilla and I found her slowly practicing footwork by herself not far from the several rings of Ora'suns and Ronians eating their dinner and talking quietly amidst the camp.

"Very methodical!" I teased in Skyyan as I returned to my spot by the fire amongst a handful of Ora'suns, my meal now void of any heat. "You have spent too much time in the courts, my Queen."

"If I could move as spirit as you do, even with our spines, you would not be so bold as you are now," Egret said, pivoting in her footwork to strike her sword through a thick branch which effortlessly removed it from the tree.

"Impressive," Aquilla said.

"Even more so after a long day's journey," I said, taking a generous bite from my cold pelafahn meat as I watched her, the gloom of Lucien's conversation fading in her light. "Perhaps you had a greater teacher than I did. Was it your father who taught you?"

Egret smiled at the mention of her father, sheathing her sword to join us by the fire. Her Ronian escorts followed closely behind, though they knew not the tongue in which we spoke and stood at a distance to give her space.

"Initially, yes, he taught me much of what I know," Egret said, her eyes sparkling from the flames and reflection. "But upon his passing, my mother forbade me from training, even with a stick. Swordplay was the only thing I had left to connect me to the memory of my father, so… I just had to find a way to continue, even if that meant I would have to do it in secret against my mother's will."

"How did you manage to get away with it?"

"Well, it wasn't easy," she said, beaming with joy as the memories of mischief most likely flooded her mind. "It mostly involved practicing forms from my father's copies of Liberio di Montarii's *Bloom of Battle and the Seven Scales of Mastery* late into the night when I probably should have been in bed."

"You must have been exhausted."

"Yes, indeed I was, so I even found a way to secretly train during the day last sol."

"How did you escape your other daily studies?"

"I didn't have to. I simply convinced my mother that I was interested in learning a new Hurinzvalese dance that I made out to be all the talk in the courts of Renborg and Hurinzval."

"Footwork disguised as dance," Aquilla noted, nodding his head in appreciation. "Clever."

"Why thank you, Aquilla," Egret responded, pleasantly surprised at his sincerity. "Before I came here, though, it had become more difficult to find the time. My mother had known about the wedding arrangement for a while, and I think she wanted me to be as well versed in Ronian history, language, and customs as humanly possible."

"No breaks?"

"None," she said, her emerald eyes lowering to look at the grass. "My mother is a hard woman to please, but I know she means well. She did what was necessary to make me… to make me strong and ready for my new life."

Egret's beaten-down composure proved otherwise.

"All Queens and those in authority must be stern if they are to produce resilient heirs," Aquilla said, trying and failing in his own way to aid in Egret's sorrow.

"Your mother is proud of you," I said, offering her a smile instead of Aquilla's unintentionally abrasive words, which she tried to reciprocate with her own.

"I hope so," she said, her voice burdened with the same heaviness I often saw in Lucien when he spoke of Gulmund. "It's why I must be strong and loyal to the marriage she chose for me, Morgan."

Egret's eyes met mine with such a gentleness that I could have remained locked in them forever. Quickly, she looked away, giving my lungs a chance to breathe again.

"Though," she continued, her voice softer, somber even, "sometimes I wish Lucien felt the same of our marriage. Felt anything at all towards me."

"Egret," I said, her melancholy gaze returning to me, "Lucien needs time."

"That is what you said before!" she said, anger rising with her tone.

"I know, but it still holds true. I truly believe that after we defeat the Drakin, he will behold you in awe as you deserve."

"Why would he do that then if he expresses no interest now?"

"Well, how could he not? You have boldly risked your life to save him in Ludsala and Laconnia. Not many can say they faced both Lycan and Spindler yet lived. You were astonishingly wise in navigating us here safely by the sea and by horse throughout all of our travels; many would be clueless in such situations. You are relentlessly determined in your devotion to your family, even us. Your soul is fascinating to discover, humorous at times, albeit slightly frustrating from your passionate will.

"But it is your passionate strength and the way you hold yourself with such graceful regality that is mesmerizing. Yet even despite such royalty, you provide care for those who deserve it least, for lowborns like myself."

Egret's mouth was agape as she slightly shook her head.

"Morgan—"

"Lucien will love you, adore you even because of who you are. With enough time with you, it would be impossible for anyone not to."

Tears swelled in her glistening forest eyes that I wanted to look into for the rest of my life, whether for four more days or one hundred sols.

"Morgan," Egret began, her words finding difficulty in their delivery, "What exactly are you—"

"Aela Zaeim!"

The three of us jumped at the quickly approaching Ora'sun who had gone with Alcharion. The Elf had been sprinting through the forest, fear coloring his dark flesh.

"Drakin have been spotted, Aela Zaeim!"

Aquilla translated for Egret as she and I looked at each other with worry. It was going to be a long night.

"Where's Alcharion?" I said, fatigue threatening to overwhelm me.

"He was surveying the perimeter just north of the camp," the Ora'sun said. "He is unaware of the Drakin's presence."

"Quickly, gather the others and send for someone to redirect Alcharion to join us," I said, thankful to still be wearing my Shepherd robes, and my Klyr spear was within reach.

Immediately, as the scout addressed the Ora'suns and the

Ronians, the camp exploded from its peaceful quiet to the sound of warriors preparing themselves for battle.

The scout held up his hand as Egret and I indicated we were ready.

"There's one more thing," the scout said, his face furrowed in worry.

"Tell me," I said, anxious to end the threat.

"I spotted a woman and a man resisting the Drakin, both young. We overheard the younger man scream 'Karlata' if that word means anything to you."

"Karlata?" Aquilla said unbeknownst to the Ora'sun.

"No," I said quietly, fear threatening its violent course once again in me, "that can't be. Show us!"

Once the Ora'sun guided us to the hill where he saw the Drakin, Egret and I outpaced the assassin in the dark, curiosity and fear propelling us through every step.

"Do not wait for me," Egret said as we ran.

Nodding, I Wyled most of my weight into Aquilla's spirit, leaping effortlessly up the hill and landing next to a gurgling brook.

"There," I said, pointing to the flaming-haired Drakin in the corpse-ridden fields below. Using Aquilla's sight, I could see the dark silhouettes of two figures struggling against the Drakin.

"Karlata and her brother shall fall beneath their blades unless we intervene," Aquilla said, right before a blood-curdling scream pierced our ears.

Karlata's scream was undeniably familiar as the Drakin began tearing at her clothes.

"Let us make haste, Morgan!" Aquilla said.

Without a moment to lose, I leaped across the hill. It felt like I was flying as I descended into the war-torn fields of Bränfält from the incredible speed Aquilla's spirit granted me. Fear grew evermore that our speed would not be enough to save them as the Drakin were about to begin their unspeakable deed to her.

Though Karlata had deeply wounded me before, and her brother was as pure as bile, they did not deserve to suffer the ravages of the Drakin.

Too many had suffered already.

My feet carried me faster when I saw what remained of the dying Ronian escorts further behind them, who must have recently been slain by the ten or so Drakin cavalry, many of whom were dismounted and assaulting Karlata while abusing her brother.

Mercy was briefly set aside as I phased most of my upper body, allowing me to leap over Karlata while delivering a deadly and simultaneous strike through the face of one of the four Drakin who greedily wrestled for her. There was no time to grapple with taking the life of another as I landed behind the fallen Drakin and quickly cleaved the side of another. The brace drove into my back upon landing and seized my hands in pain as I retreated before the two towering Drakin, who collectively turned to face me at once.

"Morgan?" Karlata said through tears while in a Drakin's grip, to which I nodded.

The two Drakin closest to me hesitated upon seeing my spear, but as the others formed behind them, they grew in confidence and began to advance on me.

Perhaps to ensure she wouldn't run away, one of the Drakin drove his head into her skull, rendering Karlata unconscious and tossing her behind them. Before I could react, each of them began feigning strikes in every direction, their hands mirroring the nervous twitching that mine displayed as I attempted to destroy their weapons with the spear.

"Do not get too close," Aquilla said as I retreated, blood

oozing down my arms from the multiple cuts the Drakin were able to deliver. "Even with my spirit, we cannot evade the speed of their strikes."

"Stay by my side, Morgan," Egret shouted through heavy breaths, running to join beside me as she engaged the other Drakin who had almost ended Seifred's life.

While heroic, she would soon be felled by their blades, as would I; for even if we could parry all of their multiple thrusts and discern their feigned attacks, which many of them gouged deep wounds along our arms and shoulders, we were both still severely weakened by our healing spines.

We would be slaughtered in seconds.

"Sister!" Seifred yelled as he saw her motionless form, all facade of boldness now gone in the face of battle. He was right to be afraid, for we were severely outnumbered, even with the Spear of Mythraelyon.

"The wind, Morgan!" Aquilla said, showing me the word for air in the Tongue of Tihrrvyith.

Though it was my first time drawing the word for the air, it obeyed my command and swept against the Drakin who charged me. Several of them were thrown to the burnt grass and some were knocked off their horses. However, the wind was not powerful enough, as they quickly recovered and surrounded the four of us for slaughter.

Death seemed inevitable as the Drakin concentrated their attacks on everyone else besides me because of the deadliness and reach of my spear. Egret took the brunt of their attacks, and she grew tired with each strike she deflected with her sword and Godstone knife.

Even if I could sweep my spear against all of the Drakin who faced me, I would leave myself open to their blades and risk harming Egret, who shouldered beside me.

One of the Drakin riders screamed from behind the horde and galloped towards us through the pack.

What do we do?

"Focus the wind on the horse!" Aquilla said.

At once, I Waed the wind to steer the horse away from our path, but a nearby Drakin threw off my focus when he batted my spear aside with his shield and slammed his defense into my face.

"Aquilla!" I said, panic consuming me as pain exploded in my nose and left me temporarily blinded.

Another scream roared into my ears, but it was not from us or the Drakin.

Cuerian curses slew from Alcharion whom I could hear rushing behind us to unleash his fury.

I had barely enough time to move out of the way from the Elf's wrath, whose greatsword cut through and battered down many of the Drakin with ease, his anger and size making him an unrelenting force that took the Drakin by surprise. Even the Drakin on horseback could not withstand his unbridled fury.

Alcharion's rage gave Egret and I just enough of a distraction to deliver the Drakin before us to the judgement of the Author above, who would surely despise the end of their stories as they included the great intended evil for Karlata.

But Alcharion's immense hatred blinded him, for tears clouded his eyes as his uncontrolled slaughter found him advancing back to us with the few Drakin who remained, their lives and possibly ours about to end as the great Elf heaved his sword for one last blow.

"Morgan, look out!" Aquilla said.

Phasing my upper body and head just as Aquilla warned me, I pushed Egret out of the way to avoid the sword of Alcharion. His blade cut through the Drakin before us, passing through my spectral neck. But such luck extended only so far, for his blade cleaved into Seifred's shoulder and stopped only when it reached his spine.

Horror seized my soul as Seifred stood for a moment, choking on the blood that flooded from his trembling lips, before collapsing with the sword into a sleepless death from which he would never awaken.

Alcharion dropped to his knees upon seeing what evil he had unwillingly done.

No words could surface in me from the shock of seeing such unnecessary carnage.

Aquilla was similarly speechless as I looked to Egret, whose emerald eyes were streaming with silent tears at what had befallen Seifred.

Without a word, Alcharion retrieved the sword of a fallen Drakin and placed it slowly before him, tears pouring down his unmoving lips. As I realized what he was about to do, I lunged forward and placed an iron grip on his shoulders, pushing against his struggle and shock at seeing me stop him.

"Let me die," Alcharion whispered.

"No," I said, lowering myself down to him. "It was an accident."

Alcharion shook his head, his thoughts lost in his shattered mind.

"He is too far gone," Aquilla said.

No!

The dark Elf lifted his swollen eyes to me; in them, I saw myself not too long ago.

"I didn't see him," Alcharion began, his words catching in his throat. "I just… I just couldn't let the same thing happen to that girl."

Alcharion's eyes looked painfully at Seifred's corpse but rested when he saw Karlata untarnished, though she was bleeding from her head.

"She will live," I said, though I only guessed. "Egret, please retrieve a few Ora'suns to carry Karlata to the camp. We will return shortly."

"Of course," she said, wrapping her own cloak around Karlata for comfort before departing quickly back to the camp.

Egret gave me one look of encouragement before she raced up the hill. As our eyes embraced each other, there formed a bonding of our souls which only shared suffering could intertwine.

Alcharion looked down as we were left alone, his sorrow and shame weighing him down as if he were about to be beheaded himself.

"I have… *become* the very thing I swore not to be," he continued, though I wasn't sure if he was talking to me anymore. "I'm sorry, mother. I failed you. *Curse the Kira Naz'ka*!"

Suddenly, I understood.

My heart was horrified by the deduction that his mother had been completely consumed in every way by the Kira Naz'ka, that her soul, her eternal essence, was no more; *forever*. And as I looked upon Alcharion's grieving and crushed soul, I knew that if I did not grab his hand from the edge of the cliffs, he would soon join his mother in the sea of destruction.

"Alcharion," I said, readjusting my grip on his shoulder and catching his attention from the dark abyss of his mind. "Alcharion, if you give up now, it will have all been for nothing, and

Seifred, her brother, would have died in vain. But I myself do not condemn you, but I plead with you to join me in ensuring that such suffering does not befall anyone else. I cannot undo what has happened, but I can offer you a chance of redemption: help me save my baby sister from the Dragon who wishes to consume her soul."

The tears in Alcharion's eyes slowly began to dry, and in his silver pupils there emerged a fiery passion that had become so annoyingly familiar that I now rejoiced to see.

No one is too far gone, spirit.

Alcharion grasped my arm, and I helped pull him up to his feet.

"Though I do not understand you, I will serve you and keep your secret," the Elf said, bowing his head low in respect. "But first, let me bury the soul who has been taken in the gentle arms of the Mother, whose strange power She has graced you with."

Aquilla and I stood and watched as Alcharion slowly took the fallen Seifred in his arms and carried him to the top of the hill, where the dark Elf buried him with the gentle love of a father.

Chapter 27
Klyr the Dragon!

In the early morn's mist, Akaidius and his men came upon us as winged spirits of death. At first, I thought they were Averties of fowlish nature, nothing but Fhaolin mercenaries that the Polisians had scraped from the barrel. But their back-mounted wings danced in the sun, revealing a different origin, and a destined doom. Their rippling feathers cut the air in a deafening rush as if the ocean were coming over the hills to wash us away. Their holy aura was an irony for the graves they sent us to. They were impossible to defeat, and there was only one solution for their ferocity.

It wasn't long before our Ronian King Tormund III decided to do what was necessary for the survival of Renborg: incorporate a similar elite cavalry into our ranks, naming them the Akaidian Brotherhood.

Diary of John Beckham
"Reflections on the 1st Polarch War 790 DE"
Vyilhein Printing

The night before the slaughter at Feldrem began, four days after we had rescued Karlata, she stirred restlessly in the Ora'sun medical tent. Aquilla and I waited with her during the waning night, closely watching Nizari who attended to Karlata's broken vessel.

Aquilla eyed the ancient leader with suspicion.

"I do not trust her Nox heart," he said as he watched Nizari rub a potent ointment on Karlata's head.

She ensured that Egret received care, I thought, pushing my eyelids up to keep awake.

"My mistake. I didn't realize Humans found those who feed on souls to be trustworthy."

We do not know her reasoning if she did.

"'Only evil can be kindled by evil, and purity by those of

purity.' If from your heart you could not conjure purity to wield the spear alone, then how can one of a wicked design create anything that is holy?"

I gave no answer to the Medjaib as we waited for hours longer.

Nizari wheezed as she labored tirelessly without complaint over Karlata. There was merit in Aquilla's perspective, but as I watched the candle-dripping and perfume-ridden woman deliver exceptional care to someone she did not know, I couldn't help but think that Aquilla's understanding of Humans was not of the depth to reach truth.

After what felt like an eternity, I awoke to a withering gasp from Nizari, not surprised that I fell asleep.

"She will live!" the ancient woman slithered.

"Dark magic has many such false promises," Aquilla said, but to our great relief, Karlata's cheeks flushed red and vibrant like a pomegranate.

Karlata would live.

However, despite this momentary burst of relief, she would be crushed upon awakening and realizing her brother was gone forever.

The spear of Mythraelyon choked in my hands at the thought of telling Karlata of Seifred's fate, which soon approached; though this weight was overshadowed by my heart's affliction in knowing that tomorrow could very well be the day that I either removed Thadius' pet or lost the souls of all whom I loved in the flames of my failure.

The weight of the battle hadn't fully gloomed upon me until now.

"We shall not hesitate when the moment comes to strike true," Aquilla said, his words bringing no encouragement to my heart. "We shall do whatever it takes, at any means."

You keep telling me that as if that makes it any easier.

Looking up to see Karlata stirring again, my eyes were caught by Nizari who silently stared at me through her Nox mask.

Chills ran down my spine as she drew nearer.

"There is a darkness about you," Nizari wheezed in particularly raspy breaths. The long voyage across the volatile sea and our ragged trek on land had left her as weathered as the restless road was beaten.

Who knew if she would even survive this journey? Perhaps even she didn't know.

"Do you fear the path ahead?" Nizari continued.

"I am not afraid of death."

"That may be. But, for those you love... *you* fear their deaths."

My eyes shifted uncomfortably from her sightless mask.

"Destiny often has its unwanted but necessary evils," she continued. "Especially when the Shadow is the only way to save them."

"I don't believe that," I said, frowning at her pessimism.

"Do you not?" Nizari said, but for a moment I thought it was Aquilla who asked, who watched me silently across the tent.

"No," I continued, "too often have I read of and seen the results of those who chose the *necessary* evil. In most cases, their choices prove to be of destructive convenience, not compassion."

Nizari shook her head slowly, wax dripping down her silver armor. "As long as there is power, there will be those who are destined to wield it, whether for good or evil, regardless of intention. However, one who leads would be wicked to choose personal morality before the well-being of those they are charged to protect. 'The sacrifice of the self shall serve the many.'"

"But must not a leader *lead* by example?" I said, leaning back in disgust from her disregard for morality and ill-usage of a Cypherian Proverb. "Should a leader betray their people by succumbing to the very wickedness that they are entrusted to protect their people *from*?"

"Can the shepherd protect his flock without bloodying his hands?" Nizari said, her tone sharpening in defense. "Does he permit the wolf to parlay? Or when the mother wolf comes near, does he not slay her with the swiftness of sling and stone? Better yet, should the shepherd happen upon the wolf's den, is it not better that he smothers the young pups, or perhaps they too be piously permitted to grow strong and hungry for vengeance?"

Nizari let out an exasperated rattle as she strained to speak, her cloyingly sweet perfumes permeating the air with each battled breath. But when she spoke again, it was with a greater stillness than I had ever witnessed prior.

"Tell me, does the lamb truly care how the wolf was slain?"

Looking away from her, I took a long pause in an attempt to ascertain her indecipherable tone which carried either an alarming indifference or complete sincerity.

Which was worse I could not tell.

"You play a dangerous game, Nizari. Where then is the line to be drawn when separating monster from man?"

"There is no such line. Each of us in our own time will and must be monstrous for the sake of our own den of pups. This world is full of monsters, my Zaeim, the least of which are those beasts of land and sea. Live long enough and you shall see them, from without and within."

"Then I suppose you agree with Alcharion, that I am unfit to lead the Ora'suns and thus unworthy of your faith?"

"Alcharion may be a skilled lieutenant second to none, yet often he can be just as much a zealous fool, second to none.

His zealotry, while passionate, ultimately stems from a heart that wishes to do what is right. As to your question, the answer is no. Although it is difficult to release control of my flock that I have tended so long, I do have faith in you, my Zaeim, but know this also…"

Leaning closer, drips of hot wax fell upon Karlata's cheek, causing the slightest of stirrings.

"I would see these old bones turn to ash before I let destruction befall my people."

The words hung in the air like an anvil held aloft by a frayed and twisting rope, the tension of which was only cut by a single soft word.

"Morgan?" Karlata said, her voice weak and strained. "Morgan, is that you?"

"Yes, I'm here," I said, pulling myself closer, wiping the hardening wax from her cheek, and holding her extended, weak hand.

Nizari stood, departing from us with a graceful bow and a reverent, "My Zaeim."

"Where are we?" Karlata's frail voice whispered. "Wait… where have you been?"

"It's a long story," I said, offering a reassuring smile. "Essentially, I had to leave so that I could call upon the aid of the Ora'suns to fight the Dragon."

"Oh," she said, confusion swimming across her face, but also a gentle warmth as she squeezed my hand.

This warmth illuminating her face was only temporary, however, for when she reclined back into the bed, her eyes glazed over. All joy vanished as she lay in a trance, in what I could only surmise were her memories unfortunately dawning upon her.

Karlata's eyes began to swell with fear until they poured out with tears.

"Wait, where's Seifred?"

My head bowed low.

"I'm sorry. Seifred… he died in the skirmish against the Drakin who attacked you."

Karlata's hand squeezed my own as I delivered the horrifying news. Though I never liked Seifred, I truly felt sorrow for her at the revelation of her brother's demise.

Tears continued gushing from her eyes as she pulled away into the sheets.

"It's my fault," she whispered to herself.

"What?" I said.

Karlata shook her head, her eyes wide with shock.

"I made him stay with me at Brännfält."

Aquilla cocked his head as he listened.

"Why?"

Karlata looked down, her eyes heavy with shame. "I was desperate, Morgan. I have searched in vain for a novel discovery for the College, to at last become a Cormag and not just be another bride married for political gain. When I heard of the Dragon in Brännfält, I begged my father to let me come with him to look for any scales it could have shed and examine the destruction it left behind. I knew I would have been the first at the College to report on the beast thought long extinct."

"Volsung allowed this?"

"Only for two days once we reached Brännfält, so that we might rejoin his army that marched to Feldrem. And Seifred… he chose to stay behind with me with a soldat of twenty of his men, to ensure I would be safe. I didn't think we would be met with any resistance. But now… now he's *dead* because of me."

"That's not your fault, Karlata."

Karlata closed her eyes, the pain behind them unbelieving of my words.

"But I'm still alone," she whispered.

The longing in her charcoal eyes was like hooks in my soul,

and I found myself pulling closer to her. But I stopped myself before we were a breath apart, not wanting to make the same mistake as before.

Not wanting to betray…

"I must go," I said, pulling away from her soft hands and moving towards the tent's opening.

"Morgan?" Karlata said, her voice hanging on a dwindling hope that I would stay.

Turning to look at her, my hand caught in the opening crease of the tent.

Karlata looked almost identical to my reflection in the waves that I gloomed over not too long ago, her dark hair hanging low as she tried to smile, as she pretended that everything was alright.

"Thank you."

Nodding, I left her longing eyes quickly before I would fall for the pursuits of a familiar soul.

"We must avoid her if we are to remain in the Light," Aquilla said as we stood beneath the ever-increasing stars.

"I know," I said, following his gaze to the Void above.

A white glimmer streaked across the corner of my sight, drawing my attention. The folds of Lucien's tent rustled quietly in the night.

He had been watching us.

By the following afternoon, the whispering trees of Renborg and the soft stomping of our horses were slowly replaced by the song of shadow darkening ahead of us.

Shortly after my vision met the plumes of smoke on the horizon, the distant screams and clashes of steel were the second terrors that scraped my ears. Not long after, the battle of Feldrem stained our eyes as we emerged from the forested hills overlooking the war-torn city by the Ren River.

Tens of thousands of Ronians were already engaged in a bloody cleave of halberds and spears with an almost equal amount of Drakin. Their bloodied canvas of survival was a rocky terrain before the crumbled and blackened walls of Feldrem. The destruction of Belial was apparent from the cindered plains to the smoking city that had been captured weeks ago; and now, the fiery serpent polluted the cotton skies above.

Strapped to the now terrifyingly massive Belial was Judux himself.

But even more bewildering were the archers who were surprisingly capable of driving the Dragon back from getting too close to our army.

At least five hundred mercenary Laconnian archers were stationed at regular intervals behind the rear of the Ronian forces. Their Delphian bows loosed arrows with such a force that while not deadly to the Dragon, they landed crippling blows if they found their mark on its scales.

Judux, however, would be easily torn apart from the superior draw weight of their bows, and he kept himself and his beast far from their deadly reach.

"My eyes must betray me," Egret said in Ronic alongside Lucien and I. "I didn't expect your uncle to hire the Lycan for war."

Lucien said nothing as his face twisted into anger.

He must have swallowed his pride when he realized trebuchets would be severely ineffective against the Dragon, I thought.

"'The rot which is pride cannot be removed cleanly,'" Aquilla said, quoting another Cypherian Proverb.

Our banter came to a swift end when a small but slowly growing gap emerged in the right flank of Volsung's men, which was slowly but surely being taken advantage of by the Drakin's left. They relentlessly pushed the weakened flank and in time would no doubt be able to curve it dangerously inwards.

It wouldn't be long before the Drakin could overwhelm the Ronian flank and force a chain route to devastating effect.

Judux must have noticed this too, for he and Belial focused the remaining fire from the Dragon's belly on the weakened flank. Hundreds, if not a thousand or so men, including a few Drakin, were incinerated by the flames before Belial's reserves puttered out. The toxic fire burned so hot and the sight of scorched and screaming men was so vile that even the Drakin were hesitant at first to re-enter the fray.

All would soon be lost.

"Halt!" a Ronian scout yelled as he rode swiftly towards us.

A ring of cavalry followed close behind him as they blocked our approach, followed by two Knights of Kyllian who headed their advance.

Our horses bridled at the potential conflict as I searched through their wall of steel and horses. Relief flooded my heart as I could just make out that behind the soldiers sat a mounted Volsung and a weary Kolstok, both of whose faces were somber as they watched the failing battle.

Quickly, I gave a signal for the Ora'suns behind us to hold their gait and to stay their blades.

Ignoring my call to approach with caution, Lucien rode boldly past me and cast aside his helmet, meeting the eager blades of the Knights of Kyllian, Sirs Valrok and Alduaura by the looks of the engravings on their helms.

"Uncle!"

The longswords of the two Knights lowered before Lucien in recognition of their King.

Volsung and Kolstok quickly turned around in their saddles. Both men squinted in speculation of Lucien. He was almost apprehended by the other guards, but they suddenly froze when they saw him clearly.

"Have some sense you fools!" Lucien yelled. "Do you not

recognize your Sovereign and the Lord of all my father's empire? Your King is returned! I am come to retake my army and save this wretched day from destruction!"

For the briefest moment, a mixed look of shock and anger flickered across Volsung's face as the Knights of Kyllian stayed their blades and sheathed their swords. However, it was quickly set aside and replaced with one of well feigned relief, and even tears.

Volsung waved the guards aside and allowed us to approach, the Ora'suns carefully following behind.

"Your Grace," exclaimed a dumbfounded Kolstok, his weathered and tired face now ecstatic with tears of joy. "I… it's—"

"It's good to see you too, old friend!" Lucien said with watered eyes.

"Lucien, thank the Mother!" Volsung said. "I am overjoyed to see that you are alive and well, my nephew. We thought—"

"Your King will discuss what has befallen him after we slay the Dragon and win this day," Lucien interrupted, the gentle water of his eyes turning to a simmer. "Now, where do we stand in the battle?"

Volsung bowed his head slightly in submission, though I doubted it was anything but painful.

"Lucien bodes well in his newfound strength," Aquilla said, to which Egret nodded and I agreed with sorrow.

Lucien the boy had died in the wolf's den.

What emerged was no longer a boy, but his shadow.

Or perhaps just a man.

"As you wish, Your Grace," Volsung said, gesturing to the war before us. "The battle is swift at hand. While it appears we are losing ground, precisely is the opposite. We have drained the Dragon of its fire with the soft target of a false gap on the right. Now, as they press our right back, they are prone to the death that rides swiftly from behind. By Her mercy, if he has any sense, Prince Aelric should be advancing any moment now."

Lucien, Egret, and I maneuvered our horses to stand beside Volsung and Kolstok to see if this Akaidian Prince of Edahnia harbored such instinct. Aquilla also watched carefully within me. Sharing his incredible clarity of sight, I could see what no other mortal could.

In a few minutes, it began.

Like bees swarming from a shaken hive, the Akaidians emerged from a wooded brook half a mile from the faltering flank. They were magnificent to behold. The shine of their armor was pristine and the sound of their advance terrifying as seven hundred horses shook the earth. The white feathered wings fixed to their back plates rippled through the air.

Five hundred paces away now, as they drew near to the exposed Drakin, they picked up their gait from a trot to a canter.

Three hundred paces. Their loose formation began to draw into incredibly close order with the knees of each rider nearly grazing the other.

One hundred paces now. Letting out a great cry, the Akaidians raised their long lances to the sky before couching them to brace for impact as they broke into a full charge. The Drakin, so sure of victory moments ago, had turned in a desperate attempt to form rank.

Fifty paces. Panic consumed them as many prepared to embrace their fate. Some even tried to flee before the wall of death that rode to meet them all.

Too late.

At once, a crack of broken lance and shattered bone erupted amongst the Drakin left wing, each Akaidian finding his mark with terrible precision. Like iron caught between hammer and anvil, the Drakin were trapped. Sensing no need to retrieve fresh lances for a second charge, the Akaidians that had broken them drew swords and war hammers to begin the bloody work of rolling up the breaking Drakin flank.

As quickly as victory had entered Judux's sights, it vanished—the tide of battle rapidly shifting against his favor.

"Impressive," Egret whispered to herself.

Belial roared in frustration above the chaos, shaking every heart with its fury.

"I must commend Aelric for his precision and his Akaidians for their bravery," Lucien said. "You are aware that nothing can penetrate the Dragon's scales?"

"Yes, Lord Kolstok has made that quite clear to me," Volsung said, to which Servillius lowered his head in bitter remembrance. "Which is why I have purchased the aid of our Laconnian mercenaries. They will do what they can to ground the beast—"

"If it is at all possible," Servilius interrupted grimmly.

"Who will slay it when it has been brought down?" Lucien said. "The Akaidians?"

"No, Your Grace", Volsung answered, his tone as condescending as one who spoke to a child. "I judge they are too valuable and too scarce a commodity to be wasted on such an undertaking."

"Who then?" inquired an increasingly irritated Lucien.

"I acquired the Lycan for more than their bows. Thrice the usual fee they demanded when I told them what they were truly needed for, though I wager there won't be much left of them to collect once all is said and done. All they need do is render it blinded."

"And what of Judux?" Egret said.

"We will topple him from the Dragon once it is brought low," Volsung said. "The Lycan carry both pike and rope. We will have their king in chains and end this war quickly with negotiations."

"Bold, but cunning," Aquilla said.

"That still doesn't resolve the Dragon," I said, drawing ire from the glance of Volsung, whose careful eyes widened as he observed the Spear of Mythraelyon in my hands. "A blind Dragon is still a threat, but in my hands is the solution. It is made of Klyr Godstone, and I can pierce its heart with it."

"Indeed," Volsung said, the plans in his mind shifting as he took into account the weapon that would silence the heart of Belial.

"Judux shall also be silenced upon Belial's death," Aquilla said. "Volsung shall be most displeased with bringing less to the post-war negotiations."

I know, but that is of least concern to me. The Drakin will still disband without their leader, and negotiations will still be highly favorable. The Drakin states will care only for themselves, and their disunity will once again be their undoing.

"The selfish pride of their Dragon and Elvish ancestors burns deeply within them it seems."

I don't want to think about that, I thought, pushing the image of their unnatural conception from my mind, focusing instead on Volsung.

"We also bring with us Kaptilolian ballistae that should prove more capable in grounding the Dragon," I continued, turning now to Lucien. "Your Grace, how should we commence?"

My question aimed towards Lucien threw off Volsung, who realized the control was slipping from his hands amongst the other Kriga and Marshalls, as was the glory if we won this battle.

Lucien smiled briefly as he realized my scheme; a brief respite from his earlier gloom.

"How quickly can the ballistae be engaged—"

"No!" Volsung said, his impatience pouring through his seemingly calm facade. "There is need to reinforce the right flank where the Drakin are now faltering."

"Uncle," Lucien said, confidence driving his steed towards him. "I think it's best that you comfort your daughter at this time. Karlata is here with us and is grieving over the loss of your son, who perished at the hands of Drakin not four days ago in Brännfält."

Morbid perplexity stunned Volsung as Karlata came weeping amidst the Ora'suns behind us. Lucien strode past his grief-stricken uncle who quickly unsaddled and knelt to console his daughter, taking complete control over the battle.

Aquilla and Egret both looked at me in shock at Lucien's cunningly dark ploy to regain power.

"Morgan," Lucien said, "order your men to set up their ballistae on the lip of the hill, and have the majority of your men reinforce the right flank."

In Lucien's command there mentioned nothing of me, which I guessed was because of his unwillingness to see me join the fray.

"But you must lead them," Aquilla said, the galaxy of his eyes gazing into mine with utmost seriousness. "It is your destiny."

Nodding to Aquilla's words, I quickly ordered the Ora'suns to begin setting up their ballistae behind our army's lines before turning back to Lucien. "I will take them to the flank myself, for I am the only one who can slay the Dragon."

Lucien's face bent in disagreement, his worried brow begging me not to go, but the screech of Belial swooping down onto the battlefield silenced his differing thoughts.

What further drove me to deny Lucien's request was the ghastly appearance of Rolloc, his orbed and clawed helm noticeable in the storm of war. He and a small band of his mounted Drakin warriors stood suicidally before the charging Akaidians, appearing unafraid of the death that came for them.

For a moment, I thought Rolloc would drown in the black grave in which he had sent so many into. Part of me hated him so strongly for the evil he brought upon Sigmund that I yearned… no, *prayed* that he would be crushed by the Akaidians.

But my prayers were not answered.

Instead, Rolloc and his group of Drakin heaved mightily within themselves, their dark grey skin turning just as molten red as the magmic veins that webbed their bodies; and like their ancestors, they breathed a wave of fire before them.

The horses of the Akaidians reared and threw many to the corpse-ridden ground where they were quickly sent to the Mother by Rolloc's red axe.

"Go, Morgan," Egret said as she offered a brave smile. "Go save Philomela."

All fear of the Dragon vanished at her encouragement—for a moment at least.

Afraid to reveal too much of my heart for her amidst our company, I simply nodded my speechless thanks to her as a river of words was dammed within. As for Lucien, I embraced him quickly. Before he could command me to stay, I rode in haste to where Alcharion and my Ora'suns awaited me.

Nizari solemnly nodded to me, her mind a mystery as ever.

"Let us ride!" Aquilla said, his spirit awaiting eagerly before us.

"Ora'suns," I said in their Cuerian tongue, "form a wedge and let us extinguish the heart of this fell serpent!"

The Ora'suns moved organically as one, Alcharion taking the second position of the wedge beside Enor while the others formed behind them in cohesion upon their lightly armored steeds. Dread washed over me as I realized what I had inadvertently commanded.

They expected me to lead the charge.

Time seemed to slow as I led my horse reluctantly to the tip of the spear. The eyes of the men and elves who trusted their very lives unto me met mine with reverence and even excitement.

How could they believe so willingly… so zealously, *in me?*

"They have faith, Morgan…", Aquilla said gently, "faith that the Mother has led you to them for a greater purpose than death alone. 'Trust in the Author,' Morgan, 'and She shall deliver you from harm.'"

Closing my eyes, I spoke within.

Deliver us.

Without hesitation, I spurred my horse as we thundered down from the hills of Feldrem, our hearts beating against the rhythm of war.

"Breathe, Morgan, and listen to my voice," Aquilla said as we neared the flank that would decide the fate of thousands.

Air sharply flooded my lungs from forgetting to breathe in the dreadful anticipation of my first charge into battle.

Though Belial didn't see me as we drew closer, its monstrous presence above was almost petrifying enough to strangle me with fear. Rows of bloody teeth the size of shields tore through metal and flesh, rendering execution to any that dared attack as he repeatedly dove towards weak points in the flanks before departing from the sea of spears into the clouds above.

My thoughts were pulled back to the screams of war as we rounded the flank. Giving a moment to reform the arrow of our formation, I nearly vomited before I felt a hand on my right shoulder.

Looking back I was met with the eyes of Enor who simply nodded with a calm assurity.

"Aela Zaeim," Enor said solemnly. Then, turning in his saddle, he cried out to the others, "Aela Zaeim!"

They responded, over and over, shaking their spears with pride as they shouted my name.

Even Alcharion.

Masking my tears, I closed my visor and spurred us onto the impatient chaos, the feel of lightning rippling through my veins as we thundered forward. Akaidians and Rolloc's cavalry desperately dueled before us as we came on. Fifty paces away, I was riding harder than I had ever ridden before, my spear leveling to greet the first mounted Drakin I saw.

On the periphery of the stalled Drakin formation, I met my first target.

As he turned in his saddle, my eyes were met with those of a young Drakin whose excitement instantly melted into terror. Klyrstone passed through his neck with unsettling ease, spraying my helm as I was just as soon met with the revolting rust and bowel-ridden scent of battle. Sifting through the increasing gaps of the breaking formation like a raging river around rock, I could think of nothing else but staying alive.

The sound of war was deafening as I quickly learned all races sounded alike in death. Frantically, I thrust my spear through anything that looked unfamiliar, staving off attacks or rogue arrows with my rounded Ora'sun shield.

Suddenly a sharp pain shot through my right arm below the shoulder. An awfully bruising blow that, had I not been armored, I knew would have cost me permanently. In haste, I turned to see a massive, mounted figure with boiling eyes dressed in deep Bludh red and finely adorned scale armor readying the sword in his left hand for a second strike.

Someone important, I thought, stunned to inaction as my short life lay in the path of his rage.

As his arm reached its zenith, my nameless executioner's life was abruptly ended by Enor's spear passing under his unarmored armpit into his heart, his last breath.

Nodding to Enor quickly, there was no time for words as we both reared on, any halt in movement threatening death.

Alcharion and the rest of the Ora'suns pierced through the Drakin cavalry with terrible efficiency. Paving slowly through the mounted Drakin who were caught in surprise by our charge, we soon found ourselves engulfed in the flank, much to our advantage, for it threw what remained of their cohesion into complete disarray as we slaughtered our way through.

My legs pressed against the Ora'suns surrounding me as I followed Aquilla's lead in striking the Drakin that I could with the Spear of Mythraelyon, its Klyr blade slicing through bone and armor alike with bitter ease.

Just ahead I could see Belial trying to avoid the volleys of Lycan arrows peppering the air. Over the course of the last few hours, however, many had found their way into the Dragon's wings. Belial struggled to stay aloft but threatened to fall upon the Drakin infantry below where the Akaidians were engaged in fierce resistance to Rolloc and his dwindling fire-breathers.

Belial's grounding would be our only chance at stopping his heart, but the beast seemed so far away in the midst of battle.

Every second we fought seemed eternal as we pushed against the Drakin and their ally's cavalry. As soon as one mounted Drakin was slain, another would take his place, be they Drakin or an allied Dwarf or Elf. My arms began to fatigue as I focused on phasing, blocking, and striking alongside the Ora'suns, who were silent as they delivered death without hesitation. This was their profession, their life.

Only a few of the Ora'suns fell.

"Phase!" Aquilla said, which I did with my head just in time as a spear from a mounted mercenary Dwarf clanged against my temporarily empty helm.

I returned the favor by swiping my spear across the Dwarf's heavily plated chest. The Klyr spear tore cleanly through, from which he fell dead into the sea of scorched and slaughtered bodies below.

My eyes caught the revered gazes of Ronian soldiers nearby, many of whom appeared much younger than I was. As I looked upon them, I could see that younger and significantly older Ronians made up the remnants of the weaker flank which Belial had previously taken with ease; their deaths had drawn the Dragon close to the Lycan volleys and Akaidians.

Many of those young and aged Ronians were now charred remains that were stomped upon by the feet and hooves of both sides, including mine.

Did Volsung plan for the lesser abled soldiers to be sacrificed?

"It seems so," Aquilla said, reading my black thoughts.

Acid rage boiled in my stomach and I felt sick at the thought of such precious lives being wasted so *strategically*.

This strategy, however evil, began to pay off. The Drakin facing our flank began to flee from the slaughter of the Ronians, Akaidians, and Lycan.

"Aela Zaeim," Enor said, turning to me as a dark figure flashed obscurely behind him through the carnage of war. "Shall we pursue—"

Multiple flames engulfed Enor who began to scream, cooking beneath his armor as fire spewed from Rolloc's warriors behind him. Enor's horse panicked as his master burned. The beast slammed into the Ora'suns behind him and sowed chaos into our wedge formation.

A shout startled me amidst the flames.

Rolloc burst through the smoke of Enor's body, his horse coming from behind me. Turning just in time, I raised my shield to block his axe. In anger, the Drakin pushed me down into the saddle of my horse, almost throwing me off. In desperation, I thrust my spear into his neck. With ease, Rolloc deflected my spear with his shield before driving his axe down into my calf.

A white-hot pain erupted in my leg. All the breath to scream had been stolen from the pain that almost overtook me. The Drakin's axe had gouged deep into my calf before being yanked painfully back to him.

"Aquilla!" I could barely scream, not caring if anyone heard.

"Phase as he grabs you!" Aquilla said, which I tried to follow as Rolloc grabbed me from my horse while his Drakin fended off the Ora'suns trying to save me, but my mind was focused too much on the fire in my leg to phase.

The world was thrown upside down as I was forcefully held on Rolloc's steed that thundered away from my Ora'suns. The Ronians surrounding us were soon replaced by Drakin who were fleeing as blood gushed from my leg.

He was taking me with them.

"Phase from his grasp!" Aquilla panicked.

Pushing through the blinding pain, I Wyled into Aquilla's spirit, slipping from Rolloc's steed and crashing onto the charred battlefield below.

My tender back exploded with pain that mirrored my leg.

A slew of Drakonnian curses erupted from Rolloc who pivoted his steed against the fleeing tide of Drakin to retrieve me, but his fury was cut short when a Lycan volley of arrows eviscerated his horse and some of the Drakin surrounding me.

"Stay down, Morgan!" Aquilla warned as several more arrows from their powerful draw cinched the flames of more Drakin who fled in a panic around us.

Hearing not another volley, I began to rise before any fleeing Drakin could end my life with sword or steed. Before I could even stand on my only good leg, my helm was torn violently off of me and cast aside by Rolloc who pinned me to the ground with his foot, crushing my stomach and ability to phase.

"Why are you leading them?" Rolloc said through his orbed helm, shifting the Godstone axe in his hands as he quickly withdrew rope from his side. "It doesn't matter. She can still use you."

Though his words slithered into my ears, my mind was focused on what Aquilla wanted me to do to escape.

As Rolloc grabbed my hands and began to violently bind me, I phased my hands through the ropes to the Drakin's surprise, grabbing my spear with all of my might and heaving it into his chest. The blow did not kill Rolloc, for his Gyldur armor was mightily forged and carried many layers that absorbed most of the blade, but it gave me enough time to rise up and strike the hilt of the spear into his helm.

Rolloc collapsed without another word.

"Aela Zaeim!" Alcharion yelled as he and our band of Ora'suns cut down the Drakin between us.

Relief flooded my heart as they surrounded me. However, as Alcharion glanced upon Rolloc, he hefted his own spear to sheathe into Rolloc's heart.

"Spare him!" I commanded, just as Alcharion was inches away from ending the Drakin's life. "We shall take him as a prisoner."

"As you will, my Aela Zaeim," Alcharion bowed, but his eyes caught something just behind me.

Belial roared in the near background of war. Turning too slowly, I could see the Dragon soaring through the sky towards me, much against the protest of its master who yelled at Belial to return its focus to saving their soldiers.

It would descend upon me in a matter of moments.

"Vorim!" I cursed, frantically picking up the Spear of Mythraelyon.

"Drop to the ground!" Aquilla said, but unlike our attempt with the Eldrake before, I was not so lucky.

Belial's claws forcefully engulfed me and dragged me to the sky. Chaos threatened to consume me as I feared what grisly and pointless end I would meet. In my violent struggle, I sliced through the claws of Belial with the spear, to which the Dragon involuntarily released me and sent me plummeting to the River Ren distant from the battle.

The water refreshed me as it caught me in its cold embrace, saving me from the fall. This grace lasted only a few precious moments, for as I staggered out from the waters, Belial crashed into the muddy river shore before me.

"Belial!" Judux yelled from atop the Dragon, noticing the Lycan mercenaries who departed from the battle line. The Averites began loosing arrows at him, carrying pikes and roped hooks in their pursuit. "Return to the battle at once! My people perish in your absence! We must organize a retreat!"

"*Cypherus*," Belial seethed, completely ignoring Judux as the Dragon slowly advanced on us, looming larger than a ship as Lycan arrows whistled past it.

Aquilla nodded to my spear. "Though we are wounded, you can still thrust the spear into its heart. The Lycan shall aid us if we stand our ground."

Belial made no sounds as it loomed hungrily before me. Slowly, Belial opened its bloody mouth, but instead of preparing to bite, the Dragon's mind spoke in the wordless imagery of the Shiveric tongue that penetrated my mind.

Through Belial's mind, I could see the thousands of Ronians that Belial had eviscerated, and with these memories came feelings of immense guilt and shame; but it wasn't just Belial's mind that spoke. Writhing through the images of Belial's mind were countless Dragons who were slain by Cypherus in the Ancient Era. Though many of the Dragon were rightfully slain from the terror that they had unleashed upon the ancient peoples, there were other Dragon whom I could feel Sh'eol's hatred for that had not rebelled against Cypherus or enleague with Thade, but were still slain regardless by Cypherus and Nazrioch.

Wrestling against Sh'eol's mind, Belial's memories emerged again. This time an image of Philomela emerged: glowing before her was the Tongue of Tihrrvyith's word for Belial's soul, which was painfully weaved into her heart like Judux's.

"No!" I screamed, my hands cold around the spear.

Judux looked at me, confusion straining his face. His confusion quickly dissipated as he began to draw the word for the Dragon's soul in anger.

Belial's memory flashed through my mind again, this time the words of the Dragon roaring through them.

"You tied my fate to the child's?" Belial yelled, snapping at Judux amidst the scorched remains of Renborg's garden which had hosted Lucien's wedding.

"Unfortunately, yes," Judux said as he held a confused Philomela, his face not stern or sinister, but saddened. "I didn't want to attach her fate to yours. You give me no choice, Belial: it is the *only* way. Your life is not enough to ensure cooperation with me, but this little girl is. I noticed your strange affection towards her, and because of it you will obey me, young Dragon, lest you damn another to share in your suffering."

Belial released a maddening growl, bowing its head in unwilling submission before slithering, "How righteous…"

"I do not see myself as righteous, Belial, but as a savior!" Judux said, his chin held high as he soothed a crying Philomela. "My people cannot afford to be torn apart by the Ronians or each other anymore, and you are Yarahm's only hope for a brighter future which I will bring forth as their deliverer, as their Shadow of Cypherus who corrects the wicked hands of history that care not for us!

"It is a costly path, I admit, both to myself, you, and others, but it is a price I am willing to pay, for it is the only way for the greater good of all. And once I birth more of your kind into this world, fully in my control, then I will at last bring peace for us all, and I will release you from my service."

Belial's memory faded from my mind as horror seized me in the present. My plans to kill Belial tore apart at the seams, for now Philomela would suffer the same sleepless death if I killed the Dragon. Hopeless and helpless, I stood before Judux and Belial as the Dragon crawled towards me to drag me below the sea of despair.

"We must slay the Dragon," Aquilla pleaded as they drew towards us.

Turning in shock to Aquilla, I was aghast that he would even continue to recommend such an evil choice.

I can't, I thought, tears choking me as my world and my destiny fell apart.

"Morgan, you must! There is no other way!"

Judux was seconds away from Waeing the Dragon's soul, but as he began to grasp the dark word before him, a Lycan arrow nicked the scales of his gauntlet. The Lycan would take him in mere moments.

Belial reared his serpentine head to devour me.

"No, Morgan!" Aquilla said, reading my thoughts as a desperate hope emerged in my mind.

If I could not kill the monster, at least I could stop it from harming anyone else.

Forever.

Phasing most of my body, I lunged underneath the Dragon as it struck with its terrible teeth to where I was previously standing.

Being almost weightless, I gained much more ground then Belial would have guessed I could make, and I landed right beneath Belial's right wing. With everything inside of me, I prepared to launch my spear into the blood red shoulder of its wing, to clip it of its power.

But as I lifted my spear, reality itself shifted like falling sand into the Tongue of Tihrrvyith as I burned within from the Ancient Word that seized my mind and plagued Philomela.

Belial's wing would have been completely severed from its joint had I not faltered in my thrust, but the precious seconds I wasted in mental agony gave the monster enough time to thrash away from me quickly into the skies; but as it did so, my spear still managed to cut through half of the right foot of the Dragon, leaving it hanging on only by a few inches of flesh.

Belial landed several feet away from me but roared so loudly that my ears almost burst from the pressure it produced.

"You fool!" Aquilla yelled. "We missed our chance!"

You think only of yourself and not the cost! I cannot kill Philomela!

"You are too ignorant to trust the Light!"

The Light you trust is only yourself, which you make impossible to trust in your aim to do evil for good like your brothers! Like Judux!

The Dragon turned in rage upon me, ignoring Judux who yelled for the beast to avoid attacking me because of the spear and my powers that were before unknown to him.

I thought that it would be over in that moment, that the last thing I would see before the judgment of my failures would be the rows of teeth that shred apart my destiny of Shadow.

But a javelin sank into the right eye of Belial, causing the Dragon to scream as it thrashed off of one foot.

Alcharion surpassed the oncoming Lycan while the mercenaries launched their own at Judux who barely avoided them.

Belial didn't wait for the other eye to be blinded. Abruptly turning to escape, it tore through some of the Lycan with ease, uncaringly crushing them and barely missing Alcharion as it launched wearily into the sky above. Once airborne again, the Dragon nearly faltered in its flight but managed to make its way back to the city with Judux barely holding fast.

Having witnessed their King and sacred Dragon flee before their very eyes, the Drakin finally began to follow suit in segments as word of Belial's retreat flooded across the field of battle.

The mounted Drakin fled quickly, leaving behind the less fortunate steed-less infantry who were forced to engage in a fighting withdrawal. But with the advance of vengeful cavalry on both wings threatening to engulf them, their tactical retreat soon turned to an outright route as Ronians, Akaidians, and Ora'suns all nipped at their heels and swung for their heads.

Alcharion rode swiftly to the riverbank where I knelt unmoving before him.

"Thank you, Alcharion," I barely managed to say through the pain as it threatened to consume me, as did the Tongue of Creation.

"Couldn't let you keep all the glory to yourself, Aela Zaeim," the dark Elf said, the slightest grin present on his blood-spattered face.

And though the joy I shared in his rescue was great, the

Light within me waned as I looked upon Aquilla, who was without words as his cosmic eyes glared at me.

But then slowly, very slowly, his swirling eyes lessened in their anger, until there was a sorrow that glowed within.

"There's something I need to show you," Aquilla said, before I descended into the dark sleep of pain.

Chapter 28
The Truth and the Lie

Seeing that he had inadvertently become a savior to thousands, Cypherus knew he must protect those whose lives were destroyed by the Dragons of Thadius from those who sought to conquer what remained of the old world before the war. Though Cypherus had no desire to be anything more than what he was before: a simple farmer, a father, and, most grievously, a husband, though his beloved wife had perished from the flames of the first Dragon he slew.

And so Cypherus declared that a city should be built in the valley of his victory; one with great walls of stone defensively held on the great cliffs named for Asculum by the mountains and the sea, near the cinders of his home. Thousands came from all across the land to join and aid Cypherus and his Taldarii, including the King of the Dorianites, Hezakias, who had been Cypherus' closest ally in the Eldren Wars. Hezakias provided much of the needed resources for the construction. When the walls were finished, they wanted to name the city after Cypherus, but he would not be deified in any such way, instead choosing to name the city after his lost beloved, for whom he sacrificed everything for: Renua.

The Tale of Cypherus the Great: The Ten Tomes
"Tome V: Birth of Renua"
Asculum I, Heir of Cypherus

W**hat** followed the battle of Feldrem was a blur.

All I could remember through the haze of pain was being carried safely by Alcharion back behind our Ronian lines, my Ora'suns defending us as we pushed through the retreating Drakin forces who fled in terror once their Dragon and King deserted them.

The battle is surely won, I remember thinking.

The last memory I had was of Lucien in shock when he saw

my suffering state. He promptly ordered the nearest doctors to bring me to a tent for healing.

"Rolloc is with the Ora'suns," I barely muttered, closing my eyes from the pain, letting them shut out the burdensome world.

Egret nodded in understanding who stood beside me.

It was her emerald pearls that I last glanced upon before closing my eyes. Though, it was a look of pity; yet seemingly, I thought, one of pride also.

Was she proud that I had fended off the Dragon?

If she was, she would soon share in Aquilla's disdain that I had failed to kill the beast; that fear of this fated Shadow for the greater good had overcome me.

I could sense Aquilla next to us as I was carried away, silently. As I lay drowsy to the lullaby of war that carried on outside, the Medjaib's glowing eyes watched me silently within. Aquilla wordlessly whispered to me a sense of guilt for his actions, but to which I could not decipher as I swooned to the waves of exhaustion that soon overtook me.

In the unconscious dark, there appeared Solstein.

Burning brightly in all of its Klyr glory, Solstein was brighter than a star as I held it before Lucien in the Bludhwood tree, the strange markings of the Tongue of Tihrrvyith glowing strongly before me as we beheld the blade before the sunrise of Renborg.

Philomela laughed in Lucien's arms as she looked playfully at the sword, reaching out her delicate hands to grab it.

"Don't touch the sword, little one," Lucien smiled as he pulled her away from it. "The sword can hurt you, but Morgan won't."

"Can I play with it?" Sigmund said below, trying to jump onto the tree to reach us.

"Get down, Sigmund!" Valena said, picking up her son as she stood next to Gulmund.

"Only the true King gets to wield such a dangerous power," Gulmund said beside them, his eyes downcast as he looked with great sorrow at the arm rings of his eldest but late son, Kyllian V. "The cost of its power is worth it, for the *greater good.* Even at the cost of one's self."

The King's words sounded forced, as if he were trying to convince himself that it was true.

"The price for love was worth it, wasn't it, Morgan?" Egret said, who stood at the edge of the sea cliffs, her hair long and startlingly blonde, but her eyes more rich than Bludhstone itself, more red than the blood that trickled from her teeth and lips.

But my eyes drifted from her to the thousands of families who looked at me from the sea cliffs on the outskirts of Renborg.

Solstein suddenly burned like a hot white blade in my hands, the flames of its power bursting forth and catching the tree on fire.

I was speechless as I fell from the flaming tree.

Solstein sheathed itself in the red skull of Belial, who lay silenced before me, a fallen Judux and Rolloc on either side of the beast.

Disbelief held me as I backed away from the slain Dragon, my hands spectral and transparent like Aquilla's as I released the blade from my hands.

"Lucien?" I said, turning around to the Bludhwood tree that was now engulfed in flames.

Lucien stood alone before a lifeless Philomela, who lay silent next to her family, all of the Mordrakes quieter than the grave beside him. Upon his head lay the dark and broken crown of Judux, his eyes more Nox than the dark aura around him.

"She is no more Shadow than I," Lucien said, his voice dark and unrecognizable, full of jealousy and hate. "Join me, forever, instead of her. It is only a matter of Time."

"Lucien?" I pleaded, tears running down my face.

"Morgan," Aquilla's voice echoed through the nightmare.

Turning to Aquilla standing behind me, I could see through his cosmic flesh and robes the thousands of families still alive in Renborg, going about their daily business in the city, spared from the destruction of the now silent Belial and fallen Drakin. But though they toiled with life in their bones, there existed no joy among their hardened faces, their faces which seemed too old for this world, much like the Elves.

I didn't realize it at first, but also missing from the crowds were children.

Strangely, even the red-robed Valkryn Cormarchs were missing, though they were normally a constant presence in the city, preaching a return to the Tree of Truth found in the text of Solbok and a message of repentance through the prophecies of the Morythial.

It was as if the once faithful and passionate Ronians littered the ground as living tombstones in the grey fields of Renborg.

Alive yet deceased.

Awake yet asleep.

"It is the only way," Aquilla said, but when I looked at him closer, I could see he looked like a different Medjaib entirely. Somehow I knew he was someone far older and with more experience, clothed in shades of white, ethereal robes.

As I analyzed his differences, through him I tried to make out the families again, but there appeared no city or people: a sea of bones from Dragons far mightier than Belial littered the fields and hills. While some bones were black with evil, many of the Dragon corpses lay curled around cracked eggs as if defending them from a different kind of evil.

"A necessary kind of evil," Nazrioch the First Medjaib said before me, and in his eyes, I could see who I really was: the Shadowed Reflection of Cypherus the Great.

"Please!" cried the young Drakin lying on the ground before me, the spear of Mythraelyon pressed to his neck by my uncovered hands. His face was familiar: my first victim in the Battle of Feldrem.

Before he could say more, I ended his pleas as malice filled my terrified heart.

"*Sleepless Death…*" the Void above hissed, and all became black.

"Morgan?" Lucien whispered.

I screamed from the nightmare which he had awoken me from, grabbing onto my brother with trembling arms and wincing in pain from my sudden movement.

"Morgan, what's wrong?" he said, but I couldn't answer as I buried my head in his arms.

Tears could not be held back as I wept in him, his finely crafted shirt-sleeves crumpling tightly in my grasp.

"It's alright, Morgan, I'm here."

Time became irrelevant as I drained myself of tears in Lucien's arms. The dream had felt different than any I had before.

It felt more real.

It felt like a warning.

Looking inward to Aquilla, he was watching me with a heavy sadness, but he spoke nothing of his thoughts; instead, he kept them quietly to himself.

"Was it of the Dragon?" Lucien said.

Pulling myself up from his arms, I looked deeply in his blue eyes, and for just a moment they reflected the boy I once knew.

"Something like that," I said, wiping the tears off with the fresh white shirt that I had been wrapped in as I was asleep.

"Well, you will be pleased to know that the Drakin fell without their precious Dragon, thanks to you," Lucien said, his soft voice offering a smile. "Though, while I believe you were exceedingly foolish to attempt something such as that, it did help to win the day. Although we lost nearly four thousand men and two thousand are being treated for their wounds, I'm told the Drakin losses stand at perhaps eighteen thousand dead and at least another five thousand captured.

"And Morgan, we captured that bastard who slew mother and father. Rolloc, his name was. By the Mother's Might, I will see him perish deeply for his sins after we drain him of his insight into the heathen horde. But it could have been far worse, and for that I am grateful."

Memories of the elderly and inexperienced youth being used as bait by the Dragon burned through my mind, the scars of war finding no mercy on me.

Not wanting to keep such revelations to myself, I relayed to Lucien of my suspicions of Volsung's treacherous plan that cost the lives of hundreds, if not a thousand.

Lucien shook his head with distaste.

"I expect nothing less of that man," Lucien said. "Though, his callousness may have prompted our only chance of victory; for it was a necessary evil for the greater good."

"Please don't say that," I said, fear beginning to sprout within me as the dream of the dark crown of Lucien tore at my mind. "That can't be the only way."

"Sometimes it is, Morgan."

I shook my head in denial of a hideous fallacy, of the choice I tried hiding from with Belial.

But maybe he was right.

Not wanting to discuss ethics anymore, I said, "So, what are you going to do with Volsung?"

Lucien's eyes closed with annoyance at his uncle's mention.

"Well, as much as I absolutely despise Volsung, in truth, it would be unwise to be rid of him so quickly. After all, the empire was kept intact, and he has the respect of most of the provinces' Kriga, Marqs, and Principates, along with a callous intellect that we can use to our advantage. In addition, he would make for a fine teacher for Egret's and my children."

"What?"

For a moment I didn't believe I was speaking to Lucien; merely, a shadowed reflection whose heart was not in the words that he spoke. In fact, Lucien's smile seemed to waver as he looked at me, as if he danced with all of his might to keep up the facade.

"She may not be the fairest, like you said, and I may not love her yet—but we have a duty."

The thought of Egret being with someone else entirely, even if that was, to my inner shame, her own husband and my brother whom I loved, was like a knife plunging slowly into my heart which beat only for her.

Looking down at his hand, Lucien touched a newly placed emerald ring that I instantly recognized as Gulmund's: a sacred heirloom passed from Mordrake to Mordrake for two hundred sols. Somehow, it had survived the fall of the citadel.

"Father died before he could see me as a man," Lucien continued. "As a worthy Prince… as a worthy *son*. Renborg needs her King, and I owe her the stability of an heir. To carry on the Mordrake line and safeguard her people for generations to come."

Simultaneous grief for the love I bore my brother and confliction for trying to take someone who didn't belong to me added further to the bottomless pit of pain I felt growing in my stomach.

"That reminds me," Lucien said, pulling out a rolled piece

of parchment from his garment. "When I went to go see Karlata after the battle, I found this that had fallen just out of her cloak."

Holding the parchment in my hands, I was unsure of whether to read it before Lucien, whose intentions I could not unmask.

"I don't think she ever got over your childhood frolic," Lucien smirked, standing up from my bed to leave. "I'll let you get some rest now, for we have some time before more reinforcements arrive from Kriga Tyrediam. They will help us storm the walls of Renborg. In the meantime, please rest."

For several breathless seconds, Lucien looked at me as I fingered the parchment, and his eyes glistened as if burdened with something heavier than he made known.

Before I could inquire further, he embraced me gently and quickly, leaving Aquilla and I alone shortly after.

"Do not read the note," Aquilla said as he emerged from the shadows to sit beside me, his spectral and galactic flesh a mesmerizing contrast to the white tent.

"Why not?"

"It wasn't intended for you to read. And I trust it will breed only discord before we face Belial for the last time."

Thinking of the Dragon which would befall Philomela was the very last thing that I wanted in my mind. My heart was also barren for the impossible hope of Egret, which felt so eternally out of reach at the abysmal reality that her hand was already taken in marriage.

"Trust me, Morgan," Aquilla said, but my heart took the lead of my insatiable and lonely curiosity.

"I'm sorry. I just… I feel so weak… so *alone*."

"I know," Aquilla said, "but this will not help."

Unrolling the parchment gently in denial, I read the words inscribed:

Castles need weapons of war
To tear down their barriers of stone.
Yet no man has conquered
This fearless fortress.
With royal rubies inside,
Its strength and desired treasure.

These walls are kept fortified,
Guarded safely for a queen
Like the matriarchy demanded.
Never to open its private gates.

And then you arrived.

Declaring war on first sight,
You relentlessly lay siege.
At first, you lustfully miscalculate,
Mistaking my throne like all the others.
But when I locked my gilded tower,
You changed tactics, realizing my gold within.

Now, my mother's strategy is threatened.
Your soft words, a piercing trebuchet,
Your kindred spirit, a battering ram.
Inside, my priceless fortune
Trembles in its chest.
But after persistent battles, a gentle knock.

Do you carry the keys to set me free?

I know I hide behind deep defenses,
But do not leave the war for my kingdom
To easily acquire a brothel.

Don't be like your breed of barbarians.
For I await a victorious, righteous king,
And to be held tightly

Like a white flag of surrender.

The beautiful words from Karlata perplexed me that she would even write them. My soul wept in the bitter truth of knowing that Egret would always be out of reach; but nonetheless, the words of Karlata's familiar spirit were satisfying enough to feed my starving soul.

Or maybe I would endure this life alone, as Cypherus did, after losing his only beloved.

And whatever it was that Aquilla wanted to show me was hidden away in my dark indulgence of the Shadow of love and longing that consumed my thoughts.

Chapter 29
Lessons from the Past

In dream you spoke to me, whispering destiny
Awake you called to me, bright amidst the olive tree
Upon the mountain I shall see a gift to set your people free
Of Dragon flames of tyranny

Blood I found upon the stone, forging stronger than Dragon bone
But as I returned, I learned what my spirit knows: I was not alone
Awakened Shadow shook the sky, my family helpless down below
Ka'Zaeir sang flames upon my home

The life of others more great, I ran to trade my family's fate
The fire I did not taste, but it consumed Renua, my only mate
My sword burned pure in sacrificial state, I fell the beast with a heart of hate
For her every Dragon I would desecrate

Then all would be safe, so thus my spirit spake

Solbok
Eldren Wars, 40:10-12
"The Grief of Cypherus"

The waiting was almost as terrible as the war itself. For the next eleven days we waited for the Kriga Tyrediam and his reinforcements to arrive before our army could even advance on Renborg's capital.

Time dragged by agonizingly slow. But it wasn't just the enduring of time that daunted my spirit: it was the anxiety that had first begun to form like a subtle wave in the sea, only to rise each day, every second, almost unnoticed, until its shadow was enough to consume every thought in my mind, blocking out even Aquilla's ponderings; it was the anxiety of the unknown.

Would I fail again before the Dragon or extinguish the innocent flame of Philomela?

Regardless of the path, would I walk it alone, envious of those whom the Mother deemed worthy of a beloved?

Was there any hope of escaping this sleepless death?

Time itself was its own curse because of how it nurtured these thoughts, grew them like weeds that suffocated me, choking my soul. The only upside to this daunting game of patience was the added preparation with Aquilla for my final encounter with the Dragon. Since we couldn't spar until I was on my feet again, Aquilla continued to have me practice Wyling my body into his spirit repeatedly, though it continued to be only partially complete since the battle of Feldrem.

Aquilla no longer chastised me for not being pure of heart to completely phase my entire being.

Instead he simply watched me, speaking not a word for a long time. Many times I would catch a glimpse of his spirit staring off into the Ren River besides our camp or gently touching the wings of a butterfly that fluttered throughout the camp, watching as it danced free in the skies.

What most perplexed me was his silent ponderings on the soldiers of youth and age who lay suffering from their wounds from Volsung's scheme. Aquilla even left my vessel several times to stand and observe a few of the younger soldiers who slowly died from their wounds of fire and steel.

For his prolonged silence, I was grateful; my soul was too heavy and torn from the Dragon that would inevitably devour my heart if I stopped its own, leaving me with no one to give it to, save someone who my flesh desired but my soul rejected.

Aquilla's training was the only thing keeping my mind together, asleep from the thoughts of Shadow that lurked in the corners of my subconscious.

Perhaps in spite of my cursed fate, even in the quiet moments of training, I was plagued by the Tongue of Tihrrvyith. Every so often, my reality would morph into its whispering sea of ancient words that constructed everything in existence.

Though it further plagued my mind the more I used it, training with the Tongue of Tihrrvyith was another necessary evil, a necessity.

I could not fight if I could not stand.

With Aquilla's guidance, we were able to draw the word of Man over the gaping wound of my calf so that we could Wae back together the torn skin to heal faster, enough to leave even the Ora'sun healer surprised who came to tend to it often. After the healer washed the wound with boiling water and wine before wrapping it, he was astounded at how little honey, herbs, and dedrim sap he needed to pour into it to help it mend properly.

The healer beheld me with a strange curiosity, muttering a slight prayer underneath his breath and bowing in reverence before leaving us alone.

As my leg recovered its strength in the weeks before the impending confrontation at Renborg's capital, we watched Judux and the Drakin prepare through Soul Sleep.

Part of me wished I hadn't.

Judux was barely resisted in Feldrem and it cost him more lives than the Ronians. It was only by sheer luck that I was able to sever Belial's claw and hinder the Drakin's ability to overwhelm our army. But now, as tens of thousands of reinforcements arrived in the Ren Valley from Yarahm via the Ilarkoi Mountains of Laconnia, Judux's forces swelled to a sea of formidable, determined Drakin and allies.

Not wanting to dwell on doom further, I let my spirit drift to my old bedroom tower. To the greatest of all joys and pains, we found Philomela locked in her room; she was tossing restlessly and crying.

No one tended to her needs.

Grief clawed my heart as I held her small hand with my galactic fingers.

I forgot how long I stayed there with her, wishing I was not some Shadow who would fail her.

Aquilla placed himself before her, a silent downcast nod informing me that it was time to return.

"I know," I said, bowing my head before kissing Philomela gently. "I'm sorry."

Aquilla didn't respond, for the apology wasn't for him.

Luckily, Alcharion almost never let us have time to be crushed by the burden of helplessness that threatened to overwhelm me when we were alone. The dark Elf was determined to make me stronger, almost annoyingly so. Once a few days had passed, and my leg was bound and healed enough that it wouldn't open on horseback, he was relentless in having me train with the other Ora'suns.

Every day and night.

As the lanceliers of the Ronian divisions were drilling maneuvers and charges in the sprawling fields, we trained alongside yet separate from them, sparring on horseback with the rest of the Ora'suns. I was thankful for the distraction, as the calm before the storm truly was a lie: there was no calm within before a battle, before a slaughter of innocents.

The persistent training with Alcharion further helped to quell the aching of my heart in the drastic reduction of time I had with Egret. No longer was I free to speak with her at leisure as we had before, nor could I train with her in public or private. Such actions would be without question seen as covetous and inappropriate, especially since the women from the fields to the courts of Renborg did not take hand in combat, queens in particular.

Egret would most likely have to train secretly once Renborg

was restored as she did in Skyya. Though, it would likely be without me.

Fortunately, Lucien brought Egret and his royal guard to join us occasionally in training. As always, my heart warmed every time I was blessed to see her, though Egret was reduced to remaining as a bystander by a quick dismissal from Lucien. She obeyed much to her silent chagrin, sitting in the shade of a tree that surrounded the sparring grounds.

A few servants began to approach Egret, most likely seeking to refresh any of her needs, but a glare sharp as my spear warded them off before they could ask.

I laughed only slightly at the sight.

"You've taken too many days of rest," Lucien said as he joined me on horseback, smacking the flat of his arming sword against my shield arm as he galloped past me before pivoting back around.

"You should have blocked that,"Aquilla said, which I frustratingly agreed with, though it was pleasant to see Lucien in a jovial mood again despite the circumstances we faced.

"I was only just fighting for my life against an ancient monster," I said, sweat dripping from my ungloved hands as I recklessly thrust my practice spear into his shield.

"You slept almost until the afternoon, dear brother," he said, allowing my spear to come within his defenses before knocking it aside with his shield and thrusting his sword to my neck in one precise movement.

"Indeed, you sleep too much," Aquilla said.

"Come now, Morgan," Lucien said, his tone of playful mockery, "you really must train a little harder, unless you want to surrender?"

His shield hand just deflected my spear as I uncalculatively thrust it at him again.

Sword in hand, Lucien surprised me at the same moment

by gripping my exposed wrist, and with not much resistance, pulled me off of my horse. But not wanting to fall so easily alone, I dropped my spear to grab his own wrist and we fell off of our horses together, laughing all the way down.

Any pain that erupted in my spine was quickly forgotten as Lucien and I both laughed on the trodden grass, the faces of mortified Ronians of every rank surrounding us only bolstering that laughter.

For a moment, I forgot all of the sufferings that had burdened Lucien since the wedding. He seemed like himself again: mischievously joyful.

I missed it.

"My King!" a mounted soldier yelled from across the camp, startling us to our feet as he moved through the crowd of Ronian and Ora'sun bystanders to reach us. It was Mathis. The Marshall had survived his visit to the Ren Valley to attack the Drakin's supply line, much to mine and Lucien's relief.

"The Kriga has arrived, Your Grace," Mathis said as he approached us, bowing his head to Lucien before looking at me with a slight grin. "Still alive, my boy?"

"Just a scratch," I said, offering a smile in return to Lucien's and my old friend.

Walking behind the soldier were Karlata and Volsung, one of which made my heart drum with anxious intrigue as she swept her dark curls behind her ear, while the other spiked my sense of caution; the wolf of Renborg was none too pleased with being under Lucien's command, though his obedient stoic face displayed none of it.

"Lord Jaerris Tyrediam yearns to begin strategizing immediately," Volsung said.

"As do I," Lucien said, before turning to me while brushing himself off from the summer grass. "Morgan, I'd like you to join us in the meeting."

"Of course," I said, handing my practice spear to Alcharion who, bowing at my departure, took both our horses to be watered.

Egret's eyes caught mine as we began to return to Lucien's tent, rising to join us.

For a moment, we just looked at each other, saying nothing.

I couldn't help but release a smile.

"Oh, Egret, you will not be needed in this meeting, dear wife," Lucien said, turning from her almost stunned face and walking swiftly to his green and gold, kingly tent. "Come, Volsung and Karlata, I would like you to join us. Karlata, would you fetch some water for Morgan?"

Egret now stood in shock, as did Aquilla and I.

"Am I nothing to you?" she said in Skyyan, her eyes red with brimming tears and wrath boiling at their surfaces.

"What did you say?" Lucien said in Ronic, turning to her in annoyed confusion. "Speak Ronic, if you will."

"Please excuse me, *husband*," she said forcibly in Ronic, striding angrily away and disappearing into the sea of tents before I could say anything of comfort. Unbeknownst to Lucien who shook his head and turned away, Egret glanced quickly at me as she fled shamefully in humiliation.

What escaped my understanding was the divisive subtleties of Lucien's actions; his continual effort to exclude his wife from even non-military matters made no sense, but the time to ponder them was put aside as the Kriga arrived with his hosts.

The victorious mood of the Ronians and even the Ora'suns grew ever stronger as Kriga Tyrediam arrived at the head of five infantry hosts, more than a few battalions of mercenary pikes and archers, and three divisions of cavalry, numbering close to twenty-five thousand foot soldiers and three thousand mounted men and Lanceliers.

The bulk of Tyrediam's force had been drawn from the midland provinces of Gedon, Edahnia, and Messina, with the majority of his mercenaries coming from the western coast of Kapria and Vargroth.

The tired Ronians who won the Battle of Feldrem welcomed them with cheers as the men of Lord Tyrediam slowly settled alongside the peripheries of Lucien's encampments.

Volsung smiled in relief as Lucien welcomed the Kriga into the King's company.

Lucien's tent was packed full with the Kriga, Marshalls, and Grand Marshalls of both Grand Hosts that, once combined, would soon form a great Kingly Host.

Lucien had me sit next to him and Karlata at the roundtable where a map of Renborg lay before us, very crude in comparison to the shape I had witnessed when amongst the stars.

Once everyone had settled into their seats, he motioned for us all to be silent.

"Kriga Tyrediam, thank you for your swiftness in joining us today," Lucien said. "Much praise is owed unto you for keeping the Drakin at bay from reaching further south than the Amon Fork of the Ren River. I'm told your frequent and ferocious skirmishes with them saved much of the farms of the valley and southernly midlands beyond from destruction. The grain houses and crops you have secured may well save tens of thousands from starvation in the sols to come. Thank you for your loyalty and service."

"It is my honor, my King," Tyrediam said, his head bowing low into his wooly but well kept beard that grew long from his hardened face.

"I would also like to give thanks to my brother Morgan, for it was his mercenaries and his Godstone spear that fended off the cursed Dragon, which will soon be cast back into the pit from whence it came. Least I should mention, it was also Morgan who saved Karlata from the ravages of the Drakin as well, who unfortunately took the precious life of my cousin Seifred before he could save them."

The roundtable erupted into applause for me, but I simply nodded my head in thanks, concealing the abyss my heart felt in knowing what would happen to Philomela if the Dragon took its last breath.

My eyes caught the downcast and weary gaze of Volsung, who looked at me strangely before returning to his own gloom. Though I hated him for the things he had done, I found that my heart still pitied him.

He hasn't slept in days, I thought.

The brown jewels of Karlata's glance similarly watched me closely, efforting a weary smile when I looked at her.

Neither has she.

Aquilla was the only one not to glance at me. The spirit stood alone on the other side of the long table, staring intensely at the map of Renborg, saying nothing in spirit or in mind.

"We have just enough to defeat the Drakin who have murdered my family," Lucien continued, strength rising in his voice. "It is true that the Drakin will soon receive significant reinforcements from Yarahm, though at this time it is difficult to say if they number twenty thousand or even fifty. Our fleets, aided by the Skyyan navy, have stopped any further reinforcement from our blockade of the Strumma, but it seems that Judux never intended to challenge the waters after his first crossing. Our scouts report his war dog, Raa'thah Hakarah, has taken the coastal route around the Strumma."

"*General Wrath,*" I overheard, the whispered chuckle behind me from one Grand Marshal to another before being silenced by the glare of Servilius.

"He has broken through the east of Laconnia with more ease than he could have possibly hoped for, no doubt thanks to the chaos the Lycan now suffer," Lucien said, gritting his teeth before continuing. "Now, Raa'thah Hakarah advances along our northern coast in full view of our helpless blockade."

The staff of Kriga and Marshalls looked low as the grim reality of present circumstances lay so naked before them.

"Nothing it seems has or will hinder his incredible pace," Lucien proceeded, "and thus we must prepare for the eventuality that Judux's numbers will replenish in the coming week to some fifty thousand at least, and perhaps even beyond that. Lord Tyredium, where does the count of our forces currently stand?"

Jaerris straightened to attention, his King's request shaking him out of a trance of seemingly deep thought.

"Your Grace, combined we have twelve hosts of infantry numbering some forty-seven thousand, factoring our battalions of pike mercenaries. Mounted, we have a cavalry host and three divisions numbering seven thousand lances. And in archers, we have ten battalions numbering roughly five thousand. In all, almost sixty thousand strong, Your Grace."

"Thank you, Kriga," Lucien said, giving him a respectful nod before returning his gaze to the rest of his men. "Now, I have called you all here today to aid my decisions in the next careful steps we must take to root out Judux and his Drakin horde. My Lords, I *beseech* you. Our capital is held ransom by a cunning enemy that holds sway over a wounded beast we thought to be but a tale of the old world. What is to be done?"

The room was as still as the grave before Lord Tyrediam cleared his throat to speak.

"Unfortunately Your Grace, there is more," Tyrediam said, his tone weary. "We may need to halt any more reinforcements moving north and send them back south. To date, we have lost between fifty and sixty thousand soldiers and have, by necessity, redirected much of our military presence throughout the empire north in response. Our instability in the heartland and lack of strength elsewhere has given rise to old and fresh discontentments in the southern provinces and the coast of Tyberia.

"Rebellions have sprouted in Redhoran, and the Prince of Loraen may follow suit and declare himself king like his grandfather if he is not challenged. But most pressing is the state of the Andohrian province. In the provincial capital of Renee, our garrison was ousted and the Marq, Gidion Rhondel, was tried and executed. Even his family was murdered. Now, their rebellion has declared for itself a new republic of Andohr and has even called for the aid of Hurinzval to protect its former province as an ally."

"Their own republic?" Lord Kolstok said, his grey hair growing ever more white from the suffering he had endured for Renborg.

"I would almost guarantee the Hurinzvalese Prince Jean-Marque D'vignier is aiding their revolt in secret, if not leading it himself," Volsung said.

"Indeed you are correct," Tyrediam said. "My spies suspected as much while I was near Mittoras."

"His father would not have approved such a reckless action," Volsung said. "Do they forget their alliance formed through Valena and Gulmund's marriage?"

"Indeed, King Charles does not approve of his son's reckless ambitions nor the amassing of his own forces, and has outright rebuked him for it," Tyrediam said. "But Renborg's friends and enemies long and not long subdued are seizing the opportunities provided in this war. We must act and show our strength soon."

"Hmm," Lucien said, his brow furrowing deep in contemplation. "It would seem my father was right. No true friendship can exist between states but that of temporary allegiance. We have much to discuss."

And discuss they did.

For days, they continued long and agonizingly slow into the nights, filled with arguments and conflicting perspectives on how to proceed forth with an empire that was poised to fall apart if Lucien could not regain control. These often opposing viewpoints were paired with a tired but encouraged army that was now likely outnumbered in its approach to reclaiming the heavily fortified capital from Judux.

I understood partly why I had been asked to join the meetings, largely for the congratulation and appearance of unified strength, but I did not comprehend the point in keeping me there. Nor did I desire to be present, for my heart was burdened in knowing Egret was shut out yet again and that we were apart.

In being alone to my thoughts, my anxiousness grew as I thought of Philomela and how her life was ever closer to being extinguished by the revolting necessity of war.

By the extinguishing of my own, worthless hands.

One of these meetings lasted unbearingly long into the night, and by the time it was over, I was exhaustingly grateful.

As the procession of leaders disbanded, Lucien gave me a quick embrace before departing for the night.

"Thank you for being here, brother," he said, his hair glowing a pale white in the moonlight as we stepped out from the tent. "I could not do this without you."

"Of course, Lucien," I said, offering a weary smile in return.

"Good night," he said, lingering just a moment before turning back into his tent.

Alone in the fresh air, Aquilla emerged slowly from the tent behind me, his cosmic face downcast and thoughts hidden from me. It was not like him to remain silent for so long.

Saying nothing, we made our way back to where Alcharion, Nizari, and the Ora'suns were camped.

From afar, I could see Egret partaking in her evening meal beside a Ronian campfire near the Ora'suns.

Egret saw us emerge from the tent as she finished her dinner. She paused, a gentle smile flowering as she saw me, though I could see she was tired and beyond frustrated through the effort she used to raise her rosy lips.

My heart led me forward to be with her, but I caught myself from plunging off the destructive cliff of such a selfish destiny, turning instead away from her and from what would forever be an impossibility.

All melancholy thoughts vanished as cold fingers suddenly grasped onto my ungloved arms as I turned around.

"Morgan?" Karlata said as I stopped myself from running into her.

"Karlata," I said, my thoughts completely thrown off guard by the tears that were welling in her eyes.

"Can we talk?"

Hesitation gripped me.

Denying her would seem impolite and it would hinder any love that could be felt from her, but the denial seemed right as my heart lay elsewhere.

But I know Egret could never be the one for me. Is she not the Queen to my brother?

"Of course," I said, lowering my head and abandoning my selfishness to follow Karlata.

Turning to look one last time at Egret, her smile had disappeared into a bleak stare.

Aquilla watched me quietly as Karlata led me into her tent that was a little ways off from Lucien's. Entering her quiet and warm abode, she sat me down on her bed.

"What did you want to talk about?" I said, my heart pounding in uncertainty through my chest.

Karlata blushed and looked down.

"I don't know if it's obvious by now… but I wanted to be honest with you…"

Karlata seemed unsure of how to proceed, so I weaved my voice in with hers.

"It is well," I said, "I've already read the words you are about to say."

Karlata looked at me with a tinge of confusion, but she must have understood that I had read her Skallgend for me, for she nodded slowly and pleaded her eyes with mine.

"So you know how I long for you," she said, placing her hand on my cheek.

"I had a feeling," I said, my stomach filling with faeries but my mind wrestling with the thoughts that plagued it, for though Karlata was beautiful, my heart did not feel peace.

"I know you still feel for me," Karlata said, her hand slowly sliding down to the side of my neck.

I don't know what to do, I pleaded silently to Aquilla.

My heart felt torn in every direction that I could no longer hold onto what I believed was true.

All I wanted was to be loved and to give that love to another. But that choice felt more impossible than finding land for safe harbor in the middle of a storm-blown sea, the way clouded by darkness and rain.

"Yield to the Light, Morgan," Aquilla said softly.

You only want me to yield to your destiny, just like your brothers.

"No longer is this what I seek, and I was mistaken to do so. Yield to the Light that your heart now knows, Morgan. 'Even in the darkness, the Mother's Light shall guide me, as does the moon in the blackest shadows.' All you must decide is to *trust* in it."

As I looked at Karlata, I could see everything that I was not: my heart did not lead to her lonely and lustful embrace, no matter the similarity of her motives that I once shared.

Instead, my heart drummed a path for me that led away from her, and to the strong and caring arms of Egret. Even if Egret would never be able to love me the way that I yearned for, just knowing her would be enough.

"I'm sorry, Karlata," I said, placing my hand gently on hers.

As I stood up, I kissed her gently on her forehead before swiftly departing from the tent.

The soft cries of Karlata grew faint behind me as I followed Aquilla through the sea of tents back to the encampment of the Ora'suns. Though it pained me to hear her weep, I knew it was the right choice, the necessary one.

However, upon arriving at the campfire where Egret had been eating, I found only Ronians partaking in their dinner where she had been. Next to them, Alcharion and Nizari, along with a handful of Ora'suns, were still awake by their own fire.

"Aela Zaeim," a chorus of Ora'suns said.

"Where's Egret?" I said, my heart pounding with anxiety.

"She has retired for the night," Alcharion said, closing his silver eyes as he rested by the fire.

"She seemed troubled," Nizari wheezed, but she spoke no more of what had disturbed her.

Before I could race back to Egret's tent, Aquilla moved to block my path.

"Talking to her now shall only hinder our destiny," the Medjaib said, his galactic face showing no emotion as my inward consciousness wrestled with his. "We must be of a clear mind before we face Belial."

Finally, I surrendered and joined Alcharion and the others by the fire.

It took an endless amount of time to fall asleep as my mind and heart battled with each other, but I succumbed to the dark whispers of my Shadowed fate and the cold night at last. When I awoke still in the twilight hour of the darkness, I could see my hands were transparent like Aquilla's who stood brightly before me in Soul Sleep.

"It is time that I show you something you need to know," Aquilla said, before launching into the moon-lit sky with his glassy wings.

The haunting waterfalls and ruins of Ludsala came into view shortly after we had begun our flight in Soul Sleep.

Aquilla did not answer my barrage of questions as to why we were returning to this place of evil and failure, and I winced to look upon the grisly sight of Sigmund's end.

Thankfully Aquilla did not suffer me to look upon that.

Instead, the Medjaib took me to the base of the city by the river that flowed from underneath, fed by the dozens of waterfalls above.

Phasing through the gushing waters that would have swept an army away by its power, we approached two doors that were at least a hundred feet tall and corroded by water damage from the nearly two thousand sols they had existed. However, the doors still looked imposingly firm, and it appeared as if no one had been to this secret entrance in a long time because of the crushing waterfall that shielded its opening.

"What is this place?" I said, but Aquilla gave no answer as he phased through the ancient doors.

Coming to the other side, it would have been completely dark had it not been for Aquilla's crystal sight that led the way down the huge steps that ran with water to the unknown below. When we finally descended the grand staircase, we came to an enormous cavern that was filled with the water from above, drowning what was most likely an area for worship.

What appeared before us was a small lake where a silver tree glittered with Godstone leaves atop of what was most likely a moss-ridden tower of a temple.

Carved entirely of stone and standing before the tree were two figures, both of them clasping a familiar sword that protected the tree.

"Cypherus and Nazrioch," Aquilla said as I landed beside him before the statues and tree.

"And the Tree of Truth?" I said, beholding the untouched relic of the past.

"Indeed."

The tree was mesmerizing, for I had never seen so much Godstone all at once, given its mysterious rarity despite the ancient stories of its abundance. The silver bark that constructed the tree glimmered far more beautifully than any precious ore I had ever seen; part of me even doubted if it was real silver and not something more significant.

If the Valkryn Faith ever discovered this holy site, this beautiful representation of the Tree that bore wisdom for the created, they would view this place with reverence.

Piluch had never let Lucien and I forget of the Tree's importance to the ancient world, though I didn't believe at the time that a tree taller than the clouds could have sprouted from the middle of what was now Kapitol. Nor did I believe in the Battle of the Gods which tore the tree apart as the world shattered in supposed ignorance.

But all was different now, and such a truth of the ancient past seemed plausible.

"Such a tragedy I fear will also befall us if we do not follow the Light," Aquilla said, observing my thoughts.

I sighed in fearing another lecture from the Medjaib.

"I know what you're about to say—"

"Morgan, I did not come here to berate you for following your heart. I came here to… *apologize* for trying to create you in my own image, just like my brothers had done before; just as Nazrioch did."

"What do you mean?"

"Let me ask you this: how many Dragons did Cypherus slay?"

"All of them."

"And were all of them evil?"

"Well… yes? Did not Thadius make them to destroy the world?"

"He did, but not all of them obeyed. Many wanted to live quietly to themselves and be the masters of their own immortal lives, as Dragons were not blessed with a fate of eternity as we are. They feared death. Cypherus believed this truth as well, and it was his primary intention to slay only the Dragons that had sided with Thadius in his rebellion. But Nazrioch was of a different mindset, and that was to destroy all that Thadius had created, even the ones that did not obey him. And so, the Medjaib coerced Cypherus into doing what his heart believed was wrong for what Nazrioch thought was necessary. Instead of working together for the Mother's purpose, they served only the Medjaib's own.

"So has it been for every Medjaib since, and I swore to myself to not become like my brothers. However, because of my foolishness, I too became just like them. I… I *saw* what suffering it birthed when I looked upon the young men whom Volsung sacrificed to win the battle in such callous calculations that either ended their lives or crippled them forever. And I saw it when the hope in you died before Belial when you were shown Philomela's fate intertwined in the Dragon.

"Morgan, you have shown me the error of my ways. I grieve in knowing that I almost forced you to kill the Dragon and so destroy your beloved sister, which would leave you haunted the rest of your days as it did Cypherus. For that, I am truly sorry, and I thank you for still trying to have faith in me even when I have failed you."

I was speechless by the touching yet shocking vulnerability of the Medjaib.

Aquilla's raw expression of his lunar heart was refreshing to my soul that mourned the seemingly inevitable fate of Shadow before me.

"I—I don't know what to say," I whispered, the words heavy. But after a few moments of silence, I finally managed, "Thank you, Aquilla."

"Of course," Aquilla said, giving a slight bow of respect.

The drum of my heart seemed to beat ever more in tune with Aquilla's as we set our pride aside and humbled ourselves before each other in forgiveness and trust.

For a long time, we stood before Cypherus and Nazrioch. We were not perfect, but neither were they.

We were not their darker Shadow doomed to sleepless death. No, we didn't have to be. Instead, we were their glimmering hope, determined to live beyond the failings of the past and grow brighter than some mere Shadow of it.

Though I did not know the way, I trusted that there was another path.

And so for the first time in my life, I prayed, looking up and past the temple's darkness and to the Mother above. Though I couldn't feel her, I could sense She was there.

What followed after my prayer was something I could never explain.

Pain erupted in my skull as the world glared again into the glowing world of Tihrrvyith. This time, the whisperings of the words that constructed reality were no longer quiet, but loud and painfully clear in their ancient symphony.

Hirwa…

Dzaera hirwa khaelihrvyyihrrae!

Destiny…
Your destiny of becoming complete love!

To grapple with the words was nearly impossible as an ocean of murmerings from the ancient language barraged my ears with their whispering shouts, this time beyond unbearable as they had been before. I could barely hear Aquilla's soul amidst the chaos, but there was one word that was more clear than all of the rest, and it lay etched into the replicated sword of Solstein which I now understood.

Vyyihrrae.

"Love in its entirety," Aquilla and I both said in unison.

Then suddenly, something far more deep and painful than any words of Creation could surmise struck our innermost being.

We both dropped to our knees before the ancient statues of Cypherus and Nazrioch. The two were no longer silent statues in an ancient ruin, but, as the world swirled before us, were now disagreeing sharply with one another amidst a mountain top laden with scattered snow.

"You know their kind can never be trusted not to fall willingly under his command," Nazrioch said, to which the face of Cypherus flushed more vibrant than Godstone in anger and confusion. "He was loyal to him once. What is to say he would not be again if Thadius returns?"

Cypherus said nothing as he finished the trek into the mountain pass, where an elongated Dragon of grey and silver scales watched carefully from his boneless and hordless den.

"You return, Shepherd?" the older Dragon said in Shiveric, his colossal head the length of several carriages turning to the side to greet him. "Have you come for counsel or just to see a friend?"

Cypherus said nothing as he withdrew a glowing white Sölstein from its scabbard while Nazrioch stood carefully beside him.

"I'm sorry, old friend," Cypherus said, his eyes brimming with tears as he took slow steps to the old Dragon, his sword raised to the level of his shield.

It was unclear if he was preparing to strike or defend himself.

The Dragon snorted deeply in what I could only think was disappointment, the sharp exhaling of his nose creating a snow flurry around them.

"A shame, I had hoped we could play another game of Caldurrian Ahn'shar," the silver Dragon said with what I almost thought was a smile before his face changed to one of sorrow. "I expected more from you, but it seems you are just as blind as my Father."

Cypherus looked down in shame as he ground his teeth.

"Don't make this harder than it needs to be, Rai'El," Cypherus said, but but his tired voice lacked any threat.

"*Need*… no," Rai'El said, the mountain quaking as he lifted himself from his rest, an avalanche of snow cascading from his mighty wings and rising castles taller than Cypherus. "I will not live a sleepless fate enchained in that sword as Sh'eol's replacement. So, there will be no *need*. I will go."

"*What*?" asked a confused Cypherus.

"If even you of all, Cypherus, cannot tolerate my small corner of peace, then for the sake of our friendship I will not burden your soul with the stain of a friend's blood on your sword. I shall leave forever unto lands yet untouched by your kind."

Rai'El then turned to Nazrioch.

"There is more to the Mother's will than the order of the greater good, Medjaib. I hope in time your new kind will learn to see that. Goodbye, my friends."

With those last words, clearly eating at Cypherus' heart, snow exploded atop the mountain as Rai'El heaved his mighty wings and launched into the haze of the winter sky.

Solstein dropped from Cypherus' hands and sheathed into the snow, as did his buckled knees. The hero's face was cold and emotionless, the inner turmoil that consumed him from within still evident.

It was a familiar look I often portrayed, and my heart grieved for him.

For an uncomfortably long time, not a word was said as Cypherus grieved and Nazrioch watched. The Medjaib's expression was indecipherable, yet there was a heaviness to his gaze as he watched his closest and only friend fall apart.

"Cypherus," Nazrioch finally said, his voice gentle now as he knelt beside the man.

"No!" Cypherus said, turning harshly from the Medjaib. "I do not wish to hear it. Rai'El did not deserve our betrayal, nor did the Dragons who refused to serve their Father."

After a long silence, Nazrioch nodded his robed head and said, "Forgive me, Cypherus."

Cypherus slowly looked up to Nazrioch, his eyes furrowing in confusion.

"What?"

"Cypherus, I was… wrong in my pursuit to control you. I

see now… I *feel* the torment of your soul from what I deemed was necessary. I was too blind to see it before."

"See what?"

Nazrioch took hold of Cypherus' shoulder, looking deep and strongly into his friend's eyes before beginning to write a familiar word in the air before him.

"That there can be another way, one that does not indulge in either path of destructive necessity, but instead in the path less traveled, the more challenging road. If I have any wisdom left at all, my assumption would be that this alternate destiny is only born from the Mother's strength in which I have deviated from in controlling you: love, in its completion."

The ancient word glimmered in the air before them: a reminder.

Vyyihrrae!

The blaring whispers of the ancient tongue consumed my mind again, so jarringly painful that I had to close my eyes to its burning severity. When my bleary eyes could see the returning world again, I could at last make out the stone statues of Cypherus and Nazrioch before me.

We were back in the forgotten temple.

"Morgan?" Aquilla said.

"Aquilla? What happened?"

"I… I do not know that I shall ever be fully able to comprehend what has passed. But I saw everything you did."

Our hearts both drummed anxiously with nerves as we took deep breaths to calm ourselves. In our connected consciousness, I could feel both of our minds unearthing a revelation that I believed was intended for us to know.

"I—" we both said, but I paused and motioned for Aquilla to speak first.

"Thank you. I truly believe whatever that was, was from the Mother Herself, though I cannot explain it. And Morgan, I now understand my purpose in all of this and why I was sent to you. The people of the earth need the Medjaib to help save them. But as Nazrioch demonstrated, and as I've painfully learned, we Medjaib need *you* to help save us too."

Aquilla held out his star-ridden hand to me as I rose slowly to my feet.

"Together," he said as I shook the hand of his spirit.

As I embraced his spirit's hand, I couldn't help my growing smile that defeated the darkness of the night in my soul, much like the warming sun after a long and cold night. The memory of Rai'El and his words of Sh'eol felt like the key to a fate that was not one of Cypherus' Shadow, but of Cypherus' triumphant successor.

"There can be another way," Nazrioch's words whispered in my soul.

"I will not live a sleepless fate enchained in that sword as Sh'eol's replacement," Rai'El promised.

My heart trembled with hopeful joy in the idea that sprouted within my mind that would spare Philomela, even Belial itself from the sleepless fate that was promised for the lie of the necessary evil.

And maybe Judux as well.

I looked at Aquilla with a calming assurity, much like he did when we first met. The Medjaib's soul understood and agreed with my words before I even said them, and at last we had a plan to thwart the darkness of a hopeless fate.

"One is not dead if their soul remains in Godstone."

Chapter 30
Destiny

Upon the slaying of the Dragon Ka'Zaeir and the death of his wife, Cypherus began a relentless quest to silence the breath of every Dragon in the land, to fulfill that which was the only way for peace. Thirty of Cypherus' closest companions joined him, bringing terror to every Dragon and hope for every child. It is even said that a Dragon of no color nor creed joined with Cypherus and aided him, but such claims are a falsehood and only serve to deny his glory.

Sh'eol, the mightiest of Dragons, soon met the wrath of Cypherus and his companions high in the mountains of his lair. Using the blade of spirit and the words of power, Cypherus brought Sh'eol to his knees where he stole his soul. But upon slaying the beast, Cypherus found a sight that bewitched him: the Elvish King of Ezorelai, Elduin Tokindell, standing before the corpses of ten Elven women, all of whom carried children of fire in their hollowed chests.

The men of Cypherus encouraged their captain to undo this abomination, and so Cypherus went forth to bring about their deliverance. But when Cypherus looked upon their deceased mothers, mercy stayed his blade, and he let them escape under the cover of darkness.

The Tale of Cypherus the Great: The Ten Tomes
"Tome IV: End of the Eldren Wars"
Asculum I, Heir of Cypherus

It had been over five months since the night when my destiny almost came to a meaningless end.

The darkness and colorless waves of a life void of purpose almost drowned me then. Even after the Light had found me, the Shadow of a sleepless fate far worse than death itself almost buried me beneath the sea.

But now, hope rekindled the flame of my heart within, even

despite the oncoming winter and deadly confrontation with the Dragon.

For the first time in my life, I didn't feel ashamed: I felt *confident.* The burned flesh of my vessel was something I was less afraid of showing, and now I even forgot where I put my gloves that once concealed my deadly birth that I had tried so desperately to forget before.

Egret had been the one to show me, whether she realized it or not, that our flaws did not deny beauty but instead helped to form its uniqueness.

The sickening sirens of the oceanic abyss that sorrow once held over me had its powerful sway no longer. For now I rode my horse boldly to face the fate that once seemed impossible to defeat.

To save Philomela, to redeem Sigmund.

To prove my life was worth living.

Heart of flesh rots to death
Ignite with love of Light above
Heart of fire world is brighter
Shine forever in surrender

I hadn't realized it then, but the Skallgend Aquilla had me say after my greatest failure as we plummeted from the Amon Bridge had been true all along, though I could not see it in my ignorance.

And all it took was just a leap of blind but desperate faith.

My heart swelled with this confidence, and my mind rested at last in peace as we finally approached Renborg's capital amidst the fall breeze of the month of Thaelas.

Renborg, the beginning and end of all my sufferings.

It had taken a month of rest and another three weeks on the road to finally return to the capital. Seeing the autumn-defying cherry-colored hills and forests of the Bludhlands that I had grown up to know was a comforting sight despite the devastation wrought on the valley by Judux's hungry armies.

Knowing that Philomela's life was just in reach of being saved from such an ancient feud, I could almost feel the peace that would soothe our hearts if we were successful.

Though, upon seeing Renborg in the distance, my heart began to beat faster again. The Drakin presence lay all about the city's outskirts, from fortified wooden encampments to a dual wooden wall ringing the entire city. One wall enclosed the city, and the other provided the Drakin a defensible position to ward off reinforcements such as those we now brought.

But most ominous of all was Belial.

Perched atop the tall spires of Renborg's citadel, the great red Dragon watched our approach with hateful eyes and screeched a ferocious cry of vengeance upon seeing us. The battle for Renborg could commence and end any day now, as could our lives and all that we fought for.

The unknown gnawed hungrily on my mind as we slowly began setting up a fortified encampment a few miles from the sight of the city, in sight of Belial.

Aquilla used this time wisely to instruct me, guiding me through training with the Ora'suns, giving me a good distraction as we waited evermore.

In the quiet times between training, I often found Aquilla studying the faces of the young and old men of the empire.

"It is good to fight for one's home, yes, but so many of them call home someplace else entirely," Aquilla said, his spectral being still in contemplation. "So afraid, yet here they remain. Why?"

"Well," I said, perplexed by the difficulty his simple question posed, "I suppose some fight because they believe in the stability of the empire. If Renborg falls, war will spread throughout its entire domain, consuming everything until hundreds of thousands or even millions perish. All to see who can gather the most from the scraps and build something new."

"'Thus is the course of empire,'" Aquilla said to my surprise. "'Not a wheel but a ladder, each rung a civilization built upon the ruin of the other. The unseen climb of millennia scaling desperately back to paradise lost.'"

"You've read Apocolus?" I said, dumbfounded by Aquilla's knowledge of the ancient writer and his political classic *The Way of the World*. "That's grim material for a spirit of Light like yourself."

"Well, what else is a Medjaib to do when living on the moon?" he said, the hint of a smile upon his voice. "My whole life, I sat and marveled at your world. So bright and beautiful, full of color and life. I did not expect all of this. Though we of Akhorus have watched you suffer the endless climb up Apocolus's ladder, we could not truly feel that pain nor understand why. I knew *of* sorrow, but I did not know of its weight."

"Perhaps that is why the Mother chose you to bond with me."

"Perhaps," he said, letting the silence fall again between us before we resumed training.

Each day and night, the camp was permeated by a cacophony of noises and a frenzy of activity. Officers barked orders, smiths hammered away, soldiers trained or kept themselves busy with song and drink, priests preached, and healers gave aid to both soldier and civilian alike. All maintained careful preparation for the conflict to come, which was a never-ending discussion amongst the Kriga and Marshalls of Lucien's Council of War.

A Council which I was nightly invited to, much to the grumblings of more than one or two of its members.

"We've been here for a week!" I said, my voice edging upon

a shout as I interrupted a rather stunned Grand Marshal, Tarren Lauront. An inquisitive Aquilla hovered unknowingly behind him and admired the intricately embroidered lion on his shoulder cape. "How much longer shall we wait? The Dragon grows and heals each day that we waste. But I have the spear that will cease the breath of the beast. The time is now to strike! Have you not feared that any night Judux could send forth his beast to awaken your slumber in flames?"

"Don't you think we have interrogated his brother on that very account?" Lucien said, his tone not of hostility but weariness. "Rolloc refuses to answer."

"I understand your haste, Morgan, and my spirit agrees with you," Qai'phus Giabhor said, whom I was surprised to see was still alive and wearing his finely flowing white Primarchal robes that he had somehow managed to *bravely* escape with during the invasion. He had arrived a week beforehand, and everyone but myself and Aquilla was grateful to see him. "For the Prophetess Morythia and her Paethian Sisters are still entrapped in Renborg's lower district, along with tens of thousands of the Mother's children. And though we long to rescue them, we should use the Mother's careful wisdom lest we lose all of them in thoughtless passion."

"I agree, Your Eminence," Volsung said, his calm demeanor soothing the tension of the room like a pleasant fragrance. "We cannot waste our smaller force on a direct attack of the walls that Judux constructed to surround Renborg's own impenetrable defenses. Our men are already tired and need more time to rest and prepare for war."

Then, turning to look directly at me, Volsung continued, "And though you can wound this Dragon, to place all of Renborg's hope in just one man is foolish."

"How else do you suggest we end it?" I said, desperately holding back my contempt.

"We need not end it, for now," Volsung said, "we need only cripple it. First, we will commence earth and timber works to form another ring of circumvallation about the city, cutting off their access to forage and leaving them only with the supplies they hold between their own walls. Whilst they are constructed, we shall send forty or fifty of our bravest and most capable men to infiltrate the city in darkness. Once inside, they will find the beast and wait for it to rest, as it must, followed by the breaking of its wings or even killing it if possible.

"Perhaps then," Volsung said, raising his brow, "you and your men would like to share in the honor, Morgan?"

"Perhaps indeed," I said, frustrated with the calm sensibility of his plan. "But what is to be done after? A siege will take months at the very least. And what of those that remain in the city?"

"They will be unharmed," Volsung said, dismissing my concern with a wave of his hand. "My spies reported last that the Drakin have not broken into the military district where our grain reserves lie intact, leaving the citizens that remain with enough provisions to last them at least two years at this point. I would not knowingly endanger our people for the sake of victory, young Master Krios."

"I'll be sure to relay those sentiments to the men of the thirteenth host of the Tarrow Vale that litter the fields of Feldrem," I said, the small chatter in the tent dying completely.

Volsung's eyes did not blink as they bored into mine. Though he looked pained by my words, his brow furrowing in contemplation, he uttered not a word, even silencing one of his Marshals with a gently upheld hand as he tried to protest.

Looking to Servillius for support in my accusation, I was met with an unexpected reaction as I saw the old Kriga staring blankly out the tent's entrance, tears threatening to break from his grey eyes.

Had he known… had he approved… had he ordered?

No, he couldn't.

It was only Lucien who broke the silence to rebuke me.

"Brother, we must be wise in our approach, lest we should lose all of what we had fought and died so much for in a single unplanned engagement."

"Berating them further will do nothing for us," Aquilla warned, seeing my anger swelling within. "See what they have planned first."

I listened to the Medjaib's wisdom, inquiring further about what other strategies might be implemented. Volsung, having spoken his piece, was mostly silent.

"I agree with Volsung," Tyrediam said. "Building another wall of circumvallation is likely our best approach. However, it will not be easily done. The reality is we are the inferior force by about ten thousand, not to mention the Dragon."

Kriga and Marshal alike cringed at the mention of their odds.

"So at least it'll be an even fight," said the grinning Kriga, laughter returning to the downtrodden officers for a brief respite before he continued on. "This Rolloc has confessed that Judux's aim in this invasion was never to retain an acre of land on our side of the Strumma. All he seeks is to bloody Renborg's nose for the persecution of the Primarchal Wars; a way of showing us as equals while unifying their semi-tribal states under his singular rule.

"Because of this, I believe Judux would be receptive to a bribe. Godstone, gold, and his brother would be a good start. Though it's no easy thing to say, Your Grace, I don't think he'll be satisfied without a complete renouncement of claim to our foothold province of Renvyr in southern Yarahm. All this in exchange for Solstein, the capital and its people, and the ending of hostilities immediately."

"But what of my father, my mother, and my brother?" Lucien said, his voice rising in anger. "All of them were slain by their hands. Am I to let them go without justice? What will the people think of their King if he cannot avenge even his own family, let alone retake his own keep?"

"I know Your Grace is passionate," Tiberius said, the Elven Master of Coin I thought certainly dead suddenly appearing from the tent's entryway. "And he is rightly so. There will be a time for the mighty coat of justice to be dawned when Judux lays prostrate at your feet. But it is the humble rags of prudence that will save Renborg today."

"Tiberius speaks truly," Tyredium said, receiving a nod of approval by the Master of Coin as he joined us at the table. "The loss of our northern forces would be devastating to the stability of the empire."

The fact that some of the other Kriga and even Lucien himself considered this was unbelievable to me.

"What are we, *a court of Sommerians*?" I said. "Do you truly think that they will just leave us be after we give them everything we have? What's to stop them next sol when they decide to come back with a Dragon and an army twice the size? You think Judux will give up Solstein after achieving so much with it? You are all fools if you believe it will not be so."

Lucien looked sternly at me before standing abruptly from his chair, to which everyone also followed.

"Thank you for your contributions, Morgan," he said, his frustration concealed with gratitude. "We will reconvene here within an hour. Let us get some fresh air to clear our minds and hopefully give us a new perspective on the many matters at hand. Thank you all."

Aquilla and I were the first to leave the tent at our dismissal, even against the surprised Lucien, who shouted for me to wait.

I did not want to harangue him further, nor did I wish to hear what he had to say. If anything, I don't know if I could trust what he would try to tell me, for my mind still pondered whether the supposed note was really Karlata's at all.

Instead, Aquilla and I took a brisk walk in the cool summer evening. Much to my dismay, it indeed gave me a fresh perspective, though I did not want to admit it.

Walking throughout the Ronian sea of tents, I received frequent praise from the myriad of Ronian soldiers who smiled at me and cheered as I walked by. But I could see through their smiles that they were exhausted, many suffering from wounds from the previous battle.

Most noticeably, some of them kept their heads lowered, weighed down by the terrors they'd witnessed and the gruesome loss of countless friends and colleagues.

There was also a deep fear that hid behind their eyes.

It didn't help that the Dragon could be seen from our encampment. Whenever I would pass them by, the Ronians would return their gaze to the monster that watched them like a serpent about to strike. The soldiers couldn't seem to keep their eyes away from Belial, and part of me wondered if that was Judux's intention.

But then again, why did Judux not send Belial to destroy us as we slept in the night? What held him back from such a potentially advantageous strategy?

"We must be quick to steal the soul of Belial," Aquilla said as we walked through the maze of campfires and soldiers talking amongst themselves. "The longer we wait, the more it shall frighten the soldiers. Cinching its flames shall make the Drakin balk in fear at its downfall."

I agree.

"Let us accept the Council's request to steal the Dragon's

soul as it sleeps. We shall provide Renborg with a great advantage in our success."

Lucien would not let me go.

"That hasn't hindered you before."

Sighing, I submitted to his counsel. *Very well. But we will not inform him beforehand. When should we embark?*

"As soon as I trust that you are ready."

To ensure I would not falter before the Dragon nor alert the Drakin of my intentions, Aquilla encouraged me to train day after day with Alcharion near the border of the tents and the newly constructed wall of dirt that encircled it. We sparred deep into what felt like endless nights with a blunted spear and shield, using every spare moment to prepare myself for a potential fight with the Dragon if it awoke amidst our robbery.

Aquilla also had me practice with the Ancient Tongue by using water to fight against Alcharion. He strangely enjoyed the challenge despite me blinding him several times with it.

Given the Drakin were weakened by water and how it could help thwart Belial's fire, it became a useful practice that I worked tirelessly to perfect.

Thankfully most of the Ronians took to bed when we practiced and did not witness my use of the Tongue, except for the patrols on watch who whispered to themselves of what they were witnessing. The word *sorcerer* escaped their lips into my ears upon many occasions.

"Ignore them," Aquilla said one particular night.

As we trained, my thoughts repeatedly drifted to thinking of Egret.

I hadn't been able to talk with her since Karlata had invited me to her tent. As each day passed apart from Egret, so too did my melancholy grow. Unfortunately, the only one I was privileged to speak to was Rolloc, who yelled at me from his closely guarded cage.

"Morgan!" Rolloc said, banging the metal cage he was locked in before being struck with the butt of a spear by a Ronian guard to keep quiet.

Looking to Aquilla for guidance, his spirit gave no answer as he was also unsure if I should engage with the hybrid Drakin.

Shrugging, I decided to inquire about what Rolloc wanted.

"Take your time, Aela Zaeim," Alcharion said, his voice strained and his entire body soaking wet from our practice beneath the moon.

The guards gave a slight bow of their helms before stepping aside for me to speak with Rolloc. Though his coarse red hair was unruly and covered part of his pale and cracked face, Rolloc appeared completely serious and grim as he stood alert in his cage, his dark yellow eyes concentrating solely on me.

"What do you want?" I said in Ronic, my voice showing no care for him. "Will you finally explain why your brother refuses to send his Dragon amidst the night?"

Rolloc held me in his deadly stare for a long time before answering.

"If it troubles you so, let me ease your sleep," he said in Ronic. "My brother wants victory to belong to Yarahm, not Belial. But truly, my brother would have no victory but his own."

His revelation of his brother's ego ironically brought relief, though I doubted he could be trusted.

"What is your real connection to all of this?" Rolloc continued. "I know you are no Akaidian. I've faced real warriors before, and you are not even close. But now, you are leading these Ora'suns and making a name for yourself. Were you some nephew to Valena?"

"You should ask her yourself," I said, the vile feelings of bitterness towards Rolloc's actions almost overwhelming me.

Rolloc grimaced at my response.

"She deserved it, as did her wretched husband. They were no more innocent than I am, or you."

"Me," I asked, annoyed with his confusing accusation, "what have I done?"

"No more than any soldier, I suppose," Rolloc said, his eyes a menace in the fading light. "He would have been no more than fourteen in comparison to the number of your sols I reckon."

"Who?"

"Imrael's son. Or have you already forgotten, given the ease with which your blade ended him?"

"Who is—" I began to ask, knowing too late I did not want the answer.

"His father nearly took your head before your man speared him through his heart. Though can one blame a father for avenging his child?"

"I—"

"Save your breath," Rolloc continued, turning from me, "whatever your relation is to the Mordrakes, you will follow in Gulmund's fate soon enough."

"You were a slave under Gulmund's dominion from your own folly. But did that necessitate the death of Valena as well?"

"You don't know what they took from me!" Rolloc said, his hands squeezing what looked to be a small Gyldur scroll tied about his neck that I hadn't seen previously. The weathered metal parchment looked worn beyond sols.

"This conversation is proving fruitless," Aquilla said, to which I agreed.

As we turned to leave Rolloc in his cage, I was surprised to see Egret standing only a stone's throw away.

"Egret?" I said, walking quickly to her as her eyes took a moment to look away from Rolloc behind me.

"Why were you talking to him?" she said.

"I don't know," I said, glancing at Rolloc who seemed almost transfixed by Egret's appearance and bright emerald eyes.

"Is that also true for Karlata?"

Before I could answer, Egret turned from us to leave.

"Princess!" Rolloc said, catching us both in shock.

"I am *Queen*," Egret said, her anger flaring as she turned back to look at him.

"You are the one from Skyya, are you not? I remember our engagement. You are the daughter of Nera."

"What have you done with her?" Egret said, stepping closer to the cage.

"Come closer and I will tell you what has become of her."

"That is not wise," Aquilla said.

"Egret don't listen—" I began.

Egret snapped, her hand flashing to Rolloc's chain in an attempt to bash him against the cage.

Rolloc didn't budge, only smiling at her attempt.

"Speak quickly, or I will remove your tongue," she said despite her failed attempt, the guards shuffling uneasily around us as they were uncertain if they should intervene.

Rolloc showed no fear as he was held hostage by her iron grasp.

Instead, he suddenly grabbed her arm, breathing in heavily as if engulfing the air with his nostrils. As his lungs filled, his yellow eyes squinted in certainty before the guards struck him again with the butt of their spears and halberds, forcing her release.

"Why did he do that?" Aquilla whispered.

I don't know, I thought, just as confused while Egret quickly backed away from the Drakin.

"You are stronger than you look, *Princess*," Rolloc said.

"What have you done to Nera?" Egret yelled.

"Nera is safe, I assure you. Judux has seen to that himself. But the past of your father is not as secure. Especially of your father's… *passions* of the flesh."

"Your lies will not discredit my father's legacy. He was a good man, and you are nothing but a liar who is dwarfed by his shadow."

Before I could react, Egret stormed past us, leaving her Ronian escorts far behind.

"Wait," I said, catching her arm gently and leading her away from Rolloc's prying eyes beside the opening of the fortified wall.

To my surprise, she didn't shrug me off as I led her there. Instead, there were tears in her eyes.

"Egret, what he said of your father is not—"

"I know what he said was false!" Egret said, her furious eyes brimming with tears. "My anger does not lie with that beast nor his falsehoods."

Egret didn't have to say anything further for me to understand.

"You are angry because Morgan engaged with Karlata," Aquilla said, receiving daggers from both my eyes and Egret's. "What? He chose not to become intertwined with her, and you are already married. Is not this tension between you both from your desire for the other?"

"Aquilla!" I yelled.

"Am I wrong?" the spirit said, his head cocking to the side in confusion. "Am I not constantly in your head hearing you bemoan the same feelings over and over again?"

Egret turned away to leave, but not before I caught her again with my hand. "Egret, please wait!"

Turning back to me, Egret shone with anger. "Give me a reason, Morgan."

Not wanting to impose my feelings on her again, I gently

took off my Godstone necklace and placed it firmly in her hands with my own, the hands which she had called *beautiful.*

"Something to remember me by if my destiny ends in the battle," I said, switching to her Skyyan tongue. There was an ocean's worth more of what I wanted to say, but all I could manage was a brief goodbye. "My world has been a brighter and more joyful place with you in it."

Before she could respond, I grabbed my Klyr spear and left through the opening in the camp wall. My heart pained in every step as I sought to find solace in the early red Bludhlands that stretched out before me. They were drenched in morning autumn mists before us, the River Ren a babbling melody of loneliness to my soul.

Aquilla was silent as I found a place alone by the river, far away from the camp.

For the longest time, Aquilla and I sat quietly by the river. Aquilla allowed my heart to grieve and harden itself with resolve for the almost certainly suicidal mission that lay before us.

At least she would be happy with the children they would bring into the world, even if Lucien did not love her. But I hoped someday he would.

At least she would know that I loved her and that even just the privilege of knowing her was enough for me.

The tears that ran from my eyes and disappeared into the river below were without limit as the day slowly awoke from its slumber, though I hardly noticed it. It wasn't until I heard the pounding hooves of a horse not far from me that I was startled awake from my solitude. Thankfully it was only a Ronian scout, but there was a trembling fear and urgency in his eyes as he rode with great haste beyond me towards our camp.

My gaze stretched to Renborg from where he had ridden, and I could see a dark mass moving from its walls into the fields before it.

Belial was above the sea of darkness that spewed from the gates of Judux's wooden walls.

"What?" I said, my heart racing as I rose immediately to sprint back to Lucien, my mind perplexed by Judux's sudden tactic. *Why is Judux leaving the walls of Renborg to meet us in the field?* I thought while panting my way through a maze of awakening soldiers and tents. *Volsung hasn't even sent his men to break Belial's bones nor us to steal its soul.*

"There is no strategy in this, only fear and pride," Aquilla said. "Judux is losing his mind."

Maybe, I thought, almost toppling a rack of halberds. *The Drakin are only under his rule if he leads them to victory. He must be afraid that his power is slipping from his fingers after his defeat. He almost lost the symbol of his prophetic legitimacy at Feldrem.*

Belial ripped the morning skies with a fearsome blood-curdling roar that must have woken up everyone and everything from our camp to as far as Hebsund.

"It is time for the end," Aquilla said.

~

The confused cacophony of fifty-nine thousand rudely awoken Ronians began as they armored themselves immediately in the early autumn morning; no orders were given where none were needed.

Finally, amongst a maelstrom of squires, men at arms, and officers, I found Lucien already well aware of the current situation. Three servants raced to buckle and lace the last facets of his magnificently adorned full plate harness of solid Godstone as he stood with armet in hand.

"Morgan," Lucien said once he saw me, his face full of concern, "why aren't you armed?"

"Right," I gasped, turning like a fool to run back to my own tent. My heart drummed rapidly as I hastily dawned my Gyldur laced robes.

"Breathe, Morgan," Aquilla said as Alcharion entered my tent. "The Mother shall guide us to victory today."

"Let me aid you, Zaeim," Alcharion said, strapping my belt tighter and taking some extra weight off my shoulders.

Ready for war, we both exited the tent to mount our horses when we were suddenly stopped by Mathis, himself mounted and holding the reins of an impressive white steed armored in metal plate from nose to tail.

"A gift from his Grace," Mathis said with a smile. "Oh, and Morgan, your Sovereign commands you not to die."

"I'll try," I said as the three of us rode to the front of Lucien and Egret's guard with the rest of our Ora'suns whose horses were pulling the ballistae before us on specially made wagons.

Alcharion nodded to me as we made eye contact again. We proceeded with approaching death, which flew haughtily in the sky in wait for us, along with its servants, whose various tribal banners were countless grains of sand by the sea.

Twenty Ora'suns, a thousand Ronians, and Nizari were left behind to guard Rolloc and the nearly ten thousand other artisans, traders, and healers that remained in camp. Five hundred Ronians still remained just outside of Feldrem to keep guard over the six thousand Drakin prisoners left behind while everyone else converged on the forming battlefield.

Joining us as well were two Knights of Kyllian and a hundred Royal Guard Lanceliers who had surrounded Lucien everywhere he went.

Sir Alduaura said not a word to me as he saw me ride before him, but he nodded in respect.

Aside from a few farmhouses and crops, the fields that Judux so hastily chose for his seventy thousand Drakin and mercenaries were vast and open. Despite his haste, he had positioned himself on favorable ground with no forests around us to conceal any Akaidians or terrain advantage to hide reserve troops from Belial's eye who roared above us.

"It seems that Judux has learned from his defeat at Feldrem," Aquilla said, and I nodded in agreement.

Watching us silently with his dark crown was Judux upon the Dragon, his Eldrakes keeping close guard to him and Belial in the air like a swarm of bats.

Oddly, his winged Kiagor was nowhere to be found.

"Perhaps Judux does not wish to risk its life in the throes of battle," Aquilla said.

One less threat is fine with me. I hope we don't have to face it. There's not many of their kind left in the world.

"Indeed."

"Take your strongest infantry and place them in the false right flank there, and have them create an opening at my command," Volsung said to a nearby Grand Marshall who rode off from our party after receiving orders.

"Why are you risking the same strategy?" Egret said from behind us.

"Judux will not go for the bait this time," Volsung said.

"And why is that?" Lucien said.

"If he's this erratic to hastily leave the safety of Renborg's walls, then fear will deter him from committing the same folly as before. I only wish we could have had more time to discover how many cavalry and archers they have, but such is the tide of war."

Though Volsung was repulsive in his deeds towards Lucien, I was thankful that my brother kept him around: for the plan sounded entirely coherent.

"May it give us enough time to take down Belial," Aquilla said.

Time was also an enemy.

The force of chaotic darkness flapped its mighty wings before us. Its unpredictability derived from partial disobedience to the will of its master was something we tried to plan for, but it was uncertain if and how it would work.

All I could really hope, and what Volsung had also strategized, was that as both of our armies engaged in the dance of death and destiny, our mobile ballistae manned by the Ora'suns would be able to penetrate the wings of Belial before it destroyed our army.

We needed to ensure the monster fell from the Void so that I could steal its soul on the ground.

"Morgan, are you ready?" Lucien said from behind.

Turning to him, I no longer saw a boy Prince who was not as strong as his older brother nor too weak for his father's empire, but a man who had been reborn by the suffering of the wolves and who now rode forth as a King of kings.

I smiled as I looked at him, for my love for him had never changed, only deepened, though my heart still worried that he had lost something along our journey.

"I am, brother," I said.

"Good. Volsung, give the order for the infantry when it is to our advantage. I will see to it that they are strengthened. Qai'phus, would you do me the honor of accompanying me to remind our men of their faith and their destiny."

"As you will, Your Grace," the Master of Faith said.

The King, along with the Primarch, rode to the front of the infantry and cavalry as the Knights of Kyllian accompanied them. Lucien's royal green cloak stretched in the gallop as Belial flew back to the Drakin lines to most likely report on our military's lines.

The battlefield was eerily still as Qai'phus began with the boldest Skallgends found in Solbok of faith and familial duty.

All movement and activity ceased as we beheld the lush Bludh-fields of Renborg that would soon be stained, letting the poems sink deep into our hearts.

Then as Lucien took over the speech, the message transformed from a kindled fire to a blazing inferno. And as he spoke, I swelled with pride.

"Men of Renborg! Today is not the day on which our destiny dies, but the glorious day of Renborg's triumph! Today we make a stand to avenge the suffering of our families, of those we love, for we have all tasted the bitter steel of Yar-ahm's hordes who seek *nothing* but destruction. But they will not have it this day, for before them stands you, oh men of Renborg; you with spear in hand and families behind who say *no more*. We will march forth in strength, fearing not the fell beast of the sky, for we hold a champion more powerful who will silence its fury.

"My countrymen, let us return to the peace we once enjoyed, to our families and our homes; for Ronians do not ask for permission; we take what is rightfully ours! We are *Forged in Fire*!"

There was a great roar from the Ronians as they repeated the Words of House Mordrake that had been with them for centuries.

"*Forged in Fire*!" they said, shaking the plain itself.

Looking at Egret, she smiled at me for encouragement while my Godstone necklace shone brightly on her forest green dress, her royal garment and headdress matching Lucien's cape while outlined with gold.

She chose to wear it, I thought, returning her grace with my own smile which bloomed from her kindness.

At least she would know that my heart belonged to her if the sea of death overcame me. But I longed to live, for just to see her smile again was enough reason to endure.

And I prayed her smile would be accompanied by Philomela's, who awaited on the other side of the Dragon.

"We will save them, Morgan," Aquilla said as Egret was escorted to a safer distance from us, my heart warming in his encouragement.

As Belial neared the Drakin's rear lines, Volsung gave the signal.

In organized cohesion, the Ronians shifted the formation of their lines at the commands of their Marshalls, creating the false weak line where our strongest soldiers lay in wait, thus making Judux's report inaccurate and preying on his fears of another weakened flank. Belial must have heard it, for the Dragon arched its wings to turn around at the commotion.

"Now, Morgan!" Volsung said.

"Alcharion!" I yelled, who nodded at my signal before yelling in Cuerian to the rest of the Ora'suns who were stationed at the ballistae. The war machines stretched for a mile behind the lines of our army.

At the dark Elf's command, nine steel bolts pierced the sky with blinding speed towards Belial. Joining them were five thousand arrows from the Ronian archers and Lycan mercenaries. The heavens were darkened by death that was soon to befall the Drakin.

Belial roared as it rolled in the sky to evade the steel bolts, just barely avoiding them.

The rest of the arrows found their deadly homes within some of the airborne Eldrakes and the Drakin lines who quickly responded with their own array of arrows.

Forty-seven thousand Ronian infantry replied with a unified roar as they slowly marched forth. Incoherent cries mixed with vulgar taunts filled the air from both sides as they drew closer and closer, now but a stone's throw away.

It was a challenge to determine where the front line, more

than twenty ranks deep, would meet the Drakin. But once I heard metals meet and the roar of defiance turn to screams for mercy, I knew.

More than a few men in the rear emptied their hastily eaten breakfasts onto the ground about them as they witnessed the carnage that may soon come to find them. Particularly I noticed a young halberdier, no older than Lucien, turn south to look in doubt at the open fields that lay behind. But his face hardened in resolve and turned northward, drawing a small vessel from his side and shakily swallowing its entire contents.

Something to dull the fear and pain, I thought.

Even the Eldrakes seemed timid to strike them from above and face the assorted sea of spears, halberds, and pikes that awaited them should they dare.

A volley of arrows responded from the Drakin as the men of the ranks, no shields at hand, snapped down their heads, trusting their armor to spare them. Many missed, but some found purchase in even the smallest avenues of any exposed weakness, the shrapnel of one arrow shattering upon a soldier's sallet and blinding the pierced eyes of another behind him.

Thankfully, none reached Lucien as he rejoined us from behind the lines. We were far enough away not to be pelted by their sting, though Sir Alduaura still shielded his King regardless.

Half an hour later, hope began to build within me as I watched the false Ronian right flank actually begin to push aggressively into the Drakin's left flank. It seemed that Judux had put most of his best troops behind their center line instead of the Ronian's much stronger right flank.

I knew our cavalry on both wings must have been engaged with theirs by now, but I could see distressingly little from my vantage point as the air filled with smoke and the eruption of a low cloud of kicked-up earth.

How any Marshall or Kriga could make sense of all this chaos, I did not know.

However, what I did see through the haze of war in which the warring Eldrakes concealed themselves was the approaching red shadow of Belial.

"Again!" I yelled desperately to Alcharion as Belial swooped down and aimed for the center of the Ronian line, who, for the moment, were dealing a deadly strike to the Drakin.

Before another volley of steel bolts could be loaded and fired at the Dragon, Belial engulfed the center line with his fiery doom.

In seconds, hundreds had been consumed in flames, fire incinerating their dying breaths. Ronian and Drakin lines, both seemingly horrified alike, still engaged in a clash of spears and halberds on either side of the burning middle. But amidst the dying flames, I could see the Drakin infantry marching through it unharmed.

"Belial does not fall for the bait," Aquilla said as we watched a Drakin commander lead his troops to focus on the opening in the Ronian center line. "Judux seeks to drive a wedge down the center to overwhelm them."

Aquilla's observation proved ever more terrifyingly true when Belial circled for another barrage of his fire onto the Ronian center line, who braced for the death that consumed their friends before them.

"Loose again!" I yelled.

But every bolt missed again.

The Dragon unleashed another torrent of death, sending hundreds more Ronians slowly to their ends. However, Belial's fire sputtered out soon after the second.

Servillius murmured something to himself beside me.

When I turned to look at him, I could only see a shell of the man he once was before the war. The old leader's eyes snapped back from his sorrow to the red death that abandoned the battle and came thundering towards us from the sky: Belial.

"Morgan…" Lucien said, his tone one of surprise and doing his best to hide the fear we all felt.

"The ballistae, Morgan!" Aquilla said as I was already riding towards one, weaving through the commanders before dismounting hastily near one.

The Dragon was ten seconds away as I commandeered my Ora'sun's ballista, swiveling it with all my might to aim it above Belial's path in the sky. Trusting in Aquilla's guidance, who pointed to where I should aim, I loaded a bolt into place with shaking hands.

"Cypherus!" Belial roared in Shiveric, coming to a halt in the air as its eyes twitched uncontrollably, mirroring a surprisingly nervous and agitated Judux upon its back.

"Return to the battle, you fiend!" Judux yelled.

Belial snapped its head back in writhing anger, connecting with the Drakin's body. The force of the blow threw Judux from his saddle and down into the enemy lines. Though the fall was great and most assuredly fatal, Judux must have lived, for Belial did not die.

The bolt clicked into place.

"What are you doing, Egret?" Lucien screamed, robbing my focus as I hastily turned to see Egret galloping towards us on her steed, followed by twenty panicked royal guards who asked the same thing. "Go back!"

Why is she coming here? I thought, anxiety rippling through me.

"There's no time," Aquilla said, his voice impatient with fear as the Dragon resumed its flight towards us. "Loose the bolt!"

Holding my breath, I fired the ballista.

Despite Belial's enormity, the Dragon swerved with frightening speed to dodge the bolt as he had the others that were fired with burgeoning hopelessness. Only my bolt had any luck in hitting Belial, but instead of crippling the fell serpent, it merely bounced off of its shoulder.

In sheer desperation, I picked up my spear in preparation for having to abandon my plan of stealing its soul if Belial aimed to crush us with its weight in the few seconds we had; there would not be enough time to write the ancient word for Dragon in time to do so.

The spear was a boulder in my hands as I pulled it back to thrust it into the heart of the Dragon, and, in turn, the innocent life of Philomela.

"Forgive me," I whispered, tears dragging down my face as the shadow of Belial overtook me.

Sleepless death was inexorable.

So would I be the Shadow of Cypherus, destined and damned to slay the Dragon, extinguishing innocence and being no better than his Shadow.

From the corner of my right eye, a bolt whistled past suddenly, its path finding its home in the armpit of Belial's wing.

"Yes!" Alcharion roared from his ballista as the force of the bolt threw Belial backwards over the clashing armies, desperately trying to sustain its descending flight.

Despite being spared from the Dragon's wrath and the Shadow of Cypherus, any sigh of relief was destroyed as Belial plummeted behind the center of the Ronian front lines, crushing almost half a battalion of men. The Ronians were already failing to keep the advancing Drakin at bay. And now, as Belial thrashed from where it landed, thinning the ever-depleting lines of the Ronian center, a Drakin victory seemed inevitable.

"Morgan, we must strike Belial now!" Aquilla said.

In seconds, my feet were in the stirrups of my white and fully armored steed. Without a word, Alcharion had ordered the rest of the Ora'suns to mount and follow us in haste.

"Morgan!" Volsung said, halting us before we rode into the

field. "I need some of your men to reinforce our cavalry on the left and whatever else can be spared towards the center line! They are about to be overrun!"

Repeating the words to Alcharion through Aquilla's translation, the Ora'sun nodded dutifully.

"Morgan!" Lucien said as we turned our horses to leave. "Don't forget the command I told Mathis to give you. I love you, brother."

For just a moment, as we beheld each other, I recognized the boy who had watched the sunset with me over these very fields in what felt like forever ago. My heart ached to know that all would be different after the dust of this war had settled.

"I love you too, brother," I said, hoping to keep his command.

Lucien was counting on me to succeed, as were Egret and Philomela.

I would not fail them.

"We shall rise!" Aquilla reaffirmed as Egret joined us on horseback, much to the dismay of Lucien and her guards who followed.

"May the Mother give you victory, Morgan," Egret said, her stern gaze softening as she looked at me one last time before I drove my boots into my horse's sides. Before she disappeared from my sight entirely, her eyes glistened with unspoken emotion, mirroring mine.

The horrendous melody of scraping steel and dying screams of men soon penetrated my ears as our horses charged behind the Ronian lines. The vile smell of battle's blood, bowels, and defecation was more rank than the ashy reek from the burning corpse-ridden field ahead of us.

Alcharion ordered a company of Ora'suns to reinforce the Ronian cavalry as he led the rest of the Ora'suns close beside me to engage Belial at the center of the storm.

The Ronians parted like a sea as we rode through.

"Are you sure you won't need me?" Alcharion said as we neared the Dragon.

"No, I need you to help hold the line."

From my elevated position, I could see that the Ronians would fall soon to the red Drakin knights, infantry, and hooded spear warriors as the Eldrakes brought unholy wrath upon them from the air.

Alcharion nodded gravely.

"Good luck, my Aela Zaeim. May Ora guide your heart!"

As Alcharion dispersed with the rest of the Ora'suns amidst the lines of Ronians, Aquilla and I were left alone along the opening from the soldiers, leaving a direct path before us to Belial. The Dragon took a snarling bite out of Ronian lancer as it tried to lift itself up to fly again amidst a sea of spears that prodded it. Belial made quick work of the eviscerated soldier, its fiery red eyes snapping to me in the opening.

"*Cypherus*!" Belial mocked, its bloody teeth snarling wide as the Dragon raised its head to devour me in its Shadow, standing taller than siege towers before me.

All was still for a breath as Aquilla and I looked up to the red Dragon, our Klyr spear humming in our hands.

"Are we ready for this?" Aquilla said, showing me the symbol for Dragon that would harness Belial's soul.

"No," I promptly said before kicking my horse to charge against the monster, though neither I nor my valiant steed wanted to.

"Breathe, Morgan," Aquilla said as we were seconds away. "Wae the water into its unblinded eye when—"

Blood exploded beneath me as Belial darted in for a killing bite with its swords for teeth, my legs phasing just in time, or else they would have been as lifeless as my horse.

"Gah!" I yelled as we were lifted high into the air by Belial's rotting mouth.

Belial's red eyes were pools of blood as it stared into my air-bound soul.

Images of a dark being flooded my mind as Belial's Shiveric tongue slithered into my consciousness. On the figure's head was a dark and very broken crown, whispers protruding from a faceless evil reflected in the Dragon's eyes.

A reflection I had glimpsed before.

"Drop, Morgan!" Aquilla said.

Not a moment too soon, I phased the lower half of my body and pushed away from my lifeless horse as Belial swallowed the rest of the steed into its gored teeth. The Spear of Mythraelyon still firm in my shaking grasp, I sliced through Belial's stronger left wing on my way down, severing half of it.

Belial screeched in pain so loudly that my ears felt as if they were about to burst from the intensity. But the pain from its cry was momentarily forgotten as I fell to the fire-scorched grass, landing upon a burnt corpse that collapsed in ashes beneath my sudden weight.

Images of a child crying in the burnt ribcage of its mother flooded my mind.

"Do you think of me as not deserving of personhood?" Belial said as it turned on me while I struggled to my feet with the spear. "Is that how you justified your genocide, Cypherus? Is that what will amend the little one's death?"

Belial gnashed out with its teeth to where I stood before I rolled out of the way, my spear tasting its teeth and causing the Dragon to pull back again.

"Fool!" Belial hissed. "Are you so blind as to not see the same Shadow within?"

"What are you talking about?" I said, circling the Dragon

as I watched Aquilla draw the word for Dragon in my mind, waiting to find the right time to grab its soul before opening its heart with my spear.

"Destiny has no other way!"

Fire erupted quickly from Belial's glowing throat, bursting onto me without warning.

Instinctively Waeing the water from my spear, its power clashed against the oncoming fire from Belial's throat.

Realizing my resistance, Belial increased the power of its fire, the flames pushing back the water inch by inch until the funnel of water was only a breath before me. Before the last of my water gave way, the fire of Belial puttered out, leaving only a boiling mist all around me.

"Shadow!" Belial slithered as it limped towards me on one wing.

"We shall live no longer if we do not take its soul now!" Aquilla said, shaking me from my paralyzed state.

"Kill me and take my place!" Belial said, swiping its remaining wing at me before I barely phased my body to vault over it. "But you shall crush her as you kill me, for the Father has whispered, 'Peace shall they purchase with blood!'"

Pity stayed my hand as I dove out of the way from another lunge from Belial.

Underneath its blood-red scales, the Dragon was merely a boy encaged in a destiny of Shadow that it did not want.

He did not deserve death.

"I will not kill you," I said as I rose beside the Dragon, quickly drawing the ancient word for Dragon and Human over Belial.

Over the boy who did not ask for a fate of sleepless death but who chose it in his refusal to surrender to the Light above instead of the colorless waves below.

Belial turned his head just as I finished the word with Aquilla's hand. But before I could strike with my spear and Wyl in his soul, the Dragon lashed out with his teeth and grabbed hold of my spear. Belial screamed as its purity burned through his mouth. The Dragon threw the spear far away into the midst of chaos, violently throwing me back as I lost my grip on his soul without Godstone.

The back brace pierced my flesh from the force of Belial's throw, leaving me breathless on the battleground.

Belial snapped his head back to me.

"Wait for me in the Void," Belial said, his voice more somber than the colorless waves that once haunted my soul.

Aquilla was speechless as Belial tore his bloody mouth open to swallow me into a sleepless fate.

And so I believed the end of my story had arrived.

The one good eye of Belial glared at me before he struck, and if Dragon's could have tears, I believed that he was shedding them.

But a steel-tipped spear sank into its remaining eye.

A terrible scream exploded from the blinded Dragon.

"To the Void with you!" Egret shouted as she dismounted from her white horse, her Kalypto knife and shield equipped, her dress torn at the knees for mobility.

"Egret!" I said, both in thankfulness and fear as she was now within the presence of the Dragon in which we could not kill.

"Egret?" Aquilla said. "Why are you here?"

Egret's eyes embraced mine for just a breath.

In that eternal moment, as my necklace glowed a burning ember upon her breast, I understood why she had come: there was truly no word to describe my death-defying joy.

"Morgan—" Egret began.

But Belial cut her off, blindly swiping Egret aside with his bloody snout, sending her flying to the other end of the burnt arena in which we danced. Her shield shattered as she dropped her Godstone knife mid-flight.

"No!" I yelled, watching helplessly as Belial turned to her instead of me, preparing to finish her off.

Aquilla!?

There was no way to further harm or kill Belial, and any hopes of taking his heart were dashed as I could not penetrate his heart to let it out. My heart seized in fear as I saw the love of my eternal soul lay helpless before the Dragon that would soon destroy her, the only one who had ever shown me how beautiful I was and who believed in the Light within me.

And that's when my eyes found Aquilla's, who was standing before Egret's Godstone blade that lay sheathed in the dirt before him.

"*Rise*, Shepherd!" Aquilla commanded, his voice bold and without fear. "Wield this blade and follow me."

My knees trembled as I rose to my feet, my shaking hands grabbing the Godstone knife in one last desperate attempt.

Aquilla wasted no time as we sprinted faster than the wind across the scorching battlefield through his spirit, stopping a short distance in front of Egret before Belial could begin his final descent upon her.

"Sh'eol!" I screamed in ancient Cypheric as Aquilla instructed, pronouncing his name with precision and writing the Dragon's soul quickly in the Tongue of Creation.

Belial halted mid-charge, roaring in a feral and blind rage as I grasped his soul's name, though I didn't see why it would be of any use since I could not pierce his heart to siphon it from him.

"Morgan, close your eyes and stretch out the blade with both hands," Aquilla said.

"What?" I said, panic resuming as the Dragon shook his head to charge again, Belial's eyes blinded, but his anger focused on me.

"*Trust* in me, Morgan. Do not be afraid."

Aquilla's voice was calm, like a whispering river in contrast to the violent thunder that would end our life in seconds.

And though I had no way to kill the Dragon, to save Egret and Lucien, nor to spare Philomela, though all was hopeless, I released my unbelief, trusting not in myself anymore but in the spirit who found me in the colorless waves. Even if this foolish trust in Aquilla meant death for myself, one last look at my beloved was reason enough to surrender it all for the slightest chance that she might be saved.

For all I knew, all I wanted, was this very chance to lay down my life for her, not because my life wasn't precious, but because she had shown me that it was.

Her heart of gold was worth dying for.

Exhaling fear, I stood my ground, trusting Aquilla as I lifted the Godstone knife with both hands and closed my eyes, the Dragon only a moment away from me as his soul's name glowed brightly beside me.

Though I would die by the teeth of the Dragon, I would not have to live a sleepless death. Instead, I would die in rejection of the Shadow of Cypherus, embracing the Light as I laid my life down for another.

The Light that Aquilla had shown to me.

A violent explosion shook the earth before me. Opening my eyes just in time, I could see Belial had bit into the ground before me where Aquilla's spirit stood unharmed.

Clarity dawned upon me as I looked in surprise at my Godstone blade, which was now burning Klyr. Belial's charge continued its path, his momentum carrying him forward as his head raised momentarily in confusion before his chest slammed into me.

With shaking hands, I thrust the Godstone blade into Belial's heart as darkness crushed me, Wyling Belial's soul into Kalypto.

Chapter 31
The Sleepless Shadow

And so it was that in the winter of his seventieth sol, after a long and full life, King Cypherus the Great went unto his eternal rest, lying in his bed surrounded by three generations of his progeny and Taldarii companions who obeyed his every word. In the final moments of Cypherus, as he told his sons of their mother Renua with tears in his eyes, his eyes began to glow a blinding white. Lifting slightly from his bed, he spoke these sacred words from the God who called him long ago to slay the Dragons of the enemy, of the Shadow:

Cypherus, savior of souls, ruled as your thesis,
His shadow, sleepless death, will reign antithesis.

As Cypherus descended to his bed, his eyes returned to normal, but in them were not the fear that his sons shared, which all kings would possess in the wait of the one who would be their eternal undoing, but a calm assurity. The peace in which Cypherus slept is the hope in which we cling, trusting not in the shadows of this world which will have its way eventually, but in the Light which will ascend triumphantly upon it, as the sun will reign upon the moon.

The Tale of Cypherus the Great: The Ten Tomes
"Tome X: The Shadow of Cypherus"
Asculum I, Heir of Cypherus

The colorful waves that appeared slowly before me were glowing white from the Klyr morning sky that radiated upon the horizon.

As I stood upon the sea cliffs of Renborg, no longer wanting to waste my precious life that I had almost thrown away, a cosmic being stood beside me, but it was no Medjaib.

There were millions of words that weaved in and out of its

being, galactically regal in the golden splendor of an ancient tongue that dazzled brighter than any sun or star.

In that moment, I realized the light upon the ocean, upon the whole world, and even within myself came from this one being.

"*Shepherd*," the familiar being said, the voice feminine but majestic, terrifying yet kind.

The hand of the Light pointed to a door that stood before us upon the sea cliffs. A very familiar door, with a very familiar word etched upon its scorched frame.

Hirwa…

Destiny…

"Will you Shepherd her?"

My hand mirrored the Light, grasping the handle in response. But as I gripped the door handle, instead of pulling it open, the door pulled me into its embrace as it swung into itself. The world suddenly became dark again, but within the darkness glittered a small light just beyond.

"You live!" Aquilla said within, joy beaming throughout my soul. "Phase if you can hear me!"

Relying only on trust, I Wyled my entire being, save parts of my chest and heart, to phase through as I was pulled forward. Within moments I emerged from the scales of the unmoving Dragon and onto the burnt battlefield, light flooding my eyes once again.

"I knew it!" Alcharion said, pulling me from underneath the belly of the beast. "The Dragon Slayer lives!"

A cheerful roar erupted around us from the Ora'suns and Ronians who circled us. The excitement was so encouraging that our warriors fought with even more feverous zeal around us. From where I emerged, I could see our lines were holding strong and that the battle was in our favor.

A wheezing sound caught my attention. Turning around, I saw Egret collapsed on the dirt and struggling to breathe.

"Egret?" I said, my heart faltering in seeing her withering form.

Not even caring to look at the slain Dragon, I dropped the Klyr blade of Kalypto and held her gently in my arms.

"Egret," I said, my tears like rain upon her soft cheeks as the screams of war faded in the background. Her eyes were completely shut. "Egret… I love you."

Those beautiful sea green eyes that I had come slowly to adore opened up joyfully to my words.

Egret's hand shook as she lifted it to my face, gently holding it, her fingers warm and kind upon my smile. For a moment, it was just the two of us in the world, our backs bearing the same scars and our souls singing the same melody as we rested in each other after defeating the Dragon *together.*

There truly was no word to describe it.

Not even the Tongue of Tihrrvyith could fully describe how my heart felt in that eternal forever.

The only word that could ever come close was the one which I remembered was carved onto the blade of Solstein: *vyyihrrae.*

Love in its completion.

"Judux lives, and so too Philomela," she said in Skyyan, her words barely a whisper. "Go… save Philomela for me… and my *mother.*"

Egret smiled before collapsing back into my arms.

"I will," I said as I gently laid her down.

"And Morgan?" Egret said, the light in her eyes fading as she struggled to say one last thing.

"Yes?" I could barely say, my voice a whisper.

Egret beamed with joy as she looked into my soul, into the heart that was hers forever. "Thank you… for speaking to me in my own tongue, for wanting me to join you on your quest… for healing me. You make me feel… treasured."

As the words left her lips, she closed her eyes, becoming still.

"So do you," I whispered, tears streaming from my eyes.

The sound of horses riding swiftly towards us from behind reminded me of the war still proceeding all around us. It was soon followed by a familiar voice.

"Morgan!" Lucien said as he dismounted his horse near us, followed by Kolstok, Volsung, and an entire host of Ronian cavalry and Knights of Kyllian who surrounded him from the ever-present war.

"Morgan, you did it!" Lucien said, joy radiating from his face as he wrapped his arms around me. "We will win back our home at last!"

It surprised me that he didn't take notice of Egret, who lay silently in my arms.

"Lucien, Egret needs healing," I said as he pulled away from me, his face contorting into concern.

"Of course," he said before ordering Sir Alduaura to take her back behind our infantry lines to our camp.

As Sir Alduaura swooped low to pick her up, I could see through his helm that in his eyes there glimmered a newfound respect that he had never shown me before.

"Dragon Slayer," he whispered as he picked up Egret before carrying her away, along with my heart.

"Well done, Morgan," Volsung said. "Now, if you can advance with your Ora'suns on the center—"

"No," I said, "I will end this war by dethroning Judux myself."

"What?" Lucien said, along with a shared disbelief of frowns from Volsung and Servillius. "You don't even know where he is! Even we haven't seen him since he fell from the Dragon."

"I will find him."

"Morgan, you cannot just ride through the battle yourself looking for him. Even if he did somehow make his way back to the city, Judux still has Eldrakes and soldiers garrisoned within the city's citadel walls. Such a task is foolish, Morgan. You are in no state to do so."

"If Judux was this reckless to rush into battle, then who knows what he will do in light of total defeat," I said, grabbing the glowing white Kalypto from the dirt and leaping onto Lucien's auburn steed. "I will save Philomela before his fearful mind can unleash more harm."

"But Morgan—"

"I love you, Lucien. I'll be back with Philomela, along with your empire."

Before he could protest further, I kicked his horse into a gallop towards the right flank of the Ronian cavalry in the near distance. Searching for the dark crown on the battlefield, we saw no sign of Judux amongst the Drakin or the fallen.

He must be in the citadel, I thought, putting as much space in between us so that Lucien couldn't see what I was about to do.

"We shall not be able to ride through the battle, Morgan," Aquilla said as we neared the clashing battle of Ronian cavalry and Drakin riding their ferocious snapping Anakrum, their beaks bloody from the chaos of battle.

"Good thing we're one," I said, dismounting from the horse and sending it back to the rear lines, the war before us an impenetrable wall for those trapped in the flesh.

"Ah, I see now," Aquilla said, reading my thoughts. "Now you shall experience what it is truly like to be as free as a Medjaib."

"I learned from the best," I said, phasing all of my body except my heart as I sprinted faster than horses, leaping higher than eagles past the carnage of war in the hope of saving Philomela.

"Very good, Shepherd," Aquilla said. "Come now. We are on a tight schedule!"

Our hearts drummed in unison as we quickly moved past the raging battle, for no Drakin or Eldrake was fast enough or even aware of our presence as we soared past them. When the closed city gates of Renborg appeared before our lightning steps, all it took was one leap to sail over their mighty dual walls.

And just like that, we were in the city.

There were thousands of disheveled men before the walls, only a few thousand of them armed, but all of them sharing a look of shock as we landed before them.

They had been trapped here since the invasion.

Before the Ronian militia could react or detain us for questioning, we leaped onto the tavern's roof that was adjacent. The red-bricked rooftops of Renborg were a blur as we dashed from building to building with ease, our carefully placed steps taking us deeper into the city as we spared not a second in our rescue of Philomela.

Fear threatened to cripple me as I worried what Judux might do at the demise of Belial. But I suffered not these thoughts as we pushed forward to save her.

In minutes, we flew past the burnt Tormund Theater and the thankfully intact Great Library of Cypheria, with the great Keep of Renborg just ahead in the royal district.

Before I took another bounding leap in Aquilla's spirit, an ear-splitting roar penetrated the sky before us. The mighty Kiagor, in all of its terrifying glory, flew past us and away from the battle we left behind.

"I didn't see Judux on the beast," I said.

"Neither did I," Aquilla said.

"Strange," I muttered, looking back to the glass overhang of the throne room that loomed mightily before us.

Using Aquilla's eyes, I could see a handful of red figures through the glass, including one on their knees and another the size of a child.

And in front of the child was a Klyr blade.

Solstein.

"Morgan, behind you!" Aquilla yelled, moving as one to pierce a killing blow to the Eldrake who had caught us unawares and had swept down from the sky to strike us.

"We're out of time. We have to move," I said, the other Eldrakes screeching in the air as they saw their fallen ally dead on the rooftop beside us.

Readying our feet, we took several steps backwards before we threw our entire being into one giant leap up onto the walls of the royal district before jumping weightlessly again up to the glass wall of the throne room. Before we slammed into the glass, we arced Kalypto down, shattering through unharmed and landing softly on our feet amidst the wreckage, ready to silence all who stood against us.

Judux, who stood wearily before us with his hand to his hip, gloomed darkly as he grappled with our shocking entrance and the blade of Kalypto I held high in front of me.

But then, a darkness within his clouded eyes vanished, revealing a clarity I had not seen in him before.

It wasn't precisely a physical clearing of his eyes but rather his spirit that I could sense through Aquilla. And as Judux looked at me, perplexion riveted throughout his core, as if he doubted his own sight.

That's when I saw the fiery blood dripping from his hand onto the floor; Judux looked pale.

Regardless, we would not wait to be formally welcomed.

"Together," Aquilla said.

As one, Aquilla and I cut through the spears of the Drakin Kebri Knights armored in red and scaled armor who moved quickly to apprehend us with their now useless weapons. The first threw an overhand strike that passed through me as I phased, confusion filling his eyes before my knife swept across his neck.

The others hesitated for a moment before lunging forward, each baffled by their sword's lack of bite and each receiving a deadly response.

Amidst our dance with the Drakin, I saw Philomela squirming unharmed in the remaining hand of Piluch, who sat watching us in dumbfounded awe near one of the many pillars of the room.

Seeing her only increased my fervor.

"Enough!" Judux bellowed, staggering between the Kebri just before we maimed another in the neck. "I will not see another drop of our blood spilt."

There was a haunted look in Judux's eyes as he motioned to the Kebri to back away from me.

They quickly obeyed, though with backward glances through their helms, as Judux returned to the marble throne laced with emerald. However, the Drakin King did not sit on the throne; instead, he grabbed the sheathed Solstein from it with one of the Godstone gauntlets of Kyllian I, keeping his back to us as he held it for support.

"Leave us," Judux said in the Drakin tongue, his voice calm and sounding no fear. "Go… negotiate what peace you can, and if you cannot achieve that, then do whatever is necessary to withdraw my soldiers from this place."

"*What*?" one of the Kebri said, removing his red helm to reveal his fiery hair, whom I slowly recognized: Ephraeos, the eldest son of the fallen Drakin General Kesch. "What of the battle that rages still? It is not yet decided. We can still win without the Dragon, or we can make another! All of Renborg lays in our grasp—"

"Our purpose here has been served!" Judux said, the broken crown looming on his brow as he tilted his head down at Solstein. "Renborg has been bloodied, and they will pay handsomely for us to leave, knowing never again to so arrogantly intrude on our lands from the wars their priests invent. We are equals now, and at last our tribes are unified in purpose."

The room was silent as Ephraeos, along with myself and Aquilla, were perplexed by the words of Judux.

I could not say whether his hopes would manifest in time, but the likelihood of continued war stretched far in my mind. Renborg had been bloodied and wounded, yes, but Yarahm would suffer more. Without her dying Deresar's vision to unite the discordant peoples of Yarahm, they would soon resign themselves to warring within as they had for millennia.

And Renborg would not forget those who stained the fields before Brannfalt, Feldrem, and her capital.

Looking to the surprisingly well-kept Piluch, who gently rocked Philomela, my old teacher nodded as if he understood that what Judux was saying was indeed a false hope but to go along with it anyway.

"Is his mind broken?" Aquilla said softly to himself.

"Take their Master of Histories to negotiate the terms," Judux continued, "generous terms of course. If the battle does not remain in our favor, order a full withdrawal behind our walls. We will return promptly to Yarahm along the coast if need be and have no more of this war."

The decision to end the war looked to trouble both Judux and General Kesch's son.

For a few tense moments, Ephraeos ground his jaw as if he were about to refuse the order. But thankfully, Ephraeos nodded gravely and carried out his task, though it would be a long time before the rest of the tribes complied, for not all would have taken kindly to Judux's rule or his swift denial of their plunder.

The red knights, still seething at the loss of their fellow brethren, reluctantly gave us the room with only Philomela abandoned on the floor.

Given no time to lay her in my arms, she immediately began to cry once Piluch had been escorted forcefully away.

Before I could rush to Philomela, the doors to the throne room burst open again, but this time it was a different red knight who approached Judux.

As soon as the Kebri removed his helm, I recognized him from the Battle of Brännfält as General Kesch's younger son, Jeshum.

"My Lord," Jeshum said, taking grim notice of me before approaching Judux, who turned to look at the young Drakin. "Will you be returning with us?"

Judux looked down before returning a smile to Jeshum, though it was the type of smile one would give when a child asked a newly widowed man how he was doing. All he could procure was a smile steeped in suffering.

"I will be joining my sons."

Jeshum embraced Judux, much to Judux's surprise but also gentle delight.

"Let me protect you!" Jeshum said.

Judux took Jeshum into his fiery and cracked hands and

said, "Make your father proud and hold these tribes together in unity, no matter the cost. Now go."

Jeshum bowed his head low before turning to leave and carry out such an impossible task. As the red knight walked past me, he refused to look at me, though I hoped that he would learn there were more than just two paths ahead of him.

The doors to the throne room thundered shut as Jeshum departed. At once, I moved to rescue Philomela, but Solstein rippled through the air and blocked the path to her.

"You know, I realized you were not the Shadow of Cypherus when I saw the child still breathing as Belial fell," Judux said in the Ronic tongue, moving with pained steps in between Philomela and I. "And now, I realize I too am not his Shadow."

"What are you talking about?" I said, Kalypto gripped tightly in my hand.

"He is wounded and troubled in mind," Aquilla said. "Let us proceed with careful steps."

Easing himself down onto the floor, more of Judux's fiery blood began to seep out beneath him, steaming on the floor.

"Though, what is not clear is how you stole Belial's soul," Judux continued, "for the Ancient Tongue has not been known for almost a thousand sols. Only the One who whispers in Shadow knows of it."

"There is more to this world than Shadow," I said, pity withholding condemnation for his blind service to Thade, whose grip was more substantial than I had realized.

Judux smiled as he looked at me, but it was one of deepest grief and sorrow. Releasing Solstein to the floor before me along with his gaze, Judux seemed almost lost in its holy splendor.

"I realize now that I was guided by such Shadow, though I thought it for a righteous cause," Judux said, almost to himself. "I believed I was chosen, picked from the mud and mire to lead my people in unity despite the Shadow I was enslaved to. To guide them away from disorder into a nation of brothers, not selfish bandits; to build a home for my sons to be proud of, even in the grave.

"But now, seeing my brother's words come true, I realize I was nothing but a pawn, being slain by my own creation which should never have been born. My destiny is only the stepping stone for someone far greater, for the one far more… *terrible*."

A horrendous cough overtook Judux, fiery blood spewing from his lips as hopelessness seized his fading eyes. Judux laid back against the base of the throne in exhaustion, a rasping gasp his only words. The broken crown upon his head slipped off, landing with an unnaturally heavy thud before the throne.

A look of relief passed from Judux as he looked upon it.

"At last," he said, his molten eyelids relaxing as he laid himself down onto the floor in his simmering blood.

"Wait!" I screamed, looking to Philomela in terror.

If Judux's fate was tied to Belial's, then so was Philomela's. She only had moments to live.

"No no no!" I said, rushing over to Philomela who began to cry in agony. "What do I do?"

"Just as Judux tied their souls together, you must unweave Philomela from Belial!" Aquilla said. "It is impossible to do so while he lives. We must pull them apart just as he approaches the Mother's embrace when his soul is weakest."

"Show me!"

With trembling hands that followed Aquilla's, I hastily gripped Philomela's precious soul which glowed white before me, her breaths becoming labored and nearing a final gasp. However, her soul wouldn't unwind from Judux's nor Belial's; they were stitched firmly together, soon to share in the same fate.

"Live!" I screamed in desperation. "It's not working, Aquilla!"

Their souls became fainter than the rays of a setting sun.

"Now!" Aquilla yelled, his word a breath to my choking lungs.

Using all of my strength and Aquilla's guidance, Belial's and Judux's souls slowly but surely untangled from Philomela's as I performed Wae, letting Belial's soul leave Kalypto's embrace to receive the Void instead.

"Well done, Shepherd," Aquilla said as color returned to Philomela's reddening cheeks, her cry a beautiful melody of life as I embraced her gently. She was heavier than she was five months ago now that she was halfway to her second sol of life, but not as heavy as my heart would have been had the Shadow stolen her light.

"Thank you," I whispered, holding her close.

"You are no Shadow indeed," Judux said faintly.

Sharply turning to him in anger, Philomela in my arms was the only thing holding me back from sending him to his fate sooner.

"If you don't believe me to be Cypherus' Shadow, or yourself, then who is?"

"You are the Shadow, Morgan," Aquilla said, but even he did not sound sure.

"I should never have trusted that half-bred bastard," Judux said to himself, his eyes wandering afar.

Placing Philomela gently upon the throne, I quickly gripped Judux by the shoulders, phasing my face to reflect Aquilla's.

"Answer us!" we said.

Judux's molten eyes were dying embers that had lost all flame, but as he looked at us in his final breath, a glimpse of terror glistened in his weakening eyes.

"Cypherus…" Judux whispered as his story came to an end.

My hands released Judux, and I backed away from the deceased Drakin, his fiery blood forever cooling. Upon my hip, Kalypto lightened as Belial's soul was similarly released from its vessel, his fate unknown given his unnatural combination of Human eternity and a Dragon's lack thereof.

The thought of Belial's endless future sparked an unsettling inquiry of the Drakin's fate as well given their common ancestor. From what Aquilla had confirmed, it was possible that they ceased to exist permanently.

But then again, maybe their eternal fates weren't such rigid destinies of necessary shadow.

Wherever they are sent, may they find rest.

A frightened glance towards Philomela soon turned to one of joy, as she did not join them in judgement. Instead, she rolled lively upon the marble throne, enchanted by the green swirls that comprised it.

Breathing a sigh of relief, I looked to Aquilla, who stood in confusion next to me. However, our thoughts were in disarray from Judux's final words that troubled the shadowed destiny I thought was mine, which I thought I bested.

Though the Deresar's words were haunting, in that moment I decided to not let another soul be burdened with such a trial that we had faced because of the incredible temptation of power that a Dragon's soul had permitted. Grabbing the handle of Solstein, the familiar presence of Sh'eol infested my mind.

"Cypherus!" the deranged Dragon shouted, both of sheer hatred and desperation as the purity of Solstein endlessly purged his soul.

Carnal images of the Eldren War flooded my mind, along with a conglomerate of garbled words that could only come from a creature which had long since lost its sanity. Mercy found my heart as I Waed Sh'eol's soul from his prison, releasing him to rest at last.

And so the last of the Dragons departed from the earth.

Forever.

Philomela shook me from the finality of my thoughts with her sudden cry.

Releasing my hold of Solstein, I scooped her up into my arms, holding her tightly to my chest as I did so often before the night when I stood upon the cliff of destiny that churned in chaos before me. My tears sprinkled her short but burgeoning hair as she quieted alongside my chest, the gradual rocking putting her back to sleep.

"I can see why you love her," Aquilla said, smiling in essence at the child and, for the moment, forgetting the words of Judux.

I sighed in the deepest relief knowing she was safe, that it was all over.

~

The Drakin left in groups of five thousand at a time.

Finally, after a month of heated negotiations, threats, scheming, trading of hostages, and the Council's confirmation of a treaty from Yarahm's Sahri'ah, the Drakin began to depart from Renborg. It wasn't until the last week of the month of Lakburry, long after the Ronians had written their annual Skallgends for the new sol amidst the winter flurries, when the last of the Drakin left upon the Strumma Sea in the ships they had stolen from us.

Though the war in Renborg was over, the war in Yarahm was far from it, with the province of Renvyr in Yarahm still hotly contested but, for now, mostly quiet. However, a temporary peace was better than none at all.

Following the death of Judux, Aquilla and I attempted to return Philomela safely to Lucien, along with the revered Solstein, but we were stopped immediately by Jeshum and his Kebri Knights who waited just outside the throne room.

"The child and the sword will remain," Jeshum had said roughly in Ronic, clearly wanting to retain bargaining power for the negotiations but trying his failing best not to appear nervous before Solstein, which glowed in my grasp.

"The Dragon has been released from the sword, so it is of no use to you," I said, much to the horror of Jeshum, who stared at me with disbelief. "I am taking the child as well. I don't want to have to end your life."

"And I don't want to hurt the child," Jeshum said, his Kebri inching nervously closer.

"Let us avoid needless shedding of blood," Aquilla had said, though still prepared to fight with me if the confrontation went awry.

"If you let me go, I vow to tell the King of your generosity, and I will convince him to be more lenient in the negotiated terms," I said.

"And why should I trust in your word?" Jeshum said, his eyes cinching together in mistrust.

"Do you think the King would deal with you more kindly if you troubled *both* his greatest friend and sister?"

The Kebri Knights looked to Jeshum for an answer, and for a few breathless moments, I prepared myself for a fight. But much to my relief, Jeshum ordered his Kebri to lower their weapons, instead asking them to retrieve a cloak to conceal us.

"You will be escorted to the gates and hidden from sight," Jeshum said. "And once you return to the Ronian King, you will remind him of how generous we have been."

Nodding in respect, I let the Kebri lead us to the gates while Philomela rested quietly in concealment within my arms. A look of relief was my last glimpse of Jeshum, and it was one that I shared as well.

Once we had returned safely to the Ronian camp, we received the worshipful applause of the Ora'suns and the cheers of our entire army. Lucien gave me a warm but weary smile. The King of Renborg embraced Philomela, holding her for a long time and saying nothing but silent tears that he hid from Volsung and the rest of his Krigas.

Peace at last, I thought, looking at Aquilla beside me. But as I looked into cyan eyes that glittered like the stars, there reflected the same fear within mine: doubt.

What had Judux meant by the Shadow being another?

My ponderings of his final words were put aside as I tended to Egret in her medical tent, spending most of my time with her and Philomela. Lucien began the arduous process of negotiations and careful planning on how to proceed with the empire that had been shaken; and still was, for though the Drakin were put to heel for the moment, rebellions flared uncontrollably across the realm like wildfires.

Egret slept most of the time in recovery. The wounds from the Dragon were less of the flesh and more internal damage, much of which I slowly weaved unto myself through my recovered Klyr spear.

Aquilla did not rebuke me for doing so.

Philomela lay softly beside Egret as she slept before us, a smile blooming from her rosy cheeks as she too received the much needed love that she was denied for so long.

Aquilla's spectral hand traced over her tiny head, beholding her innocence that was saved.

Egret's recovery, though encouraging, was slowed in part because I would not allow the Ronian nor Skyyan doctors to use dedric sap to help her recover, for I feared it would only worsen her addiction for a temporary relief. Though, I did allow Nizari and several of the Ora'suns to treat her wounds with a strange white balm glimmering in gold that they used to soothe her flesh.

"It is made with the blood of an Inor siphoned long ago," Nizari whispered through her rotting stench, watching Egret's skin glow from its powerful potency. "We should not move her from here, for I fear her wounds may worsen. There are many bones which have shattered in the Dragon's wrath."

"I know," I said, feeling part of those wounds in myself.

How I wished she could wake.

Though, the world in which Egret would wake to would be one without the love of her mother, for Nera had already returned to Skyya as soon as she could. At first, Nera had often visited Egret's bedside after the Drakin released her from captivity. However, Nera quickly departed for Skyya along the icy sea once her appearance of care was well seen amongst her people and ours.

Part of me wondered if she truly cared at all.

Fear of how Egret's heart would break in the absence of her mother's love was only set aside as we frequently spoke of Rolloc before his upcoming execution.

"We should investigate what he knows of Judux before he is executed," Aquilla said as half of the Ronian army began to return to the city once the Drakin had finally departed, celebrating with the tens of thousands of Ronian citizens and militia who were finally free.

"Let us do so after we return my sister home," I said, holding Philomela tightly to me, not letting her leave my sight once we had saved her. "The battlefield is not a place fit for a Princess."

"Very well," Aquilla said.

Giving Egret one last silent embrace, I placed a gentle kiss upon her forehead, longing for the moment she would awaken and brighten the world again with her light.

"Morgan," Aquilla said, his tone a gentle rebuke.

"I know," I said, turning halfway to him before returning my attention to her. "I won't be long."

Gently, I placed her Klyr Godstone knife beside her.

I walked out the entrance and towards Alcharion, who similarly had not left my side since the Battle of Renborg and who stood just outside the tent.

"Alcharion, order a guard of Ora'suns to watch over Egret with Nizari," I said. "Have the rest aid the doctors and care for the wounded. You shall come with me to return Philomela to her home. We will return later today."

"At your will, my Shepherd," he said, bowing before me.

As we rode into the city with Lucien and Philomela, surrounded by an entourage of soldiers, Ora'suns, and the two Knights of Kyllian, we passed by the heavily fortified cage in which Rolloc was ensnared, much like an animal with the only freedom to despise his onlookers. His feral eyes glowered as we passed by him, never leaving mine for a moment.

I quickly looked away from him, not wanting to engage with a monster.

"He shall yield to the Light," Aquilla said, to which I nodded.

The citizens of Renborg exploded with praise as Lucien and I paraded through the battle-torn streets of the city, their cheers sending weary smiles to both our lips.

Lucien halted our journey many times to reach out his hand, a sign of favor for any citizen who was able to kiss the hand of their savior, of their crownless King. Lucien did not look proud or somber as he gently greeted the citizens who looked as though the weight of the world had been lifted from their shoulders. Instead, he kept his words to himself, displaying only strength to the Ronians who lauded him as we ascended to the royal sect that was now rid of Drakin.

Even I received the trembling kisses upon my hand from

many of the freed citizens, though it felt unnatural, as word about my slaying of Belial spread faster than the flames in which he had spewed.

Peace filled my lungs as I took a deep breath in its relieving and sweet aroma, so much so that my eyes glimpsed ever so briefly into Aquilla's.

I almost wished it hadn't.

At first I thought it was another Valravn, its shadowed essence perched upon the rooftop of a distant shop in the city. Tensing, I looked closer, only to stare into the bottomless Nox eyes of a Mara.

The shadow disappeared faster than I could blink.

Did you see that? I thought, two seconds away from disbanding from the entourage to chase down the Mara.

"Indeed," Aquilla said. "The spies of Thadius shall know of the failed plot in Renborg. He shall not be pleased."

Every part of me wanted to hunt down that vile instrument of evil, but that would cause an inexcusable scene.

Restraining myself, I decided to hunt the foul creature later in the night.

"A good plan," Aquilla said, reading my thoughts.

Lucien cursed under his breath as we emerged into the royal keep: for everything of value was either destroyed or stolen, no doubt hidden amongst their wagons of supplies and wounded when they departed. All that was left in the citadel were the fire-polluted halls and the careless debris of an invading force. When we strode through the ajar doors of the throne room, I was not prepared for what the Drakin had forgotten.

"At least they were courteous enough to leave us their crown," Lucien said as he stood before the dark and broken thing that lay silent before him, reaching down to grab it.

"Don't touch it!" I yelled, catching Lucien off guard.

"Why not?" he said, eyeing me curiously as he stood back up.

"Be careful," Aquilla warned.

"I—I just think it would be wise not to engage with an item which sat upon an accursed leader. They must have left it here for a reason."

Lucien smirked as he picked up the crown. "It's just a crown, Morgan. You need not be so superstitious."

My smile managed to remain jovial, but my spirit was unsettled in remembrance of the dream in which he wore it.

In which Philomela was dead before him.

"Please, let the crown burn along with Judux," I said, gently shaking Philomela in my arms, who began to cry, my thoughts distracted by the memory of seeing Judux's funeral pyre ablaze for over a week upon my triumphant return. "She needs rest."

"As do you," Lucien said. "I will be in the Councilroom for most of the evening today, for there is much to be done. But I was thinking, after you see to Philomela's rest, how about we take a dip in father's private bathhouse later tonight that he had kept locked away throughout the sols? I've been dying to see it, and I doubt the Drakin touched its cool waters. It can just be us."

I had almost forgotten the Soulis that lay silent in Gulmund's hypocrisy, his shame. Not wanting to burden him further, not until he was ready, I said, "Let's save that for another time. I think I would like to watch the sunset instead."

"Sunset it is then," Lucien smiled.

"We shall have to be rid of the crown from Lucien," Aquilla said as we walked alone with Philomela along the silent hallways of Caer Mordrake, Alcharion trailing slightly behind us to ensure there were no assassins left in the citadel.

I couldn't agree more, I thought as we approached the stairwell that fed into the bedrooms above. But before we did, my eyes caught hold of a simple wooden door just a stone's throw away.

The room of my mother.

Philomela giggled alongside my chest, reaching out her arm to the room.

"Ma-ma," Philomela said in a delicate voice, surprising both Aquilla and I by her first word.

"The child must be guided by the Mother's spirit," Aquilla said.

She does that?

"Well, it is not impossible."

Rolling my eyes at Aquilla, I let my sight focus on the door, which was only one of many servant doors along the hall.

"It belonged to your mother, but why does fear birth within you at the sight of it?"

I… she left something in there for me.

"And you never opened the door?"

No.

"You would have made for a poor Medjaib with such curiosity," Aquilla said as he walked towards the door.

What are you doing?

Aquilla looked at me in surprise. "Waiting for you on the other side."

Without another word, Aquilla disappeared through the door.

Sighing, I took heavy steps towards the door, my heart pounding louder than the drums of war I had already faced.

"When you're ready, she left something for you in there," Valena had said, her eyes glistening in remembrance of a close friend.

With trembling hands that squeezed into strength, I gently pushed open the door with Philomela in my arms.

My mother's room wasn't very big. It was modest with its low arches, humble in its lack of grandeur and decorations. It was, of course, not left in the charred state in which I was born, its ashes long since swept away.

There was, however, a small wooden chest, placed quietly below the single window, almost unnoticeable in the empty room.

Aquilla waited patiently beside it.

Falling to my knees and placing Philomela beside me, I gently opened the box. Inside was a faded letter on parchment, its corners blackened:

My beloved child

A sunflower doesn't choose its seed
Instead, it grows brighter than what came before
You will bloom brighter than gold in Renborg's crown
Though I mourn I cannot be the one to nurture your light
Therefore be gracious to your father
Who fears not the shadow of his destiny, but its cost

For we both knew the price of love

A farmer who finds juva
Will sell all she has to purchase it
As with your heart
My greatest treasure ever found
I chose to buy your life with my own
So the world could be richer still

Your mother

My mother's words were colorful waves refreshing my soul,

yet similarly a tempest thrashing my thoughts in disarray as I compared them to what I thought I knew of my birth.

She chose to die for my birth?

How did she know she would perish?

And how could she ever expect me to be gracious to my father? What purpose did the fire serve if he knew she was going to die?

Questions churned without end in my mind as I read her small but elegant words.

"As it is written, 'The joyful breath of a child may sometimes steal the soul of the mother,'" Aquilla said as he looked fondly upon Philomela, who unknowingly smiled at him. "Mortality is a common fate amongst those who bear children."

I said nothing as I inscribed her words upon my heart.

"I don't—"

"Morgan!" Alcharion yelled, slamming the door open as he rushed towards us, fear at once startling my heart and stealing my focus. "My Shepherd! The Queen has been taken!"

"What?" we said, turning to Alcharion in shock.

"It was the prisoner, my lord!"

"The Mara must have freed Rolloc!" Aquilla said.

"Stay with Philomela!" I shouted, tucking the letter in my pocket after handing my sister to the Elf.

Wyling every part of our being into spirit, we ran faster than the wind, escaping the halls in mere moments. Emerging from the royal sect, we could see nothing until we frantically climbed the winter walls of the palace.

As I feared, our vantage gave confirmation.

Looking upon high, our eyes became one to see the entire Ronian camp in disarray. Hundreds of cavalry were riding across the rolling fields of snow, all scattering in different directions as if they had no idea where Rolloc had taken the Queen.

She was gone, and no one knew where she was or where

she was going. Suddenly, the words of the Mother came roaring back into my mind, a knife sliding slowly between my ribs.

"Will you Shepherd my Shadow of Cypherus?" the Mother had whispered.

Aquilla looked at me with sorrow as understanding also coursed through his being: I was not the Shadow.

"Will you Shepherd her?"

The world became quiet as my beloved was taken from me.

As Rolloc tore my heart from my soul.

"Egret?"

Epilogue

The Coming Winter

Snow buried the student before her, concealing the teeth marks on his neck in the growing darkness of the setting sun.

It had been hours since she had drained every drop from his feeble vessel, for the woman in midnight robes had been watching the College of Man from atop the mountain with an unbroken gaze since she replenished herself from his nourishment.

Planning.

Waiting.

Hungry for more, much like what was below the unsuspecting college.

It was almost time.

Her Thadanites in Renborg whispered to her of the crown that had at last made its way from Yarahm, only to end in the hands of the Ronians from the Dragon's defeat and the Drakin's pride.

That didn't worry her much, for she knew the boy who

would inherit it would be ruled just as easily as Judux et Cadullum.

But there rumored of the spirit who had befallen the resurrected Dragon, and how he moved as the wind and led the Ora'suns with their sacred spear. He would be a threat to overcome if the world were to receive the eternal gift that she had long prepared for, that the Shadow of Cypherus would bring to its completion and fruition.

But fear the woman did not give in to, for she had dealt with such Medjaib and their pets before throughout the centuries.

He would fall like the rest.

And so Egret Thyna would soon reach her destiny.

The woman in black smiled, not of malice nor insanity, but hope, thinking of the promises that Thade had made to her almost a thousand sols ago.

To Be Continued...

Made in the USA
Coppell, TX
04 October 2022

84072220R00372